A FABLE OF WOOD AND STRING

Contents

For
FREEDOM

This novel is dedicated to those who resist evil.

Foreword

Foreword

Dear Reader,

What's in your hands is a spin-off from my middle grade novel *The Mermaid and the Unicorns*. a novel written for my niece Scarlet when she was about eight; she was close to thirteen when I finally published it. She wanted to know what was going on with the puppeteers, and I had some idea, but I had no grand plan at the time. When I started *A Fable of Wood and String* she was a young teenager, hence my decision to aim this story at young adults.

You do not have to read *The Mermaid and the Unicorns* to read *A Fable of Wood and String*; conversely, reading the other book is like reading *The Hobbit*—it can be read before or after *The Lord of the Rings* or just generally acknowledged. Seth and Lily have no idea what transpired before their adventure began. If you're looking for a sequel to *The Mermaid and the Unicorns* and are a younger reader, know that I have plans to tell another story with Daphne, Esperanza, and Sean as the leads. You may not be ready for this novel because of one of the story's themes.

This is a story that deals with mental trauma and abuse.

This is a work of fiction, not a primer on how to deal with PTSD or Survivor's Guilt. At one point in this story, one character mentions another character's resolve finally shattering and an attempt at suicide. It was my goal to discuss absolute despair in a respectful manner.

If you or someone you love is struggling with your mental health:

reach out, get help. You are not alone. If you or someone you love are considering self-harm or suicide, please reach out and ask for help. No matter what's happened or what you've done, know that your value is intrinsic. You matter.

When things seem at their worst, remember evil is not the only player; sometimes hope and goodness presents itself in unexpected ways.

Foreword

A FABLE OF WOOD AND STRING

L. GETTY

Black Unicorn Books

One

Lily woke to the patter of small paws on her window. Starlight spilled around the satin curtains and illuminated her way to the continuous tapping and the occasional yip. No sooner had she opened the window from the bottom, a small kit jumped through, much to the nattering of his mother.

Boscoe was the most mischievous of his siblings, but he was harmless and knew better than to rouse the dogs, even though only old Chester was given a place of honour by the wood stove on chill spring nights such as that one. Lily poked her head out the window, and saw Mama Fern's other two kits lurking around the nearest shed not far from the coop.

"Everything okay?" Lily asked, wiping night sand from her eye. Mama Fern chattered, then bit, tugging the sleeve of Lily's night dress. The fox relinquished when Lily gestured she'd follow. Lily propped the window open with one of the leather-bound books from the nearest shelf and quickly donned the simple day clothes laid out on the back of a chair—a working split skirt, a pale chemise with long fitted sleeves, then an overdress. Her staff and rod were out in the barn, but she quickly strung her bow and the standard quiver was always at the ready.

Glancing at the chest at the foot of her bed where she kept her wooden training swords along with the real one, Lily decided she wouldn't need it to retrieve a wayward lamb, instead belting the standard utility knife and satchel. When she was ready to hop out the window, the only real sound was Boscoe rummaging through the wicker basket of mending.

She followed the fox, and realized just how quiet it was. She should be hearing crickets, or frogs down by the creek; it was too early for the roosters to rouse her family, but she expected to hear a distant owl or some sound besides the faint wind rustling the spring buds. The beginning traces of dew tipped the grass, but while she saw no tracks leading to the barn, there was a sudden large indent before it, then huge foot prints. She could not determine the animal. "Ginger? Zigg?" she called the younger sheep dogs.

Quiet.

Lily booked it back to the house. She went back through the window and didn't bother to close it. Their oldest dog raised his head with a grumble as she raced to her parent's room, then banged on the door.

"Something's wrong," Lily said once her mother, Sylvia, opened the door. "I saw strange tracks outside."

There wasn't any light in her parent's room, but she heard Elias moving around. Sylvia nodded. "Rouse your brother and wait for us."

"Seth!" Lily shouted from the base of the stairs before rushing to the kitchen to fill the lanterns. Her father muttered *that boy would sleep through an avalanche*—not that they were so close to the mountain that they needed to worry about those.

Still grumbling, Chester went to one of the windows and put his massive paws on the sill. His ears perked, he barked loud and growled; going to the main door he barked again.

Taking a lantern, Lily opened the main door leading to the patio overhang, but instead of lighting it let her eyes adjust to the night. Chester sped off towards the main barn. "Wait!" Lily called after him. Her guardian wolfhound stopped and barked several times, let out a peculiar whine.

This time, she smelled slaughter. Following after Chester, they discovered speckled blood on the grass. Lily hopped the pen and found the barn door ajar. Her sheep huddled together at the back of the barn, save for several ewes and their new lambs separately penned, the youngest sheepdog Zigg whimpering and cowering among them, tail between his legs. Her sheep normally would have come to her, but for the most part only her bravest sheep wagged their tails in recognition. The family mare Stella whickered and tossed her head from her stall. Lily stroked several noses and scanned the barn for clues.

She called for Zigg to join her and Chester, but the sheepdog remained with the flock. The guardian woofed and followed Lily before plodding ahead.

Eventually, Chester led her away from the barn. They didn't enter the woods leading towards the creek before they found another dog, Ginger, lying in the tall grass panting.

"What did this to you?" Lily asked, stroking the sheepdog's face and noting frothing at her mouth. Ginger raised her head and momentarily wagged her tail, but whined in pain. Lily did her best to address the deep cuts but her standard gauze was for wrapping superficial injuries, she wasn't sure she could stymie the bleeding so she pressed hard on the wounds. Chester licked Ginger's face. "There's a good girl," Lily said. Chester whined. "Ginger?"

Lily's eyes watered as her dog lay still. Lily stroked her and then clenched the fallen dog's fur in a fist. "Let's get the wolf that did this, Chester." Lily gave Ginger a consoling pat and stood. Blinking back tears, she followed after Chester as he led her through the bent grass leading to denser bush. More yipping. Mama Fern warning her not to go.

"I know what I'm doing," Lily said. She heard a shrill whistle from the house, and Chester sped back. She didn't need him; they'd moved here when she was a toddler and had this backwoods practically memorized. Her family would catch up in a minute or so. A chill down Lily's spine gave her pause, but she nocked her bow, and pressed on down the familiar game path. She frowned at the claw marks on the side of a maple tree.

She heard a sickening crunch before laying eyes upon bat-like wings and green-brown scales over bony ridges reflecting starlight. The sound of teeth severing meat from bone, before a leg fell to the forest floor.

The wyvern consumed one of the stolen sheep, another ram laying dead at his feet.

The wyvern bent its serpentine neck to pick up the leg, but before it did it paused, sniffed the air and flicked its forked tongue. The left eye was badly damaged. It turned, snake-like fast, and rearing spread its wings and roared. Startled, Lily loosed her shot. The arrow sailed to the left of the beast and Lily moved to redraw and aim at the good eye. It appeared to be a mountain variety. Almost all wyverns had leathery wings for forearms and were usually poisonous as opposed to fire-spitters. It roared again; Lily stood her ground, and she was still far enough away that most of the spittle didn't touch her.

They tracked by smell and movement, so she imagined herself frozen in place. If she turned and ran, it would almost certainly kill her, if not by the fangs or claws it would grab and carry her into the air and drop her, then finish her off after she was wounded. That was assuming it didn't incapacitate her with the poison, and carry her back to its nest to eat in a few days.

The one good eye locked on the arrow glinting off the moonlight. The aggression display suggested it didn't want to run. "I thought you'd value your own life more than your sheep, human," it hissed. Lily got the impression it was male. He reared up and batted his wings, but Lily kept her arrow trained on the good eye.

She slowly backed away. "Easy, easy," she said, mouth dry, keeping her aim level in spite of her racing heart. "My sheep are dead, you might as well finish."

The wyvern lowered several ridges of scales and spikes. She assumed she was being permitted to leave but he charged, and Lily loosed a shot that struck the wyvern's open jowls and rolled to her right. Arrows flew out of her quill as she reached for another and shouted a warning. Enraged, the wyvern clawed at his mouth and sunk his claws into the oak tree where she'd been a moment prior, and turning he knocked her down with his tail. Lily rolled with the force, and landing on her tummy, laid still until the wyvern's head was turned before pushing up and sprinting to cover beneath a mossy space under a large fallen tree.

The wyvern reared, looking around wildly. Lily crept behind his back, nocking another arrow even though she was down to four shots.

Voices sounded from the house.

"Wyvern!" Lily shouted. The wyvern turned to the sound of her voice, but Lily darted behind another tree. She heard shots sailing at the wyvern, bouncing off his scales.

"Seth, no!" Elias shouted, but her brother charged ahead. Elias tackled Seth; they hit the dirt and the beast sprayed a mist of venom in the air. Lily was upwind and could taste the bitterness. Both Seth and their father covered their faces with the crooks of their sleeves, and Sylvia let loose a clay jar no bigger than her fist, which exploded with pitch when it struck the wyvern's face. Undeterred, the creature advanced on her brother and father.

"I'm over here!" Lily whistled and waived her arms. The wyvern turned its head back and forth between her and her family.

Light flared and Sylvia readied her fireshot, but the wyvern honed in on the uneaten sheep, and gathered the fallen ram into its jaw. Lily then saw that it had a tear in one of the wings; it scaled a tree, and scrambled into the canopy until it was hidden by shadow, breaking twigs and branches and bending the lesser trees under its weight as it leapt from branch to branch away from the ranch.

Elias let Seth up, but they all watched in silence after the direction the wyvern had gone. When at last they could no longer see the twigs falling, Sylvia put out her flame arrow and raced to Lily, pulling her into an embrace before she looked her over. "Are you hurt?"

That was stupid," Elias said, looking at first to Seth, but then to Lily. "Both of you go back to the house and protect Tiffany. Syl, did you get a good look at it?"

"Not really," Sylvia said.

"It might have been a Half-Ridged Broadjaw," Lily said. "Can't be certain."

Her mother nodded. "Jot down what you think you saw while it's still fresh, we'll compare it to our old journals later." Sylvia turned her head when Elias started after the wyvern. "Elias, you'll need a better bow, that pitch wouldn't have been enough."

Elias paused. "I'm just listening to the wind. It'll be easier without all of you blathering."

Lily gestured to her brother to follow her back to the house, but Seth ignored her. "I can track it," Seth offered. "That'll give you time to gear up."

"Go home," Elias said. "It's wounded, it'll be erratic."

"I'm not going to confront it like Lily," Seth pointed out.

"I thought it was a wolf, not a wyvern," Lily snapped.

"We will discuss this later," Sylvia informed them. "If you want to hunt this sort of game, you obey your seniors. Elias, I'll saddle up Stella; we need to warn the Orells and the Phorsythes."

"You'll warn the neighbours?" Elias confirmed to Sylvia. "I'll double back and gear up. Not to engage. Just precautions." He gave Sylvia a warm smile, but that quickly became something darker, though he didn't look at his children. "You two are lingering."

"I'll saddle Stella," Seth groused and sauntered behind Lily. They didn't completely obey; they went to the barn and assessed the damage to the door, checked on the flock. Seth managed to close the door, and Zigg finally came out from hiding. Seth's twin, Tiffany, watched from the patio.

"You're letting all the cold air in with the door open," Seth told Tiffany when they finally approached the house.

Folk joked if anyone were twins it would have been her and Seth for the red in their hair like their father, though Lily's was the most brown. Lily would be eighteen before harvest and was often mistaken for the youngest; her face was rounder than either of her siblings and, while people claimed Seth resembled Elias and Tiffany a taller Sylvia, Lily reflected neither. Tiffany had thick, raven-dark hair like their mother, and though people often remarked how Tiffany and Lily looked like sisters, she never saw it. Tiffany was also tall, standing eye to eye with Elias though she and Seth had been sixteen for barely two weeks.

Seth only came in for a moment before heading back out to help saddle Stella. Sylvia never came back into the house before setting off to warn the neighbours.

Lily stoked the wood stove and boiled water, starting dough for the daily bread, and knowing she wasn't going back to bed made oatmeal for breakfast. When dawn broke she went outside and collected eggs, checked on her sheep. Thankfully the wyvern hadn't killed erratically, and counting only losses, it was short two rams.

"You can do the mending and make bread," Lily told Tiffany, who was reading a play she'd finagled from someone in town. Lily looked at Seth, who spoke up before she could assign him anything.

"You're not in charge," he said. "I want your sword in case that thing comes back."

"Last time you borrowed it, it took Jasper a week to unbend it."

"I need to be able to protect us," Seth told her.

Lily frowned. "A spear would be better. Or something with range."

"You'd know that, if you ever read up on how to hunt those beasts, Seth," Tiffany agreed. "It's a little late now."

"I don't need to memorize trivia," Seth informed his sisters. He was reading something from their mother's study.

"Was it a big wyvern?" Tiffany asked.

"I don't know," Seth said, showing his sisters the old journal. "I'd say it was two Stellas when it reared." Lily wished it had held still long enough to span its wings or stretch out its tail.

Lily quietly made her oatmeal and ate it while she boiled eggs for later before she put the bread in the oven and headed out to weed the garden. Seth tagged along, munching on a hardboiled egg, though it wasn't long before he wandered off. He was in and out of the barn trying to fix the door so Lily said nothing.

When Lily returned to the house, the bread was cooling on the counter and more dough was rising; Tiffany was busy on some piece of embroidery when Victor and Rhett from the neighbouring farms appeared. "Where's your father?"

"Out tracking," Seth offered. Both men were a little older than Elias, and looked nervous. "What did my mom say?"

"Nevermind that," Rhett said. "What direction are we likely to find Elias?"

Seth and Lily glanced at one another. "I'll take you to him," Seth said finally. "You got things here?" Lily nodded. "Have you eaten yet?"

"This isn't the time for worrying about food," Victor told Seth.

"If we're following after my dad we're not coming back for hours," Seth said. "I'm going to the root cellar. Just remember, when he asks you're the ones who insisted."

"Seth, gear up properly I'll get the food ready," Tiffany offered, so Lily and Seth led the elder men to the shed.

To her surprise, Elias returned while they were going through the old equipment in the shed. He arched an eyebrow at them, but then nodded to Rhett and Victor. Elias gestured for them to put the tools away so they left the weighted net and hunter's bows, closed up the shed, and returned to the house.

"How far did you track it?" Tiffany asked Elias as the others settled around the kitchen table.

"I'll explain later," Elias said. "Where's your mother?"

"She was just at our place, she said she was going to town," Victor said. "It killed two rams?"

"And one of our dogs," Lily offered, but no one seemed to care.

"It's a shame you couldn't kill it," said Rhett.

"I still have a bow that would have done the job, but I didn't have it on me." Elias gestured to a large bow on his back Lily could never draw. Granted, she hadn't tried in a while.

"I doubt you'd be able to do it on your own," Rhett said. "Syl's all right? I wouldn't let my wife be out on her own right now."

"We've hunted them before." Elias nodded. "Syl's got Stella; our mare will alert her if anything smells off. The wyvern ate; it would be hard pressed to attack again so quickly, given its injured and how much of a fight we put up. My land is probably undesirable unless it's desperate."

"How long do they go between meals?" Victor asked.

Elias looked contemplative. "A few days? It's injured; it'll want to eat more if it can."

"How injured?" Rhett asked.

"Not sure. Bad wing, looked like a bad eye," Elias admitted. "It had missing scales. It must have battled something on the mountain."

"We'll write to my brother," Victor said. "You and him can make short work of it."

"He's at least a day away if he's not frittering off on the mountain," Elias said.

"You have the tools?" Rhett asked. Elias nodded. "Should we write and request rangers?"

"Of course," Elias said. "They'll take their sweet time getting here. We need to deal with it before someone else's daughter stumbles onto it." He caught Lily's gaze, and she felt taken aback. How was this her fault?

"The neighbouring counties should be warned," Victor said. "You've a horse. And a son. He could ride to..."

"You write to your brother," Elias said. "*I* will track the beast down and *we* will kill it—or at least make it realize it's not welcome *here*, but I'm not about to let it attack another farm if I can help it. Lily, keep the sheep penned until this is all sorted and your mother and I tell you otherwise. Feed them like it's a rain day."

"They've been fed already, and we've minded the chickens and—" she began.

"You know how to run things," Elias said, looking back to the others and discussing who in town would be useful, and who would be more trouble than mucking about for a few days in the bush.

Lily left them talking around the trestle table and made her way to her room. She wasn't sure how much good it would do, but she attached the sword to her belt. She checked her window before going back outside; her father said nothing as she continued out to the main barn and chicken coop. No sign of Mama Fern and her babies.

Her sister's voice startled her, Tiffany had followed after her into the barn. "It's not safe to be out here."

"You heard dad. It's not likely to come back any time soon. Besides, I have to deal with Ginger."

Tiffany nodded. They pulled their sheepdog to the side, had a brief cry about her, and covered her with an old saddle blanket. "You should go back to the house, Tiffany," Lily insisted.

"I don't like you out here by yourself."

Lily nodded. "Let me check on the sheep, and I'll work the garden by the house so you can see me."

Lily returned to the barn and to check on her flock, the dogs and sheep knew the routine but for the most part the flock didn't seem to want to leave the safety of the barn. Returning to the house, Lily found her father and the others had left; Seth went with them so the animals were her responsibility. At least her brother had somewhat fixed the barn door.

Besides the lambing, running the ranch wasn't anything Lily and Tiffany couldn't handle by themselves. Thankfully none were born. Just before sunset, Sylvia returned to let Lily know another two sheep had gone missing the week before, not from Stagmil but from another county. The house smelled of mutton stew as well as Tiffany's delicious strawberry-rhubarb pie.

"Think dad will be back tonight?" Tiffany asked. Sylvia shook her head. "How'd the neighbours take it?"

"Not happy we let it escape," Sylvia said. As always, Tiffany's stew and biscuits were delicious, but Sylvia was distracted, thumbing through the book Seth had gotten earlier, plus another faded journal. "When you have a chance, Lily, think you can redraw these?"

"It'd be nice if I had something that wasn't so smudged," Lily said.

"You probably could have touched it," Sylvia snapped. "You can handle a simple drawing."

"I didn't mean to alert it," Lily said.

"It doesn't matter what you meant to do," Sylvia said. "You not only put yourself in danger, either. Seth and your father would have tried to save you. Think before you act next time."

Lily tried not to get flustered but felt the heat rush to her cheeks. "Well tell them not to try to save me next time!"

"Next time?" Sylvia asked, brows arched.

"You know what I mean. I'm a shepherd," Lily told her. "I've been confronting wolves and bears since I was ten."

"Not by yourself, and not without tools," Sylvia replied. "You weren't equipped to face a wyvern."

"Neither were any of you," Lily pointed out.

Sylvia let out a frustrated sigh. "I don't want to hear it. Tiffany made supper, you can clean up and do the drawings I asked you in your room. I have work to do." Sylvia got up wordlessly, disappearing up the stairs, likely going to her study.

"Wow," Tiffany said, waiting for their mother to be out of earshot. "You actually got in trouble."

"Don't start," Lily said, gathering the dishes. Tiffany had been baking but hadn't done dishes all day, so of course there was a pile for her to do. Tiffany followed after her but didn't help her pump water or heat it.

"I'm just saying they're mad at you instead of Seth for once." Tiffany sat at the table while Lily washed the dishes, working on that same beautiful embroidery.

Lily finished cleaning and didn't feel like doing the drawing, but knew her mother would hear if she practiced music. She went to her room but didn't feel like mending the sock pile, either.

Most of her oaken furniture was second or third hand she'd had since before he could remember. She'd added a canopy to the tall posts, and had her own bookshelf as well as a cherry-stained bouzouki on the wall near her bed.

Lily lit a candle and heard a, "Brrr?"

"What are you still doing here?"

Boscoe yawned and rolled on his backside. Lily thought he'd slept all day on her bed, but the evidence of crumbs showed the little fox had found at least one of Tiffany's biscuits. She was surprised Mama Fern wasn't at the window, chattering again.

Lily opened the window, and pointed. "Get going." Boscoe got up with a stretch. "Tell your mother thank you." Lily gave him a scratch under his chin before he jumped out the window. He stopped to look back at her for a moment when he got to the side of the shed, but scampered off towards the creek.

She got the sudden idea she ought to go see Zin, but knew her mother wouldn't let her go much further than the barns. Practicing her form with her wooden training sword, she envisioned what would have happened if she'd used her steel one against the wyvern. It was probably a good thing she hadn't; the sword might have wounded the wyvern but she imagined a dozen scenarios that involved it biting her arm clean off.

"I thought you said something with range might help?" Tiffany asked from the doorway.

"Stop spying on me!" Lily snapped. "Don't you have anything better to do?"

"You're so dramatic," Tiffany said, flicking her hair. "Tea's ready." She didn't bring Lily a mug. "They're not really mad at you. You scared them."

"It was an accident," Lily said. "Tell mom I'll do the stupid drawings in a bit. I haven't practiced my form today. Not that I'm ever going to get good around here."

Sylvia cleared her throat and made herself known. Lily bristled. "Tiffany, go practice on the mandolin."

Tiffany left, but the sounds coming from the living room sounded much more like her flute.

Sylvia seemed annoyed, but addressed Lily. "Things went well here today?"

Lily nodded. Her mother didn't need to hear any report unless there was something that needed her attention. "Seth managed to prop the barn door; it'll work until dad can look at it. I'm sorry about this morning. I didn't think it was anything I couldn't have handled."

"How did you know something was amiss?" Sylvia asked. "Did the dogs wake you?"

"One of our farm foxes woke me up," Lily said. Sylvia chuckled. It was that distinct family; Mama Fern and her babies. They never stole chickens or bothered the sheep, the neighbours tolerated them, but both of her parents walked past Mama Fern with as much concern as one of the barn cats.

Sylvia nodded. "I'm going to set out tomorrow for Longhorn and let them know what happened." Longhorn was one of their neighboring villages to the South; it was even smaller and off the beaten path than Stagmil. "Keep things running smoothly while I'm gone."

"If the neighbours take out theirs, can I take the sheep to the field tomorrow?"

"No, keep them penned," Sylvia said. "Your father and brother are not likely to be back tonight. I won't be gone more than a day. Try not to cause any more trouble."

Again she wanted to protest it wasn't her fault, but knew it didn't matter what she said. "I'll bury Ginger in the morning."

"Better her than you, love," Sylvia said, re-entering the room and embracing her daughter. "It's likely to be a very busy few weeks. Stay on top of your chores, get those drawings done before you turn in, and get some rest. I'll want copies tomorrow."

"What for?"

"To warn the other villages," Sylvia said, leaving Lily's bedroom.

Two

Sylvia left early the next morning and was gone for the next two days, returning with news that another sheep and three goats were killed up near Gilda the week prior, as well as another farm dog. Two days later, it struck again south of them at a more isolated farm, but news carried quickly through the county.

Thankfully, the wyvern struck at night when people were asleep. The people didn't know what to make of the creature's attacks and had only told their neighbours. Seth wondered if some of the other claimants weren't just looking for sympathy or if perhaps they were wolf attacks, but kept his mouth shut when they made their way to the town hall. He felt bad that they left his older sister behind, but figured there was less chance of Lily getting mobbed with questions.

Stagmil was the centre of a collection of farms, just far enough from the City of Taralee that meant they couldn't go often. The proper village consisted of a general store and a handful of tradesmen, such as Jasper the smith. Nearby farms brought their wheat to the mill, and though many folk lived in town, they drove their sheep to the various hilly fields on the outskirts of it.

Arriving at the town hall, an overly-large log house that was used for auctioning livestock, Seth abandoned his parents almost as quick as his twin did. Tiffany hurried off to be with her best friend Molly, who Seth considered the prettiest girl in Stagmil, and not just for lack of options. Molly had thick chestnut hair and stunning brown eyes. Molly was older than the twins by almost two months but for as long as Seth could remember, it was always his twin who was the leader.

He sought out Frederic, who saw him and left his kin to go speak to his father.

"Heard your firstborn's got nerves of steel," Uncle Freddy said. Phorsythes on the whole were built strong, and Uncle Freddy was no exception, though he was shorter than his older brother Victor.

"Got way too close, you mean," Elias said, giving Uncle Freddy's wife Juniper a nod. Juniper and Sylvia were cousins, but Seth reckoned half the people in the building were somehow related to the Brathwell side of the family. "Of course Lily knew what to do. I trust that girl more than myself some days."

"Where is she? I only saw Tiffany," Juniper said, scanning the crowd.

"Didn't want anyone else thinking their daughters would be fine with a run in," Sylvia explained. "She's minding the ranch. We've got lambs due."

"Seth!" Louis called over. Besides the mother, Seth got along with the Phorsythes great; Louis' oldest brother was his age and apprenticing as a cooper at Port Redmaw. Louis was thirteen, had constantly tussled golden blond hair and looked like he'd pudged out in the past few weeks, something that was supposed to accompany a growth spurt. Louis was with Tobias, another local boy the same age as Louis, though he was lean with dark brown hair. "I heard you hit the wyvern!"

"Yeah, bows and arrows not meant for scales like that," Seth said. "What did Lily call it? Half-Ridged Broadjaw."

"And your uncle is going with his dad to make short work of it, right?" Tobias asked Louis. "Are you going with the hunting party, Seth?"

"Of course," Seth said, crossing his arms. "It must be pretty injured to come off the mountain. That's what my mom said, anyway."

"Louis' uncle said the same thing," Tobias said. They watched others arrive from neighbouring communities. Most youths Seth's age were either apprenticing or manning the homestead while their parents attended this meeting. "Think you can ask your dad to let us come along?"

"If my dad said no, the answer's no," Louis said. "You're lucky, Seth. Is Lily going?"

"I don't know," Seth said. "Better her than half of these guys here, but they won't like taking orders from a girl. I don't think she's strong enough for a true hunter's bow, neither."

"Are you?" Louis asked.

Not with much accuracy. Elias made it look easy. "Jasper can fix up a few crossbows and make it a moot point. They're slow on the redraw, though. Come on, let's get seats."

They were summarily booted to the standing room in the back as the meeting came to order. They had no mayor in Stagmil so much as a council of elders, as well as folk who were leaders from their own communities, so they groused who ought to be the ones running the meeting.

Folk from different communities relayed information that Seth already knew. He knew more than others by merit of hanging around his parents. Elias and Freddy stood near the front to answer questions, though Seth knew his mother should probably be up there for technicalities, no one wanted to hear about nesting habits or other minutae.

"Why's it here?" one of the villagers asked once the floor opened up. "I thought they liked being away from people. We're not the easiest to kill."

"It's injured. It likely was driven away from its territory and wants to get its strength back," Uncle Freddy said.

"What could drive off a wyvern?" Louis asked as the grousing continued up front.

"Another wyvern or a big unicorn," Seth offered.

"How do we stay safe?" a woman asked at the front.

"A single man is easy prey for a wyvern," Freddy began. "But they're smart enough to know they don't want to be hurt, so stick to travelling in pairs, with small children staying in groups. They're part of the wyrm family; they're more active at night than during the day, so try to keep your people and animals indoors after dark. The days are growing longer, so there's some hope in that."

"You've hunted them before, haven't you?" a man Seth didn't know asked Elias.

Elias gave a solemn nod.

"Are we going to place our faith in those two?" another man asked, standing. "You abandoned your last hunt."

"That was a long time ago," Freddy said.

"So? Elias let the beast go, and now it's preying on our village!"

"I'm not asking for your help," Elias said blandly. "I'm asking for you all to listen to my wife and keep your families safe. Wyverns can roam; the trick will be to figure out if it's got a nest at all. With that injured wing, it can't range as far."

"What hunt are they talking about?" Tobias asked Louis.

"Seth's dad and Uncle Freddy caught and killed a unicorn," Louis said. Seth shot him a look, and Louis understood. "I'll tell you more later. It was before Seth was born."

"Mom was pregnant with Lily," Seth muttered just loud enough for the pair to hear. "And they trapped it, they didn't kill it. My mom some others were there too."

"Why?" Tobias asked, but things were heating up at the front of the room.

"Elias is a coward and Frederic Phorysthe is a glorified tour guide," snapped one of the townsmen from Longhorn. "I'll kill the beast."

"Perhaps we should have two parties, and see who fells the beast first," Freddy suggested.

"It's not a competition," Elias said, low and quiet, yet his voice still seemed to carry throughout the hall. "If you would like to lead a group of men into the bush, be aware that a wyvern can run almost twice as fast as a man, and that doesn't include flight."

"Sounds like you've been studying it," said Jolene, one of the Stagmil elders.

"I learned to hunt by listening to other hunters who came before me. Unlike a dragon, a hunter who knows what he's doing can fell a wyvern by himself; but ideally it's handled with a team. It's not like hunting a moose. A wyvern can fly and are clever enough to incapacitate you before killing you. I can't tell if it's a male or a female but we do not want it laying eggs. We think it's north of here."

"Away from your farm!" someone accused. "You drove it to us!"

"We need to gather everyone's livestock," said another of Stagmil's elders, Amos. "As it stands, we're too spread out, the beast could peck off a sheep and move around."

"I'm more afraid for my children than your goats," said another townswoman.

"We can move the sheep and goats into town," one of the men said. "Keep them all together. We can share fields."

"We don't normally have all the sheep penned together."

"We have before," someone said. "We have enough who have farms close to town."

"Wouldn't that bring the beast closer to town?" asked another.

"The wyvern is acting like a thief, not a robber. The wyvern won't attack a crowd for fear of further injury," Elias said. "Keep together in groups. Keep small children away from the flocks."

"Gathered all into town, wonderful," Louis muttered as the plan was solidified. Remote farms would drive their flocks to larger communities. Not everyone agreed, but they would take their chances. "I wish I was old enough to go with you, Seth."

"Maybe in a few years, Lily can lure a basilisk down off the mountain," Seth said with a grin.

They did decide to have two hunting parties—one led by Elias, the other by Guy, a loudmouth who wasn't a bad hunter by any means, but he was familiar with deer and foxes and acted like a wyvern was practically the same thing. There was a lot of territory to cover, so technically his father's group was going to split up again once they had a better idea of where it had gone since leaving their farm. Guy's party left before the meeting concluded, without the aid of crossbows or nets. *Some of them might be eaten,* Seth shivered, recalling the stories his parent's old friends used to tell him as a boy.

Folk were planning on staying overnight; the O'Connells had a large house with spare rooms but they didn't take any extra boarders as most preferred to stay with their nearest kin. "Who's going to help Sylvia?" Rhett asked.

"My daughters," Elias said. "If we're completely wrong, and it attacks here with the women and children, Sylvia will keep your families safe. It'll be with tactics, not arms."

"Juniper said she'll help me make pitch while you're gearing up," Sylvia said. "She'd stay if I needed it, but Lily and Tiffany are old enough. We can stand to lose a few more sheep so long as our neighbours are kept safe."

Sylvia stayed in town to discuss plans further with several of the elders, Elias took the twins home to ready the ranch for the next day when both would have preferred to stay and be social at the hall. Lily wasn't happy with her assignment, and Seth couldn't blame her. Not only was she being left behind, she wasn't even allowed to stay in their own home. After helping make the fire pitch, they boarded things up, though Sylvia would be back to check on the chickens and weed the garden. Tiffany groused about driving the sheep and that without Ginger it took more work. Thankfully, Louis and Tobias came to help and they brought the Phorysthe's sheepdogs. Seth gave his mother a hug when their party was ready to set out.

"Try to keep everyone's spirits up," Sylvia said, before she took Elias's hands. "Take care of Seth. I know we were both hunting around his age, but . . . oh, he reminds me of you Elias."

Lily of course was sullen and stiff when her father hugged her good-bye. "Listen to your mother. Keep the villagers safe."

Lily nodded, and Seth set out with Elias, Freddy, Juniper and others, Chester at their heels. Seth thought they should take Zigg as well, but Elias didn't want to leave his herds with at least one familiar dog, though. Seth was glad to go; after all, nothing exciting ever happened in sleepy Stagmil.

~*~

Tiffany was well pleased, mostly because she and Molly somehow wormed their way into a different house, whereas Lily and her mother were to stay at old Greta's.

Greta had a large house situated not far from where Lily needed to drive sheep and her neighbours' goats every morning, though thankfully Louis and the other shepherds were keen to do the driving so they could take the far off quadrants in the fields.

Greta was a widower with grandchildren, and it always seemed that there was some child in need of cooing or a diaper change. Lily busied herself with the flocks by day, and after the first night of crying children and not being able to turn around without being tasked asked her mother if she could have a cot and stay at one of the barns with the sheep, citing concern for her lambs. Sylvia said no, instead giving the task to Louis and Tobias.

Most folk returned to their respective village to inform their fellows to do the same thing as in Stagmil. One family came driving their flocks unexpectedly, and they were brought in all the same.

The only one from Stagmil who didn't stay in town was Zin Booey. He arrived unexpectedly in the fields where different flocks intermixed, and kicked off the dirt on his boots. "Here's my apprentice, lazing about during the prime of the day."

Lily got up from playing the family mandolin with a stretch. She was working on an original song; it wasn't coming along and she'd almost drifted off for a nap. "I thought you'd have joined one of the hunting parties."

"I thought you'd be with them too," Zin replied. He plopped down a wicker basket of delicious fresh rye bread and lightly spiced ham and cheeses that always seemed too good.

Even though she knew him years before he took pity on her and made her his apprentice, Lily had no idea what Zin did. Typically they met at the village square or the pastoral fields and he instructed her on what she ought to do for exercise every day. She never knew when he was coming and sometimes he'd be gone for a day or two, but seldom more than that.

Zin had a lean sort of musculature that gave off the impression that his youth likely involved a lot of running. His hair had faded into white and while his hairline had receded he kept what remained long in a pony tail, yet his dark eyes often sparkled when he was up to something.

"You have to tell me who makes your food one of these days."

"I told you, my mysterious wife who only comes out at night," Zin said with a chuckle. "Heard you tried to face the beast yourself."

Lily almost choked on her sandwich. "I saw it, I didn't provoke it."

"Your brother ranted something fierce when they passed by my way," he told her with a chuckle. "Finish your snack, you're behind on your training."

He told her she'd never be that good because she didn't have anyone to train with besides an old man. Every time Lily thought she'd caught up, Zin improved, but in a way that made it possible for her to compete. She had the impression that he was toying with her years ago. "Have you ever dealt with a wyvern?"

"Your mother wrote the book on dealing with those, not me."

"She didn't write it. She compiled other people's accounts."

"Sounds like a writer to me," Zin told her.

They trained for form before they sparred. Louis came to inspect. "I thought you were done apprenticing," Louis said.

"Lily is far from a master swordsman, O' Louis of the Grey Sheep," Zin said. "In my opinion she's regressing."

"I'm watching Jolene's sheep. They're mostly white."

"We're watching everyone's sheep," Lily said. "Are you joining us?"

"Take a walk and shepherd while I conduct an assessment," Zin instructed. Lily nodded, striding in the direction Louis had come from, and saw Tobias and another boy their age pretending to be interested in shepherding while Zin gave Louis basic instructions on grip and stance. She was younger than Louis when she'd started her training, but Louis was bigger than she was at his age. She did her rounds, the sheep were milling about contentedly. She circled back and geared up for sparring again, Louis laughed when he was told to take a swipe at her. She held in a receiving, then obeyed Zin when he told her to knock Louis off balance.

"I don't want to hit a girl," Louis said once he regained his footing.

"Don't worry, you won't," Zin said.

The training blades were made of a segmented wood. Lighter than swords, training blades could still break bones. Zin didn't carry the full armour, just shin and shoulder guards, as well as chest plates and helmets, and after Louis practiced Zin allowed them to spar. Towards the end, Louis grew frustrated, so she lowered her guard and let him get a strike towards the end.

"Got you!"

"She let you. Lily, don't patronize the lad he doesn't need it," Zin said with a sniff. "Louis, you'll be powerful in a few years, but you can't always bash your way though things. Focus on the technique and the speed will come."

"You sure you want to teach me your secrets? I'll be bigger than you in a few years," Louis told Zin.

"That may be, but until you can beat me I run the lesson," Zin said. "Don't look pleased with yourself Lily; as of right now if you were to square off against a knight or even his squire you'd be split from sternum to your belly button. Blade master's Quick Tip: Try to not let your insides get on the outside."

Louis chuckled, Lily doffed her gear. "You good if I do my rounds?"

"Get to it. Louis, let's practice form."

Lily strapped her mandolin on her back and began her patrol. She didn't get far when she heard Argo bark. Zigg and the larger dog raced towards the woods nearest them and woofed, making the four sheep grazing together race from the hill to rejoin the larger herd.

"Wolves," Lily muttered, and whistled and waved for Tobias or anyone near. She stopped to string her bow before following after the dogs. Cresting the hill, she found the dogs barking at a blonde woman.

The stranger stood by the edge of the forest, her red velvet dress looked travel-stained and her heeled boots unfit for hiking. Lily placed her about the same age as her mother, someplace in her early forties. She was tall and lithe, giving Lily the impression of a dancer.

"Are you all right?" Lily asked as she approached. Tobias and the other boy weren't far behind her; she heard Louis hollering to wait for him. The woman stepped towards Lily, but raised her brows at the dogs. Lily heard a 'hyah' behind her. Zin was riding away on his goat chariot.

"Where am I?" the woman asked. She backed towards the woods when the dogs barked at her again.

"Zigg, Argo, stand down," Lily ordered. "Tobias, get the dogs back."

"Enough." Tobias tapped his staff besides the dogs. "Go find some coyotes to scare, we can handle some lady." Argo looked mournfully at Louis when he approached, but Zigg continued to have his hackles up.

"Do you know where Dale is?" Lily asked, grabbing hold of Zigg. Her dog looked to her and licked his chops, but then focused his gaze on the woman.

"Yeah, with his girlfriend," Tobias said. "Let's bug 'em."

The youths scampered off; Argo followed but Zigg stayed with Lily. He grumbled as the woman approached. "Are you hurt?" Lily asked, giving Zigg's collar a slight shake.

"No. Where am I?"

"Not far from the Village of Stagmil," she said. "I'm Lily O'Connell." Judging by the fine clothing, the stranger had likely come from Taralee or was travelling there. "Are you in trouble?"

"Not any more," the woman said, looking down at grumbling Zigg. "Are you a musician?"

Of all the questions to ask! How was her mandolin the first thing she noticed? "Just a shepherd. Who are you?"

"Call me Madeline."

Before Lily pressed further, she heard the others returning. Dale and his girlfriend Brigid were of her year, both were a few months older than she was. Dale was tall with inky-black hair and usually worked the mill in town. Brigid stayed with the boys and they all watched. "Lily, what's going on?" Dale called as he approached them.

"This is Madeline," Lily gestured.

"You okay, ma'am?" Dale asked. The woman nodded, and shifted several large leather satchels over her shoulder. "Are you travelling alone?"

"I am now," the woman said.

Dale nodded before catching Lily's gaze. "You taking her to town or am I?"

"Watch my territory, and I'll go," Lily offered, then looked to the newcomer. "I'll bring you to Greta or Jolene. Whoever I find first, I guess. I'll be back and help you bring the flock home. Louis, take Zigg."

Louis nodded, and approached to leash the dog to his belt, who whined and watched Lily take the stranger towards town. Lily unstrung her bow as they traversed a few hills and made their way to more flat ground that would be easier for the woman to traverse in her city-shoes. "I must have smelled off to the dogs," Madeline told her. "Normally they like me better."

"How long have you been out of doors?" Lily asked, but the woman didn't answer.

They approached town. A few children jumped rope, not sparing them a sideways glance, though one of the friendly neighbourhood tabby cats approached Lily, and then quickly sped off when he caught sight of Madeline. A few chickens wandered the streets and Madeline commented that the old pig sleeping on a patio was "quaint."

Lily found Tiffany and Molly and several other young women at the fountain in front of the town hall, gossiping and churning butter, though one girl was sewing something yellow. Tiffany didn't give Lily a second glance until her eyes fell upon the stranger.

"You don't get too many passersby, do you?" the woman asked.

"Not outside of shearing season," Lily said. "Tiffany, do you know where mom is? Or Jolene or Greta?"

"I don't know about mom, but the other two should be home," Tiffany said, abandoning her task to approach them. "Who's this?"

"Madeline. The dogs were barking at her at the fields."

"The fields?" another woman asked, standing. "There's no decent path that way."

"It's a long story," Madeline said. "I can't help but notice that you're referring to women. Are there no men in your village? There were youths in the field."

"Most of the men are hunting a wyvern," Molly blurted, before her cheeks reddened. "It's not a secret, is it?"

"It's fine, Molly," Lily said. "There's some men left but they're busy working." Lily gestured for the woman to follow.

"A wyvern?" Madeline asked once they were out of earshot of the others. "You mean a small dragon?"

That was close enough so Lily nodded. "It killed and ate some livestock. We think it came down from the Greenbrier Mountains, but we're not sure. Most of the men are dealing with it."

Lily spotted Amos, and when she called his name he stopped trying to fix a gate, his brow furrowed as they approached.

Lily said, "This is Madeline. She stumbled into us from the woods, and so I brought her here."

Amos opened his mouth, but it was Greta who spoke, hollering through the open window of her house. "She's a guest! Lily, bring her in at once."

For once, it seemed that the house was in order without a dozen small children running around, any and all banished outside. Once Greta assumed care of the woman, Lily started a fire in the woodstove. She went out back to pump water as the others sat the woman down around Greta's trestle table and pelted her with questions.

Lily found out by the by that yes, she was from Taralee, and had a business and had left with her husband to go east and sail across the sea—she didn't give further details, except they were attacked by bandits. She and her husband escaped at night. "I must have gotten turned around in the woods," Madeline concluded her story.

Greta nodded. "I'll mention it to my son, when they return. Wyverns and bandits. We live in strange times."

"Bandits are everywhere," said Amos. "Which ship were you to take across the sea? To Tavore or Ivancia? And your poor husband must be worried sick!"

"My husband handled the details. The ship was . . . some sort of nautical name. And our destination was the Kingdom of Ivancia. It's my husband's uncle who is ill. We made preparations in haste. I didn't bother him for details."

"What's your husband's name?" Lily asked. Madeline ignored the question, but so did everyone else. Lily went to the kitchen and found fresh scones, half of which she plated, and placed them on the table. After she pumped water and put on the kettle, Greta beamed in approval. "Water should be boiling soon," Lily said. "Do you mind if I take the other scones to the fields for the others?"

"Absolutely. And take them some cheese, do you know where to find the wheels? We'll take care of the stranger from here. Toddle along now."

Lily rolled her eyes but gathered the food as instructed. Returning to the fields the hour was later than she expected. Everyone asked her about the woman, to which Lily explained her name and that she was from Taralee, and the rest she wasn't certain. "I don't know what's for supper," she admitted as the scones and hunks of cheese were gobbled up.

It was almost warm enough to keep the flocks out overnight, but given the wyvern situation, it was deemed more prudent to round them up. Hers were all accounted for but there were several stragglers from Dale's quadrant, so Lily accompanied Louis and Tobias to find them. Lily missed Ginger; she was good-natured and clever; as soon as her father was back her first order of business was to get a sheepdog puppy. The wayward sheep were found without incident but Dale grumbled about unlocking the door for three wayward sheep. Lily didn't like the pen system; far too many sheep in one place to be comfortable; but then again, she thought the same thing about staying at Greta's.

By the time they arrived at the town hall, most folk were already eating. Not Louis' mother; Mabel was a tall woman, built naturally strong even before rearing four boys or managing a ranch, most folks who heard her speak found her intimidating. Mabel waited in the main foyer by the door, her lips thinned when her gaze locked Lily's. It was only then that Lily noticed that Louis and Tobias had wandered off around the back as opposed to following Lily through the main doors.

"Zin was teaching my son the sword today?" asked Mabel, her voice carrying over into the hall. The din noticeably quieted and a good few turned their heads in their direction.

"Yes ma'am," Lily said. "Just some technique. We hardly sparred. Zin'll teach whoever's keen, you just need to tolerate his jokes."

"I don't know why your mother lets you walk around with that thing on your hip," Mabel gestured to the sword. "It isn't proper. We're farmers and ranchers. Besides, if some knights came charging down the road, do you think they'd ever pick you if they needed help? Some slip of a girl who reads too much and doesn't have enough sense to mind the sheep instead of playing soldier in the field."

Lily felt her cheeks burn, and she was about to let Mabel have it when Sylvia spoke up. "In the unlikely event that wyvern returns, a sword is better than her hand. Besides, weapons training will teach Louis some discipline."

"Louis is too young!" Mabel sputtered. Lily looked around the woman; Louis and Tobias were loading up two plates apiece before sneaking back the way they came. "Besides, that Zin Booey is a strange duck. I'd think you were smart enough to start distancing yourself from him —his swashbuckling nonsense isn't going to bring in the shearing or land you a husband now, will it? Ah well—go get supper while it's still hot."

Lily was tempted to not eat in protest, but Mabel was already off nattering at someone else. Lily wasn't particularly hungry given the snack from Zin, but looked around; people were back at their conversations now that the excitement of watching her get chewed out had passed.

Glancing about she spotted Madeline in someone else's clothes, the woollen skirt not so fine as the velvet dress she'd arrived wearing, but she looked proper, her hair styled into a chignon. Surrounded by people, Madeline appeared to be the guest of honour.

Lily plated corn bread, roasted root vegetables, and herb-roasted chicken, glancing up when Tobias snuck back in to grab dessert but said nothing before going back out the door. There was no room for her at the table with the others her age, so she snagged a seat next to

Jasper and his family. Jasper was their town blacksmith, about a decade younger than her parents.

"How goes the my mother's order?" she asked.

"You're the tenth person to ask me this hour," Jasper muttered. His wife Amber gave him a look so he softened. "I'm tired of being asked. My apprentices are out with your father instead of giving me a hand. Weighted nets are not difficult but time consuming."

"Can I help in the evenings?" Lily asked.

He let out a guffaw. His wife Amber was no taller than Lily was, and she helped Jasper in the shop plenty. "I think your talents lie elsewhere. Have you given any more thought to selling that sword? I could make you something a little more your size."

"It was a gift," Lily said. "If I get you the metal would you make me another blade?"

Jasper nodded. "Speak to me—not anyone else—before you go trotting off to get material." The blacksmith gestured towards Madeline. "Did you bring us trouble or a blessing this time?"

"I don't know," Lily admitted. "We're not the first one that wyrm stole from, I just happened to see it."

"Worm?" asked one of the girls, scrunching her nose.

"Not all hunters agree, but most journals I've read classify them as part of the dragon family—" Lily began.

"A fat lot of good knowing that did her," Amber interrupted, looking to her children. "Your father is making spears and weighted nets, Elias and the others will bring the beast down." Lily didn't feel welcome; she quickly finished her meal and excused herself, sitting at the main fireplace and pulling out her mandolin and finger plucking. She practiced the chorus she was working on.

"Lily, as much as we appreciate your idle strumming, can you play something good?" Jolene called over.

"Let her alone," Amos said. "Warm up girl, I'll join you shortly."

"Don't you need to warm up, granddad?" asked a dark-haired youth named Benny.

"I don't need the practice," Amos informed him.

I'll work on this tomorrow, Lily decided, and started to play one of the livelier songs people called out. Several of the children started to sing along, *Dew and Barley* and *Around the Oaken Tree*. She wasn't so good at sadder songs, such as *A Ballad for Cornfell*, or *Indigo Woods*, though the older folk seemed to like them. She started *Old Man on the Mountain* and Amos piped up to wait, stopped carousing and took up his fiddle and one of the young mothers picked up a hand drum. Lily switched back and forth from melody to harmony depending on what Amos directed, singing mostly backup vocals. Lily didn't mind; several of the local women had beautiful and even powerful voices she couldn't compete with.

She was enjoying herself before suddenly voices rose near the front of the hall. From where she perched she couldn't see, but was surprised when Seth arrived with Rhett. Seth looked sheepish, and Rhett marched him to their mother. "What's wrong?" Jolene asked Rhett.

"Young Seth here doesn't know how to handle directions," Rhett said. "You can explain it to your mother in private, boy. Don't spoil a good supper."

"Someone get Rhett a plate," Jolene said as Sylvia directed Seth to speak with her off to the side.

No one requested music anymore, though Lily did her best to try and take some heat off Seth with more popular songs. Rhett stayed long enough only to eat and converse briefly with his family before he set back out, with a handful of letters to warn the hunters of bandits and to be on the lookout for Madeline's husband.

"I thought you said you weren't a musician," Madeline said to Lily when the band finished—Amos cited his hands were sore, but at least Lily didn't have to help with dishes.

"Not like from the city," Lily said, placing her mandolin down near the fire. "My dad's better than me. Where are you staying?"

"Constance's home. Thank you for bringing me here," Madeline said. "I wasn't sure what to expect."

Constance was the wealthiest widow in town and had a large house. It made sense to treat an outsider well. "I'll take you to Taralee myself if I can." Lily then remembered her brother was back. He could pull his weight, take over her job in the fields and Lily could escort Madeline to either Taralee or Port Redmaw. "I'll ask my mother if I can take you tomorrow the the next day."

"Do you ever write your own songs?"

Lily felt taken aback. "Sometimes, but they always sound so derivative and flat. Not like when I hear bards and the like in Taralee."

"I might be able to teach you something," Madeline said and stood, gesturing for her to follow. "There's an old piano just over there."

Lily picked up her mandolin and followed after Madeline. "It's kind of broken."

"It'll work," the woman told her, though seemed unamused when she ran a finger over the accumulated dust on top. Lily didn't understand why the elders didn't fix the piano or be rid of it. Madeline gestured, and Lily grabbed a chair, Madeline sat on the bench. "Just listen while I play."

Lily nodded, and closed her eyes while the woman began the song. For the most part, people had cleared out or were still chatting. She listened to the song; more regal than the usual jigs and reels, but began to plunk along. The woman began to play faster, Lily was tempted to tell her to slow down, but it was almost like there was a strange pulse in the air. Lily's fingers began to move like she'd known this song forever, that she'd only forgotten. The woman played faster and faster, but she somehow managed to keep up with it.

"You are a fast learner," Madeline said, stopping. Lily felt light headed. Where did that come from? She'd never been able to hear a song once and play it. Her mother called; it was time to head out.

"Not much soul but, that's to be expected. Here, look this over tonight." Madeline pressed several sheets of music into Lily's hands. "This piano needs more than tuning," she muttered, straightening her skirt.

Lily nodded, bid her good evening, and joined her mother and brother. Tiffany was already off for the evening. "What happened?" Lily asked Seth.

"Never you mind," Sylvia told Lily. "I'd appreciate it if you both were more like Tiffany—she's not going out of her way to embarrass me."

"How have I embarrassed you?" Lily sputtered.

"I'll have Mabel at my side for every crooked stitch. You know how the town feels about Zin Booey."

"What happened?" Seth asked.

"Louis joined me for my training session this afternoon."

Seth snickered. "Mom, you shouldn't care what Mabel or anyone else thinks of Zin."

"I've got to keep them trusting in my judgement until your father deals with the wyvern," Sylvia said.

Lily said nothing while Seth protested that it wasn't his fault. He saw an opportunity and took it. "We shouldn't be having this conversation at all," Seth said. "We should be with dad out there. Most folk aren't hunters beyond a buck or a wild boar."

"We're protecting this village," Sylvia informed them. "Your father can think better when he doesn't have to worry about you. You both know your duty."

"Protecting it from what? That stranger who staggered into town? What possible harm could she cause?" Seth demanded. To their mutual disgust, they were made to share a room in the attic. It was away from the others, but it was a bit draughty.

Lily couldn't sleep, so lighting a candle she glanced over Madeline's music. She hummed, tapping her fingers to try to imagine what it could sound like on her mandolin or bouzouki. The second sheet had a different song and when she hummed it she felt strange, not like before, but all at once her eyes started to water and her throat ached, and suddenly the page burst into ash in her hands. Lily yelped and fell backwards, eyes watering.

"Are you okay?" Seth asked, bolting upright. He poked at the ash. "You hurt?"

"No," Lily said, shaking her head and dusting herself off. "It just . . . exploded."

"Please don't burn the house down while I'm in it," Seth said, leaning back into his pile of blankets. He was unconscious again in a few moments. The attic had a sloped roof and Lily had to stoop, but she went to the wash basin and cleaned her face. There was no smell; she didn't set it on fire . . .

She picked up the remnant pages. Nothing amiss or burst into ash, but they felt dirtier than they had. She gathered up the sheets and put them away.

She didn't feel any better once the papers were out of sight, the strange song played over and over again in her head; she got the impression of dancers swaying to the beat, faceless on a stage before an audience of applauding dolls. *What is going on?* Her heart raced and she tried to think of another song, to get that one out of her head. But it thundered back, harder. She had no where to pace, no where to go other than back to bed.

When at last sleep took her Lily felt heavy and dark, dreamless and hollow. She woke with a cold nose and someone shaking her shoulder. "Lily?" her mother asked. "Are you all right?"

"Mum?" Lily asked. Lily felt a strange pressure behind her eyes.

"Seth couldn't wake you. He's already had his omelette and is on his way to the fields." Sylvia was already descending the ladder. Lily sat up; black spots danced in front of her eyes. "Hurry up."

"My head hurts," Lily called.

"Don't think you can play sick just because your brother is back," Sylvia called back. "Get a move on or you're not going to market after shearing." Her mother made a tonic that helped, but warm breakfast was already eaten and dishes washed, so Lily was handed toast on her way out the door.

By the time she arrived at the field, the others had already driven the sheep. Her headache was nearly gone and she felt better in the fresh air. Seth stole the mandolin sometime before lunch, making up his own lyrics to a song when Zin arrived, this time with a sandwich for Louis as well.

"Your mother doesn't approve, Louis," Seth said.

"I know," Louis said with a mischievous look in his eyes. "Last I checked, that's Lily's problem."

Another two boys came over, and Lily found herself doing their jobs while Zin instructed, but she didn't mind; though several of the lambs wandered off a little ways she had Zigg on them. She was only summoned towards the end they all needed to face her, but before they could square off, the boys more or less stopped emulating Zin's form and started wailing on one another. Seth, the oldest, was the worst.

"There's a reason I prefer teaching girls," Zin snapped at the lot of them. "Louis, you need to work on your running. Tobias, good show but we'll work on your nerves. Seth, you need squats and lunges, remember no one likes skinny calves." He clicked on the reins and the goats began to carry him away on his chariot.

"They're not that bad," Seth grumbled, but looked over his backside.

"Let's eat the snacks he brought," Louis said, and they descended upon the apricot bars. When they were summoned for the evening meal, the boys were happier than the other shepherds who were eager to drive the flock back to town.

Thankfully, Mabel was dealing with the shenanigans of one of Louis' younger brothers and Lily managed to make it to the potluck with all sheep, goats, and others accounted for; another family of farmers had joined them by then. Lily wasn't sure where they were going to put their animals; they'd have to start using the outlying barns.

Mutton sausages and herb-roasted goat with sweet peppers as well as buttered cabbage made up the main dishes, with fruit cobblers for dessert. Lily thought she'd hate to go back to the farm because she was enjoying the variety. One could say many negative things about Stagmil, but not concerning their hospitality or the quality of their meals. Lily managed to snag a seat at the table with Dale and Brigid.

"You were in town today?" Lily asked Brigid, who nodded. Tiffany and Molly joined them "Any news of the stranger?"

"Madeline? She used to be a performer. A dancer, I think," Brigid said. She was tall but not as tall as Tiffany, with dark blonde hair. Growing up, people often called her the pretty-one of their friend group though Lily was closer with another girl who'd gone to apprentice in Taralee at eleven. Both Brigid and Dale were chosen to apprentice as well, Brigid chose to return to Stagmil, citing she found the city too busy. "She's rather vague on details."

"Has anyone take her back to Taralee?" Lily asked. Brigid shook her head. "I'll ask my mom if I can do it tomorrow."

Seth pulled up a chair and forced Lily to move over, jamming out his elbows. "Enough boring talk. Lily and Tiffany, I need you to talk mom into letting me deliver Jasper's order to dad."

Tiffany arched an eyebrow at Lily before she looked at her twin. "Who was going to deliver it?" she asked.

"You got sent home because you couldn't follow directions," Dale laughed at Seth. "They'll send Lily out before they send you."

"I think that's the plan," Seth admitted. "Lily, tell them you don't wanna go and I'm more than willing . . . " Lily had her mouth full, but rolled her eyes and listened to her sister say he was sent home for a reason, her brother counter how it wasn't his fault. He was scouting like he should, but came up on the wyvern. It was wounded, and some of the scales were missing. "I could have made the shot. I just needed to get a little closer. Then that stupid idiot Victor shouted—"

"How close are we talking about?" Tiffany asked with a laugh. "O Mighty Hunter with the lousy shot."

Seth sailed some cabbage across the table, and got it in Tiffany's raven tresses. "Looks like my aim is perfect."

Tiffany picked up her mug and threw the water in Seth's face. Lily grabbed her brother's arm when he went to throw his dinner roll and Dale grabbed Tiffany. "Calm down," Lily told her brother. "Tiffany, that was uncalled for."

"He got cabbage *in my hair*."

Molly looked uncomfortable while Brigid was saying soothing words to Tiffany. Lily's reprieve was getting the dinner roll in her face instead. Jolene squawked. "Stop rough housing at once."

Lily stared her brother down into a sit while Tiffany and Brigid went off together. Thankfully, no one else was saying anything because

Madeline was enthralling the small children with a little puppet show. Molly was already lost in it, as opposed to going with Tiffany and Brigid. Dale sat back down and gave Seth the stink eye.

"Grow up."

"You'd have punched my lights out if I had gotten it in precious Brigid's hair," Seth snapped, drying off his face with his sleeve.

"You're right—then after I would have picked you up and thrown you outside with the pigs where you belong. No wonder your father sent you home for us to babysit."

Seth stormed off. Lily was glad for the puppet show. Knowing Louis and a few of the other boys, they were waiting for an excuse to start a food fight. She was certain she'd hear about it from her mother later.

Lily finished her supper in silence, Molly watching the show, captivated.

Madeline had used a few ragdolls for her puppets. Small children clapped, wanting more stories. "Oh, if only I had good puppets. The stories I'd weave," Madeline said with a laugh.

Lily tuned her mandolin now that she'd gotten it back from Seth, but instead of working on the chorus or the verse, started to hum. Her mother interrupted her thoughts. "Come help me teach numbers."

"Can't Tiffany or Seth do it?" Lily asked.

"No. And when we're done, you should turn in early. You weren't feeling well this morning."

"Tomorrow's supposed to be my free day."

"We'll discuss it," Sylva said. "Right now, I don't think anyone's getting a day off."

She instructed as her mother asked. She didn't see the point, the children were less enthused about it than she was. Madeline came over while Benny struggled with some basic equations. He could do it, he was trying to convince his mother otherwise. "Did you have a chance to look over the music I gave you?"

"Yes . . . but something odd happened."

"Odd?" the woman asked, smiling at Sylvia.

Lily stammered. "Yeah . . . it seemed familiar I learned it quickly. Uh . . ."

"How modest," Madeline said. "I see you're busy, I look forward to hearing you play tomorrow. You practice music in the field, correct?"

"When I can." There was plenty of downtime watching the sheep, but that didn't mean she could just sit around strumming while everyone else tended to the herd. Besides, Seth had the mandolin and she didn't much feel like stealing it back. "Actually, I was thinking I could take you back to Taralee tomorrow. Do you know how to ride?"

Madeline nodded. "The others are stretched quite thin, they said they'd find an escort in a day or two. If you'll excuse me." She left and Lily felt odd, and that same song that burned her eyes came rushing back. Her head started to ache, and she felt . . . strange. Like she was too light, and something inside of her wanted to burst.

"Lily, are you all right?" Sylvia asked.

"Just a headache," Lily said.

Her mother frowned. "I don't know what gopher-dodging foolishness you've gotten yourself into," she said, "but whatever it is, be done with it."

"Tomorrow's my free day," Lily said. "Let me take Madeline to Taralee."

"She can wait another day or so."

Sleep came easy that night. Again Lily dreamed, but could not recall anything but the song.

The next day, Lily didn't get a day off per se, but the following day Seth was given Lily's charge in the field. Lily was assigned helping prepare the day's meals, peeling carrots and, when those were done, potatoes. She snuck out of the house before lunch, knowing another thankless task awaited her. Seth had the mandolin; she figured she could sneak off towards the house and get her bouzouki and perhaps something good to read besides checking on the chickens and the garden, but got sidetracked by one of the local mothers.

"You're not doing anything? Excellent!" she said. "I just need you to watch the kids for just a minute."

"Actually . . ." Lily began, but the woman rushed off. The children weren't super young, but Lily did as she was told. She and her siblings were often out at that age, but then again, some of them weren't from here. Of course the women took more than a minute, and Lily was managing a nose-bleed when finally an adult addressed her.

"There you are," Zin said. "You want to come to the field this afternoon for a lesson with the boys?"

"If I don't get tasked with anything else," Lily said. "What do you think of them?"

"Louis is a natural, but you'll have to wait for him to catch up. Tobias needs more confidence. If only I could siphon some from your brother."

"Tell me about it," she agreed, inspecting the child who's nose seemed to have stopped. "I'd like to take Madeline to Taralee, but I might be off to deliver supplies, if Seth doesn't weasel his way into a second chance. They might need me to wipe a snotty nose."

"Delivering supplies is so much more important than minding children," Zin snorted back. "Your problem, Lily, is that you don't appreciate your town."

"I do!" she protested. "It's just that . . ."

"Well?"

"My parents came here to escape. Nobody means to end up in a place like Stagmil. Look at you," she said. "One day I'll figure out why you're here, but it's not for the company."

He snorted, then sat down. "I don't know which of the rumours you're referring to. I'm rather fond of the one where I'm hiding from the seven women I married in a single day. Could you imagine the timing on seven ceremonies and my guests not saying *anything*?"

"So it's just the five, then?"

Zin gave her a wheezing laugh. "There's nothing wrong with a simple life where they get to decide if they want to raise sheep or pigs. You're worried that adventure won't come knocking. That was your chance, with the wyvern. Oh, to think life is over at seventeen!" Zin laughed. "When you have a chance, speak with Molly, she needs a friend."

"What does she need me for when she has Tiffany?" Lily frowned, and heard a kit bark. Boscoe. What was he . . . one of the boys threw a rock at him. The little kit yipped, Lily ran over and grabbed the boy's arm. "Don't do that."

"Foxes are vermin, they steal chickens," he said.

"If the wolves stay away from our sheep, we don't hurt them," Lily said. The little kit scampered off. "He's just a baby."

"He'll be trouble later," one of the girls told Lily matter-of-factly.

"So will all of you given enough time," Zin said, clapping his hands. "All right, children, enough free range play. Time for a structured learning environment."

Three

Zin had the children doing push-ups, stretching, and had them run a sort of gauntlet around the square, a series of hops and jumps, which wasn't hard but once they mastered it the children raced the course, in addition to see who could jump the furthest. The woman who'd tasked her to watch them returned with a basket of mending, and she and her sister shared a laugh at the children seeing who could do most of a given exercise.

Lily was not permitted to join in the athletics. Instead she was assigned to sit cross-legged and breathe on the side of the fountain, to which Dulcie, passing by, took interest. "What are you doing, girl?"

Lily opened her mouth but Zin answered. "I'm teaching her to control her breathing."

"I suspect she knows by now," Dulcie told Zin. She was Constance's youngest daughter, Lily knew her better back when Constance was teaching her the piano, Lily didn't care for it as much as the mandolin so she only studied it for a two years. "Do come by for supper if you like, Zin. We do worry about you off on your own, especially with that monster at large."

"World's filled with monsters besides the scaley kinds. I get my fill of company when I'm out and about," Zin said. Lily peeked slightly. "I'm paying attention over here."

"This hardly seems like a practical exercise," Dulcie said.

"So did lifting all the rocks when she was younger. And now she can lift bigger rocks." Lily's unintentional giggle got her a poke in the back.

"Focus, senior apprentice. When you feel dread and panic, you focus on your breath. Master yourself before you take on the world. Understood? Miss Aurora, is that a frog in your apron pocket?"

"It's a toad," Rory clarified. Her brother tried to swipe it and the toad jumped free. One of the girls and two of the boys stopped their push ups to chase after it and laughed as it jumped into the fountain.

"Lily, I suspect you can breathe and help set up the hall for dinner," Dulcie said. "With this weather they'll be driving the sheep back early, let's get a move on."

"I'm not dismissed."

"She's right," Zin said, waited about three seconds then said, "*Now* you're dismissed. Go help and be cheerful about it." Before Lily could protest, Zin turned on his heel to help break up the fight over who got to hold the poor toad. "Who wants to learn shield formations?"

"Me me me me!" the children chorused and hopped, probably not knowing what Zin meant.

"You know you're not being a good influence," Dulcie said to Lily, gesturing at the children.

"It's just exercise and some self-discipline."

Dulcie's eyes widened when she glanced back to the fountain. Lily followed her gaze; Zin had them processing in a wall; she wondered how he knew to bring enough shields for everyone. "Wonderful. As for you, go make yourself useful for once."

Lily was tempted to take off once Dulcie's back was turned, but spotted Molly with Tiffany. Tiffany was chatting with the usual gaggle of gossipers, Molly seemed quiet. Lily entered the hall and moved tables and chairs, putting out dishes and the like.

Thunder rolled in the distance, and she heard several women argue as to whether or not they should just eat at personal residences on days such as that one. She wondered how her father and the other hunters faired in the damp. She managed to sneak a note to Molly, who blanched when Lily gestured. They met at one of the closets where Lily was pretending to look for cleaning supplies.

"It's not what you think," Molly blurted.

"I don't know what's going on, but Zin Booey told me to talk to you. Is there something you don't want to talk to your mother or Tiffany about?"

"I can't talk to them!" Molly said weakly. She bunched her fists. "Oh, what would you know?"

"Try me," Lily said. "Seth says I'm a know-it-all, I can only imagine what Tiffany says."

"You can't tell Tiffany," Molly said. "Or anyone else. You can't let my mother know I spoke to you."

Lily nodded. "You have my word."

"My parents want to marry me to some stranger," Molly said quietly.

She wasn't expecting that. Then again, Molly was pretty, and . . . well, she was sixteen; barely. "I'm so sorry."

"I shouldn't have said anything. Forget I told you."

"Have you told anyone else?" Lily asked.

"No," Molly said, shaking her head. "And they can't know. I burned the letter. But they're coming here in a month. What am I supposed to do?" Molly's voice was getting progressively louder; Lily gestured to be quiet.

"I don't know. What if we were to convince them you had another beau?"

"Lily, they want the money."

Lily wasn't sure what else to say. "Let me think."

"Yeah, okay," Molly said, bobbing her head. "Lily, what if he's old? What if he has bad breath?"

"Molly, your parents will probably let you meet him. If that's the case, we'll just have to convince him to chase after Tiffany or something."

"What if they don't let me meet him?" Molly asked. She looked at Lily. "People are looking at us."

Let them look. What they didn't want was anyone coming to ask questions. "I have some money at the house but I have more in savings in Taralee. After shearing, it should be enough to help you move out and get a job. I have friends who are apprentices, we'll know someone, so it's not like you'd be with strangers."

"You'd do that for me?" Molly asked.

"I'd like to pretend someone would help me if I needed it," Lily said. "Just . . . don't do anything rash. My mom can write you a reference, she trained as a lore master in Taralee. I can't leave until my dad gets back, but if Seth takes Madeline to Taralee I can give him letters explaining the situation."

Molly nodded. "Just promise you won't say anything."

"I promise." Lily didn't want to sit with the others, and even though dinner was a delicious shepherd's pie, she found that her stomach was curdled. What if her parents tried to pull the same stunt on her? *I need to talk to Zin.* She frowned, thinking he would just tell her to tell Molly to be as undesirable as possible in a comical way. *Besides*, Zin would say, half-joking, *your parents would have to pay someone to take you off their hands.*

For once she was glad she was ignored and, retrieving the mandolin from her brother she took her place by the fire. "Play *The Ram and the Eagle*," said one of the women, and Lily began the familiar tune that usually inspired dancing. Her mother shot her a look—mothers were trying to get their children to finish their food, but more than one of them said, "You can't go until you're done your supper." So most quickly gobbled down their supper.

After several songs by Lily and Amos, Madeline performed a story with shadows and another with rag dolls. To her surprise, Zin showed up after the meal. The village women offered to make him up a plate, but he declined.

"What are you doing here?" Lily asked.

"Oh, just making sure things are not out of the ordinary," Zin told her. "You seem a bit off."

"Why hellooooo Zin," said Mabel. "I didn't think you were coming. Are you doing well?"

"Well as I can be," Zin said, giving her a charming smile. "I want to speak to my apprentice," he pulled Lily to the side. "Whatever happens stay out of the way."

"What's going on?"

"Details forthcoming," Zin said. "Now if you'll excuse me, I need to lay on some charm."

As fun as it was to watch folk pretend to like one another more than they did, Lily spotted Madeline's leather satchels, which were open. Curious, Lily edged towards them while she watched that the woman was still heavily involved in a game of cards, now, with the village women. There were plenty of crossbars and strings in the second bag—a lot, really, and a leather bound journal in the first. She jumped when Tiffany said, "Didn't mother tell you it's rude to snoop?"

"I wasn't," Lily stammered. It was then she realized that Madeline was walking towards them. The children were playing with her make-shift puppets.

"I caught my sister snooping," Tiffany said to Madeline when she was closer, loud enough so anyone who wanted to could hear.

"I wasn't," Lily insisted again.

"You might like these," Madeline said, going through another bag. Tiffany ogled the beautiful face mask. Exaggerated features of a chubby-cheeked woman with bee-stung round lips. The next she pulled out was some sort of grotesque warrior with his tongue jutting out.

"These are real theatre masks," Tiffany said, looking another over. In addition to the normal eye slits, it had several glass black eyes racing up the forehead; Lily found it strangely alluring and feminine and . . . *familiar*.

"Of course," the woman said, donning the woman's face. "In this, I am the lovely young courtesan, off to see her forbidden lover." Her voice sweet and airy, she made grand sweeping gestures. The woman removed it, and gracefully replaced it with was that of a handsome young man with prominent chin and nose. "Where are you, my love? You said you would meet me?" Madeline stood taller, her shoulders seemingly more broad. She switched back again to the chubby-cheeked mask. Her composure changed to something meek and demure. "Oh, my shining star! You know that if the prince catches you, you'll be executed!"

Several of small children giggled. Madeline stopped her performance. "Perhaps something a little more appropriate?" She went through her satchel, and handed Tiffany another beautiful face, that of a painted sad clown, whereas she gave Lily an evil old hag with an exaggerated nose.

Tiffany twirled. "I do hope nothing happens to me on this fine sunny day—oh Lily stop being a prude."

It didn't smell bad, but looking through the eye slits obscured her vision. It didn't fit her face particularly well.

"That one needs to be locked in place so it doesn't fall," Madeline said. Lily backed off when the woman went to adjust it. "I don't bite," Madeline said, and Lily let her fasten it so that stayed put. She whispered something in Lily's ear and it was like a bolt shot through Lily.

She bent low and a voice that wasn't her own spoke out."Who dares come to me on a night such as this?" she hissed, hunched over, reaching out with her hand, her fingers seemingly longer and twisted. She tried to stop herself, but something compelled her.

"You're not outperforming me," Tiffany said, and suddenly her sister's voice became low and simpering. "You are the hag of the woods. I'm told you can give me a face to force any man to fall desperately in love."

"Have you not seen my own complexion, fool?" Lily boomed. The children *ooh'd* and their parents stopped their card games and sewing to gander. "'Tis better to be feared than loved."

"My true love will wed another. Please, make him love me and only me."

"Fool! Forced love is not any sort of real love; but if you simply must have him I will give you something to make him your obedient slave. Keep your face and give him this."

Lily didn't know it, but one of the boys, Louis, was goaded into putting on the mask of the handsome young man that Madeline wore a moment before. Lily mimed giving Tiffany an elixir. "Make him drink it, and then just whistle and he'll come running."

"Oh thank you, crone!"

Lily exited the makeshift stage left and Tiffany mimicked running and came across to Louis, who was miming chopping wood. "I ask again, why did you chose my sister over me?" Tiffany crooned, back of her hand to her forehead, laying it on thick.

"For you are both fair of face, but she is kind of heart. You will find another."

"I will never love another!"

Lily reached for the mask. Her arms—her body—was not her own. She moved in obedience to the play, but the minute she thought of ripping the mask off, her fingers became numb and unresponsive. She wanted to scream at the folk watching to help her.

At last the young man accepted a drink from his spurned lover. "What poison!" Louis reached to heaven, clutching at his throat he collapsed motionless.

"Witch!" Tiffany wailed, her crying figure all the more tragic. "I asked for him to love me!"

Lily came back when she wasn't ready. "Behold! I have given you what you desire. He'll love you unconditionally."

The face of the handsome man fell and beneath that was that of a dog. The children laughed as Louis raced around on all fours. "Bow wow! Woof woof! Awwoooo!"

"All you need to get him to come running is whistle! Aahahahahah!" Lily cackled and left the wailing clown to her fate. The children laughed and cheered, and Lily found that she could reach for the mask, but couldn't get it off; her fingers were shaking and clumsy.

"I want to be in the next one," said Molly. "What other masks have you got?"

"Did the three of you rehearse that?" Zin asked as Tiffany took off her mask, laughing and bowing to the applause of the crowd. Louis was still acting like a puppy before the bouncing children.

"Let me give you a hand," Madeline said to Lily, helping her get the mask off. Madeline gave her a coy smile once she removed it. But Lily went on touching her nose and cheeks, making sure she hadn't really taken on the form of the grotesque hag. It seemed that Tiffany and Louis had enjoyed themselves, but one of the children had stolen the mask Louis had worn and was barking at his mother.

"Lily, that music I asked you to learn," Madeline said suddenly. "How's it coming?"

Lily bolted for the door, and barely stopped to grab her cloak. She didn't run to Greta's house, and despite the wax on her cloak she was drenched by the time she got to her homestead. There was a slight layer of dust on the window sills and table, but the house was as it should have been. She raced to her room and the mirror. Normal skin. Normal. Ordinary.

But something was lingering, something she couldn't touch but was present. And in the back of her mind, that music played over and over again. Where was it? The one page burned, the rest was back at the attic. She wanted it burned, for real this time. She knew she'd catch it from her mother, later, for leaving the way she did, but she didn't care. The rains really began to come down, so she lit a fire, and dried herself and changed her clothes and put up the soaking ones to dry.

Four

Seth thought the play was dumb but the moral was funny. If he was forced to be a dog, he'd hardly be obedient. The first thing he'd do was dig up the garden of the people who cursed him, then he would likely seek vengeance on people he didn't care for; howling at all hours and pooping on their front step. He wondered if he was allowed to keep his human intelligence as he followed his mother back to the house.

Happy to be home, if he couldn't be out hunting he might as well be in his own bed and the woods around his house were better to roam besides. "We know you're here, Lil'. Your boots are at the door," Seth hollered before ascending the stairs while his mother checked his sister's bedroom.

Lily looked like she'd fallen asleep reading in the study. Lily was usually a light sleeper, but he needed to shake her shoulder. "What time is it?" Lily asked, feeling her face. She'd been doing that a lot over the past day or so.

Seth got out of the way as their mother rushed to her, looking her over in concern before her expression hardened. "What got into you?"

"I . . . I needed to check on something here," Lily lied.

"Get what you need and we'll return to town once the rains let up," Sylvia said. "Seth, go check on the chickens." He'd just wrenched off his soggy socks.

"I don't want to go back to town," Lily said.

"Me either," Seth agreed. "I can do chores around here before we go back to the fields in the morning."

"It's not the pair of you who need saving. The townsfolk are afraid," Sylvia informed them, directing her gaze at Lily. "After Seth got sent back here, I thought you would have the sense not to embarrass us."

"Why are you so worried about what those idiots in town think?" Lily demanded. Seth was taken aback by Lily's tone.

"Do not speak about them that way," Sylvia said.

"Why? So they can be nice to my face but talk behind my back?" "Don't get ahead of yourself, Lily, no one really thinks about you at all—" Seth started.

"Seth, be quiet," Sylvia said.

Seth took it as a dismissal, but after ducking into his room to retrieve dry socks, waited in the hall just outside the study for the two of them to have it out.

"That's how they are with Zin. You think we're really any different?"

"It's not all of them. It's a handful of busybodies. And what they think doesn't matter. Lily, I can't do this on my own."

"Do what? The work they don't want to do and push on me?" Lily asked. "Hurry up, grow up, do as you're told: pump out a bunch of kids so I can slough them off on some other teen girl you'll bully into the same thing?"

"Lily—"

"I didn't know it was a wyvern. I kept my cool. I deserved to go," Lily said.

"It's not about what you deserve," Sylvia said. "What's important is helping our neighbours, regardless of whether or not you think they deserve it. You can hunt all summer long after shearing season."

"No. I'm going to be stuck here cleaning up someone else's mess. Someone's going to need help shearing, someone's lamb will be sick, someone always needs something but no one cares what I need. Maybe you and dad are happy to live this way but I'm not."

"This is a good, honest life," Sylvia said. "You know why we gave up hunting. People ask more and more until you're in a position where you're in too deep. You have it so much better than so many others . . ."

"So that makes it all okay? Someone else out there has it worse than me, and so I have to live someone else's life? I'm not you or dad. I'm not the twins, or a *natural* like Louis whatever that means."

"I know this isn't enough for you. This wasn't enough for me growing up, either," Sylvia said. "The odds of that wyvern coming back here are slim, but not zero. I said I'd look after their families. Your father and the other hunters can focus knowing their loved ones are safe."

"I didn't give my word."

"This is our home, Lily. Is getting what you want worth someone's life?"

"What's my life worth?"

The silence that followed was thick. "We'll talk after shearing season. For now, you will help the people here. Don't be angry with them; they haven't had the same opportunities as you. I know they can be . . . short sighted and shallow. But you did bring it on yourself, training with Zin."

"Zin's the only one who cared that I never made apprentice." Was Lily crying? Her voice was quivering.

"You wouldn't have been happy as a cooper," Sylvia said. "One day you'll appreciate unanswered prayers. Come here. I love you. No matter what you do nothing will ever change that. I know you feel like you got left behind, but you need to look at the good and be grateful as opposed to cherry-picking the best out of everyone else's life."

"I'm not. Mom, something weird happened during the play."

"You're just tired," Sylvia said. "We'll stay here the night, we'll tell everyone you were feeling a little unwell. Go to bed."

"I'm not a child!"

"I'll still be your mother when you're my age. I know how hard you're working. Get some rest. I'll put the book back. If you can't sleep with that headache, drink some tonic."

Lily left the study and didn't notice Seth. She went to the kitchen to stoke the fire, though he'd make it a good blazing hot one; hers were always far too conservative. He glanced at his mother, who was frowning, reading the book Lily had been. He couldn't see the title, but he moved on before Sylvia caught him. Lily was outside, checking on the chickens and gathering eggs. She didn't say anything when she caught his gaze as she approached the house.

"I was just going to do that." Lily didn't answer, and it wasn't raining enough to hide the tear-stains on her face. Seth took the basket from her as she passed to go to the kitchen, then looked up the stairs. Their mother was predictable—she knew most of his tricks, but Sylvia could get lost in a book worse than anyone else. "They didn't want you on the hunt because dad would have been worried the whole time. That's why they sent me home."

"Sure."

"You looked scared before. Now you look sad. None of us like sitting around waiting for dad and the others to take out the wyvern, but dad's the best person for the job."

"I know."

"So stop moping."

"Moping?" Lily demanded, nostrils flaring. "You threw away an opportunity I never had. Don't lecture me."

"Come on. Do you really think dad or the others would let us do more than assist?"

"What's it matter what I say?" Lily asked, finishing tidying up and starting towards her bedroom. She paused. "I'd give anything for someone to listen to me for once. Goodnight, Seth."

She was a little too obedient and dutiful, but he didn't want to tell her that right now. Not with his mother in a mood, and the fire was nice and toasty. Those eggs would make a tasty omelette . . .

Securing dried chives and morels, Seth raided one of the cheese wheels. He cracked open a jar of last year's sundried tomatoes and was appreciating his fine culinary skills when his mother caught him. "I told you to *gather* eggs!"

"And they're dee-licious," he said.

~*~

Seth slept in and Lily had to wake him after she'd already fed the chickens. Sylvia dismissed them after they tended the garden. The one benefit to staying in town was that they didn't have to walk nearly as far, but the fields were getting awfully crowded around the town, no doubt the revelries of defeating the wyvern would be met by bickering when the wrong sheep mated or imagined insults about which flock got to graze in whose fields.

"So what spooked you?" Seth asked once they were a few minutes down the winding path. "You looked like you saw a ghost last night."

"I wasn't in control of my own body," Lily said. He looked at her sceptically, but Lily was undeterred. "I doubt Louis knew the play, either."

"I'm sure he got the gist of it," Seth said.

"Does that woman's story make sense to you? Why would she be out here but have that stuff? Why isn't she worried about her husband?"

Now that he thought about it, it did seem odd. "Why don't you ask her?" Seth asked. They made it to the pens before the driving. The paths and fields were wet but they decided that they'd still let them out, in spite of the cloudy weather. Zigg raced out to meet them, and Lily gave him a hard boiled egg. Seth wondered what other treats she had, but called the furthest quadrant; he liked being away from prying eyes, so he could find an excuse to slip into the backwoods. They'd patrol and move around anyway, though in truth the dogs did most of the work. Normally he'd just lay in the grass and catch an early morning nap, but it was damp and he needed to double back and swipe Lily's blanket after he made a fire to poke at.

The rains never let up enough for him to play cards with the others. He was bored watching Lily try to correct a renegade ram lamb who kept picking fights with a tree. Seth thumbed through the books their mother had packed them before when lunch arrived; thankfully it involved warm soup which chased away the damp chill.

The winds picked up by early afternoon, light showers threatening real rain. They moved the sheep back to the pens early. It was decided there would be no large banquet in the hall; instead everyone retreated to their homes, Seth and Lily staying at the barns until one of the ewes delivered, and Seth was glad for an excuse to stay the night with Louis and Tobias and be out of that attic. They left for supper, but Sylvia was absent so Seth and Lily made awkward conversation with Greta's family. "Where is your mother?" asked one of Greta's daughters.

"She's probably doing work back at the house," Lily offered. "I know she's been going back there to take care of the chickens and tend the garden."

"Or enjoying a nice rainy day to read," Seth said. That's what Lily would have done if him and Elias were around to muck out the stalls. Not that he minded; on cooler days there tended to be more baking.

"I hope to see another performance," one of Greta's grandkids said to Lily. "Tiffany's more of a witch than you."

Lily gave a muted smile. "I think I prefer playing music."

"Did you bring your mandolin?" Greta asked. Lily shook her head. Last Seth checked, he'd left it back at the house. He'd make an excuse to go get it and sleep in his own bed tomorrow. "Well, bring it tomorrow. You can give my Polly a music lesson. Music is the highest of all the arts, I think."

"Chicka-dee-dee-dee-dee," little Polly crowed.

"No, not that one," even Polly's mother had had enough of the cutesy version of the song.

"Thank you for supper. If you'll excuse me." Lily stood and took her plate with her; she didn't take a very big portion and had mostly pushed it around her plate. Lily washed up her dishes, grabbed her cloak and headed out the back door. Seth shovelled down the rest of his meal and trailed her to one of the biggest and most expensive houses in town. He watched her hesitate before entering the gate and speaking up. "Going for music lessons?"

Lily used to come here for piano lessons when she was younger, Tiffany still played the piano but preferred the flute. Seth was twelve or so when Constance's husband died, and Seth enjoyed hearing the old guy's exploits at the community hall. Shipwrecks made for better education than fractions and sums.

Lily scowled at him, pulling back her hood when she approached the overhang and knocked on the great blue door. It started to pour, so he joined her to get out of the rain. "You can go away."

"Is this a 'face your fears' sort of thing?"

"This is a 'mind your own business Seth' sort of thing."

"Maybe I just want to see the inside of the rich . . ." Seth trailed off when the door opened. The house was grand on the outside; inside was like staring into a wealthy stereotype; intricate carpets and well-crafted wooden banisters led to a large staircase. This was the only building in Stagmil with three floors. Dulcie gave them a disapproving smile, as if they controlled the weather.

"What do you want?" Dulcie was a little older than their mother, and that evening she wore an expensive looking blue dress with white lace at the sleeves and collar, something most folk from Stagmil would only wear with company or if they were going to Taralee on more formal business than selling raw fleece.

"Is Madeline here?" Lily asked.

"Of course. Come in and try not to get the rug all wet." Despite Dulcie having a home in town, it seemed Dulcie had moved in to 'care for her mother.' "Take your boots off and your cloaks. Come with me but keep your voices down. My mother is asleep."

Seth tried not to ogle at the embossed depictions of wildlife and some more fantastic creatures carved into several door frames and even racing up the staircase, or the baby grand piano in the large sitting room where a crackling fireplace heated the house. There were cheerful voices on the main floor, and the spices from supper smelled fantastic.

Dulcie led them upstairs to where Madeline was reading by a candelabra, though the room was well lit by many candles. The vaulted study was filled not only with books but other treasures. A ship in a bottle as well as maps decorated the shelves, and a pair of twin duelling blades were attached to a plaque on the wall. Everything from the tasseled curtains to the real oil paintings, depicting ships or distinguished men in naval uniforms, screamed expensive.

"Seth?" asked a young voice from behind them, looking to be delivering laundry. Dulcie's youngest, Rebecca, wouldn't be fifteen for another month but was already taller than Lily. She was plump in a pleasing way and had her mother's dark hair. "Oh, Lily, you're here too. We can play Longman's Bluff and—"

"They are not here to play games with you. Rebecca. Go fetch tea," Dulcie said, not bothering to announce them. "The good kind."

Rebecca hurried off to do her mother's bidding. Madeline locked eyes with Lily. Seth got the impression she more or less tolerated him. "Ah, the hunter's children. Any news from your father, or does your mother give you permission to escort me to Port Redmaw?"

"Not yet," Lily said. "I thought you'd be at the piano downstairs."

"My mother has a bad headache and is resting," Dulcie said. "You didn't come here to ask for music lessons, did you?"

Lily shook her head. "Do you mind if I speak with Madeline in private?"

"Oh?" Dulcie asked, now interested.

"It's quite all right," Madeline said, standing and straightening her dark skirt. The new dress was likely one of Dulcie's; although their physiques were quite different, the stiff neck and padding at the shoulders gave her an air of refinement Dulcie could never touch. "We can have a chat and then you can show Lily and Seth your lovely home."

"It's my mother's home, and today is not the day for tours. Perhaps if you'd bring your mother for tea after your father slays the beast. I'll go help that child of mine with the tea." Dulcie gave a sniff, leaving the study in a hurry.

Madeline ignored Seth and smiled at his sister. "How can I help you?"

"What happened last night, at the play?" Lily asked.

"You performed very well."

"I couldn't take the mask off. Those lines came pouring out of me."

"There's familiar versions of the story in every village. I'm sure you remembered from some place. I despise improv that goes nowhere for the audience, since it usually devolves into crass jokes or a whole lot of nothing." Making crass jokes while doing a whole lot of nothing appealed to Seth. "I think it's best to stick to the script until you understand the magic of theatre."

"She wants to try on that mask again," Seth offered.

"No I don't," Lily said, glaring at him.

"They're in my room at the moment," Madeline said. "Is that all?"

"And I wanted to return this music to you," Lily reached into her satchel and produced papers. Well, the ones she didn't set aflame. Seth figured it best not to mention that. "Thank you, but I think it's a little too hard for me."

"Nonsense. You just need a bit of practice."

As they kept talking, Seth lost interest, walking to the bookshelves . . . to look at the ornaments and treasures, at least. He wished the old guy was still alive. If he'd offered to teach Seth to duel no one would say it was improper, and Seth would easily mop the floor with his sister. He wondered if that sword on the plaque was really attached or . . . no, too many witnesses.

Madeline laughed. "Where's the mandolin now?"

"Back at the house," Lily said. "Constance has a lute; they're not the same and she's resting."

Madeline nodded. "Lily, why don't you read this new song while I go get the masks?"

"That's not necessary," Lily said.

"Nonsense," Madeline said, not unkindly, but almost in a challenging way, as if anything Lily said was silly. "I'm quite certain that you'll find some of them very interesting. Constance loved the theatre; I'm so lucky there are so many plays for me to enjoy." She left through a door on the far side of the study Seth hadn't even noticed before.

Lily seemed hesitant, but eventually looked over the new music. He noticed her drumming her fingers, humming slightly. He was honestly sort of jealous how good she was, though Tiffany cited it was because Lily practiced; Seth just had important things to do . . . The fireplace crackled violently, and there was a strange hum in the air. He looked to his sister, and he thought there was a strange glint of candlelight in her eyes. In fact, for an instant, they seemed to be glowing.

Seth turned his head when he heard a bang on the main door. Dulcie returned with the piping tea and her daughter carrying cranberry scones while Madeline was gone. "Where did she go?" Dulcie seemed put off to be wasting the *good* tea on the likes of them.

"To get some of the theatre masks," Seth blurted.

Lily was touching her forehead, eyes closed and brow tensed, as if in pain. He made his way to her and tapped her shoulder. When she looked in his eyes, there was a faint hint of gold glowing in the iris.

"Your . . . " Seth tapped below his own eye, and Lily frowned, but there were no mirrors present. By the time Lily took a few steps, the light faded. "Nothing. Just a trick of the candles."

Tea was not poured until Madeline returned, her theatre masks in a large bag, no longer leather but looking of better quality satin. Rebecca wandered over to Seth. "I'm surprised Tiffany's not with you. Grandmother lets her borrow plays sometimes."

"Rebecca," Dulcie snapped. "Stop bothering our guests with your yammering."

Rebecca gave Madeline a finely painted tea cup. It seemed that Rebecca knew she took honey and cream, and then served her mother, and finally, to Seth's surprise, they were given the beautiful tea cups as well. Madeline handed the masks to Dulcie and Rebecca, who tried them on and laughed, mimicking voices and lines they'd no doubt heard from plays in Taralee. One looked like some strange warrior, almost horse like, reminding Seth of the old sketches of centaurs.

"There's more to getting in character than just putting a mask on and making a silly voice," Madeline said. "Try different voices, imagine what makes your character unique."

Seth found the same witch mask Lily wore the night prior, and he clipped it without help. "Welcome, my pretties," he said in a shrill tone, before one much lower. "Welcome to your doom!" He took it off just as quick, and replaced it with a horrific mask with a blue face and jutting tongue. "Kiss me, my love! Mwa mwa mwa!"

Rebecca, giggled, and Seth chased after her. "Oh no you don't!" she said, retaliating with the horse faced one. Seth chased her into the hall. He heard Dulcie yelling after them to behave, but he didn't care.

"Show me where the cool stuff is without waking your granny!" Seth told Rebecca, happy to be away from her mother.

"She's half deaf and sleeps through storms," Rebecca said, seemingly relieved that she was out from her mother's thumb. He followed her up the stairs. "Come on, I'll show you where granddad kept his treasures, the real ones!"

~*~

"So precious, the transitioning from childhood. Their imaginations are truly wonderful," Dulcie said with a forced laugh. "Well, Lily, have you settled your business with Madeline? I wouldn't dream of chasing you out."

Lily was grateful the teacups didn't hold much. The sooner she was done, the better; her headache was creeping back. "I'll just be a minute more then I'll grab—"*CRASH* "Seth and be on my way."

"What's the rush?" Madeline asked. "I appreciate her companionship, Dulcie. If you've other duties, there's no need to host."

"Oh I'm always happy to be spending time with you and this lovely young lady. I'm having some real issues turning my Rebecca into a proper lady—" The voices upstairs were muffled, but the hurried footsteps were anything but. "I'm afraid young Seth doesn't bring out her better qualities."

"Perhaps what she's in need of is a little discipline. Shorten her leash—in a loving way," Madeline suggested. "You really ought to think about sending her to one of the larger towns or finishing schools, where she can receive proper instruction."

"I spent most of my life here," Dulcie said. "Father hired tutors, until they sent me to study in Taralee. Neither of those options are cheap."

That surprised Lily. "What did you study?"

"That's not important," Dulcie said hurriedly.

"Perhaps I can be of assistance, since you're helping me," Madeline said. "I know people. I'm certain someone I know from Taralee who would be happy to take Rebecca under their careful guiding hand and make her behave." She blew on her steaming tea before sipping it, giving Dulcie a warm smile, and the woman relaxed. "It's not good to discuss it here without her father, but I could introduce your daughter to the world beyond Stagmil."

"That would be lovely."

Lily tried to listen politely, but whatever new song Madeline had given her was now superseding the other one. She massaged her left temple. What was going on?

"May I have more tea please?" Though the cups were small, the tea pot was also small. Dulcie apologized, giving her half a cup. "I'll fetch more. If only that daughter of mine could do her one and only job. She didn't change out the candlesticks today either . . ."

Lily watched her go, and was about to get up and apologize for bothering Madeline, but when she turned her head Madeline forced a mask onto her face. It seemed to bind to her skin; Lily felt her muscles contract and she couldn't scream.

"Be quiet," Madeline said. "Don't make any more noise than you absolutely must. Be as a shadow. Now relax." Lily felt a rush of cold take over, and her vision changed. It was like viewing the world through a harsh shade that dimmed and made everything more angular. She wanted to raise her hands, scream for Seth or Rebecca or anyone to help her, but she couldn't make a peep. She felt like dead weight in the chair as Madeline fiddled, then pulled another mask out.

"Lovely," she said, and put it on top of the first mask. Lily felt her vision distort, and then felt the new mask merge on top of the first. Madeline gestured to the far door. "Go to my room, and you'll find clothes on the bed. Put them on, and then wait for me." Lily tried to yell, tell her no, but she found herself rising in obedience, cat-like quiet. "Third door on the right. It'll be unlocked."

Lily couldn't look back but she could hear her brother's voice when she was in the far hall. "Where'd my sister go?"

"She didn't say. Sit, Seth, and have another scone."

Lily was compelled down the hall and found the door slightly open. One of the larger guest rooms, with lace coverings on the matching nightstand and dresser. Lily found the dark attire laid out on the bed. The room held Madeline's bags, as well as a sewing mannequin with a half-finished project; it looked like some sort of riding garment. Lily hated that her fingers could gracefully undo buttons and lacing but couldn't reach for the mask as she obediently exchanged her clothes for the dark fabric on the bed, and folded her own ever so crisply. What concerned her were the boots. They fit perfectly. Everything was tailored for her.

The first sign of movement wasn't from Madeline. Instead, a small creature came into the room. Lily could only see it with the periphery of her vision; it was a patchwork toy made of lace and what looked like scrap material from some dress Lily had seen Constance wear around town. It wasn't very big, standing to about mid-calf, but the toy brought in Lily's old boots and cloak, and stashed them on the far side of the bed. Then it went back to working on the riding clothes on the mannequin.

Madeline took her time coming. Lily stood there, only able to control her eyes as she stood in the room. There was a mirror just outside her vision. She wasn't sure how long she just stood there before Madeline opened the door, and bolted it behind her.

"So nice you came to me. I thought I'd have to spend another day or two in this tacky little town." Madeline pulled off a mask and looked over before trying another on. Lily couldn't scream as the woman's features became her own, but it wasn't perfect—in fact, there seemed to be a crack on the lower left jaw. The woman noticed as well and poking at it frowned, then took it off and put it down on a nearby nightstand. "No one will notice until they're up close." She pointed to a chair. "Sit."

Lily obeyed and saw that her own face was covered by a strange wooden blank one, eerie in how emotionless and plain, neither male nor female. She still couldn't move. Madeline unbraided Lily's hair, and then pinned it in a tight bun. She pulled out a mask that reminded Lily of shadows. There were eye slits, some holes for the nose. When the hood was up, Lily seemed to almost melt into shadow.

"If you haven't already, memorize the second sheet of music. Have you done so?" Lily found herself nodding. "The first thing I want you to do is return to your home and retrieve your mandolin. Do not be seen by anyone, especially your mother or brother. You're going to leave a letter, explaining you've run away and are seeking your fortune elsewhere. Be vague. Belt your sword, and wait for me outside your home. You'll play that second song when I tell you." Madeline tilted Lily's chin up to force Lily to look into her eyes. "And if anyone tries to stop me, kill them."

Five

Seth and Rebecca received a tongue-lashing about behaving when company was present and both were made to go through the motions of being sorry. Seth endured their chewing out with just enough faux-concern to fool Dulcie, which really wasn't all that much. The woman had about as much imagination as a toadstool.

Seth abandoned Rebecca to her mother when she was being punished with more tasks and returned to the study; he hoped whatever Lily wanted was done with so they could skedaddle. Madeline was flipping through a book, but stopped abruptly when she saw him. Lily was absent. "Where'd my sister go?" he asked.

"She didn't say," Madeline replied. "Sit, Seth, and have another scone."

"She didn't wait for me?" Seth asked, grabbing two scones, wrapping one and stuffing it onto his pocket for later. He normally didn't care for cranberries, but these were excellent.

Dulcie entered the room with theteapot while Seth was halfway done his other scone, Rebecca in her wake. "Where did Lily go?"

"She left," Madeline said. "Lovely girl, Dulcina. You should have her over more often."

"Yes, well, that O'Connell can behave properly when she puts her mind to it. Time to go, Seth. I'll see you to the door," Dulcie motioned him to leave as thunder rumbled the house, and it sounded like the winds and rains intensified.

"Mother, maybe he should wait until the weather improves?" Rebecca asked, but Dulcie waved her off and Seth found himself at the foyer. Lily's boots were missing, as was her cloak. He recognized his own slightly muddy boot print following Lily in, but there was no indication of her leaving the house. Thankfully, the winds sounded worse than it was outside and there was only a slight drizzle as he was ushered to the porch.

Lily's more devious than I thought, Seth mused, looking back at the door that locked behind him. He got an idea where most of the family was—the majority of Dulcie's kin were in the dining hall, most of them playing some very involved card game Seth would have loved to join in. He walked around the house and to his surprise, a window on the second floor opened, lit by only a flickering candle that hissed in the wind.

"Wait for me!" called a female voice from the second floor. Rebecca had obviously done this before, before he could yell at her she was rappelling when she could have gone over a few windows and scaled down the tree like a sane person.

"What do you think you're doing?" Seth asked.

"I don't think Lily left the house," Rebecca said. "No one saw her go."

"You think she's hiding and will explore after you all go to bed?"

"I don't know. That woman is odd," Rebecca said. "Not like Zin, either. She's an actress; she puts on a smile and she's got most people fooled. I don't think her real name is Madeline, either."

"Isn't that what actresses are supposed to do?" Seth was more put off that Lily was sneaking around the house without him. "Well, you should have stayed in where it's dry. Go climb your tree like a good squirrel."

"Maybe this chicky-munk wants to see what the local nuts are into," Rebecca countered, leading the way to a back shed. Rebecca's companionship wasn't without benefit. She had a satchel with most of a peach pie wrapped in cheesecloth. She also appeared to do this regularly, probably to hide from her mother, and had some wooden mugs hidden and somehow smuggled out tea.

"You normally sneak out?"

"You're not the only one who spies on Dale and Brigid. Of course, I probably do it for a different reason than you," Rebecca said.

Seth snorted. "There's nothing better to do in this town. I sneak back to the hunters with the wyvern's head on a platter, and my dad would bring backnext to my tanned backside for display." Rebecca giggled a little too much. "If I happen to spoil the escapades of two lovebirds and get 'em in trouble: oh well. Thank you for the snacks, now go back to yer granny's and if you find her tell Lily that the jig is up and we know what she's up to."

"What is she up to?" Rebecca asked.

"Not a clue," he admitted.

"You're not ditching me that easily." She followed him and Seth didn't discourage her.He just figured most girls would whine and complain about getting cold or wet, but it seemed that the rains were finally letting up.

They made their way from the large manor towards the town square. Frogs croaked and a few birds stirred now that there was finally a break in the weather. Seth always waited outside where Brigid was staying, mostly because if she didn't find a way to sneak out he wasn't going to spy on Dale. She was staying with her mother's friend in town and as if on cue, after the lights were out the backdoor opened a little, and the mysterious cloaked figure snuck out the back, not chiming the bell or alerting the dog, because she tossed the hound a pork knuckle.

Rebecca gave them away. Seth didn't watch her because she seemed to know what she was doing, so when he found a nice shadow to watch from he wasn't expecting her to walk out and approach Brigid.

"My mother watches the main floor like a hawk," Rebecca said.

Brigid gasped and turned around. She was almost as pretty as Molly and very sweet, and completely wasted on a putz like Dale. "Rebecca? I was just—"

"Out for a rainy midnight stroll," Rebecca said. "Care for company on your way to meet Dale?" she cast a sideways smile at Seth who remained hidden, and when Brigid tried to deny she was out doing anything but using the privy (Constance had one of those new-fangled indoor ones, Seth thought them loud and bizarre) Rebecca pointed out that meant there was no reason to bribe the dog.

"The whole block is going to hear you," Brigid pointed out. "Fine, I'm off to see Dale. You can leer but he'll be lucky if he gets a peck on the cheek." Seth had to bite his tongue from asking which set. The girls hurried off together, Seth followed behind.

Jasper's workshop was the meeting place. To Seth's surprise, it wasn't Dale that was present, but two younger, smaller figuresnear the forge, trying to stoke it.

"Tobias? Louis?" Brigid asked.

"Brigid, you minx," Rebecca chimed.

The two boys had a long wooden box in front of them, as well as something else longer, rolled up in a thick brown fabric. "What are you two doin' here?" Louis asked, scrunching his nose.

"I told you we're gonna get caught," Tobias snapped, clutching whatever was in the roll tighter.

"Well, the two of you can help," Louis said, pointing. "You're not strong enough to use that hammer over there. Work your feminine wiles and summon Dale for me."

"That's a sledgehammer," Rebecca said. "What have you got?"

"None of your business!" Tobias protested, before grabbing the box before them, and running into the night, missing Seth by mere inches.

"Get back here!" Louis shouted in the direction Tobias had sped off towards, far too loudly.

"Shush!" Brigid snapped. "You want Jasper to hear you?"

"Not especially, but now I don't care as much," Louis said. Seth looked to the house. There weren't any lights on or raised voices, but he assumed everyone turned in early because of the weather. Seth left his hiding place to go have a listen for snoring, and ran smack into someone else hiding in the unassuming shadows.

"Ooof! Watch it you nitwit!" Tiffany snapped.

"Tiffy?" Seth asked. "What are you doing here?"

"Trailing you, O Mighty Hunter," his twin informed him. "We saw you lurking. Imagine our surprise to see you sneaking off with Rebecca to make out in Jasper's workshop."

"I wasn't sneaking around with . . ." Seth thought about it. "Well, I'm down if she is."

"Shush!" Of course Molly wasn't far off. She hissed at them both to hide, and though Seth couldn't see her, he recognized her voice. Seth grabbed his twin's sleeve and pulled her to the shadow. The others had found decent hiding spots by this time; Seth realized they were running out of shadows to lurk in.

Dale arrived, about as subtle as a bull in a tea shop. "Brigid?"

"Here I am, big boy," Louis sang out in a scratchy voice. He stepped out of the shadows, in a mock bombshell stance and proceeded to wiggle his hips. "*A boom chicky-boom boom!*"

"Very funny. What are you doing here?" Dale asked.

"I was trying to bust a lock before you idiots showed up and scared Tobias off," Louis said. "Can't you go roll around in the hay like civilized people?"

"Idiots? More than one?" Dale asked.

"Let's see . . . Brigid and Rebecca split when Seth started a fight with his sister. Not the smart one."

"Hey!" Tiffany snapped, stepping out from the shadowand storming over to them. "Lily isn't as smart as everyone thinks. She probably doesn't even know that you're trying to break into that safe from Zin Booey's."

"It was too obvious, he left it out," Louis admitted, the youth's left eye twitched for a fraction of an instant. "But I have to know: what secrets lie within the box?"

"I'll box your ear. You should be at home," Dale snapped. "There's a wyvern out there."

Countering Dale seemed like a great place for a one-liner, so Seth crossed his arms, stepped from the shadows, and leaned against the doorframe. "I'm pretty sure that the wyvern isn't lurking in Molly's apron, so for the moment you're safe, Dale."

"Ugh, the failed hunter. Can't expect a circus without the clown," Dale said.

"You're thinking of the Ringmaster," Rebecca interjected, evidently having *not* split.

"Tobias and I would be the clowns," Louis agreed with Rebecca's shadow. "Rebecca could be a knife-juggler . . . "

"Can I be the trick horse rider instead?" Rebecca asked.

"He said circus, not rodeo," Louis said.

"There's trick riders at circuses," Rebecca insisted.

"Enough!" Dale snapped. "All of you: Go home."

"Oh?" Tiffany asked, hands on her hips. "I'd hate to tell your mother about this little nightly rendezvous."

"For the last time, you're very pretty but I picked Brigid," Dale told Tiffany. "Maybe you should tell your parents to put your name in for Molly's suitor; they're bound to find someone who can tolerate you."

"What are you talking about?" Tiffany demanded, turning towards her best friend. "Molly, you have a suitor?"

Dale scoffed before Molly could explain. "Some farmer up near Twinpeak is looking for a wife, but your parents ought to get *you* out of Stagmil and give the rest of us some peace," Dale snapped at Tiffany.

"You knew?" Molly shrieked, stepping forward.

"Oh, hi Molly," Dale said, not seeming very surprised. "A bunch of people know we have several girls available for courtships. Molly and Lily will be easy to marry off compared to Tiffany."

"Are we courting?" Brigid asked Dale.

"Not formally," Dale said. Brigid winced. "Oh come on, you know my meaning."

Tiffany snapped her fingers in front of Dale's face. "Focus, we're talking about Molly being married off to a stranger, not your awful taste."

Seth cast a glance at Molly, who looked mortified. "You don't have to marry anyone you don't want to."

"Tell that to my parents!" Molly said. "We're not all rich like you!"

"We're not rich," Tiffany scoffed. Seth agreed—they had their own land, and their house was nice, but they got up early and worked hard, the same as everyone else in town. Well, old matriarchs and weirdos with their goat chariots not withstanding. "And when were you going to tell me? Was I going to be the last person in town to know?"

"I . . . I . . ." Molly stammered. It was hard to see, but Seth could tell she was tearing up.

"What's that sound?" Louis asked, wandering towards the forge's main doors.

"We could have made a plan!" Tiffany scolded.

"I told your sister," Molly blurted. "She was going to help me get a job in Taralee or get someone to pretend to be my beau after shearing."

"What's the problem then?" Tiffany asked.

"They'll marry off Ayleth if I don't!" Molly squeaked.

"What?" Rebecca demanded. "She's . . . she's almost a year younger than me! They can't do that."

"Can everyone shut up for a minute?" Louis asked. "I'm trying to listen. There's a funny sound in the wind."

"Louis, this is important," Tiffany said.

"I hear it, too," Rebecca said.

"Who cares?" Tiffany asked. "Molly, you give me the name of this so-called suitor and I'm gonna march right up to him—"

"It sounds like music," Brigid pointed out.

They all shut up. It sounded like a distant song, hollow and lulling. Voices—two female ones, a haunting harmony, entwined with a . . .lute? Mandolin?

"Brigid, let's get out of here," Dale said, grabbing her arm.

"Wait," Brigid said, shrugging out of Dale's grip and addressing Molly. "I'm sorry. Is there's anything I can do to help?"

Seth couldn't hear Molly's reply over the sound of Louis yawning. This was comical, how could he be getting . . . tired? Seth hated that yawning was contagious. His own eyelids were growing increasingly heavy. Looking over to his sister, she was shaking her head.

"Is . . . anyone else having a hard time keeping their eyes open?" Tiffany asked, and to Seth's surprise, she slapped herself. "What's happening?"

Seth pinched himself to wake up better, and saw that Louis had found a comfortable corner to lay down in. Brigid gasped and Dale had fallen into her arms. "Dale?" she asked, shaking him. Seth and Tiffany helped put him down, and dragged him towards Louis.

"What is happening?" Rebecca asked, yawning heavily. "I feel . . . I don't even want to go home. I just want to pass out."

Seth's brain seemed to be trying to lull him to sleep, make him think of other things and just relax, that there was no danger, that it wasn't important. The corner over there looked downright comfortable, but he bit his tongue. There were animals that could lull people to sleep. What else had followed that wyvern down the mountain? *Where's Lily when I need her?* Seth did what he remembered from listening to tales from his folks and their friends. He took Louis' candle, and dripped the hot wax onto his arm, only a few drops, but his brain alerted him to the pain. He then he took the warm, malleable wax, and stuck it in his ears. Tiffany did likewise.

They tried to put the wax into Rebecca's ears, but she was beyond rousing. They even used the hot wax, which was quite painful, to try to rouse the others, but no amount of pinching or prodding would wake them. The only one who hadn't fallen was Molly, and they found her standing outside. She no longer wept. Instead she faced the night, her eyes half-closed, but strange, as if a dull blue glow was residing in her chocolate brown irises.

When he shouted, Seth could sort of hear himself, but it was unnerving to be otherwise deaf. He ducked around Tiffany to grab Molly by the shoulders and try to rouse her. Her eyes opened and there was a change, not only in Molly but the air. Seth didn't dare remove the wax. The blue light in the ring of Molly's brown eyes pulsed suddenly.

Tiffany was trying to tell him something, but he did his best to restrain Molly as she pulled away and started to walk from the workshop. "Wake up!" She was a lot stronger than she let on, and that wasn't to say he wouldn't slow her down or stop her, but she consistently tried to fight him. Tiffany raced back to the shop and that was around the time that he realized that the others were coming. Well, shuffling. Tiffany returned with rope, and she gestured. Seth grabbed Molly's wrists and

Tiffany bound them, then he picked Molly up and Tiffany bound her feet together in a seated position. He realized that if they struggled with Molly, everyone else besides maybe Brigid was going to be a more difficult. Molly struggled as the O'Connells dragged her to the side.

Of course, big old Dale was first and though he moved in a trance, there was no picking him up and tying him, so they opted to trip him. When the others saw Tiffany and Seth sitting on him, they stopped being slow moving and ran to the others, while Louis shuffled to Molly and cut her free, the others simply held back Seth and took the rope away and helped Dale get up. None of them were violent, but they were being . . . summoned by the strange music on the breeze.

"Where are they going?" Seth asked. Tiffany responded by pointing to her ears and shaking her head. Tiffany ran to the nearest house and banged on the door. It looked like she couldn't get in and no one was coming, and Seth trailed after the others. Tiffany went to another house, tried to open a door, then another, until finally finding an unlocked door and entering the dwelling. Seth kept after his friends. Seth looked down the streets, expecting to see Amos or Jolene shuffling with their grandkids, but so far it was just them who were caught out of doors. A cat hissed from under a chair on a patio when they passed, that was all they saw concerning animals.

To his surprise, Tiffany caught up with them, cheeks flushed. She tried to tell him something he didn't catch; she didn't pick up a pad of paper or a quill and ink, so short of hand signals their communication was limited.

His mind peeled over stories. There were monsters and sorcerers who had enchanted entire towns by the sound of a flute, stories of someone who played a magic fiddle and made townsfolk dance to unholy jigs for days until they died. The longer he was deaf, the better it seemed that his brain was working. He had his bow and shepherd's supplies; he hoped they'd be enough.

Seth and his twin followed the others out of town to the east towards the forest, away from the usual fields, but they would have to go miles for Seth to be unfamiliar with the wooded area around Stagmil, though he knew the eastern area the least. For the most part, the others left Seth and Tiffany alone, but several times Tiffany tried to grab Molly's hand and she was pushed away effortlessly. Seth wondered if he wasn't also being summoned. He was also going batty not being able to rely on his ears in the forest; little details he took for granted, like the hoot of an owl or the sound of snapping twigs.

A dark-clad figure was in the woods ahead, and he was glad for his bow; his utility knife was little more than a joke. He shouted a warning, and in the darkness, the figure removed her hood.

Lily? No—from a distance it looked like his sister, but she was wrong. Her hair was too light, her expression was cold, and she seemed too tall. It was hard to see from a distance and in the dark, with the moonlight illuminating their way, but something from deep down told him that this wasn't Lily, that it was trying to mimic her. If his brain was still touched by that song, he might have been relieved to see this fake. Instead, when he neared and saw that there was a crack in the bottom left side of her face, he knew not only was this not right;regardless of whoever she was, she was a threat.

This Lily reached out and grabbed Louis' arm—now he was in the lead—and for a moment he seemed to wake up and look around. He said something, but the imposter pulled him along, though not before she made eye contact with Seth. The eyes were all wrong, in a way that made Seth think *predator*. Louis looked around, not fighting back but not as hard as he ought to, following after the woman as she led him deeper into the woods.

"No, don't go with her!" Seth shouted. Tiffany said something too, and Louis tried to pull away. Whoever it was had a firm grip; when Louis pulled she did something, sang perhaps, and Louis hesitated, and followed without being coaxed. Seth went to stop her but Dale got in his way, blocking him. Tiffany shook Molly's shoulders. Rebecca and Brigid seemed to be waking up; they looked around, eyes wide in confusion and terror.

Tiffany took the wax out of her ears and started to talk. Seth had enough, socked Dale in the gut and slipped around him, careful to evade his grasp, and followed after Louis and Not-Lily. "Get out of here, all of you! I'll get Louis."

The others shouted but Seth couldn't make sense of what they were saying. Chasing after Louis and the phony, it seemed to be leading him deeper into the woods. Part of him knew this was a trap. Part of him wanted to save Louis, but most of all, Seth was curious as to what the game was.

Not-Lily was leading Louis to a valley. Seth knew this glen well enough, but what he wasn't expecting wasanother figure in black waiting for them.They worea strange, wooden mask and played either a lute or a mandolin, he couldn't hear it or see well enough in the dark to be certain. A hand on his shoulder. He didn't hear Tiffany creeping up on him. She gestured to his ears and he shook his head. The others were right behind her, their eyes no longer glazed; Brigid looked terrified. When Seth looked ahead again, he saw that the black robed figure was still playing. Louis stood before the figure, stumbling backwards but the boy was braver than Seth expected, he looked to be peering at the dark-clad figure.

"You should all have wax in your ears," Seth told Tiffany, to which his twin made a sour-puss face.

They were all trying to talk to him. Maybe he'd stuff his ears more often. "Louis! Did you see where that person wearing Lily's face went?" Louis backed off from the hooded figure.

Tiffany looked taken aback. Brigid was pulling on Rebecca's shoulder, gesturing that they should leave.

A strange silence filled the air as the wood-masked figure stopped playing. Something made the small hairs on the back of Seth's neck and knuckles stand on end and sent a chill down his spine.

Molly lifted the candle and looked up, blanching. He could barely hear it, but one of the girls screamed. Seth saw the reflections of silver and white in the trees and bushes all around them, except for the narrow path where they all emerged. *Spider webs?* They were next to invisible against the starlight.

The figure in black started to play something else, and the other's eyes widened, and Tiffany shouted something, and they all reached for the soft wax of the candle but didn't know what they were doing.In the haste of grabbing the candle, it was knocked to the ground.

Seth ignored his companions and nocked his bow. "Stop what you're doing or I'll shoot!"

The figure seemed undeterred. Seth knew he was about to commit murder, but he didn't care and he wouldn't leave Louis or any of them to whatever that doppelganger was, and this thing was obviously part of this plot. He loosed the arrow, and the figure only stopped playing to bat it away with the sword hidden under the cloak. *Impossible*, Seth thought, nocking another with a second between his fingers for quick redraw. He might not be the finest archer—but at this range he didn't have to be, and no one could deflect arrows in succession for long.

Someone screamed. It looked like Rebecca was caught in a web when she tried to bolt from the glen between two trees. Seth unsheathed his long knife and went to help her, but the figure of Not-Lily appeared, taking off her face and standing near Rebecca. The face was completely blank underneath; Seth let out a surprised gasp before she replaced that face with something with six red eyes, two in the normal place with another four running up her forehead.

Then he saw it—her—grow. The lower half of her body swelled and became massive, bulbous, like the back half of a centaur; her body remained about the same size, but rather than fur and four legs, shimmering black hair and eight legs protruded from the torso, longer at the bend than Dale was tall. She towered over Rebecca. A giant spider . . . woman? There was something eerily feminine about it, a sort of terrible beauty that froze him when his instincts told him to move. She stepped over Rebecca, barrelling down on Seth. He loosed another arrow at her head, but she dodged and shot out webbing from her hands that knocked him backwards, pinning him to the grass. More spider silk flew and pinned his arm to the grass,

As Seth tried to wriggle free the monster chased after Dale, and to Seth's horror, caught him with long strands at his wrists, and wrangled him like a marionette. Dale wriggled against the webbing and she dragged him back, and it seemed that he was transforming in the shadow, shrinking and becoming . . . something *else*. Seth unbuttoned his overshirt to try to free himself.

Dale was reduced to the size of a doll, and the spider had shifted him to a web in the canopy before going after Tiffany. Brigid flailed between two trees, seemingly stuck in a giant web.

Louis cut Seth free and thrust the bow into Seth's hand. He shouted something and Seth realized that if he got her attention, there wouldn't be another time. Louis released a rock from his sling. Seth couldn't see the rock's trajectory but the spider reeled, leaving Tiffany and moved with intent on the pair of them. They darted in opposite directions, and by luck the creature honed in on Louis, giving Seth enough time to fire. The arrow bounced off the creature's bulbous body.

Out of the corner of his eye, Seth thought he saw a fox or coyote dart from the bush and bound through the grass. It ran behind the mandolin-playing creature and bit it in the butt. Suddenly there were two people, but Seth couldn't watch them.

Seth let loose another arrow, narrowly missing the torso, and shouted at the others to run—he wasn't sure who it had now, was it Rebecca or Molly? The light was too poor for him to be certain, but whoever the spider held she was shrinking fast.

The creature turned, six red and black eyes focused on Seth, and came down on him with full force. Seth found his limbs caught by two bands of silk and forced above his head, and he was hoisted into the air. He locked eyes with Louis who was looking not only smaller, but . . . wooden. Against his control, Seth raised his hands to his ears and removed the wax, and sound same rushing back.

No sound of a mandolin, the spider sang and the world grew bigger as a strange fire coursed through Seth, he felt strangely numb and altered, but just as suddenly the spider suddenly reared and screamed and Seth was cut free, flung from the monster. He landed and rolled in the grass and saw Lily scramble, sword drawn, rolling under the beast and struck the under belly. She was dressed in unfamiliar black clothes and she never styled her hair that way, but instinctually Seth knew this was the real sister. *Where were you?* He gaped in horror as the spider tried to bring her massive tendrils down on his sister, who narrowly dodged. She tried to slice through a tendril, she hammered through hair, but the creature's legs were like armour, and Lily was knocked off balance after the strike.

Seth stood and the world was bigger – his body didn't move normal, and looking at his hands, he saw they were clunky segments of wood. He realized just how small he was after he'd ran towards his bow, which was by-the-by standard, but now was gigantic.

I'm a puppet.

His horror jarred when he heard Lily call out. The spider struck at his sister, and sent her sprawling, losing her blade in the process.

Dodging like he'd seen her with Zin in the fields when silk came down to pin her, Lily reclaimed her sword and jabbed it into the bulbous lower body again. The spider reeled and Lily dodged, cutting into the armoured body. "Let Louis go!" Lily ordered.

"You do not give me orders. *You* obey *mine*." The spider's voice sounded very different from Madeline's, but Seth knew this was her. "No matter. No one is coming to save you; everyone in town will sleep for three days. You'll sing every child from their bed before the night is done. Throw down your sword, or I'll burn this one in front of you." Seth couldn't tell who she held, the marionette hung limp from Madeline's silk.

A strange but not unfamiliar war cry sounded to the clip-clop of several irate goats and iron wheels crushing grass and twigs. By the time Seth figured it out, there was a master's blade to the spider woman's throat and a figure on her bulbous back.

"Leave my apprentice be," Zin snapped. "Lily, run!"

"Zin, the others!" Lily gestured to the marionettes suspended in webs.

"I can't hear you!" Zin shouted. He pointed to his ears. "*Wax!*"

The spider bucked violently, though Zin landed like he'd meant for that to happen. "Sorry I'm late. Kind of a tricky first real fight, isn't it? I would have specialized your training if I knew."

Lily's eyes widened and she backed off. Zin met the beast with his blade.

While the town recluse fought the abomination, Seth looked in horror at what had been done to him. Seth barely came up to Lily's knee at full height. His bow hadn't been transformed with him, but he had a toy version of his knife at his side and most of his arrows were still in his quiver—a fat lot of good that would do him. The spider climbed up the nearest tree, almost hiding against the night sky and canopy before spitting webbing at the old master and his apprentice. Zin moved with grace and agility like he'd perfected the art of such maneuvers and was just a smidge rusty. The back of Lily's boot became stuck in the spider's silk, which pinned her until she loosened her boot and propelled herself forward, hurling herself into the bush to avoid the spider's attack.

Madeline scaled a tree and seemingly vanished into the dark canopy. Seth got the impression she was plucking victims from their respective webs.

"Come on down here," Zin challenged as Lily untangled herself from the shrubbery. The spider landed in front of him with a *thump.* "Oh, you're listening, good. Release the young people and explain what you're up to."

"Stand aside, old man," Madeline ordered.

"No."

Seth might have been little, enchanted, and at the time wasn't sure what else, but he could move. When he ran he had proportionately longer strides that felt funny at first, but he could jump much further into the air; his centre of gravity was off but while the creature focused on Zin and his sister, Seth scrambled up the side of the tree, which was easier as a puppet than as a boy. Coming up behind the spider woman, Seth launched himself and jumped on her head, blinding her main eyes with his hands.There were four others but he disorientated her as he pressed inward; he wasn't sure if he was doing much more than irritating her so he pressed hard. She reared and thrashed, and Seth looked for the little latch that held that cursed mask in place.

When at last he found it, she seemed to collapse inward, the parts of her that were tendril and bulb shrinking and wisping away like smoke. Seth crashed to the ground on top of what was left: a faceless woman who fell. Before Zin or Lily were on her, she slipped on a different mask and transformed again, but this time her face lengthened and her hair became like a horse's mane. She reared, a male centaur with very powerful legs, making the other two back off—and though she tried to kick Zin with those back legs he was ever more nimble. The centaur looked around and Seth abandoned the mask to the forest floor and high-tailed it for cover. How many monsters did she have?

She didn't seem to want to hurt Lily; when Lily took a swipe Madeline backed off, then galloped away into the woods. Lily and Zin were not nearly as fast though Lily sprinted after her. "Get back here!" Lily screamed. "Tiffany! Molly!" Lily tripped suddenly and scrambled back to her feet. Zin laid a hand on her shoulder. "Zin, how did you know we were in trouble?"

"What?" Zin shouted in her face, cleaning an ear with his pinky. "Someone poured warm wax in my ears. Very rude," he said loudly towards the bushes. "Okay, talk into my left ear."

"What did she do?" Lily asked.

"What did you help her do?" Zin asked back. Lily's lower lip quivered. "I never said it was your fault," he said, shining his lantern in Seth's general direction. "And don't complain, we got one back."

"Oh my gosh," Lily said, paling. Seth resisted the urge to dive into the bush as opposed to letting her see him. "Seth? What did she do to you?"

"Uh . . . good question." Seth looked over his wooden fingers and body. He hadn't seen himself, but given what he'd seen happen to the others, he suspected he was a marionette without strings. He looked around, and retrieved the spider mask. "What happened exactly?"

"Lily, remember those breathing exercises? Do those," Zin instructed, and Lily closed her eyes and took several extended breaths. Zin didn't wait for her to calm before he spoke again. "Whatever you do, do not put that mask on again."

"I don't think I could if you tortured me," Lily said.

"Lily," Seth spoke up. Wow, he sounded annoying. "Was that you playing?"

Lily looked incredibly guilty. "What's done is done," said another woman, her dark hair put up in an elaborate bun. She had a strange but beautiful sort of pinched face, wore brilliant white and scarlet robes well-embroidered with cranes and bullrushes. Lily aimed her sword at the stranger, and Seth gaped at the brilliant white and red fox tails that followed after her.

"Put down your sword, Lily. You know me." This new woman had strangely familiar amber-gold eyes. "Not a good look, Seth."

"Is that . . . is that the fox?" Seth asked Lily.

"Zin, darling," Mama Fern said, golden eyes sparkling on Seth, "it appears we have a problem."

Six

"I'll say," Zin said. "Our son bit me in the butt!"

"I had to wake you up somehow," said a little kit who sat just on the edge of the woods.

"Mom bit Lily's behind and you don't hear her complaining," said another.

Zin waived his hands at the kits before he gestured at Seth and Lily. "I saved the apprentice, didn't I? My feet are cold. Oh, you're missing a boot! Let's go, O'Connells two."

"Lily, what is happening?" Seth demanded at his sister as she picked him up and stepped onto the goat chariot. Mama Fern changed back into her fox self, and jumped onto Zin's shoulders.

"Weee!" one of the little foxes said, the first to jump onto the chariot after retrieving Lily's footwear. Seth rested on one of Lily's shoulder while another kit jumped up and rested on the other, and gave Seth a sniff.

"You still smell like you," she said, wagging her single tail.

"Great," Seth said. "I'm short, wood, sound awful, but my body odour hasn't gone away."

"It's your clothes, dear," Mama Fern offered.

"I think things worked out for the good." Zin said. Mama Fern nipped him in the ear. "Right, right. Hang on."

"I'm not riding in this dumb . . . woah!" Seth began, but then clung on for dear wooden-life. The goats really knew how to peel from a stop.

Boscoe eyed Seth. "Can I chew him?"

"No," Mama Fern said.

"Why nooooot?" Boscoe whined as the goats picked up speed and took them around the hilly brush.

Lily held on like she'd done this far too often. "How did you know to help me?"

"I had my suspicions the whole time, dear," said Mama Fern, riding on Zin's shoulder. "I can sense certain magics when they enter my territory. Don't ride with your mouth open, or you'll catch a bug."

"I won't—*kkkkk!*" Lily coughed and spat.

"Most lady like," Mama Fern commented.

"I don't even have spit," complained Seth. "Why did you wake *Zin* of all people?"

"Well, he is my husband, and so I suppose I'm a little biased. Most of the village dreams because of the lullaby; Zin's slumber was due to a generous second helping of schnitzel."

"It was the potatoes," Zin clarified.

"Lily, what happened?" Seth asked, and almost went flying when he ignored Zin's, "bump" warning. "How long am I going to be like this?" Seth looked at his little wooden hands, and started to take apart the screw that held his thumb to the rest of his left.

"Don't do that!" Lily snapped.

"I have a scientific mind," Seth informed her. "You're right, the way Zin drives I'll lose something. I'll wait until we get somewhere decent." Pause. "Where *are* we going?"

"My place," Zin said.

Seth had been to the property before, but he'd never been in the house. Zin's acreage was in the woods with no water from a creek or river like the majority of the farms in the area, but there was a well. His stone cottage was small but comfortable enough for a bachelor. The stable for the goats was larger, and there were a few other smaller buildings in the backwoods. Several buckling *baah*'d when they arrived.

"We have guests," Zin addressed the kits. "You may come in once the goats are fed. No wandering."

One of the girls spoke up. "We aren't supposed to talk around the humans."

"Mum will make Lily forget. Won't you mother?" asked another. There were at least five of them, and they all only had single tails.

"Their mother allowed some friends to stay over," Zin explained. "I told her it wasn't a good idea with all the goings on."

Mama Fern changed before their eyes. Striding towards them, she was suddenly middle-aged and a little on the chubby side, but she had the unmistakeable sharp features of a fox, and five luxuriously fluffy tails followed behind her. She took Lily's face in her hands, and had Lily look down while running a finger into her hairline. "I don't think I'll need to wipe her mind. We'll try to minimize the bruise."

"Bruise?" Lily asked, gritting her teeth when Mama Fern found it.

"How is this night getting even weirder?" Seth asked, but no one really paid him any attention. He turned to Boscoe, who followed after them to the house. "Aren't you going to transform into a human?"

"I'm not old enough to without help," said the kit. "But *why* would I want to be human?"

"You have chores to do, youngling," Mama Fern scolded, and Boscoe slunk back to the goat pen, tail between his legs.

"Are they all celestial foxes?" Lily asked.

"One's just your average garden variety fox kit, but yes, the others kicking around here are what I believe the nomenclature would call *kitsunes*," Zin explained. "You pair should be used to them, they're constantly playing near the creek by your house. Three are mine, one's a cousin here for a sleepover."

"How do you keep them from talking?" Lily asked, but Seth forgot the question once they were led inside the house. It was magnificent— much bigger from the inside—the ceilings were vaulted and it seemed to glow with an unnatural light that Seth couldn't find the source of. It was fantastically decorated with strange vases and exotic flowers and hanging baskets. Lily stood, eyes wide, and was reminded to take off her remaining boot.

"Is this really Zin's place?" Seth asked Mama Fern. "Or do you just let him live here?"

Mama Fern handed Lily a pair of wooden house sandals and guided them to a human-sized chaise where they looked around. There were no tiny sandals for Seth, and he refused the booties, but he wasn't all that dirty anyway. "I know it looks so much smaller on the outside. Space and time are funny things." The kitsune started humming to herself like it was not a big deal.

"So you're an enchantress?" Seth asked. "You can fix me?"

"Not exactly." Mama Fern went to the fireplace and used small sticks which ignited before she disappeared into the kitchen and returned to put on a large black kettle. Zin still picked at his ears. Mama Fern glided over and gave a quick yank.

"And now we've also taken care of the excess hair problem," Mama Fern pointed out when Zin gave a yelp. "You'd be under the lullaby and sleep for three days if I didn't help; now be a good host. Oh, Lily, let's get you out of that get up."

"She's can wait five minutes," Zin grumbled and went to the only piece of uninspired furniture in the room: his comfy chair. He crossed his arms and motioned for Lily to sit on a much fancier chaise. Seth jumped up beside her as Zin said, "So, Lily, do you want to explain what happened?"

"You and your fake," Seth said, scowling.

Lily licked her lips, but looked at him before looking at Zin. "I went to see Madeline. Seth came with me." She looked to him for support. Seth rolled his eyes but nodded. "Remember when you raced out of the room with that mask on? Madeline sent Dulcie for more tea, and when I wasn't paying attention to her, she put a mask on my face," she said. "I lost control of my body. She told me to go to another room, and put on . . . this." She gestured to the dark clothes. "Before that, she gave me some sheet music and I learned it. I . . . think I lulled the village to sleep."

Zin nodded. "Sounds about right."

"I can't get these songs out of my head," Lily said, bending forward and putting her head in her hands. "It's my fault . . . "

"Moping won't do you any good," Zin said. "What's done is done. Now, what are you going to do about it?"

Seth watched Lily's, waited for her to say, "And here's my plan." For once, she looked like she didn't know. "She made a copy of my face, had me write a letter saying I was running away."

"You mean this note here?" asked a little girl fox, holding it up, before Boscoe took it and shoved it in Lily's face. Kitsune paws seemed awfully dextrous.

"You followed me?" Lily asked.

"You were more interesting than the lovebirds," Boscoe said, before ripping up the paper and joining the others in a little confetti dance on the expensive-looking carpet. "I sent the others to go get mother, but I wasn't going to let you out of my sight until I knew what her game was."

"Game?" Lily asked.

"Need to know the rules before we play," said one of the girls.

"Humans don't think like that," Zin informed the little kits. "My daughter's not wrong though."

"What are your real names?" Lily asked.

"No offence, O'Conells, but one big revelation at a time," Zin said. "They'll go by whatever you call them."

"Last year you called me Snowball," one of the girls offered. "The year before that, I was Posey."

Mama Fern returned and gave Lily a tiny glass cup. She used the hot water from the kettle and mixed a lime-green concoction. "This will make you drowsy but let me take a gander. I'll wake you up right after."

Lily looked nervous, but nodded, and sipped. She didn't drink half before the spark left her eyes and she sank down a little on the cushion. Mama Fern set the remnant drink on the table and titled Lily head back and had a look in her eyes. Mama Fern frowned, but that quickly melted into a smile.

"Can you fix her?" asked Seth. "Or better yet, me?"

"All in good time, Seth," Mama Fern said. "Besides, it's useful to get used to other forms."

"How is *this* useful?" Seth demanded as Mama Fern took Lily's face in her hands. She stroked between her brow and Lily came to with a jerk.

"That, young lady, is a strong spell," Mama Fern said. "Should wear off in a few days without reinforcement."

"Thank goodness." Lily's brow relaxed. "But we don't have a few days. Where is she taking them?"

"You want to stop her?" Mama Fern asked.

"Of course!" Seth sputtered.

"Seth, calm down," Lily said.

"You're not the one turned into a little wooden man," Seth said. Now that he thought about it, he hadn't really examined himself. "I'm still a man, right?"

"Well, you have an energy of intrinsic masculinity about you, " Mama Fern assured him. "Very fetching."

"Uggggh." Seth would check later. Most of the kits sped off, but Boscoe jumped on the chaise and sandwiched himself between Seth and Lily, his puffy tail in Seth's face. Lily stroked him behind the ears while Seth tried to elbow the little fox to move.

"Zin, how are they your family?" Seth asked.

"Don't look at me like that," Mama Fern said. "Zin was quite the looker when he had a full head of dark hair." She cast her hooded eyes in Zin's direction. "Not that he's too sore on the eyes now."

"I was told looks aren't important when you've been married forever, but sheeesh," Seth said to Lily. He was under the impression that Celestial Foxes were uncannily lovely, with the sort of blinding beauty to drive a human bonkers. Seth considered: if marrying a dumpy one to spurn the greatest beauty would be like the Zin he'd grown up knowing or, more simply, this *was* Zin's ideal woman. "What the heck are you doing in Stagmil?" Seth asked.

"My darling Seth, absconding with me barely makes the short list of the heroic and incredibly foolish things my beloved Zin has done," Mama Fern said. She put an ointment then a poultice on Lily's goose egg. Lily grimaced. "That's better. I'm sorry I bit you on the rumpus, dear, would you like some cream for it?"

"No, uh, no thank you," Lily said. "If you knew the woman was magical, why didn't you warn us?"

"We were watching," Mama Fern said. "I warned you about the wyvern, Zin told you to stay out of it. Besides, I needed to learn the game."

"Game? Look at me!" Seth snapped."Why don't you use your magic to fix me?"

"Can't, dear," said the kitsune.

"Then why are we wasting time here?" Seth asked.

"Are you up for another round so soon?" Mama Fern asked. "Tell me about your plan."

Seth wasn't about to let her defeat him with logic or reason. "We get some really, really big clubs . . ."

"Which will be instrumental in bringing down the spider," the kitsune said with a smile that wasn't quite right. "Go on."

"She's the thinker, I'm the doer," Seth pointed to Lily. Beating that thing up would be easier if he wasn't so small. He supposed the first order of business would be turning back human and getting some of his parents' old equipment. He wasn't good for much like this. "We could find dad and the others. A team of us, prepared, could bring her down."

"And in the days it takes to find them and form a plan, how far will she have gone?" Lily asked.

"If you're so smart, let's hear your plan," Seth snapped.

"Her plan was to steal every child in town and turn them into something like you, I think," Lily said quietly. "She must . . . she transformed you because it make you easier to move. Or control."

"Go on," Mama Fern said.

Seth spoke up. "To sell us in some shop? Not likely. Maybe some wizard wants a bunch of slaves and this is the way to move people around without anyone noticing. I mean, who cares if you're moving a bunch of toys around?"

"Oh look dearest, he's a thinker and a doer," Zin said.

"Hey now," Seth said. "Don't lump me in with her. All right: strange lady shows up in town and steals a bunch of kids and turns them into puppets. She waited until our guard was down. If she was invulnerable she wouldn't have played nice for a few days. She'll probably high-tail it out of town . . ." Realization struck him. "East leads to Port Redmaw, Lily. She's going to catch a ship and sail someplace. If she does that we may never find her."

"We'll lose her if we wait or try to find dad," Lily said. Zin nodded.

"As to why, your guess is probably not as good as mine, and I have no clue. Lily, would you like something to eat?" asked the kitsune.

"What about me?" Seth asked.

"You won't need anything to eat or drink for some time. I doubt you could even taste anything." The kitsune returned with a crystal bowl of fresh strawberries—not only were they not in season, but they were perhaps the most beautiful berries Seth had ever seen. The kitsune cut off a sliver of one and handed it to Seth, who crammed it in his mouth. It had no where to go, since his mouth was a cavity.

Mama Fern handed the rest of the berry to Lily. Lily's expression of pleasure annoyed Seth all the more; strawberries were *his* favourite, while Lily preferred blueberries. "These won't be in season for another month," Lily protested.

"Believe me, that'll be the least of your questions before we're done tonight," Zin said. "Are you feeling like yourself again, Lily? You still have that song in your head?"

Lily blanched and looked to Mama Fern. "You said the hold on me will diminish?"

"It should unless you or she keeps reinforcing it," Mama Fern said dryly. "Music without magic is powerful, and many a spellcaster has woven a spell in a song."

"If she has magic then how are we going to stop her? She'll turn into a monster if we get near her," Seth said. "Few horses can keep up with a centaur, none of which are in Stagmil."

"She's not all-powerful. She needed Lily," Zin said.

"Need is a strong word," Seth said.

"The point remains, she played weak and docile and worked in the shadows. She could be overrun," Zin said. "She's likely run off and will try again in another town."

"But why?" Lily asked.

Mama Fern shook her head. "That's what I was trying to figure out. I think part of her story is true—she's on the run."

Lily nodded. "I'm going to free them and bring our people home."

"All of them?" Zin asked.

"I meant our villagers," Lily said quietly, catching Zin's eyes. "How many people do you think she's done this to?"

"I suspect this isn't her first time. Not with the puppets, or the masks. We'll help," Zin said. Lily nodded and tried to stiffen her lip. Seth didn't realize she was so upset. "Don't thank us yet," Zin continued. "Focus on getting your sister and the others back, that'll be a start."

Seth stopped feeling sorry for himself and started to feel bad for the others. Was Madeline going to sell them for children's shows? No, that didn't make any sense. Artisans could make good puppets. Why go through the act of kidnapping? There had to be another motivation.

"As to what she wants—people always want other people to control. Hardly a new concept," said Mama Fern. "Besides, who's to say that the buyer isn't aware of what they really are? Maybe they're being used by selective buyers."

Seth couldn't feel cold but he suppressed a shiver. "I want my body back," he said lowly. "How about it? We four set out?"

"Who said we're going?" Zin asked. "This village is vulnerable; the lullaby ensured that."

"So you're going to bum around here while Lily and I take on a monster?" Seth demanded. "Real heroic of you there, Zin."

Mama Fern frowned. "The Village of Stagmil sleeps. If she returns to steal anyone else we'll be ready for her. You weren't equipped to deal with her magic."

"How am I supposed to fight her when she puts a mask on? She had other masks," Lily said. "Or what if she puts a mask on me again and takes me over?"

"You mean this mask?" Mama Fern asked, producing the spider face. Lily paled and backed away. "It doesn't do anything without the right prompt." Mama Fern put it on herself for emphasis. Nothing happened. "See?"

"One creature down," Seth muttered. "What was that thing, anyway? I think I've heard stories about things like that. They're not common in these parts."

"Maybe we have something back at the house, but I could spend days pouring over the journals," Lily said.

"A jorogumo," Mama Fern informed them. "And you're right, your mother isn't likely to have a journal on them, maybe a story here or there. You'd need your mother's help. You and I both know that's not happening." Lily bowed her head.

"What did I miss?" Seth asked.

"The first person I put to sleep was mom," Lily said. "She was still at the house. I didn't have a choice. Is there no way to wake her?"

"We'll try," Zin said. "Can't make promises; odds are the more time passes, the weaker the hold on everyone will be."

"Is mom okay?" Seth asked his sister. Lily nodded.

Zin cleared his throat. "We'll stay put until the villagers awaken. When they rouse, I'll make my way to Taralee, try to figure out what happened."

Mama Fern nodded. "Zin, get the magic chest."

"I'll get it, mother!" squeaked a kit.

"No, me!" said another.

"*Your father will get it.* Lily, I'll give you something to help. It won't look like much, but while you wear it, you'll be immune from most forms of enchantment. It can be broken, and there are some powers that are greater, but this should be a useful ward."

Zin returned with a large black and red jewellery box. Inside were amazing treasures—rings and brooches with amazing gemstones that sparkled, and others that filled Seth with dread or at least some general irritation, like an itch he couldn't scratch. The kitsune produced a slender bracelet, plain compared to everything else in the box.

"Put your wrist out." Mama Fern said. Lily hesitated. "It will lock on so no one can slip it off. We'll give the key to your brother."

"Why?" Seth asked.

"That way, if anyone grabs you, they'll need to get him to get the key. If anyone grabs him, they'll have the key but not you. Understood?"

"Could it undo my curse?" Seth asked.

"It may lock you to your curse," the kitsune cautioned. "For those already affected, it'll trap an enchantment."

Lily nodded, and Mama Fern locked the bracelet in place.

"Okay, what's that raven pendant with the ruby eyes do?" Seth asked.

"Makes your chicken extra crispy," Zin said. "Mind your own business."

They fastened the key to a leather chord and Seth took it. "Well, we can't have you going out like that." Mama Fern gestured, and Lily followed her out of the room.

~*~

The walk-in closet had formal dresses, stunning robes, and general gardening gear. Mama Fern helped Lily into a crimson blouse and black trousers, with a brown overdress that would allow her to ride. "When you get back, I'll let you come play dress up."

"I don't need to . . ."

"Are you okay if I burn this?" Mama Fern gestured to the black clothes Madeline had made for her. The fit of the new clothes were next to perfect. It was like Mama Fern knew all of Lily's favourite colours. Then she realized that the fox had been her friend all this time. This was the same fox who had come to her for years. She wondered if those kits were the same ones, just changing shape and fur pattern enough to fool her. "Did you ever have human children?"

Mama Fern selected some practical footwear. "Fully human? Yes. My current litter will one day be able to take a human form, but it's not the same thing. You're going to return home and get a few changes of clothes for yourself and Seth? Bring something nice."

"This is a chase," Lily pointed out.

Mama Fern cocked her head. "I'll make you something for when you return. I was making Zin some new clothes, because he needs them . . ."

"This shirt is nicely worn in, woman," called from down the hall.

Mama Fern gave her a once over, and to Lily's surprise, put silver hoops through her ears and styled her hair in a fancier braid than Lily was used to. "There. Now the bracelet won't look out of place," Mama Fern said, and gestured for her to follow. "Just a young lady going about her business. Don't make eye contact with the little wooden puppet, he bites. That bracelet will be helpful, but don't stand in the way of a fireball. Once the magic manifests into flame, it'll be fire, even though the origin is magic. And yes, you and your brother are welcome here after your quest."

"*She gets new clothes and a magic bracelet, all I get is this key*," Seth pointed out upon Lily's return.

"I haven't forgotten about you," Mama Fern said, and got him some string and crossbars.

"Get that away from me!" Seth said.

"You may find them useful," Mama Fern lectured. "You may be in that form for some time, so I would learn how to use it."

"I do jump higher than I did before," Seth said, then took the string, and made a lasso. He had skills from hunting and rearing sheep, but so far he wasn't getting tired, and he never felt cold or pain. He could see much better in the dark, what else could that body do?

"You get a call to adventure and . . . that's not going to cut it, is it?" Zin asked. He pulled out an old crate. "Want some grappling equipment?"

"No," Lily said while Seth crowed, "YES!"

"I'm a hunter and a ranger," Seth said. "Got any enchanted arrow heads?"

"No, just some highly explosive powder, and these throwing knives. I wonder what this does . . . " Zin picked up some sort of strange musicalbox, only for Mama Fern to quickly take it away.

"Darling, I love you, but keep that abomination closed," Mama Fern said. "Or I'm taking the kits and going back to my mother."

"You'll be back."

"I mean it this time."

He shot her a smile, and before Lily and Seth knew it, they were nuzzling each other and whispering sweet nothings in each other's ears.

"We should go. Time is of the essence," Lily said, standing.

"And my non-existent stomach wants to vomit," Seth said.

~*~

Passing through town Seth checked a few houses, everyone they found was in a deep sleep. Many were in their beds, while others were in their chairs, or even sleeping where they stood.

Entering their house, both wrote letters for their mother, even though Zin and Mama Fern said they'd make sure they'd let Sylvia know what had transpired once she roused. It was bizarre because Sylvia slept feet from them, Lily stroked their mom's hair when they got up to leave.

Lily took rations of pemmican and dried fruit and nuts as well as oats for Stella and some of the fire-pitch she'd made. The small clay jars were designed to shatter upon impact so she packed them among her changes of clothing so they wouldn't rattle or break. Monster or woman, everything alive short of a firedrake could be burned.

Lily took the best bow she was consistent with and some of her father's better arrows; he'd taken the best ones with him but he made plenty of good ones on rainy days, as well as oil for her lantern.

The plan was that they'd track, and if the trail took them towards the hunters, they'd signal Elias or at least send word that way if there was a reasonable chance to find someone they knew. If they needed to split up, Seth would track Madeline while Lily would speak to the hunters before rejoining him. He'd notch the trees or leave clues to ensure the path wouldn't go cold, his sister left tracks his little marionette form was too light and unfamiliar to even their trained eyes.

They set out into the night and to the glen where their friends were stolen. The spider webs gleamed under the moonlight, collecting dew as dawn approached. Seth urged Lily to continue east to the main road so they could catch up. Lily took her time, and pointed out that yes, it appeared she was going east, but there was another, different set of tracks. The centaur form trailed south.

She was right. Still, the idea of setting out in the wrong direction irked Seth. "If she makes the port and boards a ship we can't track her," Seth said. "She won't give the same name."

"There's another port to the south a few days," Lily said. "She's trying to trick us into going east. You can go that way if you want, but I'm going south."

"Those tracks were obvious," Seth said.

"You got good eyesight in the dark."

"The only thing good so far. Let's go."

They travelled south, notching trees every ten minutes to make their path evident for whoever would follow. The centaur tracks faded to human ones, smaller female-sized tracks, and he was glad for his sister's earlier stubbornness. Catching someone by foot wouldn't be a problem, but the tracks changed back to hooves. It seemed Madeline couldn't stay a centaur indefinitely.

For the first day, Lily only stopped to feed and water Stella and attend to nature, eating in the saddle.She looked exhausted by the time the sun set on the first day, but both she and Stella pressed on through the forest. Seth realized she hadn't slept the night before, while he was bright and chipper. "We need to make camp," he said when he saw her jerking her head to try to stay awake. "You and Stella need to sleep."

"I'm good," Lily said, rubbing her eyes.

"She'll put her guard down and we'll catch up. We're making camp," Seth told her. Lily looked unconvinced. "For all we know she can turn into something with wings. You're no good to me exhausted, Lil'. You're gonna make a mistake and I'm going to have to make a living telling jokes for peanuts at some carnival."

His sister was normally a light sleeper, and they were so far away from anyone he wasn't worried about keeping watch. Both his sister and Stella slept but Seth couldn't. He could enter a lessened state of awareness. It was boring, as it gave him time to think deep thoughts, and he realized that he'd rather be out mucking about in the bush than examining his life choices. If he left Lily no doubt he would catch up with Madeline; both of them needed to rest, but he didn't. The problem, of course, was he'd end up captured with the others.

They should have noticed the kit hiding in the saddle bags. Seth found Boscoe stalking a rabbit.

"I knew it!" Seth declared, and Boscoe glared at Seth when the rabbit scampered into the bush. "How long have you been following us?"

"I wasn't about to miss my chance for adventure," Boscoe told Seth, giving him a sly smile. "Besides, grandma won't even notice I'm missing." He wandered towards Seth, and gave him a sniff.

"Well, if you're going to be here, you might as well be useful," Seth said, grabbing onto the kitsune's fur and climbing onto Boscoe's back. "Hyup!" He clicked his heels into the little fox's ribs. "Get going!"

Boscoe sat down and looked over his shoulder at Seth. "I will gnaw on you," he said eventually.

"What good are you?"

"Stop thinking like a human, for starters," the kitsune said. "Your new form has new capabilities, and you need to use them. I bet you can scale that tree in front of us."

"I could as a boy."

"Not the same way."

Lily slept through their training session. Because he was so much lighter, Seth could easily rappel and use the string and crossbars to swing from tree to tree. He already knew how to lasso and shoot, the scale made it tricky but he relearned old skills and learned to flip and collapse then pick himself up, launching and propelling further. He wasn't getting tired, so he gave himself a goal and didn't stop until he became agile and then proficient. He also could take himself apart— with his arm off he made it go do his bidding as he sat there, but realized that it was really only good until it was out of sight, then it would fall over and be mostly useless.

Lily woke to the pair of them laughing, reminiscing because what boy doesn't like to make fun of their sisters? "Boscoe?" she asked, sitting up in her sleeping bag. "You shouldn't be here!"

"*You shouldn't be here,*" Boscoe mimicked in a high-pitched voice, wiggling slightly and falling over in a fit of giggles.

"Ordering him around is a losing battle," Seth agreed.

"How long did you know?" Lily asked.

"I thought something stank. Boscoe ate all my jerky from home."

"It was delicious," Boscoe said, smacking his jowls.

Lily walked to the pair of them, arms crossed. "I'll take you home the minute we find the others. What should I call you?"

"I like it when you call me Boscoe. And I'm a kitsune; we help heroes. Haven't you heard stories?"

"Mostly the ones where celestial foxes lead fools to their doom," Seth offered.

"Besides all of those," said Boscoe, rubbing his chin and cheeks on Lily's boots and pants affectionately. "The pair of you need help on the magic part of your quest. Besides," he paused to chuckle. "Seth needs all the help he can get."

"Oi!"

~*~

In the days of tracking that followed, while Stella and Lily slept, Seth trained. The few times he fell he found that he wasn't really hurt, but he didn't want to test the theory and determine at which height he'd break. He practiced hogtying his sleeping sister—she was not amused, but he could easily incapacitate her if the ropes were strong enough.

One night, they squared off and he tried to fight her her, jumping and slicing. If she caught him, the game was up, but first, she had to catch him. He learned to grab onto her sleeve and run up her arm, and the best trick he learned was climbing behind someone and blinding them. He tried to incapacitate Lily, using the string in an attempted choke, but Lily pulled him off and sent him flying. He wasn't particularly strong but he could trip her and be irritable.

Seth wasn't sure how many days they journeyed, because he never ate or slept. For the most part he rode on Stella's head or Lily's shoulder, though he and Boscoe passed the time in the saddle bags telling riddles and bad jokes, sticking their heads out to ask Lily how she was doing and offering their brilliant one-liners. Lily occasionally got consternated with the path, but then Boscoe would leap out, and sniff, and gesture.

"How are you at sensing magic?" Lily asked.

"Wouldn't you like to know," Boscoe sung. "That spider mask stinks something fierce though."

Seth could smell fire, dew, and fox no problem, but the mask smelled just like wood and plaster to him.

Eventually the trees thinned and they found a path, there were more marks but Madeline's feet no longer resembled a centaur's but a woman's. They journeyed down the road, speaking to the odd passerby before they spotted the coast and a castle in the distance. Seth had been to Port Redmaw; he wasn't sure the last time he'd been this far south. Normally their business took them north to visit their grandparents or west to Taralee.

The path took them to a small town southwest of the castle. Shelkie's Bay was on a sign; they could have asked the folk coming and going, with people driving their herds and wagons.In a way it felt not so different than Stagmil. Before they entered the town, Boscoe jumped out of Stella's saddle bag and fox-trotted towards the tall grass besides the dirt path.

"That place's not fit for kitsunes," he said. "Be careful."

"You want to go steal a chicken," Seth pointed out. The kitsune didn't deny it, instead he bounded away, the ripples in the tall grass growing distant until they were no different than that of a gentle breeze.

"You better hide too," Lily said, and Seth nodded, making his way to the saddle bag, but leaving his head out so he could still see and talk to her.

"What do we do if she's already sailed?" he asked as Stella took them past the outlying houses. For the most part, the town seemed well-kept and clean and folk didn't look sideways at them.

"Follow, and hope mom and dad won't be too far behind," Lily said, prompting Stella towards the town and docks.

Seven

The coastal town of Shelkie's Bay was some distance from the castle they'd spotted from the main road. Fisherboats launched near the town or even from one of the nearby beaches. Massive reconstruction was underway at the docks; they learned that the port was nearly destroyed a few weeks prior, so while merchant vessels and passenger ships were coming and going, it was in a much reduced capacity.

Lily had no idea what to ask when she approached the dock master, but apparently only two cargo ships launched that day with another set to go that evening—one south along the coast, the other across the sea to Ivancia. No passenger ships had left for the past two days; she doubted Madeline had that much of a lead on them.

Lily decided to find a tavern and a hot meal; she'd been to pubs in Taralee where people talked freely and her parents regularly made business deals over pints. The town was bigger than Stagmil and had more variety of building and businesses, but there was really only one inn in town. There was a large fountain before several large businesses, and there Lily and Seth found the woman who they'd been looking for, performing a puppet show before a crowd.

Madeline wore a new dress of black and yellow, and her hair was pinned in a loose chignon. Seth popped his head out of Stella's saddle bag and they studied the performance and the crowd. Mostly children and the elderly. "We didn't think this far, did we?" Seth asked.

"We can't accuse her in front of this crowd." Lily dismounted, not wanting to draw undue attention, so she led Stella to a side street where they could continue to watch. The town didn't seem large enough to warrant guards in any real force, but with the port and the castle less than an hour's ride from town, no doubt there was someone who was trained within a reasonable distance. Stella wickered and folk cast glances at them; Lily wondered if she should tie her down and get closer. Assuming she and Seth managed to capture Madeline, then what? Take her to the woods and wait for her parents for three days? Start trekking home?

"I say you string me up and we join her little show," Seth said. "I'll attack her and you pretend it's all part of the act. *Hey kids, do you like violence?*"

"Let's not do anything rash," Lily said. "That passenger ship's not leaving for a few days. She's probably staying at the inn."

"I can sneak into her room and rummage," Seth offered.

"Are you a puppeteer too?" asked a voice belonging to a boy about nine or so. Lily was watching Madeline so intently, she hadn't noticed him. He was dark-skinned and dressed like the farmers' kids back home. "Can I see yours?"

"Sorry?" Lily asked, glancing down at Stella's saddlebag. Seth had disappeared into it.

"I saw your doll."

"Puppet," came from the bag.

"Can I see it?" the boy pressed.

Lily smiled and knew this was a terrible idea, but figured this was the best way for the boy to sate himself and be gone. She whispered, "Just pretend to be a toy." Into the saddle bag, Seth protested but went limp like a rag doll. "He doesn't have any strings," Lily said, producing Seth. The young boy smiled and held Seth gently.

"He's so lifelike. He's not for sale, is he?"

"No, I'm sorry," Lily said. "He's uh . . . very *precious* to me."

"Gustav!" Another boy called from the market square, moving towards them. They didn't look like brothers; this one had blond hair and big ears, Lily thought he was kind of cute, though he looked younger than Seth. "Don't wander off like that."

"The story's for little kids," Gustav said. "They should tell stories about knights and dragons!" He gestured with Seth, making chopping motions. "You know, good stuff!"

"Wow, that's realistic," Sean said, his upper lip curling as he examined Lily and took her brother from Gustav before Lily could retrieve her brother. Sean bent Seth's limbs at awkward angles, and Lily thought Seth would poke him in the eyes but remained Seth limp. "Where did you get this?" His nostrils flared, tone hostile.

"None of your business," Lily said, feeling her heart racing and heat rushing to her cheeks. "Give him back." She tried to grab Seth, but Sean jerked his hand away.

"I'm serious, where did you—ow!" Sean dropped Seth, who hit the ground cat like. Seth then did a dance where he crouched, kicked, did several cartwheels and flips before he hightailed it to the nearest fence and jumped over it, disappearing from sight.

"Huh, that was weird," Lily said, ignoring Sean's glare and grabbing Stella's reins, leading the mare away.

"Gustav, go find your brother," Sean said, walking towards Lily with intent.

"He's right there," Gustav pointed down the street where Lily was headed. A taller, lean youth with a similar complexion to Gustav was walking towards them.

"Alfred!" Sean called. Lily froze in her tracks. "Stop her!"

"Who's your friend?" Alfred asked, stopping in his tracks, gesturing to Lily.

"This is not my friend," Sean snapped. "I thought that woman looked familiar!" He grabbed Lily's forearm. Lily shoved him off. "Help me!"

"What?" Alfred asked, but grabbed Lily's other arm before she could reach across her hip for her sword. She tried to use her weight to drag them off, but thought better of screaming for help. The two were locals, and she was a stranger. "Sean?" Alfred asked, the concern in his voice obvious. "What are we doing?"

"Let me go!" Lily demanded. "I'm warning you!"

"You be quiet," Sean told her.

Stella nickered and reared, and the boys released Lily. Once the mare calmed, Lily tried to mount, but Alfred was faster than he looked, and grabbing Lily he dragged her from Stella, who whinnied and charged him. Alfred let go and stumbled backwards; Lily clambered into the saddle. Alfred reached for her again, but Lily kicked his arm away.

"Gustav," Sean said. "Go back to the others, and call for help."

"Boys!" said a very large, burly woman wearing a bright yellow skirt. "What on earth has gotten into you?"

"Aunt Catarina, I can explain," Sean said.

"Please do," Alfred said.

"This girl is in league with that puppeteer in the town square."

"Oh?" asked Catarina. "And you don't approve of the programme?"

"That woman back there turned me and Espy into puppets back in Taralee. This girl is with her," Sean said. Lily protested but Sean continued, "Didn't Uncle Terrance and Aunt Siona mention what happened back in Taralee?"

"They mentioned lots of things," Catarina said.

Lily reached for the reigns and didn't dare dismount. "That woman and I have unfinished business," Lily snapped through gritted teeth. "Get out of my way."

"What are you, some sort of bounty hunter?" Sean asked sceptically.

"Her? *Hah!*" Seth called from behind Catarina. Seth was with Gustav, holding his hand. "Don't make me laugh. *Hah!*"

Alfred's eyes widened and he walked to his brother. "Espy said . . ." His gaze turned towards the crowd. "Bedelia and Yolonda are back there."

"She doesn't work her real magic in front of a crowd," Lily said, scowling at Sean. She licked her lips, grateful she didn't actually hurt either of them.

"Love," Catarina said. "How exactly are you planning on confronting her?"

"I'm working on it," Lily said, dismounting. The mare tossed her head, Lily consoled her, but kept her eyes on the strangers. "Let's go, Seth."

"Nuh-uh. I've been waiting days for this."

"For what?" Sean asked.

"Pow! Right in the kisser!" Seth crowed.

Lily pinched the bridge of her nose. "You are not selling this."

"We just need you and her to get arrested until mom and dad catch up," Seth pointed out.

"I wouldn't take advice from a little wooden boy if I were you," Catarina said.

"Little wooden *man*," Seth clarified.

"All of you be quiet and stop getting in my way," Lily said.

"Is violence your first choice?" Catarina asked.

Lily shook her head. "I'd rather not make a scene until I find my people."

"I have a plan that won't make that necessary," Catarina said. "You didn't by chance bring your banjo, Alfred?"

"Yeah," said the tall youth. "It's back in the wagon."

"Excellent. Go find a nice spot away from her but in the square and play something when she's done her performance. Draw the crowd's attention. I'll handle the puppeteer," Catarina said. "I suggest the young lady isn't seen. In fact, until we get to the bottom of this, it's best not to let her wander." Catarina marched to the town square. If she wasn't so tall she would have blended right into the crowd.

She felt a hand on her shoulder from behind. "I still don't trust you," Sean said. "As for you," he looked to Seth. "the spell should start to wear off soon."

"I've been like this for days." Seth said. "Now get your mitts off my sister."

"What are you doing to—ow ow ow ow!" Seth shot a blunt arrow into Sean's kneecap. He and Sean bickered, so Lily looked to Alfred.

"Do you know what she's going to do?" she asked.

He shrugged. "If she recognizes you she may take off," Alfred said. "That goes for you too, Sean. Don't draw attention to yourself."

Sean gave Seth the stink eye. "Come on, Gustav. Let's grab your sister and Yolanda." Leading Stella, Lily waited where Sean gestured. Seth watched from Stella's head.

Madeline had moved on to more woodland creatures and another tall tale. Part of Lily wanted to see her sister or one of the other human puppets, but so far all of her marionettes were animals.

Sean left them and blended into the crowd. Alfred hopped into his old wagon, drawn by a pair of donkeys, and pulled out a red banjo that looked well-used but cared for, and began to tune it quietly.

Lily's heart raced when a human puppet was introduced. It wasn't obvious who it was at first, but hope kindled. The marionette wore a red skirt and matching bonnet. Lily resisted the urge to rush over, crowd or no, but told herself there was no do-over and, Seth wasn't one for subtlety.

Sean moved to another girl that had a resemblance of Alfred and Gustav, and a tall girl wearing a homespun blue dress with puffy linen sleeves, and gestured for them to go a different way. As the show concluded and people tossed their coins, Alfred started to play from the back of his turnip wagon. Most people went from one entertainer to another. Madeline looked sour that some of her coin was to be split up with another opportunistic busker, but continued to pack up her equipment.

Sean returned with the others he was speaking to. The younger girl peered at Lily quizzically, though she smiled at Stella. "I like your horse," she said. "Oh, you have a puppet too! Where's his strings? How is he standing like that and rolling his eyes?"

"Yolanda, can you take the kids home?" Sean asked the tall girl with the puffy sleeves.

Yolanda nodded, but then looked back to the wagon. "Is everything all right?"

Lily stopped paying attention to the exchange, as Catarina's massive shadow fell upon Madeline. "Excuse me," Catarina said sweetly. "I just wanted to say I really enjoyed your play."

"I'm glad to hear that I brought joy to your day," Madeline said, looking up at the much bigger woman. "I'd love to do something a little more refined, but I noticed there were mostly children playing in the square. I really ought to be going, excuse me."

It almost seemed like Catarina could will herself even bigger when people were doing what she didn't like. "Are you staying somewhere in town?"

"Moving on, I'm afraid," the woman said with a smile. "Now if you'll excuse me."

"I've actually been working on a play. Not for puppets but the stage. We have a stage built every year for our spring and fall festivals. I'm wondering if I were to buy you a pint, that you might look it over."

"I really don't consider myself an expert on the writing. I do my best to bring the scripts to life," Madeline said.

"Nonsense," Catarina said, embracing the woman from the side like an old chum, lifting her off her feet. "I insist you come with me. I won't take 'no' for an answer."

"I couldn't say no to a friendly drink at the pub, one artist to another," said the puppeteer. "Isn't the tavern back that way?"

"I thought you weren't staying at the inn."

Alfred was joined by a fiddler, and several of the smaller children started jigging when someone started to blow on a jug. No one seemed to notice Catarina kidnapping the puppeteer they were all gawking at a moment ago. Lily and Seth followed Sean back to Catarina's wagon, which had several sacks of flour and sugar as well as some apples and other fresh produce. Catarina had the woman in one arm, and the bags in the other.

"Unhand me this instant," Madeline said. "I'll . . . I'll *scream*."

"Go ahead. I'll gather all the people who know me and you can explain the little yappy puppet," Catarina said, gesturing to Seth. "Now behave or I'm emptying my floursack and stuffing you inside. I don't want to go wasting food if I can avoid it."

Sean walked right over to the woman as Catarina set Madeline down on the driver's bench. "Remember me?"

Judging by her expression, Madeline did not. She did, however, recognize Lily and Seth, standing a few feet behind them. She gave a sly smirk when her eyes landed on Seth. "You caught me," Madeline said to them. "Now what are you going to do?"

Seth was already diving into the bag that Catarina had barely put down, and he resurfaced. "It's Rebecca!" he said, hauling out the girl by the strings.

"Who else is there?" Lily asked.

"Just her," Seth said. "Where's my sister?" he demanded of Madeline, who caught Lily's gaze, and smiled, as if in approval. Lily bristled as the puppeteer remained completely silent.

~*~

Lily wasn't sure where they were going but had Stella follow behind the wagon as they plodded along north of town, Seth sat on Stella's head and glaring at the back of Madeline's. The puppeteer sat next to Catarina, Sean relegated to sitting in the back with the supplies. The masks were absent, and besides the puppet of Rebecca there were several animals.

Besides the occasional grunt from the oxen they travelled in silence, eventually arriving at a large cottage-style dwelling in a wooded area. Madeline didn't didn't look amused as Catarina told her to follow her into the house, and Sean unhitched the oxen and said she could leave Stella with them. Lily hauled water for all three of them before removing Stella's tack. "You did good girl," Lily said, stroking the mare's nose. "I hope I can give you a day of rest, you deserve it."

Lily brushed her mare down and gave her oats, though Stella was content with the oxen's feed of hay and alfalfa. By the time Lily finished, Sean was almost done putting away the supplies they'd picked up from town so she assisted where she could before following him into the house where Seth, Madeline, and Catarina had already gone. It was like everything was built to a slightly larger scale. Lily felt tiny as she followed Sean in and he told her where to put her boots. The sturdy furniture was of a golden stain and the blue curtains were drawn back to allow in natural light. There were hand-crafted wooden figures as well as a loom and spinning wheel in the main seating area. Seth scowled, sitting on the round kitchen table, inanimate Rebecca beside him. Madeline sat there like she was a guest while Catarina worked the oven.

A big dog woofed at them when they entered the dining room, however a tiny fluffy kitten curled up in the big dog's bed mewed at the dog, so it whined slightly and laid back down mournfully on the hard floor.

Sean pulled up a chair so Lily did likewise. She wanted to break the silence, but didn't know what to say until Catarina asked the woman what she took for her tea. "You do know she's kidnapped people," Lily said.

"There's no reason to not be hospitable," Catarina said. She thrust a warm cup of something that boasted cinnamon and cardamom at Lily and asked if anyone would like muffins; she had poppyseed and blueberry. Seth muttered how much *he'd* like a muffin. "We'll be having stew and fresh bread later. *No one* needs to give me a reason to be inhospitable."

"You're going to fix us." Seth left Rebecca and stormed over to the bags, producing a puppet wolf and crane in addition to the squirrel she'd seen earlier. Rebecca only moved when she fell over, which Seth quickly remedied. "If you try to do to me what you did to Rebecca, Lily will chop your head clean off."

Madeline arched an eyebrow. "I don't have the supplies to restore you here," Madeline said lowly.

"Where are they?" Seth demanded. "Tell me or I'm giving you splinters!"

Madeline sipped her tea and ignored Seth.

"When you turned me into a puppet, you couldn't do the same to Daphne," Sean said. "She was already under a spell. You had a special pair of scissors."

"Who's Daphne?" Seth asked.

"A friend," Sean said before turning his attention back to Madeline. "Where are their villagers?"

"It's too late for them," said the puppeteer. "I've already sent them in a ship across the sea."

Lily's heart raced.

"So the spell *is* reversible," Catarina said. "There' no reason to be inhospitable. Yet."

"Look what she did to me!" Seth pointed out.

"*Yet.*"

"What? Oh," Seth said, then nodded.

Madeline looked impassive, like she was trying to pretend she was there of her own free will and they were annoying her. "It wasn't anything personal," she said eventually.

"Personal? You put that mask on me and took me over," Lily snapped. "You said you were going to steal every child in our village."

Sean wrinkled his nose in confusion, but the woman shrugged. "I wasn't after anyone specific. I did what I had to. You were my first choice; as for that old swordsman I didn't buy that doddering old man routine for a minute. As for what I did in Taralee—they all wanted to be on the stage." Madeline smiled at some secret joke. "To be free of a mundane peasant life toiling away in the fields."

"There were masks back in her studio," Sean said lowly. "She didn't use them, though."

"Now Sean, you didn't expect her to have played all her cards then and there, did you? Why don't you tell me what happened as you remembered it?" Catarina said. "And don't be embarrassed—why, if I had a ruby tiara for every time your uncle Larry crossed a wizard and was stuck in an enchanted form, I'd have at least four of them."

"She used a pair of golden scissors to cut the strings on Daphne, but Daphne moved and she cut the giant mannequin's strings instead," Sean said. "It came to life and attacked her. Then Daphne started freeing everyone else in the toy store with those scissors."

Madeline nodded. "The others I worked with fled. Two of us were arrested and taken to a cell, but there I made more puppets out of scraps and was able to animate them for a short amount of time. We escaped, and made our way back to the shop in the middle of the night. I grabbed what supplies I could and left town and journeyed east, got off the beaten path and stumbled into your *quaint* little village. My associate . . . doesn't matter. Like I said," she looked to Seth. "Nothing personal."

Around that time, Alfred arrived with a man of about forty or so years of age. There was a strong resemblance between the pair. "Good to see you Isaac. How is the farm?" Catarina asked.

"We're doing well, thanks to you," Isaac said, taking off his coat, familiar as to where to put his boots and hang his hat. "Alfred told me everything, Sean."

"I don't think I told Alfred everything," Sean told the older man. "Is Espy home?"

"No, she's off with her friends," Isaac said. He welcomed the warm mug of tea. "My name is Isaac Sprites," he said, looking levelly at Madeline. "Did you do this," he pointed to Seth. "To my daughter?"

The woman's lips thinned. "I can't remember everyone I've ever enchanted, but I do remember the last set before being forced to flee. Petite thing with big eyes? She wanted the stage, and the fools at the academy didn't want her."

"They're fools all right," Catarina said. "That's why my Larry walked away. It's tragic, really," she let out a sniff. "but a tale for another day. Well, you knew where the inn was so I assume you have a room. Now, both Isaac and I know innkeeper. If you lie, we will find out."

"And if you do, what then?" Madeline asked, a thin smile still on her lips.

"We'll keep you nice and safe and I'll write to my brother Terrence who lives in Taralee. I'm sure the authorities are wondering where their prime suspect has gotten to," Catarina said, her voice dripping in kindness. "I'd imagine many folks are wondering where their loved ones are. There's not a bounty on you, is there?"

Madeline's face soured. "If I help you get your sister, I want to be free when this is over."

"There's still the matter of Louis and Brigid," Seth pointed out.

Catarina shook her head. "You can't be trusted not to go out and kidnap more children."

"You're going to hand me over to the authorities regardless, so I don't see what's motivating me to help you."

"You're repenting for your wrong-doings," Catarina said. "As a sign of good faith, you helped us rescue the others. You're a changed woman, and are throwing yourself on the mercy of the courts."

"I'm in room four at your inn," Madeline said. "I didn't lie; your friends have already been sent out. I only kept one of them."

"They've already been sold," Seth muttered. "How much are we worth to you? I want a number."

"It doesn't matter," Isaac said. "We're getting them back. I know we just got here, Catarina . . ."

"Go on," Catarina obliged. "Tell them I sent you."

After they left for town, it was just Lily and Catarina watching Madeline, and part of Lily wanted to go with them, but she knew that the woman could try something, and Catarina shouldn't be alone. She wasn't sure what she could do that Catarina couldn't, but still. With the bracelet on Lily's wrist, Madeline couldn't take her over. "You would have laid low if you had enough money," Lily said.

"I wasn't expecting you to track me all the way here."

It was an awkward silence, and Lily felt like Madeline's was almost approving that Lily had found her. She helped Catarina, mostly cutting vegetables. When the boys returned, they'd pulled the buns from the oven and Seth was still looking still small and puppet-like.

"I couldn't find the others," he told Lily. Madeline's bags held masks and string and cross-bars, a few changes of garment and some items that looked like they'd been taken from Constance's home.

Catarina picked up a long-faced mask. "These things took you over, dear?"

"Yes. Not immediately. She did something. Better not put one on." Lily suggested. She didn't doubt that Catarina didn't have to be trans-formed into a monster to be a menace. "At least, not until we know what we're doing." When Lily touched the mask, she felt the bracelet on her wrist grow heavy. *A warning?* Lily certainly wasn't going to put one on.

Cutting Rebecca's strings, she fell forward in a tumble, away from

Lily's hand before she picked herself up off the table. She looked around at everyone wildly, her once-muted features as animated as Seth's. "Holy smokes," she said. "Why are you all just sitting there having tea? Look what she did to me!"

Lily grabbed her and despite Rebecca's size, she wasn't the easiest to hold. "I don't like this either," Lily told her. "Until we find the others, we need her."

Rebecca ignored Lily. "You monster! What did you do to me? Where's Molly and Dale?"

Madeline smiled. "You should be back to normal within the next half hour. Then all evidence against me will be gone."

Lily felt a strange dread, but she seemed to be the only one remotely taken aback. "Oh? How about kidnapping?" Rebecca demanded. "You explain what I'm doing down here! My uncle is a lawyer in Taralee!"

"Children run away from home all the time," Madeline said with a shrug.

"You are wearing my grandmother's earrings," Rebecca said. "And that's my mother's dress. You took other stuff from my grandmother's house. If kidnapping me won't stick, I'll get you on theft. We took you in! Where is Brigid, huh?"

Rebecca was rapidly growing. "Rebecca, I don't think the clothing will hold," Lily pointed out.

"What? Eee!"

"I've got some spare clothes in the saddle bags, come on." Lily had gotten so used to Seth just climbing on her she had to double back when Rebecca dangled from the table, uncertain how her puppet body moved. Seth made it look easy, but thankfully Rebecca wasn't so big she was awkward to carry.

Rebecca brightened when she saw Stella muddling around with two large oxen. She didn't turn her nose up at Lily's clothing which had lacing to allow their differences in heights and figures, but it was strange to see Rebecca wearing her things.

Returning, Seth was back to normal size and looked almost normal. He was still sitting at the table topless, his pants and small clothes hadn't ripped, he was holding the remnant of the shirt he'd made himself as a puppet in his hands. "Odd." He also didn't appear to care that he was going to sit around topless until Sean offered him a tunic.

"All right, now that I'm back to normal size." Rebecca stormed towards the table. Both Seth and Lily restrained her, but Rebecca was stronger than she looked. "Let me at her, O'Connells!"

"Rebecca, we're not supposed to use that last name outside of Stagmil," Seth snapped. "Use my mom's maiden name."

"Why?" Sean spoke up.

Lily opened her mouth but it was Catarina who spoke. "Elias O'Connell travelled from the west to hunt in the Greenbrier Mountains, and made a name for himself before he . . . upset the wrong people." She paused to chuckle. "Should have known with that hair."

Lily's heart lurched as she caught Seth's gaze, who looked equally surprised. Sean spoke up. "How do you know that?"

"You know how your uncle Terrence married Siona? Sylvia and Sonia are first cousins. Can't chuck a stick without hitting a Brathwell in Rosehill County," Catarina stated matter-of-factly.

"We're from Stagmil," Rebecca said.

"We were born up in Rosehill," Seth clarified. "Brathwell's a pretty common name, by the by. Wait, so your brother is married to my mum's cousin?"

Catarina nodded. "Distantly, we're family."

"I don't understand," Rebecca said. "You use the Brathwell name when you sell fleece, but lots of people use old names for trade."

"We . . . can't talk about what my parents used to do," Lily said.

"Didn't your dad panic on a hunt?"

"No," Lily said. "Both my parents were involved. They kind of met because of the business."

Catarina nodded. "Syl didn't stop until after she was pregnant with . . . I suppose that would have been one of you," Catarina said to Seth and Lily. "Yes, I suppose we ought not discuss the perils of refusing a prince. That was years ago, mind."

Rebecca frowned. "What aren't you telling me?"

"We are not talking about it in front of her," Lily said, gesturing at Madeline. "We shouldn't be talking about it at all."

"I think I understand," Rebecca said. "But that doesn't change what that woman did."

"We need her to find the others," Lily said. "I haven't sent a letter back home yet; I think maybe you should do it so your parents aren't so worried."

"Oh, my penmanship will be singed with righteous fury! And how dare you name me *Babette*?"

"That is the name of the girl in the play," Madeline said with an indifferent shrug.

"I," Seth said lowly, "am starving." Catarina served the former puppets bowls of piping hot soup before handing out bowls to the others, bringing out the crusty buns and citing Larry should have been home by now.

Seth normally had a big appetite but he was gobbling the fodo down like he hadn't eaten in a week. Rebecca was much more reserved. Lily enjoyed the warmth as well as the creamy broth; she'd made fires at night but really hadn't made any complicated meals. "Sean and Alfred told me about what happened, though it seems when they're done explaining one thing they gloss over another," Isaac told Catarina. "It seems that your sister had quite the adventure while I was locked up."

"We didn't really think much of Daphne showing up in time for the contest," Sean said. "A lot of girls from farms and other towns like to compete in the contests, or dance jigs." He looked to Madeline, who was eating quietly. "You weren't doing it just for the money."

Lily frowned. "Who gave you the power to do this?"

Madeline looked pensive, but nodded. "I sent your friends across the sea to the one who gifted me . . . certain things. I sent them to Mirador, but they may not stay. That is up for my master to decide."

"Where's Mirador?" Seth asked his sister.

"I've never heard of it," Lily said.

"It's a castle in the Kingdom of Ivancia," Madeline said. "Once your friends arrive, they cannot get out. Of course, they may be sent elsewhere. The ship I sent them on sailed this morning. You will never get to them in time."

"Who is your master?" Lily asked.

"What does he want with puppets?" Sean asked.

"Do you have any salt and pepper?" Seth asked.

"The name he uses is Asmodean. A dancer does not question the rhythm the song, neither does a puppet know why the master's hand moves him a certain way," Madeline said. "I am fulfilling my part of the bargain."

"Which ship did they board?" Isaac asked. "They may still be in the harbour."

"*The Marigold Dinglett* sailed with the tide this morning," Madeline explained. "I'm no expert, but depending on the wind they'll arrive tonight or tomorrow morning. From there, they'll be taken by carriage to the castle. Normally they'd wait in storage and be brought in a few weeks, but I had a message to deliver."

"I already put in a request," Isaac said. "I'll know which ships have left the harbour in the last week by morning." Lily and Seth looked at one another. They missed their friends by mere hours. But, technically, they weren't in the castle yet. There was still a chance.

"All right, over the sea I go," Seth announced. "Lily, you double back the way we came; odds are someone's on their way down here and will meet you halfway. I'll write to you when I get to Manydoor."

"We left plenty of notches in the trail, mom and dad'll be here in a few days," Lily said. "We'll go together. How long does it take to sail to Ivancia?"

"Depends on the winds and the ship," Alfred offered. "Larry says it's usually faster coming back this way. Some ships can do it in eight hours, but Larry's ship's never done it faster than ten. Also depends on where you're sailing to, there's plenty of ports along the Ivancian coast."

"Who's Larry?" Seth asked.

"You're in his house," Sean said.

"They ain't gonna let a girl just tallyho across the pond into a different kingdom," Seth said. "I'll get a job on crew then make my way to wherever she sent them. I got two good legs."

"And then what?" Lily asked. "You've never been overseas before."

"Neither have you, but it'll be easier without you slowing me down."

"Stop both of you," Isaac said. They hadn't even begun to bicker. "I'll take you both to Mirador myself."

Lily and Seth were stunned into silence. This man didn't owe them anything. "Dad, we just got you back," Alfred said.

"I couldn't help Esperanza before," Isaac said. "I'll help them."

"Okay, I guess," Seth said to Isaac before he turned his gaze to his sister. "Do you really want to leave Rebecca here by herself?"

"I'm not made of glass, Seth," Rebecca snapped. "It makes sense if you're sailing off for someone from home stays here to let folks know where you've gone. Why do I have to be the youngest?"

"It's important to let your family see you for themselves," Lily said, "It'll help Brigid and Molly's family too, let them know we're going to find them." She smiled at Catarina. "Seems like we're not leaving you with strangers."

It was around that time that a large man came in through the main door. He was broad-shouldered and had an impressive flannel-shirt and a debonair tricorn hat. "This doesn't look like your sewing circle."

"Hurry up, we're eating already."

"Isaac, good to see you," Larry said when he joined them. "I'm surprised Nora is letting you out of her sight."

"She understands," Isaac said.

"You know the Sprites, but this is Seth and this young lady is Rebecca, the other is Lily," Catarina gestured as she introduced them. "The woman—"

"Is the puppeteer who did that to him," Larry gestured. "Don't look at me like that; his hands are still wood."

Seth paused, put his spoon down, looked at his hands, shrugged, then went back to eating.

"Don't tell me you knew—" Catarina began.

"I listen to your brother once in a while," Larry offered.

They got Larry up to speed, who nodded and confirmed that it would have been a normal day at sea, and yes, there were plenty of ports in which that vessel could have sailed. He didn't know of any Mirador, though he thought the name sounded somewhat familiar.

"This Asmodean," Sean pressed Madeline. "What exactly was your bargain?"

"He approached me when my career as a dancer was ending. I wasn't one of the chosen ones. I was getting older—but I could still glide better than girls half my age. I was assigned to take in dresses, but never to design them. To be the back up, but never on centre stage.

"He said I couldn't be anything other than a useful tool, no matter how hard I worked. He said if I agreed to help him in the future, he'd give me the power to be acknowledged." She snickered. "Suddenly, I was noticed. For two years, I was finally getting the recognition I deserved." Her eyes and smile were distant, like she was reliving better times. "And one day, my ankle gave out. My time in the sun was over, and the same shallow fools who fawned over me were on to their next up and coming, never caring about the dancer so long as she performed the way they liked." She chuckled. "I thought we were done, but I had to pay the toll. In short, all Asmodean wants is for me send him puppets. He wants young folk and no one pays attention to me, so it's not that hard. If I don't obey, I lose what power I have."

"That's no excuse for what you did," Larry pointed out.

Madeline shrugged. "Being a dancer was my passion. For years I watched the talentless get propped up and the good struggle. Life's unfair; I learned that too late. But power. . . once you develop a taste for it, there's nothing quite like it." She chuckled. "If I stopped, Asmodean would still collect. In the meantime, if I happen to kidnap a little idiot who didn't deserve the stage, so be it."

"Lady, I used to teach at the academy," Larry said. "I know every little crook and problem about them. I left when I had enough of their politicsand started my own business. I'm my own man and didn't have to make a deal with the devil to get here."

"You?" the woman asked, incredulity in her tone. "Did you teach the new hires to use a broom?"

Larry cleared his throat, then let loose a low melody that shook the house. His insanely beautiful voice made Lily shiver. Seth was so enchanted he almost put his spoon down. Catarina joined him for a little bit—she had a lovely voice, but nothing could compare to Larry's larynx.

"You're not—there was a Larry and they said he was a tall man but . . . you can't be *that* Larry. They said he gave up his career to be with his one true love." Madeline looked from Larry to Catarina in confusion.

"Oh, I liked Taralee right enough. Larry was the one sick and tired of playwrights banging on our door at all hours asking them to cover their bad lyrics with his beautiful voice. A distraction, I think it's called," Catarina mused.

Madeline didn't seem deterred. "If only I could bottle your voice . . ."

"I got no strings on me, lady, and I intend to keep 'em that way," Larry said. He looked to Seth and Lily. "So, you think you're going to manage her across the ocean and rescue your people?"

"Well yeah," Seth said.

Isaac nodded in agreement. "This woman tried to kidnap my Esperanza. I can only imagine what your families back at home are going through. We can send a letter to your village. Where is it?"

"East of Taralee—I don't think you've heard of it," Lily said. "It's called Stagmil."

"Oh not as familiar as we'd like to be. We'd visit that way more often, if someone wasn't such a homebody." Catarina poked Larry in the ribs. He harummphed. "In fact, I think I could use a holiday."

"So go," Larry said.

"You know full well I am a delicate flower in need of protection."

"Someone has to be sensible."

"Good, you can keep us on course. We're going. Larry's just putting on an act but he's tickled pink," Catarina said. "Sean, watch the house while we're gone."

"What?" Sean demanded. "She turned me into a puppet too, you know."

"And we don't want you being rash. In the meantime, we all can't just leave our oxen unattended," Catarina pointed out. Sean gave a reluctant sigh, but nodded.

"Well I'm not being left out," Alfred said. "How about it Larry? Teach me to do real sailing?"

Isaac turned to his son. "I'm going to insist you stay home."

"When you were arrested, I promised mom I'd protect Espy," Alfred said.

"Which is why I need you here where she and your siblings are," Isaac said.

"We just got you back," Alfred said. "You know I want to crew up this fall."

Isaac looked contemplative. "I am trusting you to look after the family while I'm gone. I don't know how long that'll be. Besides, won't you miss Yolanda?" Alfred's eyes widened at the mention of the tall girl. "Their people will come this way and if they no longer need me, I'll come home."

The others looked at Larry expectantly, who eventually let out an exaggerated sigh. "We'll take my sailboat in the morning, are you all happy?"

"Oh, Larry my sweet!" Catarina beamed, before addressing Seth and Lily. "See? All solved. Sean, dig out our tents, including the kitchen one. Oh, I best get to baking before the journey."

Rebecca would stay at the Sprite's farm, so Lily went with her for the evening. Seth, Alfred, and Sean were put to task by Larry so they could sail the next day. Any misgivings about leaving Rebecca with Isaac's family vanished when they walked in through the door. Besides Gustav and Bedelia, there was another girl about Rebecca's age named Esperanza, who adopted Rebecca immediately; the pair of them raced off to Esperanza's room while Lily had tea with Isaac's family, though she was advised to turn in early as it would do her good to rest up before the journey. Lily had been in the neighbours' canoes plenty, but she'd never been on a real boat before; the cramped sleeping quarters wouldn't be nearly as restful as the spare bedroom. There were two spare rooms. Lily took the one in the attic giving Rebecca the roomier one downstairs.

"You're going to be okay here by yourself?" Lily asked Rebecca as they settled in for the night, both of them in borrowed nightdresses, Lily washed her clothing and laying out to dry.

Rebecca nodded. "They seem kind. Lily, what if you lose the trail?"

"I don't know," Lily said. "Seth's good at improvising, and I'm stubborn."

"I want to give you this," Rebecca said, handing Lily a ring with a brilliant square-cut gem. "It's white gold and a diamond. It'll be useful for a bribe, if you need it."

"I can't take your grandmother's jewellery."

"My mom will be furious," Rebecca said. "But Grandma will be mad if I don't. If it was me over there, and . . . I don't know. You'll bring them home, won't you?"

"Of course."

In addition to the ring, Rebecca gave her some bracelets so the one Mama Fern gave her was less noticeable. Madeline took valuable items as opposed to actual money, as it weighed less than coin, though tracing it back to Constance would be too easy.

Lily woke with the roosters and most of the family were about their chores. Rebecca saddled Stella and was instructing Bedelia on riding. When the Sprites declined her help, Lily penned a message for when her family made it to town.

Before midday, the family gathered supplies on the turnip wagon and went through their land towards a cove, where a sailboat lay anchored. She wasn't surprised to see her brother wearing some of Alfred's old clothes already aboard deck, but there was another girl besides Yolanda. She had damp blonde hair that hung loose in beachy waves and introduced herself as Daphne, but lost interest in them and inspected the sailboat much to Alfred's consternation.

"What's that?" Daphne asked Alfred, pointing.

"That's the rigging system," Alfed said, storing supplies in the hull.

"And that?"

"A sail," Alfred said.

"And that?"

"An oar. Daphne, you were already on this boat."

"I know but Larry hasn't let me near it in weeks. And this?" She just kept going.

Esperanza giggled, but was hesitant to approach the boat herself. "Where's the woman . . . the puppeteer, I mean?" Esperanza asked Larry.

"On board with Catarina," Larry explained. "Below deck, hopefully sitting quietly."

Esperanza nodded. "I was hoping it was over when Daphne freed that knight back at the toy shop. I still have nightmares about it."

Lily nodded. "We'll find our people. Hopefully my dad will only be a few days behind us."

"What are you going to do if you get to the castle and your friends are already inside?" Esperanza asked. "Castles aren't easy to break into."

"I don't know," Lily admitted. "I like to pretend someone would come for me and wouldn't give up."

Esperanza smiled. "We heard that Seth needed new clothes, so Rebecca and I made this up last night. It's not fancy, but it'll be warm." She produced a long-sleeved red shirt and a waxen cloak of a darker shade. Seth blushed to his ears.

Sean didn't like Seth being so gracious about it. He immediately went to Esperanza's side and all but put an arm about her. "It's too bad you're going so soon," he said. "You're a sore loser, so I suppose a rematch is in order."

"You cheated," Seth started.

"Don't you start again," Larry said. "And no parties at my place while I'm gone," Larry told Sean.

"*Oh we won't,*" the teenagers chorused.

"Come on, Rebecca," Daphne said, grabbing Rebecca's arm and giving her a playful tug. "Let's go explore the nearby beaches before game night at Sean's. Espy packed us a picnic lunch."

"We'll keep you busy so you're not worried," Esperanza agreed. The girls ran off, giggling with Sean protesting that they needed to wait for him. Lily thought Daphne ran kind of funny.

Sean watched them go, but caught Lily's gaze before he addressed her. "I'm sorry about what happened when we met."

"I know why you did it. I need to get my sister back," Lily said.

Sean's eyes looked wounded at the word *sister*. "Isaac said he'll send updates when he can. When your people get here, I'll tell them what you told me."

"Thanks. Remember, no parties," Lily said, glancing over her shoulder with a grin.

After their party boarded, Sean and Alfred rolled up their pants and led the sailboat to deeper water. Larry hollered as the sails caught the breeze. It only occurred then to Lily that this was really happening; the next time she stepped foot on solid ground it would be in another kingdom. This was already the furthest from home she'd ever been.

Isaac and Catarina seemed to know what they were doing, but Larry stopped Seth from leaning against the railing almost immediately. "This isn't a pleasure cruise. I'm making a sailor of you." Seth obliged.vHe was better at knots now than he was when he was younger.

Lily felt uneasy as the coast drifted further from sight. She couldn't recall the name of the port they were sailing to. Were they doing the right thing? Should they have waited for the others? It was one thing to chase the woman—they had Madeline and Lily saw herself that she was below deck. There was a cot for each of them, but there wasn't much extra room.

"Oh!" she exclaimed.

"What are you going on about?" Seth asked, enjoying the breeze through his hair. The others were having a nice sit down on deck while Larry took the helm.

"We forgot Boscoe."

"I wish," Seth said. He gestured to just behind Larry. Boscoe was throwing chicken bones into the sea. Whenever an adult turned their head, the kitsune seemed to be aware and moved just out of sight, hiding behind someone's leg. "We're still stuck with your annoying sidekick."

"I love you too," Boscoe said, stretching as he walked past the pair of them on the side railing, giving Seth's nose just the tiniest little tweak with his tail as he stalked by.

"I'm glad you made it," Lily said.

"I was temped to stay. The chickens at the Sprites' Farm are plump and juicy," Boscoe said with a sigh.

Lily went below deck and inspected the sleeping quarters—with luck they'd make port before midnight, but still spend the night before setting out the next day. She'd imagined setting sail on a much larger craft. Most of their supplies were in storage for the journey, but they'd left her mandolin out. She picked it up, and all at once it seemed Madeline's songs came rushing back. She put it down, and fought back the headache. Her headaches were getting softer. The strange melodies were becoming less painful, and strangely, almost like they were part of her.

She tried to hum other shanties and tales, and she dared not ask Madeline what songs played again and again in her head.

Eight

When she was in the box she couldn't move, but Tiffany was aware. Madeline took her out only twice and both times were brief; most of Tiffany's initial experience with her kidnapping was in utter darkness.

To keep herself from being bored, she dreamed out stories, illustrations from her mother's books intermixed with plays she'd read, typically she cast herself as the princess or heroine, Molly another princess or damsel in need of rescue, Seth on more than one occasion became a comical evil stepsister or troll in good humour. How long was she there? Was life ever real before being in the box?

Feelings came back to her fingers and toes, but in general she felt odd, her sense of touch was overall diminished; she couldn't really feel cold or warmth. She realized that she was no longer flesh and bone but wood and screw, save for parts of her that were glass like her eyes and a thin layer of paint and she never quite figured out what her hair was.

The lid to the box slid off, and there was a light not above, but from the far side of the room. The room was cast in shadow, the ceiling tall, and she was shrunken to about the size of her lower leg, so she couldn't be certain of scale. She reached up. The strings seemed to guide her, almost invisible. But they were there. They were . . . part of her, somehow.

"Tiff, you okay?" asked Molly, leaning over, taking Tiffany's hand, and helping her out.

In addition to being with her best friend, she spotted Louis, Dale, and Brigid. No sign of Seth or Rebecca—was Lily there? She thought she saw her sister in the woods, but somehow knew that wasn't really her.

Dale was comforting Brigid, who wept. Louis was the furthest away, spying out of the door, comically small compared to the real door frame. He was adorable; it seemed that they were all changed into some aspect of themselves. Caricatures of what they looked like, but because she was an attractive young lady, Tiffany didn't have a bulbous nose or squinty look. As far as marionettes went, she was lovely.

"Is that the dress I made?" Molly asked, peering at a wall.

There were several outfits on display pinned to the wall opposite the door. Not just the ones they'd made, which now that she was shrunken down, it was plain to see Tiffany's stitches weren't as nice as Molly's. A jacket for a fancy lady pirate, a suit of knightly armour, as well as a pair of fairy princess outfits, one pink the other blue. An outfit for a woodsman and a dark-cowled attire for some ne'er-do-well. Clothing for milkmaids, a goat herder, as well as a farmer.

"Think it's a test of some sort?" Tiffany asked. Molly grabbed the pink fairy outfit and doffed her village girl outfit. Tiffany looked down at herself. She was still wearing her clothing—the details of her embroidery were there, including a small stain and a patch-job. She even had her wooden clogs from home.

"Shouldn't you go change some place private?" Dale asked.

"Why? I'm made out of wood," Molly pointed out. "There's nothing to see."

"I've got an overactive imagination," Louis offered, but at the same time, seemed a little disappointed. Given Molly's curves were only slightly exaggerated in puppet form, there was nothing exciting about their puppet bodies, in fact they were lacking what Seth would consider critical anatomy.

"I want to go home," Brigid wept.

"Why didn't I think of that?" Tiffany snapped.

"Don't be cruel," Dale snapped. "Where's your idiot brother?"

"If Seth escaped *and* he's the idiot, what does that make us?" Louis asked. They heard barking coming from the other room. Louis gasped as he was tackled by a puppet dog, brought to life with strings. "Down boy! Down! Haha! You're more of a caricature of a dog than a real one."

The wooden dog *arfed* and chased his tale before he and Louis became tangled in each other's strings. Tiffany helped get them untangled, as Dale wouldn't do much other than comfort Brigid.

"I don't want to get tied up with the pair of you," Tiffany cautioned. "A pair of scissors would be nice."

"Yeah," Louis agreed, moving his arm and looking up at the mist where their strings disappeared. "So what's happening?"

"I don't know," Tiffany admitted. "I suppose we ought to figure out where we are and why we were brought here." She looked back at Molly, who gave her a muted marionette smile and a twirl. "All you're missing is a tiara and a wand," Tiffany said. She helped Dale make Brigid stand. "We're all scared, Brigid. But we'll stick together, whatever happens."

"Yeah we're all in this to—woaaah!" Molly took a step and launched into the air.

"Woah! No fair!" Louis said as Molly's wings frittered and she almost flew into what Tiffany could only see as a strange mist. She crash landed, but quickly got up and straightened herself out. She took off a second time with a jump, hovering just out of Tiffany's reach.

"There's another fairy outfit," Molly pointed out. The blue had a longer longer skirt and there was a tiara, but something in her told Tiffany *trap*.

"I'm good," Tiffany said finally. "Anyone else want to play dress up?" She cast Molly a cheeky grin, who scowled back.

Louis looked like he was going to strap on the wings, but hesitated, only to take the pair of knives from the dark-cowled attire. "This'll be good," Louis said. "Dale, Brigid?"

Dale took the axe from a woodcutter outfit. Nothing launched out at him and told him that he must take the whole thing or nothing. "Well, let's get started," Dale said, and without warning, cut the string attaching Louis' wrist. Louis' arm went slack but with the exception of the dangling arm and Louis's squawking, nothing happened.

"What did you do that for?" Louis demanded. He picked up his limp string with his other hand to try to make the dead arm move.

"Stop with the chopping!" Tiffany told him, getting in Dale's way. "You have no idea what you're doing."

"And don't test your theories on me!" Louis quipped.

"Do you think it'll be like that forever?" Brigid asked, stopping her weeping. Tiffany realized they couldn't really cry, but she was going through the motions.

"We won't know for a while. Let's . . . be cautious until we know what's going on," Tiffany said. "Keep the axe—are there other weapons?" The knight set had nothing. That was odd. "I guess we should try to figure out where we are." She looked up at Molly. "How far can you fly?"

"I'm not sure," Molly said. Like them, she could be tangled up in her strings, and they found physically they could jump both higher and further and move quicker than they could proportionate to when they were human, but she wasn't sure how much of it was their off-scale world. Molly seemed to be getting the hang of flying, but if she tried to do a loop she'd get tangled, but she didn't come down to Tiffany to get untangled. She hardly ever touched the ground, hovering just above the others unless she wanted a better vantage.

"Why don't you be useful," Dale said, "and fly up and see who's pulling our strings?"

"What's in the other room?" Tiffany asked Louis as Molly frittered, and hovered below the mist, hesitating before flying into it.

"Mostly looks like fake hills and sheep," Louis said. The wooden dog *arfed* and sniffed Tiffany.

"We're not even breathing, can you . . ." Tiffany learned she could still smell, of all the silly things. Rolling her glass eyes, she called up to Molly. "You okay up there?"

"I'm fine!" Molly called back.

"Any sign of Seth?" she asked.

"He got away," Brigid offered. "I saw Lily fighting that creature. Zin showed up, and they almost freed us."

"I don't think so, Brigid," Dale said. "Rebecca isn't here either. I saw her when Madeline pulled me out. Rebecca and Seth are probably together."

"Anything?" Louis called up to the mist.

"I can only fly so high!" Molly shouted down. "It keeps going, but I can't go higher." She descended. "You're more than welcome to strap on a pair of wings yourself."

Brigid alone seemed to be hesitant to leave that room. "What if it's a trap?"

"You want to stay here?" Louis demanded. "I'd rather explore than sit around pouting." The dog *arfed* and raced ahead. "What should we call him?"

"Huh?" Tiffany asked.

"Our dog. He needs a name."

"He probably already has one," Tiffany said, then pursed her little lips. "He's kinda weird like Zin. Maybe Lil' Booey?"

Louis guffawed and the name stuck. The next room led to a tunnel that was just a little taller than Dale and Tiffany. The tunnel led them to a bright room that was much taller and spacious than she expected. She was tempted to rush back there and grab the blue fairy outfit, because they bobbed along on the rolling hills. Molly would fly and describe what she saw, and give a general direction. It seemed that it was daytime in this world, and there were puppet sheep and other critters, such as squirrels. Not everything was on strings, for many small creatures were anchored to the ground, brought up on their tracks with wooden poles and the like.

The sheep skittered away when they neared, and Brigid even raced ahead when they found a stream. Real water, though the flowers near it were made of silk. Dale bent down, and inspected the grass. It was all fake, made for the scale of their marionette forms. The walls were painted to make it look like the world ended in forest in the background, but it was well-painted. Given Molly could fly, she could tell where the perspective was and so they navigated.

"Think we're in Taralee?" Tiffany asked Dale.

"We were on a boat," he told her. "I was on one when I was about

Louis' age. I was in darkness but I felt us rocking and I could smell the salt of the ocean and other port sounds."

Tiffany frowned. Her parents would track them . . . but if they were put on a ship, it would be next to impossible to find out where they'd been sent.

"Woah!" Louis shouted as he and Lil' Booey started to run around, seemingly at random.

"What's the problem?" Molly asked, hovering, her wings a twitter.

"That string is following me!" Louis was still cradling his arm.

Molly rolled her eyes and sighed, and grabbed Louis' arm. "Stop struggling." Louis didn't listen, and almost smacked her away, but the string reattached itself, and the old string fell apart. Louis seemed to get the use of his arm back. "Was that so hard?" Molly asked, unkindly, and flittered back into the sky.

Tiffany wanted to call her down, tell her to not be that way—they were all afraid, and Louis was only a kid. He was taking things in stride better than any of them, but maybe he didn't have the sense to be afraid.

The sheep began to flock together. Part of her wondered if this was real, if this was just to make her think this was her. When she looked at the others —little details like Dale's cowlick, or Brigid's scowl, Tiffany knew these weren't replicas. There were sensations coming from the strings, but she could move to her own accord —as much as her body would allow.

An arrow shot from a tree and took out Dale's leg string. "I can't move my leg!"

More arrows from the same direction. Most missed, and although one did strike Brigid's actual leg, she didn't even cry out, though she did use herself as a crutch to help Dale.

Tiffany bounded faster than she ever could as a human, jumping from hill to hill, though there were limits and it seemed that Dale and Brigid were falling behind. She turned to help them. "Go! I'm stronger than you!" Tiffany told Brigid, who protested but the pair of them grabbed Dale's arms, and that seemed to give the speed they needed.

Pale green goblins laid in wait in a craggy ravine among pale rocks that hid their strings, about two dozen or so. The horde had exaggerated noses and pointy ears, but the proportions weren't right on many of them; some looked like goblins from the old journals with heads too large for their bodies, but many were shaped more like humans, only painted green. Most dressed in loincloths of fur as well as a lone piece of armour, such as spiky metal spaulders, or wore talismans of bone and pale runic tattoos decorating their arms and legs.

"A fairy! Get the fairy!" One squealed, taking their attention from the trio. One arrow did succeed in taking out one of Molly's arms, but her wings kept her safe. They realized then that they were not outrunning the horde, nor did they know where it was they were going. Molly flew high and shouted.

"Abandon me!" Dale told the girls. Neither did, so to their surprise, it was Louis who let out a war cry and charged the horde, only to be completely dog-piled on. The goblin horde cut Louis' strings and he fell down, limp. The dog whined and barked and several of his strings were cut as well, and he limped away, but the goblins weren't after him.

Molly shouted a warning. One of the goblins threw an axe, and cut most of Molly's strings, and she came crashing to the ground. Tiffany released Dale to help her.

Arrows severed head-strings of the ones nearest them and the creatures crashed,suspended in a half-slump. The goblin nearest Tiffany shouted a warning to the ones behind the group before another shot took out that goblin's head string as well.

Tiffany felt someone behind them. This marionette was human, tall and almost comically slender he wore bits and pieces of armour, though she could see his face and he wore a jester's cap. He hauled Dale to his feet. "Drag him that way," he instructed Brigid before leaping far too high into the air, and throwing his spear. More shots came from behind, and Tiffany wondered why there was no bow in that collection of silly outfits before she spotted the shooter. He was dressed in dark armour from head to toe, and leapt like the longer marionette. There were embellishments of a wolf's head on his breastplate and shield, but he was fully visored and she could not see his face.

The Wolf Knight landed before them, raised his shield and backed up, guarding her and Molly. "Get going," he ordered. The Wolf Knight stayed with them only a few seconds, but made a gap between them and the goblins. "You good?"

"Does it look like we're good?" Tiffany demanded.

"Too bad," the Wolf Knight said, then rushed into the fray.

Tiffany knew every second she watched those two was a second a goblin had to break through or go around, and she had a limp Molly in her arms. Molly wasn't as heavy as she would have been so carrying her was easy, though it was still the matter of the two good strings that made moving difficult.

Tiffany caught up to Brigid and looking back, the pair were fending off the horde, but there was so many . . .

"Let's go," Tiffany instructed.Somehow, moving Molly was easier than Dale because she wasn't trying to help. They made it through the pass to an open clearing before they heard a shout and the sound of hooves as opposed to the heavy chattering on the ground of heavy cavalry. Puppet horses and riders, their colours bright and each knight had his own emblem—mostly animals, but one had a crescent moon and another a rose. Strings were severed on both sides and monsters retreated, only to try to swarm one knight who'd broken off from the fold. Their horses encircled the newcomers while knights landed blows and struck down goblins.

Tiffany protected Molly with her body when an opportunistic goblin tried to seize her, fighting him off by throwing her tiny wooden clog at his head. It stunned the goblin and he seemed more surprised than hurt until a rider with a boar motif chased him off.

After he beat back one of the goblins, one finally raised his visor, and Tiffany saw that not only was the Hawk Knight about the same age as she was, but he was cute.

"You girls okay?" asked the Rose Knight. He also raised his visor. Tiffany had a hard time deciding which one she liked better.

"My friend's strings have been cut," Tiffany said. She cradled Molly, and attempted to pick her up, but Molly was singing. Tiffany thought she knew that song; not like the one in the valley, but there was something about it, a strange vibration that shook Tiffany to her core, now more intensely. All at once the strings shot down and struck Molly violently. Tiffany let go of her in surprise, but Molly was flying again.

"A fairy?" asked the Boar Knight, raising his visor. He was gorgeous, but he had glasses; to Tiffany that immediately knocked him down about three pegs, even if he was the first to come to her aid.

"Protect the fairy!" another knight shouted. Several formed a barrier between Molly and the horde. She didn't fly high—but if all the goblins had to do was cut their strings, she would be in trouble.Several knights had sustained injuries to their own strings, and Molly's wordless song restrung the knights who were injured, though Dale's leg remained unstrung.

Abandoning their stringless counterparts, the goblins raced off from whence they came, though their strings prevented them from peeling off under the trees and other such barriers. Tiffany didn't put up long with the knight's huzzah's. "Our friend's been stolen!" she shouted. No one seemed to notice. "Molly, where's Louis?" Molly didn't answer, Tiffany brushed by a puppet horse and went to check on Dale and Brigid. He was easier to move with both of them helping him.

A lady knight with a crescent sigil slowed down to speak to the trio remaining from Stagmil. "How was his leg severed?"

"His leg's still attached!" Brigid sputtered.

"From the string," the Crescent Knight clarified.

"An arrow. I'll go after Louis," Tiffany said to Dale and Brigid. The lady knight moved her horse in front of Tiffany, then another did the same, this one with a sun sigil. "Let me through!"

"Your friend was taken by the horde," said the mace-wielding Sun Knight. "There's nothing you can do."

"What will they do to him?" Dale asked.

"Make him one of them, I suppose," said the Crescent Knight.

Tiffany pushed through the horses, spotting the pair that had gotten to them first.The jester was the easier one to recognize. Several of the knights were speaking to them. "Who are you people?" Tiffany demanded as the pair joined the group, the one in wolf armour going to the Boar Knight's horse, who protested. Wolfie led the animal to Dale and Brigid.

"It's easier than riding a real horse," Wolfie explained and still Dale hesitated, so without so much as a word, Wolfie hoisted Dale onto the horse.

A man in golden armour astride a white horse approached them. "Justin."

"*Sir* Justin," said the golden knight with a lion motif. "They still lost one." Wolfie shrugged. Wolfie and Jester started to make towards the forest. "Come back and speak with your lady mother, she hasn't seen you in days."

"Are we still measuring in days?" Jester asked, and the two snickered. They dashed off towards a wall of trees, and strangely, their strings released them.

"Lucky," one of the knights said.

"That'll be us soon," said another.

The golden knight glared after them. "Sir Hector, order those two to—"

"Oh, let them roam," the fat knight said. "Where are they going to go?"

"Not the point, Hector. Just wait for the rest of them to catch up, they'll all be off in the woods all the time."

"Yes, well, so far the only thing they've managed to collect are more scratches," Hector told Justin.

"You can ride my horse," said Hawk Knight to Tiffany.

"Mine's better," said Rose Knight.

"What's your name?" Boar Knight asked her.

"You three can fight over the pretty girl in five minutes," said the golden knight, removing his helm. At first Tiffany thought he was good-looking, at least as far as marionettes went. Justin, The Lion

Knight, wasn't as handsome once you got close; he had dark hair and a bit of a beak for a nose.

"Who are *you*?" Tiffany asked the Lion Knight.

Hector had the emblem of a horse, but it looked more like a donkey. When he put up the frog-guard of his helm, he revealed an impressively bushy moustache. "I am Sir Hector, once Knight Champion of Castle Mirador."

"Ahem," snapped the Lion Knight.

"And this is Justin, once courtier—"

"It is Sir Justin now," said the Lion Knight. "I lead these knights who came to your rescue."

"Slapping on armour does not make you a knight," Hector told Justin.

"You lost the battle of the baked goods before you were turned into a marionette, Sir," Justin snapped.

"Thank you for helping us," Tiffany said. "Can you tell us where we are?"

"I'll have the people of the town explain everything," Sir Justin said. "What are your names?"

Tiffany wondered if they ought to give their real names. She had no idea who these people were, still she decided it prudent to make friends. "I'm Tiffany, and we're from the village of Stagmil. You've probably never heard of it, but it's east of Taralee."

"So you're from The Kingdom of Merilon?" Rose Knight asked.

"Yes," Tiffany said, glancing at Dale and Brigid. "Where are we?"

"The Kingdom of Ivancia," Sir Hector said.

"Where's that?" Brigid asked.

"Across the sea," Dale explained. "It's only about a day or two to sail, but still . . . I was hoping we were just taken south down the coast. There was another girl we think was taken, possibly another boy. What happened to them?"

"Hard to say," said the Boar Knight with a shrug. "Wait, you're all from the same place?" He glanced at Hector, who shrugged. "Sorry, normally they drop a mix. I've been here since the beginning."

"Beginning of what?" Tiffany asked, confused. "And who's *they*?"

"We'll answer their questions after we return to the castle," Sir Justin instructed. The three young knights were still trying to offer Tiffany their horse. Tiffany couldn't really pick a favourite, so she accepted Hawk's horse but paid more attention to Rose Knight, and continued to throw sweet smiles as Boar. He wasn't that bad, but those glasses . . .

"Why did the goblins kidnap Louis?" Dale asked.

"They always manage to nab someone from time to time," the Rose Knight said. "I'm just happy it wasn't one of you fine ladies." He flashed Tiffany a brilliant smile. Tiffany knew if he was like this as a puppet, he was downright dangerous as a real boy. "I'm Braden, this is Jayden," he gestured to the Boar Knight, "and Caiden." He gestured to the Hawk.

"What is going on?" Brigid asked as they continued along. "We woke up back there." She pointed in the general direction. The world had walls and rooms, and she was starting to get disorientated. "I'm wearing a version of what I did in the village."

"Ladies, you've been transformed, and now you're more or less stuck here on our little merry adventure," Braden said.

"Doing *what*, pray tell?" Tiffany asked.

"Well, given none of you reached for that armour back there, hanging around the village until the next shoe drops is my best guess," Jayden said.

"I'm really surprised they put out a fairy outfit though," Caiden said, looking up at Molly. "Those are rare. Looking good, though."

"There were two," Brigid pointed out.

"Really? And you didn't take it? Well, I suppose you wouldn't have known," Jayden said.

"Should we go back and get it?" Tiffany asked.

"Nah, the door will be closed. There's different entry and exit points, and we have no idea when we're getting new people," Caiden said. "My cousin was signalling us and saw horde movement, so he let us know."

"Who's your cousin?" Brigid asked.

"Ethan. He was wearing the jester cap. Hard to miss him; he's a tall skinny guy with big sideburns," Caiden explained, then laughed before continuing, "Well, tall for being like this, I mean."

"Oh!" Tiffany said. "So er . . . Jayden, Braden, and Caiden, right? Are the three of you related?"

"No. Why do you ask?" Braden asked.

"Nevermind."

"We want to go home," Brigid said.

"If you can find a way out of the castle, take me with you," Jayden said. "My cousin can de-string on command and he's still stuck here."

"De-string? What are you talking about?" Tiffany demanded. "What castle?"

"I'm sure you'll figure it out," Weasel Knight spoke up, before adding flatly, "Probably through song."

It was then that there was a melody starting by the birds in the trees. None of the knights had musical instruments, but Tiffany recognized the sound of a lute and a hand drum, before a cheerful wooden flute sounded. Molly and Tiffany locked eyes. "Could it be?" Molly asked, flittering to Tiffany. They took each other's hands, then they squealed in delight, Tiffany flying slightly out of sheer will-power.

"What are you two going on about?" Weasel Knight demanded once they finished.

"Are we trapped," Tiffany squealed, trying hard to contain herself, "in a *musical*?"

Something stronger than a pleasant melody seemed to emanate from the trees. Little squirrels popped out—not that they could go far as they were part of the scenery. They were singing a welcome song.

"How can you be okay with this?" Dale asked as little rabbits serenaded them.

"If we have to be trapped some place," Tiffany said,"we might as well dance to some catchy music." For the duration of the number, Tiffany forgot her predicament. "Oh, Seth would *loathe* this."

The town boasted an oversized watermill that did nothing, and the castle had a pinkish tint to it.She'd learn later many of the towers were just for show but looked splendid. The buildings varied, and people were going about their variety of chores, sweeping dirt that wasn't there and a smith was using his hammer.He had a very nice tenor voice when they passed by on their way to the castle.

"Is this the usual welcome song?" Dale asked.

"Unfortunately, yes," Weasel Knight said, brushing off a tweeting-bird of unnatural blue that tried to land on his shoulder. It had a rather deep, baritone voice.

Tiffany thought the little details here and there were fitting, but she realized many of the buildings had no roofs because that would prevent them from entering, but most people milled about on the street, little more than pieces of the scenery.

The town was, admittedly, adorable, and there were plenty of fixtures, but to Tiffany's surprise, there were no doors, just bars that went overtop if the person inside wanted to close it. She realized that she couldn't cross with her strings, so there was no need for actual doors to keep everyone out. She soon determined that that strange fog did exist inside several the buildings, but things were almost built so people could easily see one another and what they were up to.

The knights took their party to a large building with stairs on the outside; several women in nurse outfits waited for Dale to get off the horse and he was helped inside. Brigid wanted to follow him, but a bar quickly appeared over the entry 'door' and she couldn't follow. "Where are you taking him?" Brigid asked.

"To get his string back," said the jolly round knight. "It'll take some time, but he'll be right as rain before you know it."

"I kind of miss the rain," said another of the knights, quietly.

"Nonsense!" said a villager. He looked like a blacksmith. "It's always Spring and sunny."

Several villagers gathered and mostly gaped at Molly who was fiddling with her hair and seemingly getting all the more self-conscious.

The knights promised they'd tell more once they got to the castle and, she certainly wanted answers. *I hope Louis is all right,* Tiffany thought, though part of her acknowledged that if one of them was separated, it was probably best it was Louis.

"Excuse me," she said to Jayden. "Er . . . what ought we do now?"

"Right. I guess you don't really know how things work around here," he said. "So . . . were you like, taken at a carnival or . . . ?"

"I thought you were supposed to be smart," Caiden said. "There's five of them from the same village."

"Maybe it's from the same village festival or something. I was here from the beginning," Jayden said. "When the castle was cursed, I mean."

"That castle?" Tiffany pointed to the magnificent pink structure.

Caiden shook his head and gestured all around them. "We're in Castle Mirador. At least, we think so."

"And this castle has been cursed for how long?" Brigid asked.

"It's hard to tell time, but we figure it's been a little over two years," Caiden told them.

It was around that time that beautiful carriage arrived containing a magnificently dressed lady. Tiffany wondered how her strings didn't get all caught as she stepped back. The people went quiet as the lady descended the carriage.

Her dark blonde hair was pinned and styled by a pearl-lined snood and her grey and brown dress boasted a high-backed collar. "I trust you found the fairy and she came to no harm," she said to Sir Justin. She barely spared a glance towards Tiffany and Brigid.

"We did. Thankfully, two of my scouts were able to intercept, only one was lost to the horde this time . . ."

"Your scouts?" Braden asked. He started to snicker, then most of the rest of them did as well.

"Enough," Hector barked, making the others shut up. "We rescued the fairy. No real injuries were sustained."

The lady nodded. "Girls, go to my carriage," she ordered. "I'll explain things without the likes of them filling your head with rubbish."

Moving into things without obstructing their strings wasn't second nature yet. It wasn't a very comfortable ride, and Brigid didn't want to leave Dale. The Lady waited for the impressive looking carriage to start moving before starting to talk. She looked to Molly. "What is your name?"

"Molly," she said. "Not sure that's fitting for a fairy."

"What would you like to be called?" asked the lady.

"Molly," Tiffany answered. She clenched her fists. "What is going on here?"

The lady nodded. "My name is Lady Chrysta, I was a courtier before all of this happened. We're not exactly sure what this place is, or what happened. We think we are still at Castle Mirador. No one has been outside the game board to check."

"Game board?" Tiffany asked.

"That's what we call the areas we can access," the lady said. She pulled on one of her arm strings with the other hand. "I'm sure you've noticed we can only go in certain areas."

"Those knights that helped us," Brigid spoke up. "Two ran off into the woods. No one could follow them. How did they lose their strings and move around without them?"

The lady snorted. "I wouldn't pay much attention to what those two are up to. Stay away from them or you'll get hurt. In the meantime, welcome to our kingdom within a kingdom. So long as you don't make waves, you're free to do whatever you like. You can write songs and dance, make beautiful outfits as well as build up our town—unlike most villages, our woodcutters make trees!"

"Why are we here?" Brigid asked. "What's the point of all this?" She gestured to the town.

Lady Chrysta shrugged. "Do folk in plays and stories know the why? You're here, and you ought to make the best of it. There's advantages to being here: you'll never be sick, never grow old. We live in forever Spring, and seldom have night. Our brave knights protect us from whatever danger threatens. You'll never go hungry or need to work another day in your life."

"We'll . . . be this way forever?" Brigid asked.

Lady Chrysta laughed. "I don't know about forever. If you're hurt, say you accidentally cut a string or the like—you go to the infirmary and it'll be restored. As a puppet your parts can be destroyed, but generally speaking they can be replaced. You'll be pulled up if you get too damaged." She pointed up to the mists above them. "If you cause a ruckus, you might be punished. Heaven knows they ought to be punishing the pair you mentioned. You might be turned into a mermaid or . . . a monster." She gave an indifferent shrug. "Think wisely before you act."

Tiffany remembered tales about maidens enchanted into the forms of harps or cursed to sleep a hundred years. What if they were there for two, five, or a hundred years? She liked singing and dancing just fine, but there was more to life than that. What would they do while the knights were farting about? Just . . . hang around as part of the scenery?

Lady Chrysta continued, "You are made of wood and screw. This town is relatively safe, and if anything bad happens we send the knights to deal with it. Understood?" Tiffany realized they weren't heading to the pink castle, the woman was talking to them in the carriage so no one could spy and hear what they had to say, as people avoided the carriage. "All right, fairy, you're coming with me to the castle; you other two should introduce yourselves to the villagers."

"Just . . . go mingle and find a hobby?" Brigid clarified.

"You'll have ample time. Paint, write, learn a new language; I don't care so long as you don't cause trouble," the lady said, as the carriage stopped in front of the castle, her attention fixated on Molly. "There's much we need to discuss."

Tiffany and Brigid got out as they were instructed, and watched Molly and the lady converse as the carriage continued on towards the castle. That's it? Just do as we're told and if we get in trouble wait for someone to come and save us?" Tiffany asked.

Brigid frowned. "Let's find Dale and see if he's got any ideas on how to rescue Louis."

The town was bigger than they expected, and in general the girls found that unless they spoke to someone, no one was really going out of their way to befriend them. After wandering around they cornered a villager who seemed to be baking, onlyhe was really painting plaster pies and putting them on display. "We don't have to toil for food or shelter," he explained. "I go through the motions, but for the most part

I've gotten really good at playing chess. My friend is writing a hum-dinger of a play, you ought to read it."

"That seems silly," Brigid said.

The man shrugged. "For the most part I'm left alone. Thing is, if I don't, well, they put me on restrictions. You'll learn soon enough."

"*They?*" Tiffany asked.

He gestured to the mist. "The ones pulling the strings. Don't look up too much, it'll draw attention. You girls should keep your heads low."

They wandered a while before they befriended a boy doing archery. Tiffany asked if she could shoot a few rounds; the scale was off but within a few moments she felt proficient again. He had dark hair and was slender in build. "Lemme guess: you're new," he said.

"Is it that obvious?" Tiffany asked.

"We're looking for the infirmary," Brigid pressed.

"Want me to sneak you inside it?"

"What'll it cost us?" Tiffany asked.

"I'm bored," the youth replied with an indifferent shrug. They fol-lowed him through the streets; he knew where he was going, but the backdoor was still barred. "Don't draw too much attention to your-selves," the boy repeated. "And don't trust Geraldine, she's a spy for *Them.*" He fiddled with a pole in a back alley, and managed to move the bar, so their strings would allow them to enter. "I'll close it when you're up the stairs. Look for strings, but most of us forget they're there."

The boy was gone before Tiffany could ask more questions. She didn't even ask his name. Bars over doorways prevented their strings from entering into some of the rooms, so they made their way up the stairs, before bumping into a young woman of about twenty dressed as a nurse, startling her. "Oh! Who are you?"

"We're looking for Dale," Brigid said.

"You're . . . Brigid or Molly or . . . ?"

"I'm Brigid. Is Dale okay?" Brigid asked.

"Keep your voice down," the woman said. She led them to a side room, bade them wait, then came back for them and led them to a larger room with mostly empty beds.

Dale was sitting on a bed near a window; his strings were much more limited, strung overhead to a set of crossbars. Brigid rushed to him; they got a little tangled but they figured it out. "You girls okay? Did you find Louis?"

Brigid shook her head. "Oh Dale, it's worse than I thought. Whatever is going on is affecting the entire castle. They've been trapped here, they think for about two years."

Dale looked grave but nodded. "Where's Molly?"

"Embracing her role as the Pink Fairy," Tiffany muttered. Tiffany got up when an elder gentlemen entered the room. It was hard to place his age but he was stout, and wore a green coat.

"Relax, they never should have barred the door," the man said. "Must be quite a shock, arriving here. Dale will be all right in a day or so."

"This is Demetri," Dale gestured. "He used to be the royal physician for the prince who used to rule this castle we're in."

The elder marionette nodded. "To the best of our knowledge, the boys have scouted and it seems consistent."

"Boys? You mean Jayden and Caiden . . .?"

"Take your pick," the doctor said with a laugh. "All things considered, how are you doing?"

Tiffany and Brigid glanced at one another. "I suppose we're all right," Brigid said. "One of our party was taken by goblins."

"We're sorry for your loss. We could ask Ethan or Caleb to rescue him," the young woman offered. The doctor frowned and shook his head. "Why not?"

"Leave it alone, Esther," the doctor said before looking back to Brigid and Tiffany. "How are you adjusting?"

"This is an infirmary, but you're not really doing anything," Tiffany pointed out.

"Why do we have a butcher or a baker or a candlestick maker?" asked the physician. "It's a false sense of normalcy."

"What's really going on?" Tiffany asked. "Are *they* making you act out plays?"

"That's what we thought at first," Demetri admitted. "Had quite a few capers which were shameless reiterations of stories of yore, and then some lesser known ones. Several squires went completely off script, it was dreadful to watch. Of course, when you're part of the background, the ones pulling the strings pay less attention to you, so I've had a chance to experiment. I discombobulated myself, for instance."

"It was unnerving," Esther said. "And you were just yapping at me, same as always. I had half a mind to reattach it backwards."

"I'm not convinced you didn't," Demetri said with a chuckle.

"Can we die?" Brigid pressed.

Demitri nodded. "We can be destroyed. I'm not sure how much damage we can take."

"You better sit, we'll tell you what we know." Esther gestured. Tiffany didn't really get tired, but it was comforting. "See the strings?"

"Hard to miss them," Tiffany said.

"We're not being controlled, but at any given time, we can be," Esther said.

"What does that mean?" Brigid asked.

"There's something, or someone, who's controlling all of this," Esther said. "We're not sure who or what, but we do know that for the most part, it seems . . . it doesn't want to really hurt us. That being said, if you draw too much attention to yourselves, or you start causing trouble, then you could get pulled out. Sometimes you will regardless, but it's best to try to go unnoticed. You're completely helpless if that happens."

"Have you been pulled out?" Tiffany asked.

"We all have. They decided to change my hair," said Esther. "It was quite long. I also used to be in a cook costume, but then Danielle disappeared about oh . . . four or so months back."

"Disappeared?"

Someone called him from another room, and Demetri said. "Excuse me. Esther are you good?" Esther nodded and the older puppet left them.

"Who was Danielle?" Tiffany pressed.

"People who were originally from the castle, such as Demetri, tend to stay, unless they cause trouble. Some like me come and go. Danielle was put in before me, and worked as a nurse before I got recast here."

"What did she do?"

Esther shrugged. "Not sure. Might have been something Ethan did, but it's hard to say. They were sweethearts."

"Ethan?" Tiffany was having a hard time keeping track of so many people. "Is that the guy with the jester hat?"

Esther nodded. "He didn't start out that way; he beat up a boss and kept his hat. The squires have a strange sense of humour."

"I thought they were knights," Brigid said.

Esther looked pensive before she answered. "Demetri was once royal physician to the prince who ruled here, but I'm not really a nurse. I worked on my parents' farm. The ones who rescued you play the role of knights. The only one who was a knight before was Sir Hector."

"I have to ask, out of Jayden, Braden, and Caiden," Tiffany began, "who's the tallest in real life?"

"Focus, Tiffany," Brigid said. "No one knows what happens up there?"

Esther looked like she was contemplating an answer. "Some people claim to be more aware when they're pulled. Caleb said he was able to see what was going on upstairs for a little while before he got caught, but I don't know what else to tell you," she said finally.

"So how come they can't just waltz out of here if they're not on strings?" Dale asked.

"They can't, they've tried. There's other obstacles—oh, hello Geraldine."

Tiffany looked over to a stern-looking nurse standing in the doorway. "This isn't a social club, Esther. What are these two doing in here?"

"Checking on Dale," Brigid said.

"We'll release him when he's all healed," Geraldine said. "Really Esther, you know better."

"I didn't let them in," Esther said truthfully.

"I'll see you ladies out," Geraldine said.

Tiffany wondered how often they would 'turn off' or be pulled. It didn't sound painful but she didn't like the idea of being seized at any time.

She and Brigid explored the town together. It wasn't that people were unfriendly, but nervous about talking about strings or where they came from. They inquired about Molly, but no one gave them a straight answer.

They found the gate leading to the world outside the village. They couldn't leave if they wanted; they could see the rolling green hills and trees in the distance, but there was a bar, blocking their strings. "We should find that kid again," Tiffany said. "Maybe find some weapons."

"Without Dale?"

"You want to wait for him before we look for Louis?" Tiffany asked. They assisted in painting flowers. Other marionettes were out of earshot before she heard Brigid mutter. "Decorating our prison."

Several musicians were practicing their instruments, but no sound came from their props, only from above. Perfect music, no mistakes. Tiffany cast a glance overhead, to the mist which swallowed up their strings. "Who do you suppose is up there?"

It was around that time that several of the puppets started shrieking and to 'take cover' but Tiffany wondered how anyone could if their strings wouldn't allow them to go anywhere with an overhang. The next thing she knew, she was staring at a great red dragon, breathing what appeared to be real fire.

"Run, Brigid!" she shouted, and grabbed Brigid's hand, pulling her towards the castle because she had no idea where else to go. Marionettes scattered and people shouted, and though Tiffany knew they didn't have flesh, the world was on fire, and the wooden people were putting it out. Knights ran out on their chargers and they started throwing stuff at the dragon, to a negligible effect. One severed a string and the back leg went limp, but the wings propelled it through the air.

It swooped down on her and Brigid.

Tiffany fell forward, and though she didn't feel burned, she could smell it. She smacked out the fire on her dress but screamed. "Brigid!"

Tiffany cried. The strings where she was a moment before hung slack in the air, and the dragon was carrying limp Brigid up and away.

Tiffany tried to run after her, but despite her increased speed and stride the dragon was moving away ever further. She came across one of the knights—this one had a crane emblem. "Where is that thing taking her?"

"I don't know," he said, nonchalantly. "Don't worry, we'll get her back."

"Like you'll get Louis back?" Tiffany demanded.

"Feisty," one of the other knights said.

"If you *like* fiesty you'll *love* me in about another moment," Tiffany snapped. "Now do something or give me your armour and you can prance around in my village dress." She looked back at where the swooping had taken place. The strings suspending Brigid from the mist were gone.

People seemed more intent on fixing the scenery and repainting the backdrop where there were scorch marks than consoling her or explaining what had happened to Brigid. The knights were slowly amassing, so Tiffany sought out the three 'Aidens.

She found them goofing around, shooting a target. "It's Tiffany!" one snapped, and they stood to attention. "Just training. How was your talk with Lady Chrysta?" Caiden asked.

"Not as eventful as my chat with your dragon," Tiffany snapped. "It would have been nice to have one or three of you around when he showed up. Now, are any of you going to save my *friend* or do you want to show me where I can find armour?"

"Really, you want some?" Braden asked.

"Not too many people want to go that route," Jayden said, and gestured for her to follow. They had a little storehouse of goodies as well as a lot of junk, but they delivered.

"No one else thought to ask?" she demanded.

"You want Good or Evil?" Caiden didn't appear to hear her.

The good motif was silver plated with gold; she seemed to remember something about those metals, especially gold, being awful in terms of actual protection and weaponry. The evil armour, conversely, was black with jagged paldrons and pointy shoes. No animal sigils.

"Do I have to wear the whole thing or can I be like what's-his-name?"

"You mean Ethan?" Braden clarified. "I guess you can try wearing bits and pieces."

As tempting as it was to mix and match, when she was done, she'd donned part of the black chest plate, retrieved a hammer and banged out a more ample bosom than was needed. The result had a bare midriff, pointy boots, and a single spaulder. From what she could tell it looked decent; she wondered what the point was if all her foes needed to do was cut her strings. *Let's see Brigid pull this off,* she mused, and when she was finished donning the armour, asked them what they thought.

She didn't get so much of a verbal answer as the three were practically panting. "I like it," said Braden.

"Me too," said Jayden.

"Derp," bleated Caiden.

"All right, give me a horse, and let's go save Dale's girlfriend." Tiffany hated the words tumbling out of her mouth. A dark horse awaited for her and she followed the trio through the city gate into the strange marionette world.

Nine

They were attacked three times as they journeyed, but Tiffany barely got to learn to use her weapons. At the end of the second skirmish, Jayden pointed out she needed the practice so they stopped and they taught her a little swordplay.

While both Tiffany and Seth had previously stolen Lily's sword, Tiffany lost interest almost immediately once the thing was in her grip and pretended like it was all Seth's idea. It's not like there were only swords, but she decided on it as well as a bow and arrows because besides a sling or a shepherd's staff, that was the closest thing she was used to.

"So how much actual sword play matters?" she asked. "They were aiming at our strings."

"I suppose we could be using scythes," Jayden pointed out. "Boss fights are different. We lose our strings in some areas and we can be damaged. We need to actually destroy a target, if that makes any sense."

"Hey Tiffany, check this out!" Caiden said, standing on top of his horse's saddle. He didn't have to worry about low hanging branches; nothing really could be above them.

"Very nice," Tiffany said. "So you were all here when the spell hit the castle?"

"Yeah, we were squires," Caiden said. He furrowed his brow. "There was a fight almost a week before the curse hit the castle, several of the knights were really injured. Three people died."

"Sir Justin and his band of brave knights were left?" Tiffany asked.

"Nope—Justin isn't a knight, he comes from money. You can buy a knighthood, but he was never a squire," Braden said. "Some nobles and princes train with us, but he never did."

Once they were satisfied Tiffany could use the sword with some proficiency, they continued on. Tiffany wondered if she was a heroine in a tale, that she should learn to make the best of her scenario, but she didn't want to believe for one second that any of this was normal. "That is such a pretty forest!" she chimed as they rode, forking away from an area blooming with yellow and white flowers.

"Yeah, the prettier stuff is, the more dangerous it tends to be," Jayden said. "We can take you later, after we save Brigid, I mean."

"Okay guys, mini game time!" Braden announced when they came to a stone bridge. The horses stopped, and Braden got off, and bounded down to the riverbed with his fishing rod.

"Wait, what?" Tiffany demanded.

"Let him go," Caiden said.

Within a few seconds Braden pulled out a fake red fish. "Oh," he sounded disappointed and chucked it back in. Eventually, he pulled out a pearly-gold one, and seemed pleased.

"What is he doing?" Tiffany asked. "We need to do this to proceed or something?"

"He just likes fishing. He's convinced there's a point," Caiden explained.

Though apparently they had eternity, this was taking too long. "My friend Brigid is in peril!"

"So?" Caiden asked.

"You may be used to damsels being in distress while you going about fishing or whatever, I'm not," Tiffany huffed. "I'll help you fish after we save her."

"Really?" Braden asked, casting again. "I know where we can get a rowboat . . ."

"Want to go see mermaids later?" Jayden asked.

"After we save What's-Her-Name," Caiden said.

Tiffany crossed her arms. "If you can get Louis back," she said. "I'd be forever grateful and would make a tapestry of your animal or whatever." They didn't need to know her general embroidery skills were abysmal.

"You got it!" Jayden crowed.

"Let's hurry up and save Tiffany's viallgers!" Caiden hollered at Braden.

Muttering, Braden trudged back to them. "One of you's just gonna be back in peril in ten minutes anyway . . ."

She'd already forgotten they had actual names before they caught up to Jester and Wolfie. They were at the base of a tall mountain of grey and pinkish rock. It went so high up the mist parted and she couldn't see overtop it. They didn't seem to be going over a plan as to how to rescue Brigid. They were building something made with wood and string, almost like a catapult.

"What are you doing down here?" Tiffany asked, startling the pair. "My friend is up there!"

"What is she talking about?" the blond jester asked Caiden. She couldn't remember who was cousins with who, but Caiden and Ethan had similar pale-blond hair though Ethan's was longer and he'd large sideburns.

"New batch," Braden offered, "the short one got nabbed by Peanut."

"You named the dragon *Peanut*?" Tiffany demanded.

"We didn't name him," Jayden, Caiden, and Braden chorused.

"You're going about that wrong," Jayden offered.

"No one asked you," Wolfie said.

"But if you were to ask me, I would tell you you're using the wrong kind of wood."

"If you can get the right kind to me I'd be forever in your debt." Wolfie didn't even look up at them.

"I think Jayden may be on to something," Braden said.

"All of you focus," Tiffany snapped. "My friend has been captured by a dragon. You're all in shiny armour. Will someone please remedy the situation?"

"Peanut flew off about ten minutes ago," Wolfie offered. "If he had her, she's probably still up there. You guys can handle a fetch quest?"

"Why can't you, you shiny Gopher-Dodger?" Tiffany said.

Wolfie sputtered, but turned out he was laughing. Irked, Tiffanyreached over and turned his helmet askew—it spun around easily, and this made the others cackle. Wolfie took off his helmet to put it back on properly. Other than the puppet face, he looked just like a normal guy. Not as cute as one of the Aidens, with dark eyes and hair—if she was being generous, she could say he had nice cheekbones, at least as far as marionettes went. "Don't know why, I'm surprised you *have* a head."

"I'll put in request for a skull with flames for eyes," Wolfie told her. "Is that supposed to be a euphemism?"

"Yeah, what's wrong with dodging gophers?" Braden asked.

"It's a saying from home," Tiffany snapped. "Now one of you get up there and save her!"

"You're new to this, calm down," Wolfie said, attempting to fluff his helmet hair.

"Well maybe you should just stay down here and let the real heroes do it," Tiffany snapped. "I'm here to make sure they don't get side-tracked."

"You *are* the sidetrack," Wofie said.

"Yeah well, you didn't help Louis, and I'm not about to let another person from my village end up missing if I can help it," Tiffany told him.

"Tiffany, is it?" Wolfie asked.

"You may refer to me as *Lady Theophania I*. And maybe you should switch hats with your friend."

"Tiffany, just stay down here and stay out of the way," Wolfie told her flatly, putting his helm back on. "They can handle a climb."

"We don't mind," Braden said.

"Are you saying I can't handle a climb?" Tiffany asked. "My parents were taking me into real mountains since before I could walk."

"So you were carried?" Wolfie asked.

"Is he always a jerk?" Tiffany demanded following the other three to the obvious path leading up the mountain.

"Cay'll help us if we need it—which we won't," Jayden said. "This doesn't feel like a boss fight."

"They said the dragon's not even up here," Tiffany pointed out.

"They're wrong a lot," Caiden said.

"If we finish too early something else'll be thrown in our faces," Braden pointed out. "It's not a bad idea to do some minigames in the mean time."

"We are not going back to fish!" Caiden told Braden.

Tiffany hesitated slightly, and looked over her shoulder. "Aren't you coming?" she asked the Jester.

"Be careful," Ethan called. "If it's too much, just come back down here and let them handle it. We can teach you some stuff later."

The older pair didn't follow, and Tiffany found that while she wasn't becoming tired from the climb in the puppet body, there were other challenges. Some ways were barred because of the overhanging cliffs, and she still wasn't used to strings. They were forced to climb and jump, then go back and try a different way.

"Did they remove the ceiling to put this in?" she asked Jayden.

"I think this used to be a stairwell," he told her.

Tiffany peered. She did see a door, and was tempted to jump, but realized that her strings would keep her from getting into the hallway. She was stuck in this cheerful little world. "Have you guys ever tried cutting your strings and throwing a person through a door?"

"You betcha," Jayden confessed. "Didn't work. Someone or something always finds us and puts us back."

"I saw them lose their strings."

"If they could get out of the castle, they wouldn't still be here. Do you like jousting?" Braden asked.

"I've never seen jousting," Tiffany admitted. "I probably would like it."

"We had the most amazing tourneys before the castle was cursed," Braden said. "People would come from all over to see Hector in action, before he hurt his knee I mean. I placed third in the last squire melee for our age group."

The trio argued about who was better at what. Tiffany wasn't certain how long they climbed, but she got nervous looking down. "So if I were to fall. Would I get dashed and get . . . put back together?"

"I don't know. I don't recommend jumping off the roof of the castle," Jayden said. "Well, the castle within the castle. Cay had his arm burned off, but ain't none of us shattered."

She was tempted to ask if he still had an arm under the armor, but he seemed fine. "How do you know you're still in the castle?"

"I got nibbled pretty badly by a rat, and they fixed me up, but I was kind of . . . aware for some of it," Caiden said. "It's hard to explain. You're sort of aware but sometimes you can't hear what they're saying or doing."

Tiffany nodded. She was sort of aware when she wasn't in the box, but in the box she was in a deep dream. "So you don't eat . . . you sort of sleep . . . you mostly just meander about and save damsels?"

"Not for lack of trying," said Caiden. "When we have more spare time, people get uncomfortable with what's going on."

"Well at least I won't be bored," Tiffany said."So what's the plan on beating the dragon?"

The trio looked at one another, mostly at Jayden, who was the one who spoke up. "Be very, very quiet. If the dragon's there, grab your friend, and get out."

"Oh for the love of—you're supposed to be heroes," Tiffany groused. "I should have waited with Joker and Sir Grumpy."

"You guys want to go back down and train her some more while I fish?" Braden asked.

"No!" Jayden and Caiden chorused.

When they entered the tall mouth of the cave their strings released them, allowing them to enter into the area. Though she never explored them to the same extent as her siblings, Tiffany had been to caves before.This one was very big and spacious, allowing them to jump around, and was so well-lit they didn't need lanterns. It only occurred to Tiffany later that her eyes had adjusted to the dark.

There weren't a lot of ways to get turned around, but eventually the path forked and something moved. One of the 'Aidens went after it, and it scurried away.

"It was a big dragon," Tiffany called after him.

"Tiffany?" Brigid asked, hiding behind some rocks. She was still attached to strings; her prison was the small area she could move around. "Be careful! What on earth are you dressed as?"

"Relax, we're here to save you." Tiffany said, posing to accentuate her midriff; as it was wood it had never been firmer. "Stylish, no?"

"Hyah!" Caiden brought down his sword, and something squeaked.

"Look out for the rats!" Brigid squealed.

Tiffany had grown up with rats and mice in the barn.Between the barn cats and the farm foxes if there was ever a problem her parents typically dealt with the pests. These were on a completely different scale. The rats weren't puppets; they were regular, barn variety, with very strong teeth that could easily chomp through the wood of their arms.

One overwhelmed Caiden, and two more fell on top of him.

"Do something!" Tiffany squeaked at Jayden, who was fighting them off, his sword sticky with rat blood.

"We were prepared for a dragon, not a dozen rats!" Jayden said.

"Grab your friend, we'll hold them!" Braden told her, rushing the rats atop Caiden with his shield.

"Brigid, let's go!" Tiffany called.

"I can't! My strings won't let me!"

"One of us has to go and save her," Braden said, so Tiffany huffed and shot at the rats. Tiffany at least had to touch her so they held hands, and now that the boys needed to do all the fighting, Tiffany needed both hands to use the bow—and if she wasn't holding Brigid, Brigid's legs couldn't move. She and Brigid raced towards the mouth of the cave, and once they were in the open, Brigid's strings lengthened again and Tiffany could let go of her. Tiffany's own strings seemed hesitant, uncertain if she was going to rejoin the boys in the cave.

"There's two more knights goofing off below," Tiffany said, thrusting Brigid into the path.

"I'll fall," Brigid protested. "Tiffany, don't leave me!"

Someone bowled out a rat, almost knocking into the girls but it squealed and fell, disappearing into the mist.

"Look out below!" Tiffany called, more than the pair down there deserved. She went back into the cave. "We got Brigid, let's go!"

Caiden was overwhelmed and the other two were trying to help him. Tiffany shot a rat in the butt when it tried to bite Jayden's sword. Jayden hauled a rat off of Caiden.

"Thanks," he said, and threw another rat at her, out the side of the cliff.

"You almost hit me!" Tiffany shouted.

"Almost doesn't count."

The surviving rats scurried back into the cave, and suddenly the boys couldn't follow, strings threatening them. The real rats had no such restrictions and retreated deeper into the cave.

"Is the dragon back there?" Tiffany called.

"I don't think so," Caiden replied.

"You didn't say there would be rats," Tiffany snapped.

"Well, it's not like they let us patrol the hallways to get rid of them," Braden said. "It seems like they're getting bigger. Come on, we can explore that way."

"That dragon will be back. Oh, Brigid!" Tiffany raced back out, to where Brigid was sitting, looking like she was trying to get over a panic attack. "You all right?"

"It just left me, and I could only move around that little pen," Brigid said as the boys continued to argue in the cave. Tiffany hadn't noticed, but the strings snaked down and struck her. She felt strangely invigorated, and didn't like that she instinctively welcomed them. "Thanks for coming for me."

"I didn't want Dale to worry," Tiffany said as the boys dragged out a wooden chest. They couldn't unlock it, and they were finding a way to strap it to Caiden's back.

"Brigid and I are climbing down now," Tiffany shouted. "I'd be ever in someone's debt if they were to assist us."

To her surprise, what came to their assistance was the wood end of a spear from the path leading down, which was extended to help Brigid down a tricky part. "You girls all right?" Ethan asked.

"About time. Did you just climb up now?" That was way too fast. He must have grown a conscience and not been that far. "Where's Sour Puss?"

"He has a name, you know," Ethan said, taking Brigid's hand. "Easy, I got you. Tiffany, you good?"

"Peachy," Tiffany said, falling behind. "I'm waiting for them. Don't let Brigid fall."

Somehow, getting down was trickier and part of her was tempted to just jump but she didn't want to end up damaged. "Ew," Tiffany stated when she saw Wolfie butchering the rats, harvesting some of the long bones.

"She all right?" Wolfie asked, continuing to work.

"Ask her," Ethan said.

"I'm . . . it's just a lot to take in right now," Brigid said meekly. "I want to go home."

Wolfie took off his helmet and cleaned his hands on the fake grass before walking to Brigid. "I'm sorry you were brought here." He cast a sour look at Tiffany while she scoffed. "I'd say try to make the best of it, but I find that condescending."

"Look what I got!" Caiden crowed, showing off a wooden chest on his back, appearing with the other trio unceremoniously.

"Very nice," Ethan said. "It's probably cursed, though."

"That's what I said," Jayden agreed.

"Any sign of the dragon?" Ethan asked. Jayden shook his head. "You good here?" he asked Caleb, who was now tying strings to rat carcasses.

"We don't need your help," Tiffany said, but then realized that unlike in real life, they couldn't sit multiple people on the horses. Fortunately, Ethan and Caleb had horses stashed, so they led Brigid to a steed and helped her on. Ethan got on the other horse, Caleb went back to his rat pile after giving Ethan the bones he'd harvested.

"You're going to be out here alone?" Brigid asked.

"Cay'll be fine," Ethan said. "We figured out most of the traps and dangers. Maybe something for Day 2 in Ethan's school of *Don't play in the Enchanted Forest, and other fun games that'll make you lose a limb.*"

"Take your time," Wolfie said. "Meet me back here?"

"I could go fish," Braden offered.

"No," Ethan said, and prompted the others to start moving back towards the village. "How many keyholes were in the cave?"

"Multiple. Might be a new dungeon in there," Caiden said.

"Limited string access?" Ethan asked.

"Yeah, but maybe we could just dig a hole in the mountain and get the treasure?"

"They don't like it when we cheat," Ethan said.

"Is he going to be okay by himself?" Brigid asked, looking over her shoulder.

Ethan nodded. "Don't worry about Cay; we found everything that could possibly hurt us the hard way. I'll go back for him when you are safe in town."

"We were safe in town when Brigid got yoinked," Tiffany pointed out.

"Well, buddy back there won't forgive me if I need to save him." Ethan chuckled a little bit. "It would be fun if a bunch of maidens came and saved the knights for a change," he called a little loud, looking up at the sky.

"Oh would it ever," Caiden crooned in agreement.

"I'm good with powerful evil maidens too," Braden joined in.

"That is precisely why you don't get to chose your own adventures," Tiffany said with a snort.

"What's the rush to go back to town?" Braden asked.

"We are not fishing," Jayden told him.

"No one's making any of you fish . . . " Braden muttered under his breath.

"Could we look for Louis?" Tiffany asked. Ethan frowned, then looked to Jayden, who shrugged. "He was taken by goblins, but he's only thirteen."

"We've been studying the goblins for a while," Jayden said. "They've got multiple caves and you'd need to un-string on command, so good luck . . ."

"He can," Tiffany pointed at Ethan.

"Ethan's not invincible," Braden pointed out.

Something leapt out from the ground; Tiffany saw a flash of brown and it was at the two horses from the front, so she only heard Caiden and Braden gasp. At first, she thought it was some sort of wyrm, for it was long and snake like, and then saw the double set of arms, each holding a curved blade coming from a human torso and near-human face, only without a nose. They struck down Caiden's strings, then Braden's, then the horses.

Ethan and Jayden leapt forward from their horses, Tiffany watched before realizing maybe she ought to help, and there was another one coming up from behind. The snake-women were covered in shiny scales, a dark red-brown with black striped patterns for the most part. Brigid screamed in surprise but went limp as her strings were cut—again—and another went for Tiffany. She narrowly dodged out of the way. While Ethan and Jayden were distracted away, Tiffany shot one trying to make off with Braden, which lost use of one arm and hissed and threw something at her. Why were their strings still attached? She didn't know, but the third one didn't bother to grab Caiden, instead they disappeared with Braden and Brigid into the river, which diverted underground.

"Tiffany, are you okay?" Jayden asked, helping her up.

"What just happened?" she demanded.

"New event," Ethan said with a shrug.

"We didn't even get back," Tiffany protested.

"We don't make the rules," Jayden told her. "Think you can take Caiden back to town?"

"You want me to be out here by myself?" Tiffany demanded.

The pair glanced at one another. "I suppose you can tag along," Ethan said. "Odds are we'll run into someone else and they can take you back to town." They bound Caiden to his horse. It was almost unnerving to see how they bounced and flopped when they weren't animated by strings. "Any ideas as to where to start looking?"

"Nagas are water guardians; any good rivers or streams you think they'd make use of?" Jayden asked.

"Is that what they were?" Tiffany asked.

"I think so. Looked like ones," Jayden said. "Well, people made to look like nagas, anyway. I don't know enough about real ones and it's easier to make people look like monsters than catch real ones."

"How do you know that?" Tiffany asked.

"Castle has a very good library," Jayden explained. "Not that we can access it now. We sometimes get hints about things in our loot, but being able to spend fifteen minutes in the library would make some of these quests a lot easier."

"Ugh, you could use my sister right now, not me," Tiffany groaned.

"Why's that?" Ethan asked.

"Because I liked to read good stuff," Tiffany said. "Plays and novels about girls forced into marriage, not dry journals like how to trap a gryphon."

"That's too bad," Ethan said. "There's a really grumpy one guarding something south of here."

They travelled a little ways through an enchanted forest, and because Tiffany and Jayden couldn't de-string, it took a little longer for them to get through it. There were beautiful flowers and more than once Tiffany triggered something that started Ethan getting strung up by an ankle, but by the end of it she knew the yellow ones were the dangerous ones. Eventually they arrived at a nondescript cave, but as opposed to climbing it seemed to lead down. "How do you know this is the place they were taken?"

"We don't," Ethan explained. "Sometimes we get cryptic little clues but it's a lot of trial and error." Tiffany was about to complain, but they heard the sound of fighting. The boys told her to stay put and watch Caiden, and she almost followed after them anyway when they ran off, de-stringing and charging into the bush.

A strange, squat creature of brownish dark green charged out of the bush. It was not unlike pictures she'd seen of alligators, but it was much boxy face and she quickly led the horses away from it. It seemed more keen on getting away then attacking her, but someone threw an axe and severed several of the creature's strings, it dragged its back legs as it attempted to flee.

The Weasel Knight appeared and severed the head string. He was older than any of the 'Aidens. Tiffany would place him in his mid-twenties with dark hair. She couldn't be certain of his real life features, but a far as marionettes went, he was a more than a little funny looking.

"You all right, chicka?" he asked, but didn't wait for a response.Instead he ran back into the fray. Tiffany groused, and looking at Caiden realized he'd be helpless if she left him, so she waited for them to return.They looked pleased. "What was that?"

"We had to save Martin," Jayden gestured.

"I never asked for your help," said the Weasel Knight.

"Well, you could stand to not stir up a nest of critters," Ethan said.

"I haven't been here as long as you," Martin told them. "Pardon me for not knowing the intricacies of how your precious world works."

"I didn't make it," Ethan pointed out.

"Hardly my world," Jayden agreed.

Martin harrumphed and peered at Caiden all bundled up. "That's not good."

Ethan and Jayden looked a little flustered. "I can take her and Caiden back to town," Jayden offered."Go find Cay and we'll meet you back here?"

"We can tie him up so that nothing can get him, rescue your people and mine, and be done with this misadventure," Martin said. "Sound good?"

"And bring Tiffany along?" Jayden asked.

"I think I ought to get a say," Tiffany said. "Surely you three can protect me. Why don't we wait for Caiden to go back on string?"

"Unless the watchers pull him we need to take him to the infirmary. Don't know why, they make us go through rituals," Martin explained. "We'll do our best to protect you. On my honour."

"Honour of a sell-sword," Ethan said with a grin.

Tiffany followed them into the cave after Jayden and Ethan bound up Caiden and unceremoniously hoisted him on a high branch, out of harm's way, like hanging meat on a tree. The cave's ceiling was quite vaulted, pointed with stalagmites of pink and red, so they couldn't be on string to progress. Tiffany felt good to be off of them, even if only temporarily. The sound of rushing water intensified as they descended.

"So what's your story?" Tiffany asked Martin.

"I might as well ask yours, but it's always the same. Kidnapped at carnivals or lured by promises," Martin said with a laugh.

"We helped a woman who kidnapped us," Tiffany said.

"Same thing," Martin pointed out.

"Martin and his team broke into the castle," Jayden explained to Tiffany.

"Oh yes, it was as simple as that," Martin said. "Break into a castle. I've done it before, but this situation was . . . *delicate*. We were hired to find a prince. Can't remember his name."

"And you were caught and transformed into puppets?" Tiffany asked.

"Not exactly. He turned us into puppets to break into the castle," Martin explained. "I don't normally hold with magic, but the pay was considerable, you understand."

"Did you come in boxes?" Tiffany asked.

Martin shook his head. "The wizard made a path leading under the castle. I'm sure he destroyed it after he abandoned us. We had a vague idea on what to expect, but, once we were discovered just about everything turned on us."

"That could be our way out," Tiffany said to Jayden.

"Si, if we could reach it," Martin said. "I cannot de-string like him, but my sister and I have told him where it is if he can get there. He says he goes so far in the halls and then poof!"

"More like *bzzap*," Ethan offered. "For all I know if I get on the outside, I'll lose life after a few days of being off-string."

"So you're not even trying?" Tiffany asked.

"I'm saying that assuming that tunnel is still there, I can't reach it," Ethan clarified. "Enough chatter, game faces on. Tiffany, stay in the rearguard and try not to shoot us. Jayden, think you can fill in for your cousin?"

"I don't mesh as well as you two do," Jayden said, but lowered his visor.

"Hopefully this won't be complicated." Ethan stopped. Humanoid figures exploded out of the water, knocking back Ethan and Martin and another and grabbed her. The naga almost succeeded in carrying her back to the stream they walked beside, but the Weasel Knight exploded into action, taking out the headstring. Funny looking or not, he was very good.

"I like having bait," Martin said as Tiffany clambered to her feet.

"I'm not—!" Tiffany screamed instead of reaching for arrows, but the other three seemed comfortable and took out the new naga who appeared. They were outnumbered, but as the boys had no strings to cut, they were at a decided advantage.

"Leave that one for questioning!" Ethan told Jayden as they finished this challenge. He and Martin paired up to take out one who'd lost his arm strings.It ended with Martin stepping on his throat.

"We're looking for people," Martin said. The slithery, once-human face hissed and licked the boot in a mock gesture with a forked tongue. "You wouldn't happen to know where we ought to look, would you?"

"Jayden?" another voice asked, sounding human. "Ethan?"

"It's a trap, Jayden," Ethan cautioned.

"Ethan, it's me," the voice said, the voice not at all serpentine. "It's Peter. Come on . . . "

"You can't trust him," Ethan grumbled.

"You know him?" Martin asked.

Ethan addressed the naga. "Peter, I know you aren't in control. If you know where they took Braden and the others, tell us what direction to go."

"I'm sorry," Jayden said, leaning in, and the naga pushed up suddenly despite having his strings severed, and struck Jayden with a strange knife which caused Jayden to shake and fall down. Ethan struck the marionette naga through the torso, then Martin; they cut the arms off.

"I thought he couldn't move his arms if his strings were cut," Tiffany said, rushing to Jayden and cradling his head. He was completely limp.

"Don't trust anything. There's little patterns here and there but what works on one quest won't work on another," Ethan told Martin. He bent down and shook Jayden's shoulders.

"Great," Martin said.

"We should think about circling back, dropping off these two and Caiden," Ethan said. "We could get Selene and Cay and come back . . . "

"Who do you think I'm here to save?" Martin asked. "Jace's little troupe got ambushed, Selene had to get involved."

Ethan muttered something she didn't catch, taking Jayden from Tiffany's arms. She initially protested but Martin helped boost him, then began to tie him around Ethan's frame in a sort of piggy-back style.

"What about the others?" Tiffany asked.

"They'll be fine until we save them, I suspect," Martin said.

"You mean like Louis?" Tiffany demanded.

"Who?" Martin asked. "You're new, why don't you—"

"Be bait and follow you schmucks around? I like the idea of getting more people, you two seem to be doing a fabulous job."

"This isn't as easy as it looks, you know," Ethan said, he seemed bittersweet around the one he'd called Peter; and put him to the side gingerly.

"Do you recognize all of them?" Martin asked.

"No," Ethan admitted. "They're all real people. I try not to look at the faces." Martin muttered under his breath. "If you have any ideas on how to help them, I'd love to hear it."

"Wait . . . these are all people?" Tiffany asked. "Why are they attacking us?"

"They don't have a choice," Ethan told her. "None of us have real choices in here." He scowled, looking back the way they'd come. "Where'd your marking rope go?"

"Crap," Martin muttered.

"Tell me we're not lost," Ethan said.

"I won't tell you, then," Martin offered.

Before she could muster a response, the pair were distracted by something shimmering in nearby water. "This doesn't feel scripted," Martin mumbled.

Tiffany thought it was a trap, but she found herself compelled towards the water. Something struck the pair, and Tiffany felt her body seize, numb—not unlike how she was in the box, only this time she was aware. She ascended.

Tiffany wasn't sure what happened; light shifted and she was in a real castle. She looked down and she could see the world below in a sort of strange set of orbs. They shifted, scanning certain areas, like she was looking at a stage from above.

Looking up, Molly had her crossbars. Her best friend was fully human and wearing a sky-blue dress with full draping sleeves and puffing at the shoulders; it looked like something she would have designed but never had the fabric to make herself. Tiffany looked at herself—she was still in the assortment of dark armour.

"Can you hear me?" Molly asked, human. Blue butterflies flittered around Molly's head almost like a halo but they flew off. "I don't want you like that." Molly was a little abrupt and swung Tiffany, but Molly realized her error and became more precise. She lifted Tiffany to a set of crossbars. Tiffany couldn't move but she could see the room after after Molly awkwardly placed her into an upright position. The room was lovely; it was about the same size as her own living room back home with a canopied bed with a matching nightstand and some chairs. A full-sized variation of the fairy outfit graced a mannequin, as well as others in the open wardrobe behind the pink garb. Behind that were canvases and paint; Molly had been busy, designing clothing and monsters and the like.

Molly took off her armour and dressed Tiffany in a rich gown, sleek and emerald green like Tiffany's eyes, then put her on the bed and Tiffany felt her movements and sensations came back. Sitting up she was human again; she was still growing, just a little smaller than Molly but within a dozen heartbeats she felt restored.

"Molly," Tiffany said, feeling her face. It felt weird how her lips could squish and her nose could wriggle. Now that she had a heart again, it was racing like mad. "What—where—? What's going on?"

"I cheated. I really wanted to talk to you," Molly admitted, looking bashful. Tiffany grabbed Molly's hand and bolted for the door, and found it locked.

"Calm down. You want slippers?"

Tiffany's feet were much bigger than Molly's but small, strange machines came through a dumb-waiter and brought some dark slippers that fit.

"They have you locked in this tower without so much as a mat, you poor thing!" Tiffany said, embracing her best friend. "Is that a full harp?"

"I think so," Molly said. "I'm still learning how to play it. Tiffany, I'm fine."

"Fine *fine* or FINE *fine*?"

"I was taken to the master," Molly offered. "The one in charge of all of this. Come on."

Molly directed Tiffany to the strange orb. The surface was more like a pool shimmering. Using her hand, Molly scrolled over the area, was able to zoom in and out, but for the most part they couldn't make out small details. Dale was still in the infirmary. It was hard to really zone in, but Tiffany recognized the back-alley where she and Brigid had snuck in. Molly scrolled again, across hills of sheep and fantastic creatures, of goblins looking like they were up to something and saw that Ethan and Martin were still fighting in that cave. They hadn't made it very far from the river where she was pulled.

"You want to control one? It's easy," Molly said, and suddenly a control bar appeared, and she took control of another lesser knight. The others around him backed off. Molly had him direct course, then offered the cross-bar to Tiffany, who shook her head. "Help them find one another. Not much of a story. I'm making a better one for another session; you can help if you like. Oh, we could make you a secret princess or your kiss could break the spell—"

"Molly," Tiffany said. "What is happening?"

Molly released the crossbar and the marionette fell forward to a knee, the others around him hesitant to approach. Molly used her hand to scan over the area. Tiffany saw that one marionette was speaking to goblins . . . Wolfie. He was colluding with the monsters. *Of course.* Molly noticed her annoyance and arched a brow. "Some of them are off-limits, Asmodean hasn't explained why."

"Who is Asmodean?" Tiffany asked.

"I'll introduce you, but we need to talk. Would you like to wear something else?"Molly gestured to the wardrobe. It seemed like she didn't get much company, but the couch and side tables were lavish and meant for company.

"You have great taste. Well, mostly," Tiffany pointed out. "This belt."

"Ugh, I know. Short notice," Molly said, rolling her eyes. "We'll fix that before you go. But do you know what would look great?" She had a chest full of cute shoes. Too bad none of them fit Tiffany.

"Besides one of those cute boys?" Tiffany asked.

They giggled. "I like Braden best."

"No way, I like him. Well, okay you're my best friend. If you get Braden, I want Jayden."

"But Caiden's cute too!"

"I know! Maybe Lily can have a boyfriend too! Or Brigid when she realizes Dale's a goober."

They giggled like mad before the realization dawned that they weren't back at home and their situation was serious.

"So . . . what happened? Why aren't you down there?" Tiffany asked.

"Fairies are special characters. I wouldn't be put in play very often. Asmodean talked to me. From what I can gather, he's the one in charge. There's others. I'm not a true puppeteer—not yet, anyway. I'm mostly observing."

"You're a puppeteer?" Tiffany asked. "Molly, I . . . we're all puppets down there."

"I had a choice. Stay a puppet and be put aside until they needed me, or become a puppeteer," Molly said with a shrug. "Easy."

"What do they want with us?" Tiffany asked. "Will he let us go home?"

"Why should we want to go home?" Molly asked. "No one listened to us or let us do what we wanted. Tiffany—we're in a story like we always dreamed about. And we can direct the way this goes. We can have everything we've ever wanted."

"I don't want to be a puppet or a puppeteer," Tiffany said, shaking her head. "We don't have to go home. Let's escape with the others. We can go to Taralee or anyplace we want."

"I understand this is a shock," Molly said. "We can be more than just bakers and farmgirls. We'll be young forever, just that is enough to make me want to stay. In the meantime, you can be the heroine in the stories we grew up loving!"

"I wasn't going to let you marry anyone because your parents said so!" Tiffany said.

"How benevolent," Molly sneered. "You've never had to worry about when the shoe's going to drop; maybe this'll do you some good to know what it's like."

For the first time, Tiffany became afraid of her friend. "This isn't right. Do you at least know what happened to Seth and Rebecca?"

Molly shook her head, then put her hand over the orb. Several puppets lit up—two were hiding, seemingly off-string. Molly frowned, strung a goblin, and seemed to be pulling him out, when Wolfie and another goblin attacked the one she was trying to pull, and cut him from the strings. Molly strung Wolfie, but the other goblin raced off with the body of the one she'd initially tried to nab. Molly breathed deep and focused, started to move Wolfie towards the event where Ethan and Martin were fighting. He was a good distance away. Molly made him walk.

"Why don't you always control them?"

"Takes a lot of energy and focus," Molly said. "Most of them learned what they ought to be doing; we punish the ones who don't behave. Different things work for different people; threatening their friends makes most fall into line."

"You should be punishing that one a lot more." Tiffany said, gesturing at Wolfie.

"He doesn't have that many friends," Molly said blandly.

"Molly, my parents will track us down."

"We were on a ship," Molly pointed out. Tiffany frowned. Dale had said the same thing. "Even if they were to somehow know where we've been sent, they can't enter the castle. No one is coming to save us."

"That one guy broke in." Tiffany gestured towards Martin.

"Doesn't matter; the tunnel on the outside was filled in. That was months ago.Besides the main drawbridge, no one gets in or out. The one that brought us in will be loaded and gone by the end of the week, then there'll be nothing for several months. We were a special order. Madeline gave a message to the master—I don't know for sure but I think their operation in Taralee was compromised. There was something about Lily . . . " Molly shook her head. "They wouldn't tell me."

"Molly, please," Tiffany said. "I'll find a way out. Or maybe you can, from up here?"

Molly looked at her sadly. "Why don't you spend a little more time as a puppet, Tiffany? Then you can decide how you want to spend the next century or so."

"Century?"

"Kingdoms aren't built in a day," Molly said with a shrug. "It's okay, I won't let anything bad happen to you." Molly released her grip on Wolfie. He encountered another group and they rushed ahead into the cave. Scrolling ahead, she witnessed Martin and Ethan struggling with some sort of large beast. It looked like a giant toadstool. "You ready to go back?"

"You said you'd introduce me to Asmodean."

"I'll ask for an audience. Impress him in the meantime."

Molly touched Tiffany and she felt light, then she was falling—a controlled fall, through the mist but back in armour; she had a better bow as well as a whip. She touched down and heard the skirmish in the other room. Looking herself over, she noticed that her armour was more stylish and tailored.

Wolfie racing ahead barely spared her a glance. "You shouldn't be here."

"None of us should," Tiffany said. They came up to the others; the giant mushroom ripped one knight from his strings; and just as he was about to consume his limp body, Ethan leapt up and threw his spear, striking the giant toadstool through his forehead and making him drop the fallen knight. The toadstool retaliated by swiping Ethan like a fly, and he went flying backwards. Martin went in to grab the fallen knight, but the toadstool let out a bellow which resulted in a dark cloud that obscured him from her view.

Wolfie stopped and took out his bow.

"Aren't you going to help?" she demanded.

"Can you be quiet? I'm trying to focus." He aimed his bow.

"Oh, like this? Stop doing this? Is it bothering you when I'm doing—" He aimed above the toadstool and fired, hitting the rocky ceiling. "How could you miss? He's enormous." The stalagmite fractured and fell, impaling and pinning the giant toadstool to the ground.

"What took you so long?" Ethan demanded before the dust settled.

"Keep your distance. It's only stopped for the moment," Wolfie called back, then reloaded and shot behind Ethan. The fight was far from over; a gate opened and a swarm of naga creatures slithered up, but soon they were outnumbered.

Wolfie shot their head strings and Ethan raced to the giant toadstool and retrieved his spear. Thankfully, the other team arrived, and Tiffany held back, watching them work. Wolfie and Jester in particular seemed to work well in conjunction. Finally, some of the creatures slithered and lost their strings in the river, and swam off.

She thought it would be over, but one of the knights lurched forward suddenly. Tiffany could tell he was being taken over.

"What's going on?" another knight asked.

"I don't want to . . . !" the knight sputtered. He seemed to be trying to resist but was compelled forward, shaking. Tiffany couldn't see his face but he sounded young. Tiffany watched in horror as the youth walked towards one of the already defeated naga puppets. The youth took out a bludgeoning weapon.

Ethan grabbed him from behind, and Wolfie took his mace. "I'm sorry," Wolfie said, but brought the mace down on the puppet's head, shattering it. It was over fast; the hold on the younger knight broke as the head of the puppet splintered.

"I saw that!" snapped another knight. He marched over, but then him and Wolfie and Ethan all jerked; strings striking the latter pair violently. Everyone else backed off; eventually the reprimand coming from above relented.

"Jace, calm down," another knight spoke up once the trio were themselves, though Wolfie and Ethan remained on string like the rest of them. "Let them do the actual killing."

"How do you think they got the ability to go off-string at will?" demanded another knight.

Wolfie turned to the younger knight. "You okay?"

The younger knight nodded. "Why did you do that?"

"So he can get more powerful," snapped Jace. "He wants to keep us on strings!"

"Shut your face, you don't know what you're talking about," Ethan snapped at him.

"Or you'll what—smash my head in? I'd like to see you try," Jace snapped.

"Take it up with *them*," Wolfie snapped, pointing up.

"Ease up, all of you," Selene spoke up, she'd led a small faction to bring out their captives. They had Brigid and Braden, who were brought to life suddenly when they entered the mist and were restrung. Brigid looked around wide-eyed, only relieved at seeing Tiffany. Selene and Martin were the oldest of those present, seemingly giving them some authority. "Let's not forget who the real enemy is."

"And the ones who are only too eager to do their bidding," Jace snapped, going back to his cohort. It only occurred to Tiffany then that there were factions among the knights.

"I like your new bow," Braden told Tiffany. "Where did you get it?"

"Uh . . . I'm not sure," Tiffany lied. He didn't seem to notice. "Are we done here? Can we go back to the town?"

"Yeah, let's get Brigid back to town for real this time," Ethan agreed. "Braden, you ain't gonna catch anything, let's go."

Braden was just getting ready to cast his line into the glowing river. "Five minutes!"

Tiffany's group went to leave while Jace's team explored the area; they didn't get far when the ground started to rumble, and it was as if fate intervened to free the giant toadstool. Tiffany had muted senses of smell, but the putrid stench was thick.

"Brigid, stay with Tiffany and stay behind us!" Jayden ordered, and they formed a protective barrier. Tiffany nocked an arrow. The other knights fanned out as the new threat emerged, but to her surprise, Jace's faction turned on Ethan and Wolfie. Wolfie's head string was cut and he fell, but Martin and Selene aided Ethan.

"Don't fight us, fight the monster!" Jayden ordered. Selene grabbed Wolfie and severed the rest of his strings, and dragged him away from the fight.

"Idiots," Ethan yelled at Jace's team, but he worked well enough with two 'Aidens and Selene. The younger knight guarded Wolfie and Martin as the beast reared up; everyone stayed on string, and it cut through arms, rendering the knights helpless. Martin went to aid another, and he lost the use of his sword arm, unable to get to a safe distance before his head string was struck.

"This would have been easier if we had our stronger fighters," Ethan told Jace. "Who can we thank for that?"

"We can handle—"Jace began, but he suddenly lost his sword arm and needed to back off from the fray.

"Brigid, stay back. I am going to help," Tiffany said. The horrific mushroom monster had a gaping mouth and it would consume any puppets it could grab hold of. She was glad for a bow, she had range on the creature.

It seemed like all was lost and the creature was going to make off with its puppet captives.It had consumed four of them and was beelining deeper into the dark cave. Molly descended, in fairy form. She raised a hand and banished the creature. So long as their headstrings weren't cut, those who had their arms and legs were rendered whole again.

"Nice timing," Ethan told her, getting up and dusting himself off. He watched the toadstool beast retreat deeper into the cave. "Are we getting them back anytime soon?"

Molly gave an indifferent shrug, but she looked to Jace specifically. "You wanted a challenge, the beast is yours. Take a team of your choice with you."

"I want to be able to go off-string like him," Jace gestured to Ethan.

"You will be satisfied with the reward you are given," she said.

"Let's go!" One of the knights in Jace's cohort cheered.

Jace looked pensive before he spoke. "I pick Ethan and Martin."

"What?" his friend snapped. "That's the thanks I get?"

"Pick someone else," Ethan snapped, picking up Wolfie's slack form, pulling him on his back like he'd done with Jayden earlier. "I don't need you stabbing me in the back."

"Fine, I'll take Paul," Jace said, then looked to Molly. "Restore Martin."

"Thanks a lot," Paul muttered.

"I'll lead the rescue party once you're eaten," Ethan assured Jace. Molly revived Martin, who came to with a jerk, and was given the gist of what had happened via his sister. Molly nodded, and blessed the three chosen; they alone were permitted to continue deeper into the strange cave off-string. Ethan eyed Molly, then Tiffany, but focused on securing Wolfie. "Can you fix him so I don't have to lug him?"

"The rest of you may go," Molly said. "Let his mother see him."

"Can you please . . ." One of the girls started, but Molly's now larger wings opened and she ascended.

"What did you want?" Selene asked once the pink fairy was gone.

"I just wanted to know if it would be okay if I wrote a letter to my family. Told them I'm all right," the girl said quietly.

Selene put a hand on her shoulder. "I'm sorry. It might be best for them to forget about us altogether. Hearing from you might open an almost-closed wound." Selene looked to Ethan. "You need help?"

"Nah, we're good," Ethan said. "Might fill in and paint some of his scratches while he's out." He glanced at Tiffany, but didn't approach her. "I ain't coming back for any of y'all until he's back."

It was a sombre ride back to town, but they were met with a beautiful song and people applauded their return, though several of their number were missing and Wolfie and another knight were taken to the infirmary. Dale was still unable to leave his cot, but Brigid rushed to him.

A woman with dark hair didn't seem to care about the infirmary rules. She dressed like a lady and seemed a bit older. Tiffany assumed that was Caleb's mother, who after briefly checking on Wolfie, took pains in berating Ethan. Tiffany left before the chewing out got heated, but couldn't recall the woman's name so she could let the woman know when the pair were annoying her in the future.

"Congratulations on becoming a knight," said the boy who'd led her and Brigid in earlier. "Must be nice."

"Tell you what: If you want, you can have the armour and I'll hang around town and practice the day's choreography."

"It won't fit," the boy muttered. "Some people get to be forever twenty; I get to be forever twelve."

Tiffany found herself being escorted to the castle. There she found she had her own chamber, which was silly because she didn't need to sleep. It was a bedroom from a dream, a miniature version of what Molly had above. There were several romantic novels in addition to a surplus of sewing equipment, besides that lovely emerald dress with a much better belt, and a note.

You did so well! Keep it up. I've got my eye on you.

Tiffany shuddered. If escape was possible, it just got a lot more complicated with Molly being ever-vigilant.

Ten

Though the small sailboat didn't allow him to roam like he did back at home, Seth didn't want the journey to end. The sun was just setting when the Ivancian Coast came into view. Seth had hoped he'd get to do a little navigating by the stars, but the promise of warm tavern food ashore curbed his disappointment.

The two kingdoms for the most part got along; Ivancians spoke the same language as they did back in Merilon and they had a similar climate. Still, he'd been lectured by everyone about keeping a low profile and not advertising that they were outlanders. He didn't see the big deal; sailors and merchants from Ivancia often had business in Taralee or at least Port Redmaw. On the whole, Seth didn't mind them.

"What's the name of the town?" Lily asked Isaac.

"Port Garendell," Isaac informed her, he'd a map in his hands. "With luck your sister and the others are still awaiting transport."

Coming in was trickier than Seth expected.He had no idea who was allowed to dock where. Their sailboat was small compared to many of the more modest merchant vessels, but there were a few other humble boats such as theirs on the north end of the dock, which was where they were directed.

Unlike Stagmil, after dark the town lit up. The taverns were numerous, especially close to the docks, and there were many taller houses ranging from grungy to magnificent, though Seth didn't get as good a look as he would have liked.

"We can sleep overnight here," Isaac said as they finished tying off.

Larry had already departed to speak to the dock master. "Do you ladies mind watching our charge while we make inquiries?"

"I wouldn't mind stretching my legs," Catarina said.

"I'm doing all right," Lily said. That surprised Seth. He figured she'd be the first one to want off the boat, but remembered she wore the bracelet. If Madeline tried anything, it made sense that Lily, who couldn't be taken over, be present.

"I won't be long," Catarina said. Isaac stayed with Lily while he set out with Catarina; Larry's business with the dockmaster was brief as he was told to come back in the morning. Most of the vendors and shops had closed up, but Seth almost lost Larry and Catarina when he stopped to watch some travelling minstrels performing songs, but Larry doubled back and retrieved him.

They found a pub and Catarina cited she had her leg stretch, then he was set back to escort her and retrieve Isaac. He was grateful Catarina relayed instructions to Isaac. Seth felt turned around in big cities, and this busy port was no exception.

Seth and Isaac set out and met Larry at the pub and Seth enjoyed the most delicious bowl of chowder while Isaac and Larry went over what they'd found. Seth found the pub a little chilly, being near the sea and boasting open walls, but the chill wind didn't seem to bother the other patrons.

Larry was chatting up sailors; the *Marigold Dinglett* was still in port; the crew said some items were offloaded and the vessel would be in port for another day before eventually heading back west. Isaac inquired about supplies and Seth wondered why they'd need a wagon; they could carry everything they needed, couldn't they? Several pints later, Larry and Isaac were chatting up a man who was willing to part with a decent wagon as well as a pair of donkeys on loan. The man said he would need them in a few weeks, and Isaac agreed to sell them back at that time, after determining that their first destination was Mirador.

"Hope you're not staying in Mirador long," the man said with a laugh. "That place is cursed."

Seth noticed Boscoe, just always out of sight, nibbling on someone's half-finished plate, scampering under the table to enjoy the bones when another pub goer passed near.

"What can you tell us about Mirador?" Isaac asked the barkeep.

The old gent looked a little nervous, but the pub activity continued on. Seth reached for Isaac's beer, only stopping when Larry slapped his wrist and continued on to the sourdough bread like he meant it. "It's not a secret. I'm not the right person to ask about the Castle. Er . . . they're both called Mirador, the town and the castle, I mean. The castle's been abandoned."

"What happened?" Isaac asked.

The man shrugged. "A little over two years ago, a strange curse fell upon the castle. The royalty and most of the knights escaped, see? There were people left behind—and they haven't been seen since. The castle was built near a lake and there was a moat around it. But after the one attempt to find some royal brat, the nobles abandoned the place."

"What happened to the royal family?" Isaac pressed.

The barkeep gave another shrug. Another man, this one clad in a long leather coat and wearing an impressive tricorn cap, joined them. "Evacuated—they knew something was wrong, but not enough to warn the common folk or even some of the courtiers. They even hired wizards to try to reclaim the castle. I saw a wizard and his team go in and, but only the wizard made it out."

"You are?" Isaac asked the new stranger.

"Herald," the man offered. He had a lean, prematurely weathered look about him. "A bunch of us were hired to be on standby; the wizard's job was to rescue some princeling. A bunch of hurrah for nothing. So much for his so-called *heroes*."

"How did the wizard get in?" Larry pressed.

"Wouldn't you like to know," Herald said, grinning into his ale.

"He transform into a bat or something?" Seth asked.

The man's eyes widened in surprise, then shook his head.

"Mirador used to be a decent place. I miss the tourneys," the barkeep said, sighing wistfully. "I stayed as long as I could, but there wasn't any use."

"You're from there?" Larry asked.

"Aye—the castle kept most of us in business. Almost everyone knew someone who lost someone. Shops closed up, people moved away. Local rangers and the knights and their squires kept us busy," the bartender paused, his eyes twinkling at some private memory. "I heard something about what you were talking about. Seven men entered the castle, only one came back out."

"Six men and a woman," Herald clarified. "She didn't fare so well, if you're curious."

"You saw them go in?" Isaac pressed.

Herald nodded. "My information isn't free."

"I'll pay for your beer and supper," Larry grumbled.

"My thanks," said Herald. He tipped his mug at the barkeep, who filled it with ale. The barkeep didn't fill up Seth's extended mug. "Last I checked, about every month or so someone arrives by carriage with goods. We intercepted several packages—nothing of importance. No letters. Some bundles of fabric, and food stuffs . . . not much, but I'm told the castle had good stores. Toys."

"Toys?" Seth asked.

"Dolls. Nah, they've strings. What did the captain call them . . .fancy word."

"What did you do with them?" Seth pressed.

"I'm not sure. I suppose that isn't true," Herald said after some hesitation, licking his lips and mulling over his words before he continued. "Captain allowed me to keep one, so I cut the strings and gave it to my daughter."

"Where is it now?" Seth asked, standing.

"At my home. It's one of her favourite dollies."

Seth exchanged glances with Isaac and Larry. "Can we see the toy?" Isaac pressed. "And do you know where the rest are?"

Herald shrugged "There were about a dozen of them. If they're as hard as my daughter's is, most are likely firewood." Herald said with a snicker. "This was probably about eight or so months back."

Seth studied the roaring fire. He imagined Rebecca burning in that limp puppet form. When he made some harsh landings as a puppet it didn't really hurt. Would burning be painful? Would she be aware?

"How'd the wizard get in?" Seth asked.

"Not by a means you can manage. I don't want any funny business, understand?"

"We just want to see the toy," Isaac said.

Herald shouldn't have been drinking at the tavern. His home was small and dingy. Seth never understood why anyone would live in town when they could get land and not have to constantly deal with neighbours. Herald's wife didn't offer them tea; she looked ready to tear a strip off of her husband when they arrived in the mud room. Herald's daughter was about the same age as Isaac's younger son Gustav. She didn't want to bring the puppet. It was probably once quite a beautiful doll—her skirt was of cascading shades of lavender, but dirty. The strings were long since cut and the hair matted; there were plenty of scratches across the face, too.

"There aren't any strings to cut," Larry told Isaac. To Seth's surprise, Isaac produced the scissors. Isaac did the same ritual Madeline had done over Seth. Seth realized he himself didn't have any strings to cut and he was still restored to his humanity. He wasn't sure it was going to work, but the little puppet let out a gasp. She looked around and tried to run away, but Seth grabbed her.

"It's okay," Seth insisted. "We're friends."

"I hate tea parties!" the little puppet cried. "Let me go!"

"Papa, what is going on?" the little girl asked Herald, who along with his wife had visibly paled.

"Blimey . . ." Herald sputtered.

"I'm Seth. What's your name?" Seth asked.

"E-Elinor," the girl sputtered, looking around. "Is it true? I can interact with you? Or am I dreaming?"

"Y-you mean to say, all this time?" Herald asked, covering his mouth, backing away.

Isaac looked to the man. "We'll be leaving now, with the girl. If you have any leads to any others, you'll let me know?" He took Elinor from

Seth, and coddled her. "It's all right, Elinor. I'm Issac, this is Larry and Seth. We'll take you to Larry's ship. Larry's wife and Seth's sister are there, you're safe now." They all turned to go.

"Wait!" Herald sputtered. "There's a small passage, near the southeastern wing of the castle. Take the ferry across the moat and, and . . . what's the point? When I say it's a small passage, you can't possibly . . . "

"Is there a way in?" Isaac asked.

"Not for the likes of us or we would have marched in! The wizard turned himself and his team into puppets," Herald said. "Only the spell-caster made it out. I'm sorry."

"What's going on inside the castle?" Larry asked.

"I don't know."

Seth saw Boscoe peeking from behind an alley. He didn't say anything, leaving the light of the porch as Isaac and Larry pressed the family for more information. "What do you want?" Seth asked the kit.

"This is very strange magic," said the little kitsune, wriggling his nose, jumping on a barrel. "I don't like any of this. And that woman . . . she's not normal. I can't explain it very well, but my mom might know."

"I know all of that," Seth said. "Do you have anything useful to add?"

"She did something to Lily. It's not wearing off like mom said."

"Don't worry about Lil'. Just stay out of the way," Seth said, then furrowed his brow. "Unless you can try to find the other puppets like that girl?"

Boscoe's ears perked but he let out a whine. "Maybe, if I snuck into every house. There's a lot of dogs here. You might as well break into them and look as well. Something doesn't smell right."

"Yeah, it stinks like fox," Seth said with a huff and returned to the others to wait for Isaac to finish questioning Herald. He found the night chilly, but found sleep easy on the little sailboat as Catarina spoke to Elinor, the new girl wearing a spare set of Lily's clothing. Seth slept on deck with the other men, as doing so made Elinor less nervous. He roused the next morning at the sound of sailors and seagulls calling and his back was the least sore.

Catarina was already up and moving; she'd left Lily below deck and smiled when she saw Seth. "Excellent. You can watch Madeline with your sister."

"Where are you going?" Seth asked.

"To make inquiries." She and Elinor left with Larry. Isaac was retrieving backsacks from the hull.

"So now what?" Seth asked. "We just hang around and wait?" "I believe the day before yesterday you said it best: you've got two good feet," Isaac said, loading a backsack with a bedroll and dried food, belting a hatchet and utility knife. "They'll catch up tomorrow or even later tonight. Let's get a move on. The walk will take us most of the day."

Seth wasn't expecting this, neither was he comfortable leaving Lily alone with Madeline until he saw that Madeline's ankle had been secured to a bench below deck. Lily kept her distance and with that bracelet . . . well, Seth figured hanging about wasn't productive.

He and Isaac stopped only to grab street food, fill their water flasks from a well, speak with a caravan who'd just travelled that way. Soon they found themselves on the road to Mirador.

The path was well-maintained and the woods they passed through weren't as thick here as they were back home. It seemed the way was well-patrolled and two men were hardly worth robbing. At least Seth hoped so; he would be embarrassed if they were ambushed. Isaac had some coin but had left the majority of it with Catarina.

He liked Isaac but hoped the others wouldn't be more than a day or two behind them. "What do you suppose they're going to do with Elinor?"

"Larry talked about sailing her back, but he'll need Catarina or me to crew," Isaac explained. "Catarina said she'd see if she could find the girl a job, but we'll bring Elinor with us when we sail for home."

"Boat's going to get crowded if we rescue my people from home," Seth said. "Me and Louis might have to catch a passenger vessel."

"We'll cross that bridge when we get to it," Isaac said. "Thankfully, Mirador's not that far inland. Larry said once we have a plan, some of us will sail back and get your folks. None of us feel comfortable splitting up given what you told us about Madeline, but there's a chance we can get your sister before she's in that castle."

Seth hoped Isaac was right. He'd heard of stuff waiting for days in a shipyard before being moved to Taralee. Then again, his world was fleece and flour, and those didn't spoil quickly. "Think she's got other tricks?" Seth asked, meaning Madeline.

"I know she does."

He chatted with Isaac but for the most part they trekked in earnest. Seth wondered if Madeline was leading them into a trap. And why she thought the castle she sent their friends and sister to was impenetrable. If it was abandoned, there wasn't anyone to guard it. He didn't know much about castles, but he did know plenty about finding alternate routes to try to sneak in and out of caves and other buildings. Perhaps not fit for normal people, but he and Lily could climb and rappel so, if there was a way, Seth would find it.

They saw the castle before they saw the town, for the castle had tall towers and was built on an incline, and at its closest there was more than a moat that separated them. A lake was to its north, parts of the castle wall extending almost to the water nestled amongst trees.

Thick briars consumed the walls, like something out of a child's story. The castle was of a darker stone than the ones Seth had seen back at home. The town of Mirador felt smaller than Port Garendell but like the place had once thrived. The streets for the most part were cobbled and there were signs of businesses that supported a larger population; fountains with figures of water-bearing beauties on them still worked though there was a growth of moss and algae.

They had sleeping rolls but made their way to a tavern with straw flooring just as it was getting dark. Their roasted quail was slightly bland but warm, and the bread and vegetables were decent. He and Isaac couldn't pull off being father and son but no one seemed interested in them or their business. Isaac was friendly enough but the locals weren't as welcoming to outsiders as the port. Seth supposed that made sense; ports were expecting travellers. Seth was more than willing to explore the area outside the castle, but Isaac said they'd turn in early and explore during daylight.

The straw bed was more comfortable than the forest floor. Seth normally would have stayed up for hours and enjoyed the atmosphere below but he drifted off quickly, and when he woke to the sound of local roosters, for a minute he thought he was back home. He quickly donned a fresh set of day clothes and they set out, Isaac citing that he'd gotten more useful information from the port than the locals.

Breakfast was fruit from a vendor. They travelled east from the town towards a spot that was apparently favoured by peddlers in the past, only about a ten minute walk from the last real house. It would make a good camping site if they had tents with them. They got a better view of the castle from here, and walking around they found that the briars didn't extend to the drawbridge. The castle did not seem to be in ruin.

"Well, if the carriage comes only once every other month," Seth told Isaac, "Tiffy and the others ain't in there yet."

Isaac nodded, then said. "Madeline said she fled Taralee with others. Odds are she's letting whoever know that as well—your sister and the others might have been delivered with that message."

Seth would have liked to spend a day or three poking around Taralee and learning what had transpired there. "Doesn't mean that the message needed to be delivered here," Seth pointed out. He frowned, thinking Madeline might have sent it to a completely different place than where she'd sent Tiffany and the others—assuming they were sent together. They spent much of the morning exploring up the road and the countryside. It would have been pointless if Seth didn't chance upon a wild turkey. Isaac went back to town while Seth sat around their prospective campsite; he made a fire and was plucking the bird when he heard braying. Catarina and Madeline sat on a wagon pulled by a pair of strong donkeys. Lily and Larry had walked; they'd caught up, sans Elinor.

Larry came over. "Where's Isaac?"

"He went back to town to do more inquiring," Seth said. "Where's Elinor?"

"We had a good chat. We couldn't find a ship that would sail her for a few weeks, so I promised we'd take her back to Shelkie's Bay with us and help her get home from there. We asked if she wanted to come camp with us or stay in Garendell, so we helped her find a job with board until we returned. She'd stay on our sailboat if only the docks weren't so rowdy at night. She'll be keeping an eye out for your folk from Stagmil." It didn't feel right leaving her behind, but she didn't know them; no doubt Elinor didn't want to be anywhere near Madeline.

Seth cleaned his hands and helped them unload the supplies from the wagon. Catarina directed where she wanted her kitchen tent in addition to the sleeping one; Seth would have groused that he knew more about camping and sleeping out of doors than she ever did, but the tents were Catarina and Larry's—or Isaac's, he was never quite certain.

They gathered firewood while Catarina finished plucking his turkey. "Mind if I make us a soup?" she asked. Seth didn't think twice about what it was going to be other than cooked on a stick, so he agreed.

When the camp started to take proper shape, Seth was about to offer to go find Isaac in town, but Larry spotted him coming up the road. From their vantage point, they would see if anyone was coming with plenty of warning so long as they weren't lurking in the bush.

"Any ideas about what's our next step?" Lily asked Isaac.

"Not all the lands are covered in briars," Isaac said, pointing to the castle grounds across the lake. It wasn't super far away but he'd be hard pressed to shoot an arrow and not lose it to the water. Madeline was usually all but chained to Catarina, assisting in whatever she was doing.

"What do we do if Tiffany's not in there?" Seth asked Lily.

"Are there other places they could be sent?" Lily asked Madeline. The puppeteer nodded. "Where?"

"One's not far from Taralee, there's two other places on this side of the ocean."

Someplace not far from home? "You're not particularly helpful, you know that?" Seth asked. To his surprise, he heard a familiar *baaah*, and then a dog bark. He shouldn't have been surprised to see sheep on this side of the sea.

"Get back over here," a shepherd called. He was probably Louis' age, though shorter and skinnier. "Sorry about that."

"No harm done," Seth said.

"You staying long or just passin' through?" the shepherd asked.

"Haven't decided," Seth said with a shrug. They hadn't really rehearsed what they were supposed to say, but he didn't like the idea of letting everyone know what they were up to. The youth turned his head when his grandfather called him. The older man was tall, lean though he'd thick forearms. "You don't look like peddlers," the older shepherd muttered. "If you've come to see our enchanted castle, it's not terrible exciting, is it?"

"What makes you say it's enchanted?" Isaac asked.

"Most princes don't give up their castles, much less one like Mirador," said the youth.

"I don't suppose you were there when it happened?" Isaac asked.

"I was at home, but blimey I don't doubt that folk from the next county knew something was wrong," the older shepherd said.

"I was in town," the youth said. "Sky turned green! Well, it was green for like, two hours before. That's when the royals left. Clouds were funny for two days before that."

"It was like lightning struck the castle, we heard it from the farm," the older shepherd offered.

The youth nodded. "We heard screaming from across the lake. A handful made it out by the skin of their teeth, but after the briars went up, no one's been in or out of the castle."

Seth bit his tongue; they didn't need to tell them what they knew, at least concerning Herald and the wizard. If he was to be believed, six sellswords were still in there. If Tiffany was there, there had to be a way to save her.

"Anything odd happen before the curse?" Isaac asked.

The youth shook his head, but the older shepherd looked contemplative. "There was an incident."

"They couldn't have been related," the youth pointed out.

"Several knights and rangers were killed days before those strange clouds appeared," said the older man. "Word is, one of their ghosts knew it was betrayal, and cursed the castle. The curse trapped everyone inside it, and everyone outside has been looking on ever since."

"Has anyone tried to use ladders and climb over the briars?" Lily asked.

"There were two attempts to take the castle back, before they got mixed up with that . . . sorcerer," the old shepherd almost spat out the final word. "I supported them before he got involved."

"People bring packages back and forth," Lily said. "How do they get them in and out of the castle?"

The older man shook his head. "Those carriages are supposed to be stopped. What's left of the law is dealing with other problems. Besides, they intercepted a few and to what end?"

"Are there any puppets from the carriages in town?" Seth asked.

The man's jaw clenched and he sneered. "I don't understand what it is with people asking those questions. Why would we collect those?"

"Not you personally," Seth said. "Are any still around?"

"Darned if I know," said the old man. "You folks should move on. There's something evil going on in there. I can't put my finger on it, but when I look at it, and think about my Gwendolyn." His eyes watered, and the grandson put an hand on his shoulder.

"It's okay, granddad. Let's go," the youth said before addressing their group again. "You'd best press on; everyone who can already has."

"Thank you for the information," Isaac said. More words were exchanged, but Seth saw Lily enter the bush towards the lake. He would have thought she was going to attend to nature, were it not for the familiar tail sticking up from the tall grass.

Seth followed after his sister. The woods here weren't thick, though it wouldn't be difficult to hide if he needed to lay low. To his surprise, Isaac followed after him, leaving Larry and Catarina to mind Madeline.

Lily stood before a small wooden raft, a dark rope running across the lake to the castle. Boscoe was on the raft, pointing at a long stick and looking like he was telling her to get to work.

"That little fox is more useful than I thought," Isaac told him quietly, startling Seth.

"How long have you know about Boscoe?" Seth asked.

"Since he stole two chickens and I'm not sure how many eggs," Isaac said.

"You're not mad?"

"They're usually a sign of luck," Isaac said. "Good or bad I'm not certain. Why didn't you mention him?"

"He doesn't really belong to us, he just shows up when he feels like it," Seth told Isaac before he followed the older man towards his sister and the kit.

Boots snapping a twig startled his sister and Boscoe trotted away, jumping into the bush, but Isaac called out. "We saw you talking to her just a moment ago."

"Yip yip!" Boscoe barked unconvincingly from the bush. He came back, eyes wide, and he rolled on his back, exposing his belly for a rub.

"You fool no one," Seth told the kitsune, who got up and shook off the dirt. "Should we go check it out? Secret tunnel sounds like fun."

"Yeah, it does," Boscoe agreed.

"Maybe one of us should keep an eye on Madeline while Larry and Catarina are busy," Lily suggested. "Tell me if you find anything." She made her way back to camp as Seth jumped on the raft. The ferry seemed a little neglected but was otherwise sturdy. The kitsune jumped on with them, and Isaac seemed to know what he was doing, though half way he let Seth take over. It wasn't hard to move the ferry along the line, there was hardly any breeze and the lake was for the most part calm. Isaac looked back at town. People pointed.

"Great, we've been spotted," Isaac said.

"Who cares?" Seth asked. "We aren't doing anything."

"People know we're not from here, and the folk won't be as friendly if they think we've got business with the castle. We should have stocked up on supplies first," Isaac said, but then gave a deep breath as if acknowledging there wasn't a do-over. "Let's check out the grounds surrounding the castle."

The briar didn't reach the shore, and they were able to easily dock and tie the raft on the far side; Seth wondered why the folk didn't cut the ferry's rope. Boscoe scampered ahead towards the denser collection of trees. Seth patrolled as near as he could to the castle, parts of the wall were exposed, but they were sheer and so high up that they couldn't be scaled.

"All right, so all we need to do is break into a castle," Seth said. "That's assuming Tiffy and the others are here. Madeline said there's another place she could have sent them to."

"If you wriggle names out of her let me know," Isaac said. The kitsune sniffed about on the ground. "Well, how about it? You good luck or bad luck?"

"It's strange magic," Boscoe affirmed. "The castle reeks of it. But . . . there's something old . . . something different. . ."

The kitsune led them away from the walls into a wooded area, and though they could no longer see the ferry the could see the lake. The kitsune sniffed, looked consternated, then walked away, and sniffed again. He kept going to the same grassy area, and Seth would have thought nothing of it until Boscoe started to dig. Boscoe disappeared beneath the earth before he let out a yelp, then backed up. He held up a hurt paw, his eyes wide and sad.

"I'll take you back to Lily, she can kiss it better," Seth offered as Isaac removed the thorn.

"I found the secret tunnel, what have *you* discovered?" the little kitsune said, then stuck out his tongue.

Seth lowered his head, then had to use his lantern. It was dark, and full of roots, but it led under the briars. How . . . did it go all the way into the castle? "We can't go this way."

"If I could clear out the briars, I could fit," the kitsune said.

"You'll be scratched," Isaac said. "Let's keep looking."

They investigated the area. Nothing of note—they were never sucked into the briars, but Seth got the idea that the briars were very thick.

They returned to camp before sunset. Catarina had turned his wild turkey into the most amazing soup, with potatoes and carrots and spices he'd not thought to bring along.

"Well, we found the tunnel," Isaac said, mostly watching Madeline, who had a frozen expression. "It's too small for any of us to use, including the kitsune."

"Where is he?" Catarina asked.

"Off pretending to be sneaky," Isaac replied.

"I am sneaky!" Boscoe harkened from a nearby shrub.

"So what, we wait for this carriage or Mom and Dad?" Lily asked. "That carriage could be well-armed, assuming we could get the jump on them."

"We've enough money to camp out for at least a month," Isaac said. "I suppose we could split up and sail back, and return Elinor to Shelkie's Bay."

"There's not enough of us as is," Larry spoke up, mostly because he was glaring at Madeline. Seth was glad someone else wasn't buying this demure act either.

Before he finished his soup, Larry put his bowl down, and Boscoe stalked out and licked it clean. Madeline scowled at the kitsune, but said nothing. Boscoe finished, then jumped into Larry's lap for a pet.

"Two weeks is a long time to be doing nothing," Seth said. "Maybe we should go back to town, get more information."

"How small is the tunnel?" Lily asked.

"I couldn't fit," Boscoe said, licking his paws and cleaning his ears. "Seth could have, if he was still a puppet."

"Yeah, too bad I'm back to normal," Seth said. Everyone else went quiet and exchanged glances. "What are you all thinking?"

"Herald said they entered through the tunnel as puppets," Lily said.

"He also said only the wizard made it out," Seth pointed out. "He went in with six sellswords. There's six . . . seven of us including the kitsune. If a wizard and his hired thugs couldn't make it out, what do you want me to do?"

"We shouldn't do anything rash. Besides, I don't want to be turned into anything," Larry said.

Isaac looked at the fire before he spoke to Seth. "You and I could transform, and take a look around."

"I don't want to be a puppet again!" Seth sputtered.

"You don't have to. I'll go," Lily offered.

"You're a girl," Isaac countered. "It's not safe."

"I didn't come here to be safe," Lily replied, "I came here to find my sister."

Seth stared at the fire and at Madeline as the others conversed. "We're trying to get people out, not send more people in," he said finally.

"Do you have a better idea?" Lily asked. "I can scout. We'll figure out if this is even an option and come right back. We have the scissors, you can turn me right back."

Seth felt his cheeks burn as the others conversed. They hadn't any idea how the castle was laid out; a map would be handy. So long as he had an open sky Seth was fine but he wasn't the best in cities, and castles were sort of like small cities. Lily and Isaac didn't have any experience as puppets. He was the best candidate to undergo the change and scout. It also made sense to send two people; if one person got trapped the other could go back and report what happened or attempt a rescue. Why did he get the idea that everything in there was meant to keep puppets in? Besides, what was he going to tell his father if they sat around waiting for a week? That he was brave now that Elias showed up?

"If anyone's going it should be me," Seth said eventually. "Isaac, you don't know what our sister or the others look like. If this is what we're doing, Lily and I should scout. We're shepherds. There's not enough of us to leave *her* unattended, either." He gestured at Madeline.

Isaac looked contemplative. "I don't feel comfortable sending you."

"I'm seventeen and Seth is sixteen," Lily pointed out.

"I spent time as a puppet before," Seth said. "It's . . . weird, Lily. You get the hang of it but you don't move the same as we do now. I should go." He bit his lip before he caught Isaac's gaze. "Mr. Sprites, after we figure out what exactly is going on in there, we can come back and come up with a more solid plan. After that, it shouldn't matter who goes so long as one of us is there to recognize Tiffany and the others."

"I'll sketch out a map," Lily said. "I'm not much of a cartographer, but it'll be better than nothing."

Isaac nodded slowly, but then his expression became stern. "You go in and get information. No rescue unless it can be done safely. We come up with a plan to save your sister and the others, understood?"

Lily looked through her book, ripped out some pages and handed them to Isaac. "In case I'm captured, I don't want anyone to learn anything sensitive." Seth was more hesitant—how could she easily be asked to turn into a puppet? He realized that he was much more autonomous than Lily was when that mask was forced onto her.

"All right," Madeline said. "You'll be free puppets. You'll have to remove that magic bracelet," she told Lily.

Seth produced the key and Lily unlocked it from her wrist.

"It's my mom's," Boscoe said. "Don't ask how it works, but it's meant to keep you from being cursed. If the curse is already on you, it'll lock it in place. You ought to wear it, Mr. Sprites." He cast a glance at Madeline. "Keep her from doing anything to you, anyway."

Isaac furrowed his brow, but upon a moment's consideration nodded, and locked the bracelet, but he kept the key on the same leather thong that Seth did and placed it around his neck. "All right—let's wait until it's nearly dark. No one will see you crossing the lake."

They helped clean and Catarina and Larry spoke at length with Lily; it seemed that they'd bonded during their trip with the donkeys. He looked to Boscoe, then the castle. What if Tiffany wasn't in there? What if she was, and they couldn't find her?

Time that had been crawling before now seemed to go by quickly.

When at last they'd gone over supplies and were ready, Seth stood by his sister facing the lake. Madeline sang. Seth felt the air around them change, and the fire spat and hissed more than it ought. The trans-formation was relatively fast—not as fast as when Mama Fern changed shape back and forth. Everything they had on them shrank, but they were still useful: his real bow, their utility knives, Lily's sword. Despite having a good few inches on her, as marionettes Lily was only a little smaller than he was. She opened her eyes, and gasped and immediately stumbled backwards. She looked cute, whereas Madeline seemed to be making fun of his nose.

"Are you yourselves?" Isaac asked.

Seth assumed he mostly looked like he did before. He despised being that small, but he did a few practice jumps and swung his arms, then did a backflip. "Still got it," he said. Lily went to look at herself in the lake, but they barely had enough light for a reflection.

"I don't know how long we'll be in the castle," Lily said. "If we lose track of time, I don't want you to worry about us."

"Try to return by dawn, but if you're late still make your way back to us," Isaac said.

"Will we be able to use the ferry like this?" Lily asked.

"We won't need the ferry, just the rope," Seth said. He went to the line, and not only monkey-barred it, but ran across it and even did a few flips. "See? We can get back and forth no trouble."

"Speak for yourself, Seth," Lily said, jumping, but she didn't try to flip. "I'm new at this."

"If you're chickening out, turn back and I'll take Isaac instead," Seth said. "I can draw a map."

"I've seen your spelling." Lily shook her head. She pet Boscoe.

"Take good care of Seth," Boscoe yipped. "I don't know who I'll bother if anything were to happen to him."

"I'm sure you'll move on quickly," Seth muttered. "Times 'a-wasting, and I want to spend as little time like this as possible."

Lily nodded. "If we're not out after two days, assume we're captured and come up with another plan. One that doesn't involve turning any-one into puppets."

"I'll be working on that plan until you return," Isaac said, and gestured to the castle. "Try to go unnoticed, so far we still have the element of surprise."

Seth led the way along the rope; it was almost annoying how slow his sister was, but he helped her across. She didn't bound like he did when they made it to the other side, so he had to wait for her and led her to the cobbled tunnel. They had to bend, but they continued without lighting the lantern. He'd forgotten how well he could see in the dark. The occasional thorn pricked them, but it barely scratched their paint and it didn't hurt.

There was a faint blue glow ahead, and they quieted their movements. The room was dark, and hard to make out, but it seemed like they were in a spare room with furniture draped in fabric; cobwebs climbed along the corners of the ceiling. The long path led them behind a mirror that wasn't broken but laid against the wall at an angle, and there was no getting around footprints but Lily was careful to walk in his footsteps to minimize their presence. The door was locked but they had rope and Seth tossed a grapple to the open window that would have been about face level. He quickly scaled, then helped Lily up. Looking to the hallway, the castle had vaulted ceilings; that part seemed a little more maintained. He looked at Lily, who seemed nervous at the climb down.

"It's just the scale," he told her, then slid down quickly. She was slower; they left their rope to tell them which door they used, and in the dark Seth doubted anyone would even notice it. The place seemed abandoned. "All right, we're in," he said. "Now what?"

Lily took out her book, and made an X. "Let's try to navigate." She gestured towards faint light as opposed to darkness—candles or lanterns. He nodded, and they moved quietly, though it felt like he could scream and no one besides her would hear him. There were multiple closed doors, eventually they found one ajar and he ducked in to investigate. Lily waited in the hallway.

There were a lot of boxes stacked. He sped towards them, and opened one from the top pile, it was empty. Frowning, he pulled one from several rows down. Empty again. The next one, which they took from the top, not so much. The puppet looked somewhat like they did, a knightly fellow, dressed in black armour and he seemed like a villain with an excellent yet ugly moustache and pointy beard. Another box revealed someone who looked like a chef, with a white coat and top hat. Their eyes were glazed but Seth could tell they were in some sort of subtle-awareness. He frowned, and put the box back.

"Try not to disturb the dust too much," Lily told him.

"You're supposed to be keeping watch," Seth told her. "You don't think these are all . . ." Seth said, but despite her diminished marionette expression, he could tell she did think that yes, these were people. There were fifty or so boxes stacked along the wall. They quietly went through them; none had anyone they recognized. They also found there were several rooms holding such boxes. "We can't go through all of these," Seth pointed out. "At least, we should know how many there are."

"I marked the ones we've searched," Lily told him. Seth frowned; they could spend hours checking every box. Besides, what if they changed Tiffany's clothes like Rebecca had, and they missed her? "The ones with heavy dust have been here for a while. Tiffany wouldn't be there."

He nodded, and led the way down the hall. He wondered if they ought to free some of the people they found, but the scissors were back at the camp, and dragging someone . . . and who exactly was the best person to help them? Suits of armour and old banners decorated the walls. Benches and other furniture became nicer once they moved under torch light.

"All these halls look the same. I could see us getting turned around," Seth told her.

"We'll just have to travel slow and . . ."

While her head was in the book, Seth saw something strange and blue down the far end of the hallway. He shushed her and grabbed her arm, and they took shelter behind a suit of armour. Butterflies? Butterflies of a brilliant blue entered the corridor, about a dozen in total.

"They're beautiful," Lily whispered.

"Beautiful trap," Seth agreed. They remained perfectly still; he was thankful they had no beating hearts or breath to hold so the butterflies continued down the hall. When they were on the move again, Seth let Lily do the counting and the sketching.There were multiple doors and the next one they entered gave them pause.

It looked like a craft room of some sort, with hundreds of bolts of fabric on shelves and a work space and sewing equipment, paints and rows of buttons organized by colour, half finished projects as well as papers showing how to make a certain coat or hat. A figure sat on a chair, regular size, wearing a long, flowing robe of grey but the face was in shadow. They were painting a figure on strings;some sort of terrible sea beast puppet, controlled by wooden poles and wire from below as opposed to marionette strings.

"Let's go," Seth whispered in Lily's ear. She nodded, and followed him back into the hallway. The castle was strange, cold, and dark, even though there were brilliant stained glass windows and moonlight shone through them, casting coloured light into the hallway. They found another room—this one was full of countless spare parts: arms and torsos, eyes and wigs, all marionette sizes. Seth wondered how many of them were taken from real people, and what was made, but noticed that the workshop was building monsters.

"So many," Lily said, barely above a whisper.

"Hey, you!" someone called from . . . behind glass? He was on strings and dangling from a metal stand, but he'd swung and was kicking the glass. It was hard to hear him.

Seth gestured. "I'm not sure he's friendly."

"He's someone to talk to," Lily said. "Come on."

She entered the room and jumped from the floor to the ledge, and Seth realized that there were an awful lot. The man was suspended, and he seemed to be shouting in excitement. It wasn't even that hard to lift the glass off of him.

"Thanks—er," he was far too loud, and he realized it as he hushed the rest of his words. Seth walked over to him. "Get me down! We're not on the playing field, I'll help you escape!"

"Shush!" Lily gestured. "Someone's working down the hall. Keep your voice down." The marionette nodded.

Lily unsheathed her sword and Seth grabbed her arm. "Don't get too excited," Seth said. "Who are you?"

"Name's Bernard," the marionette said. "Pleased to make your acquaintances. Now could you cut me down?"

"Lily, this could be a trap," Seth said.

She hesitated, but Lily cut the man's leg strings, then his head, finally his hands. Bernard fell unceremoniously, and for a moment Seth thought his sister broke him.

After an instant, the man picked himself off the ground and seemed unfamiliar how to move without the strings, but after a few motions, relaxed. "Finally," the man said, looking at his wrists. He slapped Seth's hands away when he went to poke the strings. "Get away from those!" he said, and quickly made them back up and flip the glass lid atop the crossbars. "Sorry, can't be too careful."

"Voice down. Bernard, we had our sister stolen," Lily tried to explain, but Bernard cut her off.

"Well, you just rescued someone, let's go."

"Wait—do you know where they would have taken her?" Seth asked.

"More merchandise arrives from time to time; I've never figured out a schedule. No doubt she's in storage." The man did have a very theatrical voice. "I for one don't want to waste my first chance for freedom in over a hundred years of going back there!"

"A hundred years?" Seth demanded.

"Well, more like two, but you have no idea how the theatre world works. One minute you're the crème de la crème, the next you're chopped liver and a has-been, or a never-was."

"We need information," Lily said.

Bernard nodded. "Follow me."

Seth didn't like how trusting Lily was, but neither did he complain when Bernard climbed off the table, all of them making a clattering sound when they reached the ground. Thankfully, no one inspected their sound. They followed Bernard down the hall, away from the torchlight. Bernard seemed to know where to go and where not to.

"I haven't been out of that room in months, and it's all coming back to me. Yes, yes this way." He led them away from the place they'd come in. Seth was certain that if he wanted to trap them, he could have made noise and drawn far more attention. He seemed flabbergasted when they came to a door. Using his rope, Seth lassoed and pulled, opening the door, which creaked but nothing came to investigate them. They entered a room that looked like it hadn't been used in a while, the furniture was draped much like the room they'd entered.

"Who are you?" Bernard asked.

"I'm Lily, and this is Seth. We're from Stagmil, it's a small village you haven't heard of."

"Why, Stagmil isn't far from my hometown of Gilda!" Bernard said. "I've been to Stagmil in my wayward youth, but up until my untimely kidnapping I was residing in Taralee."

Gilda was north of them, about a day or two's walk. A rougher territory, not so many farmers but many trappers and mountain folk lived there. Seth mostly met guys coming down to trade their furs. "A hopeful?" Seth ventured.

"Nay my good man, I was quite the rising star in the theatrical world," Bernard professed. "I was the leading man in several shows, but where I really shone was in the role of antagonist. I excelled as a cruel prince or shook audiences when becoming a jealous god. I believe one of my many rivals paid good money to be rid of me. I have been cast in the most odd roles here, mostly in a despicable light, but ofttimes the leading second-in-command when the monster de jour was unable to enunciate the plot. Not that there is one, half the time. First I was a jester who only spoke in rhyme. Then I was shelved for sometime before I was a wicked wizard who turned a maiden into a swan . . . lovely girl, but not my type."

Seth supposed villains had to be entertaining. "So you haven't seen Tiffany?"

"No sir, I've barely had a chance to exchange words with the heroes I am thrown against. It's always scripted, my lines, you understand. Clearly the so-called heroes are improvising, their dialogue is quite juvenile . . . "

"The woman who did it to you," Lily explained, "she's at a camp across the lake."

"Lake?" Bernard asked. "I don't even know where *here* is! And it was no woman, but a man. We were imbibing a good amount of spirits, and arguing philosophy."

Seth realized that there were more people involved in this scheme then Madeline, but more importantly, Bernard didn't know a thing. They had effectively rescued a clueless narrator. "We need to look around. Either you're going to help us or you can wait here and we'll bring you with us when we leave."

"You said you'd help me," Bernard said. "I mean, you look rather young and I ought to be helping you, but as you can imagine, my nerves are quite frazzled."

"We're here to scout," Lily said. "Several people from our village were kidnapped and we think they were brought here. The way I see it, is either you can come along, you can wait here for us, or you can take your chances out there on your own, but you need to be quiet."

"Lily, maybe we should take him to the camp," Seth said. "He must know something of value."

"You've a camp? " Bernard asked.

Seth nodded. "Come on. We'll take him across to Larry, otherwise he's going to get us caught. "

Lily frowned, but didn't verbalize her disagreement. They navigated back the way they came with her map, Bernard seemed to understand the need to be quiet. Their travel was uneventful until the ground before them suddenly started to glow.

Seth slowed down, it was a narrow band of pale blue but it circled the width of the hall. His instinct was to jump over it. He heard his sister call his name, and she was holding Bernard, who had not only collapsed, but was glowing much like the strange markings on the floor.

"Don't touch that! " Seth insisted, and jumped back, then realized Lily had a foot on it. She was fine. Seth hesitantly touched the glowing, it wasn't really there. Seth wondered what sort of sorcery this was, and why it effected Bernard but not them. He and Lily were fine, whereas Bernard was as motionless as Elinor and Rebecca when he first encountered them. "What just happened? Why isn't it effecting you and me? "

Lily shrugged and pulled Bernard to the side, then away from the glowing. Seth didn't follow at first, it dimmed for a minute, then disappeared completely as Lily moved Bernard away. Seth followed after her then helped cart Bernard. "Think he'll be like this forever? "

"I doubt we'd be that lucky," Seth said, Lily shot him a dirty look but he dragged Bernard to better cover under a chair. "There, we can pick him up on the way out. "

They left Bernard, until they saw a glowing room, and though they had to climb up stairs, they found that, eventually, there was an open expanse in front of them. Forests, fake mountains, and trees. From their angle, they couldn't tell where the background was painted. There were strings moving in the distance.

"How large is it?" Seth asked.

"Look," Lily gestured. It looked like a red dragon flying in the distance. The dragon never got close, but there were more creatures—some didn't have strings, but moved around on sticks. In fact, some of the sheep could only move in restricted areas, popping out of the ground.

"Well, we didn't come to look at it," Lily said, readying the rappelling equipment. He went to tie the knot, but she declined and tied it herself.

"Come on, that was like five years ago," Seth pointed out, Lily rappelled down after she was satisfied that the knot was secure. Seth let her reach the ground before following after her.

He gathered the rope and glanced at Lily making notes and sketching where they were going—crude drawings, but better than nothing. "Okay —operation let's not draw attention to ourselves is a go." Seth gestured and they set out, avoiding strings when they could.

Eleven

When they spotted the castle it made for an easy target to walk towards. They encountered creatures, but for the most part while Lily worked, Seth kept an eye out and they avoided anything hostile. When at last they arrived before the town Lily said it didn't seem like a good idea to proceed.

"We came to scout, didn't we?" Seth asked. "Why don't you keep doing the cartography thing, and I'll do the heroic thing and meet you back here?"

"We should wait for someone to come outside the town, and if they're not friendly, we can hide from one or two people," Lily said, gesturing to the rocky incline and the woods around them. "We could get mobbed in there."

"I'm faster than you, it'll be fine," Seth said. "If Tiffy and the others are anywhere it's probably some place like this. Wait for me in this area. I won't be long."

He strode into town like he owned the place and the people marionettes went about their business and ignored him. Everything was just a little too storybook cheerful, and several people were repairing buildings, obnoxiously, to song.

The marionettes were dressed like common folk; there was a butcher, and Seth wondered what the point was if they didn't need to eat, because in his transformation he'd certainly tried. He spotted knights in polished armour—often with the emblems of animals as motifs. Their horses seemed to be limited in where they could go, attached to the ground on tracks, and a gilded princess-style carriage passed him.

Peering at faces, he realized there was a flaw to his plan: how was he going to be certain it was Tiffany if he found her? There were plenty of girls with dark hair. He thought of that room of remaking. That was to say nothing if perhaps they wiped her mind and . . .

"Hey Tiffany, I got you this neat hat!" said a marionette in shiny armour.

"I got you this axe," said another.

"Why would she want an axe?" asked the first.

"You're all very sweet. Put it with my other presents, we'll compare them all later, both in number *and* quality."

Found her. It looked like Puppet!Tiffany and Puppet!Brigid were hoisting banners. They were also dressed like maidens fair, their gowns a far cry from anything they'd be allowed to wear in Stagmil, Tiffany in an emerald green and Brigid in a ruby red, both wearing tiaras of silk flowers. People put out fake food on a long table and Brigid shooed away a small puppet chicken. Seth knew he wasn't really hungry—but the hint made him want to go over and spoil their little tea party or at least mess with a chicken.

"Will you enter the tournament yourself?" Brigid asked Tiffany.

"Ew! That sounds like something dirty Lily would do."

"Even the dirt is fake," Brigid commented.

"It's easier to clean."

Seth waited for Tiffany to be out of eyesight of her admirers and grabbed her from an alley, clasping a hand over her big mouth. He turned her around and made the 'shush' gesture. Her eyes widened but she nodded and to his surprise, grabbed his arm and pulled him away from the crowd and Brigid.

"I can't believe they caught you, too!" Tiffany said. "Don't get me wrong, I'm glad to see you—wait, where are your strings?"

"Lily cut me free. We tracked you here and we're trying to figure out a way to get you out," Seth said. "I saw Brigid. How are the others? How are you?"

"All things considered, I can't complain," Tiffany said. "Louis got taken by the horde and Brigid didn't last the day without getting kidnapped. Dale's got an injured leg that is taking forever to heal, and Molly is a fairy princess."

"That's a lot to take in. I'm going to get you out," Seth said, then gestured towards the way he'd come. "Get Brigid and we'll get you out of the castle."

"'We'?"

"Lily's here. There's a small path that leads under the castle. I'll explain later, let's go."

Tiffany nodded, but hesitated when Seth took her hand and started to lead her. "Molly is off the game board."

"What?" Seth asked. "We'll figure that out later—"

"Seth, if we leave, Molly may be stuck here. As for Dale—they're not letting him out of the infirmary. I don't even know how to begin looking for Louis!"

"We can come back for the others," he said. "Whatever's going on in this castle is evil. There were hundreds of boxes with inanimate marionettes, and we saw rooms for remaking puppets. Paint, fabric, you name it. We need to get out of here."

Tiffany shook her head. "It won't work. If our strings are fully cut we can't move. We just fall down."

"Lily and I will carry you."

"What if I don't come back to life?"

"We saved Rebecca. She's across the sea waiting for mom and dad. We restored her, and we can fix you."

Tiffany nodded. "Seth, we're all spread out. I'm fine for now," Tiffany said. She caught Seth's expression. "Seth, Molly is watching me. If I disappear, whoever's doing this will know. Dale and Brigid will fall apart if they think I've abandoned them. I will talk to Molly and . . . I'll drag her if I have to."

Seth looked at Tiffany. If she could get the others to them, that would be the best but one in the hand, two in the bush was better. "I don't know if another chance will come. You need to think about this."

"I have," Tiffany said. "Molly will change her mind after I talk to her. Tell Lily I can get all eight of us, just be patient."

Seth frowned, but nodded. "Eight?"

"Jayden, Braden, and Caiden," Tiffany said. "One of them's my future husband, I just haven't narrowed it down yet."

"You just made those names up. Look, grab who you can and I'll be back tomorrow night. Be careful."

Seth ran off, oblivious to the fact they were being watched.

~*~

Tiffany nonchalantly went back to look for Brigid. "Who was the guy without strings?" Ethan asked, startling her.

"I don't know what you're talking about," Tiffany said, ignoring him and Sour Puss, who went in the direction her brother had taken off. "Glad to see he's back up and running, or do you just slap whoever is in the armour while he's down?" Tiffany hated that she couldn't go warn Seth he'd been noticed. Seth was better off without her trying to tail him.

"Be careful who you trust," Ethan told her. "Stages are made for deception, afterall."

"I saw her first!" Caiden said, marching over.

"If my little cousin or anyone else is bothering you," Ethan said, grabbing Caiden in a headlock. "Let me know."

"We're not *bothering* her . . ."

"You're annoying *me*, by proxy," Ethan informed his cousin.

"*Unhand him!*" Tiffany ordered, retrieving her 'Aiden. "You happen to be bothering *me* at the moment, Ethan. Besides, good men don't just fall from the sky."

The sun knight fell off the ladder with a yelp.

"Ew," Tiffany said.

~*~

Seth wasn't sure when he knew he was being trailed, but he got the inkling.

Of course, it wasn't just a matter of laying low. Everyone wore bright colours compared to his common clothing and, in general, seemed to be happy. Then he got a glimpse of the guy in grey armour with a wolf motif, and quickened his pace. To his surprise, a musical number erupted on the street. The townsfolk were singing about. Seth joined in—mouthing along, dancing and twisting, shaking his backside in his pursuer's general direction.

> *I appreciate this safe city!*
> *We're all so truly blessed*
> *With the knights here to protect us*
> *We can lay down our heads to rest!*

Wolf Guy had some taste and stood near the edge of the dancers, defiantly refusing to join in the lame-duck choreography or even tap a toe. Seth couldn't help himself, so he waltzed near his pursuer and sang his own lyrics:

> *Hey Bub it's nice to meet ya*
> *But I can't chit-chat over tea*
> *You can stalk you can grab you can try all ya like*
> *But ya ain't ever ever gonna catch meeeee*

The armoured guy swiped but Seth pirouetted away to the opposite alley and split before the song properly ended. He ducked and went back the way he came, and ran up the hill. *Did I lose him?* He got the distinct impression that even if it was temporary, Wolf Guy wasn't going to let off. Seth got a little turned around but recognized the rocky slopes as the way he came in, resisted the urge to jump atop buildings and scrambled back mostly the way he came. He was glad his other sister wasn't out in the open. What was worse, he knew that the guy was not only trailing, but somehow gaining.

~*~

Lily saw Seth sprinting from town and got the impression he was in trouble, so she started to walk towards him. She stayed under the cover of the trees, and observed someone in dark armour chasing him. Like her brother, the other marionette wasn't on strings, and he appeared to be gaining. She tried to wave to her brother but he sprinted past her. The dark knight paused when he crested a nearby hill looking back to the village. Lily hid behind a tree, but was still able to watch and see Seth get away.

Rustling from the woods stirred her attention; something strange and ugly was coming from the woods, but instead of at her, it and another creature were creeping towards the armoured marionette. Seth's pursuer faced back towards town and appeared to signalling; she wasn't sure but he was reflecting light. There were two creatures, and they had clubs and . . . the creatures conversed, then burst from the woods while his back was turned.

Lily nocked her bow and shot one before shouting. "Look out!" and shot again. Her aim was off but she managed torso shots on both, the figures didn't even slow down or appear injured. She knocked again and managed a leg shot, below the knee but it didn't even slow the things down. The armoured marionette drew his sword and was on them.

Something encircled her wrist, pulling her backwards, and dragged her from the cover of the trees. Lily lost the bow and pulled her sword, cutting herself free. They tried to lasso her again, but she scrambled backwards out of range. There were another two creatures, ghastly pale who looked humanoid but emaciated. Long faces with bulbous noses, eyes too big with stringy hair; they wore rags so worn out they were mostly see-through. She thought for a moment they were ghouls, but they couldn't exist in sunlight. She frowned; they weren't exactly in sunlight now, were they?

She wondered if her sword would do any better when she felt a heavy hand on her shoulder. "Be absolutely quiet, stringless," Wolf Knight ordered, "They can't get you under this cover unless they drag you into the open." He nocked an arrow, but rather than aiming for their bodies, he shot above, at their head strings. One tried to peel away and run, but it collapsed into awkward half-suspension when the arrow severed the string. The marionette took a few steps from her and appeared to be looking around. "Do you see any others?"

"No," she matched his volume. "Um . . . thank you?"

"Stay here; do not run. I will be right back." He went back out to the vantage point he was previously; he wore a visored helm so she couldn't tell exactly where he was looking; he moved his head when she moved, and she resisted the urge to sprint in the opposite direction.

Returning, he retrieved her bow and the smattering of arrows she'd lost. "Ghouls always attack in groups of three to five. I don't see a fifth one. You hurt?"

She shook her head. "Who are you?"

"Let's save pleasantries until you're out of harm's way. Don't shout again unless you have to, understood? Nod so I know it's getting through your skull." He handed her back the bow before gesturing to her sword. "Sheathe that thing. I don't want to take it away from you. How many of you are there?" She wasn't sure what he meant. "What are you doing in the castle?"

She glanced towards the town where he'd just come from. "I'm not in the castle."

"Castle Mirador, not that joke down there," he clarified.

"I'm just going to go . . . " She backed off from him and he grabbed her arm.

"Answer the question, stringless."

She straightened, trying her best to pretend she wasn't afraid. "Just out of curiosity, what happens if I scream for help?"

"Odds are you'll be strung or burned. Listen to me and I'll do everything in my power to keep that from happening," Wolf said. "Why are you here?"

"Someone I love was brought here," she said quietly.

Another figure came up the hill. This one wasn't fully armoured but looked like he had bits and pieces, wearing a jester's cap. His glass eyes widened at the sight of Lily. "Two of them?"

"Maybe more," Wolf said before gesturing after Seth. "Other one went that way."

"You're scaring her," said Jester. "Take your helmet off."

Wolf muttered something she didn't catch, and obliged. She didn't know why, but she wasn't expecting them both to be about her age. "Personally, I think the cold dead eyes are scarier than a toy helmet," Wolf said, tapping them; they made a *tink tink* noise. "Get her someplace safe. I'll look for the guy."

"He's seen you," Jester said. "I'll look for him. Meet up in fifteen nearest . . ." The Jester trailed off, then gestured up. Lily followed their gaze to some black bird, likely a raven or a crow. Wolf took out his bow and took out the head string, making it crash to the ground. "They're not far," Wolf told Jester then gestured at Lily. "This takes priority. If you don't find him in the next fifteen minutes, meet up at the nearest burrow west of here. Try to stay off-string."

"No kidding," Jester said before looking to Lily. "Whoever you are, stick with Caleb. Do not get caught or draw attention to yourself. I'll hopefully find the guy before he gets into trouble."

"Stringless, try to keep up." Jester was gone and she was amazed at how fast they could move—she wasn't getting tired, but the pair were notably faster than her. Wolf seemed to expect that, and leading her through the dense trees, often waited for her to catch up. Wolf slowed down when they came to some rolling hills littered with puppet sheep. "Nice wide open patch—we walk like we don't care—get to that set of trees, then we run again."

"Are people watching from above?" she hesitated at the tree line, looking up at the mist.

"Sometimes, but they're kind of neglectful. So long as you don't draw attention to us we should be okay." She wasn't sure what to say. He grabbed her arm as soon as they were back in the treeline. "Tell me if I'm hurting you. Come on." This brush was thicker. He warned her several times to avoid something or follow in his steps exactly, and even then once she stumbled and triggered a trap of sorts, he grabbed her and moved her out of harm's way.

He led her to a treestump, and he fumbled around, and there was an entrance leading down. She felt very trapped suddenly, she didn't know why, but while his attention was turned, she started to slip backwards. There was a lot of cover here, she could . . .

"Go first so I can close it." Wolf looked over his shoulder. "You snuck into a cursed castle, and you're scared of a little hole in the ground?"

"How do I know I can trust you?"

"All I had to do was shout and you and the other guy would have been caught," Wolf said. "There is no 'safe' while you're in this castle, but I can get you safer. I don't want to see you get hurt. If they string me I won't have a choice, but we can discuss all that down there."

"I don't understand."

"Just hurry up."

It felt like steel—not that feeling anything was normal. Lily climbed down to darkness and her eyes adjusted. He was right behind her, closed the hatch and jumped off while she was still descending, helping her down. She didn't need to breathe, but she let out a startled gasp.

"We don't have any bones to break or blood to spill. That's why your arrows didn't work on those ghouls. You make the arrows yourself?"

"No, my . . . someone from my village makes them. I didn't think ghouls could be active during daylight."

"That's not sunlight sweetheart. They would also be a lot tougher in real life. You want some real light down here?" Caleb used the lantern and lit a standard candle. There were mirrors down here to help light the place, and what looked like a table and chairs as well as some sort of cabinet filled with miscellaneous gear, broken pieces of puppets. He took off his helm and left it on the table. "I'd say get comfortable, but I know what it looks like down here. There's no mist in here, so they can't see in these burrows, so you should be relatively safe. Didn't catch your name."

She wasn't sure how to answer; there wasn't a manual on outsmarting humans but, in her experience, making him think she was docile was probably her best play. People got overconfident and he'd let his guard down. He cocked his head when she hesitated. "Lily," she offered.

"My name is Caleb, the other guy's Ethan. We're squires serving in Castle Mirador. Who was that guy you were with?"

He's just a squire. You're scared of nothing. "You're not going to hurt him?"

"Might have to incapacitate him, but I don't want to hurt him or you."

"Seth. We . . . I snuck in here after several of my villagers were turned into . . . this." She gestured to herself.

"How'd you manage to sneak in?"

"It's a long story."

"I got time, stringless."

"No offence—Caleb right? What do you mean, *stringless*? You're not on strings."

"I can go off them for a long time but not indefinitely," Caleb said. "Stringless means someone who isn't bound by strings. I can go off for hours but eventually I'll slow down and need to be back on them. I haven't really figured it out. Just about everyone out there is stuck in that world, and you don't belong. You haven't been at this long, the other guy seemed to know what he was doing."

It never occurred to her that maybe they were being spied on while they were attempting to scout. She also didn't like that he was controlling the questions. "You were . . . *are* human? Not . . . "

"I'm not a bunch of scraps turned to life, if that's what you're getting at," Caleb said.

Noises from above. Lily was relieved Seth wasn't with the blond jester; Ethan joined them when he finished securing the trap door. "That is one slippery guy." He seemed friendly. "Mind if I see what model you are?" He was very fast, and before Lily knew it he'd popped her arm out, and was looking it over. "Yeah, I mean, check out this joint here—"

"Ethan, you cannot just take someone's arm off."

"Lighten up, will ya?"

She got her arm back but neither of them noticed Lily's utter mortification that, one, she had no idea how to put it back, and two, when she thought about it, she could waive her unattached fingers. She attempted to jam the arm back in (it did not stay) and realized the pair had retreated to argue a little bit.

"I don't want to put some girl in danger," Caleb told Ethan.

"We're not really boys and girls at this point," Ethan said. "She put herself in peril sneaking in here."

"Excuse me," Lily said when they got a little heated. "I can hear you."

"See? She doesn't even know how to put her arm back on. Don't look at me, you popped it out."

"Sorry," Ethan said, and just as smoothly put Lily's arm back in place. "See, we do this all the time . . ."

Caleb spoke up. "Sorry Miss Lily, we were expecting . . . someone else."

"Who were you expecting, exactly?" She knew the answer was not Seth.

"If people could sneak into the castle they would have already," Caleb said. "How did you manage?"

"We tracked down the woman responsible for kidnapping our villagers and are forcing her to help us," Lily said. "If we had waited for the people of my village to come around, the trail would have gone cold."

"How did you get into the castle?" Caleb clarified.

Lily bristled. "Apparently some wizard made a tunnel. He entered with his bodyguards as puppets."

"Yeah, that was eight months ago," Ethan said, before his puppet eyes widened and he looked at Caleb before addressing her. "You found it? Then you turned yourself into . . . this?"

"There were some additional steps but essentially," Lily said. "You're squires? I mean, I don't really care who you were—but what is this place? Not the castle, but what's going on?"

"We're just two guys trying to find a way out," Ethan admitted. "I'm thinking you can help us with that." He gave Caleb a playful shove.

"All right, all right," Caleb grumbled. The pair crossed their arms and attempted to look authoritative. "First things first. How many of you are there?"

"Just me and Seth. We wanted to scout and report to the others back in the camp."

"There's a war camp outside?" Ethan squeaked. Their sense of authority melted away almost instantly. "How many people are outside? And why did they let you . . . er . . ."

"Four. Counting the woman who kidnapped our people. Nobody *let* us, the townsfolk didn't like us asking about the castle. We decided to come in and scout. I wouldn't exactly call what we have outside a warcamp, either."

"Four," Caleb sounded incredulous.

"It's more than three," Ethan offered.

"It technically is three because one of them is a hostile," Caleb pointed out. "Aren't you a little . . . young?"

"I might ask you the same thing." Lily crossed her arms. "I don't know what's normal for people who live in prissy castles but I'm old enough to have made it this far. What is going on in this castle?" Lily asked. "We rescued Bernard but he says he's only allowed on what he called the 'theatre floor' once in a while."

"We call it the game board," Ethan said. He looked to Caleb, who shrugged. "Bernard?"

"He's . . . kind of theatrical. Said he was forced to play the part of a villain? I guess it doesn't matter. What happened? You said you were regular people two years ago. I heard something from townsfolk about the castle being haunted or cursed. I wasn't expecting all this."

Ethan nodded. "Two years ago we were squires in this castle. Strange clouds started appearing overhead. Two days of slow, but when things happened, they happened real fast."

"Sounds like what they said in town," Lily said.

"Where'd you stop and ask for information?" Ethan asked.

"Uh . . . I think Seth called it *The Cat and Fiddle*."

"Declan's is better," Ethan offered.

"Anyway," Caleb glanced at Ethan, "they evacuated the royals and a handful of others. I missed most of it."

"Nothing you could have done," Ethan said. "Saw the beginnings of the briars before . . . this happened." He gestured to this wooden hand. "Strange clouds went funny green, fell on the castle and BOOM! First time in my life everyone ever said I was short. We're all running around panicking, strings struck the back of most of the knights and guard's heads, ripped 'em out. The rest of us were easy pickings. Cay here was in the infirmary, so him and a handful of others were free range a little while longer."

"She doesn't care about that," Caleb said before he turned his attention to her. "You need to know about the dangers out there. Be careful around strings. Anyone on string can be turned on you in a heartbeat. Including us if they think we're helping you. We're currently off-string, so no danger, but we can't be off indefinitely."

"We jerk a little bit and stutter, eyes get kinda weird. If that happens, if you were more seasoned, cut our strings, but in your case: run and get somewhere our strings can't go. We're completely aware, just not in control the whole time. Don't trust us, they'll slack up enough for us to sound like ourselves to put your guard down, then we'll get you. Make sense?" Ethan waited for her to nod. "Second thing: Anyone in authority back there is a potential danger. Don't trust anyone. Some of the watchers become puppets and spy, they can go off-string like us."

"If we get under control, we're much more dangerous than just about anything else out there," Caleb said. "We're ... kind of ... "

"Upgrades." Ethan offered.

"More like enforcers," Caleb said. "Like I said, we don't have bones to break or blood to bleed out. We can be destroyed."

"So you take out the strings?" Lily asked.

"Yup. Headstrings render the puppet unconscious, others take out that limb," Caleb explained. "I'm not opposed to you being armed, but you should avoid fighting if possible. It draws attention. Attention means they will try to string us. Not our choice. With us so far?"

"I think so," she said.

Caleb paused before he spoke again. "If you can cross the barrier, I would like to ask for your help."

"What barrier?" Lily asked.

"Did you notice any of the floor lighting up when you came to it?" Caleb asked. Her face must have betrayed her. He cussed under his breath and turned away.

"Yeah, it lit up when we tried to cross it, it struck Bernard. Seth jumped right over it," Lily said. "Are you saying we're trapped here?"

"Wait, the other guy got across it no problem?" Ethan asked, Caleb looked back at her.

"Bernard started glowing and went inanimate, nothing happened to Seth and me. We stashed Bernard under a chair," Lily said.

The squires looked at one another before they looked to her. "Do you know where you came in?" Caleb asked.

She reached into her satchel, and pulled out her notebook to look at the map. Rather impolitely, Caleb tipped the sketchbook so that they could see. "It's not exactly done. I can't tell east or west in here, but—"

"Not bad," Ethan said.

"Can I borrow this?" Caleb asked, not waiting for an answer, taking her book and moving it to the candle.

"Of all the gopher-dodging fiddle-faddle . . . "she muttered under her breath.

He paused, smirked, and glanced at Ethan. He rotated her map to the left and said,"There's your north. It's mostly accurate. This is the eastern wing of the castle's main floor. What does this symbol mean?" He flipped through the book. She tried not to get flustered.

"That one's pretty good," Ethan said. "Think you can draw me?"

"You sure like foxes," said Caleb.

"Excuse you," she said, putting her hand out.

"I can finish the map or, probably better, do a proper one," Caleb told her.

"You don't have the halls memorized," Ethan said.

"No, but we can point the big things out for her."

You came in here for information. These guys are loaded with it. "Fine," she said, giving him the satchel with ink. "How about on another page? You can do two pages, make it as big as you can."

He nodded, ripped out the page she was working on and used it for reference. His felt more to scale and made more sense. He wasn't a great artist, but it was clear enough.

"These are common drafting symbols. I'll make a key on the page over," Caleb said. "You probably aren't familiar with battle plans, but it'll translate. How literate are you?"

"What do you think?"

"Just asking," Caleb said. "We'll get you out of here as soon as I'm done this."

"I thought you wanted my help."

"I think I'll ask your big—"

"I'm the older sibling."

He rolled his eyes. "If we can we'll find your brother and escort you to the barrier. Hopefully Seth is already long gone."

"He's probably waiting for me."

Caleb studied her. "I think you have the same nose."

"What?" Lily asked, covering her nose with her hand. She and Seth most certainly did not have the same nose!

"You see our beaks? You have the cutest most delicate nose in the room," Caleb said, going back to the book. "I swear they make all you girls look the same."

"Yeah, this puppet face is not the most flattering," Ethan agreed. "Hey, what's that mean, anyway? Gopher dodging. You got me stumped."

That's what they got out of it? "It's a euphemism."

"That's a big word," Caleb snickered.

"For a peasant or just in general?"

"I didn't mean to insult you," Caleb told her, "and for the record both of our moms were common folk. We aren't that different if you think about it."

Ethan slapped Caleb's shoulder. "We could have pretended to be long lost princes," Ethan said with a snicker. "There's a barrier there."

"She won't trigger it, your highness."

"You said you needed help," Lily said. "What do you want?"

Caleb showed her the finished map. "I want you to get out of this castle safely. Wait for your villagers, send in someone a little more . . . experienced."

Maybe it made sense to wait for her father—how long would he be? If others were with him, he'd be delayed. Then again, their kin who had a boat were on this side of the sea. That would hardly stop her father; if Seth could weasel his way onto a ship as crew, her father could be much more resourceful. "What's the purpose of turning you into marionettes?"

"You got us. We just get to live with it," Caleb said. "Be nice if the wizard or whatever came down to explain himself as opposed to throwing creatures at us. So you're from the same village as Tiffany and Brigid?"

"How did you—"

"*Gopher dodging* and your little shnoz. Where did Lady Theophania say they were from?" Caleb asked Ethan.

"My cousin said some little backwater place. Buckhorn?"

"Deerston?"

"Stagmil!" Lily blurted, before realizing she got played.

"We can probably sneak out Tiffany, Dale, and Brigid without too much trouble. Get them to you, anyway," Ethan said as Caleb continued to sketch. He dipped his finger in ink and drew something she didn't see. "They shouldn't be hard, that one kid got taken by the horde; Molly will be a trick but not impossible."

"You can sneak people out?"

"We can get them so far," Ethan said. "We know how that world works. If you can run the barrier, you can get one of us out too."

"Is that what you want?" Lily asked.

"Yeah, pretty much," Caleb replied. He looked to Ethan who was gesturing for him to continue, then to her. "If you take Ethan, will you restore him?"

Ethan was long and lanky but . . . they were puppets. They weren't physically the same as they were as humans. Seth had lifted things much heavier than he should have while they were tracking Madeline. "Probably. The woman changed Seth and Rebecca back. This is my first time being like this but the spell's reversible."

"Cay, if I leave you'll be on your own," Ethan pointed out.

"I'll manage," Caleb told Ethan.

"We have better options now than we did last week," Ethan said. "People are going to start asking questions if I vanish."

"I can lie," Caleb said. Ethan looked sceptical. "What do you suggest?"

"She's got at least three people to pull out, and it'll be easier if you got someone watching your back. If she's willing to come back, that's a game changer. Let's help her get her sister, then she can drag me outside the castle. Besides, what happens if I ride off for help and no one will help me?"

"I don't know," Caleb said. "Figure something out, but maybe there's nothing anyone can do. Not expecting you to come back here just because people we know are here."

"If they notice, they'll be on the alert," Ethan said, pointing up. "We might have to wait weeks if not months for things to calm down to attempt another rescue."

"We haven't been able to come close to escaping," Caleb pointed out. "I don't know if there'll be a second chance."

"How many could be snuck out before anyone notices?" Lily asked. "Why are there rooms filled with boxes of puppets?" The pair glanced at one another. "You . . . don't know about them?"

"We're stuck in a relatively small part of the castle," Caleb said. Ethan looked disturbed, even with the muted puppet features. "How many would you say there are?"

"We didn't search them all. Maybe . . . fifty in that one room? More? Then there's that room of . . . let's just call it a crafting room. Spare arms and eyes and heads, sort of thing." That was the first time she made Caleb wince. Ethan took a little walk.

"And you've only been in that eastern wing," Caleb said quietly. "You didn't run screaming back the way you came because . . . ?"

"She obviously cares about her people," Ethan said. "Like we care about ours."

Caleb nodded. "Once Ethan is out, we can pay you."

"I don't want your money," Lily said. "If I can help you, I will."

"Thanks. Let's return the favour by helping you get your sister,"

Caleb said. "My best guess is we should sneak out the doc or Sir Hector. People will listen to them."

"Hector would say there's lots of us squires, only one former royal physician. Half the courtiers will know Demetri. Let's get her out, and her brother if we can, then we go talk to the doc. See if he's got a better idea. If he says it doesn't matter, we'll get Brigid and Tiffany ready for tomorrow night, then you won't be seeing much of me around here," Ethan said. "That sound fair?"

Caleb nodded before he looked to her. "Where on your map did you say you were supposed to meet your brother?"

Lily hesitated. "Do not betray us," she said. "Where we first met."

"All right. He won't approach if he sees us. We'll try to keep an eye out but keep our distance. If things go sideways, you beeline it for the exit and stay out for a few days. Understood?"

She wanted to tell him he wasn't the boss of her, but they appeared to know what they were doing. They led her back towards where she'd first encountered them, the squires took cover in the woods. Lily wondered if she was a fool for trusting them, but they seemed earnest. Seth came sprinting down the way she'd seen him go, looking no worse for wear. "Okay, hope you took notes. We're out of here!" Seth said, grabbing her arm.

"Stop. Darting around will draw attention. I managed to get a decent map."

"No time! I have been dodging weirdos since I left you," Seth said. "First it was this guy with the dog motif, then there was this guy with the fool's cap, now I have goblins on my butt."

"Goblins?"

"Don't worry, I gave them the slip."

They heard a twang and Seth took an arrow in the leg. "That doesn't even hurt," Seth professed, grabbing his sister's arm, and dragging her into a section of rocks into an ambush.

Arrows came from behind them, and several goblins fell from their respective perches in the rocky places. Seth continued to pull them up the incline, but Lily wriggled free and took her sword and parried a goblin's thrust, but striking what should have been a killing wound to the throat realized: they cannot bleed, they are solid wood. She struck the goblin's hand string; he seemed surprised, then backed up and another took his place and she went for his head string.

Ethan landed on one, breaking through their wood with his spear, and grabbing Seth, danced back the way they came.

"Let go of me!" Seth ordered. Ethan did and lunged forward, cutting a headstring off another who was on string before taking out a hand string, then absolutely bashing another, splinters flying.

"Both of you stay behind me," Caleb told them, shattering a goblin limb and darting around. "Ethan, don't go too far ahead!"

"I spent the last hour running from these guys," Seth said.

Seth grabbed Lily and more or less carried her, "Seth, wait!"

"No time!" Seth wasn't as fast as the knights, but he seemed to know the area.

It took her a minute to wriggle out of Seth's grasp. She planted her feet and her brother pulled her along anyway. He turned and looked like he was going to yell, but his eyes bulged and he pushed her down an incline, tried to dodge but a net took him. Goblins riding rats dragged Seth, but one stared down at her, and Lily thought they'd shoot her. "Run back to your knights, lass," one of them said. He was uglier than the others, and had a milky eye. "The boy is ours."

"Wait!" Lily called. She knew Caleb said not to fight, that would draw attention. She removed the ring Rebecca had given her and held it so the light would make the gem twinkle. "I'll trade you this for him!"

"That's a pretty trinket," said one of the goblins beside the one with the milky eye.

"Give it here," Milky-Eye said.

"In exchange for him and safe passage."

"Leave them on the stump." Lily did, then backed away. One of the goblins brought Seth down in the net, and took up the ring. He went to drag Seth, and Lily chucked the jar of fire-pitch at the goblin, and it covered him. Lily lit one of her arrows on fire and aimed it.

"I said," Lily said lowly, "In exchange for him and safe passage."

"You'll burn him, too. You may burn yourself," Milky-eye said.

"Did I stutter?" Lily asked.

"Leave him," Milky-Eye ordered.

The large goblin released the net, and backed up, Lily waited for him to be a healthy distance before she doused the fire. The burly goblin wasn't right; he looked like a person painted green. There weren't that many good pictures of goblins in the journals; her parents never hunted them. On the whole, goblins were smaller and weaker than the average person, their heads were bigger and they tended to have larger eyes and noses in addition to the obvious green-tinged complexion.

Milky-Eye looked over his shoulder. "You shouldn't have let them run around so much." He whistled, gestured to two of his number, and two headstrings were severed by arrows, several members of his own party falling. Ethan appeared behind Lily, and released Seth from the netting. Seth went to strike Ethan, who casually knocked him down with the wood of his spear.

"Don't do that again," Ethan told Seth. "I'm going to let you up, but do anything I don't like and I will take your limbs off. Understood?"

"Stop," Lily told him. Ethan glanced at her, and relaxed slightly. "Seth, do not fight."

Milky-Eye called down. "Bring the stringless up here but keep them in the cover, squire."

Seth batted Ethan's hand when he went to grab him, Lily wondered if she was a fool and they were betrayed, but almost could tell that the goblins were . . . human. That, and judging by the looks, they meant them absolutely no harm. Curious and hopeful, they were intermixed amongst those who appeared to be real goblins.

"Put an arm around my shoulder," Ethan told Lily, crouching slightly.

"Okay." She did so hesitantly, he scooped around her waist and leapt up the incline, and put her down gently once she was almost face to face with Milky-Eye. "You okay back there Garett?"

"Let's go," the big goblin told Seth. He and the others down there couldn't jump as high as Ethan and needed to jump from several ledges to catch up.

"What is it with you and headshots?" asked a female goblin to Caleb.

"Your husband suggested I get good at something while we're stuck here," Caleb replied.

"I meant writing poetry or painting. Learn an instrument," said a tall, skinny goblin. "If only I had access to my library, I could turn you into a mathematician."

"Squire, I don't mind if you roll your eyes at the courtiers, but you'll remove your helmet," a lady goblin said. "Introductions, please."

"Lily, what is going—"Seth started, but a goblin shushed him.

Caleb introduced them, "Sir Percival, Lady Beatrice, this is Lily of Stagmil, and her little brother Seth."

"Younger brother," Seth interjected.

"Younger brother, you are quite difficult to apprehend," Lady Beatrice said.

"I know, right?" Ethan said.

"Excuse you, you're representing this castle," Lady Beatrice said. She handed Lily back the ring. "Not bad, for a beginner. In the meantime, we're borrowing your stringless brother for a small mission."

"I'm not helping you—" Seth began, then squinted at the lurking goblins in the surrounding woods. "Louis?"

"Heya Seth," Louis said, stepping forward, painted a beige-green and wearing naught but warpaint and a loincloth. His prosthetic nose and ears fooled no one. "And it's not Louis anymore. It's Lugvar Toothrattler."

"A cliché name, but we let newcomers chose their own," Beatrice informed Lily.

"Check out these tattoos!" Louis gestured to his arms and legs. "He wants you to take members of our clan to the library. Why not the armoury, or—"

"Toothrattler, you'll mind your tongue while I'm on knightly business."

"You're a knight?" Lily asked, then felt an idiot for saying it out loud.

Percival nodded. "When whoever took over this castle, most of my brothers were taken and never seen again. Because of my . . . previous condition," he said, pointing to his milky eye. "All they saw was the makings of a monster. So, to the best of my knowledge, we have six pages, a dozen squires—" He gestured at Ethan and Caleb, as well as two goblins in his party. "—and two knights in this castle. Handful of men-at-arms—" He gestured, and several goblins sheepishly raised their arms. "But for the most part my personal horde consists of cooks, farriers, stable workers, and others who did not escape the castle."

"Luckily, the entire castle library staff is here," beamed the one who threatened to turn Caleb into a mathematician. His group made the most convincing of the goblins.

"Where's the other knight?" Lily asked.

"We'll get you caught up to speed. Let's go, stringless," one of the librarians said to Seth. "All you have to do is get me over a barrier."

"Can I enforce?" Ethan asked. Sir Percival nodded, so Ethan gestured to Seth. "Meet back here?"

"I'll leave a messenger. If we have to move, we'll stash the other stringless someplace safe. Do not lose him," Percival said. "My love, do you mind speaking with the young lady while I converse with the squires?"

"Of course," Beatrice said, sliding off her rat. Caleb and Sir Percival went off to the side to talk with several others, including the burly one still trying to wipe off the pitch. "Don't mind the formalities, Percy likes to remind them what they really are. Do you have any news of the outside world?" Beatrice asked.

"I'm not even from this country. We sailed across the sea from Shelkie's Bay." The woman didn't appear to know where that was. "We're from a village not far from Taralee in Merilon."

Beatrice nodded. "A lot of new arrivals come from there."

"Caleb and Ethan told me a little," Lily said. She glanced at Percival and Caleb. "They told me they don't know what is going on with this castle. They wanted me to smuggle someone out as well, but . . . seemed hesitant to leave themselves."

Beatrice nodded. "Unfortunately, most of the high-value people the prince would listen to are missing. I'd sent Percival or one of the older squires, but things may get . . . rough if the watchers above suspect we've discovered a way in or out of the castle." She gave Lily a weak smile. "Were the squires cordial? If they weren't, I'll tune them up."

Percival and Caleb came back. "It's not prudent to wait for your people to arrive. We'll put feelers out but I think you've gone mostly undetected.If we suspect otherwise we'll let you know. Would you be willing to come back into the castle and bring tools with you?" the knight asked. Lily nodded. "Do not approach the goblin hordes, we're not all like this. You might as well smuggle Toothrattler out."

"What?" Louis demanded.

"I told you, keep out of my knightly business," Sir Percival told Louis. "We can be anonymous in a large group but we're better served causing distractions away from where you'll be. Caleb and Ethan will help you get your people out." He looked to Caleb. "Hector should stay where he is. Update him when you can."

"Once our people are out, we'll pay you back for the tools you bring in," Caleb told her. "Shouldn't be expensive: shovels, hammers and chisels."

"Rock busting equipment if you can manage," another goblin interjected.

"Well, squire? I'll send an honour guard, but they'll keep their distance. We'll send Seth as soon as he's done his mission. She can take Louis, I'll send someone with Seth to help us on the outside."

"I don't like sending her by herself," Caleb said.

"Squire, I didn't ask what you like," Percival said, before turning his attention to Louis. "All right, Toothrattler. It's been a pleasure."

"Don't I get a say?" Louis demanded.

"No," Sir Percival said, and struck down Louis's headstring uncere-moniously. Caleb took out the other strings, and more or less used them to bundle Louis more effectively before hoisting him over his shoulder. "You'll find that you can manage another puppet's weight rather effi-ciently, we're not heavy. Get them out of the castle safely as far as you can manage, squire," Percival ordered, mounting his rat, and all but two of his goblins followed him. The two remaining goblins offered to carry Louis for Caleb, but he had a hand free, so he declined the help.

"I'll scout ahead," said the bigger one. "I'll trill if anything's interesting."

"Thanks Garett," Caleb told him. They walked as opposed to the goblin's sprint. Lily followed Caleb with the other goblin trailing them, and wondered if Isaac was going to be pleased or upset with everything she'd learned. "How's Louis?"

Caleb shuffled him a bit. No response. "This is all for nothing if you can't cross the barrier." He led the way out into the hallway, handed Louis to the other goblin, and went ahead before signalling that it was clear for them to proceed. He seemed to know where they were going.Lily looked to the goblin behind her, who was staring at her, but then looked away like he wasn't. "Can you all de-string?"

The smaller goblin shook his head. "Only for short periods of time. Cay and Ethan can go way longer than us," he said. "I'm Darius, by the way."

Caleb shushed them and they continued down the hall, keeping to the edge of the corridor, sprinting now from furniture to another useful object to hide behind but it was uneventful. They saw Garett up ahead. When they neared, the goblin moved ahead and Lily saw the barrier again—there was a strange glowing mark on the floor in a strange set of circular patterns, which brightened in intensity when either the goblin or the squire approached.

"When you bring Louis over," Caleb said. "It should affect him, but not you. We'll lasso you back if you're hurt or immobile. Once you cross we can't follow. Understand?"

"I think so. Where's your list?" she asked. Caleb handed her a scrap of paper. It wasn't fancy—hammer, chisels, a shovel. She hadn't really gone to town to procure supplies, but she didn't doubt she could trade for those items at nearby farms. "Um, Bernard's just that way." She gestured, Darius raced ahead and dragged him out.

"What do you want done with him?" Darius asked.

Caleb and Garett were obviously older, and looked to one another.

"Might be useful to have a near-stringless marionette in the horde," Garett offered. "I'll take him back to Percy for questioning. She can smuggle him out another time."

Caleb looked like he was going to address them, but looked to her. "Lily, you shouldn't linger. Leave the castle directly and wait for Seth outside. I'll get him to you as quick as I can." Caleb gestured to the map in her book. "Do you have any questions?"

"I don't think so. It's probably not even all that late out now," Lily said. "I'll come back for Seth."

"There's no need for that."

"Percy said he'd send someone out," Lily pointed out. "Pick someone. You said the horde is anonymous." She looked to Darius. "They won't notice him, will they?"

"She's got a point," Garett said.

Caleb looked contemplative. "Don't rush, we'll time you and wait here. If you're not back by the time Seth's here, we'll send him out with Seth. Be careful," Caleb said. "I'll show you how we carry each other so we keep our hands free. Kind of a piggy-back style." He more or less lassoed Louis to Lily, and tied his wrists around her neck. She had no windpipe to crush. "I can't promise where we'll be but either Ethan or I will be near that big red cave after next sunset. Don't go to the same places all the time, and try not to disturb things too much. If we're with anyone else, do not approach. Got it?"

She nodded. She looked to the goblins, felt Louis's head bob against her shoulder. "Take care of my brother."

"I'll get him here safely," Caleb said. Lily was hesitant to run the barrier when it lit up, but she felt nothing even though Louis lit up. "That's normal," Caleb called. "Keep going."

She ran the hall keeping towards the one wall, paused when she came to the bend, and looking back saw that the squire and two goblins were watching. She felt terrible for leaving them, but found the room where the map had indicated (at least it was accurate) and their rope was still there. She again followed their previous footsteps and found the tunnel. She crawled, realized she was scraping Louis, so she untied him, dragged him behind her but he was better off that way than being scraped by thorns. She was surprised it was still dark out when she made it to the other side, and put Louis back the same way. She couldn't scurry the rope with the same speed as her brother, but she got over the lake without faltering.

Larry idly poked the fire. She called him, and he stood and raised his eyebrows. "Where's your brother?"

"Back in the castle. He'll be along shortly," she said. "This is Louis."

"He looks awfully green."

"What time is it?"

"After midnight," Larry said. "The others are resting. Well, let's change you back."

"I'm going back for Seth, possibly others," Lily said. "Take care of Louis."

"Are you sure?" Larry asked. Lily nodded, and before they could argue, trekked her way back through the bush and did they ferry line. It was bizarre, how much more she was afraid now that she wasn't thinking about Louis. She missed Seth's company, he knew where he was going whereas she hadn't landmarked and struggled to find the tunnel leading back, but once she found it hesitated. Then she knelt, and crawled.

Emerging back in that same room she returned to the halls, and assumed that they'd given up on her, but to her surprise, Caleb stepped out from the same hiding place they'd stashed Bernard. "The others had to go back on string," he said. "Try to be a little less noticeable."

"There's no one here."

"I saw you coming from down the hall," he told her. "I can't help you on the other side." He gestured, and she followed him and they sat beneath the chair where they'd previously stashed Bernard, and waited.

"How long do you think they'll be?" she asked

"Don't know . I'd be helping them now if I didn't have you to worry about."

"If the others can't stay off string long, what good is sending them to the library?" she asked. Caleb shrugged. "Did you have a chance to talk to my sister?" He nodded. "Well, how is she?"

"She's okay, I guess," he said. Caleb wasn't much of a talker, Lily got the idea that he was irked she didn't listen to him and stay out. She supposed it was better to be quiet, so she hugged her knees. "Sorry, I have a lot on my mind." He offered eventually. "Merilon, huh? We're not at war with you or anything, are we?"

"Wouldn't you know?"

"We get news slowly if at all."

"No, last I checked you haven't invaded us," Lily offered. "I never gave this kingdom much thought until a few days ago." He nodded, said nothing. "So you were injured when all this happened?"

"Yeah."

If he didn't want to talk, Lily decided maybe silence was better. "I don't know who's left in town," he said eventually with a sigh. "I know some of the rangers, I don't know if saying my name will make anyone help you though. They probably think I died before the castle fell."

"We're managing okay."

He frowned and Lily heard voices, they were being way too chatty considering how muted she and Caleb were. "You won't be able to do this, but you can absolutely cut your own strings and swing," Ethan said to Seth, another goblin in tow that was too small to be Garett. "I like it when I put some weight on a guy's arm, force him to hold an axe, and just launch..."

"Can you be louder?" Caleb asked, climbing out from their hiding spot.

"Sorry, geez," Ethan said. "Don't take this act seriously, Seth, Caleb's fun once he puts his guard down." He cocked his head, Lily realized she hadn't climbed out but Ethan had spotted her just the same. "You two need a little more private time?"

"We were waiting for you," Caleb told him. He offered her a hand up, she didn't need it but took it anyway. "You let the entire castle know they're here?"

"Oh, ye of little faith," Ethan said. "Well, I guess we can send out two people."

"You and Tristan?" Caleb asked, looking to the other goblin.

Ethan frowned. "Percy said once Demetri's out, we don't have to be as stealthy. Doc doesn't even know yet." He looked to the goblin. "You going to be all right out there?"

Tristan nodded. "What if this doesn't work, and when I return I'm stuck here?"

"They aren't triggering it," Ethan pointed out, gesturing to Seth and Lily. He looked to Lily. "Did it work on Louis?"

"I returned here before he was restored," Lily said. "It's hard to keep track of time like this. Look, there's two of us, why don't we bring one of you with us?"

"Not so fast, Lil'," Seth interjected. "They said they're gonna get Tiffy tomorrow night. Let them do that, and I'll shuttle whoever they want."

"I told you there wasn't a reason to return," Caleb told Lily. Then he looked to Ethan. "I'll be right back. Stay here if you can." He ran back the way Ethan and Seth had come.

"He being moody?" Ethan asked, but didn't wait for an answer. "Don't take it personally he lives in his own head. If for whatever reason, you don't make it back, Tristan, you take care."

They didn't wait long, Caleb returned with Garett and Darius in tow. "I can't be off much longer," Garett said. "You take care."

Darius nodded, then looked nervous. "I'll be your guide, Tristan'll help you around camp. I'm older, afterall."

"Alright. You're not on strings, you'll have to just run the barrier," Ethan pointed out.

The pair nodded, and were initially hesitant, but eventually Darius walked right into it, one arm died before the rest of him lurched over. "Bring him back and I'll tie him like I did Louis," Caleb offered, and saddled him on Seth.

"Wait, she's going to carry me?" Tristan gestured at Lily.

"Someone has to," Ethan said, then realizing Tristan wasn't going to go, just shoved him. The goblin let out a surprised shout but lit up all the same. "He'll forgive me before he's popping his first pimple," Ethan said with a grin.

Tristan was only nominally longer than Louis was, but the weight difference was negligible. Caleb checked her over. "Sorry if I scared you earlier," he said. "We're not what you need to be afraid of in here."

"Yeah yeah, get our sister good and ready," Seth said, and charged off down the hall before Lily was ready. He waited for her around a bend in the hall.

This time, they brought their repelling equipment with them after they climbed through the door. It was little wonder the people in the castle never found the tunnel from the inside, the room was so cluttered and dusty they needed to follow their footprints to find the hole behind the mirror.

Crossing the ferry in the dark, to her surprise Isaac and Catarina were up. Louis had mostly grown back to his regular size, stuffed in a bedroll.

"Who are these? Folk from your village?" Isaac asked. Seth didn't need to sleep as a puppet but they transformed back when they freed the young goblins. They weren't fully grown when the taller of the pair started to shiver, so they found more blankets and kept them near the fire to try to warm them.

"We better make some tea," Lily told Isaac. "We have much to discuss."

Twelve

Tiffany wanted to find those idiots and demand to know what happened to Seth, but decided if she was being watched, it was best to wait a little while. She returned to Brigid and went about the motions of helping. No one noticed the difference.

It felt like hours of not knowing, when suddenly Brigid brightened. "Dale!"

He was moving around like them, seemingly whole, and had come up the street still wearing the marionette version of his clothes from home. The pair embraced; Tiffany would have felt jealous but she went to her boyfriends. "Braden, Caiden, I'd like to properly introduce you to Dale," Tiffany said, then squinted. "Where's Jayden?"

"Ethan grabbed him like five minutes ago, said for us not to go nowhere." Braden gestured to a nearby alleyway.

They're back? She'd gotten the impression that Wolfie and Jester didn't spend any more time in the village than they had to. Wolfie and Jester were speaking to Jayden, but before she approached them that boy that snuck them into the infirmary ran over. Jester took him to the side to speak to him.

"Hey," Tiffany snapped, getting Jayden and Wolfie's attention. "I got some words for you."

"I wanted to speak to you anyway," Wolfie said.

"Remove the helmet. I don't want you making stupid faces at me," Tiffany ordered. He muttered but obliged. "How dare you spy on me," she snapped. "Who I talk to is none of your business."

"We spoke to your siblings. Shut up, they're here for you," Wolfie told her. Jayden's eyes widened. "We said we'd help get you out when they come tomorrow night."

"You know you really need to work on your people skills."

"I'm not here to be social," Wolfie snapped, then looked to Jayden. "Understood?"

"Yeah, I can pass the message on to Hector. What can I tell Braden and Caiden?"

"Need to know," Wolfie told him. Jayden nodded, then left them to get the others. "Tiffany, when they come for you they're either going to take Ethan or Jayden out."

"Molly's my best friend. I'm not abandoning her," Tiffany told him.

"I'll get my fairy-trapping net," Wolfie said.

"*That* is why no one likes you, Caleb," Tiffany said. "You should really consider becoming the strong, silent type. At least one of those is possible."

"I think we saved that boy who was with you when you first arrived," Wolfie said. Tiffany brightened, but he continued. "I'll work on getting Molly, but I promised your sister you'd be rescued."

Jayden returned with Caiden and Braden. "What did you want to talk about?"

"Big change—I'm not going to discuss details, but I need you guys to manage any quests they throw at us," Wolfie told them. "Other than that, don't do anything to trigger an event. Several horde factions will be acting up, do not engage them. Can you handle that?"

"What's going on?" Braden asked.

"We might have a way out. Percy's going to have his officers act up away from us, you just need to keep things calm. Don't do anything to trigger an event. Understood?" The pair nodded. Jester returned with the boy.

"Come on, why won't you tell me?" the dark-haired youth asked.

"Need to know for the time being," Jester said. "Be patient. We got some stuff to take care of. Keep a low profile and don't make waves, got it?"

"Yeah," Caiden said, annoyed. "We're not idiots."

"Don't tell anyone what's going on," Wolfie said. "This may be a trap." He studied her, then looked to the others. "Keep a cool head if things go south."

Wolfie and Jester walked off, the youth in tow pelting them with questions. "Where are they going that's so important?" Braden asked.

"Don't worry about it," Jayden said. "I guess you and I will be hanging out a lot together, Tiffany."

"What?" Caiden demanded.

"Is this some plot by your cousin to steal Tiffany from us?" Braden asked.

"You heard them: you go do the quests, it is my solemn duty to protect the fair Theophania I."

They started to argue, so Tiffany started to make her way back to Brigid and Dale. She wondered how much she ought to tell them. To her surprise, Braden and Caiden followed after her.

"Tiffany, want me to teach you how to fish?" Braden asked. "We can do it right here in town."

"No one cares about fishing," Caiden told him.

"Oh yeah?" Braden asked, reached into a small satchel, and showed them a green shiny fish. "Check this out." He squeezed it, and it coughed out a key.

"In the real world that would stink. How many hours did that take you?" Cadien asked.

"It's not like we're aging," Braden pointed out. Caiden scooped up the key. "Hey, give it!"

"Finders keepers!"

"Guys," Tiffany snapped. "I know what they said, but here's what I'm saying: will triggering an event bring Molly down?"

"I dunno," Caiden said. "Maybe. We can't know until we try."

"And what's the best way to trigger an event?" Tiffany asked.

"They kind of just happen," Braden said.

Tiffany rolled her eyes. "They were telling you to distinctly not do something."

"We're not in control," Caiden insisted. He looked a little sheepish. "Sometimes, we can do things to open up the map or find a new boss."

"There you are!" Jayden exclaimed. "Guys, you know your assignment, now leave me to mine. So Tiffany, what do you like to do in your village for fun?"

"Date boys who help me rescue my best friend," Tiffany said. "I don't care what those two said. If we get Molly down, can one of you nab her?"

"I guess," Caiden said. "We can use it on that chest we brought down from the mountain. Don't know what it'll do."

"No, absolutely not," Jayden said. Caiden and Braden looked at one another, then at Jayden, their eyes seemed bigger and sadder.

"That's fine," Tiffany said. "Braden, want to take me fishing? Who knows what we'll find."

"Milady," Braden said, offering an arm.

"That's not fair," Jayden said as Tiffany accepted it.

"I'd kiss the guy who helps me get Molly," Tiffany said.

Caiden stared down Jayden. "Alright... just... nothing too big," Jayden said. "We can't promise Molly will come down. Might be someone else."

"It's worth a try," Tiffany told him.

They made their way to the castle. She'd not really been in any of their rooms; theirs were much like hers in that they had a few items of luxury and interest; beds for the sake of normalcy none of them ever slept. Caiden's room was red and black and he evidently enjoyed building things, with a lot of scraps on a nearby shelf of unfinished projects. She didn't ask. Instead, he went to the chest they'd taken from Peanut's Cave.

"Did it ever occur to you to just start calling the dragon something else?" she asked.

"Yeah, but the name stuck, you know?" Braden asked.

Caiden opened the chest and all that was in there was a tiny bottle with a ship inside. "This is it?" Caiden sounded disappointed. "There's gotta be something else." He handed Braden the bottle. There were tiny people inside.

"Woah, woah, woah," Jayden said, trying to take it from Braden. "That looks like a big one. They'll kill us."

"We're like the main characters," Braden said.

"No, I mean my cousin will stuff my head in a box again," Jayden said. "Give it!"

"I'm not going to break it," Braden said, and in their struggle the bottle fell and smashed, including the little boat.

The boat disappeared and the people inside vanished. "That was anticlimactic," Tiffany said, crossing her arms. "Any other ideas? And how long will Martin and the others be going after that giant mushroom?"

"I'm kind of surprised that's taking as long as it is, to be honest," Braden said. "Come on, sometimes it takes a little while for the new event to trigger. Best way I see it, we start fishing . . . "

"No," Caiden told him as they made their way back to the town square.

Tiffany considered gearing up, but instead sought out Dale and Brigid. "There you are," Brigid said when Tiffany approached. "Dale says he asked about smuggling tools outside of town, but they almost always break when they exit through the gate."

"I was thinking of tunnelling," Dale admitted. "If we don't get tired, who cares how long it takes?"

"Never mind that," Tiffany told them. "Seth's here."

"Did he get turned into a monster?" Dale snorted.

"No. He said he and Lily followed us. He . . . somehow found a way in. He's working on a plan to get us out. He wanted to sneak me out. I said I'd speak to you first."

Dale and Brigid looked at one another. Dale looked sceptical. "You're sure it's your brother? We don't exactly look like ourselves."

"He's my twin," Tiffany said. Besides, who'd want to pretend to be Seth? "Also, those two knights who helped us before are aware and want to get us out. You two should escape tonight. I'm going to try to find Molly."

"Where is she?" Dale asked.

The sound of screaming directed their attention. Instinctively, Tiffany looked up, but there was no dragon or other strange monster flying over the town.Instead the threat came at them from floor level. Puppet strings weren't cut, but nets were launched at people, and they were dragged towards the strangers . . . pirates? Tiffany wasn't certain.

"Come on, let's hide," Tiffany told the pair.

More than once they tried to run down the streets where the strings wouldn't allow them. It never occurred to Tiffany to look up and see if there were bars blocking the way. She didn't have any weapons on her, but she didn't want to risk losing Dale or Brigid.

It was a moot point when she felt her body start to shake, then seize. She could hear and see everything. "Tiffany?" Brigid asked.

"Let's go!" Dale said.

Tiffany felt herself turning around, and walking back towards the fray. She grabbed a pole that had been used to hold a banner, and she struck a pirate with it. He went down far too easily. She stepped on his throat. He was a big bloke; in real life he easily should have been able to get up. "Where's your captain?"

"To me, my fellows!" said an impressive figure with a long coat and tricorn hat. The fellow Tiffany was standing on did what he should have from the beginning, and forced her off. "Back to the ship." The pirates had captured what seemed like the vast majority of the villagers, and to her horror, Tiffany was forced to just . . . stand there and allow it to happen. When she was allowed to move again, she found the streets nearly deserted. There were only a handful of people left. "What happened?" she demanded when she found her 'Aidens. Like her, they weren't allowed to pursue. "What was that?"

"Well, we triggered an event like you wanted," Caiden said.

"I wanted to bring down Molly. Brigid! Dale!" Tiffany ran in the general direction the pirates had come from. The gate was still closed, and she was impeded by strings. Her 'Aidens were behind her. "How do we open the gate?"

"We don't," Caiden said. "We're stuck here until we're allowed to proceed."

"When will we be allowed to proceed?" Tiffany demanded.

"Dunno. Might take a while for us to find Dale and Brigid, assuming they're together," Caiden offered. "Don't worry, we'll get them back. Caleb and Ethan put us in charge of quests while they're gone."

"They're not going to help?"

"Well, if this was a small one, but—oh, you missed the dialogue between the captain and Justin, didn't you? Odds are they'll be marched back here and forced to help," Braden said. "Pirates, huh? Think they'll have any new fish?"

~*~

Once he woke, Louis donned a set of Seth's clothes and happily ate the fritters and bacon that Catarina made and seemed like his normal self.

The other two were . . . odd.

They explained the spell froze their ages, so while technically they were both older than Seth, they appeared younger. Darius looked strong, was blond with hazel eyes, his face was still boyish. Fourteen year old Tristan was taller and more slender, had a tinge of red to his brown hair and a lot of freckles dusting his cheeks and shoulders.

Both fit into either Seth or Isaac's spare clothes. They didn't have much for extra footwear so they used spare fabric and Catarina made them something that would keep their feet warm, but they weren't practical for running around. For the most part, the squires from the castle kept to themselves and eyed the people at the camp suspiciously. Darius was the more sullen of the two, whereas Tristan looked lost, but seemed content about the fire.

Lily wondered how many people they could comfortably care for with what they had. She had brought money with her from home but she'd pooled what she had with Isaac to help get the donkeys and the wagon. She idly played with the ring she'd received from Rebecca, and wondered how much she'd get for the silver bracelets and earrings. The people in town probably wouldn't be able to pay what it was worth, but still.

"If you're insisting on going back," Catarina told Seth and Lily. "You best be getting some sleep during the day."

"We were puppets, we didn't need sleep," Seth pointed out.

"You're human now," Catarina said. "I don't want you dead on your feet. It'll be less cramped if you rest now, these boys can help us."

"I already had a nap," Louis pointed out. "I should be great for tonight's mission."

"You are not going back," Isaac said.

"Why not?" Louis asked.

"Because you're thirteen," everyone said.

Lily went to the tent and brushed out her hair before Seth joined her."Maybe we should have stayed puppets," Seth said with a yawn, stretching into his bed roll. He was snoring within minutes.

Boscoe curled up at Lily's feet. "What are you thinking?"

"It's something that shepherd said when we got here. It didn't seem important at the time so I didn't write it down. Why can't I remember?" She realized she was getting overwhelmed with information. She thought about the meeting with Caleb and Ethan, then the goblins. They were people, and despite their muted features, they were . . . so incredibly hopeful. "I hope Tiffany's okay." She settled down, and wished she could fall asleep as easily as Seth did. She was tired, but her mind was restless, starving for information she knew was back at that castle. She tossed before she drifted to sleep, those terrible songs again playing over and over again.

She dreamed she was back in Stagmil, watching her flock, only these weren't her normal sheep, they were marionettes. She was human, and the skies were strange with clouds that weren't right.

She played her mandolin to a strange song.

Her sheep bleated and then she heard the growling of a wolf.

He was black with massive paws; she'd seen big wolves many times but this was something out of a storybook. Her flock scattered, those whose strings he didn't cut, anyway. She had no bow, only her staff, and went to strike him. He dug his sharp teeth into the wood, and pulled it from her grasp. Her heart quickened, but suddenly the wolf backed off.

She grew, never losing her legs but long tendrils out of her back made her tower over the creature. The wolf tried to run, but she called down webbing. "Leaving so soon?" she asked, as the big bad wolf whined and struggled against her.She made him stand on his hind legs.

She thirsted for something the wolf couldn't give her, but he could bring others. "You're mine now." She sang, and slowly the wolf transformed from fur to wood, but unlike the marionette, somehow this thing was more terrible and real than any dog or wolf that could have existed. Releasing him, he was little more than her obedient dog. She stroked his snout. "Bring me a present."

The wolf howled and ran off into the woods.Lily thirsted and moved on her tendrils, ignoring the cries of her sheep as she picked up her mandolin, and played those strange, familiar songs to lure, to lull . . . to . . .

~*~

Seth woke up needing to take a leak. Lily's eyes fluttered, but when he got up Boscoe got up with a stretch and followed him out. Exiting the tent, the only people he saw were Catarina and Madeline, busy sewing. He went to the thicker brush.

"How you gonna catch a rabbit without a bow?" Boscoe asked.

"I'm taking a wiz," Seth said. "Go away." The little kitsune bounded along undeterred. Seth ensured he was out of eyeshot of the main road but he heard a rustling in the bush. Boscoe appeared to be smelling something but perked his ears.

Something leapt from the bush. At first Seth assumed it was Boscoe's mother, but this kitsune was a little bigger, his colouring mostly white with black tips at his ears and up his legs. Two tails trailed behind him. He pinned Boscoe with a paw.

"Lemme up!" Boscoe demanded. "I'll tell mom!"

"Who do you think sent me?" the white kitsune asked.

"You taking him home?" Seth asked hopefully.

"He's not taking me nowhere!" Boscoe sputtered. "Seth, help!"

"You need me to tie him up for you?" Seth ventured.

The other kitsune cocked his head in Seth's general direction, raising a paw he allowed Boscoe to stand. "Seth?"

"Yeah?"

"Seth!" the kitsune exclaimed, and fox trotting towards him, releasing Boscoe who bounded into the nearest bush to presumably hide. "I should have known. An enchanted castle, wow. Do tell how you got in."

"Don't tell him nothing!" Boscoe poked his head out from tall grass, then quickly disappeared.

"Secret tunnel you can't fit in," Seth said. "Now can a guy pee in peace?"

"Not a bad idea," the white kitsune said. He went up to another tree and raised his leg. "Mom mentioned Lily, but not you. But look at you! You reek of bad magic. What's going on in there?" The kitsune gestured towards the castle once he finished.

"I've answered you twice, now I get one: how'd you find us?" Seth said.

"My brother's scent took mom to a port. We weren't sure where he sailed so it took a little prying to figure out where you went. I caught Lily's scent. My little brother doesn't have enough tricks to evade us for long."

Seth thought about it. They'd both ridden Stella, and despite both acquiring new clothes, Lily's had a chance to pick up her odour. He hadn't really ridden the mare since arriving in Shelkie's Bay, he probably smelled more like the sea or the donkies. "If you're brothers, how come you're so much larger?"

"We're not littermates," the white kitsune said. "You don't remember me at all?" Seth shook his head. He frowned, then staring at the kitsune, backed up, suddenly remembering . . . tunnels, only it wasn't like the cave, they were bright and . . . Seth couldn't remember. Only, they led to places they shouldn't have. "Right, you had your memory wiped pretty good. Too bad."

"Wait, we . . . we were kids together," Seth said.

"Simpler times," the kitsune told Seth. "We got into so much trouble. The fun kind, of course."

Seth tried to think about all the times he'd spent just mucking about in the woods, they all sort of blended together. He was fine with the foxes, but . . . this new batch wasn't the same. They were little, this one was . . . this one and him did something. "Your mom wiped my memory?"

"Yeah, I guess it was my fault for letting you into the tunnels," the kitsune said. "It seemed like a good idea at the time." He turned his head when there was rustling in the bushes. "I have something I need to take care of. See you around, Seth." He bounded into the woods.

Seth listened, but more sounds were coming from the camp than the lake or the woods. He tried to remember, but everything was coming up blank. How could he not know? It smelled like they were cooking something decent on the fry pan. Someone caught rabbits. He emerged, listening to the squires laughing with Louis. Darius saw Seth and became sullen. "Don't mind me," Seth said, squatting near their fire. He'd be greatful if they shared, but there probably wasn't enough meat to satisfy one of them.

Louis and Tristan seemed to be getting along great, and were talking about some commander they'd pranked. "Tonight while they're in the castle, we can head up to a great hunting spot. You don't have much good fishing equipment," Tristan said.

"We got some time now," Seth pointed out. He frowned, those miserable little hossenpfeffers wouldn't make much of a meal by themselves. "Be ready to cause some trouble tonight."

"Trouble's the opposite of what Percival wants. Sounds like we're rescuing your sister," Tristan said. "Then Demetri, then I guess Ethan. What do you think the plan will be once they're out?"

"We're going to get caught if we go back," Darius said, looking at the castle.

"Relax, I've got this," Seth said, flexing his arms behind his back.

"You got lucky before," Darius said.

"I make my own luck," Seth said. "Don't worry, I'll protect you."

Darius picked up the nearby axe and pointed it at Seth, making Louis and Tristan back away from him. "I'm not going back!"

"Darius, don't!" Tristan said.

Catarina and Madeline stood. They were going to make this worse. "I don't need your help, coward," Seth said. "I'll save Tiffy without you."

"I am not a coward," Darius said, backing away from everyone, aiming at whoever was nearest. "Come on, Tristan."

"Sir Percival said—"

"Sir Percival is an idiot. We're free. I'm not going back there. None of you can make me go back there!"

That hatchet wasn't as good as a great splitting axe that Larry had in the wagon. They used the hatchet for making kindling. Darius no doubt had been training since he could walk if he was a squire.

"Darius," Isaac said levelly. Seth thought he'd gone to town with Larry. "Put it down." Isaac put his hands out, then approached him, keeping his distance. "Relax."

"What's going on?" Lily called, ducking out of the tent.

"Lily, stay back," Seth ordered, watching Darius. The young man's eyes widened at her. Seth was tempted to wrestle Darius for the hatchet, but he suspected Darius was stronger than he was and they'd both likely be injured in the struggle.

"We are not your enemies," Isaac said. "Put it down."

The youth shouted, faced away from Isaac, dug the hatchet into a nearby tree and popped into a squat, running his hands through his hair. Seth raced up and took the hatchet, whereas Tristan raced to the other squire. Darius was breathing heavily. Lily rushed to Isaac. "What brought that on?" she asked Isaac.

"Nothing. He kept getting anxious every time he looked at the castle," Isaac said. "These boys are terrified."

"We're not," Tristan said, though his eyes were wide and his voice quivered. "It's just . . . we don't know what to do. Everything is so . . . so . . ."

Seth didn't notice the riders until the squires saw them, and they raced off to hide. The riders appeared to be woodsmen, with green cloaks and leather hauberks. They slowed down to look over the camp with interest. The younger of the pair, a blond, was eying Seth's sister a little too much.

"Hey," he called when he stopped his horse. "What's your name?"

"Gillam," the older one called.

"I know my own name."

"You can talk to her when you're off duty," the other ranger said.

"See you around, beautiful." Gillam shot Lily a wink, and spurred his horse ahead. He glanced back at the camp.

"If you're gonna flirt, summon someone useful," Seth said to his sister. "We already have woodsmen."

She blushed. "I was just standing here."

"I was wondering when people were going to start poking around," Isaac said with a sigh before gesturing towards the direction Tristan and Darius had fled. They looked to be talking to one another hurriedly. "Don't let them, or anyone else you change back, around weapons or even cutlery until we know they're safe. That might take days."

"So anyone we save is crazy," Seth said.

"I'm not," Louis said.

"They're not crazy," Isaac told him. "I was imprisoned for almost two months and I was both relieved and terrified of an open door. Those boys were in there—if you're to be believed, for two years. Louis, you weren't changed for that long. We don't know what affect it had on them. Be patient and kind, understood?"

Isaac went to go speak to the squires. Darius seemed to calm down, but Tristan's brow tensed.

"Great," Seth muttered to Lily. "I'll bet you they'll all be like this."

"They're good guys Seth," Louis pointed out.

Isaac spoke to the squires quietly, but their voices became more raised.

"Darius, this is our home," Tristan said.

"It's not," Darius told Tristan. "It's ruined. You stay if you want."

"Please don't leave me. We can catch up with those rangers-" he gestured after the riders.

"They left us for dead. Come with me to Yarrosfeld, maybe someone can help there. If not we can go some place no one knows us," Darius said. Tristan shook his head. "Fine—I can't stand looking at that castle, even if all we can see are the towers."

To Seth's surprise, Isaac didn't try to talk him into staying. He and Catarina seemed supportive, and even gave him some coin. "Don't steal anything," Catarina instructed. "Don't hurt anyone. You're welcome back here, if you change your mind."

Darius nodded, and set out down the path opposite town. Tristan watched him leave, and even when the squire disappeared from sight he watched that way. Seth tried to be friendly, but Tristan became more agitated when it became evident that Darius wasn't coming back.

~*~

They never went to that hunting spot; instead Larry returned from town with supplies including a large chicken, and they ate an early supper. Tristan was even more withdrawn, only opening up to Louis. "I guess I'm your guide," he said quietly.

"You're too nervous," Isaac said. "I'll take Seth and Lily."

"They sent us out here to help," Tristan said.

"You are helping," Seth told him. "You and Louis can guard Madeline for the first part of the evening." Larry nodded in agreement.

"I'm letting them down," Tristan said, eyes on the castle.

"They're in there and you're out here," Seth pointed out. "We'll tell them that breaking the spell made you sick but you're the strongest bestest guy to watch our prisoner. It'll be fine." He smiled, but scowled seeing Boscoe begging for chicken at Lily's side. She obliged and fed him, and he gave Seth a sassy grin as he happily sucked on the chicken bones.

"I'll be better tomorrow night," Tristan said.

Seth waited for the others to be involved in discussing the mission before he got up and grabbing Boscoe by the back of his neck once he was behind his sister. No one seemed to notice, so Seth walked into the nearby bush. He whistled shrilly. Muffin should have been able to catch Boscoe, he wasn't that inept . . .

. . . Muffin? What kind of stupid name was . . . How did he know that?

Boscoe bit Seth's thumb while he remembered something about cheesing off a burgermeister . . . he didn't know what a burgermeister *was*. Seth dropped Boscoe, who scrambled back towards the fire.

Another fox stepped out to stop Boscoe; this one was a silver fox, smaller than either Muffin or Mama Fern but had two tails. They were shapeshifters, but this one was . . . Seth couldn't put his finger on it, but he knew this wasn't Muffin. "You got him this time?"

The silver kitsune looked at him, but gestured to Boscoe to go. The kit ran off. "So, you're Seth?"

"Who wants to know?"

She smiled at him through hooded eyes. She was pretty, for a fox. "Who would you like me to be?"

"Oi, stop that over there," said another fox. This one had a crystal pattern to him, and three tails. The silver fox bared her teeth at him.

"How many of you are there?" Seth asked.

"Wouldn't you like to know," said another, a brown fox with four tails at Seth's feet.

"My cousin said you found a way into the castle," said the crystal fox.

The silver fox nipped at the brown fox who went running back into the bush. She batted her eyes at Seth. "What are you doing later?"

"He's sneaking into that castle," said the crystal fox. "Unless he'd like us to do it for him."

Oh yes, he was going to sit around knitting with Catarina and he'd send a bunch of magical foxes into the castle instead. How could that end poorly? "If you could just take Boscoe and be on your way."

The silver fox suddenly changed in front of him. When she took human form appeared about his age, and wore silver robes not unlike Mama Fern but wore her dark hair loose and adjusted her height so she was a few inches smaller than him. She got way too close to Seth's personal space and sniffed him. "Do you like this form better?" she asked.

"No, no no, I don't care if you're my perfect woman, absolutely not."

"I'm your perfect woman?" the silver fox beamed. "Oh, I can't wait to cook for you!" She bounced slightly when she clapped. "I make the most wonderful mouse pie."

"Stop embarrassing yourself," said the crystal fox. "Humans don't even like mice."

"He hasn't tried my mice." The silver kitsune bared her fangs at the crystal fox, but then cast her hooded eyes at Seth. "What say you tell them how to get in, and you and I get to know each other?"

"I ain't stupid enough to fall for that," Seth said, trying to escape the silver kitsune.

She pouted, and suddenly her bosom became fuller. "How about now?"

Seth hurried back to the camp. For all his efforts, Boscoe was still on Lily's lap. The kitsune pointed at Seth. "He was mean to me!"

"No one buys it you little shyster," Seth snapped, but Lily was petting Boscoe.

"Leave the kitsune alone. He's not causing any trouble," Isaac said. He and the others were going over the plan: Tristan wasn't going to come with them that evening, and that was fine with Seth. The fewer people he had to babysit in there, the better.

They put the magic bracelet on Louis to keep watch over Madeline. They gathered a few supplies. Larry wasn't able to secure rock busting equipment but the smaller hatchet and sevearl other supplies that Tristan said would be useful they gathered. Isaac and Lily looked nervous when they stood. Seth just wished that Madeline could perform her spell without singing.

It was also unfair that they'd be puppets in a matter of seconds whereas changing back would take a lot longer. It would be nice to be able to shift back and forth the way the silver kitsune just went from fox to girl.

Once Madeline transformed them, Lily and Isaac spoke and Isaac got used to moving around. Seth should have known better to check his pockets before he transformed, because he felt something kicking in his satchel. He pulled out what looked like an adorable little stuffed kitsune, but it blinked at him.

"Why did you change?" Seth demanded.

"I'm an accessory," Boscoe explained. "Don't worry, I have lots of experience being an accessory."

"We're not going to commit crimes," Seth grumbled, and was tempted to leave the kitsune like that outside. Then again, he was stuck like that and he'd be safer with him. Seth put him back in the satchel.

Lily and Isaac were much slower at crossing the ferry rope than Seth was, and he was almost comically waiting for them at the other side.

He was getting used to finding the tunnel, though Lily and Isaac were slow they didn't complain, though they took longer this time, clearing out several of the noticeable thorns that scratched them. It was a lot easier now that they had a map, and entering the halls, it was almost too easy to navigate, though they kept quiet all the same. Leaving the halls to several exits he would have walked past if they weren't indicated on that map, they found the red mountain where Caleb had indicated without issue. No sign of anyone.

"How long do you think they'll be?" Isaac asked as they took cover under several trees.

"Sometimes it takes hours for prey to come into an area," Seth stated. "We'll just sit here, be quiet." He found a good place to lounge. Nothing to do but wait, hopefully those idiots would bring Tiffany and the others right to them. Easy . . .

. . . until he saw the first stringless fox puppet watching them. He disappeared on the other side of a hill. *No no no* . . . "You know, on second thought: I'll go scout and keep an eye out. I'm a lot more agile than either of you," Seth said. "Just in case this is a double-cross."

"Seth, you just said it's best to sit quietly," Lily said.

"And that is precisely what you and Isaac are going to do," Seth said. "Lily, I kept everyone at bay for hours. I'll be fine." He walked off in the direction he'd seen the fox. "All right, where are—"

Arms grabbed his and he was gagged, but to his surprise, they were all amber-eyed foxes in a humanoid marionette form. "All right, study the face," said one. He had a top-knot and appeared older than the others. "Notice the design on the hands, you want to blend right in."

The kitsune marionettes merged little details Seth didn't notice, and soon took on a form not unlike his—in fact, two of them replicated him exactly before changing hair color and exaggerating their features. They examined his hands and arms and how the joints were supposed to connect. Once they were satisfied, they released Seth. "What are you doing?" Seth demanded once he wrenched off that gag. "How did you get in here?"

"We followed you," Muffin explained. "Tunnel I couldn't apparently fit into." He snickered. He hadn't tried to replicate Seth exactly; he had dark hair and a long face, and he relieved Boscoe from Seth's satchel. "Thank you."

"Seth, help me!" Boscoe pleaded, unable to shape-shift his way out.

"All right, you got him. Now get out before you get us caught," Seth said. There were at least six of them.

"We just got here," said the silver kitsune, besides Muffin she was the only one he recognized.

"We're trying not to draw attention," Seth said.

"We're excellent at not being seen if we don't wish it," said Top-Knot. He gestured to two, who, now that they were satisfied with their human marionette appearances, melted back into marionette foxes. "Don't let anyone know we're here."

"We fit in better than him," one chuckled, and the two sped off quietly, though they studied sheep and took on their appearances as well, bounding off, the same as the others mulling about save for lack of strings.

"Think you can turn yourselves into a big horking monster to kick down the draw bridge?" Seth asked.

"Why didn't we think of that earlier?" Top-Knot asked the others, who cackled in laughter. "We've got limits. Why don't you worry less about what we're doing, and more about what you need to?"

Seth frowned; he wasn't going to let them roam around and wait for the others to rescue Tiffany. "I'm going to go find my sister," he snapped. "So help me, if you get Lily caught . . . "

"I'll keep an eye on Lily and Isaac," the silver kitsune offered. "Show these silly cousins of mine how it's done."

How what's done? Seth had no idea. The kitsunes scattered, some as human marionettes and others as foxes. He glanced back at Isaac and Lily; if he told them they'd insist on staying together. Lily knew he'd be fine, so he went ahead and found that most of the town was empty— there were hardly any strings. He followed the horse trail to an area on his map that was simply called "beach" and found that the knights and others were busy building a boat.

"Step lively," Sir Justin said, posing with a hammer but not helping. "Sooner we build this ship, the sooner we rescue our beloved people."

Tiffany was being useless, suntanning herself in parts of her armour. Her gaggle of boys were off—two of them were being fawned over by mermaids, with the third one out fishing in a boat. He was about to speak to her, when one of the other knights approached so Seth hid. "How goes the watch?"

"Fine," Tiffany said. "Hey, Braden!" she shouted to the knight fishing. "Any sign of—" It was that time that a smaller rowboat arrived carrying Caleb, Ethan, and the Crescent and Weasel Knights.

"About time," Tiffany said. "What took you so long?"

"We mapped out the area," Crescent Knight said. "Don't know why we didn't attempt at least one of the islands." She glared slightly at Ethan and Caleb.

"We need to go back to town," Caleb said. "Tiffany, come with us."

"My friends are out there, go and save them," Tiffany insisted.

There was a sudden pair of *thunks*, and Caiden and Jayden hit the sand. Ethan pointed, looking incredibly guilty. "Those mermaids!" The mermaids looked surprised and shocked at the accusation.

"I knew it!" Tiffany said, taking out her bow, shooting at them and scaring them off. She put a finger on Ethan's chest. "Don't you start, Mr. Innocent! I know you could have stopped those mermaids. Kind of glad you didn't and they're gone, but it is *your* fault my boyfriends are hurt!"

"Want to help us load them and take them back to town?" Ethan asked, batting his glass eyes. "You can nurse them back to hea—"

"BRADEN!" Tiffany bellowed. "You and I are going on a quest!"

Braden speedily rowed back to shore, and despite Caleb and Ethan trying to grab her, Tiffany jumped into the boat and sped off, Tiffany yammering on about beaches, beaches everywhere, while they disappeared into the blue.

Caleb and Ethan loaded up Caiden and Jayden. Seth crept up so he could wave and Ethan spotted him. Ethan gestured, and Seth got in the back of the wagon. "How are Darius and Tristan doing?" Ethan asked.

"Kind of crazy. Darius left this afternoon," Seth explained. "Sounded like he was going to some other town for help. Tristan's watching our prisoner, seemed like the right guy for the job."

"You came alone?" Caleb asked.

They didn't need to worry about the kitsunes. "My sister and Mr. Sprites are waiting for you where you said before." Seth said, looking over his shoulder at the goings on at the beach. "They're not that bright, are they?"

"Sorry about your sister," Ethan said.

"Tiffy's your problem until you get her to me," Seth said.

"You good?" Caleb asked Ethan, who nodded. They waited until they were out of the general sight of the beach and Caleb hopped on his horse, leading the other two away. Ethan picked up speed too.

"Things going smoothly?" Seth asked, reclining.

"I don't know which one of those idiots triggered a new event, but our village is mostly empty. We think we narrowed down where Dale and Brigid are, but we're not certain. Didn't want to miss you guys. Sucks that Darius left, he seemed decent if not a little . . . you know, weird in the head."

"I don't think Percival meant for them to come back," Ethan admitted. "He's worried about the younger ones."

Younger ones? They were the same age as him pretty much. "Couldn't one of you have stayed to find my people?"

"People start getting suspicious if Cay and I aren't together on missions unless one of us is injured," Ethan said. "We are trying to not draw attention, remember?"

Seth nodded, but it gave him an idea.

~*~

Lily was nervous when she saw the strings, but was relieved to see it was Caleb. She waved from one of the hiding spots and walked over.

"Sorry I'm late," Caleb said, dismounting. "You navigate all right?"

"That map helped," Isaac said. "I'm Isaac Sprites. Where's Seth? He's been gone a long time. Are you Ethan or Caleb?"

"Caleb Felvey," Caleb extended a hand, and the pair shook. "Seth with Ethan. Let's get you in and out. I don't have your people yet but I'd like you to sneak out Demetri, he was the royal physician. People will listen to him." He gestured to the horses.

It wasn't like riding Stella—Lily wondered briefly how the mare fared, and of Rebecca. Stella was gentle with young riders, and the Sprite's farm was the best place for her until her parents caught up.

"I thought you were going to bring Tiffany and the others to us," Isaac said.

"We had a hiccup. We'll get them. Town's pretty empty right now, but Geraldine's there. She's one of the people I warned you about. We'll distract her. Lily, you got something . . . " Caleb gestured to his hair.

She ran a hand through her hair, and pulled out a tiny, toy-style version of a twig and buds, there was only one real oak leaf on it. "I guess I can't leave this, it'll hint that I was here. The spell really works down to details, doesn't it?"" Caleb asked.

"Can I have it? I mean, if you don't want it."

"Of course." He seemed fascinated with it. The fake trees they were riding by became more apparent. They were forever green and the bark looked . . . better from the distance and the leaves . . . were all kind of generic and the same. They weren't oaks, or maples, rowans or willows. None were of particular note.

Caleb put it in what looked like a velvet draw string bag, something she'd expect to find jewellery in. He ditched the horses out of town, with others who were running about. "Is their tack always on?" Isaac asked.

"Yeah, they've been stuck like that," he said, giving his a pat and gesturing for him to join the others. Several others came up to them. "I don't have time to play with you." He gave the three horses quick nose scratches. "People gotta come first, guys." He gestured, and Lily and Isaac followed him into the town.

The village was bigger than Lily had assumed and seemed deserted. The buildings for the most part were of a cheerful design and every-thing was clean. It would have been eerily quiet if it weren't for the sound of a woman yelling at small children. Caleb seemed amused, but bade them wait in an alleyway when he saw a woman and stepped out so she could berate him "Have you rescued anyone to oversee these brats?" the woman demanded.

"We're working on it."

"Well stop loafing about here," the woman snapped at Caleb. "You have one job and quite frankly none of you knights do it well. You there, stop that!" She ran off.

Caleb gestured, and they ducked down another alleyway and the building he led them to appeared to be an infirmary. Lily never got a look at the children up close, but there were about six or so painting the sides of buildings and throwing around the little puppet chickens. "So much for subtlety."

"You said to cause a distraction," Ethan said when they met outside the building. "Seth is this way." He gestured and they followed him up the back steps.

"So they can't access half the world?" Isaac asked.

"Pretty much," Ethan offered. "Drove me bonkers when I couldn't un-string." There was an older man and a woman with dark hair in the infirmary room, withthree unresponsive puppets laying in cots.

"Before you ask: They tried to grab Tiffy. Dale and Brigid are apparently captured by pirates," Seth said, rolling his eyes.

"Pick a plot, amirite? Your guess is as good as ours as to when Molly will show up again." Ethan found a window to keep watch while Caleb guarded the door they came in.

"It's a bit of a shock, seeing them like this. They'll come around, they had their headstrings cut by . . . er . . . I'm getting ahead of myself," said the old marionette. "Caleb, get over here and introduce us formally."

"I told you about them."

"That's not the same thing," the woman said. She walked to Lily. "I'm Esther, and this is Doctor Demetri. He used to be the prince's royal physician; I was just a milkmaid."

"It's nice to meet you," Isaac said. "I'm Isaac Sprites, and this is Lily O'Connell."

"I understand Sir Percival sent two of his horde to be of assistance?" Demetri asked.

Isaac explained the situation at the camp. Lily felt like she wasn't essential to the mission. She snuck out Louis, but unless someone returned with Tiffany or Brigid, the plan at the moment seemed to be only smuggling out Demetri. With Caleb and Ethan keeping watch, it seemed that they were able to have some privacy. Esther seemed concerned when Darius was brought up, but the doc was more fascinated with how the squires reacted as opposed to Louis. "So it seems that we won't be able to bring any of my collection," he muttered sadly. "I have so many books that would be of use. I suppose I could get some spectacles to magnify them . . ."

"I have this," Lily said, handing Esther the new journal. "I haven't even written in it. It came from the town.Whoever stays can write out information and we can smuggle it out next time." Esther nodded.

Demetri crossed his arms. "It feels wrong for me to be shuttled out when you are all so much younger than me," he admitted. "You've your lives ahead of you."

"The prince who ruled this castle doesn't know us, but he knows you," Esther said. "This may be our best chance to stop this at its source."

"If he does anything at all," Caleb muttered.

"You need to be positive," Demetri said. "Brooding isn't going to solve anything. All right, we stick to the plan. Let me gather some things . . . you know, it's a sort of fear, knowing I won't get to see this place again."

"You were supposed to be ready to go," Caleb said.

The doctor rushed off into another room. "Just a few housekeeping items."

Esther also walked off, and despite their muted features, Lily saw the woman break down. Lily started towards her, but Ethan and Caleb went to her. "It's okay, Esther," Ethan said.

"If I thought only four or five people were getting out, you'd be my first choice," Caleb said.

"What about you? One of you should go."

Caleb and Ethan glanced at each other. "As soon as we save their sister, I'm out of here," Ethan said. "Cay's staying until the bitter end. We're not abandoning the people here."

"You shouldn't stay just because some of us are trapped," Esther said.

"Esther, I might go back to how I was when the spell hit," Caleb said. "I won't be any use to anyone. Don't worry about us. If you can't function without Demetri, say so. We'll figure something else out."

"I'll be fine. I have hope, but I'm scared. I don't know what I feel." Esther composed herself, looked at Lily and Isaac. They couldn't cry, not really. "I'm sorry you saw me that way."

"It's okay," Isaac said. Lily felt worse than useless standing there.

"You'll be all right, Esther," Ethan reassured her. "You were a swan for a month. Those things are deceptively dangerous."

"Scratched my cousin up real good," Caleb gestured to one of the unconscious puppets.

Ethan and Esther spoke quietly. Caleb exited after Demetri, but spoke to someone in another room.

"You know I can see your strings?"

The boy who came out looked not much younger than Louis. "You thought I was one of the little ones, didn't you?" he asked, his hopeful gaze on Isaac and Lily. "Caleb, you're sneaking people out? Can I go? *Please?*"

Caleb gestured, and walked the boy down the hall and talked to him in private. Lily almost felt like following, but Caleb took out that draw-string bag. He gave it to the boy, and bent down to look him in the eyes when he examined the twig. She had no idea what they were saying, but they both looked towards her.

"He's not making any promises," Esther offered. "Oliver wouldn't believe him."

"Little brother?" Isaac asked.

"Oliver's a page. He should be a squire by now," Esther said. "We're not aging. The armour won't fit him, and we don't think it ever will. All he wants is to help Caleb and Ethan, and . . . "

"How are there kids here when just about everyone else got captured?" Isaac asked.

"Oliver and the children have a system, he helps them hide and cuts their head-strings if he has to, then stashes the little ones out of the way. Oliver knows he just needs to get them someplace safe, with cover. They come to in a while, and usually by then the victims are selected. Less time than for them to be gone for weeks if it's . . . involved."

Caleb returned to the main room, Oliver in tow, who looked solemn, and had that drawstring bag in his hand like it was a lost treasure. Caleb didn't introduce them, but Seth got up. "Can I steal you for a minute?" Seth asked, gestured for Caleb to follow, who nodded, and they hurried off to talk to Ethan waiting at the backstairs, Oliver in tow.

"How many children are here?" Lily asked.

"Not that many. Whoever is bringing in people usually want them older, most are between sixteen to twenty. A lot of girls are as young as fourteen. I think we have twenty-three children under the age of twelve." Esther nodded. "We don't want you to have an orphanage out there, but . . . the doctor will know the children's families. Think you can help us help them?"

"Even if we can't find their families, we'll do what we can," Lily said. "If Isaac's carrying Demetri, I can take a child."

"Caleb will say children don't belong in war camps."

"I don't know what he's used to, but what we have is not a war camp," Isaac said. "We'll figure things out."

Esther nodded. It seemed that the doctor had finished writing out his orders and had returned to them. "You'll be fine, Esther. The boys know they can't bash their way through this one so they're going to have to look before they leap. Well, shall we go?"

Lily nodded, and Esther walked to a nearby window, then squinted. "Where are they going?"

Lily ran to the window, and saw Ethan and Caleb running off—both in full armour.

"I told them to tell you," Caleb said, crossing his arms at the doorway. She almost didn't recognize him dressed like a regular civilian. "The two of you are stuck with me as your escort. Seth'll be fine."

"How are you—? *Seth*?" Isaac demanded.

"His idea. Ethan said if he grunted and pretended to be sullen no one would notice the difference," Caleb said. "Ethan can handle a low level on his own, so long as they're not stupid they might even find your villagers. We'll have to walk to not draw attention." He looked to Oliver, who nodded, going down the backstairs.

Demetri nodded. "If the horde clues in, you have my permission to cut my strings and drag me accordingly."

"I thought you were allied," Isaac said.

Demetri shook his head. "They've warring factions, I'll explain it better once we're outside if Tristan doesn't."

Esther spoke to Caleb quietly, who cast a glance at Lily, then nodded. She disappeared, but within a few moments came back with a small, limp puppet in her arms. "This is Alanna," she said quietly. "Her parents were rangers, they were delivering messages when the spell hit the castle. She's four and . . . promise me you'll take care of her."

Caleb looked to Lily. "You're sure?"

"I'm sure. I'm sure Tristan can help me find her parents."

He nodded, then said, "I'll carry her until we get to the barrier. Let's go."

Demetri gave Esther a final hug and they left in silence, other children keeping the wretched Geraldine busy. "They're going to be feral if you don't get them out of here," Demetri said with a chuckle when they exited the town.

"Going to be?" Caleb asked.

The doc chuckled again, and before Lily knew it they were making their way through the woods. There were a handful of times that Caleb had them duck out of sight. Though Demetri remained on strings, and couldn't join them, Caleb tended to stay in the open with him. "All right, we're almost to the point I'm going to have to cut your strings," Caleb told Demetri. He looked to Lily and Isaac. "You both might as well change back. If we rescue your people we'll send them with Seth and he'll fetch one of you to help him with the others. I'll get Seth to help me with something."

"Maybe I should take Alanna now?" Lily asked. Caleb nodded. Compared to moving Louis, Alanna was easy. "What do you want my brother for?"

"Are you volunteering?" he asked.

"Maybe."

" . . . it would be easier while they think I'm out there . . . " Caleb sounded contemplative. "Do not come back here until Alanna is safe. Demetri?"

"Do it," the doctor said. Caleb nodded, and struck the physician's head strings. The doctor went slack, and Caleb cut the rest, then bundled him up onto Isaac's back. "All right. They'll light up like we saw before. Let's be quiet in the hallways just in case."

He led them and it was almost unnerving how she was getting used to this. She was no Seth, but Isaac was relieved when the barrier lit up. "All right, you know the way," Caleb said quietly. He looked to her. "I don't blame you if you don't come back. Thank you."

"I won't be long," she said, and followed Isaac across. She paused when he got to the end of the hallway, looking back at Caleb, then chased after Isaac. They made it down the hall without issue and found the room. She located the tunnel before Isaac, though Isaac had to drag the doctor, she could easily just move Alanna so she was cradled in her arms as she made her way through the dark.

She wasn't sure the hour but Tristan and Louis were laughing at the fire. When Isaac called, it was Larry who stood to greet them. "These don't look like your people."

"They're not," Isaac explained. "The man is named Demetri, the little girl is Alanna."

"Little girl?" Larry sputtered. Lily handed her to him. "How many children are back there?" He looked to Tristan.

"We think around twenty," Tristan said. "Occasionally more get added." He took Demetri. "I can't believe how small I was."

"Get them to the kitchen tent. Do you know her parents?" Isaac gestured towards Alanna.

Tristan nodded. Lily turned to go "Are you sure you're going back?"

"I said I would," Lily said. "You got them from here?"

"Yes—be careful," Isaac said.

To her surprise, Caleb had only moved to the side of the hall, approaching until the barrier started to light up, then backed off. "Care to clue me in?" Lily asked.

He gestured, and she followed him down the hallway, not ducking back the way they came but in through another area that looked like a desert. Caleb knew another way out and they were in a different section of the castle halls, one she hadn't seen before.

The new barrier on the second floor impeded Caleb; he said there was a library not far from where they were but he seemed relieved to just sit in the stairwell. He took her to a little secluded spot overlooking the playing field.She hadn't realized how high up they were. "What are we doing?"

"Seeing if one of my friends shows up."

"More goblins?"

"No goblins," he said. "I didn't know when I'd get here, and he can't make it obvious and hang around an area too much."

"Not good at sneaking around?"

"Not at all."

They sat in silence for a little while. He seemed attentive enough, and was constantly scanning the room below. "You doing okay? he asked after a while.

She nodded. "What happens when you hit the barrier? I mean, I know what happens, but what's it like?"

"A jolt. I freeze up, but I'm aware for an instant," he said. "Then I lose consciousness. It doesn't hurt, but it's not pleasant. I wake up back in the field, and for whatever reason it takes me a lot longer than Ethan."

"I'll bet you it's those blue butterflies," she said quietly.

"Probably," he said. "Ethan and I did runs; one of us stayed behind and shot the butterflies. We even tied ropes to each other, and when one fell, dragged the other one back to see how long we were disabled." He changed subjects pretty abruptly. "What's it like, travelling on a ship?"

"It was a small sailboat, and I liked it," she said, though to be honest she was happy to see shore. "Don't know if I have the making of a sailor in me. I prefer the mountains and the forest."

"Taralee, right?"

"Stagmil. Taralee's not far from home. Stagmil is mostly farms and sheep, plenty of wooded areas for hunting and the like."

"Don't know if I'd like Taralee," Caleb admitted. "The mountains, I hear they're amazing. Is that how you know about monsters?"

"My parents did . . . more select hunts for paying clients. I mostly read their old hunters' journals." She realized maybe she ought not be talking trade secrets with a stranger. Maybe not a stranger, but he didn't need to know. "Maybe you and Ethan can come and visit, when this is all said and done."

"Yeah," he sounded doubtful.

"You going to let a little ocean get in your way?"

"It's a sea, and that's not the problem. Ah, there's my friend," Caleb said. He took out a polished piece of glass, and used it to reflect light. The signal wasn't complex.

She looked down at the scenery. There were sheep, indications of the horde, but really, the only thing of note was large and red and, flying . . . at them.

"Is that a dragon?"

"Sure is. Pretty sure he's painted red, I don't see the usual scale pattern. I'd need reference but I think this kind would normally be more bronze."

Lily backed away and almost ran off, but he was so casual about it. The dragon didn't fly to them directly, but when he slowed down, hovered a little bit. "How's it going?" Caleb called out, petting his snout when he passed. "See? He's safe." The dragon snorted as if to remind Caleb that *safe* wasn't the proper term.

"Caleb, they breathe fire. You're made mostly of wood."

"Flesh and bone wouldn't stand up particularly well, either. Besides, he can only breathe fire when the people upstairs make him. He'd have burned everything below before we befriended him."

"How is—I mean, aren't you supposed to be slaying him in these stupid quests?"

"Yeah, and he's upset about it, too," Caleb said. "He doesn't bite." Apparently he understood them, because the dragon nibbled on Caleb's hair. "You are embarrassing me." Lily hesitated, so Caleb walked over to her, and offered her a hand. "He won't hurt you, he knows the plan."

"When were you going to explain the plan to me?" she asked, letting him lead her.

"We're going to get him out of here."

She waited for an explanation. "Okay?"

"First, let him sniff you." The dragon's eyes were dazzling and the snout had a grin.

"I have all sorts of objections to either of you sniffing me."

"He'll be able to track you outside—"

"You are doing a really bad job convincing me."

"He'll find you outside, you'll be able to turn him back to normal. Ethan and I have a hole he can fit through. I need you to shove him through the barrier. He goes back to normal size, and he attacks the castle and distracts the people who did this long enough for us to get away with as much as we possibly can." The dragon nodded vehemently.

"Oh, is that all?"

"Want to see how much I trust this guy?" Caleb asked, letting go of her hand. "Can I go for a zip?" The dragon backed off, and did a big circle.

"No please don't—!" Lily sputtered, Caleb took a giant leap and the dragon dove, and of course she ran to the edge, to see him in the dragon's claws. "See? He's not going to drop me. No, no don't—Lily back up!"

All things considered, the dragon's fling and Caleb's landing were borderline graceful, though he skidded and released more of what sounded like dragon laughter as he circled around the playing field. "I never said he was tame."

"I thought dragons could speak."

"I think they did something so he can't. Like how he can't breathe fire unless he's under control. We call him Peanut. One of the kids named him, don't ask."

"Look, he can't hang out here very long without getting attention. If anyone's looking for me they'll see Seth, so this is our best chance to break him out. If you don't think you can handle it that's fine."

"So you want my help to release a puppet dragon into the wild, and I have to turn it back to the big scaly version?"

"There's some added steps in there, but essentially yes."

"What's going to happen after it attacks a town?"

"He's a young dragon.He's hardly a scourge." Peanutroared. "You *aren't*. Look, the only other dragon I saw here was old and injured. I don't want to be responsible for another of these magnificent creatures getting hacked to pieces if I can help it. And between you and me, I'd love for him to attack the castle and tear it apart brick by brick but that's not going to happen. A nice molten hole in the wall, I think you could manage, Peanut." Roaring. "Even taking out their little briar patch. Just know I'm cheering for you from the inside.He knows to leave the people and the town alone, and we told him where to find deer."

"There's . . . an ocean west of here. I'm sure you could find some big fish," she offered. "About a little over a day's ride?" Against her better judgement, Lily slowly moved towards the edge. The dragon came back. He gave her a sniff, then opened his mouth, and gave her upper body and head a lick. The dragon didn't have any saliva, Lily somehow got the impression it was a friendly gesture.

"He likes you," Caleb told her.

"Let's just get this over with. Where's this hole in the wall?"

"Don't worry, he won't fling you. Right, Peanut? Lily's our friend? You don't have to jump, just walk into his outstretched talon, kind of lean backwards . . . "

Each talon didn't have to be regular-sized to be able to easily crush her. "How are we supposed to get back here?"

"I have grappling equipment and you already know how to rappel. We'll end up down there. Look, I can't do this without you or Seth or I would have already."

She hated to do it but she had to hold Caleb's hand and he helped her step into the claws. They tightened, and she was secure. "Let go of my hand, he's got you. I'm going to be right beside you. Peanut, nice easy flight. I don't want to hear her scream."

She closed her eyes and knew they were flying, and she never got the nerve to open them again.

"It feels like the wind, doesn't it?" Caleb asked.

"Not exactly," she called back.

"I miss it."

The bricked-up window wasn't that far, but much higher up. Caleb let himself out and helped her down. "I can't believe I just did that," she said.

"Okay, like we discussed. Take your time getting back here, I'll signal when I'm ready," Caleb told Peanut. He left her watching the magnificent dragon fly, and was moving the bricks that had already been cleared out. He had stone picks and what looked like a shovel made out of a rat skull. The bricks moved easily.The mortar was dirt and it was obvious Caleb and Ethan had done it some time ago. It was still dark out—not a great view, but she could sort of see the town from where they were. "We tried jumping. Fell to the briars, got put back in. We're trying to build a catapult, to try launching Ethan into the moat." He looked pleased when he'd made just enough of a hole. For a minute she forgot there was a barrier, until she noticed that strange pale blue light emanating from the floor when Caleb got close. When she was near and he backed off, it just looked like normal castle. "Let me handle this part," he said. "It might not go exactly to plan." He used his shiny glass to signal Peanut.

"I can bring you in a hand mirror next time," she offered.

"I'd appreciate that," Caleb said. It seemed that the dragon would hover in other areas, in case someone was watching, so that it didn't seem like he was favouring one area or another.

Returning to their cubby, the dragon lowered his head and nudged the squire. "I'll miss you, too.Cause them some grief, and go home. Maybe I'll still be here in a hundred years when you're the right size for the job. Okay, let's do this."

Caleb climbed onto his head, and the dragon dug his talons into the stone of the window sill, and tried to pull himself, but the strings only allowed him to crawl so far. Caleb cut the tail string.The dragon stretched and clawed, but parts of him went limp when the strings were severed. Caleb pet Peanut's head, "Scary part, I know." Then went for the head-string and hopped down. "I'll need you to move parts of him and then finish shoving him out. Stand there and look pretty until I need you."

"Watch it," Lily said, and got out from her brick of protection and helped him shove the dragon. She noticed the barrier light up when Caleb neared it. At one point, Caleb went too much on the barrier and his left arm lit up, then went limp. "What happened?"

"That's a warning," Caleb said. "Can you handle the rest?"

"Yes, back off. I swear, if you fall down on me while I'm stuck up here I am not going to be happy," she said.

"Pretty sure we skipped happy when you first saw Peanut. Wait," he said, going into his satchel and finding the grappling equipment. "Make yourself a harness, just in case you accidentally pitch yourself over. Let his weight do the work, don't fall with him."

"You do this often?"

"This is the first dragon I've rescued."

"How long will he be out?"

"I don't know. If he's not roaring by dawn, you let me worry about him."

She wasn't sure when the dragon would go, but suddenly he began to slide without her help and she scrambled to avoid becoming tangled. The slow became sudden and the dragon disappeared, and she approached the edge.

"Do you see him?" Caleb called.

"Don't slack the line," she called back. Looking down, she was greatful for the enhanced night vision, the dragon was sprawled out atop briar. She then realized how high she was and lurched backwards. Caleb had the string taut and pulled her backwards, steadying her when he could approach, before cradling his dead arm.

"Did you see him?" Caleb asked, and waited for her nod. "I guess now we wait."

He gestured, and found himself a perch so that he could look out the hole. There wasn't anything going on out there. A slight breeze, sounds of crickets and perhaps an owl in the distance. They couldn't see the town; she assumed the view would be better during the day. "Are the lilacs blooming or did I miss it?" he asked.

"How'd you know it was spring?"

"I have my ways. That twig in your hair, for instance."

"You didn't strike me as a floral kind of guy."

"I like some flowers better than others. My younger sister liked lilacs, made the entire house smell. I used to make fun of her, but I'd kill to be able to smell lilacs right now. I wonder how she's doing."

"You didn't always live in a castle?"

"I didn't become a page until I was seven. I still got to go home; well, my grandparents' home; it's not that far from here."

"Which is your house in town?"

"Farm about ten miles south," he explained. "My grandfather Henry was a fletcher conscripted into battle, he achieved knighthood because he sniped the right general on the other side. I'm the third one in the family after him . . . well, *would* have been the third one to get his knighthood. Besides the title of Knight, my grandfather was awarded a small plot of land. It's not much, but it's home."

Lily didn't know why, but she'd just assumed he was better off than she was. "How many siblings do you have?"

"I'm the oldest. Two sisters, then a little brother. Dad went off on a campaign just after I was born, there's a bit of a gap between me and my siblings. Ethan said they never came back to the castle after my . . ." he trailed off. "Doesn't matter. They weren't here when the spell hit. My best guess is they're with my grandmother or one of my aunts."

"It must have been scary," Lily said. "Everyone getting turned to puppets and having no idea what was going on."

"I don't remember, to be honest," Caleb admitted. "I was drugged and injured so I didn't even have the option of running. You don't want to hear it. But yeah, just about everyone was terrified. I was when I came to and I found out I was made of wood and shrunk down—I thought I died and was in some transition between heaven and hell before I heard other people calling out. Ethan said strings just came out of nowhere and grabbed people. Never seen again. Not that I mind telling you this, but I want to hear more about the outside world."

"If I get you a journal, will you or Ethan write it down?"

"I guess." Caleb shrugged. "How'd your people get kidnapped, anyway?"

"How should I start? I guess a wyvern stole some sheep from our farm. There's a point to this, I promise. My father and mother hunted speciality game. So I know how dangerous your little Peanut is."

"Not as dangerous as your wyvern, currently. He better at least roar so I know he's awake."

"We figured the wyvern came down from the mountains. Most of the men went to assist in the hunt.Those of us who were left behind needed to congregate. Wyverns tend to pick off things that separate from the pack."

"You didn't go on the hunt?"

"No one gave me the option. Seth went initially. Dad knew a handful of people needed to protect the village, my mom knows how to drive things off and how to minimize drawing them in and wanted me to help, but I really just did more of the same old. Then, this woman shows up. Madeline, I mean. She looked like she was on the run, but not like a vagabond. Town took her in, and we were going to help her. I'd have taken her back to Taralee the next day but no one listens to me." Lily sighed. "Anyway—we were having meals at the community hall and I played the mandolin and Madeline asked me to learn some sheet music. People ask me to play songs and I like learning new ones, so I didn't think it was a big deal."

"What's a mandolin?"

"It's kind of like a lute, only you play the strings in pairs. Anyway, I learn it, but it's a song that gets stuck in my head. I've barely touched my mandolin; I play something else and that song eventually worms its way back. Mama Fern said it should have wore off by now."

"Who?"

"Someone who helped us. We're skipping ahead. Anyway, another night Madeline's hosting an after-supper puppet show and I can't put my finger on it but something is off. I went to go see what else she had in her bag and she had these theatre masks. Tiffany, naturally, rats me out and makes a scene—"

"Not Tiffany!"

"You've had the pleasure."

"I want you to rescue Lady Theophania I more than anyone."

"Madeline plastered a mask on my face and I was taken over. I acted out a play I'd never read. She put masks on Louis and Tiffany too, and they improvised, but I had no control. I panicked once she got it off, and then she asked if I memorized the song. I got out of there as fast as I could."

"Let me guess: You told yourself it was all in your head."

Lily nodded. "I went to go talk to her, and Seth tagged along to have my back. I should have known better by then—and she slapped another mask on me when Seth was goofing off. I couldn't move and she made a copy of my face and ordered me to write a letter that I was running away from home, then forced me to get my mandolin."

"So your parents think you ran off?"

"Skipping ahead again, but no, we took care of that. She had me go to part of the forest, and play. I played a lullaby that put the town to sleep for days. Seth and Tiffany and the others were . . . let's just say out after hours, and because we grew up with our parents' stories, when I played a luring song, they knew something wasn't right. Seth said he and Tiffany put wax in their ears, but Louis and the rest of them were compelled. Madeline wore my face, and lured Seth and Tiffany to where I was.

"The song in my head changed," she said, "Madeline put on a mask, and became . . . if I said Jorogumo, would you know what that is?"

Caleb was casually lounging, but he sat up. "Large half-woman with the lower body of a spider who drinks the living blood of her victims. Typically prefers young men and dwell in caves or other isolated areas."

"Wow that . . . is incredibly accurate."

"Can I see your sketchbook?" Caleb could make excellent layouts and maps, but his drawing skills were just okay. What he produced wasn't perfect but he nailed the rows of eyes and thin lips.

"You've seen one before?"

"The song, what did it sound like?"

"I don't have my mandolin."

"Okay, this isn't my normal voice, but I can try to sing parts I remember."

"You mean you're taller in real life, too?"

"Maybe a little. Muted puppet features hide the sloped forehead," Caleb said. "Don't tell anyone I sung." He still hesitated like it was a bad idea, but she heard the influx in his voice. Part of her seemed to switch on what she felt was dormant before. She joined him, he nodded, but then she broke into that spider song. For a moment it was academic before it poured out of her, and he leapt to his feet and drew his sword.

Lily turned and drew hers. "What?"

He grabbed her and turned her roughly, made her look at him. "What are you?"

"What?"

"It's fading . . . " he said, letting her go. "Don't . . . sing again. Understood?"

"Why? What just happened?"

"I don't know," he said. He was studying her, Lily wasn't sure if he thought she was a threat, but he seemed to relax after a minute. "Lily, I think whatever she did to you is still affecting you."

"That was embarrassing."

"Try being a little child's toy for two years."

Her mind raced. Why did that happen? "Maybe I need to wear that bracelet."

"I don't get it."

"I have a bracelet that will ward off Madeline's transformations. We have her out at the camp, whoever is guarding her wears it." Realization struck her. "That's why!"

"Still not following."

"The bracelet prevents the person wearing it from being cursed, but if you are cursed, it locks the curse in. I can't believe I didn't figure that out until now." She looked at her puppet hands. She was cursed but . . . she still had the power to do that? She didn't want any part of that woman's filthy magic in her.

Why would Mama Fern give her that?

Fire illuminated them from below and outside. Thankfully, there was enough starlight that they could see Peanut in real flight—majestic swooping not restricted by strings. Caleb cradled his arm and walked as near as he could to the barrier. Peanut flapped his wings, doing barrel rolls and other moves that would have been impossible with strings. "If this is what he looks like as a puppet, imagine what he's going to look like when you fix him."

"Think he'll rage against the castle?"

"I hope a little," Caleb said. "I don't want him to get caught and he knows it. They'll make killing him the next quest and, I've already been forced to slay one dragon." He looked up to Peanut. "Okay, you're going to find some place to hide and wait for Lily, unless you think you can fix yourself."

Roaring, Peanut neared, and the barrier lit up; so did the dragon. He couldn't come back into the castle.

"I am not going with you," Caleb said, then looked at Lily. "Peanut can fly you back to the camp. You can jump out the window, it'll be faster—"

"No!"

"Have a good life," Caleb said to the dragon. "I wish I knew your real name, or where you're from. You must be sick of hearing about my problems. Well, what are you waiting for, a goodbye kiss? Get going."

The dragon made what sounded like kissy noises, breathed fire to illuminate his way. "Don't set yourself on fire, you stupid dragon," Caleb called, watching him go. For a moment he just stood there, and it almost looked like he was going to scream at Peanut to come back and get him. He moved his shoulders, the one arm coming back and started to put the bricks back where they came from. He didn't acknowledge Lily helping.

"That was amazing," she said. "I can't believe we just did that."

"I guess." Caleb seemed remarkably somber for someone who just shoved his dragon pal out the castle window. He hesitated at the last brick, taking another look, then closed it up. "Hopefully Seth and Ethan are back and you can get out of here with Lady Theophania." He took out his grappling equipment and started fussing with knots.

Lily teetered at the edge. "I don't think I can do this."

"Sure you can. We picked up your grapple from earlier."

"That wasn't from nearly as high," she said.

"Not a problem. I can lower you, but you can just hitch a ride with me. That'll be the safest. Climb on my back like we did with Louis. I'll rope you so you won't fall."

She felt silly for needing help, but he boosted her and made a few adjustments to the harness. "You can close your eyes if you want."

"Believe me I'm going to—you have a scar near your neck."

"Yeah, don't know why that one isn't painted over."

"Sorry."

"Nah, I could do it if it bothered me that much. Okay, eyes closed."

He backed towards the edge, Lily thought she would have strangled him if they needed air. This was somehow worse than being on the dragon.

"And we're down. Open your eyes, you're okay. You really don't like heights." He bent down and let her off. "Noted, I'll try not to scare you so much next time. I keep forgetting that you're not used to all this." He managed to not get the grapple, but got his rope, which was quite different than the marionette strings. "Good job. If you were stuck here, I wouldn't care if you came on quests."

"Is that an invitation?"

"You do not want to be stuck here. In the nicest way, I want to see you and your brother as little as possible." He gestured. They took a relatively shaded spot and he gathered up his rope properly before putting it away. "That went quicker than I expected. I can't show you too much of the castle," he said, then frowned. "What I would give to change back and storm up there and run through two or three people responsible."

"It's an option," Lily pointed out. "I could bring the scissors and transform you back in the hallway. You wouldn't have much but you'd be normal size."

"We wouldn't make it that far." He led them back to the panelling leading back to the castle halls. He paused. There was a strange sound from the far end of the game field. "Do they only play the good music while I'm not around?"

Random creatures fell from the sky, without strings. They were bizarre looking, humanoid in form but they had no strings. Thankfully, they started to run away from where they were, back towards the town. "What is that?" she asked.

"I have no idea," Caleb said. "Something's wrong. Come on, you're getting out of here."

"What about Seth?"

"I'll go back for him. If he doesn't come back, wait a few days before coming back into the castle. We can hide him in one of our crevices if it's not safe to move. Let's go."

They sprinted down the halls. "We might have to hide for a while, but let's get you out of here. You should have jumped on Peanut's head."

At one point he grabbed her hand to pull her along quicker, and they hid behind a suit of armor on display. Lily didn't ask, a figure rushed down the hall, masked she seemed so preoccupied she might not have noticed them. Caleb gestured for Lily to wait, he scouted ahead, then gestured for her to follow once he looked around the corner.

"What's going on?" Lily asked, voice barely above a whisper.

"I don't know," Caleb admitted in kind. "Your brother's with Ethan, so long as he doesn't get taken over, he'll be okay."

"Do you think they know we're here? Or maybe it was because they lost their dragon?"

"I don't think losing their dragon would have allowed those strange . . . they didn't even really look like puppets, did they?" Caleb asked. He got her to the barrier. From there, it was a quick run back out the castle. "This is where I leave you." He waited for her to go. "I'm not leaving until you're out of sight, and I have to go save your brother and probably Ethan. I hope the doc and Alanna won't be as much trouble as—" She reached over and touched his shoulder, he calmed down.

"You let me worry about everyone on the outside. You be careful too. I'll need you later," she said.

When he wasn't being cynical, he had a nice smile. "To be continued, Stringless. You got a dragon to restore and I got your brother to rescue."

"Don't remind me." She raced over the barrier. She did look back at him, realizing he wasn't paying attention to the blue butterflies coming up behind him. Lily stopped. "Caleb, look out!"

He turned and two got his arms. She wasn't that far; she sprinted back. A third one got his head, and he struck through the webbing, his back leg started to glow.

"Lily, I'll be fine! Go!" He managed to use his weight and pendulum off the wall. Jumping away he'd freed himself, but another one snagged his back leg and dragged him. Caleb cut himself free but it was almost like there were a hundred butterflies coming out of nowhere. When the barrier lit up beneath him and the green light lit him up his struggling was for nothing, his sword clattering along the floor still gripped in his hand.

There was a hooded masked figure walking towards him and —

Hot stone exploded between them, and a small, but very fire-breathing dragon puppet crashed through the wall. The masked figure panicked as the robe was engulfed.

Lily raced to Caleb, striking the butterflies and pulling him away from the fire and hot stones before he burned, though his clothing singed and parts of the paint on his arm began to crack and peel. More butterflies were still coming, but the butterflies seemed to vanish with the masked figure shrieking. "Caleb! Caleb speak me!" She tried pulling him onto her back but ran before he was secured, dragging his feet.

He can't hear you. He won't for some hours.

Looking over her shoulder the dragon barrelled towards them. She found that riding horizontal in the claws was also far less comfortable, and before she knew it, they were out of the castle, spiralling over the briars and high, higher than any tower. In a heartbeat they were diving over the lake. She had to strain, but she saw that the dragon had Caleb in the other talon. "How am I hearing you?"

With your mind. Now, calm yourself. I saved my friends. They landed in the woods surrounding the lake, not directly across from where they'd shot out.

"Let me down first, hand him to me." The dragon obliged, but then became annoyed when Lily tried to open his puppet eyes, that strange glow the colour of the barrier was present. Caleb looked like a little discarded toy, his grip fixed on his sword. The dragon nudged him. Nothing.

You can fix this? The dragon asked. Lily found she didn't have to intentionally answer yes or no. *Good. Fix him.*

"How did you know we were in trouble?"

I knew he was in trouble. When I felt them hurt him, try to block him, I zoned in on you. To think I needed to sniff you to find you, but try telling this one anything. She sensed that the dragon had genuine affection for Caleb and Ethan . . . sort of like she did for Ginger or her flock.

"He didn't want to leave."

The dragon growled. *You want to keep him in there!*

"I don't! He was going to help us from the inside. He didn't want to leave Ethan and the others," she said. "Why did that happen?"

There were things the dragon didn't know. *I can smell your camp from here. You will fix him. And me. Stay a puppet if you like. I will help him if you won't. I'll take him with me.*

"You can't have him!"

The dragon put a wing out, and simply pushed Lily away from the squire. "Hey!" She tried scrambling around. The dragon whipped his tail down in front of her. "That is enough!"

The dragon picked up Caleb with his mouth. The fit was almost a little too perfect. *I should pretend to chew on him when he starts to awaken, but that may take a long time.*

"Give him back!"

Or you'll what?

"I'm asking nicely," Lily said. "As a friend."

Snarling. *And who will look after him?*

"I will!"

The dragon snorted. *I will hold you to that, human.*

"It's Lily."

The dragon snorted hot air at her. *I am Varian. Don't tell him that, I want to tell him myself. Now, let's go to your camp. He is better off with his own kind, but you will fix him.*

The dragon outstretched his talons. Lily couldn't believe she was walking into them willingly, but she also knew she couldn't outrun Varian, and if he meant her harm he could have left her behind or dropped her.

The camp was quiet, the embers low. Larry was on watch, looking like he was whittling. She wondered if the doctor was awake yet. She directed the dragon to the kitchen tent, and he landed almost silently and they retrieved the scissors. She didn't talk to Larry.

Him first.

"He's going to grow and lose those clothes. He won't be happy."

I don't care if he's happy. Dragon laughter. *You can do me first and I'll find him a sheepskin to wear.* Varian flicked his tongue. Lily got the mental image of people running around in raw fleece, which the dragon found hilarious.

"I'm saying I need to get him somewhere private—no, I'll take him." There wasn't any arguing with the dragon. Lily did what she'd seen a dozen times with the scissors over Caleb. No movement from him, and when she checked his eyes a faint green glow lingered.

The dragon seemed satisfied. *Me next.* She obliged, then used the scissors on herself. The change was faster on her and Varian than Caleb.

What foul magic did they weave on us? Varian hissed. *You will protect him until he awakens?*

"Of course," she said.

The dragon's glassy eyes became more brilliant with each passing second. They studied her with increasing judgement, but he seemed satisfied. *Tell my friend that Peanut will return, and not to do anything too cocky in the meantime.* The dragon roared, stirring Larry from his seat, but before anyone could tell him otherwise Varian took off at a run, spreading his wings and flying away.

"What is going on over—When did you get back to camp?"

"Larry," Lily said, cradling the fallen squire. "Help me."

Thirteen

Seth supposed they were being sneaky by him putting on armour, but enough with the blah blah blah save this waah waah waaah cloak and dagger nonsense. He'd heard from not only Louis, but Ethan that there was ample stuff to whack, and if he had to beat things up to rescue Tiffany, so much the better. Ethan agreed to do all the talking and they agreed that Seth shouldn't be completely silent, but make dumb grunting noises. A little practice with extra swagger, and it was too easy.

They travelled by canoe and arrived at the island—one of many, apparently, and their job was to clear things out and rescue the poor townsfolk. Ethan seemed convinced that among the captives they'd release from 'winning' was Dale and or Brigid, but he wasn't certain. "We had to convince them to return with intel or we'd miss rendezvous. Now, we'll clear our island then we'll go find Miss Theophania, and like it or not we're getting her out. Got it?"

An affirmative "Grraaaa!"

Weasel and Crescent continued to bicker over the map.

"I wonder if they got Peanut out." Ethan said.

"Gggrrr?" Seth asked.

Ethan was doing his best to not giggle. "I'll tell you later."

"Unga-bunga." Seth nodded.

Seth knew they had to rein it in or this was going to end terribly, but it was fun to push the line and occasionally make the other pair suspicious, and then they'd dismiss it. Ethan explained that Selene and Martin were actually incredibly decent and probably wouldn't rat them out, but the less people who knew what was going on, the better. Selene's preferred weapon was a curved sword that she shone like a white beacon, which was kind of annoying but Seth didn't mind that she was drawing all the attention. Martin was proficient with many weapons today he preferred a halberd but was wicked good with throwing knives. "Hurry up you two," Martin called back.

"Urrrr!" Seth grunted. He didn't approve this castle or what was going on by any stretch, but whoever made this island did have a good attention to detail, and more importantly, there seemed like no shortage of beasties to skewer. Ethan explained that not all of them could be defeated via string, but there were other ways to outright destroy the puppets. Usually there was a glowing light or something they had to specifically strike as opposed to outright breaking stuff.

Ethan secured the boat and Seth did what he was hoping to do: go take down some low level monsters. That didn't mean it wasn't fun just bashing away. Selene and Martin were rushing off towards a temple, un-stringing to go explore it and solve some tedious puzzle.

"Hey now—Caleb's sloppy, but at least he has some style," Ethan said.

"Just tell me if you see my villagers."

"Who's the prettiest one in real life?"

"If I were to rank 'em—Molly wins in almost every category, but none of them are ugly."

"I'm starting to forget what I'm supposed to look like," Ethan said quietly.

"You serious?" Seth asked.

"Been two years," Ethan said, throwing his spear and skewering a coconut, which fell down. He picked it up, ripped it open and found something that he pocketed. They were supposed to be collecting some junk too, but Seth didn't care. "I've definitely heard of worse stories of being in prison . . . but you start to forget what it's supposed to be like out in the real world. That this is all there is, you know?"

"Teach me some fun stuff."

"All right; just don't make it obvious."

"Grrrr!"

After some random launching, shooting arrows with attached ropes, having their arms walk up the line, and other general shenanigans, they found Martin and Selene struggling with some mid-levels. Seth was having a blast, but Ethan loked bored. "This is such filler." The other pair had done all of the heavy lifting, by that Seth meant figuring out and tediously going back from one end of the map to the other with a small key or whatever to progress. It also appeared that they'd found the hostages. It didn't appear Dale or Brigid was present, so they might as well just finish it off and go try to find Tiffany.

There was a boss fight, a clam-headed monster that was more annoying than dangerous. Seth couldn't keep up with the other three but still managed a few good hits. Martin commented he was slacking today. The trapped villagers waitedin a pen that Seth thought they could clearly just jump over. Ethan chucked his spear, and ended the fight anti-climatically.

Martin took the pearl in the clam head, and held it aloft.

"Huzzah! Huzzah!" The people started a victory song, about how they were safe. Mermaids arrived and there was a cute little crab dance on the beach.

Seth wondered how they got the choreography down. *Hey, why not?* Seth thought, and joined in the chorus, dancing along in a moment where Ethan was distracted when someone knocked his hat off. Ethan figured it out and tried to stop him, but several of the villagers, very aware of which knight the one with the wolf design was, stopped singing, and Seth found himself singing by himself as the victory music stopped abruptly.

"What? Why is everyone looking at me?" Seth asked, looking around. "I step on a baby or something?"

Selene stormed over and wrenched off his helmet. "You're not Caleb!"

"What?" Seth gasped, and stole a mermaid's handmirror. "I'm gorgeous!"

"Where's his strings?" Martin asked, before Ethan took out his headstring. Martin went for Ethan, but he pushed her off balance and took out her headstring before he cut one of his own hand strings.

"Get out of here!" Ethan said.Seth didn't see why—Martin and Selene hung funny, like little dolls.

"What are you—"

"No time to—to—to—"A strange look took over Ethan's face. The previously calm and pleasant people, little birds, everything, began to jerk. Ethan came to and thrust his spear at Seth's head, who narrowly dodged. One-armed, the squire was still a force to be reckoned with. Seth managed a lucky strike and cut his headstring after dodging several thrusts, but the knight kept moving, his head limp.

Seth ran back towards the beach where the boat was. Previously defeated enemies, which were a cakewalk a minute before, grabbed at him, he grabbed easy ones and cut arms from bodies and swung them at other marionettes. More creatures crashed down; these weren't cute little filler monsters. He leapt, and started to climb their strings, then above the others, jumped from puppet string to puppet string.

As he moved, those puppets he was running towards came to life, and the ones behind him went limp. Suddenly, the puppets who he was on started to ascend quickly. Seth jumped and realized that the knights were following—they had new, strange strings on their heads and Ethan could jump really high. Seth flipped backwards and took out his leg string, but Ethan wouldn't stop following him, and it seemed that every inch of progress he made, more was being thrown at him. He jumped to another set of strings, until that puppet's strings were cut from above, and Seth fell.

Arms grabbed him, pinning him to the ground. Strings were coming from above. He couldn't move, except . . .

"You found him!" bellowed a dramatic voice. Caleb? No, he didn't sound right or . . . look right either. Seth had to wrench his neck to see. He was wearing his armor . . . but Seth was wearing the armour . . . how? And when did he grow a beard?

The strings attached to a piece of wood, and another villager, this one looking uncanny and bizarre to the others, plucked them like strings of a harp with no sound. "Let me at him," said the other Caleb. "My good people, let me put this doppelganger to mine blade." The bearded Caleb drew sword, only it was a green fish. "Curses and drat! Oh well," he said, and slapped one of the puppets nearing him with the fish. It did nothing

Seth realized that several puppets approaching those that held him him were all grinning in a way a true marionette couldn't. The kitsunes around him moved out and cut the strings of the puppets holding him. Seth pushed away and another kitsune took on Seth's appearance. The resemblance was uncanny . . . only it wasn't quite right. He drew a blue fish to the fake Caleb's green. "Have at thee, knave!" he struck.

The two battled with flounders, not even swordfishes.

Enjoying the performance?" asked a longer, leaner kit than the one he'd thrown to Seth as the other pair burst into song about how much they hated the other.

"It's not for you, silly goose. Come along," Muffin said to Seth. Seth followed him down towards the beach and their rowboat. The other kitsunes fanned out though Seth got the distinct idea they were playing with the controlled puppets, taking out headstrings. "Where are we going?"

"You got in on your own, you're getting out on your own. Oh, hope you like the jewellery."

"What?" Seth asked, following Muffin to the rowboat and helping him cast off.

"We chatted and got you a little something," Muffin said, dangling a chain with a fox head medallion. "Might find it useful." Seth snatched it and put it on without asking questions, then started to row. "Don't go that way; you'll get caught."

"There's only one way out," Seth snapped. "Wait, what about my sister?"

"Which one?" Muffin asked, lounging as Seth rowed. He was watching the mists. "Hello up there!" he called. "Yes, you who is watching. Is that all you got?"

"Are you crazy?" Seth asked.

Something fell and made a splash, and Seth stood, then realized he was holding an oar offensively. The kitsune didn't get up from his lounged recline. A small manifestation of the cloaked figure with the mask emerged from the water.

"You are not welcome here, kitsune," it said. This voice was male, low and threatening.

"You don't say?" Muffin asked lazily. "Well, if I'm not wanted I'll take my leave. How'saboot we take all the nice little puppets you have in this castle and I'll be on my merry little way?"

"We are not negotiating," the masked figure said. The clothing ruptured, and more than twenty butterflies came out. They spat strings, but Seth found that they didn't stick to him. "The knights will obliterate any form you take."

"You can't really tell the difference between us and them, can you?" the kitsune asked. "You really think we're the worst that's going to challenge you? How about you keep your precious castle, the little enforcers, and you promise to stop bringing in fresh meat? Let us have the civilians. Fair deal."

"No deals."

"Very well. We'll be on our way then. In our good time, of course. Want to really experience what you've done with the place. We've got our own scripts, so we'll be going with those. Turrah." Muffin waved him away.

"You will leave our castle immediately," the figure instructed.

For a moment, Muffin reminded Seth of Zin standing up to that spider with a single word. "No."

"Then you will die."

The water began to ripple, and the mist changed overhead from white to a strange green—sort of like that barrier. Seth got the idea that whatever was up there was going to try to trap them in, but Muffin didn't seem particularly upset. Seth started to row in earnest away from the figure, but followed the kitsunes' direction. "That's a wall!"

"So?" the kitsune asked.

"I'm not a shapeshifter."

"Yes, that's quite annoying," Muffin agreed. To his surprise, there was a hole halfway up the wall, and a rope led down.

"How am I supposed to get out if the halls are swarming?" Seth demanded.

"The Seth I knew always has another trick," Muffin said, and began climbing up the rope, and Seth didn't hesitate to follow.

What awaited them in the halls was that silver kitsune, in human form. "You're so cute like this," she said, plucking Seth up and nuzzling him. "Didn't Muffin give you the amulet?"

"Yeah, so?" Seth demanded.

"Use the amulet," she told him.

Seth touched the amulet. Nothing happned. The Silver Fox poked him, and suddenly Seth found that he was standing in the hall as a regular human being, staring down at tiny little puppet Muffin.

"You're so handsome no matter what form you take," the silver kitsune crooned, leaning into Seth's personal space.

"Ahem," Muffin chimed.

"Fine," she pouted, and shrank down to her silver fox form. "I'll find your villagers, Seth. See you outside." She dashed down the halls.

"We're going to get caught like this," Seth sputtered.

"Perhaps. Try again," Muffin gestured. Hesitant, Seth took the fox-head medallion, and twisted it again, and he was immediately back to puppet size. Again, human. Again, marionette.

"Now, that's only going to last until the end of the game," Muffin lectured, staying the same. "Keep you and only you safe from all sorts of nasty magics. If you're touching someone who's outside of the castle you can transform them back and forth with you. Won't work on anyone still cursed in the castle. Let's go."

"Where are we going?"

"We might have switched around some boxes, thank me later." He changed into his regular fox form, and led the way down the hall.

Staying human, Seth raced after the kitsune, not sure where they were going. He often forgot he was inside a castle at times, and there were doors and he came to an open area, where a dark wooden carriage was being loaded. Drawn by several tall draft horses, Seth realized the drawbridge ahead of them was down. "Don't rush ahead," Muffin said. "Think."

"What is going on in there?" asked one of the humans ahead of them. There were three or four, at least one left the carriage and disappeared into the castle. Seth wasn't certain if anyone was watching the courtyard from the walls.

"Her note said she faced off against a kitsune. One of the additions must have been in disguise," said the figure.

They weren't going to keep the drawbridge down for long, but if he approached at this size they'd most certainly see him. Seth bristled, then turned back into a marionette before racing ahead. There was a very human driver, and neither he nor the figures in the dark cloaks and masks noticed him approach under the faint moonlight

"We'll keep the gate down after you're gone for the next few weeks. Alert the other towers, burn any suspicious marionettes," said a male. "They're not worth the risk."

"What about the puppeteer?"

"She'll have to be patient. The master won't risk the gate until they're flushed out. If you get suspicious, burn the lot to be safe."

Seth barely had enough time to grab onto the back step before the carriage started to lurch. Seth climbed on and looking back he saw Muffin grinning at him mischievously as the team of heavy horses carried them across the drawbridge.

In the carriage were multiple boxes as well as other supplies and a handful of letters sealed with wax, a sleeping cot and some personal effects. "Anyone awake?" Seth called quietly, the driver ahead didn't acknowledge him so he called again.

Nothing. No one in the shipping containers was calling for help. Seth wondered if they were like Elinor or Rebecca.   Opening the first lid, he found a nondescript puppet connected to marionette strings. Seth remembered Rebecca needed to be cut properly to release the spell, but the scissors were back at camp. He could rescue one or . . . Seth didn't hear the cat watching him from the cot, and it jumped at him and scratched. Seth kicked it off, but he heard the driver snap at his feline. "Kill the rats or else, beast," he muttered, and clicked the reins, the draft horses slowed only slightly.

Seth used strings to hog tie the cat. It fussed and hissed but Seth squeezed it, the feline making a terrible yet hilarious sound.

"Wretched cat," the driver muttered.

Seth lurched when the driver bid the horses to stop, and as he got up Seth could hear his spurs as he walked around to the back door.

Seth found a cane that worked as a cudgel, and waited, human size, and when the man opened the door, brought it down on the man's forehead. Seth shrank down, gripping the rope, and jumped on the man's shoulder, then used them to trip the man. He jumped off, and was human size again. "Where were you going?" Seth asked.

"Boy!" The man pulled out a knife. Seth grabbed his wrist but the man was stronger. Seth shrunk them both down, and just as quick stepped back, and became regular sized again. The man looked at himself, Seth grabbing him as he staggered, unused to his new form. The man did manage to draw blood, but Seth quickly relieved him of the dagger.

"Where were you going?" Seth asked again.

"I'll never tell!" the man declared.

"Okay," Seth said, unceremoniously dumping another puppet out of his box, placing the carriage driver in it, and promptly wrapping it in string. The driver made a lot of noise but the string held. "I wonder how many rocks it'll take to weigh you down in the depths of the lake."

Seth climbed into the carriage seat and turned the horses around. It took a minute for him to orientate, and low and behold, there was a kitsune on the path. The drawbridge was already back up.

"Not bad," Muffin said. "They can't drown, you know."

"I know," Seth said. He gestured, and the kitsune hopped up and sat next to him. "Might make him mouldy, though." He could get much more creative than burning. Seth clicked the reins. It took a bit to get the wagon turned around properly with such a big team and Seth was unfamiliar with their commands. But Seth had led a wagon filled with fleece and supplies many times since he was younger than Louis, and within a few minutes, directed the carriage back to camp.

The silver kitsune scampered out from the shadowy bush, intercepting and leaping onto the seat next to Seth, two small puppets in her mouth. She put them down and transformed into human form.

"Did you have to save Dale?" Seth complained.

"My friend's having a party next week," she said. "You'll be the only human there, without destiny or powers anyway."

"Lay off, he's got a job to do," Muffin said. "So do you."

The silver kitsune slid close to Seth on the driver's bench. "I'll pick you up on my swan." She nuzzled him slightly before changing back to fox form, waiting until there was a soft spot to land before jumping off and disappearing into the woods alongside the road.

"You're welcome," Muffin told Seth as the carriage lurched towards the camp.

"For blowing our cover?"

"Did we?" Muffin asked. "If any of you get caught, they'll think we had something to do with it." He chuckled. "Let's focus on that castle. We'll catch up properly at the party. And for what it's worth: she does make a delicious mouse pie." The kitsune cackled, jumping off before Seth entered the camp.

Fourteen

Seth rolling into camp with a caravan full of supplies and having rescued more poor souls than Lily didn't result in any praise; from the minute he got back he had to help clear out the kitchen tent. Catarina figured it would be less embarrassing for men and women to turn back in separate quarters; Seth initially thought she meant that meant they ought to fix the men first. The doc and squire were still recovering in the main tent, so they cleared out the kitchen tent for the ladies.

Seth determined it was to keep him away from the snacks.

He didn't recognize and had to ask who Caleb was. Lily explained he'd gotten too close to a barrier and fallen, that she'd panicked and brought him out. Tristan initially was going to be that known face when the older squire came to, but confessed to the doctor he didn't want to be anywhere near Caleb when he woke up.

"He's not going to be upset with you," Demetri said. "I'll tune him up if he's being a curmudgeon. Hopefully he's not as beaten up coming out as when he went in. Not to worry, Seth is his friend. Oh, Seth!"

The doc was using sewing needles to assess pain, and whether or not people were cursed or simply sleeping. It took a while for Caleb to start to rouse, but another man moaned. "If you can, try to wake him gently. Louis, fetch more warm broth." The doc hurried to the other man. Seth was happy to kick the lummox out of his bedroll.

"Hey, get up," Seth ordered. Caleb turned in the opposite direction. Clearly he was no longer just enchanted.

Louis entered with a tray and placed it near the doc before moseying to Seth. "My mom usually baked something to get me out of bed," he said helpfully.

"I'll get right on it when the oven is free," Seth said. If he didn't get to nap after everything he did, he didn't see why Caleb got to sleep in, so Seth grabbed a water flask, and poured it over Caleb's face. The squire coughed and opened his eyes. "Wakey-wakey."

Caleb bolted up and seized Seth by his collar, but before launching a pounding, Caleb sputtered, "Seth?" and he was released. Previously kneeling, Seth fell backwards over another comatose patient.

"Before you get up," Louis offered. "You're in the buff."

Seth, the real victim, received a chewing out from the doc, telling him to be more careful or something. "He's awake." Dusting himself off, Seth looked to their patient, who was staring at his hands as if he'd not just used those meat hooks to inflict bodily harm.

"Don't forget to breathe," the doc said to the squire. "How do you feel?"

". . . F . . . .Fine," Caleb said. Seth realized he was expecting the puppets to still have slightly squeaky voices. The squire licked his lips and ran a hand through his hair, and touched the end of his nose and moved the fleshy part. "Demetri? Where are we?"

"The young lady brought you outside the castle. We're in their camp. Cold?" the doc asked, Caleb nodded. "Seth, stop goofing around and bring clothes. Caleb, you're safe. Relax."

Seth and Caleb eyed each other. Seth handed him some larger clothes that they'd managed to scrounge together. Beggars couldn't be choosers. "How'd you know it was me?" Seth asked.

"Uh . . . your stupid haircut."

"Oi!"

Caleb didn't seem to notice. He ran the fabric of the bulky tunic through his thumb and forefinger. "You didn't realize you forgot, did you?" the doc asked. Caleb shook his head. "You'll feel warmer once you're by the fire, but there are women and children about, and you need to be decent. Before you get that shirt on, let me examine your shoulder."

"I don't see any difference. Is there?" Caleb asked.

"Not that I can tell," the doc said, looking him over. "Seems to be the same length, colour." He used a pin the way he had before, poking at fingers. "Interesting. All right, you are flesh and blood, do not attempt to find out for yourself. You move differently, so try not to run around until you get used to walking again. Do not try to hurt yourself, even just to experience it. I don't remember all your injuries from before, but you seem relatively unscathed." The squire nodded. "Let's have a look at that old injury site."

The squire nodded and leaned forward when the doc prodded him. "Still there?"

"Unfortunately. We won't know what that means for a while. If you—" Caleb shook his head, gesturing towards Seth. The furrow in Demetri's brow deepened. "When you develop symptoms come to me immediately. Goodness, you must be freezing. Cover up."

Caleb nodded, pulling on the tunic and accepting the bowl of broth, and drank directly from the bowl, coughing slightly.

"You need to be reminded to swallow and breathe?" Seth asked.

"Who are these people?" Caleb asked, gesturing at the other recovering folk in the tent.

"I rescued nearly forty people who were about to leave on a carriage," Seth humble-bragged. "We are kicking you out of the tent to make room for the next victim."

"I was in a carriage?"

Seth shook his head. *"I rescued forty people. All Lil' did was rescue you.* Come on, let's go bug her."

"Take him to the fire and let him recover," Demetri instructed. "Caleb, you pretty much lost everything besides your father's sword and the belt. Don't even think about touching anything sharper than a fork for the next hour. Oh, this didn't rip, is it important?" Demetri produced a folded piece of paper. Caleb snatched it and hid it in his tunic.

"How long was I out? Is Alanna okay?" the squire asked.

He lost the doc's gaze when another man moaned. "Seth and Louis can tell you what you need to know. Louis, bring more hot drinks, and when I'm done with this gentleman, have Isaac bring in another puppet and the scissors."

"Let's get out of here," Seth gestured. Caleb hesitated at the door flap when the early sunlight hit his face. He glanced up before walking with more purpose to where others were sitting around by the fire.

"Just so you know, I ain't no nanny," Seth said. In the two dozen steps required, he'd lost Caleb, who'd wandered away and was laughing softly at tweeting birds. "Get your butt over here!" Once Seth got Caleb sitting around the fire, Seth retrieved the mandolin, and started to wail on it. "Anyone you recognize?" he asked after a few riffs, gesturing at people around the fire.

Caleb shook his head, and went back to studying his hands before getting up and trying to wander off again to look at a donkey. Seth noticed after he was petting the donkey. "Do ya mind?" He gestured to the fire. The squire rolled his eyes and came back.

"Ah, your friend is awake," Catarina said, wandering over from the kitchen tent. "Seth, cease that infernal racket."

"Why does everyone assume we're friends? Oh, Caleb, you missed an epic . . ."

"The doc wants more hot water," Louis called from the tent.

"And to think Larry thought me making blankets and sweaters was a bad idea," Catarina said, dishing up more broth and bringing it to the men's tent. "Is everyone decent?" Louis opened the flap and accepted the tray. Isaac and Larry were going over the boxes filled with puppets. Catarina returned to scold Seth. "If you're not going to be useful, change jobs with your sister. Let her and Tristan know their friend is awake at least."

Seth lounged on his stump. "I'm minding all these wayward souls I saved while I serenade them on the family heirloom. If you won't sing my praises I'll sing what I like."

Caleb stood up and extended his hand. "My name is Caleb Felvey. I'm a squire serving Castle Mirador. Who may I have the honour of thanking for this camp's hospitality?"

"Ah, someone with manners!" Catarina said, mostly at Seth. "I am Catarina, wife of Larry. He's over there with Isaac."

"Mr. Sprites?" Caleb called.

The pair stopped their respective tasks and made their way towards the fire. "Call me Isaac." Caleb shook both of their hands. "Little different in the flesh, aren't we?" Isaac gestured; there wasn't enough seating for everyone, but they insisted Caleb try to stay warm. "Gave us quite a scare when Lily showed up with you. We've been so busy we haven't had a chance to get her to elaborate."

"You've been up all night?" Caleb asked.

"We were up early," Catarina clarified. "When Seth arrived with a carriage laden with people, we couldn't just leave them."

"We could have waited until we were better organized," Larry pointed out.

"Do not start," Catarina said. "Or I'll have that woman work her charms and put you in a box."

"One thing at a time," Isaac said. "Caleb, anyone who was in that castle for a long time took hours to recover. What you're going through seems to be normal."

"It all just kept going," Caleb said quietly. To Seth, it seemed like just another road and camp near the lake. "The world, I mean."

"You're not the only one," one of the men sitting around the fire spoke up.

"It's beautiful," said a young woman, "but also kind of terrifying."

"I felt the same way when I was released from prison," Isaac said. "You'll be all right. Seems like everyone needs time to adjust. Seth, why don't you go trade jobs with your sister or Tristan?"

"Tristan insists on guarding Madeline," Seth said.

"Who is Madeline?" Caleb asked.

"The woman who kidnapped our villagers," Seth said. Caleb clenched his jaw. "Now, before you go avenging anybody, she's the one who's changes us back and forth. We kind of need her. We figured moving her behind something wouldn't make it so easy for people to get mad and do something irrational. Don't worry, we have a magic bracelet thingie.

I could explain it but I'm sure it's not really sinking in." Seth got up. "I am not sorting through clothing, just so you know. Wait here."

Now that their camp consisted of more than a few tents and a lone wagon, the carriage was a late arrival and served as a decent barricade so long as folk stayed on the far side of it. Seth found Tristan watching Madeline while Lily was attempting to make Alanna a dress from the clothing they'd pilfered from the carriage. Madeline might have been their captive, but she was given too much freedom, at least in Seth's opinion, but now, she could at least earn her keep looking through the clothing and cataloguing it. It was a bunch of useless prissy things—fine gloves, boots meant for dancing, coats with embroidery, the sorts of things people who weren't camping might enjoy. There was the odd useful thing here or there, better than nothing, but he wondered if farmers and the commoners in town would be interested in any of it.

"Hey," Seth said to Lily, "they want you back at the fire to help."

"All right." Lily said, and Seth looked, noting that the magic bracelet was around Tristan's wrist. He seemed more confident with it on, but he also suspected he'd be all too happy if Madeline tried anything. Lily finished the hem of Alanna's dress before she made a motion to leave them. "How's that?"

"Well, you tried." Alanna giggled doing a twirl. Alanna's new dress was a shirt Lily had cut down to size. Lily could sew but she was no Tiffany, and given how much Alanna wanted to run around, it was amazing she'd accomplished anything.

"Aren't you going to help?" Madeline asked once Lily and Alanna departed towards the fire. Seth got back to playing the same chord over—and over—and over again.

"Nope," Seth said, meaning every word *and* note.

~*~

"Cay!" Alanna squealed and burst into a run. Isaac warned her to watch the fire, and Caleb moved away from it and picked her up. "I can spit now!"

Lily already knew what Caleb looked like, as she'd sat with him until Larry pointed out that the squire would be confused and disorientated, and probably wouldn't appreciate having her or any other woman leering at him. She wasn't leering so much as curious; she hoped that he was at least not funny-looking. While they were within a few inches of one another, she decided he had nice cheekbones, and generally good bone structure, though it was hard to tell with that patchy growth of whiskers. He kept growing until she barely came up to his shoulder and, among other features one obtained from training with weapons, no one could accuse him of having skinny legs. All of which was all fine before he was staring at her.

He spoke to Alanna quietly, his gaze narrowed and lips thinned. Lily made her way to them. "Are you all right?"

He stammered, "What happened?"

Lily gestured for him to follow. He put Alanna down and they moved to nearby trees surrounding their camp. She was sure everyone wanted to hear what they were saying, so she kept her voice down. "The butterflies dragged you to the barrier and incapacitated you. Your . . . friend broke through the wall and saved us."

"How could Eth—" Caleb began before his eyes widened. "Where is he? My *other friend*, I mean."

"He didn't say where he was flying off to. After he got us out, he insisted I turn you back. He was going to take you with him. I said I'd look after you."

" . . . huh."

Huh? All she got was a *huh*?

Alanna had followed after them and had grabbed onto Caleb's arm. He bent down and she climbed onto his shoulders. The squire stood once Alanna was comfortably seated. Now they could *both* talk down to her. "She has a talking kitty!"

"Are you and Lily friends now?" Caleb asked Alanna.

Alanna let out an exaggerated sigh. "I guess. She's bossy and won't take me to catch frogs," Alanna told him. "You're bossy too, sometimes. Where's Esther and Ethan?" She rubbed the side of his face. "Are you trying to grow a beard? *Squires aren't allowed.*"

"I would hardly call this a beard," Caleb told Alanna.

"Alanna, I need to talk to Caleb," Lily said. "It shouldn't take more than a few minutes."

"Okay," Alanna said, beaming intently at Lily. "How long is a few minutes? Then can I show him the baby ducklings?"

"Why don't you tell me where to find the ducklings? Then I need to talk to Lily alone," Caleb said.

"Why aloooooone?" Alanna asked.

"Super secret knight stuff," Caleb said.

"She's not a knight," Alanna pointed out.

"Show me the ducklings," Caleb told Alanna. He gave Lily an apologetic look and Alanna pointed. Caleb not quite being as easy to steer as a horse, they walked into the bush towards the lake, never quite leaving view from the camp. Alanna squealed in delight and demanded to be put down. Lily wasn't sure if she ought to follow or not, but Alanna raced back after a few minutes, Caleb following at a much more leisurely pace. "There are FOUR of them! *Your kitty got one.*"

Alanna looked like she was getting ready to tell the squire to defend the ducklings but Catarina cut in. "Has she been down for a nap yet?" Catarina poked Lily slightly with her wooden spoon. "I told you she can't be up all hours."

"Four year olds don't need naps," Alanna declared defiantly.

"Well forty year olds certainly do," Isaac said.

"I told you this would be too hectic for children," Caleb told Lily.

"As for you—thinking we would be burdened by this wonderful treasure," Catarina lectured via wooden spoon, Alanna shaking her finger at him in agreement. "When you march back in that castle, you and Lily bring as many back as you can manage safely. Understood?"

Caleb gestured to the camp. "How are you going to manage—"

"You let us worry about that," Catarina said. "You do the flashy rescuing, I'll worry about where they lay their heads. Brigid!" Catarina called. Brigid ducked out of the kitchen tent. "Think you can put this one down for a nap?"

"Will do," Brigid said, going to take Alanna, who instead insisted on walking back to the lake, but Brigid quickly corrected course.

"Tell me a story," Alanna insisted. "One about talking kitties!"

Catarina watched them go before dressing down the pair of them. "Lily, if you can spare a minute help Isaac do inventory so I know how much food I can make without going to town for supplies."

"Cook up what we have," Isaac called. "Once we're organized, I'll send one of the boys or Lily for supplies."

"For forty people?" Larry asked.

"No one in this camp is a burden," Catarina said. "Seth's offered to hunt and fish, we'll figure the rest out. Food might be simple, and you might have to start heading for home earlier than later," she told Larry.

"I'm not leaving you here," Larry said.

"Half of these people were taken from Taralee," Catarina said. "That's across the sea. They're probably anxious to go home."

"I can't crew it by myself. Seth's got a knack for sailing, but he's the most capable at sneaking in and out of the castle," Larry said. "Look what he did by himself!"

"Let's get through the day first," Isaac said. "We can sell the carriage and horses to someone in town."

"The carriage is transportation and shelter," Larry muttered. "If you want me shuttling people across the sea, that's one thing, but we need to get there and not all of them are as spry as Seth."

"We need to think before we make any decisions," Catarina said. "But there's things that need doing now. If you'll excuse me, most of these people haven't had anything to eat in years."

"I don't like leaving the sorceress out of eyesight," Larry muttered. Lily knew he meant Madeline. "I'll go check on the animals and make sure Seth hasn't let her wander off." Everyone in camp could definitely hear the sound he was making, so Seth was fine.

She looked to Caleb, who shrugged, so they went back to sit at the fire. Lily waited for him to talk, say something, but he stayed quiet until Boscoe came out from the bush. She knew Seth somehow had to do with his sudden . . . *development*, but the kitsune insisted she'd known him since he was small and this was normal for kitsunes, and had changed colours and patterns to prove a point before settling on white. He took one look at them, and fox-trotted right up to the squire.

"Look at this little guy," Caleb put out a hand for him to sniff. "With two tails?"

"Caleb, meet Boscoe," Lily began, "he's—"

"Not a kitty," Boscoe said, glaring in the direction of the kitchen tent. Several of the folk around the fire backed up.

"Why do you have a kitsune? Don't you know they're bad luck?" asked a young woman at the fire.

"Not necessarily," Caleb said.

Boscoe began sniffing the squire like there were treats hidden somewhere. "Oh? An expert, are we?" the kitsune asked. "Think of the stories, of nasty tricks and cunning wiles!"

"Foolish foxes indebted to giants and chased off by farm dogs," Caleb replied. "Journeying all the way intending to betray the hero, only to fumble in the final act."

"No kitsune would ever be outsmarted by a common mutt! Consider the tales where we consume your very souls," Boscoe scolded. Caleb hesitantly pet Boscoe, who gave a playful nip at his left ear. "You taste terrible! Bleh! I'd rather have a nice goose!"

"You know about kitsunes?" Lily asked. "From the castle?"

The squire shook his head. "We have quite the library at the castle, but my mom used to tell us stories about them. She is . . . she *was* foreign; my dad met her abroad."

"Like Merilon, where I'm from?"

Caleb shook his head. "Ever hear of a kingdom called Nishan?"

"I've heard of it . . . " He did have slightly angled eyes, and perhaps his skin was of a slightly darker hue, but if he didn't say anything, she wouldn't have noticed. "So you're . . . part Nishanese?"

"Never been there. I can speak some." The kitsune didn't skip a beat and spoke to the squire in a different tongue. The squire replied in kind. The kistune and squire bantered back and forth and seemed to laugh at a joke, before Caleb glanced at her. "We're being rude, no one else here understands us."

The kitsune laughed. "I barely understand you, your accent is *terrible*."

"Lily, can you help me with the porridge?" Catarina called.

"Be right there," she replied. She handed out bowls and when she looked back at Caleb and Boscoe, it seemed that Boscoe and Caleb were speaking Nishanese, and Boscoe was helping him pronounce certain words.

"Thanks," Caleb said upon accepting his bowl. "Can I help?" He pushed away the kitsune nose.

"When you're feeling up to it, we'll go talk to Tristan," Lily said. "He's kind of nervous to see you."

"That's silly, but okay." The squire shovelled down most of his food, and as soon as he made a gesture to stand, Boscoe jumped into his lap and settled down for a snooze. "Get."

"No," the kitsune declared, lounging harder. "You have been chosen."

Caleb dumped the kitsune, who glared after Caleb while he put his bowl with the other washables, thanked Catarina, then followed after Lily as she took him away from the fire. Dale appeared to be trying to have a conversation with her brother, who was still strumming.

Tristan stood to attention when he saw Caleb.

"Relax, Tristan," Caleb said. "How are you doing?"

"Darius is just confused," said the younger squire.

"I didn't ask that," Caleb said. "Are you okay?" Tristan nodded. "How long does it take to start feeling normal?"

"It's weird, isn't it?" Tristan asked. "First few hours are the worst. I was much better in the afternoon than the morning. Still kind of surreal. Are you still injured? Demetri said most of your scrapes and bruises are gone."

"Pretty sure I look like I got run over by a horse, but I feel fine," Caleb admitted. "Guess we'll find out in a few hours. Excuse us," Caleb said to Lily, and he and Tristan walked off a short distance to talk.

Dale gestured. "He's from the castle?"

"You were in the castle," Seth pointed out.

"That's not what I meant," Dale said. He gestured at the pair of squires returning.

"Can I interest any of you in this fine gentleman's shoe?" Seth asked, the shiny footwear in question was gold and crimson with a heel and giant ribbon.

Caleb found a set of soft-soled boots that were more or less practical, besides the leather laces. Took him a while to lace them up, but they appeared to fit. "Where'd all this come from?"

"This all came from the carriage last night," Seth said, gesturing to the clothes. "You're welcome."

"Maybe after they string people they steal the real clothes and re-sell them?" Dale asked, looking through things. "This all looks unworn." There was a lot of delicate embroidery and other embellishments.

"You got me," Seth said before looking to Caleb. "You still whoo-hoo in the head?" Seth gestured with his fingers.

"I am not whoo-hoo in the head," Caleb told him, making the same gesture back.

"You're from the castle," Dale said to the squires.

The squires glanced at one another, Caleb answered, "Yeah?"

"What's really going on in there?" Dale asked.

Caleb gestured to Madeline, who was watching them all keenly. "I'll tell you what I know over there." He gestured to where he and Tristan were a moment before. Dale followed the squires, Seth got up to follow as well. "Someone needs to watch her," Lily said.

"So you do it," Seth said, leaving the mandolin resting against a treestump.

"Amazing how much things change but things stay the same," Madeline said. "You've rescued most of your villagers. I didn't think you would."

Lily kept Madeline's gaze. "Why are those songs stuck in my head?"

"You've much to learn," Madeline said with a soft chuckle. "I'd be wary—soon they're not going to trust you, once they learn the truth about your part in what happened." Madeline gestured to the mandolin. Lily didn't touch it. Madeline seemed amused before the boys joined them. "Gentlemen."

"We know you're doing this on someone's behalf," Dale said. "Who?"

"Are you going to torture me to find out?" Madeline asked.

"Just tell us what's going on in that castle," Seth said.

"I'll tell you what I told them before: I was a regular young woman who had dreams and aspirations of becoming a dancer. And I was wonderful," she said. "But, because I didn't come from wealth or breeding . . . " She wrinkled her nose at the squires.

"Nice try, we're not important," Caleb said.

"Among your class, perhaps. To those of us on the outside looking in, you have so much that you never earned," Madeline said. "*Class*. The rich and landed came in, talentless, looking to play, without passion. When they got bored, they frittered off into their next indulgence, probably to paint terrible pictures or write hackneyed plays that never should have seen the light of day. When you're a woman, your value decreases with time. I was offered . . . a chance to make my dreams come true. And I took it."

"Yeah, yeah, you stubbed your big toe and it turned out selling your soul was a bad idea," Seth said. "Lily, can we talk? The goons will watch Madeline."

The squires gave smiles suggesting that they were happy to take over this particular task. Lily followed her brother and Dale to where the donkeys grazed. "I want to thank you both for coming after us," Dale said. "As much as it scares me, I'll go back and help you get your sister, Molly, too, if we can, but I have to think about Brigid and Louis. Shoot—what is our end goal here?"

Lily's heart raced. "It was to find you and bring everyone from the village home. But we can't leave people like—" she gestured back at the squires and Madeline, who were also having a conversation.

"That's hundreds of people," Dale pointed out. "You've been lucky because you've been sneaking around. You're going to get caught."

"We agreed to work with them," Seth explained. "They'd help get you to us and we'd help them sneak some of their people out. No one's asking you to do nothing, Dale."

Dale asked more questions and Lily tuned out of her brother's replies.

They were friends when they were younger; bunching her fists, she realized Dale might hate her, and make Brigid and Louis hate her too.

"I have to make a confession." Dale looked at her quizzically. "You were both there when that woman put that witch's mask on my face in the town hall and we performed that play. I lost control, tried to convince myself it was all in my head. The next day I went to her and she put another mask on my face. She made me lure you into the woods."

"That was you," Dale said, raising his eyebrows. "In the glen, singing."

"Dale, I'm so sorry . . . I didn't mean for any of this to happen."

"None of us knew what she was doing," Dale said, scowling. "We helped her!"

"I went back!" Lily said.

"Don't beat yourself up," Seth told Lily. "I never blamed you."

"Here's the thing: last night Caleb and I were talking, and that song I sang to lure you? I sang a little bit, Caleb said my eyes started to glow yellow. I felt strange. I haven't been able to play my mandolin without accidentally spilling into her songs." She gestured to the bracelet still around Tristan's wrist. "Mama Fern gave that bracelet to me, and I thought it was to keep me safe, but I think it was to lock the curse inside me into place."

"Who?" Dale asked.

"A kitsune," Seth said. "They kind of helped us. Why would she do that? She's your friend."

Lily stammered, "I don't know."

"Do you feel like you're under her control?" Dale asked. Lily shook her head. "Then it shouldn't be a problem. Other than you guarding her, but we can do that and you can keep your distance. And no singing or whatever."

"Easy for you to say, you unmusical lout," Seth said, glancing at the two squires and Madeline. "They were prisoners stuck in there like you."

"No, him and the other knights had it better than we did," Dale said. "What's our goal here? You came to save us—and I'm grateful you did. But it's only a matter of time until you get caught. I say we rescue Tiffany and Molly and go home."

"We left messages for our parents. Ours care enough to come," Seth pointed out. "You go home with Brigid, and leave the heroics to the heroes."

"You really think you two can make a difference?" Dale demanded. "You're a lousy hunter and but because that weirdo taught you to play with a sword you can stand up to that? You aren't heroes, you're shepherds!" Dale's brow softened upon realizing how harsh that sounded. "Sorry, it's just . . . none of this is right. I mean, we're all shepherds. This is beyond any of us."

"Speak for yourself, *miller*," Seth said without skipping a beat. "Imma hitch up my ponies and go for a carriage ride, you can walk to the port."

"Excuse me, I'm going to go help." Lily started back towards the main camp but pausing, turned abruptly when Dale called after her to wait.

"Lily, you're going to get hurt if you keep this up."

"Really?" she asked. "You don't think I didn't get bruised training with Zin? If it wasn't for *that weirdo* none of us would be standing here having this conversation."

"I didn't mean—" Dale started, but she didn't care to listen to what he had to say.

That was probably the most honest Dale's ever been, she thought, walking to Catarina. "How are we doing?"

"Oh, my Larry is right about being able to help people go home. We have a sail boat! He'll need a hand to help him, and if I leave, who will run the camp if we're shuttling people across the sea?"

Lily frowned. She supposed Seth and the squires could run the missions, and she could run the camp with Isaac. Isaac was probably missing his family. Would it make more sense to send Larry and Isaac? "One problem at a time. How can I help you right now?"

"Well, you'd best ask that Demetri fellow what he'll be needing. We can send Louis or Seth to fish. What did you find from the clothing? Is there anything not covered in lace?"

"Handful of items seemed decent," Lily said. "Might make sense to try to trade them for supplies. Any idea how much draft horses eat?"

"Probably similar to my oxen; they can graze somewhat but between them and the donkies they'll pick this area clean, we'll have to move them to different locations or buy them feed. Cleaning after them's another matter altogether. When you have a chance, we're going to need more water."

Lily hadn't noticed Caleb was standing behind her until she backed into him. "Where are the buckets?" Caleb asked. "You're boiling the water?" Catarina gestured towards her bucket station. Caleb nodded, looked to Lily and said, "Dale and Tristan are on guard duty." He grabbed a small hatchet and all four buckets before heading down the road away from the town. There was a more direct path to the lake; he'd used it to observe ducklings.

"He doing all right?" Larry asked Lily, who shrugged. "I can't read your mind, but I can read your face. Go after him."

"I won't be long," Lily said, belting Caleb's sword; it seemed silly to carry two but figured he'd want it back and he seemed normal enough. Boscoe came out of the bush and followed beside her, shooting her a cheeky grin when she looked down at him. "Are you sure you're the same fox?"

"*Kitsune*. Don't worry about me, find your human."

"I don't think he's lost."

"So you say." She heard chopping, and found her squire making a pole to carry the buckets. He'd gotten a hatchet and was making notches to hold them so that he could balance it on his shoulders and carry all four buckets without spilling. He stopped when he saw her and looked to the castle.

"I don't see any movement," he said. "You?"

It was so still, she had a hard time believing that was where she'd been the last two nights. "No."

"Stop fretting," he told her, "I've been assisting in camps since I was a page. Probably before when I was underfoot."

"Are you mad at me?"

"What? No." He turned and hurried towards a stone bridge. There was a small creek they'd missed where fresh water trickled in to the moat before expanding to the lake. He washed his face before filling the buckets. "I could never argue with Peanut."

"I'm sorry, I know you didn't want to be out here."

"I've wanted nothing else but to be out here. The real world feels different than what I remembered." He balanced the pole and declined her help and started to walk back to camp. "My brain's not good enough for banter. Give me another hour."

"I have your sword. I figured you'd want it back as soon as you were able. Do you have any more questions about what happened?"

"Got any more kitsunes or other surprises?" he asked, squatting down without spilling his buckets. "I'd like to hear the story you were trying to tell me in the castle a little later. Right now it seems like you need help. I'll take my sword back."

Lily unbelted it, but Boscoe out of nowhere nabbed it from Lily, ran towards the lake, and pitched it in. Then he sat down, never breaking the squire's gaze, and scratched behind his ears.

"Why did you do that?" Caleb demanded. "That was my father's!" He tried to take his boots off, the lacing slowed him down.

"You're cold, let me do it," Lily said, sliding off her overdress. She shot Boscoe a sour look, who simply beamed at her. Caleb on the other hand turned around and shielded his eyes.

"Could you not?" he asked.

"I know you can see me, stop pretending like you can't or I'm indecent." Her chemise and trousers were dark, chosen for adventuring thank you very much; she'd learned what to wear to repell after a wayward ewe long ago. She hung her overdress on a low branch and waded into the cold water.

"Do you have any idea how long it took me to get these on?" Caleb asked the kitsune, who went, *Yip yip!* "Fine. To your left," he offered. Part of her spitefully wanted to disobey him, but figured his father's sword was important. "How's the water?"

"Refreshing," she called back, but paused when she got to about her navel. She didn't think it was that deep. "Tell me this lake doesn't have an overabundance of leeches."

"I'll help you pick them off," Caleb offered.

"You're very kind," she replied. The water was murky and dark, she couldn't see his sword so she felt around with her feet and finding it, resigned herself to the dive. Thankfully, she retrieved the sword on her first attempt, and she brought it backup tip first.

Caleb had waded out anyway, but really had only gotten to his knees. He also looked at her with wide eyes, kind of like an idiot for a half-second. "What?" she asked, wading towards him, offering him the sword. "Go on, take it—make sure I didn't find someone else's sword."

Caleb hesitated, but upon grasping the handle unsheathed it, then cast a glare back at the kitsune, who put a paw to his nose and stuck out his tongue. "You're not a kitsune or a mermaid, are you?" he asked eventually.

Lily couldn't stifle a guffaw. "You see a tail or scales?" she asked, brushing her hair behind her ears.

"Sounds like something a lake monster would say," he said with just a hint of teasing.

She flicked water at him, but the way the way the water and sunlight reflected off the blade, she noticed engraving. "It's got an inscription?"

He held it so she could read it. "Old language. Means 'Do not unsheathe me without reason, do not wield me without valour.' Hey, you got a little leech, right—" Caleb gestured to his own neck.

"Waaah!" Lily panicked and fell backwards, and upon getting up, seeing him chuckling and realizing it was a ruse, reached for the sword. "Give me that! Boscoe didn't get it in far enough." He had longer strides so she had to settle for splashing him.

He splashed her back, before it ended with them both laughing and he waited for her to catch up and practically handed the family heirloom over. "Do not throw it in," he said seriously. Before she asked, he dove in, and swam out to deeper water.

If she wasn't trusting him with his sword she might have followed, instead she watched him briefly before she waded back to the riverbank, doing her best to be stern with the kitsune. "Don't do that again."

"What? He hasn't had a bath in two years," Muffin said. "Next time, let him pick the leech off."

"There wasn't a leech," she said, wringing out her hair on top of the kitsune, who grumbled and scooched."I don't know if the name Boscoe suits you anymore."

"Oh, something more mature? Renard is a classic. Let's see how creatively you stack up."

"I think you're a cute little . . . *Muffin.*"

The kitsune gave her a canine-grin. "Call me Boscoe," he said, reaching for a folded paper sticking out of Caleb's boot.

"No swiping!" she slapped his paw.

"This is why everyone loves Seth," he grumbled, before they both turned their attention to the soaking squire coming to join them. "How was the swim?"

"Don't do that again, kitsune," Caleb said, belting his sword.

"You needed the exercise," Boscoe said. "Don't drip on me!"

The squire leaned over the kitsune more and wrung out the hem of his tunic. Soaking wet, Boscoe bounded off into the bush. "You're right: that was refreshing. Might jump in again after we get that camp running." He carried the boots and managed the pole over one shoulder.

People were moving about the camp more than when they'd left. Lily didn't think they were gone for that long. A different young man was by the fire now, and most talked to each other about the dreams that played over and over in their heads, or where they were from, and that they weren't going to be sitting around idly either.

Another man was taking care of the donkeys and another grabbed the buckets from Caleb after he dumped the water. "We decided," he said. "No offence to the people here, but you look like you're the best one in a fight by half a span. We would like for you to stay around the camp, until some of those men with the shiny armour wake up."

Catarina squawked seeing them. "When I said get water, I meant using buckets. Stop dripping all over my camp."

"The water's best at the bottom of the lake," Caleb offered. "She wouldn't believe me."

"Don't be smart unless it's funny," Larry lectured.

Lily donned the crimson blouse she'd gotten from Mama Fern and a riding skirt, before she combed through her hair and let it dry loose. Caleb changed into something more fitted; when she found him he was going through the people in the boxes with Isaac. He didn't know the people around the fire, but he did recognize several people in the boxes.

"Unfortunately, keeping people in the boxes is the best way to keep them from getting tangled." Isaac explained.

There were only four marionettes in armour out of the thirty-eight boxes that came from the carriage. Caleb's eyes went wide at one man, who Lily thought was nondescript except perhaps he had a bushy beard and hair redder than hers. "Save him next. And you won't need to put him in a tent, those are absolutely his clothes." Lily assumed the horrible tunic was some sort of bizarre house sigil. Caleb confirmed this wasn't the case.

"Do you know him?" Isaac asked.

Caleb nodded. "I should be back from town before he wakes up. You ready to go, Tristan?"

The other squire was petting the draft horses and nodded. "I'm coming, too!" Louis called, and was given a leather satchel by Isaac, who was lecturing him to get a decent pair of boots from the cobbler.

Lily pressed the silver earrings into Louis' hands. "Trade them for what you need, it'll be fine." She looked at the ring and bracelets; they were worth a lot more but it sounded like no one in town would pay a fraction of their worth. She knew Caleb had a lot on his mind, but he was probably the only one who had any idea what they were worth. "See if anyone is willing to pay for more expensive items?" She showed him the bracelets and rings. "We need food more than we need gold."

His lips thinned and he nodded, and Louis tucked the jewellery into the leather satchel as well. "I'll see what I can do, I'm going to try to find Alanna's parents. Look after her until I'm back." After the trio set out, Seth realized he'd been left behind on what he considered precious Man Time, and raced after them about twenty minutes later, taking the mandolin with him.

After two hours of their absence, Catarina became annoyed, so she sent Larry to check in on them. Most folk around the camp were useful; even if they weren't utilitarian time went faster with one older man telling stories to those waking up, and one woman was not used to such a caravan lifestyle but was a voice of calm reason and helped other women know they were safe. An hour after Larry's absence, a rider came from town. Given his crisp grey clothes he looked like a courier.

"Lady Catarina?" he asked, and Catarina walked over, ripping open the letter and looking like she was going to throw it into the fire. "The nerve of that man! I can't just leave."

"Everything all right?" Lily asked. The rider handed her packages containing clothing—simple things, a blue dress with stockings and shoes looking like they'd fit Alanna. Nothing expensive but more practical than most of what they'd found in that carriage.

"They don't have any extra money," Isaac offered. "We didn't send them with enough to purchase this."

"I assure you it's all been paid for," the courier said.

"They must have sold the jewellery," Lily offered. "I'm sure Larry . . ."

"Spent our precious funds on a box of chocolates! Fiddle-dee-dee! Here I am starved of oats and the other simple things I asked for," Catarina said, hands on hips. She handed the box of chocolates around to the people at the fire, who didn't complain. Lily took two; one for herself and another for Alanna. "Lily, go rouse Alanna, and see her in this dress."

"What does the message say?" Isaac pressed.

"My jolly husband thinks I can just waltz into town and join him at some pub! Bring Alanna, he says. Yes, right after I finish me manicure and do my hair and make pie. The nerve of some people."

"We're managing fine, Catarina," Isaac said. "Go see what Larry wants."

"No, Lily is going to march into town—with Alanna.If her parents are there, they must be worried sick—and she will bring the large children back here with the supplies I asked them for hours ago. Won't you, love?"

"I'll get Alanna," Lily offered.

"The note also says to bring some of the fine items from the carriage," Catarina muttered as Lily made her way to the kitchen tent. "What are they up to?"

The dress and stockings fit Alanna and the girl was soon happily skipping towards town, eating both chocolates as she'd misunderstood Lily's offer of a choice. Only holding Lily's hand when she balanced on an old stone ridge, she asked questions about snails and stopped abruptly at one of the trees. "It's just like from the drawing Cay showed us! Oh, an acorn!" She handed it to Lily to bring along. "Did you have your super secret knight meeting? Are you a knight?"

"No."

"Then you shouldn't listen to the super secret meetings. You'll tell all the secrets."

"I'll try not to."

"Good. Because Cay can be really grumpy sometimes." Alanna let out an exaggerated sigh. "Ethan makes him less grumpy, but Ethan gets sad sometimes. Cay got sad by the lake. He didn't want to look at the ducklings *at all*."

"How sad did he get?"

"He didn't cry; I will cry if we lose any more ducklings. Tell your kitty *no*."

Besides the first day of riding through it, Lily hadn't explored the town. At its height, Mirador was once a small city. The oldest part of town snaked around the lake, with old statues that depicted heroes and maidens, often in pairs at crossings. Some of the buildings were quite large, and she'd passed more than one large fountain. At intervals they changed, first a stone work depicting a girl with a vase, then a boy with the same vase several blocks down. People were out and about. Some looked at Lily suspiciously, but for the most part folk were about their business. There were a few stray cats and chickens, and a goat had managed to climb onto someone's roof, which reminded her of home.

The Dark Horse Tavern was a two-storey inn, featuring many carvings of horses and woodland animals such as badgers and ravens into the door frames and bannisters, as well as several portraits of folk and jousting from tourneys past. The central inner wall was encased in stone, where a large, crackling fire gave off comforting warmth.

Lily spotted everyone but Tristan in the main pub, which for the most part was made up of trestle tables and stout chairs with a handful of booths were in the back. Seth and Louis wore matching sky blue shirts and brown jerkins as well as bracers and new boots that matched. Louis looked like he'd had a haircut, and possibly shaved, even though she hadn't seen any prior evidence of needing it. They were busy doodling at a long table. There were also three people she didn't recognize, nursing drinks with them.

At a smaller table, Caleb and Larry were speaking to a well-dressed man in yellow and purple with an impressively tall hat. Caleb was signing papers and Larry, arms crossed, pointed and asked questions. Caleb seemed like he was done with everything before she got there, and when he spotted her and Alanna, leapt up.

Larry grabbed his arm. "Finish up so the he can get on with his day."

"Be right there," Caleb said, hurriedly scribbling and not bothering to sit back own. He was wearing a similar variation as the boys' new clothes, and he'd lost that stubble. He looked like someone from a castle.

"You said that ten minutes ago," Louis called. "Lily, I got to go to a real barber shop! They're letting me come by and help tomorrow."

Larry excused himself and walked to Lily and Alanna. "Let me guess: Catarina's asking what's taking so long? Tell her I'm getting everything she wanted, including what she didn't ask for."

"Did you sell the jewellery?" Lily asked.

"We'll explain shortly. Go have a seat and feed Alanna."

A server came over and put bread on the long table. Alanna went for the ink and paper while the boys went for the food. "Alanna, do you want some bread?"

"I'm gonna draw Peanut!"

"One drawing, then you eat something," Lily said, Alanna nodded and got to drawing.

"A-Alanna?" one of the men asked, standing. He walked to the young girl, who barely gave him a sideways glance now that she had copious amounts of ink at her disposal. "Do . . . do you remember me?"

Alanna shook her head *no*, and pointed to Lily. "She has a talking kitty!"

"Why didn't he warn me?" The man hugged Alanna, picking her up. "You smell like soap."

"That squire, I'll wring his fool neck." The man had tears in his eyes.

"Like my new dress? It's not as fancy as when I was in the castle," Alanna said. "But I like this one better because out here I can do this." She put her finger in her mouth and proceeded to make popping noises. She made a face when she realized she got ink on her tongue. Lily wiped her hands and had her drink some water.

"Please tell me we're done," Caleb said nearby, sounding incredibly defeated.

The well-dressed man nodded. "For you. My work has just begun. I assume you'll be taking lodgings at this inn?" Caleb nodded, rubbing his temples. "All right. Is that Catarina?" The man asked, gesturing at Lily. Caleb shook his head. "Please have Catarina come to the bank and we'll give her signing authority. We've confirmed who you are and it's acknowledged that your father has been buried these past two years. You are now entitled to the following family accounts we discussed." The man gave him a piece of paper as well as a sealed envelope, which Caleb immediately opened and took the key, handing it to Larry. "We do not have access to all of your money, as most of it is being held in trust at the City of Innesbrooke."

"Thank you," Caleb said, shaking the man's hand.

"Young man, I personally handled your grandparents' accounts, and your parents'. It is a pleasure to continue doing business with your family." He produced a small sack of coins, which Larry proceeded to count and confirm. "This should cover discretionary spending in the meantime. And I do say, exercise restraint. Young men such as yourselves have gotten much more lucrative inheritances and through cavalier lifestyles have blown through them quite quickly." The well-dressed man gathered his paperwork, declining to stay for lunch.

When Caleb finally looked at Lily, he was smirking. "That is the dumbest look I've ever seen," he told her. "What did you think we were doing? Your camp needed more supplies. I needed witnesses who recognized me. I promised them a meal and an explanation."

The eldest stranger who had recognized Alanna was on him, and Caleb's smirk vanished. "Why didn't you say she was with you? Out there with strangers? Why didn't you bring Alanna immediately to my shop?"

"She was safe in the camp," Caleb insisted. "And she wasn't with a stranger." He gestured to Lily. "This is Lily. And I didn't know if you were still in business."

"Where did you think I'd be?" asked the older man. "Do you know what they want to charge me for a hole in the wall in Yarrosfeld? Lily, is it?"

"Sorry, let's start again," Caleb said. "Wallace, this is Lily O'Connell, Seth's sister. Lily, this is Wallace Talsby. He's been cutting my hair since I was five."

"You were four," Wallace said. He gave Lily an appraising look, but he was back on Caleb. "Squire, you have a lot of explaining to do."

"You want to hear it now or wait for Tristan to get back?" Caleb asked.

"I wanted an explanation when you walked through my door over two hours ago."

"How many more children are back there?" the woman sitting with the other man asked. She wore a well-tailored green dress.

"Twenty two," Caleb said quietly, and introduced Lily to the others. The woman, Ingrid Hassaway, was a weaving and textile trader, and eagerly looked over the clothing Lily had brought. The other man was Ivan Gabbron, and he ran a haberdashery and had outfitted the boys that morning.

"This must be your jewellery," the woman said, handing the ring and bracelets back to Lily. "He wanted me to hold onto it until he paid me back, I only kept them to keep those boys from losing it."

"You might want to consider storing it in the bank if you're not going to wear it," the haberdasher offered.

"Do I get a team shirt, too?" she asked.

Ivan chuckled. "I figured making them a matched set would help us remember who the newcomers are."

"Just don't hold him responsible for any problems my brother or Louis causes," Lily said. "Where's Tristan?"

"On an errand," Larry said.

"If everything's under control, I can let Catarina know to come here," Lily said. "Alanna, will you behave or—"

"Please stay," Caleb said. "Also, you have to try these apples." Caleb had a rather large bag of them as well as some other supplies on the bench she hadn't noticed.

Caleb was done his before Lily had bitten hers and he gestured that she had to try, but in her defence she'd seen horses take smaller bites. "Did you know that we have over twenty varieties of apples in this part of the county?" He had another bag of red and green and another of golden ones. "I should have let you pick. You can try them all if you want."

"Tell Apple Jack no one cares and we were promised real food," Seth called.

"I still don't know what a retainer does," Louis chirped.

"Don't disrespect the apples," Caleb said.

"Stop making fun, Seth," Larry said. "You were a puppet for a week and you gobbled down my wife's cooking like nobody's business."

"That's how Seth normally eats," Lily said.

"Have you boys sketched out the maps like I asked?" Larry asked.

"Sort of," Louis said.

"Did you rewrite the To-Do List?" Larry asked.

"I was just about to."

"What have you been doing?" Larry took the small stack of papers.

In their defence, there were two layouts of the castle that they were told to make copies of. Then they decided to make more interesting stuff.

"Now that we're retainers, this is us going on adventures," Louis said, indicating his drawing. "Caleb's obvious because he has a helmet, and Seth has an eye-patch because the eyes weren't symmetrical." Everyone besides Seth was ridiculously jacked and, though Louis was not a terrible artist, he had no idea how most major muscles were supposed to attach.

"I like the horns," Caleb offered.

"So much better than the wolf thing," Louis said.

"No one asked me," Caleb said.

"And this is us shooting celestial meddlers with a canon." Seth was somehow a worse artist.

Larry stumbled across something in the stack of papers and his and Caleb's body language changed. "Wow, this one's really good." Caleb took the paper from Larry and showed Seth. "You should stick to drawing fox-girls."

"Gimme that!" Seth tore up the picture before Lily saw it, though Louis still let out a whistle that indicated he liked what he saw.

"Can you do one like that for me, maybe just a normal girl?" Louis asked. "Not normal but like *that*."

"I can't draw that well!" Seth insisted.

"I drew Boscoe!" Alanna said proudly with an incredibly smudged picture, more ink on her hands than on the paper.

"All right, enough goofing," Ingrid said. "And start explaining."

Caleb nodded. "I was unconscious when the spell hit the castle, but Ethan said they evacuated the royals about two hours before things got weird."

"Yes, we know that," Wallace said.

"Why were you in bed at that hour?" Ivan asked.

"He was on night shift," Ingrid said.

"No, he was dying. Anyway, continue on with your story," Wallace said.

"Oh, skip this part. We all know someone who got out just in the nick of time," Ivan said. "What happened next?"

"I came to, shrunk down and turned into a marionette," Caleb said.

"What, pray tell, is a marionette?" Wallace asked.

"It's a puppet, now shush," Ingrid said.

"Whoever put the spell on the castle wasn't worried about the handful of us in the infirmary, so we had no idea—but we weren't put on string right away. About five of us hid out," Caleb explained.

Lily hadn't heard this part of the story; he mentioned names of people she'd not met but just as it seemed that they were formulating a plan to escape by rappelling out a window, two people entered the tavern. The first one stormed over, Tristan looking apologetic in his wake, wearing the same shirt and jerkin combo as the others, though now Lily noticed there were slight embellishments on the squires' jerkins.

"I'm not selling you this, you understand? It's an indefinite loan." The man had a trim beard with hints of grey and a lean, leathery look. He slammed a gauntlet on the table, to which Caleb picked up and strapped on, seemingly impressed with the quality. The man produced a helmet with a visor that Louis declared was *his* on indefinite loan and, finding Seth's old shirt, starting buffing it. "Full suits are at my home, you'll have to come up with your own wagon!"

"That's fine." Caleb handed the gauntlet to Tristan, and gave him a smile and nod. Tristan grabbed an apple. "Would you like to join us? I've ordered plenty of food. I'm hoping the others get here soon."

The man took a seat next to Larry. "Just tell me when there's fighting. I ain't missing it for nothin'."

"This is good steel," Larry said, examining the gauntlet. "How many can you outfit?"

"None your size. So long as they ain't giants, four. My favourite set might need a polish, might borrow him," he gestured to Louis.

"Smithy said he absolutely has to finish an order,but he's got some equipment to sell us," Tristan offered. "I can get wet stones and oil—Louis and Seth can help me sharpen them."

"Lily, look what I got!" Louis said, holding aloft a sword.

"I told you not in the tavern," Larry said.

Lily gestured and Louis and Tristan took her to the fire to show their swords as Caleb tried to tell the story again. "No family heirloom?" she asked Tristan.

"We both should have more weapons and armour in the castle," Tristan said. "It's getting to it if it's still there that's the problem."

Caleb was doing his best to story tell, but people kept interrupting. A friar joined them. "Caleb?" He rushed over. "Bless you, you're the first face I've seen from the castle in two years! What happened? I have so many questions. Is your lady mother all right?" The friar then looked to Tristan. There wasn't the same sense of familiarity, but he still asked Tristan questions.

"Can we get back to what happened?" asked the man who'd brought the armour.

"We all want to know what's going on," Ivan snapped. "You're done your business with the bank, boy, spit it out."

"Are there more people at your camp?" asked Wallace.

"How many more?" the friar pressed.

Alanna had the fringe of the friar's robe and was tugging it. "Wanna see me jump *really* high?"

"Children," the friar said, eyes watering. "How many, squire?"

Caleb no longer smiled, instead he seemed taken aback.

Larry cleared his throat. "As we discussed before: The squires need to stay here so people who want to see your face know where to find you," Larry said firmly. "Senior squire: If you have a task that needs to be completed, you send *them* to do errands. If they don't perform to Larry's satisfaction, there is no more coming to the pub." Seth and Louis didn't seem to be taking the threat too seriously. Larry looked to Lily. "Junior squire, stay put unless a task requires one of you specifically. If you can manage, Lily," Larry said. "Just point him in the direction he needs to go in and don't let the others talk him into any shenanigans." Larry addressed the friar next. "I'll walk you to the camp. I want to see my leetle wife. She couldn't come here herself for a pint, as the camp wouldn't have fallen apart within the hour." He and the friar left.

"*Leetle wife?*" Tristan asked.

"What is going on at that camp?" asked the haberdasher.

An older woman entered. She embraced Tristan before walking to Caleb. "I needed to see you with my own eyes! Are you all right, and whole?"

"We're fine," Caleb sounded annoyed.

Another man arrived; judging by his cloth Lily assumed he was a farrier. "It's like looking at ghosts."

"Should I start over?" Caleb asked.

"No, you can't start over every time someone shows up," snapped the barber.

"I just got here," the farrier insisted.

"I want to know about those poor souls at the camp," one of the women said.

"That's not what's important," said Ingrid.

"Then stop interrupting him!" the haberdasher snapped.

"I don't care what happened," the man who'd brought in the gauntlet and helmet grumbled. "I want to know who is going to do something about it."

"What do you think I'm trying to do here?" Caleb asked.

"I don't know. So far I'm staring at a whole lot of nothing," the man quipped.

Caleb cocked his head before he stood up. "I need some fresh air." Despite several protests and was out the back door.

"Wonderful," one of the women told the man. The small conversations around the table died. "We can't be fractured. Let him tell us about what's needed at the camp."

"No, we need to know what's going on in that castle," the farrier said.

"I've seen that look before," the short, older woman said. "Men get it after war sometimes. Ain't no bandage for wounds like that."

"Great, we have a knightling without a spine," said the man who'd brought in the armour. "Probably ran off when things got bad."

"He couldn't have walked out, much less run," muttered the farrier.

"Don't dredge up the past," Wallace told him.

"Oh, shouldn't I? Twenty years ago his father was ransomed, my brother never made it home," the man snapped. "Now, do any of you want to tell me where my son is?" The man's anger broke and his stern demeanour softened, and to Lily's surprise, the woman he'd been arguing with got up and embraced the man.

"I should have gone back," the man said, snivelling slightly, still so angry. "I ran like a coward."

"You'd have been stuck there the same as him," another of the women said.

"At least I'd know."

"But we wouldn't."

Lily looked to Tristan; he was staring at the back door. "Watch Alanna," she said to him quietly, getting up and following after Caleb.

She found him in the alley leaning against the side of the tavern, hands behind his head, looking up at the sky.

"Caleb?" she asked. He didn't acknowledge her until she got closer.

"That wasn't two minutes," he said, facing away from her. "I'm fine. I just needed to think."

"Don't let me stop you," she said, and let him have some quiet time. She gave him at least three minutes before she spoke again. "Thank you, by the way."

"For what?"

"The supplies you sent to camp. That can't be cheap."

"I can't believe they sent you out here," he said with a snort. "People of Mirador are really something sometimes. I should get back there before they peck Tristan to death."

"He's fine. Unless it's to the camp I doubt anyone is going anywhere," she said. Another scoff. "Whatever it is, spill it."

He turned away from her, fists clenched at his side. "Four suits of armour? Might as well throw flowers at the drawbridge. I couldn't even get Catarina another tent to help her. I'm such an idiot—!"

"Hey," Lily said, ducking around, putting a hand on his shoulder, but he was doing his best to not look at her. "Don't say mean things about my friend." He was looking up at the sky, his brow tense. "Talk to me."

"It's stupid."

"I don't care."

He hesitated, but kept his eyes fixated on the sky. "I keep expecting strings to come in and rip people away. I'm not sure what real is anymore. It's like the before was a dream, that I'm just back there in that cave and it'll be another trick and I'm falling for it."

When he stepped away from her, she grabbed his hand, like he was leading her to Peanut. She didn't say anything, didn't let him go. He tensed up, but held onto her hand. "You are out of the castle," she said firmly. "You told me that if it's only a handful of people, it's worth it. Give me a good reason why you shouldn't be one of them."

"I told you I could have jeopardized getting other people out." He looked over his shoulder at her. "Are you even real?"

She wasn't sure what to say to that, wasn't sure how much of that was supposed to be a stupid joke. "I'm a little far from my lake, aren't I?"

The back door where they'd come out of opened with a slam and startled them both. "There you are, you numbskull!"

Caleb was in front of her, but when she ducked around to see him she saw the deep voice belonged to the largest man Lily had ever seen. She placed him about the age of forty, with a shaved head and square face. He had a leather-studded hauberk and stormed down the stairs. Caleb strode towards him.

"You remind me of your wretched father!" For a moment he and Caleb stared down, before the larger man grabbed Caleb, giving him the biggest hug, lifting him off his feet. "If I didn't give you up for dead I'd kill you!" He belly-laughed.

"I missed you too, Rodney," Caleb offered.

Rodney put Caleb down. "I'm supposed to talk to you about getting back there and pears or something, as far as I'm concerned, tell everyone to piss off. If I was you I'd be at the bar, not playing whatabout-whatabout."

"Watch your language around women and children," Caleb told him.

"Ah, there's your father's voice, I suppose that'll do. I'll try not to offend your lassie. Now stop running off with strange women and join me for an ale tell me what in the . . . *dickens* happened." Rodney shot Lily a quick wink.

"Lily, this is Rodney—former man at arms for the castle, currently serving as a ranger."

"Captain Rodney, squire," the big man snapped.

"I didn't know that," Caleb said.

"I suppose your ignorance to my promotion can be excused," Rodney said. "I met her brother already, no need for formality. Now get your sorry behind in there. You owe someone a minute of your time."

Another man with a similar uniform to Rodney left the main group and met them when they re-entered the tavern. There was a familiarity to him Lily couldn't place. Tears in his eyes, he embraced the squire, and Caleb was tense but returned it. "Thank you."

Lily looked over them to the crowd. A woman who also wore the green cloak and leather hauberk, was running her hands through Alanna's hair of the exact same colour as the man who'd met them. Alanna called over, "Daddy! Mummy won't stop crying! And I didn't even do nothing." There were about ten of the rangers now, their uniforms varying; some had fur-lined boots and another his bracers had a leather fringe.

"Lily's the one you should be thanking—" Caleb said.

"It was a team effort," Lily interrupted.

The man shook Lily's hand, and rushed back to his family. He picked up his daughter, who hugged him and laughed. Lily watched the reunion, then Caleb. The squire caught her staring at him, and gave her the briefest nod.

"Go see them." Lily gestured.

"I can see fine from here."

"Git." Rodney shoved Caleb towards the reunion. "Thanks for watching the squire. I'll kick his . . . anything that needs kickin' from here on in."

"These the apples, then?" one of the leather-clad men asked, holding up one of the bags. He scrunched his nose before turning to the ranger beside him. "Didn't your great-uncle eat nothing but turnips for four months straight during a siege? Refused to touch them afterwards."

"I've come back from being in the field without game or anything to forage," another offered. "Nothing but hard tack and stale water—forty-four days of maybe some boiled squirrel for flavour, or some dandelions for my tea. I gorged myself on potatoes for a week when I made it back to the first bit of landscape that wasn't decimated. Everyone said I'd be sick of them but I think there's so much versatility with the little things."

"I'm glad somebody gets it," Caleb said, still conversing with Alanna's family. She left her father's embrace only to ruffle Caleb's hair, which he returned in kind.

"All right," Rodney called over to Caleb. "I want some bloody answers."

"We just needed to make a quick plan," Lily said, then looked to the people at the table. "If you have questions about the camp, please come to my end of the table. Tristan, I need you for five minutes."

Tristan squawked but obeyed. He explained most of the stuff Larry had procured, as well as things they were having a hard time obtaining. Lily could have told the others much of what was going on at the camp, but the locals seemed to prefer hearing it from one of their own. In addition to most of the townswomen, two rangers had followed to their end of the table.

"We'll move that woman into proper custody," said the elder of the pair of rangers. "You ladies, can you accept people into your homes? At least until we get something sorted."

"I'll go see my neighbours," one of the women said. "We'll gather clothes and food before we head down. Might make sense to gather what we need, and hay for the animals besides."

While her people conversed, Tristan was paying attention to the exploits of what was going down on the far end of the table, so she sent him back. It sounded a lot more fun than planning the logistics of dealing with their camp. Eventually, her group splintered, two women and a ranger leaving, the rest joined Caleb's group, Tristan joining in was the most energetic Lily had seen him.

"Puppets?" Rodney asked.

"Marionettes," Caleb corrected. Tristan gestured with his hands for the size. "Strangers come about every other week or so. Seth and Lily told me they have rooms full of boxes of them."

"Never seen them yourself?" a ranger asked.

"They don't let us roam the entire castle," Caleb shook his head.

"So, what are we going to do about it?" one of the rangers asked.

"What I'd like to do," Caleb said. "Is figure out how I can get up there, with Sir Percival and Friends, and ask questions the old-fashioned way."

"Well, I don't know about the rest of you, but Percival is close enough to being my friend," Rodney said.

The food was delicious. Lily ate with Alanna and her parents. People mulled around after the meal though more rangers left once Caleb wrote letters. He took time to see Alanna's family before they were dismissed for the day. When she asked how much this was costing him, Caleb shrugged and said, "Ask Larry."

"Are you one of those rich people who had servants pay for things?" she asked.

He and Tristan shared a glance and they full-out belly laughed. "No. I lived in a castle since I turned seven and we never got an allowance except for when we were granted leave and on holidays," Caleb said. "Everything Tristan and I can pool together isn't going to be near what we're going to need."

"You seem to be doing okay." Someone handed him a beer from behind. "You done playing nice?" asked the blond ranger.

Caleb rolled his eyes. "Piss off, Gill."

"Come on, it's been two years—"

"Not long enough." The squire walked away, and the ranger wrinkled his nose. Lily recognized him from the day before, when he and another man, who was also present, rode up near their camp. He caught her eyes and he shot her a flirty smile, but sauntered away, watching Caleb go converse with another small group.

Gillam had bushy blond hair, and rather striking blue eyes. He'd a more wiry musculature than Caleb; Gillam was nominally taller but seemed smaller until they stood next to one another. Out of the pair, Gillam would have been the one most girls would have preferred, but Lily preferred Caleb's jaw and especially his eyes, then reminded herself she'd just make a fool of herself if she indulged in this. Gillam struck her as a flirt and she wasn't easy prey, whereas Caleb . . . *Let's not go there. For all you know he's been betrothed since before he was born*, she mused. *Then again, if he isn't wealthy, that's not likely.*

"Heaven forbid I say a cuss when it's needed and he looks ready to put Gillam through the wall," Rodney offered. "I mean, it's Gillam, so he must have done *something* . . . " Rodney looked to Tristan, who shrugged.

"Well . . . it must have happened two years ago," Lily offered.

"Ack," Rodney muttered, massaging his temples.

Before he could explain, a happily-fed Louis wandered over to them. "Caleb said he'd train me, but he's kind of busy. Think you can give me a lesson? I mean, you're no Zin, but you're the best of what I got."

Rodney crossed his arms. "Not a bad idea, though I've already sent one of my training officers to camp . . . Oh, did you mean her?"

"This old guy named Zin taught us back at our village," Louis said. "But I like stories where people travel across the seas to learn swordplay and . . . you know, stuff. This is the furthest I've ever been from home but I can hop two fences and get to Seth and Lily's place ."

"I'll get one of the lads to give you some lessons in a spell," Rodney said. "I think it would be best if Daisy stuck around."

"I'll teach him," Gillam offered. "Kid, you like fishing?"

"Yeah," Louis said. "And it's Louis."

"Gillam, it would be best if you leave him and Daisy be," Rodney said.

"I'm not doing anything," Gillam insisted. "Just being friendly." He looked to Lily and extended a hand. "I'm Gillam. Ranger."

She didn't take it. "Lily. Shepherdess." Gillam seemed amused. "What's so funny?"

"Leave it to that chump to be saved by you and Seth. Shinies are the ones supposed to be doing the rescuing. What's it really like in there?"

Louis answered, but made it sound like being a goblin puppet was where it was at if one was stuck there. Lily zoned out of the conversation; of course Seth had evaporated now that he'd eaten, and it was mostly rangers left. Both squires were speaking to an elderly couple that had just arrived; at first she thought they were farmers that had thrown on their good clothes, but the man had a sword at his side and his old boots looked more formal than anything she'd expect from a rancher.

"Oh, Sir Cabbages is here. Surprised he's not at home stroking his cat," Gillam said.

"Apologies, Sir Wilfred, I will be right back," Caleb said, and stormed over to Gillam, gesturing for him to follow.

"I've been trying to talk to you since I got here," Gillam said. "Can you spare five minutes of your precious—"

"I have business with Sir Wilfred. Now leave the foreigners alone."

"I can talk to whoever I jolly well like. Since you're ignoring them, I'll teach Louis bladework, then show him where to get fish for breakfast."

"You get fish for breakfast?" Louis asked.

"Best time to catch them," Gillam said. "Unlike shinies who get their meals served, we rangers are self-reliant. Our fish is fresh whereas—"

Caleb crossed his arms. "I know what you're trying to do and it's not going to work."

"And what is *that*, pray tell?" Gillam asked.

"Wrap it up squire," Sir Wilfred called over. There was a certain command that no one else had. "Let Rodney deal with his charge."

"One second, sir. Louis, Lily, don't go anywhere with this idiot. And if you find Seth, tell him the same thing. Lily, do you by chance have your sketchbook? Can I borrow it?" Lily handed it to Caleb, he thanked her with a brief nod and returned to the elder man.

Lily spotted the mandolin laying on a bench near where Seth had been seated. "Did you see where my brother went?" she asked Louis.

"I can help you find him if you'd like," Gillam offered. "I mentioned a few things in town that aren't completely dried up. You want to see the old tourney grounds? We used to have the grandest—"

"Do not take these two further than where we've tied our horses. I better get in on this," Rodney muttered, looking at Caleb and the older knight at the table, Caleb pointing and Wilfred asking questions. "Gillam, you can be charming when you put your mind to it, be bloody cordial to these two." Gillam didn't elaborate, so Rodney left them and joined the trio, another senior ranger joining them. They started to use buttons and coins as reference points.

"Can someone teach me sparring?" Louis pressed Gillam.

"Give Rodney a few minutes," Lily said.

"*A few minutes, a few minutes,*" Louis mocked. "I spent the morning being told this, that, and the other thing was only going to take *a few minutes.*"

Gillam laughed. "That's just knights. Take ten words to say two and then they look at you like you're the one with your head on backwards when you point it out. I have training blades with my horse. Come on," Gillam gestured, and despite Lily's protests, Louis followed him out the front door. She gave Caleb an apologetic look when she passed; he looked a little flustered but stayed seated with Sir Wilfred and Rodney.

"These are ranger horses, aren't they?" Louis asked, racing down the steps to inspect the horses hitched near a trough. They were far from uniform in size or colour, but they all had the same green and orange livery on their tack. The colours of the Ivancian flag; she realized then that meant they were royal rangers.

"Mine's Piper, she's great for endurance," Gillam gestured to a red horse. "Not as swift as Thumper here, but he gets tired easy."

"Your horse Stella could handle the mountains, right?" Louis asked.

"Mum needed her specifically for . . . atypical searches, and to be careful with a wounded rider," Lily explained. "Dad joked she was part mule."

"This one's Ferdinand, and that one's Velluvius. Don't pet the speckled one, she's a biter." Going into his saddlebags, Gillam produced two training blades. They were segmented and he tossed one to Louis unceremoniously, before he gestured to an area away from the horses, not quite a back alley between the buildings. "All right, show me what you know."

"I'm not as talented as her. Lily, show him—"

"I'm not training," Lily said. She only was tagging along to ensure Louis didn't go anywhere with Gillam. "And it's not talent, I started training with Zin when I was eleven."

Gillam corrected Louis's grip. "I guess it's different from your neck of the woods. You don't really need to train every day since you can walk with a blade. Not all of us rangers are born into it, sometimes we get lads Louis' age who show a knack."

"I'm good with a sling," Louis offered.

"I'm sure you are. We got a range at headquarters; I'm sure you'd like that. Seth gave me those vibes."

"His dad is a great archer," Louis said. Lily gestured for him to drop it. "Why don't you guys talk about it? If my parents were interesting, I'd have brought it up. My uncle and their dad—"

Thankfully, Gillam interrupted before Lily thought of a good way to change the subject. "Great archer," Gillam said. She knew he was trying to get her to elaborate, she didn't take the bait. "Win a few tourneys when you were little?"

"A wyvern attacked several farms in our area," Louis said. "Lily went after it on her own."

"I didn't know it was a wyvern," Lily said.

"What kind was it?" Gillam asked.

"Mountain," Lily said curtly.

Louis offered. "You called it a Half-Ridged—"

She cut him off. "It was dark. I can't be certain."

"Oh come on, everyone said you practically touched it."

"You charged a wyvern on your lonesome, Buttercup? What are you doing hanging around with knights for?" Gillam said. "If you're not at his beck and call, I can show you things that are more interesting than fishing." She did her best to ignore him. "Listen Sweetheart, I appreciate your loyalty to my friend but I really need to speak to him, so just play along, okay?"

"Louis, that's enough," Lily told him.

"Why? I'm having some fun finally."

"Yeah Buttercup, he's having some fun finally." Gillam never struck Louis, but went into a receiving form and had Louis strike at him. This only continued on for a minute before he gestured for Louis to stop, and proceeded to grab a bag Lily hadn't noticed he'd brought out with them.

"Are you kidding me?" Caleb asked, atop the steps, Rodney just behind him.

"Nope," Gillam said, hand-feeding the horses nice shiny apples.

Caleb didn't storm down, in fact he was rather slow—though he did snatch the bag. "You have twenty words or less, Gill," Caleb said.

"Then we're back to being friends?" Gillam asked. The squire held up six fingers. "Can we go talk in private?" Gillam also used his fingers and appeared to mull over his last set before saying, "Knights are pompous—"

"Gillam, get over here," Rodney called from the stairs.

"And you, squire," Wilfred added.

"*Me?*"

"For smirking."

"I think that's just his face sometimes," Lily pointed out.

"Daisy has a point," Rodney said, though Wilfred waived his hand dismissively.

The reaming out didn't occur very far away at all, another back alley between the buildings. "Do not try to rile him up or bother any of the people who helped him escape the castle. Understood?" Rodney informed Gillam. "When the knights are discussing their *important business*, even when we know it's some overly-polite dandy gibberish, you shut your pie hole."

"And as for you, you'll pay attention to briefings and not be distracted by someone else's idiocy." Sir Wilfred didn't seem angry, just stern. Caleb didn't make eye contact, just looked slightly up and ahead and nodded.

"Now, Gillam, do you have something to say?" Wilfred asked.

"I'm sorry," Gillam said.

"And you, squire?" Wilfred asked.

"Nothing at all, sir," Caleb said as if he was declining a cup of tea.

"I was stupid, and . . . Cay, I'm sorry, okay?" Gillam tried to get in Caleb's face, who mostly looked up and indignant. "What more do you want? Grovelling?" The ranger fell on his knees and grabbed the hem of Caleb's shirt.

"Gill, stop embarrassing us both."

"Accept the apology, squire," Wilfred instructed.

"He's being intentionally obnoxious to get attention," Caleb said. "Stop playing into this, sir."

"Do I have to cover myself in ashes over here?" Gillam asked.

"Gill, get up," Caleb snapped, pulling the ranger to his feet. "I know you're not to blame for what happened. We both have duties, and I can't be farting around with you."

"That," Wilfred said. "Is better. You have fifteen minutes to talk to the ranger. Rodney says his man will be returning from the camp shortly."

"Oooh, scheming squires and ravishing rangers converge again for the common good. Do tell," Gillam said, throwing an arm around Caleb like they were old chums again. "Can I have a matchy-matchy shirt?"

Caleb removed the arm. "Just because I'm speaking to you doesn't make us friends."

"Fine—maybe Rodney, Buttercup, and I will get matching shirts, and hats too. Buttercup, you like feathers?"

"I want a hat with a feather," Louis announced.

Gillam gave Caleb a toothy grin. "Introduce me or I will get you demoted back to page by the end of the day."

"I'm amazed you're still a ranger," Caleb replied.

"Come on, or I'm taking the boy on a three day hunting trip." Gillam sauntered back to him and Lily.

"Lily, Louis, this is Gillam, he's a ranger I've known most of my life. Gillam, this is Lily, she and her brother broke into the castle and snuck me and several others out. Louis is also from her village. He's been helping me out since I woke up."

"I met Seth and Louis while you were out back," Gillam explained. He put out a hand, she took it and they shook. "Thank you for saving my friend, even if he doesn't like me right now." He looked to Caleb sheepishly. "Now that you're talking to me, can we talk more? In private, I mean. You probably don't even remember what happened leading up to the days before the castle fell."

Lily pursed her lips trying to read their expressions. "Is this to do with that cave you were talking about earlier? You said you were hurt."

"Yeah," Caleb said quietly. "Louis, let's get you that sparring lesson. I'll try to give you one myself later. I'll be right back." Tristan came out of the building while Caleb spoke quickly with one of the rangers. Tristan walked to Caleb and mostly listened and nodded.. Louis hardly needed any help getting on one of the ranger horses and didn't look back when galloping off with Tristan and the ranger.

"When he was injured," Lily spoke quietly to Gillam. "How bad was he?"

"I didn't think he was going to make it," Gillam said. He looked to Caleb when the squire approached. "How much does she know?"

"Lily's not from here, so if you're thinking someone is scheming she couldn't be in on it. She might as well hear whatever it is you have to say."

Gillam nodded. "Okay—like I said, some place private. I haven't really spoken about this to anyone." Caleb and Gillam seemed to know where they were going in the tavern; Lily followed. "You learn any good tunes?" He gestured to the mandolin abandoned on the chair.

"This is hers," Caleb said, handing it to her. "Lily, do you think you can play—"

"I'm sure she's really talented, but I want to go first," Gillam said. "This is really important."

"So is this."

"Look, if you never talk to me again that's fine, but I have been waiting two years to get this off my chest." They went over to a side dining room, plenty big for just the three of them. Gillam waited until the door was closed. "How much do you remember? The night of that mission."

"I was fine in the cave," Caleb said. "Confusing inside, but we were all running around in the dark. The next day was okay, the day after that was when things started to get fuzzy. Why?"

"You got blinded. I remember you picking spider silk out of your hair right before they told you about your father."

Caleb nodded. "I just thought how lousy I felt was because of grief. The second day is mostly clear, until about half past midday. Third day I'm going to say I was having fever dreams, don't know how much of it was from the venom as opposed to the medicine they gave me. Day five was when the castle fell?"

"Sounds about right," Gillam agreed.

Lily felt incredibly left out. "You sure you want me here?"

"It's a weird coincidence that the same sort of creature that attacked us less than a week before that castle fell also turned your people into puppets," Caleb said quietly. "Remember when you sang that song and I drew that weird spider face? That . . . Juroguomo?" He hesitated. "It poisoned me in that cave. My other injuries were minor."

"What song are we talking about?" Gillam asked.

"I need to catch her up," the squire told the ranger before looking to her. "I didn't know if getting turned back would get me in the same state going in. That's why rescuing Ethan made the most sense. If I turned back and was still poisoned, I'd be no use to anyone."

"What?" Gillam asked. He looked at her, then at Caleb. "Are you telling me she . . . ?"

"She knows the song, and she said she was able to lure her people out to the woods. Lily, can you play it?"

Her heart raced. "I think that's a bad idea."

"I stopped you before."

Lily didn't want to, but figured he was right. "Okay—we leave weapons outside the room. And if this goes wrong you absolutely have to stop me. At least one of you ought to put wax in his ears."

Caleb obliged, they told Rodney they were up to something dumb and to check in on them but not without hearing protection. His "Eh?" found him holding their swords, bows, and whatever knives Gillam had hiding on his person. "What's the point of us both putting wax in our ears?" Gillam asked. "How will we know?"

"It's her eyes."

Lily made sure the door was closed and sat down, Gillam looking uncharacteristically nervous instead of smug, and Caleb looking characteristically unhappy but gave her a nod. She started to play intellectually, but remembered that it took a minute, then it poured out of her.

She opened her eyes when she heard them moving. Compared to Rodney or Caleb, Gillam never seemed that threatening until all of a sudden his eyes widened and he looked terrified. He grabbed the mandolin and raised it over his head like he was going to smash her with it. Caleb sandwiched himself between them and made Gillam back up. The ranger struck the wall even though Caleb didn't lay a finger on him.

"Don't ever move at her like that again!" Caleb snapped, his voice was more of a growl.

Rodney entered. "What in the blue blazes are you three up to? Gillam, put that down!"

"What?" Gillam and Caleb chorused.

"They can't hear you," Lily said, gesturing to the ears.

Rodney took one look at her, and backed up. "Daisy, you're . . . " he gestured to his own eyes.

By the time she found a mirror, it was pretty much done. There was just a faint hint of gold glowing in Lily's iris. Rodney was giving the pair another chewing out, the pair picked wax out of their ears so they got the general impression of some of it. "Do you want to explain what that was about?" Rodney asked her.

"Not really," she said, and reached for the mandolin, which Gillam raised so she couldn't reach.

"I couldn't hear it, but it sent that same chill up my spine," Gillam said. "Caleb, this is serious. How is this all connected?"

"I don't know."

"Smarten up, and I better not come back in here to any more shenanigans." Rodney let himself out.

"Lily, you need to stay away from that woman, and that castle, until we figure out what exactly is going on with . . . whatever just happened," Caleb said.

"Well now that we have more people, that's possible," Lily said. "That stupid bracelet . . ."

"Where is it?"

"Tristan has it. Maybe it's not good for him to have it on, either."

Seth popped his head into the room. "I was looking for that." He reached for the mandolin. Gillam wouldn't give it to him. Seth had shorter arms than the ranger, but was more persistent.

"Where have you been?" Lily asked.

"Off not being bossed around," Seth gestured towards Caleb before practically climbing on Gillam. "That's mine, gimme!"

"Your mandolin?" Gillam asked.

"Family mandolin. If anyone's going to break it, it better be me." Seth snatched it, before he strummed a little shanty. No glowing eyes. "See? *E. O'Connell.* There's no E in Lily or Tiffany, but there is in Seth."

Gillam briefly mouthed E. O'Connell and looked consternated, but said nothing.

"Seth, have you ever seen your sister's eyes glow before?" Caleb asked.

"Yeah, when they're on their monthlies," Seth said before laughing. "Oh come on, that was a good one." He wiped an eye.

"I'm serious," Caleb told him.

"You didn't hear it from me, but my sisters are completely normal," Seth said.

"Her eyes just lit up after she sang a spider's song," Gillam said. "Wait, would he know it?"

"Probably."

"Eh?" Seth asked. Caleb and Gillam were so afraid of Lily singing it—even as academically as possible, that they did the 'dah dah dah' parts. Gillam put wax back into his ears, before Seth played to Caleb's satisfaction. "Oh, I know what you're talking about." When Seth put his mind to it, he was quite good.

"Lose the wax," Caleb told Gillam, "there's nothing to see here."

"What?" Gillam asked.

"What happened when Lily played it?" Seth asked.

"Apparently my eyes glowed yellow," Lily told her brother. Seth pursed his lips. "I can't do any music without those songs worming their way back into my head."

"Maybe you ought to get that bracelet back on. Where is it?" Seth asked.

"Tristan has it, he was the one mostly watching Madeline," Lily said.

"Who's watching her now?"

"Rodney sent a few of us to your camp with supplies and to bring people back," Gillam said, still picking out wax. "I think the plan was for her to be brought to cells."

"Those masks she used to control you, where are they?" Caleb asked.

"At the camp, I guess," Lily said. "Gillam, can we go to headquarters and ask questions?"

"Don't see why not," Gillam said. "He's gotta stay but I can take you. What do you mean, 'control you'?"

"I'll get ya up to speed," Seth offered. "Madeline slapped a theatre mask on Lily, made her play this." He gestured to the mandolin. "She made a copy of Lily's face, but it wasn't right, if that makes any sense. Madeline's tall and skinny, like a dancer, so she didn't look right. Madeline lured us into the woods, put the spider face on and became some sort of spider monster. Lily was forced to help her; she played this and lulled the rest of our townsfolk. They were all together, only Zin wasn't affected because he's a bit of a recluse and he's got a magic fox wife."

"Madeline transformed into the spider?" Caleb asked.

Seth nodded. "Turned me and Louis into living puppets. Lily cut me free before I was completely incapacitated, I don't know what would have happened to me or Lily if the kitsunes and Zin didn't show up. Lil and I trailed her, caught her in Shelkie's Bay, made her help us so we could sneak into the castle. Guess we don't need her anymore." Caleb nodded.

"How are you planning on getting back into the castle?" Lily asked.

"Let's close the door. All right, here's our secret weapon," Seth said, taking a hint. He'd done his best to keep that fox medallion hidden. Lily saw the chain peeking out from his collar. "This won't work on her with the bracelet on, but—" He used it, and shrank down to puppet size. Came right back up. The transformation was near immediate. "Hey Gillam! Imma 'bout to make you fun-sized."

Seth grabbed Gillam's shoulder and they transformed in less than a heartbeat. Lily gaped. Caleb crossed his arms. "Yes, he told me earlier. Part of of the reason we took a little longer this morning was we were experimenting."

"You were like this?" Gillam said, before sticking his hand over his mouth. "You sounded like this?" He then broke into a ridiculous sea shanty. "It's all so . . . lame."

"Yes," Caleb agreed, then said to Lily quietly. "Don't tell him about the anatomy changes; I might actually need him."

"How did you manage this Seth?" Lily asked. Seth changed back, forgetting Gillam.

"It's . . ."

"Hey!" Gillam chirped.

"Oh, one sec," Seth had to change back, to bring Gillam back to normal size and body composition. "Short answer is our kitsunes. There's more than one. Basically they wanted me to get good in a puppet body, so now I get to chose which form I'm in. And before you suggest it, it only works for me and whoever or whatever I'm touching," Seth explained. "We haven't tried bigger groups, so maybe if I touched people riding a horse or . . ."

"You saw how fast that worked?" Caleb asked. "I could throw him as a puppet and he could transform in the middle of it. He could climb through bars and transform on the other side to unlock a door or grab something. We could sneak a dozen people into a room and bring them back to normal size in less than a minute."

Seth nodded. "Now, I'd love to go in there and fix Ethan and all your buddies, but they are under other spells. Lily and I were unaffected by the barriers. We didn't look that much different than you did in there."

"So that means you think you'll be okay to cross the barriers again," Lily said.

"Only one way to find out. Once I cross I might be stuck there again," Caleb admitted. "But I think I'll effectively be a stringless."

"What's a stringless?" Gillam asked.

"Marionettes not under control by string. I might as well tell you the plan that's in my head. Can the three of you agree to secrecy?" Caleb waited for them to nod. "If we get aid—Rodney's already sent letters —then we sneak a team in. We lower the drawbridge, outside help marches in. Seth helps change my team back to human, and we take the castle. We need more intel; no point throwing bodies at a problem until we know what sort of sorcery will hit us."

"And if you don't get aid?" Gillam asked.

"I still do the intel," Caleb said, nodding. "If it's not going to completely obliterate the team, the team goes after whoever's up there. Kick their ass, if possible."

Seth nodded. "And in the event that this is the no help coming, nigh impossible evil that will squash us into jelly?"

"Sneak out as many decent people as possible, figure out if there's a way to stop or slow down their plans. Ethan gets out towards the end, he tries to figure out what exactly is going on and break the curse."

"You and Ethan will keep trying?" Gillam asked.

Caleb nodded. "I'll stay behind and try to help who I can."

"You can't stay in there," Gillam said. "By then your cover will be blown."

"We can't abandon the people we don't save. Besides, I don't know if I'm still poisoned or not. It'll be a moot point in a week if I am."

The silence became uncomfortable. Lily was about to blow her stack at him, but Gillam beat her to it. "What?" Gillam asked. "How are you still alive?" Caleb shrugged. "And you were just going to not tell anyone?"

"I've been kind of busy, if you haven't noticed," Caleb said. "I haven't had time to worry. I'm okay right now."

"Right now?" Gillam demanded.

"Gill, calm down," Caleb told him.

"*I am calm!*"

"How do you know you're still poisoned?" Seth asked.

"I don't," Caleb confessed. "Come on, be rational. Lily agrees with me."

He looked more wounded from her scoff than she expected. She needed to change the subject. "This all happened days before your castle was cursed?" Lily asked.

"Yeah," Gillam said. "These spider things prefer the taste of young men, and people were going missing in and around a less commonly travelled roadside. One of the rangers thought he tracked it to its forest but not its lair, but we didn't know if it was a river nixie or any of the other million things that'll kill you. Called in knights for back up and to do more investigating. My job was to patrol the area around our camp. Hal was with me, and he heard a song, and . . . I was transfixed. I saw the most beautiful girl . . . woman . . . she was stunning." He shook his head. "She wasn't anywhere near the cave. It was a glen. We were miles away from where we should have been."

"Tracking you two in the dark wasn't easy," Caleb said.

Gillam nodded. "She lured us both into a cave, I thought she was going to kiss me, but instead she stung me on the back of my neck and turned my legs into jelly. Hal snapped out of it and she left me. I managed to fire a few shots before my fingers stopped working. Wrapped us up in silk, I think I screamed for help but . . . everything went fuzzy. I heard her eat Hal. She probably would have used the poison she used on Caleb to soften my insides. This guy, right here, cut me out. So I kind of owe him."

"You got a funny way of showing gratitude. All of you stop worrying.

We'll cross the poison bridge when we get to it, but until then we've got bigger fish to fry."

"But back there, that's what I need to talk to you about," Gillam said. "What do you remember? Who was on what team and who was with you?"

"I cut you down and I don't remember who I handed you to," Caleb said. "Ethan was on fire duty. Fire was supposed to keep the spider from coming at us on rescue. I got my gauntlet stuck, had to abandon it, but before I got down, she came." Caleb looked contemplative. "I got thrown pretty good and lost my helm. She gobbed me and I was blind, I stumbled around, someone eventually led me out."

"I was rousing while I was still cocooned," Gillam said. "When I saw you next, I was already at the infirmary at the castle under watch. I was fine. The brass dragged you in, and you were insisting you were fine but you were slurring. They wouldn't let me see you."

Caleb nodded. "Does this have a point, Gill?"

"You sure you want those two present?"

"Might as well," Caleb said.

"What specifically did Sir Lionel say?" Gillam asked.

Caleb furrowed his brow. "He said lots of stuff. When exactly?"

"When you got that silk in your face. He told you to do something."

"Okay . . . he told me to move."

"No. I think he told you to roll to your left," Gillam said. "I was still close enough to hear this. Then I heard you father scream 'You bastard!' Now, I'm not saying women can't be bastards, but if you had seen the curves on that spider—I mean, why would your father say 'bastard'? Edgar never cussed."

Caleb looked at Gillam. "He did say that," Caleb said quietly, clenching his fists. Gillam glanced nervously at Lily and Seth. "Just say it."

"You didn't respond to the anti-venom. I think you were stabbed in the back by another knight or ranger," Gillam said. "And that person probably poisoned your dad and the other ranger who died that night too. Their injuries didn't make sense. Who all was with you? Last I checked it was you, the guy carrying me away, your dad, and—"

"I think I'm going to be sick," Caleb said, finding a chair and sitting on it.

"You see why I was ready to mess up this pretty face to speak to you?" Gillam asked. "And you're saying Lionel told you to roll a certain way? Cay, I'm sorry."

"Who was Sir Lionel?" Seth asked Gillam.

"That doesn't make any sense!" Caleb exclaimed, visibly pale.

Lily left the room and got a pitcher of water. Rodney looked like he was going to also burst in. She said, "Five more minutes."

"Tell them fun time is over," Rodney snapped at her.

"Drink some," she told Caleb when she returned to the room.

"I'm not a toddler. I'm good."

"Don't argue with the lady," Gillam ordered.

"Give yourself a minute," Lily said to Caleb, putting a hand on his back; it seemed like something someone from home would do. "Gillam, who was Sir Lionel?"

"His father's friend. Close friend," Gillam said.

Caleb shook his head. "How could he have orchestrated that? You were lured . . . " His eyes widened. "Gillam, you didn't have a choice. Lily said when she played that music, she compelled her villagers into the woods."

"Did it not occur to you," Seth offered quietly. "That whatever stung you brought you to the real monster's cave? You were all set up."

"The fire team drove off one." Gillam nodded. "The second spider pounced on the team who thought they were in the clear. Cay, what did you see there?"

"I was blind. Besides, I don't remember clearly."

"There must have been some reason Lionel—or whoever, tried to take you out."

"Maybe it wasn't something you saw?" Seth asked. "You were a distraction."

"Seth's got a point," Gillam said. "Everyone would have been talking about this injury or who was to blame, something could have been snuck in with less eyes paying attention. The guard would have been pulling longer shifts and people make mistakes when they're stretched or worried about their friends. Cay, they knew to evacuate the royal family."

Caleb's colour improved. "Gill, have you discussed this with anyone?"

The ranger shook his head. "When I thought about it, I don't know who I can trust out there," Gillam admitted. "You have to keep this to yourself until I can do some more digging."

"You've had two years," Caleb said.

"You being here kind of helps. Others who were at the cave are in that castle. I need to speak with Ethan. I'm sure he's got some missing pieces in the back of his brain. Your friend here, he can get me into that castle." Gillam gestured at Seth.

Caleb nodded. "I'm going back tonight. I'll bring you if it's possible to get in without getting caught."

"Are you saying if you don't change back, you're going to be dead in a few days?" Gillam asked.

"I don't know," Caleb admitted. His colour had improved; he'd drank some water but was mostly staring at it. "I would be going back regardless; Ethan and Esther are on their own right now."

"Who's Esther?" Gillam asked.

"A woman who got put in about a year ago. Innocent people are in there, Gill. Including their sister." Caleb gestured to Seth and Lily. "I said I'd help rescue her."

"How many people do we have?" Seth asked.

"Rodney said if I can get him in, he's got five people who have a personal vendetta. We'll lose some of them when they see what the transformation does," Caleb said. "We might have lost the element of surprise, so we might need to lay low for a while. Does us no good walking into a trap."

"One in ten reporting," Gillam said. "I don't like it . . . can't imagine what it would be like being stuck like that for any length of time. We would have caused so much trouble in there, if I was in there with you."

"There's no promise you'd have stayed. We lost a lot of knights Ethan says he was with when the spell struck. It was almost an insult being allowed to stay. Like we weren't enough of a threat."

Gill nodded. "The poison won't kill you while you're transformed. I guess that's a stroke of luck. We just need to keep you enchanted until we figure out a way to fix you."

"I'm not staying that way any longer than I have to," Caleb said.

"It'll buy you some time," Gillam said. Caleb rolled his eyes. "Come on, being a cute little puppet's not that bad . . ."

"What makes you think I'm going to be happy watching all of you get to have real lives? I'd rather take a run at whatever's up there and hope I slow it down long enough for Rodney or Hector to beat it."

Lily felt Seth staring at her. They went to another corner of the room. "This is insane," Seth said. "Not me going back with him but . . . you know what I'm thinking? By the time he shows symptoms, it'll be too late."

"We can't be certain he is poisoned."

"You gotta ask mom and dad," Seth said. Yes, the two people who were thrilled with her.

"They'll do it if you ask. Lily, they trust you."

"They could be halfway across the sea by now," Lily told him. "They're not going to turn around because I sent them a message." She glanced at the squire and ranger, who were going back and forth edging on yelling.

"They're probably not even in Shelkie's Bay right now," Seth said. "You can go back and find them; send dad here and you and mom could get one."

"I don't want to leave you and Tiffany, or him."

"Him?"

"Them."

"Right." Seth was far too smug. Lily shot him a look. "Whatever you say." He put his hands up innocently before he ponied up the key to that bracelet. "It's your choice, Lily. I have to help them." He blinked, then added, "I mean, it's more fun than hanging with you and Dale."

She pocketed the key and lowered her head. Mama Fern woke her up and warned her about the wyvern. She didn't mean for her to engage. Mama Fern helped her get out of Madeline's control the first time. Somehow, this was help. She just didn't have all the pieces yet. "I'll give the key to Louis after I get the bracelet back. Won't do me much good with you in the castle."

"Someplace that woman won't suspect," Seth agreed. "You talk to him. We won't make it a family thing." He picked up the mandolin and let out a shrill whistle, shutting the older pair up. "Are you done?"

"This idiot has a death wish," Gillam pointed.

"Yeah, and we're following him," Seth said. "I need a beer and you're buying, ranger."

"I need more than a beer," Gillam agreed. "And last I checked, he's the one buying."

"I need two minutes of Caleb's time," Lily said. "Just Caleb."

Gillam looked at her, then shot Caleb a grin, but followed after Seth. Lily was glad to see the mandolin go. "E. O'Connell, eh? You wouldn't be related to . . ."

"Common last name from my neck of the woods. Happy to finally get out of that neck so I can meet girls I'm not related to, yet here I am bumming around with you."

"Sorry you found out that way," Caleb said lowly, arms crossed. It looked like he was expecting a reaming out. He let out a relieved sigh after a moment. "I have two years worth of horror stories. I'll try to remember to tell you the most relevant ones."

"I think I might be able to help with your other situation. This can't leave the room."

He raised an eyebrow but nodded. "Okay. Day can't get any weirder."

"My parents were hunters before I was born. Specialty game. My mom was the lore master, she understood how to make elixirs and-"

"Demetri tried using the anti-venom, but if what Gillam said is true, then it makes sense that it wouldn't work. I have no idea of narrowing down what the poison was."

"If you had an incredible purifier the origin of the poison is irrelevant," Lily said. "My parents hunted a unicorn before I was born."

He clearly had no idea what that meant. "Lily you live across the sea; even if it's possible there's no way I could get there in time unless you turned me into a puppet. I'm needed here."

"My dad snapped and refused to do any more hunts like that afterwards. They stopped several hunts after in the years that followed. They have access to several unicorn horns. I could obtain one and if you're still poisoned we can use it to cure you."

He furrowed his brow. "They just carry these around all the time?"

"Absolutely not," she said, shaking her head. "But they'll do it if I ask." His lips thinned and he looked away. "You don't believe me."

"Sorry. I got a lot on my mind. If you think it'll help . . . just . . . don't get your hopes up. Your parents don't owe me anything. Reasonable chance that whatever goes down I'll be in the thick of fighting anyway. I'd rather die on my feet than choking on my own spit over the course of a few days."

"It's worth trying," Lily said. "Don't throw your life away."

"I'm not Ethan," he said, before his eyes widened and he covered his mouth. He grabbed her shoulders. "Forget I said that."

She forced him to meet her gaze before she spoke up. "What happened?"

"He . . . he had enough," Caleb said quietly, looking away as if guilty. "I told you, two years worth of nightmares. It's not nice when you get taken over. You can be forced to hack people to bits. Ethan tried to make the best of it. He always pretended he was happier than he was. Details are not important; I need to go back for him. Understand?" His grip tightened, so she nodded. "Thank you." He released her, and backed off. "Sorry, I didn't mean to do that. Grab you, I mean. Geez . . ." He ran a hand through his hair.

"You don't scare me," she said. "Lips are sealed about Ethan." He wouldn't look at her. "They really hurt you guys in there."

"If it was just us, we could have handled it," Caleb said, crossing his arms. "I told him not to get attached. They hurt other people."

"Was it a girl?"

"Yeah," he said quietly. "I can't talk about it."

"I understand," she said. "Ethan and Esther are lucky to have you in there with them. I guess you have things to do. Back to the real world?"

He perked up when she changed the subject. "I'm buying for everyone else, join me for an ale before I have to get to work?"

"Ale is disgusting."

"I knew you had to have some flaw," he said. "Little girl lemonade?"

She laughed. "Whatever you have can't compare to the mead from Rosehill. Is the whiskey any good?"

"You'll have to tell me, Worldly Traveller." He got up to follow her, but only took a few steps. "Hey Lily . . . " He trailed off when she stopped and turned to look at him. " . . . Nevermind."

"What?" Their eyes met, and she flushed a little. She ran a hand through her hair. "Whatever it is, just tell me."

His dark eyes darted. "I . . . just wanted to give this back to you." He reached into his jerkin and produced a folded piece of paper. "I kind of stole it when we met." She took it, one side had several leaves she'd sketched while they travelled from the port to Mirador. The other side had the map she was trying to make. She'd forgotten all about her original attempt at a map.

"Is this it?" she asked. "You kept this on you the whole time?" She remembered how reverent he'd been with that silly little twig. "Well, thanks I guess, but I'm probably going to use it to start a fire."

"Don't do that!" He almost snatched it back, but caught himself.

"It's just a scrap of paper," she said, catching his gaze. She bit her lip. "If it means that much to you, keep it." She offered it up, and he slowly took it, but then took her hand. She felt a little dizzy.

He pulled her hand to his face and he kissed the back of it, keeping her gaze. She had to keep herself from trembling when he cupped her face and his kiss was softer than she'd imagined. For an instant she had no idea what she was doing; she ran a hand through his hair.

She opened her eyes briefly when they stopped, she thought he'd say they just made a mistake, but he caught her gaze and said, "I don't care if you're a kitsune or another spider." And kissed her again, harder, but after the second kiss he held her, and pressing her head against his chest she listened to his heart beating. First it was racing, but after a minute it seemed to slow. She didn't realize it, but for the first time, since that woman threw a mask on her, she was safe. "Can I court you?" He pulled away, shaking his head. "What am I saying? I mean, I'm only going to be here for the next few hours and . . ."

She took his hand. "No, it's not just a few hours. If you're poisoned I'm going to find a way to save you." She waited for him to look her in the eyes, she brushed a few stray hairs so she could see him. "Yes." He pulled her into an embrace.

"Squire," someone called from the door.

"Ignore him," Caleb said.

"I know you haven't seen a girl in two years," the burly man said. "Apparently I haven't seen the sun in at least that long. You have some explaining to do."

"We can always go steal Gill's horse and book it," Caleb muttered. He released their embrace but turning she stayed in his space. The man had an impressive beard,and wore perhaps the most garish tunic Lily had ever seen. "I see you're awake, Captain. Am I really the only one willing to speak with you?"

"That's how you greet me?" the captain asked.

"I could have left you in the box, sir," Caleb said. "Lily, meet Captain Myron Daraby of the Castle Mirador's Men-at-Arms. Captain Daraby, this is one of the people responsible for our rescue, Lily O'Connell."

Captain Daraby didn't appear to be listening to a word he said. "I send Tristan to find you and we find you canoodling . . ."

A Captain? Lily looked to Caleb before interrupting the Captain. "Are you a knight too?" Lily asked.

The man guffawed before he answered. "No, I don't have a fancy set of arms or some badger painted on my shield. Bloodlines don't matter to us, my men manned the castle. No one knows that cursed monstrosity across the lake better than me. Now, what's this I hear that you know of a way in? Lad, I'll kiss you myself if you give me a fighting chance to give a one-for to whoever slapped us in boxes."

"And the uppity squire was never seen again, after running off screaming into the night," Caleb said. "You don't have many men."

"Not yet I don't," Daraby said. "I spoke to Wilfred about your plan. Needs bodies and steel behind it."

"We need more intelligence," Caleb said. "That means going back after sunset and scouting. It'll be a game changer if I can run barriers."

"What barriers? Nevermind—grab a pint and join me in the next room and tell me how I can get in there with you and the good ol' boys and take it back."

"Yeah, we need to talk," Caleb agreed. He looked to Lily apologetically.

"Don't worry about me," she said. "You focus on your mission."

Fifteen

Tristan obviously had seen something, so Caleb paused to talk to him when he and Lily followed after Captain Daraby back to the main room. "You give Louis a decent sparring lesson?"

"I barely taught him anything before someone else took over," Tristan admitted, smiling faintly. "He's got some experience, but he oughtta keep at it for the next few days." One minute Tristan seemed glad Caleb was there, the next he seemed like he'd done something wrong and expected Caleb to come down like the brass. "I've been following Daraby around since he woke up. I thought you'd be angry when you came to this morning; imagine explaining to him he's been put in storage for two years."

"I'll let you talk in private." Lily left them and walked over to a nearby table, where Isaac sat with several locals, including the friar from Caleb's parish. It seemed that Catarina and Larry were at their own table, semi-private, enjoying pints and possibly playing footsie.

"Sounds like we have a functional war camp," Caleb told Tristan.

"Seems like it." Tristan grinned, glancing after Lily. "I thought you said none of us ought to . . . " Tristan trailed off when Caleb shot him a look, and the younger squire bit his lip.

"I know what I said," Caleb told him. "If I were you, I'd make myself scarce before I became Daraby's personal messenger boy."

"I left Louis fishing by the creek," Tristan offered. Caleb nodded and Tristan took it as a dismissal, the younger squire walking to Seth and

Gillam at the bar, though they proceeded to a round table with drinks in hand.

Caleb caught up with Lily speaking to the others. He didn't catch the entire conversation, but they confirmed that the camp was pretty much taken over by rangers and men-at-arms and there were people recovering in the rooms upstairs. Madeline was in ranger custody and had been moved to their cell block. He unconsciously slipped an arm around Lily's waist, catching several raised brows.

"Anything interesting happen here while we were gone?" Larry asked, calling over from his table.

To his surprise, Lily nestled in closer to him. "Caleb's asked to court me. I said yes."

"Oh really?" asked a young woman. It took Caleb a minute to recognize her from that morning. Her eyes were on the young man from Lily's village sitting next to her. "Hear that, Dale? They've known one another for what, two, three days tops?" Everyone else at the table seemed amused or pleasantly surprised. Caleb supposed that made it official.

Catarina chuckled before she spoke up. "Thank you for everything you did for my camp. It's still my camp, but I will relinquish ownership of it in the morning."

"Why the morning?" Caleb asked.

"We've been talking with the folk from town," Isaac said gesturing at the friar and several women who were sipping tea, looking rather pleased with themselves. He'd known many of them growing up; women from his parish or who he'd known mostly through his mother. "The folk here can care for the rescued better than we can, so we thought we could start bringing people across the sea. We have more than enough people to cram onto Larry's boat."

"We can't expect you to be back and forth across the sea taking six, seven people at a time," one of the women pointed out.

"I'm not offering that," Larry said. "I'm sure Lily and Louis' family are anxious to get over here. If I'm to fetch them, I might as well bring some folk with me. We've a lot to figure out, you see," Larry said, then turned to Caleb. "If you can save folk, do so."

The local women nodded. "We'll manage," said one.

The friar's hands were ink-stained, as he was taking notes. "The ones who are from this side of the ocean will need help too, mind."

"Rodney's riders will return in a few days," another woman said. "We'll get it figured out. With luck, some of the refugees will know a thing about shearing, or planting. We can take extra hands no problem, and if they can work they can earn passage. Hardly charity at all."

"Squire," someone called.

"You've got work to do," Larry told Caleb.

Caleb stopped at the bar for a pint and Gill waved him over, Tristan looking relaxed even when he approached, shuffling cards and casually dealing out for the three of them.

"Look into my eyes," Gill asked. "Anything weird?"

"Not more than I'd expect," Caleb replied.

"Unless you're buying supper, I think I'm going to go try to catch a fish or snatch up a rabbit," Seth said, stretching.

"I made a deal with Declan," Caleb said. "There should be food at the camp as well."

"We can catch up with Louis after this hand," Tristan offered. "I'd prefer a fish fry."

"We'll think of you while we're off having fun," Gill offered.

"Don't remind me," Caleb said, leaving them and making his way over to where Daraby and Wilfred conversed with several other senior rangers and two of the men-at-arms, though they'd removed their armour and almost looked like civilians.

"Glad you could grace us with your presence," Daraby said, though it turned out he was speaking to Rodney, who also had grabbed a pint.

"I'm told that your camp is properly furnished and the civilians have been moved out," Rodney said. "Except for that old coot of a doctor. Once we finish our drinks we can continue planning there; I might have sent a few barrels that way already." He shot Caleb a grin.

"Works for me," Daraby said. "Don't need anyone getting distracted." He said this levelly to Caleb, though Wilfred shot him a look.

"Put that drink down, I need you sober," Wilfred said.

"It takes more than a pint, sir." Caleb still did as he was told.

He'd explained the essentials of his plan already to Rodney and Wilfred, and now relaying it, they needed him to answer questions. He'd spent ample time training under Daraby and Rodney; Wilfred and his grandfather had served together, Caleb knew him the least well but he was an honourable man. Caleb tuned out of the conversation about how long the riders would take. They still had Lily's sketchbook so his thoughts drifted to Ethan and Esther, then Oliver, and then his cousin and his friends. He wouldn't give up on them; even if that meant he had to spend time as a puppet until the guard to the castle went back down, or they found another way in. Seth had jumped one caravan; would another come? It might take months. What if he was poisoned, and Lily could cure him? Not her, her family. Would they?

Someone's tone went up, asking a question, but he missed it. "Sorry, I was thinking."

"About that girl, or the castle?" Daraby asked, gesturing towards the table where Lily sat with the civilians.

"One involves the other," Caleb said. He was told to smarten up and pay attention, and Rodney pretty much relayed the plan to Daraby, who nodded and asked questions. Caleb hadn't told them everything— especially pertaining to Seth and Lily, only that they were the ones who snuck in. "I'm just thinking about if the castle's on high alert. We don't want to compromise the only way in and out."

"Won't know until we try," Rodney said. "We can wait a few days if you think it makes sense."

Caleb shook his head. "I'm going back after dark with Seth," Caleb said. "If only to check on the others. Sir Percival has his faction making distractions, so hopefully we'll be able to get in without being noticed."

"How can we be certain Percival or Hector weren't involved in bringing the castle down in the first place?" Daraby asked.

"We can't be," Wilfred said simply. They still had Lily's sketchbook;

he wished he'd made another copy of his map. Technically it was his schematic. He wondered where Ethan was on the map as he looked it over.

"Right. Well, it's a knightly matter, you two sort it out," Daraby said, snapping Caleb's attention back to the task at hand.

"Squire, you are our best choice to lead a team into the castle," Wilfred told him. "I'm going to knight you before we send you back in. Understood?"

The others obviously knew; they were reading his face. "You're serious," Caleb said quietly.

"I don't want to hear about needing this or that," Daraby joined in. "When my great-grandfather was under siege, the prince knighted all the squires over the age of fifteen."

Caleb wanted to tell them he was supposed to be knighted with his brothers. There was supposed to be the excitement of the days leading up, spending the night before in prayer (more or less) before nobles came to witness. Often it was done in conjunction with a holiday or special event. Besides perhaps the crowning of a king or his own wedding, there wasn't supposed to be a more important event in his life.

He didn't need any of that. He'd heard stories where they quickly knighted squires and even a well-deserving man-at-arms to be elevated on the eve before a battle, for the survivors to re-swear the oaths. He knew Wilfred's meaning. They needed more knights than him; ten knights with half as many fighting-age squires would be a start if they could get the drawbridge down; and no one was *sending him in*; he was going regardless of what anyone said. He looked over his shoulder at Lily. It would be nice to ask her what she thought, but he also knew she had no idea what this meant.

"Let's knight him at the camp. Less distractions," Daraby said.

"This bar is like his second home," Rodney pointed out.

"I'm not against it," Caleb said finally. "But I didn't do anything to earn an early knighthood, sir."

"If I'm to be completely honest, it's not about you, squire," Wilfred pointed out.

"If you want it to be seen as legitimate, that requires witnesses," Caleb told him.

"She's the chief distraction," Daraby gestured in Lily's direction. "There'll be time for chasing girls later."

This would have been so much easier if he wasn't feeling self-conscious about his earlier brain-fog. He knew he was still off, but at least now he wasn't staring at the majesty of the lake like a ninny, or mesmerized by the sound of wind through the leaves. Earlier, touching bark or the soft fabric seemed intense. "If you think it's for the best," Caleb said. "My only request is it's done in the parish where my parents got married. The friar's here, we can ask. And nothing big. Just enough witnesses to count, but I'm sure Wallace and the friar will vouch for me. If he says no, we go to the camp and do it by the lake."

"Fine fine," Daraby answered for Wilfred. "Shouldn't take more than five minutes and we'll double the knights we currently have."

"I'll ask." Caleb realized someone had helped himself to his pint, and he made his way back over to where the others were seated, discussing moving people to the nearest port over tea, though Larry and Catarina were slightly sequestered again.

"They let you go so soon?" Isaac asked as he approached.

"No such luck. Is it possible to borrow the parish for about fifteen minutes?" Caleb asked the friar.

The friar broke into a smile. "I knew they were going to! Yes, of course. When do you need it?"

Did they mention the idea to anyone else? "I guess as soon as we walk there," Caleb said. Everyone else at the table was looking at one another quizzically.One lady scowled at Lily. "Lily, they want to knight me, so do you mind witnessing?" He then realized that people were looking at him and their expressions were increasingly judgemental. "You can all come to if you want but it won't be anything fancy. They want to do the fast version."

"Of course," Lily said, "but isn't getting knighted really important for you?"

"Yes, but . . . look, it's an honour I don't deserve. If Wilfred or Daraby thinks it'll help, I'm all for it. I just want it to be seen as legitimate in a week."

"Does the knighting ceremony matter?" Catarina asked. Caleb nodded. Of course it mattered. "You wait here," she got up, and hurried over to Sir Wilfred.

"We've books in the parish that should contain the vows, we can just repeat them," the friar said. "Not much time for me to come up with anything original."

Caleb nodded. "I'm sure it'll be fine."

It was Catarina who objected from the other side of the room. "Are you telling me that it absolutely needs to be done, but you can't spare more than five minutes?"

"Madame, I appreciate everything you've done, the folk of this town owe you a debt, but this is knight business," Wilfred said, making his way over to Caleb and the friar. "Is the parish available?"

"Of course. I have the keys, we can walk down there now if you'd like. I'll need about ten minutes to find the appropriate materials."

"I want this done with so we can get to planning," Daraby called over.

"We've already got a plan," Wilfred called back. "You go to your camp and let me handle the knighting."

"Aye, we're supposed to let you ride off to battle, so you can tend your own wounds, catch your own food, just waving our kerchiefs and hoping things are handled, are we?" Catarina asked. "I'm not saying you can't knight him, but do it right."

"We're what now?" Tristan asked from across the room.

Seth wandered over, holding his cards close to his chest. "What's going on?"

"We're promoting the squire so it feels like I'm not taking orders from a child," Rodney said. "I'm with these woodcutters; take twenty minutes if you're insisting it'll make a lick of difference."

"You all understand why we're insisting? I would love to give you a day or two, squire," Wilfred said. "If you're going back to the castle tonight, time's not a luxury we can afford."

"It's fine, sir," Caleb said. "So long as someone who won't be caught up in the fighting can witness me taking the oaths can tell my family. They should know."

"Right, your family." Sir Wilfred seemed like he was wavering.

"I may never see them again,sir," Caleb said. "Unless you know for a fact they're here in town, seeing them is not my priority. If you think this is important, we do it. Getting people out of that castle alive matters more to me than a ceremony no one is going to remember in two days." He didn't mean to sound cynical; he'd been to several knightings. The ceremonies were beautiful and after the fact were often a lot of fun, listening to minstrels and gifted speakers telling tales of brave heroics well into the night.

Gill said something to Tristan, who smacked Seth's arm and, abandoning their game, the two sped off out the main doors.

"I'm glad we have an understanding," Catarina said. "Now, what all do you need for this?"

"Him," Wifred gestured. "I like the idea of the parish and a handful of you to witness; I don't mind foreigners but some of you knew him growing up."

"Actually," Caleb said. "Can she have me recite the vows? Catarina, I mean."

"Me?" Catarina asked.

"You ran that camp. I don't think Seth and Lily would have made it as far as they did without your help. You've been selflessly working to ensure everyone's warm, sheltered, and fed," Caleb said. "Wilfred? You said yourself this town owes this woman, her husband, and Mr. Sprites a debt. I'd be honoured if Catarina participated."

"I suppose it would be all right," Wilfred said.

"Give me fifteen minutes to make myself look like one of them fancy ladies in the paintings," Catarina said, then turned her attention to her husband. "And to think you said I didn't need a nice dress!"

"Oh, Catarina," Larry groused. "You're lovely in a potato sack. Go gussy, put those noble women who don't know how to stitch to shame."

Caleb was honestly happy whenever someone else made plans that involved him, then buzzed around like they had more important things and he could relax a little bit. Seriously though, as if a pint would have . . .

Lily's gentle hand on his shoulder brought him back. "You're okay with this?" Lily asked.

Caleb realized Lily wasn't the distraction—everything else was the distraction keeping him away from her. "I wish Ethan was here. To be knighted with, I mean. You're coming?"

"Of course. Did you want to walk together, or do you have to do anything ahead of time?"

"I don't think Wilfred's going to spot me an hour for prayer and meditation."

"He'll walk with me," Wilfred said. "No offence to the civilians here, but it's a common thing for a squire to walk into the cathedral with other squires and his knight sponsor. I'll be the stand in for Sir Marinell."

Lily nodded. "Okay, then. Someone tell us where to go, and we'll be there, right?" she asked Isaac and Larry.

"Come along, I need to dig out some material. Give me fifteen minutes, Wilfred," the friar said. "Come down when you're ready, the doors will be open to all. Do you have anything with your family colours, Caleb?"

"Not really. I nearly cleared out Ivan's supply of shirts; I'll put a fresh one on." Caleb said.

"There's more shirts?" Gill asked, too loudly.

Caleb turned on him. Gill was already walking towards the stairs. "No, those are for Ethan and anyone else we rescue." Gill stopped, they eyed one another. Gill shuffled forward slightly. Caleb matched him.

"But you're getting a different one." Step.

"For ten minutes." Step.

"Yeah well . . . I'm getting one anyway!" Gill said, and dashed. Gill was always just a little quicker, but Caleb grabbed his boot on the stairs and was ready to drag him down when he heard Wilfred call.

"Oh, let him be your brother for an hour."

"I already have a little brother," Caleb said, Gill had left him a boot and scrambled; of course he knew which door. By the time Caleb joined him, Gill had donned a forest green tunic but posed with a red shirt. "Do up the top button, no one wants to see that."

"I'll pay you back I swear. Which colour are we doing? Brown? You're boring, so that makes sense. Oh, this one brings out my eyes . . . "

Caleb washed his face, ditched the jerkin and slipped on a fresh black shirt and ran a comb through his hair. Gill acquiesced and matched him.

"Seth was telling me that it takes a bit of getting used to as a puppet," Gill said. "Can I change early?"

"We're going to run drills and see if anyone can't handle it. I'd rather have people panic and back out before we're inside."

The main dining room to the tavern was uncharacteristically quiet as they made their way to the front doors. "Does this walk have to be silent?" Gill asked, trailing after him.

"In the case of you pair," Wilfred said, Rodney also waiting for them outside. "Yes. You can talk when we get to the parish."

"Why is that?" Gill asked.

"Because I'm sick and tired of hearing your voice, Gillam," Rodney snapped.

There were multiple churches in the town. The one Caleb's family attended was a parish by the lake. Caleb liked to sneak off after services and throw rocks into the lake with his friends, but it felt good to see the familiar trees and the familiar statue of an angel in battle over a large snake. He slowed down when they approached the graveyard.

"Your father's buried that way, near your grandfather," Wilfred said, gesturing.

He knew about where that was. "Can I have a minute?"

"I'll go make sure they're ready. I'll have Gillam fetch you if you're dawdling."

They went inside. It wasn't hard to figure out where; there wasn't so much a family section as it was near where they'd buried his grandfather; both died from injuries incurred during service. Caleb wondered if he ought to be buried here himself, if that curse didn't hit the castle and extend his life. Both Henry and Edgar's tombstones were engraved with poems his father had written.

Caleb unsheathed his sword and knelt, tip to the soil with his forehead against the hilt. Many knights didn't make their way back home, buried in strange lands or faraway counties.

He thought about the last two years, the last week and everything that happened. He'd thought all he'd needed was a chance and here it was. He wasn't ready.

What if Lily hadn't called out to him to try to warn him about those ghouls, or she and Seth found someone else first? They could have allied with other people—what if they'd been detected, and the ones pulling the strings had sent him and Ethan on her and her brother? After she and Seth reunite and took Darius and Tristan with them, he worried that they had been caught and he'd never see them again. Or that there was only one chance to escape and he should have pressed Ethan to go. He was letting his emotions get the better of him. He could go mad thinking about what could have happened. *Even if all I had was one day out here, it was a good day.*

"God, I'm unworthy of this. I was arrogant, and took so much for granted. I'm so thankful that I could be reminded of what good there is in the world—the real one, I mean. Help me to be half the knight these men were. Use me to help those people trapped in that castle." He licked his lips, thinking of not just Ethan and Oliver and Esther, but everyone, even the ones who didn't much care for him, or the ones who professed to like that half-life in that fake world. "I want to be a better man, even if I'm not made of flesh and bone."

Caleb entered the church before they called him. Lit by candles, the ambient light felt familiar and comforting. People mostly congregated and chatted up in the first three rows—he subconsciously slid into the second row from the back on the left, thinking he would have five minutes to meditate and avoid small talk. He was almost immediately joined by Seth, Gill, Tristan, and Louis, who were in the very back a moment prior. They didn't go around, but told him in no uncertain terms to get out of their way.

"Too good for us?" Gill asked as they spread out, taking up an entire bench that could have easily held double their number.

"This is my normal spot," Caleb told him. He liked being near the aisle so he could duck out.

"It's a church, you ain't got no spot," Louis said.

"Ain't you supposed to march in to music?" Seth asked, shifting his mandolin over his shoulder. He played a few cheerful chords of what sounded like a children's song.

"Louis, how did you—" Caleb began.

"Tristan and Seth got me. I'm missing my fish fry, just so you know."

"Big one?"

"Meeeeh." Louis used his hands. Seth corrected him to indicate it was a little smaller. "Are you sure this is all there is to a knighting?"

"Yeah, normally there's a lot more pomp and circumstance. In a good way," Tristan said. "Still, kind of a big deal."

"So kinda like a wedding," Louis offered.

"Yeah, pretty much," Tristan said. "Alotta hoo-ha for five minutes of promising not to poison each other."

"Does my salary increase after this?" Seth asked.

"Take it up with Larry." Larry was up front talking with Catarina and Wilfred. Catarina wore a very lovely dress, cream and yellow with long sleeves. She might have been the biggest woman he'd ever seen; somehow that was Caleb's childhood impression of Lady Valour. Towering over him, impossible to reason with, and ever ready to smack him with that giant wooden spoon. Lily and Isaac were talking with Wilfred's wife up near the front. Part of Caleb's brain was still questioning the validity of the day. It still all seemed surreal . . .

. . . waking up relatively unscathed, with people who accepted him without question, only that he was known to them and somehow one of them.

Before he'd seen her as human, he'd suspected Lily was pretty—but not only was she smart and stunning, but kind and supportive. He was starting to suspect things were too good to be true; that there was a reason sailors threw themselves into the waves . . .

. . . and then Seth strummed his mandolin and produced a rather dubious set of lyrics, before being told to shush, that this was a solemn event, and the resulting, "Says who?" banter that followed between him and a lady from two rows up.

His nightmares might have fed on the insecurities and dark hollows of his mind, but Caleb knew no hypnotic man-eating spider, seductive lake monster, chaotic kitsune, or combination thereof could amount to half of what two Stagmil boys could sputter when they thought they were out of earshot, or plum didn't care.

"It would be better if Wilfred made him run a gauntlet first," Louis said. "I don't think we could make a spike pit, but we could throw big sacks of flour at him."

"Oooh! Him and Tristan! Whoever makes it get to be a knight," Seth agreed. "Whoever fails has to retrieve five finger bones from the lake."

"Leave me out of it," Tristan said. "And there's gotta be more than five finger bones down there."

"Let's go find some after this," Seth said. Louis nodded in agreement.

Several children raced in. "Don't cause a ruckus," their father said, carrying the youngest on his shoulder, their mother directing the older two. It was then that Caleb realized there were more people than he remembered speaking to earlier.

"Didn't we agree to this fifteen minutes ago?" Caleb asked.

"I don't know how long it takes for you to trim your nose hairs," Gillam said.

"*Cay!*" Alanna squealed, pushing Gillam out of her way so she could sit next to Caleb. She wore a very pale purple dress, lilacs braided into her hair. "Did you stop the kitty from getting the ducklings?"

"I haven't had a chance to look after the ducklings," Caleb said. Alanna scowled. "Should we ask Tristan and Louis?"

"Alanna." Alanna's mother, Kelsey, reached for her daughter, who shook her head. "He's not going to be sitting here. We're here to watch him become a real knight, remember?" Nicolas, Alanna's father, carried their other child, who looked to be only a few months old, swaddled and generally behaving.

"Boy or girl?"

"Boy," Nicolas said. Caleb stood to get a better look at him, and Alanna jumped on his back. Caleb gestured it was fine and boosted her so she wasn't completely blocking his windpipe. "Hard to believe we were all this size once."

Kelsey wrangled their daughter. "Do not mess up his hair, Alanna."

"Bye Cay! I'm supposed to thank you for something, but I don't know what." Alanna wriggled away and skipped ahead down the aisle.

"How do you say this word?" Louis asked, shoving a paper in Seth's face.

"Sagacity," Tristan clarified. "Fancy word for cunning."

"Wouldn't that interfere with the vow of truth?" Louis asked.

"Pursue truth and be honest in your dealings, you don't need to give away your position on a battlefield or tell every secret," Caleb stated matter-of-factly. To be fair, he tried to *Whattaboutdat* when he was Louis' age too. He looked to Tristan, he had to keep reminding himself Tristan was older than Seth; he was good in the training yard but he'd yet to fill out; it wouldn't be fair to put him in the thick of fighting. "Didn't think to ask them to do both of us."

"I'm glad it's just you," Tristan said. "Less intimidating than in the cathedral, though."

"All right, we're just about ready to get started," the friar said to Wilfred. "Those lingering outside, please come in and be seated."

Caleb resisted the urge to sink into the pew as more than a dozen people stopped their visiting outside. "What part of 'don't make a big deal' do they not understand?"

"You're the princess who wanted her fancy coronation," Gill told him.

"I'll go get him." Rodney told the friar. "Leave it to a squire to get lost in a graveyard." Gill let out an annoyingly shrill whistle. "Why are you seated in the back?" Rodney demanded. Several people turned their heads and chuckled.

"This is where I normally sit," Caleb offered.

"And you are sort of involved with the accolade ceremony. *Get over here.*"

"He's not wrong," the friar offered as Caleb got up and snuck around the side as opposed to walking down the centre of the aisle. "Besides ducking in at the last minute and out before he had to socialize, he was a regular up until two years ago. What's your excuse, Rodney?"

Caleb smiled and made eye contact with everyone, glad to see that Isaac, Larry, Lily and Alanna were in the front row, apparently having abandoned her family who were seated more or less right behind her. Offering up his sword to Catarina, she wrapped it in a piece of silky, off-white fabric she'd no doubt procured from Ingrid. "You look lovely," he said to Catarina. She beamed.

"Just remember that's my wife," Larry called.

"Cay, don't be nervous!" Alanna told him.

"Just stand there," the friar directed him to stand to the right along with Catarina as the last stragglers settled into their seats.

"Why are there so many people here?" Caleb asked Catarina quietly.

"It's not about you. Look at their faces."

He wished she was right; they wanted a knight, but for all the good he'd do he wasn't certain. He was happy to see Alanna's family. And Wallace, and . . . he surprised himself at just how many people he knew. These weren't the faces he'd expected when he attained knighthood. "They're going to be disappointed if they've seen one of these before."

"Hush up," Catarina told him. "This is what hope looks like."

"I'd like to thank you all for coming," said the friar. "I know this normally done in the cathedral at the castle, and but you are all welcome here for this knighting ceremony.

"The town's changed quite a bit in the past two years. Even if we are not missing someone personally, we can all agree that what happened two years ago changed not only the castle, but all of us who remained, hoping for answers we knew we wouldn't like for the sake of closure. Families left, businesses shut down, and we can't escape the lingering shadow across the lake.

"I for one was surprised when I overheard a shopkeeper say someone appeared to be back from the dead. I'm glad she was mistaken.

That our candidate—and others here we haven't seen in years—are very much alive, and they were quite missed.

"We still have many questions about what's going on. None save God the Almighty can see how their actions will play out fully, even if we have good intentions. All we can do is work with that's given to us. Our time, our gifts, our compassion and caring for one another; acts of valour aren't necessarily done at the end of a sword or a shield, though they have their place in protecting the ones behind them. We're here with a family reunited, in hopes that more will follow; with people who have only known this town and have never set further than a day's travel away, and with those who have travelled from overseas, united in the common goal of helping those who can't free themselves.

"The accolade ceremony is about an ideal no one can hope to live up to. The point isn't that the accolade will somehow be any better or worse than he was as a squire, or that we're to hold him to a higher standard. This candidate in particular is known to me; he was dedicated . . . *mostly*," he gave Caleb a slight grin, "in the pursuit of knighthood. We cannot grant everyone who would heartily answer yes to the vows he will accept the title of knighthood. That is a matter among those of a class most of us only see from afar or in passing. There is more to nobility than valour; more to bravery than a willingness to stand up to what makes us afraid. I do invite all who are here to look within and ask themselves how it is they can serve their fellow man, and strive to be the best version of themselves."

The friar nodded to Wilfred, who looked pleased with the speech. "Will the accolade please come forward and kneel?" Caleb did as he was told. All that preening, and everyone was going to be staring at the back of his head. "Do you, Caleb Ander Felvey of Mirador, son of Sir Edgar and Lady Maya, accept the accolade for knighthood?" Wilfred asked. Caleb nodded. "You have to say 'yes.'"

"Yes," he said quietly, then cleared his throat, and said it again.

"Do you promise to hold to ideals greater than your own?"

"Yes."

Wilfred nodded, and Catarina stepped forward, her voice more authoritative than he'd expected. "Do you accept the Vow of Valour, to show courage and protect the weak and those in need of defence?"

"Yes."

"Do you accept the Vow of Liberality, to be fair in dealings with all folk, noble and common, rich and poor? From this land, and abroad?"

"Yes."

"Do you accept the Vow of Justice, to obey just laws and see them carried out without personal vendetta or malice?"

"Yes."

"Do you accept the Vow of Truth, to be honest and forthright in your dealings? To speak the truth, even when it could mean your death?"

"Yes."

"Do you accept the Vow of Diligence, to persevere and see things to their end?"

"Yes."

"Do you accept the Vow of Temperance, to curb your desires for vengeance and bloodshed for its own sake?"

"Yes."

"Do you accept the Vow of Sagacity, to behave shrewdly and cunning when needed in defence of all these other principles?"

"Yes."

"I stand to witness Caleb Ander Felvey of Mirador make these vows in the presence of those assembled here. Let the assembly hold him to account and be a reminder of the vows made this day," Catarina said, and stepped back.

Wilfred grasped his father's blade, and tapped the flat of the sword to Caleb's shoulders twice on each side. "Be Thou a Knight, Sir Caleb of Mirador. Arise and take up your sword in service to the vows you have made this day." He handed the sword back to Catarina, who held it for him to accept. He did so, and did his best to stand tall when he turned around. There was polite clapping, until Seth let out a whistle and Louis went, "Booyah!"

"One does not booyah in a cathedral," Wilfred said.

"We're not in a cathedral. Booyah!" Gill chimed. The hooting from the rowdies made other people whistle and cheer.

"My lady?" Sir Caleb asked, offering Catarina an arm. She accepted, and he led her to Larry.

"Good. I was getting antsy," Larry said, taking Catarina's arms and giving her a kiss. "You did wonderful, Lady Valour. She did write a speech, you should hear it. Oh stop being polite, you didn't come here to see me." The pair walked off to chat privately.

Caleb gave Isaac a nod. "Mr. Sprites."

"Sir Caleb of Mirador." They shook hands.

"Lady of the Lake." Caleb smiled at the person he wanted to see most, but Alanna launched herself at him from the pew with so much force he almost had to turn to catch her.

"Cay, you're no longer a fake knight!"

"Alanna!" Nicolas scrambled from his pew.

Caleb gestured it was fine. "Full knight. Squires are like apprentice knights," he told her. Alanna wasn't listening; instead she grabbed his chin to move his head and kissed his cheek.

"Mommy said I'm supposed to do that after you're knighted. Gillam said I should slap you. Can I slap him instead?" Alanna asked.

"Only if you tell him it's from me."

"Come with me," Nicolas said, taking his daughter from Caleb's arms before shaking his hand. Alanna stuck a piece of lilac behind Caleb's ear. "Congratulations, Sir Caleb. Sorry about my daughter."

"What for?" Caleb asked. He put up a fist, and Alanna pounded it. "Thank you for coming, Alanna."

"Hurry up and kiss him already," Alanna told Lily. "We're waiting!"

"Oh, he thinks he gets her first?" asked one of the women from town. Caleb bent down and gave the townswoman a hug. "Congratulations, Sir." For fun, he picked her up and she let loose a squeal of laughter.

Other people came up to offer their congratulations. "Bless you, boy," one man Caleb didn't know said. "I didn't think anything could be done about that castle. Even if you and Tristan were the only ones who made it out, it's a spit in the eye of whatever is to blame."

"He's not, though," said Wallace, "that precious young . . . "

Somewhere in the back of the church, a *SLAP!* resonated with really good acoustics. "Ow!" escaped from Gill.

"That's for Sir Cay!" Alanna crowed. Caleb couldn't watch the exchange that followed and almost thought Lily wasn't going to wait for him, but she watched in amusement as he talked with the townsfolk. His mother and sisters and brother squires weren't here, but people who loved him were. And people he loved were back at the castle.

This had to work. He had to rescue Ethan and Oliver and no one here knew Esther but she deserved to be free. These people thought he could do something and he had no idea if . . .

Lily seemed to notice when he tensed up and his mind started to take him back to that dark place. Her gentle but guiding hand was enough to bring him out the dark. "Can I have him for a minute?" She'd waited towards the end, and pulled him into an embrace. "Thank you for protecting me and my brother in the castle, Sir." Then she gave him a look, which he later could recognize but had a hard time describing. He knew he was going to be scolded no matter what, so if everyone was watching, he might as well give them reason, so he tipped her back slightly.

"Seth, your sister is kinda . . . ?" Louis sputtered.

"I know," Seth said. "I'm all for it; if she moves out I'm turning her bedroom into my trophy room."

"Chaste kisses in the church," Wilfred told them, breaking it up. "Squire—I mean, Sir. Stop smirking."

"I'm not."

"All right, Sir Caleb," Sir Wilfred said. "Captain Daraby's waiting. We need to gather and ensure everyone knows what their tasks are. I'd love to give you an hour or two, but we don't have time to waste."

Caleb nodded. He went back to Isaac and Lily. "Unfortunately, I've got work to do. Thank you both for everything you've done."

"Can we come with you to the camp? We don't need to know specifics," Isaac said. "We can figure out what we need to do there as good as anywhere."

"That would be nice." Caleb realized then that he'd left camp relatively early that morning and now the day was almost done. Not exactly how he imagined he'd spend it, but even if all they did was get Alanna out and people knew the others were still in there, it was worth it. He wanted to spend the walk with Lily. Instead, Louis mostly asked questions about campaign work he'd done with Sir Marinell, and Tristan answered, with Rodney and Wilfred interjecting their other, more interesting war stories. It was nice so he could relax. The walk took less time than he'd expected, and it looked like a war camp now.

Ranger tents, not the large sort he'd hoped for, but they were functional. The wagon and the carriage were gone. Caleb had overheard that the donkeys and draft horses were being cared for at a nearby farm. Ranger horses were tied to an actual hitch, with several ranger apprentices busy running tasks, but most of them were playing a knife throwing game until they realized their superiors were present.

The two large tents that were there this morning had been commandeered; the main sleeping tent was the new infirmary, and the kitchen tent was now a war tent.

Daraby was speaking with several men at the low fire. They still had a few hours before dark. "It's done?"

"Sir Caleb and I are reporting, Captain," Wilfred said. The captain gave him a brief nod —before he made Captain, Myron was one of Caleb's training officers.

"Good, let's have the knights lead by example," the captain said, and gestured to the war tent.

Caleb gave Lily's hand a final squeeze, nodded to the others, and followed Sir Wilfred into the tent. He'd not been in this one before; there was a trestle table and some mismatched chairs in addition to a handful of stumps. It was bigger than the tent he'd woken up in.

Caleb's first task as a knight was making a bigger map for Daraby, who was telling him strategic points in the halls where they ought to fall back to if it came to a skirmish, and other tactical issues as Wilfred argued with Rodney about something irrelevant, before they'd go on tangents about missions that took place before he was born.

By the time he'd made something to Daraby's liking, eight people congregated inside, rangers stood by men-at-arms, chatting over pints. A handful of stragglers, such as Gill and Seth, entered as Wilfred began to speak.

"Before we get started, I want to thank everyone for volunteering for this mission. We don't know the nature of what's going on in there," Sir Wilfred said. "Our best eyes and ears is Sir Caleb. He spent more than two years in there. As most of you know, we knighted him within the previous hour. I know he's much younger than many of you, but he has seen what's gone on inside. That'll change after we get some of you in, but if he tells you something, don't argue."

"What's with the foreign boy?" One of the rangers gestured with his thumb at Seth. "You need loyal men. We're all from here besides him."

"He's imperative to the current plan," Caleb said. He found it was easy to just pretend what his father or grandfather would say and imitate their mannerisms the best he could recall. "Most of you know most of the people inside are cursed. Most are turned into puppets, about this tall." He gestured with his hands. "Not quite a year ago, a wizard constructed a tunnel that will only allow someone that size in. We've found it; the plan is to use their own magic, transform ourselves into marionettes, and sneak small teams into the castle. Once we're in there, we contact the people I know who are inside, and we determine if it's plausible to fight what's up there.

"Besides the puppet spell, there are other spells on the inhabitants captive in Mirador. Make no mistake, they are all captive. Those inside who are on strings are real people. If they start to jerk, they will attack you. You won't feel pain. You can be hacked to pieces or burned to ash. If you are caught, the best you can hope for is that they will string you and keep you on the playing board. We have allies in there, but besides Sir Percival and Sir Hector I'm not giving any names at this time. We will do our best to rescue you, but the mission comes first."

"Yes yes, most of us have caught up on this," said one of the rangers. "I want to know the plan."

"The first phase is intel. I think the curse keeping me in the castle is gone. But I don't know for certain until we reenter the castle," Caleb said. "Some of you are like Captain Daraby and know the castle. It's been . . . remodelled, but much of the layout is the same as how you knew it. We're going to sneak people in, and determine if they can reach the drawbridge. If it's deemed feasible, we're going to sneak the rest of you in. Most of you will lay low until it's time to get back to normal, but you may assist in rescuing my allies, hopefully they can join us tomorrow night. We repeat for a few nights, and we can have a small army in a few days."

"Sorcery can be strange," a ranger offered. "How do we know we won't be turned into anything else?"

"Why not go kill the wizard responsible?" asked a man-at-arms. "With lots of us shrunk down, we can swarm him."

"When things happened to the castle, initially they were slow. Those strange green clouds congregated overhead not only over the castle but over the town for days, but it was almost after the royal family left, and before the next group evacuated things happened very fast," Captain Daraby said. "We don't even know if it was a wizard. I was awake for the transformation as were several others here." He gestured to the four nodding men-at-arms. "People were making for the drawbridge and several jumped from windows. Strings hit my head, and I got pulled out; last thing I remember were your ugly mugs and learning I've spent the last two years in storage.

"Now, the drawbridge was open last night, so we know it's operable." Daraby gestured to the map. "I want scouts and intel; there's not enough of us to muscle our way in. If whatever is up there puts its guard down, we have the advantage of surprise. For all we know, we can't fight what's up there with steel, and our goal will change to evacuating hostages. We're going to scout and learn before we strike. Understood?"

"We could wait until the riders have returned with more bodies," a ranger offered.

"I need to go back," Caleb pointed out. "Sir Hector will likely notice I'm missing by now, but if the place is on high alert there's no point of us going to wait out for weeks."

"How many hostages?" asked a ranger.

Caleb's mouth went dry, but they were all looking at him. "Hundreds, if not potentially more than a thousand."

"Everyone here has a reason to lash out and be angry, but I will remind you all that there is no do over," Wilfred spoke up. "If we mess this up, the one way in could be lost. Do not lash out in vengeance. Us keeping a cool head until we know what we're up against may be the difference between getting another Alanna home."

Caleb nodded in agreement. "This first step will be crucial; if we can get other people out who are used to moving around like me, I become a lot less vital to the mission, plus most of you know Ethan and my cousin can put up a decent fight." He frowned. If only Sir Hector didn't have a bad knee; then again, that only slowed him down. Everyone here save Seth knew who Sir Hector was. "We also need to leave some who were like me behind, so it's not suspicious that everyone's gone missing. Sir Hector and Sir Percival are active and will be with us."

"Let them be as suspicious as they'd like in a few days," someone said. "Moot point if we him 'em hard."

"We have the element of surprise," Daraby snapped. "We're not wasting it."

"Why are we operating at night?" someone asked.

"Because if anyone's watching from the castle, it'll be less obvious when we're crossing the lake," Seth offered.

"Who is this kid again?" a man-at-arms asked.

"This is Seth O'Connell. He and his sister broke in a few nights ago and helped me escape. He is our secret weapon—this cannot leave this tent. We're going to show you what becoming a puppet looks like, and do it to you if you can handle it as well. If you see this and lose heart, I do not blame you. Do not speak of this to anyone, even your beloved spouse or one another outside this tent." Caleb put his hand on Seth's shoulder, and nodded.

Seth put his hand on the amulet and they transformed. It was immediate; they both practiced earlier and leapt slightly so they landed on the table; Caleb almost hated how small he was, and how people gawked at him. He nodded, and Seth let go of him and leaping backwards, resumed humanity almost instantly. Caleb did his best to not be embarrassed at how he looked; he already felt slightly numb and this body was more familiar to him. He hoped he wouldn't have that same brain fog he had, but watching Seth goof around with the amulet earlier, noted how Louis, Gillam, and Seth seemed like their normal selves almost immediately after.

"That's . . . what you . . . and I . . . looked like?" Captain Daraby asked. "For two years?"

"I mean, it looks like you, but . . . " Rodney began.

One man-at-arms visibly paled.

"Quiet. As you can see, this young man is the most valuable person in the room," Wilfred explained, gesturing at Seth. "This is how we're getting into the castle. There's a path that'll allow someone his size to get in. This man will get you back to full size."

To Caleb's surprise, none of the volunteers balked. He figured that would happen after they transformed. "Don't ask how I'm alive, I just am. There's some very obvious differences, notably I'm solid wood for the most part. Yes, you can poke me but just let me know you're about to do it."

"Pop your arm off and hand it around," Tristan offered, ducking into the tent.

He didn't know why people were so hesitant to take it. The first time was unnerving, but he'd gotten used to it over a year ago. "You got the string like I asked?" he asked Tristan, not sure who exactly he gave his left arm to.

"It's going to feel weird doing it to you" the squire said.

"I know. Okay, any volunteers? Seth'll turn you back if you can't handle it."

Rodney let out a groan before he nodded. "I'm going to regret this." He gestured to Seth.

Seth transformed Rodney and Gill while Caleb worked at putting strings on himself; they didn't really have crossbars, so Tristan tied the ends to his fingers. Once they saw that Rodney and Gill were fine, several other men-at-arms and rangers consented.

The only good news was that old aches and pains seemed to go away, and one ranger later cited he'd lost old scars. Only one of the volunteers panicked and demanded to change back, but he just needed to be human again, see how Seth did it, and rejoined. Once they got used to their bearings, Caleb gestured to not aim at him, but the strings if at all possible. He put his arm out and let them do practice swings, pretending his arm went dead.

"Remember, he'll be a moving target," Tristan said. "Caleb, next round I'll let the strings go slack, okay?"

He nodded, knowing that Tristan couldn't control him the same way as he could instinctively fight. Thankfully, Seth took half the group so they weren't all waiting to strike him. Seth taught them centre of gravity—balancing on a hand, even a finger if they got the hang of it—and how to remove screws and joints, before a more energetic method of learning how to jump and move nimbly. And because he needed to have some attention, Gill made a small archery range for those who were waiting. Thankfully the rangers were all excellent shots, and within a few rounds were able to hone in on the differences scale made.

To his surprise, it was the doc who entered the tent. Seth restored Caleb back to flesh before he approached the elderly physician. "I thought you'd be in town," Caleb said.

"I want to talk," said the old physician. "I understand you've been busy, Sir Knight. Congratulations; sorry I wasn't there, I was having supper with an old friend and only found out you were knighted afterwards."

"I wish I could splice myself into multiple parts," Caleb offered. Caleb ensured the others were doing all right—Seth was strung up now, and was a moving target.

Caleb followed Demetri to their infirmary, which was thankfully empty. "Rodney sent riders. I suppose you won't have to reach out to the prince."

"I've attended war camps before," Demetri nodded. "Have you shown any signs of being poisoned? Even something small, like a headache."

"Not really," Caleb admitted. "Why wouldn't it have launched me back into how bad I was before?"

"I don't know. I haven't experienced my old aches and pains, either. One of Daraby's armsmen said he is missing scarring. Kind of a panacea, isn't it?"

"I don't think such a thing exists," Caleb admitted. " . . . although, if one were to exist, what would you say it was?"

"I have heard of miraculous healings, but that's not my line of work," Demetri mused. "The junior physician swears she gave you the correct dosage. I was baffled, to be frank. No matter, we'll try again. Rodney promised me one of his riders would bring some back." Caleb frowned. They didn't have access to Mirador's stores; assuming anything was left and viable. Other castles might, but if Gill was right, that wasn't the cure.

"What poisons would mimic the Jorogumo venom?"

"Plenty, I would imagine."

"No way of narrowing it down," Caleb said. The doctor eyed him suspiciously. "In theory, if I was poisoned by something else, what's the best way to figure out what it would be?"

"Figure out what that other source of poison was," Demetri said. "Did you go mushroom picking?"

"No, nothing like that. Besides, the wound's still genky on my shoulders."

"Genky? Is that a word knights use?" Demetri asked.

"I thought being a knight would make people lay off."

"Ah, my naive knight, you have no idea," the doctor asked. "As for *panaceas*, I've heard of miraculous healings but the most allegedly profound one would be a pool in the far north. Freezing all around, all who descend into it would be restored to youth and health and—"

Jolly well and good assuming he could survive that long. "Potions?"

"I'm not an herbalist," Demetri said, he tended to look down on midwives so Caleb didn't press him. "My theory is that the vast majority of poisons a person could endure if they had the stamina. In your case, you would have died from dehydration. I would have to examine your organs after you perished to be certain, though."

He would, too. "What about a wizard?" Caleb asked.

"They often exact a price you don't expect. Maybe if you gave them something they'd want, but I've also heard people having a wizard laying a hand on them, and part of them goes . . . dormant, or missing."

"What would a wizard possibly want in payment? Like . . . a dragon scale, or a unicorn horn, or . . ."

The doctor laughed. "I'd be amazed if you could lay your hand on either one of those! I don't know what good a dragon scale would do, but unicorn horns are said to be incredible purifiers. Not as strong as when they're still attached to the unicorns. We seem to be in short order of unicorns in these parts. Hunting them is nigh impossible."

Caleb wondered how all of this could just be falling into place. What were the odds that the first stringless he managed to have a conversation with also had parents who would have access to something he would have needed? It wasn't perfect—last he checked, it would probably take him a better part of a week to make it to the mountains, let alone trek into them. "Would you know what to do with one if you found one?"

"Catching it? Not a clue."

"I mean using the horn."

"Do you have any idea how many people have paid for a sliver of a fake horn? I thought you had more sense than that."

"I do," Caleb said. "A guy can dream a little."

"Focus on your path, not what the rest of us need to do," Demetri lectured. "I'll do everything I can to help you. Do you think someone else poisoned you besides the Jorogumo?"

"I don't know," he said. "But the neck guard would have been lifted up, then I got stuck. That never made sense."

The doctor nodded. "It would be nice to pretend all of our enemies were external. You watch yourself."

"Don't tell anyone, it'll just upset them."

The doctor nodded. "Stay vigilant."

Leaving the tent, Caleb found Larry was waiting to speak to him. Isaac and Catarina were talking around the fire with Lily and Louis, who was frying his fish. The scent of butter and rosemary made Caleb's mouth water. "So, Sir, I suppose I won't be seeing much of you after this."

"You're going home?" Caleb asked.

"I'm taking people home. I'll be back, but you'll be there." Larry gestured to the castle. "I can squeeze ten people on my boat, which is not a lot, but ten less souls cluttering up the inn. About a day to my boat, we sail through the night, take a day or three to resupply back at Shelkie's Bay, and I'll come back for more. Your local folk will work on getting them to Port Garendell."

"Thank you, for everything you've done," Caleb said. "Seth and Lily couldn't have gotten this far without you."

"Courting. That's adorable," Larry said, producing a letter sealed with wax. "Lily gave me this letter for her family—any idea what it's about?" He studied Caleb's eyes.

"Ask her," Caleb gestured to Lily.

"Good," Larry said.

"When are you leaving?"

"After breakfast, and hopefully after an update from you on the inside. Not bad, all this," Larry said, gesturing to the camp. "Go see them."

As Caleb approached, Louis gave his fish a flip, then to his surprise, made two portions. "Just in time for fish and chips," Louis chirped. It was a very decently-sized fish.

"I won't be hungry in there." It smelled amazing.

"Might be your last meal for a while," Isaac said. "Don't disappoint Louis."

Louis didn't disappoint Caleb either, although both burned their tongue and fingers somewhat.

"Cutlery, children!" Catarina scolded.

"I won't ask details, but everything's going well?" Isaac asked.

"There's a reason why they got rid of most of the warriors in that castle. The ones they left behind are devoted," Caleb said. "I didn't think much of the people who we left behind outside the castle. Even if they didn't have people in the castle, businesses closed and people moved on."

"They've had two years of . . . what would my dad say . . . ? Steaming in their own gravy," Louis said.

"Is this before or after dodging gophers?" Caleb asked. He and Louis cackled; it wasn't that funny but Lily's expression was. Isaac didn't get it.

When he finished eating, Caleb sat on a log next to Lily. "How are you holding up? You didn't sleep since yesterday."

"I'm fine. Neither did Seth." She frowned suddenly and he followed her gaze. Tristan was returning to the war tent with a rather muddy shovel, whistling merrily, he'd a box of some sort in his other hand. "I don't even want to know."

He felt a strange, but not unfamiliar presence. A roar sounded overhead. Horses whinnied and fussed, and several people stopped what they were doing.

"Is that . . . ?" Lily asked.

"I think so."

Caleb went to the horses, and to his surprise, Lily started to unhitch one as well. "I'm coming to mind the horses," Lily said.

"They're ranger horses," an apprentice ranger cautioned, helping Lily with the tack. "You'd best take a ranger."

Lily said she had some sort of old, well-trained horse. These were notoriously hard to commandeer. "I'll grab Gill." Caleb poked his head back into the war tent. "How we doing?"

On the table, his free puppets were sparring and jumping.

Beside the table, Seth was full-sized, and looked like he and Tristan were about to give the mud-covered box to full-sized Daraby. They stared at him, wide-eyed and incredibly guilty, before they glanced at one another, then uniformly turned on Caleb. "Nothing to see here," Seth said.

"What are you up to?" Caleb asked.

"None of your business." Daraby put the box behind his back. Caleb almost thought he heard a very muffled *"Lemme out of here!"* Tristan made a poor attempt to hide the shovel, but Caleb could see the mud on the toes of his boots. "Didn't you just make poncy vows about justice and temperance? We don't need that right now: *out.*"

"I need about half an hour and Gillam. What is going on in—"

"Take an hour," said puppet Rodney, cracking his little knuckles. Caleb was right: The cold, dead eyes were very scary and they were all united, ranger, guardsman, shepherd, glaring at him. "Take two. Go write a poem about Liberality and perform it for Daisy. And don't let me catch you back in here early."

"Gill," Caleb called. Seth obliged, and Gill seemed somewhat relieved to be back to his normal self. "Is that fried fish I smell? Oh, you're running off with your girlfriend. Shouldn't you have done that earlier?"

"Come mind the horses," Caleb said, hopping in a saddle. "Lily, the commands for these ones are a little different." He scowled, noticing someone put a "NO GNITES ALLOWED" sign on the outside of the war tent, so he assumed they'd sent someone to distract and otherwise be rid of Wilfred too. *Not suspicious at all.* "Can someone tell them they spelled *Knights* wrong?"

Gillam briefed Lily on the basics. "We use different terms so over-fed shinies don't steal and break the backs of the poor horses," Gillam said. "Ours tend not to be built as big but they're like us rangers: swift and clever and know more tricks—great listeners, really. Loyal companions who'll never desert you, chosen for their skill as opposed to their breeding." He went to help her, but Lily mounted. "Oh, you've ridden before?"

"We have a horse," she said. Her horse backed up a little bit. "You're a little feistier than Stella." She patted her mare's neck, who tossed her head and nickered.

"Rein command is the same," Caleb said. "I believe the term is 'Kya' instead of 'Hyup.'"

"Where did you want to go?" Gill asked. Caleb spurred his horse ahead, and Lily gave the throaty, "Kya!" and followed after him. "All right, off with Sir Cay and his Lady Love."

They followed the path east winding around the river away from town. It wasn't the first time Caleb had ridden ranger horses or spoken to Peanut. The dragon was just getting his ability back when he got Lily across. Of course, he was ignoring the dragon's pestering because he was concerned about her, thinking about Seth and Ethan. He didn't blame any of them; it was bad timing and he let his guard down. When Lily said Peanut got him out, he didn't doubt her. He was impressed that a small wooden puppet could have burned through solid stone.

"What's the halt? Woah?" she asked. Her mare didn't slow down until Lily really seized up on the reins.

"I'll show you," Gill said. He used the reins and whistled, then made a series of clicks to spur his own mount ahead. "Oh, right, civilians. Use the term 'Yield!' And shouldn't I be leading?"

"I grew up here," Caleb called back. "Watch after Lily." He wasn't sure exactly, and if it wasn't for the mind link, probably wouldn't have chased after the dragon; he had a general sense of direction and knowledge of the area was enough for him to pick a given road without having to double back. The dragon wasn't so much talking to him but reassuring him that there was some sort of mutual affection, almost an honour debt.

The path narrowed as they detoured into a more wooded area. Gill picked out a trail when Caleb became a little flustered as to how to continue northeast. Didn't bother Gillam; the ground was relatively flat and the forest wasn't so thick that they needed to dismount so much as ride in single file.

"I understand the two of you wanting private time, but there's more scenic places to watch the sunset," Gill said.

Another roar and the horses buckled slightly. "Easy, easy. You guys stay here," Caleb said, dismounting and handing the reins to Gillam.

"Caleb, what is that?" Gill asked. "And why did we ride towards it?"

"Just wait here and be quiet. It'll be fine."

"Lily?" Gillam asked.

"It's . . . his friend from the castle," Lily said.

"Oh, good. His friends are my friends. That makes us frie—"

"Don't push it, Gill," Caleb called back.

Part of him wondered if he was being lured like Gillam was two years prior. Some part of him knew how dangerous this was. Another part of him felt there was a sort of innate fondness. He supposed it was like his affection for a horse or a dog.

The dragon wasn't red, but copper and gold and green. A very young dragon, Caleb would have stood a chance against him but not much if he breathed fire. Caleb used to pour over pictures of sea dragons and fire drakes in the castle library as opposed to learning whatever lesson was relevant, but the old illustrations paled in comparison to the rows of horns and overlapping plates. In hindsight, he would have asked Lily to draw the dragon and compare it to the library pictures.

He could hear Gill sputtering and Lily reassuring him, but once the mind link bridged Caleb had no choice but to hear the dragon.

Hello Caleb, the dragon thought out to him. *You are looking hale. Most of the sorceries are diminishing off of you. Would you like her to commune as well? You need to guard your thoughts better around her.*

Last thing he wanted was Lily getting any glimpse into his mind; he'd probably scare her off with his gushing. "I'm good like this. She said you have a real name?"

I am surprised she did not blurt it out. I am called Varian. My nickname for you was never Wolf. Until you told me, I called all of you armoured ones Kindling. Varian seemed amused at his wit. *The ocean was a fantastic place to enjoy delicacies I have long missed. The shark in particular was delicious. I didn't think to bring you any.*

"You flew to the ocean and back?"

That is your most pressing question?

"I'm glad to see you with my real eyes," Caleb said. "Can I—" He put a hand out, and Varian lowered his serpentine neck. The scales were hard to the touch. "Wow, and you're going to get bigger."

Much bigger. Your great-grand children may see me approaching full size. We are not as the great wyrms but I will live to be over five hundred years so long as I am not foolish.

"Varian, you can't stay here."

Of course not. I am not going to break into the castle another time to save you. That is your plan, then? To return?

The thoughts weren't as judgemental as Caleb expected. He felt that warmth of affection, only it was for Ethan, Oliver, Esther. The thoughts became less warm when he thought about his mother; the dragon didn't press, didn't understand. Caleb didn't want to explain it, either. There were too many people in there to count and, if he was honest, he wouldn't leave an enemy to that fate. "Can you read minds?"

Not exactly. I get inklings about what you are thinking about. You've never had to guard your thoughts or your feelings, so I will try not to pry. Your mind is still a little scattered, but it should improve with time.

"I'm a lot better than I was this morning."

The dragon laughed; it was a series of clicks. *I long for the embrace of my kind, so in four days I will depart to the South. I hope if we meet again, it be on good terms. I would hate to have to kill you. You seem a decent fellow.*

"I would hate to have to die. Those claws though . . . "

Varian flexed them, startling Gill and Lily but Caleb tapped them. If Varian wanted him dead, there was absolutely nothing he could do. *In three days, I will take my vengeance on the castle. I would do it sooner, but no doubt they expect it. Something is going on in there, something new. I may do it sooner, but I will wait until they are unsuspecting.*

"We will be crossing the lake at night," Caleb said. "I don't know where we'll be in three days. I am going back to try to get intelligence. Figure out what's causing it, and why."

If it is a wizard, chase him up to a tower. I can bite his head off for you.

"It's some sort of sorcery but . . . look, my goal is to get Ethan out to-morrow. I can't promise an update, but he may be able to speak to you. Understood? I mean, if we have someone I could throw from a tower, you could eat him or something . . . I'm not sure if we could work out the timing."

I meant to spit out the head. You humans really think you are tasty, don't you?

"A kitsune told me I tasted terrible."

Food is food, but it's not like a nice tender seal or octopus. I've always wanted to try kraken.

"Maybe if I get to be a lone wandering swordsman I'll go south with Ethan.If we find you we can try it."

You can't be alone with another person. That is the definition of a Duo.

"He'd be my sidekick."

You're both the sidekick. I advise caution and hope your foolish plan to uproot whatever captured me is successful. Ill-advised, but I suppose that is your cave, and I wouldn't be happy if some wyvern took up residence in mine.

"Castle."

It is made mostly of stone.

"Don't hurt the people in the lower levels. They're prisoners as much as you were."

Of course. Oh, I have a matter I was hoping you could help me with. And you'll have something shiny to present to your female until you have adequately impressed her with your . . . human methods. What are those, exactly? Do you sing to them or give them shiny rocks? The tail bristled so Caleb obliged, stepping on.

"Caleb, what are you doing?" Gill called.

"Climbing on my dragon. It's fine."

I am moulting in my hindquarters. You may take a scale. I will give another to Ethan when he is human again.

"You want me to pick a scale off your—"

Hind. Use a knife, you won't hurt me.

He was most certainly not moulting. Varian had scratched a section so that they were loose. Caleb had to use a knife but upon taking a scale, it glistened in his hand. "How long to regenerate?" he asked when he stepped off.

I told you I am moulting. Caleb knew the dragon was lying; he thought human hang ups about nudity and orifices were hilarious. *I will not say I longed for human companionship, however you and Ethan were more amusing than others.*

"Can I tell Ethan your name? I wanted to call you something fierce, like Stormbreaker."

That is pretentious and worse than Peanut, the dragon declared, spreading his wings, Caleb instinctually backed off.

"Have your vengeance, but just remember that castle will be a giant oven and I'll be in there."

I will do my best to scorch the upper levels. At the very least, they will be distracted and you can attempt one of your ill-advised schemes.

"I got manpower and tools this time," Caleb said.

The dragon snorted, and took off at a gallop, leaping into the air with a strange grace that did not bely the dragon's size.

"Goodbye." Caleb wondered if the words were for Varian, or if the dragon knew what he was thinking.

"Caleb," Gill called. "How do you know—"

"One of the carriages brought him into the castle. Maybe keep that under your hood," Caleb said, walking back to them.

"And you *let it out*?" Gill asked.

"There's enough other fun stuff we'll have to deal with. Remember what I said about the people inside turning on you? How about one that is ten times your size, flies, and breathes fire?"

"What's all in there?" Gill asked.

Caleb wasn't certain. "Let's . . . not worry about it too much. That was the single biggest threat I can think of." Caleb pointed to the dragon in the sky, doing barrel rolls. "And we have a common enemy. This is for you," he said, handing Lily the dragon scale.

"That's what you were doing?" Lily asked. She gaped at it. "I can't accept this. Do you have any idea what it's worth?"

My dignity. "Tell you what then: Hold it for me in trust until we either smite the great evil holed up or we all run away because I made things worse. You can hand it to one of my siblings as proof I met a dragon. Want to take the scenic way back?"

Gill nodded. "Anything the pretty lady wants to see?"

"Any place in the countryside with lilacs?" Lily asked.

Caleb had gotten his fill that morning, but he wouldn't mind more of the same with her. "Gill, any good places to watch the sunset?"

He felt alive after the kitsune made him jump in the lake (more or less), but something ignited again on the back of a horse. In an open stretch he peeled from his companions just to feel the rhythm of the canter again. Lily and Gill galloped after him at a much more relaxed speed. He'd forgotten how scenic the countryside was; the details in the oaks and maples were amazing as spring was beginning to turn into summer. Gill took them to where there were rolling hills. Caleb only realized then that they couldn't see Mirador at all from where they were.

"You've got a beautiful country," Lily said.

"This? When we're heroes we're going hunting in your backyard," Gill said. "Help your daddy with the wyvern that drove you to us. Make me some wyvern-skin boots."

Lily giggled, indicating that wasn't likely. "The mountains aren't as close as you're thinking," Lily said. "The backyard mostly has the normal variety of critters. Maybe you can borrow Louis' canoes and go fishing."

"Did you hear that? Canoe trip into the backcountry!" Gill grinned at Caleb. "Oh look: the sun is setting and I'm going to do something ranger-ish away from you pair. You're welcome." He had Piper trot away with exaggerated high-legs.

He wasn't sure what Gillam was expecting. "How long do you think before the message reaches your parents?"

"If they're in Shelkie's Bay and Larry finds them, that would be the fastest. I don't know if they've found another ship to take them to another port and they're traversing by land. They could be crossing the ocean as we speak. If that's the case, I'll speak to them when they get here." She looked down. "They'll want to stay until Tiffany and Molly are rescued, but, I'll go home and retrieve a horn. Mom'll write me a letter and we'll figure the rest out."

He took her hand. "I'll do my best to try and come back and see you."

"Mission comes first."

"I got twelve good people who are trusting me. You know what it was like first hand, now try explaining that to people who saw you as a snot-nosed kid." She gave his hand a squeeze. "I don't like you being on your own."

"I'm not on my own. I've met people. Besides, Louis is here. If I have to leave, I'm going for that horn."

They watched the sun set, just holding hands on their horses. They didn't need to kiss or say nonsense about how radiant the other one was, which was good because Caleb thought the sunset was almost as beautiful as her and he'd be a fool to try to articulate himself.

They caught up with Gill and returning to the camp, Gillam said he'd spot him a few minutes and cared for the horses, although he almost immediately whistled for Louis and sloughed the job on him. Caleb found the sign was still on the outside of the tent, but decided that meant they were doing just fine and someone would come get him.

After he and the ranger apprentices finished watering the horses, Louis returned to their throwing knife game, but he got frustrated and used a sling. Louis was deadly with it, and Caleb didn't think a rock could be that dangerous of a weapon until he saw the speed and accuracy the boy could hurl stones.

"You've got the making of a ranger," an older ranger told Louis.

"I'm opening the first barbershop back in Stagmil," he said. "But I guess I could be a ranger once everyone has a superior moustache."

Caleb became aware that someone was watching them. "Sir Wilfred? Everything all right?"

"I wasn't allowed in there." Wilfred had the misspelled sign in his hands, which he summarily threw into the fire. "What are they doing?"

"Not a clue," Caleb said. "I'll take the first team across about twenty or thirty minutes after it gets dark."

Wilfred nodded. "If I don't hear from you by sunrise, I'll wait a day then send another team in."

"If I don't return, who's going to be the guide?"

"I was going to ask her or Tristan," Wilfred said, gesturing to Lily. "I don't like it either, but the next team will just to be to find out what happened to the first team."

"Tristan wants to come in with me. We're all going to lose our physical strength in there anyway," Caleb said. Wilfred pursed his lips but eventually gave a dissatisfied nod. "If I go in there and no one comes out, wait for three days," Caleb instructed. "If they're on the alert, that'll be probably enough time to get their guard down again. We won't need to eat or sleep. I'll bring in cards and a few books to pass the time while we lay low."

"I'm just hoping boredom doesn't make them foolish. You know rangers."

"Is this a back and forth thing?" Lily asked with a chuckle.

Wilfred nodded. "Doesn't matter how many times we save their pointy feather-heads, either."

"Can't blame them for being upset that we make it in all the stories," Caleb said. "Let me say goodbye to Lily properly."

Wilfred nodded, and left them.

He looked at her. She'd helped him all day—he'd not given her much of anything but his time but, given he only had one day, that was more precious than all the coin in the bank. "Not much of a courtship," he said.

"Don't throw your life away. You want to see that mountain," Lily told him. "A real one."

"I want to see Larry's sailboat, the infamous Shelkie's Bay, and your cute little lambs," he said. "If you see your parents, tell them I said *hi* and, *yes please I want to live?*"

"I will. It would be best to pretend you're no longer poisoned."

"Slay abomination, ride like crazy to your house. Don't tell anyone why. Got it." They embraced, and he didn't want to let go of her. He was starting to understand why people wrote ridiculous songs and stories about ill-fated love. "Until we meet again."

"Be thou a knight."

She had to say something like that. It took all of his willpower to not take her hand, run to the nearest horse and pick a direction away from the castle. He gave her a smile—not a smirk, he didn't know what Wilfred was going on about—and entered the war tent.

Sixteen

The first group setting out to the secret tunnel was all rangers be-sides himself and Tristan. Daraby hated being left behind, but agreed he was invaluable as he knew the castle better than anyone. If no one from the first group returned, they'd wait three days; hopefully Varian would do as he said and the distraction would allow Seth's team a chance to investigate. In the event that they were fine but it wasn't safe to proceed, Caleb's plan was to light a candle from a pre-determined window the following evening.

Seth transformed both teams into marionettes and before they tra-versed the ferry line. Rodney, Gill, Anne, and Lyle, all rangers, followed him in through a tunnel Caleb thought smelled like fox. He hated how naturally Seth could run over the rope of the ferry. Everyone else had to walk, and it wasn't easy when it swayed in the wind.

"If you lose heart, let me know," Caleb said in the dark. "We'll double back and trade you out."

"We'll be fine," Rodney said.

Caleb wasn't sure if he would be fine, if he'd panic or taken out by the barrier. What if that was his only day outside? They had backup maps, if he fell the plan was to get him somewhere safe and Tristan would advise the best course to try to find Ethan.

It was almost terrifying to come into the dim light. Everything was as Seth and Lily described. Furniture draped in cloth, cobwebs; every-thing was still and the room was so nondescript he could have been in many rooms in Mirador and not certain where. Nothing seized them, nothing moved. He nodded, and Lyle doubled-back to fetch Tristan.

The first order of business was to ensure that their footprints wouldn't be noted, so they used the tiny brooms and very lightly swept not only their path, but the floor surrounding them. One or two of them could tread lightly, but they were going to be moving back and forth; last thing they needed was a clear path of footprints leading to and fro their only way out.

Once he and Lyle joined them, Tristan scouted ahead and confirmed Lily had gotten the details right while they finished cleaning the floor. It occurred to Caleb that neither he nor Tristan could have prepared for what was ahead of them. The room Seth described as having people in storage was accurate. They didn't explore the boxes. The room of re-making, though, the others didn't see it the way he and Tristan did. He told the squire to wait outside, but Tristan followed him in anyway.

"I'm sure they're made, not scavenged," Lyle told them quietly. Caleb wished he could believe him.

There was a hole in the castle wall where Lily said there would be, though it looked like they'd tried to board it up. There were definitely scorch marks in some of the surrounding stone. No barrier lit up when he neared. The landscape before him was almost more familiar than the town of Mirador; it almost felt like his day outside was a dream and this was the world he belonged to.

"Well, some luck," he told the others when they arrived back at the puppet world. Gill peered up at the mist, the others were a little more subdued. "No strings in sight. That means there's probably no one near us. They can watch from above, so keep your voices down and don't dart around."

"When will they figure out whether or not you've been gone?" Rodney asked, gesturing up. "Gill, stop looking up."

"Don't know. Never done this before." He'd explained the impor-tance of cover, and the rangers wore brown and green colours that were much better suited for blending into the ground; blonds like Gill kept their hoods up. They'd be more conspicuous at their level, but out of the two options he'd take it. They could easily incapacitate other puppets; he wasn't worried about the stringless spies so long as they didn't sound the alert. "I'll go ahead. Tristan, you lead them after I motion it's safe to proceed. You know the burrow Ethan and I have near the town? That's where we're headed. I'll drop the team off there. If we don't run into one of ours, I'll head to town, you go find Percy."

"We'll watch your back," Rodney told him. "We can take out any-thing if it attacks you."

He expected the world to turn on and recognize he didn't belong, but he told himself that getting in wasn't the problem; it was getting out.

"That's a pretty little enchanted forest. Has *trap* written all over it," Anne said as they travelled.

Caleb wished he was that smart when this all started. "They glued horns on horses, had them attack us. Then again, so did some of the trees."

"Tell me again why we're bringing rock busting equipment and play-ing cards?" Rodney asked as they walked in the open before they went into the dense bush area. So far, so good.

It occurred to Caleb this was where he took Lily when they'd first met. He knew he couldn't let his mind wander, but part of him allowed the indulgence. "It's just a little hidey-hole Ethan and I started to use when we were able to de-string."

"So for most of your time, you couldn't even access half of the world?" Anne asked. "Why did they let you go off-string?"

Caleb figured they'd ask, and had been thinking about some way to tell them that wouldn't be a lie. Ethan's secrets were his own. "Maybe they thought I didn't need strings any more," Caleb said. He took them down. "All right—stay put, keep the candlelight minimum. I don't know if you noticed, but we can see well in the dark."

"Where does the smoke go?" Rodney asked.

"Vented. We learned that the hard way." They hadn't been ballsy enough to start setting things randomly on fire; there was too much of a chance the fire would get out of control and take out civilians. "Keep a low profile, book it out of the castle if something goes wrong. I'll be back as soon as I can." Caleb looked to Tristan. "Are you sure you can handle being by yourself?"

Tristan nodded. "I was in here just as long as you."

"You don't have horde camouflage anymore," Caleb reminded him. "Take your time. Seth and the others know we'll be a while. I'll meet you back here with Percy?"

"So long as he hasn't been off-string a lot that shouldn't be a problem," Tristan said. "If I don't see you before you get him out, tell Ethan what to expect out there."

"I will."

Caleb made his way to the town without incident, avoiding ghouls and other pitfalls because he knew how they moved. Town seemed busier—not exactly how he had come to expect it; but there were more townsfolk about. No one was at their pointless tasks; instead the usual offenders were playing chess. He almost made it to the infirmary without being seen. Thankfully, the one who approached him was Oliver.

"I thought they pulled you!" Oliver told him, running over. He shushed down down after Caleb gestured, and followed him to a side alley.

"I know I've been gone a while. How are things here?"

"Interesting."

"Interesting good, or interesting bad?"

"I'm amused," Oliver said.

Raised voices came from the block square, and Caleb thought he was going to kill Seth, because the ginger wasn't supposed to be in the castle yet. He was still wearing Caleb's Wolf Armour, minus the helm, but he was . . . wrong. This marionette of Seth absolutely made fun of his nose and had procured a hat with an overly long feather, despite wearing Caleb's armour (or at least a cheeky simulacrum of it) made fun of his skinny legs. If Caleb had looked closer, the wolf emblem looked more like a chicken.

This version of Seth also seemed to be non-plussed about keeping to the shadows, and was strumming a tiny mandolin, singing sweet love-songs with crooning terrible notes to the townswomen, who were desperately trying to get away. Every so often, his mandolin would break a string with a *twang*, and Seth would obtain a string, via another puppet—or even a loose thread from someone's pants.

"What is going on?" Caleb asked.

"Don't know. Him and a version of you have been going at it for hours. Oh, and there's another group of jolly bandits who keep kidnapping everyone the knights have saved; Hector and most of the knights are out dealing with them."

". . . another version of me?" Caleb asked. "Never mind, where is Ethan?"

As if on cue, another Caleb appeared—his incredibly big chin had a prominent beard and he had a top knot, as well as a brow so furrowed it might as well have been a unibrow. He was also wearing the armour sans helmet, his wolf was more of a derpy puppy. "You there," this version of Caleb had much more bravado. "Stop harassing the fair women of this town! That is my privilege."

"What in the actual . . . " Caleb began.

"He got your nose all wrong, but when he's just bounding around it's a little harder to tell," Oliver explained. "The real difference is he won't wear a helmet."

"I need to emote!" snapped the imposter knight as if he heard their conversation.

"We will duel!" snapped the fake Seth. "But first . . . " He tried to grab another girl from the crowd; and when he tried to leave a trail of kisses up her arm she was ready, and slapped him with a chicken before scurrying away. "Why will no one return my affections?" The chicken gave him a peck on his cheek.

"Don't worry, I will return your inflictions!" crowed Caleb's doppelgänger.

"Inflections?" Seth's Imposter deedle-dee'd his mandolin.

"Defections! En guard! Ha!" Swing.

"Ha ha!" Parry and return.

"Aha ha!" Return and overdramatic swipe.

"Ahahaha ha!" Stupid dramatic turn with parry. The pair started to duel with some actual speed in the streets, which quickly became more of a dance, and then a song. Caleb thought the allusions to swords compensating for their personalities a little on the nose, but both really could sing better than either of their real counterparts, as he'd endured Seth's original lyrics much of that morning.

Lady Chrysta emerged sans guards, looking like her normal however flustered self. "That is enough, you charlatans!"

"My love!" the False Seth crooned.

"You crass brute! You will leave the fair maidens alone!" the Lousy Caleb declared. "And this one as well!"

"Oh don't lose your head!" the Imitation Seth jeered, and chopped off his nemesis's head.

"Which is why we wear helmets," the Real Caleb said.

The Other Caleb plucked his head, and carried it under his arm, making no attempt to put it back. "*Me amore!*" the Other Seth chased after Lady Chrysta in a fox-trot, plunking along to some other little naughty ditty.

"Stay away from me!" Lady Chrysta squealed, speeding off from her abhorrent admirer.

"Don't worry!" the Incorrect Caleb bellowed, following after them in a similar but more bounding gait, his head still tucked safely under his arm. "*I will save you!*"

"It's repetitive, but the formula works," Oliver said, checking to make sure the way was clear prior to gesturing to Caleb to follow him up to the infirmary.

"Formula?"

"The redhead causes trouble, you try to stop him. Violence happens, mostly to you." Caleb followed Oliver up the back steps into the infirmary. It seemed quieter than usual as well. To his surprise, the first person he saw was his cousin, and he seemed back to normal.

"Cay!'" Jayden exclaimed when he saw him, lowering his voice when Caleb gestured. "Have you been paying attention to your look-alike?"

"You were my look-alike," Caleb said. "Is Ethan here?"

"Yup. Tiffany is letting him have it."

Caleb recalled that Ethan had technically broken a cardinal rule: don't cut someone else's strings, because they will invariably find a way to get you back, even if they said all is forgiven.

Esther rushed to him when she heard his voice. "We were worried! How did it go?"

"And another thing—who is that guy?" Tiffany demanded, pointing in Caleb's general direction.

"You've met my cousin," Jayden said.

Tiffany rolled her eyes. "Does your cousin have a name?"

"Okay, I walked into that one. I have more than a dozen cousins," Jayden admitted. "You've seen Cay without his helmet before."

"I keep forgetting he has a face," Tiffany said. "Now if only we can prove he's got a soul." She focused back on some ornamental closet that anyone who couldn't de-string couldn't go. "You can't hide forever, Ethan!"

"Yes I can," Ethan called out.

Caleb pulled Esther to another room. "Think you can get rid of Tiffany? I need Ethan."

"Of course," Esther said, looking him over, skeptical.

"I'll explain when I have a chance."

Esther nodded and went to try and talk sense into Tiffany, Oliver managed to get Ethan to sneak out behind her. Ethan couldn't suppress his grin. "I knew that wasn't you down there. You and I should have ripped off Dalzen and Burkotta, it would have been a blast."

"Who?" Oliver asked.

Caleb had been so preoccupied, he didn't realize he'd seen those antics before. "I'm not going to say they're from a play. They reoccur in different stories and almost have no bearing on the plot."

"Recurring characters?" Oliver asked.

"Sort of. Know how sometimes, they change the sets during a play?" Ethan asked. "Dalzen and Burkotta exist to distract the audience while they're moving chairs and whatnot. They were very popular, so other theatre troupes added their versions of them. Dalzen's usually a young hapless buffoon, and Burkotta is usually a sort of an idiot law-enforcer.

Dalzen breaks a rule, Burkotta yells; they fight or do comedy routines." The best ones were the comedic fights, but there were many skits that involved Burkotta getting drenched, pied, and most notably in Caleb's mind, dragged off-set by a sea-monster.

"Yeah, our moms took us to some shows. We always asked if there were going to be any comedy like that," Caleb explained, then shook his head. "None of that is important right now. I need you to—"

"Out of the way, sister!" Tiffany caught on, and bowled over to them. "He's almost as much to blame as Ethan for hurting Jayden and Caiden."

"Please don't raise your voice," Caleb asked.

"Oh, and are you going to sprout tails and ears again?"

Caleb wondered what else his little doppelgänger had done; his vague plan of leaving the country for the next two years was sounding better all the time. "That wasn't me. Tiffany, if you don't stop shouting I will cut your strings. Understood?"

"Not if I cut yours first." She looked at him, then scrunched her face as well as she could for a puppet. "Riiiight."

"Shhhh." He gestured.

"Don't shush me!" Tiffany sputtered.

"Shhhh."

The harrowing glare told him she was going to get back at him, but for now she relented. He waited for her to nod. "Tiffany, I either need you to come with me and be rescued—"

"What about Molly?"

"Think you can get her down here?" Caleb asked.

Tiffany shook her head. "Last time I saw her was with you in that weird cave. I'm not leaving her."

"I understand," Caleb said. "Please just be patient while I talk to Ethan. I need you to carry on like things are normal. No screaming and drawing attention to me. If you want to do it anywhere I am not, be my guest."

"Will that help?" Jayden asked.

"Incredibly."

Jayden looked to Tiffany, then to Caiden and Braden. "Well . . . what say we join in the shenanigans downstairs?" Jayden asked.

"I say we improvise our own skit," Braden agreed.

"Ethan, I need you now," Caleb said as Braden pointed out he should be the lead. "Esther, I'll explain later. Keep acting like everything is normal. Oliver, I think it's time to sneak you out." He was expecting Esther to protest, but she looked at him, hopeful, hint of a smile. "I will explain everything." He promised, giving her a nod. "I'll be back as soon as I can. And after I explain things, I need your help getting every child to me."

Esther nodded.

"Hey, I don't know how caught up you are, but Seth and I kind of messed up," Ethan explained as they made their way through town, Caleb keeping under cover as much as he could. The other two were on strings and doing their best to follow normally.

"Don't worry about that. I was outside," he said quietly. "Didn't mean for it to happen, had to wait until dark to get back in. I snuck five of our people inside. Rangers. They never gave up on us," he said quietly. Ethan and Oliver exchanged hopeful looks. "Remember Rodney? He's a ranger captain now and sent letters asking for aid. I want to sneak you both out. They'll fix you, but if you choose to come back in here you'll be able to run barriers."

"What's it like?" Ethan asked.

"It's spring. The world goes on. Town's not the same as it was, but . . . guys, it's incredible. You can feel the bark and everything tastes so intense."

"And you came back?" Oliver asked.

"I couldn't leave you." There were too many people to mention. When Alanna's father hugged him, he told himself he was going back if only for another child. He'd told himself they were okay here, until he felt a gentle breeze in his hair and the smell of dew on grass; how donkeys were supposed to sound and unfortunately, smell. Skin on skin even if that was just Lily's hand.

They came to the shaded part of the forest where Oliver couldn't follow, but Ethan knew the way. "I left Rodney, Gillam, and two other rangers there. Tristan probably with Percival by now," Caleb said. "Oliver, I'm sneaking you out. You'll come to restored outside the castle, probably at Declan's. Understood?"

"Yes, sir."

Caleb realized he'd not told him or Ethan he'd been knighted, but Ethan had already departed for the burrow. Ethan would likely know by the time Caleb returned, but out of everything that happened that day, that mattered the least; he and Ethan would always be brothers and equals; Wilfred insisted he'd knight him and other squires at least sixteen years of age once he realized that they ought to have done the same thing for Tristan.

Oliver and him kept quiet, but before Caleb cut Oliver's strings at the border of their fake world, he explained: "I probably won't be out there when you come to. I don't want you coming back in here. If he's out there, you listen to Ethan like you're his squire. If for whatever reason he's not there, you listen to Lily. Remember her? There's others out there too who will take care of you, but you can trust her."

"I'm not a kid," Oliver said. "I don't need to be cared for."

"I know. There'll be clothing for you and until you can get ahold of your family, things are prepared so you can sleep and eat for weeks if needed. If this all goes south, I want you to try again when you're older. Older than I am right now. You know what it's like here; and you can train for it. We're going to try to stop this, but Ethan and I might be killed or stuck here. Understood?" Oliver nodded. "Okay. Be brave."

It was always a hard thing to cut someone's strings, even if they wanted you to. Watching the life leave Oliver's eyes, doubt started to plague him. Caleb half expected to be foiled when he approached where the barrier ought to have been in the hall. He realized he could find it from where that patched up hole in the wall was. It lit up when he approached with Oliver, but he himself didn't light up; nothing hindered him. Caleb found the tunnel and focused on the dim light on the far side and Seth whistling, annoyingly.

"How are things?" Daraby asked impatiently when Caleb arrived.

"Whoever's upstairs is good and distracted," Caleb said, handing off Oliver to a man-at-arms, who slowly made his way over the ferry rope. "You ready?"

"Wait for Eugene to return," Daraby said.

"I'll wait. Seth, you start leading the next team. Wait for us in the other room. Might make sense for one of us to run down a hall at a time." They had mirrors and real lanterns and could signal to one another; not the easiest thing to do at night and this evening was overcast. Waiting, he considered that he and Seth ought to do the ferry line runs until the others became faster and more proficient, but then realized they were going to get experience by doing it. Eugene was doing his best, and Caleb gave him the briefest nod before they descended into the tunnel. Seth had already taken three people to the hallway. This time they made no stops, and arrived back at the entrance still without incident. Lady Beatrice and Percival were waiting for them just inside the game board, a small honour guard of goblins hidden unstrung.

"Captain," Percival said to Daraby.

"Sir Percy? Not a good look," Daraby said.

"I've grown rather fond of it," Percy said. "Come on, let's get you some place safe, then we'll talk about the plan I've gleaned from Tristan. *Sir* Caleb." Caleb returned the curt nod. "Several of my officers have teams making a distraction a good distance from here but resist the urge to run, it draws attention."

"Congratulations," Beatrice said, taking Caleb to the side and giving him a hug. "Tristan told us what you've accomplished. I'm so proud of you both."

"We'll find Darius when this is done," Caleb said. "When they fixed us, we were disorientated. We got better but it took hours."

Beatrice nodded. "Focus on what's ahead right now. We'll bring our lost sheep home later."

Caleb found that once they were in their burrow, he was almost irrelevant. Percival, Daraby, and Rodney seemed to think they knew a thing or two, and Caleb didn't mind them making executive decisions and moving screws and other scraps around on the table over another edition of his map, arguing just like old times.

"So . . . busy day, I understand," Ethan said, ignoring Seth and Gill's protests that the card game was more important and Caleb couldn't be dealt in.

"I was a bit of a mess when I came to," Caleb said. "Took most of the morning fighting with the bank to access my money in an account, and get ahold of Rodney."

"And?" Ethan asked.

"Rodney sent riders to the nearby communities. With luck, help will be on its way."

"And?"

"Things sort of snowballed," Caleb said. "It was Wilfred's idea to knight me. Main thing I missed was having you there."

Ethan raised an eyebrow. "*And?*"

" . . . *and* I'm a giant hypocrite."

Ethan laughed and slapped Caleb's shoulder. "I knew it! You are human and you do have a heart!"

"I didn't want to be the creep going after someone just being nice but . . . Ethan, she's amazing."

Seth snorted at *amazing*. "Why would he be a hypocrite?" Seth asked.

"You haven't known *A Woman Would Only Complicate Things* very long," Gill pointed out.

"Shut up *Anything That Moves*."

"Somebody once told me not to get attached to anyone while we're in here," Ethan said.

"I think we figured out something was going on before he did," Gill said. "Poor Lily."

"Excuse you, she was the one flirting with him," Seth said. "*Seth, we need to work with these idiots. Seth, they're prisoners and they need my help— go do dangerous stuff, mmkay? Boo hoo hoo . . .*"

"Don't listen to this mook, Ethan. Caleb started it," Gill insisted.

Seth stood, and accentuated his incredibly flat hips. "My sister was all like, *Oh Yoo Hoo! I know I'm the first girl you've seen in two years, but that makes me the prettiest girl you've seen so far today!*"

"Ooh, I get to be him," Gill said, furrowing his puppet brow and crossing his puppet arms stuck his nose in the air and faced away. "*Away with thee, foul temptress. I am over-thinking which beer to have. I had fun once, never again.*"

"*I said yoo hoo,*" Seth kicked Gill in the back of his calf.

"*Gasp! My repulsive personality worked at charming a comely maid,*" Gill growled, taking Seth in his arms, who put the back of his hand to his forehead and swooned. "*It must be true love! We will be married first thing in the morning! But first, I must go die some place, for reasons hitherto unknown.*" Gill dropped Seth, who clung to his pant leg.

"*Don't leave me, sir knight! Is it because you've seen me without my girdle?*"

"*I'm leaving you for my horse!*" Gill escaped Seth.

Although he would never admit it aloud, Caleb found this depiction funnier than the kitsune antics. "Thank you for summing it up so I don't have to." He looked around the room. "Gillam did have some questions for you specifically, Ethan."

"Little crowded in here, come on," Ethan said, standing. "Percy, you good?"

"Sir Percy."

"Sorry, Sir Percy, you good? I'm taking Sir Knight and Ranger Roy for a walk."

"Don't go far."

"This is my playground," Ethan said. "I'll try not to lose my stringless charges."

Seth seemed to take a hint and stayed behind, getting dealt into a hand of cards with the rangers. Above the alcove, they found a quiet bit of dense brush with a lot of canopy. "It's to do with the last week before . . . everything changed," Caleb explained. "You were on fire. You saw the spider and drove it back from us on rescue."

"I guess we drove it to you," Ethan said. "I figured she was going to beeline and get out of there. Man-eating monster or not, there was over a dozen of us."

"We think there were two of them," Gill said.

"Wouldn't you have gotten eaten too?" Ethan asked.

"Did Seth or his sister talk to you at all about how he and the rest of his villagers got captured?" Caleb pressed.

"We never really went into great detail," Ethan admitted.

"The woman who captured them, turned Seth into a puppet in the first place, was able to transform into a Jorogumo—that's the spider woman. Seth and Louis said she used theatre masks. Lily knew the song," Caleb explained. Ethan's brow tensed as much as his features would allow. "Madeline forced Lily to lure out her villagers and transformed them into puppets like us."

"Why not turn us into puppets back in the cave if that was the goal?" Ethan asked.

"The goal wasn't us, the goal was the castle," Caleb said.

Gill nodded. "About two months after the castle was seized, we start intercepting carriages and wagons with puppets in them. We jumped at least three. Can't make head nor tail of it, but the marionettes didn't come back to life when we cut the strings."

"What happened to the carriage driver?" Caleb asked.

Gill frowned. "You're not going to believe this. They disappeared from their cells. After the first two, there were guards right outside the door."

"They wouldn't have been looking for anyone puppet-sized," Ethan muttered. "We've all been bored out of our minds on guard duty. Guards put their feet up. We can see in the dark, you and I could easily sneak past someone not paying attention." Ethan's eyes widened. "We were set up."

"We think it's worse than that," Gill said. "I was drugged pretty bad, but Caleb cut me down. He exposed my face, so I could see him."

"He knows," Caleb said, crossing his arms. "Skip to the relevant part."

The ranger nodded. "Caleb said when he was blind, Lionel told him to roll to the left. That was when he thinks the spider lifted his gorget to sting him. Then dear old dad shouts, *You bastard!*"

"You never went into detail about that," Ethan said.

"Ethan, I need you to think: what was going on while I was in the infirmary? Right before my dad died, Percival and Cedric pulled me to the side and started asking questions. I wasn't sick yet. They were suspicious about something, but I was so focused on my family I was kind of an ass."

"People were throwing speculations and accusations around like mad. Why was this person on that team or who sent two young men on patrol," Ethan said. "Didn't you volunteer for rescue? No one forced you."

"Everyone had a dangerous job to do," Caleb said, crossing his arms. "Anything specific come to mind once they started drugging me?"

"Well, your mom forbid Gillam from being anywhere near you. He left without Captain Jax's permission to go get more anti-venom. We all went to your dad's funeral. Your sisters and brother went off to your grandmother's place in the country, your mom didn't want them to be there when you . . . you know . . . "

"I need you to think specifics, because Gill thinks Lionel might have poisoned me."

"What?" Ethan asked.

"I chase girls in taverns, but I ain't stupid enough to follow one luring me away from my post," Gill said. "Hal woulda smacked me around. We were bait. I think they ate him first because he got injured in the struggle. If we were both dead, they wouldn't have entered the cave, they could have plugged the hole and starved or smoked her out. I was bait; they killed Hal to make you act rashly."

Ethan looked contemplative. "Sorry guys," he said finally with a sigh. "Maybe something'll come to me. I've never seen your mom so angry, but with your dad dying and you looking to join him, no one held it against her."

"Maybe it was something I saw," Caleb said. "I don't remember. I've dreamed about that stupid cave so much, if you were to plunk me in there now I'd probably get details wrong."

"Have you figured it out yet?" Sir Percival asked, startling them.

Caleb stiffened. "No."

"Sir, I can get you out—" Gill offered.

"Already been discussed. We need at least one person here who knows what's going on. Rodney and Daraby are good, but they're not used to these bodies, we are. I want you to get Ethan out and restore him so he can run barriers with you tomorrow evening. There's puppets in storage near the exit?"

They all nodded, it took Caleb a minute to realize he outranked Gill and Ethan so he spoke up. "Yes, sir."

"Prioritize rescuing fighting men. Once Ethan is back, you can sneak me out. Once I'm back, we're going upstairs and figuring out what we're up against. You do not go up there without me, understood?" Ethan and Gill nodded in agreement before Caleb did; he didn't disagree but he was thinking. "Later, I want you to also sneak out Lady Beatrice. I want her to take over intelligence operations from the outside, write letters, organize help. She won't go without our children, you understand. I'll update my lieutenants, you'll be sneaking out some of them tonight. Has Hector been updated?"

"Not yet."

"He's fine for the time being, but he should be informed when you won't be compromised," Percy said. "You're still going to behave like any mistakes are lethal, understood?"

"Yes. Where is Tristan?" Caleb asked.

"He's waiting in another location. Once Ethan and others are back he'll be able to help. As of right now, only you two are experienced and can run barriers. I'll have some of my people train these rangers; they won't be idle."

"Seth and Caleb already trained us," Gill said.

"It took us weeks to adjust," Sir Percival said. "Gillam, go with Caleb, and sneak Ethan out. Act like each person we get out is the last and will be the people we rely on if we're caught. Go in pairs; if one of you is captured, hopefully the other one will get away." He caught Caleb's gaze. "Go after I speak with Caleb." He gestured, Caleb followed him off a little ways, where Beatrice waited.

"Decent people out there?" Beatrice asked. "Tristan said they treated him well." Caleb nodded. "He also said you're . . . courting a girl?"

"Yeah, I kind of . . . didn't think," Caleb admitted. "You'd like Lily. She's smart, and kind, and—"

"I imagine I would love her," Beatrice said. "But that's not like you. Moving quickly, I mean. Tristan said the first day wasn't easy, but then his senses calmed down and he adjusted to being human again. Don't go making promises until we get our lives back."

"I didn't, I'm not stupid," Caleb said. "Besides, there isn't any going back to our old lives. Not really." There wasn't for him. His father was dead—murdered?—and he wasn't a squire anymore. The world had moved on in the last two years; he had to find a place in it somewhere. He looked to Sir Percival. "Anything else, sir?"

"I have no say in your personal affairs so long as you're not behaving like a brute. Quite frankly, the less I hear about your love life the happier I'll be."

"We are happy for you," Beatrice clarified for her husband. "So long as you are in the right state of mind, that's all."

"This is our first chance in two years, sir," Percy said. "No glory-hounding, no vengeance."

"I just swore the oaths a few hours ago," Caleb said.

"And I mean for you to keep them," Percy said. "I'm potentially sending you and your friends to their deaths. If you have to step over my corpse to stop what caused this, you do it."

"Percy," Beatrice said, her tone warbling.

"He's no boy, Beatrice. Caleb's proven himself many times," Sir Percival said. "We're not going to be rash until we understand what's up there. Not unless you have anything more to add."

"No sir."

"Good. It should be early enough that Ethan will recover before sunrise, but keep him in the town for the day; he'll be safer there and can rejoin us after sunset. Can't have any of you getting recaptured. I will go and relay orders to my men." He frowned. "Keep your suspicions to yourself. We'll catch whoever did this and hold them responsible. Any questions?"

"No, sir."

"Then get going, you have much to accomplish before dawn's light."

Seventeen

Heavy boots and voices woke Lily from a real bed for the first time in weeks. She'd drawn the curtains but light spilled through them.The single room was small but nicer in the daylight than when she'd laid out her clothes to dry; they were still slightly damp,so she opted for the borrowed items from several of the townsfolk. They were practical dresses for the most part, unfit for riding or rappelling, but they still cinched to fit her. Tiny details in the clothing made her think that she belonged. She didn't really look like a shepherd from Stagmil—not that Stagmil was big enough to have its own fashion trends distinct from the other villages.

Two letters were slipped under the door, sometime in the night. She thought she might have dreamed or woke to her brother's voice and entering before someone yanked him back to the hallway.

She read Caleb's first.

Lily,

Things are chaotic but somehow are going well. I will sneak back and see you when I can. Sleep at night; we'll coordinate so I can see you, but I can't promise when that'll be.

Please take care of Ethan and Oliver. Do not permit Oliver to come back in here.If Ethan suggests it, say I will discombobulate him and hide his head again. We sent out Lady Beatrice; she will take over your job as soon as she is able; that'll free you up soon, but she could probably use some help. Tristan is staying behind enemy lines, but do not worry about him or any of us, for that matter.

Pass me letters and I'll read them before I destroy them unless you tell me otherwise. Too dangerous to keep. I trust this team but they are new. I keep forgetting how awkward I was when I got thrown in here.

I know you are waiting for your parents, but I think I want to ask a huge favour; I'd like for someone to take a message to my sisters and brother but I don't know where they are. The friar may know—if you can please ask him to find out?

Will talk to you tonight in person, luck permitting.

Caleb

PS —Talk to Declan about what I left for you. Money is for you and Ethan.

And one from Seth.

If I die, let Louis have what's in the box under my bed. I have left him further instructions. Other than that, board up my room or at least don't let Tiffany turn it into a sewing room.

Seth

Leaving the room, she could oversee the main dining hall. Isaac was awake and chatting with a young and very tall young man with yellow hair longer than she expected. Instinctively she knew this was Ethan—she was a little disappointed he couldn't keep his jester's hat, though she found out later he did put it to the side as a souvenir.

"Morning. You're not usually such a late riser," Isaac said as she approached them.

"Lily, is that you?" Ethan asked. He almost seemed a bit sheepish; she wondered what he'd expected her to look and sound like.

"How are you feeling?" Lily asked.

"I'm . . . adjusting," said the squire. "Cay gave me a head's up and Isaac's been helping. He said it wasn't what he expected. Uh . . . I guess this is where I formally say thank you."

"Caleb can run barriers?" she pressed.

Ethan nodded. "Percy is impressed for a change. You wouldn't know it by looking," he said, tightening the woollen blanket over his shoulders.

"Let's go back to the fire," she directed.

"Caleb said he was chilly until he jumped in the lake," Ethan admitted, returning to the stony warmth. "Or did you push him in?"

Lily couldn't suppress her smile. "Would you like some tea? I'm making for myself anyway."

"They gave us the run of the place," Isaac explained to the squire.

Lily made her way to the kitchen, passing Larry and Catarina enjoying eggs and toast as they conversed with several others who would be joining them on the voyage overseas. She heard Ethan say, " . . . is it wrong to admit I'm afraid to go outside?"

"You don't have to if you don't want to," Isaac said.

"I want to but . . . it's . . . it's safe in places where there's no mist, you know?" Ethan asked. He chuckled softly. "Guess there is no mist out here."

She'd seen the tavern owners that morning in passing, but the place was busier at night so, rather than bringing in more staff, Lily and a handful of others were given permission to cook. She put the kettle on and looked around the pantry; she felt awkward rummaging, but knew where the tea was and returned with warm drinks. Ethan didn't seem to want to talk as freely with her around, but was happy for the warm drink.

"He told me about yesterday." He grinned as she tried to fight down the blush, fiddling with her hair. "I had an inkling."

"Nothing was going on before yesterday," Lily insisted. "Caleb said Beatrice and Oliver are here. Anyone else I'd know?"

The squire looked pensive before answering. "I spoke to Caleb before he returned to the castle so I have some idea," Ethan offered, but he stood when he spotted a young man descending the main stairs. "Sorry, I should really be a friendly face."

She and Isaac watched them exchange familiarities, though it seemed a little stiff. "Did you sleep through them returning as well?" Lily asked Isaac.

"I left instructions for them to wake me," Isaac explained. "I'll be sleeping in the back of a cart all day. I expect to help Larry sail through the night if the weather holds. We may sail in the morning if he deems it best. I was too excited to rest until the first team came back with news." Ethan was talking to an older man now, but then another young man opened a door, he and Ethan hooted, and the pair met middle of the stairs, fist-bumped, and did a victory dance. "Think you can handle this on your own?"

"Caleb said he sent out someone to do my job. I'll probably be her assistant," Lily said. "How many people did they rescue?"

"Twenty-eight people last night," Isaac said.

Ethan led the younger pair who had just come down the stairs to the fire. One was a fair-haired man-at-arms, the other was a burly squire with curly black hair, big hands and round features. Lily realized she was subconsciously comparing everyone to Caleb.She wondered when this *you-before-any-other* phase was going to last, but thinking about him made it worse.

"Ah, so that's what you look like," the bigger one said. "Ethan, is there any green paint on my face?"

Ethan shook his head. "Lily, do you remember Garett? He was in your goblin escort when you snuck out Louis," Ethan explained. "Where is he?"

While Isaac explained that Louis was off at the barbershop or fishing, Lily did see a semblance. Garett looked like a heavy hitter; he didn't make a convincing goblin before and wondered why they tried. "Why don't you sit down by the fire where it's warm? I'll bring more warm drinks."

The young man-at-arms nodded. "It is chilly. So uh . . . what just happened at the castle?"

"I'll tell him," Garett said. "Sit down, you ain't gonna like this."

Isaac and Lily gave them space after the castle folk were given mugs of tea. "Do you know what room Ethan was in? I suspect Oliver was with him. I won't wake him up, but in case he's by himself," Lily said.

"I'll come with you," Isaac agreed. They found Oliver sitting on the edge of the bed in the clothing left out for him,. He looked at Lily and Isaac, his eyes widening. "No way," he said, his voice barely above a whisper. The biggest grin broke onto his face. The youth bolted past them, down the stairs. "Ethan!"

Isaac briefly checked on another man who was comatose before he and Lily left the room and closed the door. They leaned on the banister to take in the reunion.

The page launched himself at Ethan. The pair laughed and Ethan spun him around. "We're out! We made it out!"

Ethan put Oliver down and ruffled his hair. "I forgot how short you were!"

"I'll catch up. Garett! Nolan! We've escaped!" They bumped fists and Garett put Oliver in a brotherly headlock; Ethan came to his rescue and thankfully the bigger pair calmed their rough-housing. Oliver stopped his antics, his eyes widening as if in realization. "Caleb's back there." He scanned the room. "Where can I find the swords?"

"Oliver," Catarina called, standing up, "the only thing you should do is comb that hair, but not until you've had some breakfast. Would you like some porridge or eggs with—"

"*Bacon?*"

Oliver demolished two plates at a rate that would have made Seth tell him to slow down.

"I can't believe Cay went nuts over apples," Ethan said, eating pickles in addition to his healthy portion of eggs and toast. Oliver stole his bacon. "These are so much better." Garett agreed, and between the two of them and nominally Oliver, ate every pickle at Declan's throughout the day.

The squires fixed their posture when a woman descended the stairs. Lily couldn't place her age; the clothing was that of a commoner but she had a severe expression. "Lady Beatrice?" Lily asked, standing to greet her.

"Lily," the woman gave her a curt nod but looked at the squires, who suddenly remembered cutlery existed. Isaac spoke to her while she was still on the stairs. Lily saw another man emerge upstairs with Demetri; he was of middle age and seemed confused, but relaxed once he saw familiar faces. Isaac and Beatrice went upstairs to talk to him and the physician.

"You have all the intel upstairs?" Beatrice asked once she was ready for Lily. "Would you be opposed if we turn your sleeping chamber into a private office? Squires, don't use your fingers to get the pickles, use a fork."

Garett did as he was told. "Where's Louis? Still asleep?"

"As of yesterday he's become an apprentice barber. I still think we should bring him with us," Larry groused. "He's your family."

"You can escort him to me next round," Catarina said. She called for Lily to finish up with the dishes; Lily took over and Catarina went outside. People congregated in the hallway, and Lily recognized several from the day prior but they looked different in the Ivancian clothes. Other townsfolk were coming in with clothing and blankets, excited to see some of people who had just woken. At least two people came in and had teary-eyed reunions; one man-at-arms left to join his family in spite of Beatrice's insistence that everyone stay put.

"I thought there would be a child," said a local woman, who handed Oliver a large leather ball. "It's not much."

"I am not a little kid," Oliver said, holding the ball aloofly.

"Yoink," Ethan took it from him.

"Give it here!" Garett called. They chucked it back and forth, sprinting out the back door before anyone yelled at them to take it outside.

"Gimme back my ball!" Oliver hollered, chasing after them.

Larry eyed them before he spoke to Lily. "You're sure you're good?"

"I'm sure. You have my letter for my parents?"

"For the last time, yes," Larry assured her. "I'll personally ensure it gets to them, if they don't come to Shelkie's Bay, we'll send word. Isaac said he might go up that way, visit my in-laws and ask some questions. You don't wear yourself out; this isn't over by a longshot."

"If she's still in Shelkie's Bay, tell Rebecca I'm thinking about her."

"She was getting along fine with Esperanza, I doubt she's dwelling on us too much," Larry pointed out. "When I return, I expect a list of who needs to go where. I ain't sailing the world, but I can go to ports other than home."

"And tell Louis his little holiday is over, I'm dragging him back next round; his poor mother must be worried sick," Catarina informed her. "I'm only allowing this because you are here and I am worried about poor sweet Elinor."

Dale and Brigid had stayed at separate houses, but arrived wearing local fashions. They looked well. The gathering was sombre. Brigid was given letters by people who were going to try to find passage on a ship in Garendell; Larry's boat couldn't fit anyone else.

Brigid hugged Lily when it was announced they were leaving shortly, to gather what was needed. "When you see Alanna, tell her I'm glad she found her parents and she's home safe."

Lily nodded. "If Rebecca is still in Shelkie's Bay, tell her we're thinking about her every day."

Dale was more sullen. "About yesterday, Lily . . . "

She didn't want to hear it. "You shouldn't feel bad for being honest."

"Can I at least apologize?" he asked.

"What for?" she asked. "I don't want you to spare my feelings and lie to me."

"Yeah, but I didn't have to be a jerk," Dale admitted. "This just all seems so surreal. I don't want you getting hurt helping people we don't know."

"I know some of them now," Lily said. "Take care of each other, and Rebecca. Tell everyone we're doing well."

Dale looked pensive. "Louis should take my place on the boat. I'll stay."

"He was quite adamant he's working at the barbershop," Brigid said, then the pair of them hugged.

"Get in here, Dale," Lily said. He obliged, and picked them both up. "Okay, strong guy, we get it!" They laughed.

"If you're not back in a month, so help me," Dale threatened. "Thanks for coming for us."

"You'd do the same for me. Not sure about the twins," Lily said, and saw them out the door.

Isaac pulled her to the side just as the others were getting on the wagon. "Your knight paid us back," Isaac said, handing her a bag of coin. "He insisted that this'll go up higher than him. Here's everything you gave me. You're a smart girl, but you don't have to do everything on your own."

"I won't. Thank you for everything, Mr. Sprites."

"Isaac. And I know Port Redmaw is closer to your home than Shelkie's Bay, but I'd appreciate seeing your faces in person when you're back on our side of the sea."

"If I have to rush home, I'll write to you," Lily said. "When all this is over, you need to come visit after shearing season. We're a little off the beaten path, but it's a big house."

Isaac nodded. "Absolutely. And you are welcome to our home any time."

By the time their wagon started plodding along, a ranger in tow to guide them, Ethan was trying to explain to the innkeeper that they needed to get to the roof to retrieve their ball. When Garett alone was taken upstairs to the hatch, Ethan gave Lily his letter from Caleb:

To Do and Not To Do

1. *Don't wallow, find something to do. Help Lily if she needs it but hopefully everything is running smoothly out there. I say find a horse and pick a direction. Louis is around, go fishing or something. I promised him a sparring lesson. I never got to make good on my word. Tell him I will if and when I can, but if you can—bueno.*
2. *Seriously though, don't go nuts on the athletics; my reactions and senses were hypersensitive even when the brain-fog cleared up. We'll figure it out.*
3. *Our shepherds have kitsunes. Remember my mom's stories? One is on*

the outside, if you come across it: pet it, feed it, and otherwise ignore it. If you upset it—like accidentally kick it, just give it a treat and don't bring up the incident. Cheese should do the trick.

4. *If you go to the bank they will waste your day and swallow up your soul and give it back wrinkled and a mess. Beatrice will assume control of funds but see Lily; I left some actual coin for you. Knew I forgot something. If she doesn't know what you're talking about I left it with the innkeeper.*

5. *Wallace has it out for your sideburns; avoid him*

There was more, but Ethan took the paper away and gestured to the stairs.

The brunette descending the stairs looked nervously at the people in the tavern. Ethan followed after her and they waited at the bottom of the steps. "Hello," Lily said. "You're in a town called Mirador. Do you know where that is?" The young woman shook her head. "It's in a Kingdom called Ivancia. My name is Lily, how are you feeling?"

The brunette frowned. "The last thing I remember, was I was at a carnival . . . bright lights . . . " Lily gestured, and the girl followed her, though she eyed Ethan suspiciously.

Her name was Colleen, same age as Lily, and was an apprentice dyer. She was from Ivancia but from the south. She had heard of Mirador once Ethan mentioned Sir Hector. Colleen relaxed with Ethan, but seemed anxious around the other castle folk.

Ethan didn't know every town and village, but he explained the situation. Lenore seemed to understand, but appreciated the offer to not be about the pub all day. Folk Ethan and the other squires knew from town came and went; some of the people she interviewed went to nearby homes after Lily recorded names and where they were going. If they lived on this side of the sea, it was a matter of figuring out a way for them to make their way home. If they were from the castle from the beginning, it was a matter of finding out where their loved ones were.

Ethan read through the lists they'd compiled so far, but who he was looking for wasn't on them.He waited until no one was near them to say to Lily, "Caleb told me he blurted out what happened a few months ago. About Danielle and . . . me, giving up." Ethan crossed his arms and wouldn't look at her. "I was in a dark place. I was better by the time you and Seth showed up. I'd appreciate it if you didn't say anything, especially to Oliver or Lady Bee."

She nodded. "You want to talk about it?" Judging by his cold expression, *no.* "Danielle, right?" she asked. His jaw clenched as she went over the papers. "Any idea where she's from? I barely know anything about your kingdom."

"She came from a seaside town called Mereth. That's south of here. She could be anywhere—in the castle or . . . " he trailed off. "There were almost forty people in that carriage. Where were they taking them?"

"I'm sure Caleb will bring her out if he finds her. You'll be able to search for records yourself when you're back there."

"If she's there, I'll find her," Ethan said, then rubbed his eyes. "I can't believe he told you."

Lily wasn't sure what to say. Besides perhaps Oliver, Ethan seemed to be the most important person to Caleb, so she wanted to get along with him. "Focus on the mission."

His brow tightened. "You don't need to tell me."

Thankfully, Garett and Oliver wandered over. "You have our allowance?" Oliver asked.

"I haven't spoken to Declan. Why don't you do that?" Lily asked. Garett and Oliver raced to the bar. Declan produced a wooden box and handed Ethan the key.Ethan counted out the coins; it wasn't a fortune but it was more money than she was used to handling short of shearing season. "How much do you want?"

Beatrice walked over. "First lesson, never let squires determine how much they get. They'll give each other blackeyes over who gets a slightly larger cupcake."

"Come on, Lady Bee—boots and stuff," Ethan said. "Besides, we're spending Caleb's money."

"Your *And Stuff* will be accounted for," Beatrice said. "Hand all of that over to me." She divvied up what she thought was appropriate.

"You're spending your own money, understood? We don't have unlimited funds. As for boots—trace your feet on a sheet of paper, I'll send the forms to the cobbler and we'll have something suitable." Lily catalogued but didn't take anything for herself; she assumed she'd be fine with the savings from home. Exchanging it for the local coin would have been nice.

"Don't you have to worry about your children?" Garett asked.

"They won't be awake for hours," Beatrice said, sitting down and picking up the papers. Beatrice didn't like any of what Lily had done, so she had her redo it. Lily didn't argue, though she found it tedious but wanted to be on her good side. The boys did as she asked, and traced their feet, each citing another had the worst smelling feet in existence.

While Lily was still copying out the information in a manner Beatrice preferred, she'd sent Oliver and Garett to pick up boots.

They returned with the cobbler, who was well-received and shook hands with many folk in the tavern while the squires brought in boxes of boots and shoes.

There was another squire who joined them; he was shorter than the others and had strawberry-blond hair and a familiarity to him she couldn't place. He mostly sat around the fire while Oliver and Garett explained to him the reality of his situation—he'd been stuck in a box while they ran around a little pretend world. "But why?" the squire asked. He was a year older than Caleb and Ethan, same as Garett. His brow tightened when Lily approached their group by the fire. "Who is this?"

"This is Lily," Garett explained. "She and her brother snuck in and rescued some of us. Caleb and and some rangers are responsible for getting you out."

"It's a group effort," Ethan explained. "Lily, this is Asher and Nolan." The new squire was Asher; she'd seen Nolan about but hadn't been introduced.

Asher didn't look at her long; if anything his lips thinned and he turned away from her. "Thanks, I guess," he said. "Two years? You're sure it's been two years?"

"Ask Declan," Garett gestured to the bar.

"I will when my head stops hurting." Asher wrapped the knit blanket around himself tighter. "Why does everything seem . . . so intense?"

"We haven't used our real eyes in a while," Ethan offered.

"Well, one thing's for certain: We have gathered here a group of inseparable brothers. Lo, I have longed for the vengeance of this day," Garett said, posing dramatically, leg up on the stone ridge around the fire.

"Absolutely. Whoever was responsible for our captivity will taste the bite of my steel," Ethan agreed, arms crossed. "Now, who wants to go to the lake and skip stones?"

"Oooh, ooh, me! I do! I do!" Oliver leaped up.

"If we can, let's go find a kitty to play with," Garett agreed. They made for the front door, but Ethan paused mid-stride.

"Do you need help?" Ethan asked Lily.

"Go, I'll catch up later."

Lily walked them out the door, then went back to her spot, and waited. It seemed like forever until Beatrice descended the stairs with the knight.

"Where are they?" Beatrice asked.

"Ethan and Garett took the others to the lake," Lily offered.

"They were not dismissed. And it's a large lake, that hardly narrows it down."

"Oh, let them stretch their legs and tire themselves out," said the knight. He cleared his throat; several knights looked up from their conversations. "Gentlemen, another four of our number are recovering, let's go discuss the matter at hand privately." They all got up from the table and made their way to the private dining room where Lily and Caleb had shared their first kiss. A lot happened there, but she kept thinking about that. "I'm sorry, Vern, but this is knights only."

The man frowned. "I've been serving Percival for two years faithfully."

"Vernon is one of our most trusted officers." Beatrice said.

"Lady Beatrice, this is not up for discussion. Vern, perhaps you could . . . bake something?"

The large man nodded and went to the kitchen. Lily thought that was unfair; if Caleb rescued him, there was a reason. Her thoughts jarred when Beatrice addressed her.

"You, I want to speak to," Beatrice said levelly, arms crossed. "I appreciate everything you've done, but don't encourage the squires to goof off. Now, do you think you can handle anyone else who wakes up?"

Lily nodded. She wanted to run upstairs and gather up her hopefully dry clothes if Beatrice was going to use the room. Instead, she tried to draw Caleb from memory; she hated it because she couldn't get his eyes right, only leaving her post to throw that piece of paper into the fire. In the time that Beatrice and the knights were gone, she interviewed two more people.

To her surprise, Vern sat down next to her. "So, were you a baker?" she asked him.

"A cook," he said. "Can you make a meal, or do you need lessons?"

She wasn't about to win a pie-making contest if Tiffany entered, but no one complained when it was her turn to make supper. "I cook all the time at home."

"That's not what I asked," Vern said. "Can you make yourself useful?"

Lily wasn't sure she liked his tone. She wanted to point out if it wasn't for her and her brother, he'd still be in there. They'd all be. Still, when he returned with a bucket she took the peeler and got to work, putting it down only once to interview another person who emerged from upstairs.

She wasn't sure how long the meeting lasted, but Beatrice approached her. "I have everything under control. I'm releasing you for the time being." She gathered up Lily's notes and ink.

"Thank you?" Lily asked. "Are you sure you don't want me to . . . "

"No offence, girl, but you are a foreigner," said one of the elder knights. "We will direct anyone else who wakes up to Lady Beatrice."

There wasn't really enough work for her to need an assistant. Lily nodded, gathered her bucket of potatoes and dropped them off, not letting Vern know. She walked up the stairs. The room didn't seem like hers; her clothing had been unceremoniously dumped on the bed so she folded and put them in a cubby shelf for the time being. Putting the mandolin over her shoulder, she figured the squires couldn't be far. She didn't want to be put to work for looking bored.

She was vaguely told where ranger headquarters was located, but figured she'd head to the lake. She was curious about the tourney grounds, selfishly she wanted Caleb to take her. She didn't make it that far; she found that the squires had stolen their ball back and Oliver and Ethan were chucking it back and forth near a fountain.

"What are the odds I've restored my humanity, getting my knighthood, and met my one true love in the same day?" Garett asked, lounging on the fountain.

"Impossible," Oliver said with a chuckle. "Considering you haven't even introduced yourself yet."

"When you know, you know," Garett said, sniffing a flower. "I wonder what her name is."

"You don't know her. Does Caleb even know Lilian?"

"Not really," Ethan said. Lily realized they hadn't seen her, so she ducked out of sight.

"What's her deal? He said he's a squire and she was over the moon?"

"I guess; you know how common girls are." She recognized Ethan's voice.

"You wouldn't," Oliver said.

"Shaddap!"

"You think we'll be heroes? Not that I want to marry a princess, but I totally *would*."

"You just showed up," Garett pointed out.

"You know my meaning. *The squires that saved Castle Mirador.*"

"I won't. I'll marry for true love!" Garett said.

"Yeah right," Ethan laughed. "Cay's probably as lovestruck as you, it'll wear off. Let him have fun with his apple. Like you said, if this works out we'll all have better options."

She heard enough. She didn't know where she was going, she just needed to . . .

. . . no, no one needed her. She didn't need to do anything. She could fritter off and no one would notice.

An apple?

Really?

Until he rescues someone important from the castle. Even if he doesn't, he'll still be a hero and I'll just be . . .

She didn't know. She went to another fountain, and sat, looking at her reflection, before staring at the castle in the distance. Hopefully, Seth and Caleb were okay. She knew they would be; between the pair of them they were capable and could improvise. She played with the bangle at her wrist. *Their senses are heightened, everything is more intense. He fell in love with apples. I wanted him more than he wanted me and I was too stupid to . . .*

"Just checking in," Mama Fern said, placing a basket of laundry next to Lily. "Mind helping me?"

"Hi!" Boscoe stuck his head out of the basket between layers of beautifully embroidered silk and some of Zin's stuff, too.

"I was worried about you!" Lily said, picking up Boscoe for a loving cuddle.

"What?" Boscoe squawked. He jumped out of her grasp, and standing on the side of the fountain stuck his posterior in her direction, tail up. "This is why everyone likes Seth better."

"I've noticed," she muttered, but scratched behind his ears. "You'd be with Seth if you could."

"Everyone says it's too dangerous," Boscoe grumbled. "They're just jealous *I* got in *first* and I can't even shapeshift on my own."

"Who's with Seth?" Lily asked.

"Another of my sons, from a different litter," Mama Fern told her. "You helping me do laundry?"

Lily wasn't sure about the rough bar of soap on such delicate fibres, but she found the beautiful fabric enchanting in the fountain water, just floating around. "These are really fancy. You sure we ought to be doing them here?"

"Get to it." The water was fresh and clean. "Enjoying your adventure away from home?"

Some parts were better than others. She blushed thinking about Caleb's kiss, but what was that, anyway? "How'd you get here so fast?" The kitsune only grinned. "Why did you give me this?" Lily pointed to the bracelet.

"To keep that woman from taking you over with a mask."

"No, I mean . . . why did you trap those songs in my head?"

"Did I?"

"Yes . . . no . . . my eyes glow yellow when I play her songs."

Mama Fern peered deep into Lily's eyes. "They look normal to me."

"This stupid bracelet locked it in," Lily said.

"So why are you still wearing it?"

"You're up to something."

"I'm having a friendly chat over laundry." Mama Fern said, and scolded Boscoe for chasing a butterfly. "As for you: You were in no way prepared to deal with that woman's magic when you left Stagmil." She chuckled when Lily groaned in frustration.

"It's not funny," Lily said. "Maybe it is for you; you aren't passed over again and again when someone better comes along."

"Oh, is that the hand you've been dealt?"

"I was the first one willing to sneak into the castle." Seth was the one better suited for it. "I said I'd help the people in there."

"Did you?"

"Yes—no—I don't know."

"Are they in better shape than they were before you were there?" asked the kitsune.

"Better, I guess, but it's not like it was all my doing. You don't understand."

"I'm trying. You're the one who can't say what she means."

Lily put some elbow grease into a faded shirt she'd seen Zin wear a hundred times. Thing was going to fall apart any day. "People get mad when I'm honest."

"So you'll lie to yourself and everyone else to keep the peace? Peaceful for them, maybe, for a little while." Mama Fern's bucket was also funny with time and space; she just kept pulling out fabric, some of which Lily wasn't even sure was clothing. "Can you be honest with yourself?"

"I thought being shoehorned into a role was just because I was in Stagmil and everyone thinks they know everything about everyone," Lily said. "I'm in a completely different country, and it's more of the same. I thought maybe all I needed was to go somewhere else. Then I could let people judge for themselves if I was . . ." Worthy? Competent?

Mama Fern let a beautiful dress float in the fountain. "Lily, have you noticed a pattern to the people you've spoken to?"

"No. They're just . . . people. Ordinary, every day people."

"The ones pulling the strings see the value of people even if you don't," Mama Fern said, pointing to the castle.

"What does that have to do with anything?" Lily asked.

"Humans are funny. Is this dress worth less because you don't know what it's made of?" Mama Fern selected one of Zin's shirts, and ripped it up with extreme prejudice. "One at a time, he won't notice if it's one at a time . . . "

"You gave Seth that amulet. You could have done more to stop this."

"If Seth had his humanity immediately restored, he wouldn't have learned to use his puppet body as effectively." The kitsune scoffed a little. "I still think it's a bit of overkill."

"What good is this?" Lily asked, looking at her hands. "If anything it's preventing me from helping them."

"Don't worry about what others are doing. You focus on what you need to do."

"I don't know what that is. No one takes me seriously. I'm always passed over for someone better."

"Assuming that's true: So? I asked for your help. Oh, you meant something important. I'm sure you appreciate clean clothes as much as the next person. Is this beneath you?"

"I've never complained about honest work. I'm saying all I ever get is the work no one else wants to do until it's suddenly important, then told *go sit over there* and *don't worry, we'll handle it.* Do this chore or carry that burden and don't whine. Track someone for days, break into a castle? Here, peel some potatoes."

"What's wrong with peeling potatoes?"

"Just . . . forget it. He's gonna be a hero and I'm just gonna be . . . "

"There it is. Speak plainly, if you can."

Lily wasn't even sure. "All my life I have done everything my parents have asked of me. They don't care how many times I've proven myself."

"You can't control other people," Mama Fern said. "How they behave is on them. I mean I suppose you could, if you were to transform them and put them on strings, then you can get everyone behaving exactly how you'd like."

Lily sputtered, "I would never! I'm not her!"

"How are you going to make people respect you, dear?" Mama Fern asked.

"I thought maybe by proving myself I'd earn respect. It never works. I mean, these people don't know me," Lily laughed. "Then again, why should they? No one in Stagmil did."

"No one in Stagmil?" Mama Fern asked. "No one thought to train you, to give you music lessons or educate you? No one entrusted you with flocks and protecting their precious children?" Kistune laughter was almost contagious. "And the people who have been trying to escape for the past two years, feeling like strangers in their own bodies; they clearly have been waiting for the chance to snub you. Highlight of their day, I'm sure."

"I'm frustrated."

"Because?"

"In spite of everything I've done, I'm just going to be some shepherd to everyone. Including me when I give up and accept it."

"Is there something wrong with being a shepherd?"

"No," Lily shook her head. "I like the work. I like my flock. I like that I can write songs and read books and Zin can train me. I just . . . wish someone would see I'm trying to help." Lily looked down to her reflection, and Mama Fern took her by the chin and tilted her head up. Those amber eyes indicated she did, and wished Lily would do the same thing.

"Mum, are you going to keep talking?" Boscoe complained. "I want action!"

"There's a nasty landlady going about town about to evict someone who doesn't deserve it. Why don't you see to it she gets some come-uppance?" Mama Fern asked. Boscoe scampered off, giggling maniacally. "Now, where were we? Oh yes, the moral: People will only see you to the level of their own understanding. Including you, young lady. What does that change?"

"Nothing, I guess." Lily frowned. "So what, I'm supposed to just step back, and let everyone carry on?"

"You keep doing what you know needs to be done, but if people don't want your help, that's their choice. You don't force it on them any more than you'd force yourself on someone who wasn't interested in you. Even if it means no one understands, or even if they think the worst of you because that's the only way it'll make sense to them. *Prove them wrong.*"

Lily supposed that made sense. "Do people ever really see each other? I mean, how they really are?"

"Yes, and then you restore him to his human form and you get distracted by the muscles and nice cheekbones. Ooops! Did I say that out loud? No, you aren't shallow. Not that I blame you. He's no Zin but there's a certain *je ne sais quois* . . . " Mama Fern nudged Lily playfully.

"Yeah well, let's see if he's still interested once he rescues a princess or something," Lily said.

"Doubt already! Or is it jealousy? You really are human," Mama Fern chuckled. "Let's pretend this little spark ends with him leaving you for someone supposedly better because she gets him a castle by the sea. Are you only going to help him because you get something out of it?"

"Helping Madeline started this mess."

"You weren't in a position to know her game."

"Do you?" Lily fiddled with her skirt. "Do you know what's going on in that castle?"

"I know this Asmodean is a powerful adversary. I know my beloved Zin's apprentice is no match for him, or anyone else I can name or at least ask a favour. I know what he's trying to do."

"Tell me."

"He's trying to turn people into his living puppets."

"I know that already! Why keep me tainted?" Lily asked.

"Darling, when you've seen generations of humans come and go, you learn to play the long game," Mama Fern told her. "His minions want Seth as a puppet? I'll give it to them with interest. No strings attached!"

Lily pursed her lips. "Those songs were meant to lull to sleep, then to summon, then to . . ."

"Transform. You have the power to turn people to puppets. Not for yourself there's a hold on you that doesn't allow you to do anything for yourself. You turned your villagers into puppets. You summoned them."

Lily nodded. She suspected she could without Madeline controlling her. That didn't mean she wanted to do it; quite the opposite. "Yes, but *why*. There must be a purpose."

"Right question. Let's ask the right person," Mama Fern said. She gathered her garments. "Let's go pay our puppeteer a visit, shall we?" She made Lily carry the basket; it should have been much heavier.

Ranger headquarters was on the south end of town with stables in the back and a large yard for training horses and an archery range nearby. The stone and brick building was larger than she anticipated, and the main building looked like a county jail, but inside was more orderly than she'd assumed. Alanna's father recognized Lily and he happily allowed her and Mama Fern to speak to their prisoner in the back cells, where they found Madeline reading.

She eyed Mama Fern when they entered. "What do you want, kitsune?"

"Lily has questions for you," the kitsune offered. "I'm here as a warm maternal presence."

Madeline caught Lily's gaze as if she wasn't the one behind bars, and was giving her permission to speak. "What was the point of using me?" Lily asked.

"I need a way to make power manifest. Song is powerful: I play the piano, but it's not the easiest instrument to bring along. Singing takes a higher toll on the body, so a diffuser was best. If you became damaged, it was no loss. You could fight and track, so it eliminated one potential threat."

She was going to be honest? "What is your master doing in the castle?" Lily asked. "I mean, why is he turning people into puppets? What is his ultimate goal?"

"Control," Madeline said simply. "He is teaching them to accept the control. Do you think if one of those rangers were to shoot an arrow at you, you could deflect it with your sword? Of course not. You could get lucky, but your impulses and desires get in the way of your potential."

Mama Fern walked to the mask collection on a shelf well out of reach.The puppeteer watched her. Mama Fern placed a mask on, the blue face with the jutting tongue—and while nothing happened, something irked the puppeteer. "I suppose I won't have to cast my spell again if you're doing it in my stead. Are you feeling the strain yet?"

Lily knew she was being baited, and said nothing. She should have written out her questions, not be led. Madeline began to whistle. Lily didn't think anything of it at first, until the chorus wormed into her head. Lily's heart raced and blood turned ice cold, and then all at once a strange fire coursed through her veins, lapping her up and overwhelming her, like a strange fever. Staggering as the shadows of the room lurched; they took hostile forms, mocking and belittling. The bracelet on her wrist grew heavy.

"A small gift," Madeline said as Lily staggered backwards. "There's much I should have been teaching you this whole time."

The bracelet wasn't working? Lily tried to steel herself, but the song nibbled away at her very core. A song of fear, one meant to terrify and make the most valiant pause and doubt. She wanted to hide; Mama Fern grabbed her wrists, pulled them from her face and tried to make Lily look at her, only Lily couldn't because of the shame. How could Mama Fern look at someone like her, and not be repulsed? "It's okay, Lily. Just breathe."

No, she had to get out; the shadows were giving way to something else. The masks were there; she'd be forced to sing and lull everyone to sleep; it was all pointless and hopeless and . . .

"Now you can force people to respect you. Isn't that a wonderful gift?" Madeline asked.

Lily focused on her breathing. She was fine. Nothing in the room had really changed, only her reaction. Her heart—which when it came right down, was the heart of a coward. "Why didn't the braclet work?"

"Oh but it did," Madeline pointed out. "If you weren't wearing it all this time, the hold on you would have worn off. Do you still trust her?" She gestured at Mama Fern with her chin. "She wanted you to learn these songs. What's your plan, kitsune?" Mama Fern cocked her head, but said nothing. Madeline locked eyes with Lily. "She's manipulated you from the start, and given you nothing. How does that feel?"

"How I feel doesn't change what you did," Lily said. "Keep your gifts. I'm nothing like you."

"You say that now. Wait until you need it. Leave us, kitsune."

"Lily, I will if you ask," Mama Fern said.

"I'm okay," Lily said, standing firmly, her breath finally under control. "She doesn't control me." Mama Fern nodded, and left them, closing the door behind her. "Why is he forcing them to accept the control? What is he offering you?"

"Power has a price," Madeline said. She pulled back the sleeve of her dress to reveal her forearm, and for a moment, it was wood. She didn't elaborate; in the time it took for Lily to get over her initial shock, Madeline appeared as flesh and skin. "Asmodean has desires above that of any mortal. You submit willingly, he will exalt you, give you power you couldn't dream of. He'll make you the best version of yourself. You won't be just a little shepherd."

"And end up like you?" Lily asked. "Kidnapping people?"

"If I teach you a song, and you go to the drawbridge and sing it, you'll be taken in. Tell Asmodean where I am, and reveal what your friends are planning. He'll give you what your heart desires. He'll give you your sister. Isn't it better, that you'll be able to protect her?" She paused. "And your knight. He can be yours."

She thought about that; Caleb would hate her forever if she even contemplated it. Part of her entertained the possibility. What if he did? Could he be forced to . . . ? *No, don't go there.* Lily steeled herself and let the silence grow uncomfortable.

"I am giving you a chance to submit willingly," Madeline volunteered, her smile deepened. "Shall I teach you another song?"

Lily pulled out her mandolin, and played Seth's naughty version of *The Chickadee Song.* Somehow, she knew his version better than the traditional. "If you think you're influential, you have no idea the effect my brother has on my nerves." The woman's songs were there, but so was her resolve. Lily knew she didn't have to pour herself out, to lose control.

Lily exited the holding bay, and asked the rangers on duty where Mama Fern had gone, though the rangers pointed that she'd left through the front door, only pausing to pick up her basket. Lily walked outside only a few steps, but didn't see her on the street. *I suppose I am alone.* Then she looked back at the rangers on guard, and reentered the building. "I know I'm not dressed for it, but if I were to change my clothes, would I be able to use the archery range out back, or get some proper riding lessons? I sort of know how to ride, but I could stand to be better."

Alanna's father got up from his chair. "I know your meaning. Of course—rumour has it you can use that sword at your hip, too. Once our riders return, we can train you up. How are things at the tavern?"

"I don't think I'm needed there," Lily said. "Could you use an extra set of hands?"

"Absolutely. Just you being here would help." He cast a glance at the other ranger. "Afterall, we still need to round up the puppets that are likely around town." The other ranger looked more sceptical, but eventually smiled.

Lily's heart lurched. She hadn't even thought about people like Elinor. "How many?"

"Don't know," said the other man. "We've got feelers out, but this is a delicate matter."

"We also can't leave her here alone," Alanna's father said, gesturing towards the cells. "If Lady Beatrice can spare a squire or a page, we'll take him. He can benefit from training and we'll benefit by having an extra hand."

"All right. Do you think Louis and I can take you up on the offer of staying at your house? I don't need to stay at the inn."

"Don't you want to see Sir Caleb?" asked Alanna's father.

"Of course, but he needs to stay focused. We'll get it figured, or I could stay here tonight."

He nodded. "I'm not going home until after the knighting. Then consider yourselves my guests. We'll feed you all once I get a head count. We'll put out cots here but we'll start your training first thing in the morning."

Returning to the pub, it was relatively quiet, though a handful of knights were playing cards, looking sombre and a little lost; Lily wondered if being angry would be better. She made her way up to the office, knocked, and discovering it unoccupied, quickly changed her borrowed clothing to her clothes from home. Leaving the room, she saw Beatrice and a knight speaking to one another at a table, sipping tea. Beatrice looked exhausted.

"Can I have a minute?" Lily asked.

"Of course. How can I help you?" Beatrice asked. Neither she nor the knight got up to let them speak privately, but Lily didn't care.

Lily licked her lips; she hadn't really thought about what she was going to say. "What's the normal chain of command I should be going through?"

Beatrice betrayed a hint of a smile. "For the time being, if you have questions or concerns, speak to me. I'll pass any messages you have along to Caleb. That'll likely change once we get additional resources."

"Okay. I've got an open invitation to stay at a ranger's house; unless anyone has a better idea, Louis can be with me. If you've a page or a squire, they could use a hand, and they said they'd train them in the meantime. I can make my way here every morning and see if you need anything. Caleb's asked me to do some polite inquiring about town, but I think he needs to focus on the castle."

Beatrice nodded and examined her remnant tea before looking up to answer. "That's fine with me. You're coming to the knighting?"

Did Ethan or Garett care? "If I'm still invited."

"Of course you are," Beatrice said. "Anything else?"

"No." Lily shook her head. Beatrice gave a curt nod, and Lily made to leave.

"Leave your clothes and everything you don't need here," Beatrice said. "I don't know you, but you're one of us now."

"Not yet," Lily told Beatrice.

Caleb didn't want her to do any of this alone, but she was one less thing Caleb needed to worry about. She went back to that fountain, looking for Boscoe and Mama Fern, and saw only ordinary people—but so was she. She sat down, and tuned her mandolin.

She watched her reflection in the water, didn't touch that song of fear. So long as she stayed away from what was trying to get her to call it, she was okay. She felt the songs try to creep, take her over. She wasn't going to let them. She played reels, jigs, and classical songs that she had to think about as opposed to the ones she could play instinctively. She watched her eyes in the pool's reflection. Occasionally, there was a hint of yellow, but she was going to wrestle it down and win.

Eighteen

Lily never drew a crowd, though folk did on occasion pause for a song or three. She didn't know all the ballads folk would request, but at one point someone joined her with a fiddle and several people insisted their local versions were superior to hers. She'd ask how the song went and tried to replicate it, usually to someone's frown breaking into a grin even if it wasn't *just so*. She played popular songs to which children sang—they had their own version of young Seth in the crowd, who belted out his own lyrics.

She was on a break when she overheard people mentioning something about riders, and went to investigate. She heard the sound of hooves. Not the sound of someone herding their pigs or sheep through town, but the sound of heavy horses. They seemed to be making their way to the ranger headquarters. The men wore armour for the most part, as well as their own halberds, which ranged in colour and complexity as much as their armour.

I should let Beatrice know. Lily made her way back to the Dark Horse Tavern. Garett and Ethan were near the fire; both looking like they were in need of a bath, given more than a healthy glow of sweat on their brows and tunics.

"Where's Beatrice?" she asked, but figured letting them know would make it so it went through the proper channels anyway. "I saw riders going to ranger headquarters. They looked like knights but I'm not certain."

A knight overheard them, and approached Lily. "How many?"

"I didn't count. More than a dozen," Lily said. The knight nodded, and raced off to speak to another knight.

"I'll let Lady Bee know," Garett said, chasing off after him but bolting up the stairs.

"Where's Oliver?" she asked Ethan.

"We left him at camp with Louis. Well, no time like the present." Ethan gestured, and she followed him outside. There were two riders bearing the black and yellow banner coming down the streets. His smile quickly died. "Lily," he said quietly. "I need you to trust me." He more or less took the steps in two strides with his long legs, looking like he was looking for a vantage point to watch but ducked out of sight. Lily followed his gaze. She saw no reason to get excited, although Beatrice and another senior knight hurried past them to speak to the riders. "That," he gestured, "is Sir Lionel."

She wasn't sure which of the pair he meant. She followed Ethan to a nearby alley, and ducked out of sight. They watched the small group enter the tavern. Ethan looked tempted to speak to the youths minding the horses. "If I can't, you need to get the message to Caleb that he's here so he doesn't . . . do anything rash. If he comes out and sees Lionel, I don't know what he'll do."

"Caleb's not stupid."

"He's the stupidest smart guy I know," Ethan said, leading her down the back alley away from the riders. "We're going to walk casually to the camp. Once we're out of sight, we're going to run."

"You start, I'll go a different way. If they stop you, I'll still have a chance. They don't know me."

Ethan nodded. She didn't know the layout of the streets, but knew the general direction and was out of town without issue, looking up at the sun. It was still way too early; she'd gleaned that those in the castle were trying to restrict movement to after sunset.She saw Ethan detained on the path, arguing with two knights. She slipped into the woods beside the road, and did her best not to stir up attention like she was trying to hide or avoid detection. Camp was manned mostly by ranger apprentices, and she found Oliver and Louis training with throwing knives.

"Boys, I need a favour," she said, gesturing for them to follow.

Louis seemed to plant himself. "We're going to the knighting ceremony," he informed her.

"I need a message passed on to Caleb." Lily looked up the path towards town. Ethan was walking, looking defeated, leading a horse coming up the path as an older man spoke to him.

"What's wrong?" Oliver asked.

"Yeah, why's Ethan coming to camp?" Louis asked. "I thought Lady Beatrice was making them take a bath."

Oliver's eyes widened. "What's the message?"

"Sir Lionel is among the knights that have just arrived."

"Is that it?" Oliver asked. "He'll be relieved! He used to be best friends with Sir Edgar. That's Caleb's dad."

Louis's frown deepened, watching her. "Please make sure whoever comes out gets that message in there. Understand?" She pressed. They nodded. "Take a lantern and some candles, go across the ferry and wait so he knows as soon as possible. Don't light them and draw attention to yourself in the dark, but . . . "

"I'm used to moving around in the dark," Louis said.

"Yeah, don't worry about us, Buttercup." Oliver affirmed. The pair didn't run off with anymore bravado than what would be expected, drawing next to no attention as they grabbed a leather satchel, and made their way towards the ferry.

Command of the camp was given to one of the men-at-arms, who identified himself as the riders entered the camp, though they'd either dismounted or were riding quite slowly, not having their horses enter into the camp as the younger ones, Lily assumed squires, spread out and got to making hitching post stations. Besides Ethan, Wilfred was also with the larger group of riders, and he was arguing with another knight. Ethan caught her gaze, and gestured towards town. She gave him the briefest nod and smile before leaving the way she came. She was pleased until several riders came up, squires slowing their horses.

"Hey cutie, no need to run off," said one. "We just got here!"

"I like your lute," said another.

"Hey, do you know *The Knight and the Oak Tree?*" another asked.

"I'd like to hear *The Squire and the Horse Brush,*" a knight snapped, gesturing, and the riders continued on.

Lily quickened her pace. She thought she got away, but one of the knights intercepted her about two minutes down the road; his roan horse was much bigger than the ranger's mounts they'd ridden the previous day. "I'm going to have to ask you to accompany me back to camp."

"Can I ask why?" Lily asked politely. She glanced at the castle, saw that the ferry had made it across the lake. She couldn't stare at it too long. She met the knight's gaze and smiled.

"We need you to answer some questions."

She couldn't outrun him on a horse, and also didn't want a scene. He dismounted and walked her back. "What's your name?"

"Lily."

"Lily what?"

"Brathwell." Ethan was surrounded by people looking to be firing questions at him; his look of defeat deepened when he saw her. It seemed the squires who'd addressed her on the road were given chores to keep them occupied, but no one made any more song requests.

Wilfred met them just before the camp. "Thank you Duncan. Lily, stay with me until I tell you otherwise. I hope he didn't frighten you."

The kitchen tent was now a war tent. It was well lit and they had a large wooden table. Ethan was still outside talking, but he and another knight entered shortly after she was ushered inside. A tall, strong-looking blond knight with greying hair eyed Lily but spoke to Wilfred "This is the girl he's courting? Where is he?"

"Sir Caleb is back in the castle," Wilfred said. "This is—"

"*You knighted him?* In front of what witnesses? The geese in the lake?" The knight scoffed. "Don't worry, Ethan, we'll do it proper for you and Caleb."

"It was proper," Wilfred insisted. "I've more than a dozen witnesses besides my Lady-Wife."

"Common folk. You had no right—"

"I had every right," Wilfred told the blond. "Both Henry and Edgar would have approved. Besides, it was common folk who discovered a way inside the castle."

"I'm his godfather, Wilfred," said the blond. "I'm probably the second or third man to hold him after he was born."

"That's enough, Lionel." Another older man entered the tent, and a large, red-headed man followed closely behind.

He was poisoned by his godfather? Lily tried to steel her expression. Neither Caleb nor Gillam knew for certain, but . . .

They'd already moved on. "Captain, how many men did you bring?" Wilfred pressed.

"Thirty fighting men; forty in total," the captain replied. "We came to investigate the claims of a ranger who appeared in Yarrosfeld towards the end of the day yesterday. I'm authorized to send for an additional five hundred men who can be here in less than a week," the salt-and-peppered haired man said, before looking at Lily. "I forgot you were here."

"She shouldn't even be in this camp," Lionel pointed out. "Sir, she's a distraction and our boys hardly need an excuse. Place her under my protection and I'll get my godson's . . .courtship sorted."

"Sir Caleb can court whoever he likes; the girl's already under my protection," Wilfred said. "Lily, may I introduce Captain Evander. This is Sir Goren, and this is Sir Lionel; Lionel and Sir Caleb's father were close, much like Ethan and Caleb are. This is Lily; she and her brother are responsible for finding a way into the castle. She's from the Kingdom of Merilon, and has been instrumental in our success so far."

"Ethan, explain," Lionel instructed.

"Merilon is a kingdom from across the sea," Ethan explained. "I assume they took a boat but sprouting fins and gills wouldn't surprise me."

"Be smart-mouthed again and I'll cuff you upside your head," Goren said, chuckling slightly. "Where's Demetri?"

"Last I checked, Declan's—but he's been frequenting an old neighbour's house for tea," Ethan said with a shrug. Ethan explained things as best and as she could tell; he seemed a little cold to Lionel. The captain nodded, though Goren seemed to think that the stories of puppets were poppycock. Evander pointed out that the stories made sense; in the beginning months, they intercepted several carriages worth of puppets. No cutting strings had brought any one to life, but several puppets were still in collections, and at least one wizard had shown interest in the marionettes.

"If you don't believe me," Ethan said. "Just wait until after the sun goes down and see what crosses the ferry line. Someone'll come back and give a report, and then I'll go join the others. They'll shuttle more people out; it'll take time for them to recover but the plan was once I'm in they'll get Sir Percival out."

"If the team can get that drawbridge open, we can take it by force," Goren said.

"I want an actual army," Evander said. He seldom looked at Lily, but when he did she couldn't read his expression when he assessed her. "When the brother gets out, he will be detained. They're too valuable to send back into there, at this time. In fact, we're going to get as many of those . . . refugees out of town before the assault. Regular folk we can send to Yarrosfeld; we'll send the girl and her brother to Fort Beldys."

Ethan's brow tensed. "They helped us. You can't treat them like prisoners."

"I didn't ask you what you thought, squire. They'll be treated like guests according to their . . . station," Evander said, looking Lily over.

"Sir, you can send her to Innesbrooke," Lionel said. "She'll be safe at my estate."

Raised voices outside the tent. Goren stepped out and a different squire with short-cropped hair popped his head in. "There's people from the town, sir. Knights, I mean."

"All right," Evander said with a nod. "The girl doesn't need to be here. Why is she still armed? Take that from her; I don't want any funny business. Keep her in camp and don't let anyone bother her."

"Gavin," Ethan said when the squire laid a hand on Lily's shoulder and gestured for her to give up her blade and follow. "Just so you're aware, if anything happens to her, I'm holding you accountable."

"Relax, Ethan, I ain't gonna let anyone hurt your girlfriend," Gavin told him. Ethan didn't correct him, and neither did Lily.

'Detained' turned out to be sent to a small tent. "Just sit there until you're called for," Gavin said. At least they had a blanket on the floor, and it didn't smell like a latrine tent. "Are Caleb and the others okay in there?"

"I hope so," Lily said. He bit his lip but nodded, leaving her. Lily paced in her small prison. *Okay, think, Lily, think. I'll wait for it to get dark and for them to put their guard down. I'll sneak off back to the ranger headquarters; maybe one of them might help me. If not . . . I'll make my way back towards the port. Larry may be a few days but he said he'd return.* She sat down. Occasionally, someone popped the tent door to make sure she was still there; Gavin was the only one who said more than two words to her, but it seemed that they sent a new guy every time.

I wish there was something I could do to . . . she realized she still had her mandolin. She could lull her guards, or make them fear her. She strummed on it, listening to the sound cascade. She could . . .

. . . no, she was not going to use it against innocent people who didn't know any better. She wasn't Madeline, she was in no immediate danger; last thing she needed was to mess up whatever was going on in the castle. She was going to wait, and when their guard was down, sneak off. If not from this camp, then some time in the night. She'd figure it out.

~*~

Seth and Anne had two marionettes strapped to their back and made their way down the tunnel. He heard a *pssst!* It was Louis. "What are you—" Seth demanded.

"I don't know what's going on, but a bunch of knights showed up," Louis said. "Something's wrong."

"Isn't that a good thing?" Seth asked, looking to Anne. She frowned; they both stared at the camp across the water. There was more noise; more horses. The fires were subdued, but it was evident to anyone looking from the castle grounds there were more people, though it was hard to make out numbers.

"Lily told me to give you a message. She and Ethan both wanted to tell you but they got . . . I don't think apprehended is the right term but, basically she tried to go back to town and people stopped her."

"Oh they did, did they?" Seth asked. "I'll transform her and we'll be out of there before . . . right, magic bracelet."

"Oliver's keeping an eye on her, she ain't being mistreated or anything. He'll come back and get me when I signal him."

"What's the message?" Anne pressed.

Louis nodded. "Tell Sir Caleb that Sir Lionel arrived in the camp."

"That's it? You had me worried," Anne said. "Seth, you go and deliver it. I can go across and give report."

"I can go with you. Save time with this amulet."

"If they've apprehended your sister, they'll apprehend you."

Seth grumbled. The camp was supposed to be safe, but he found that safe was quickly becoming another word for boring. "Try to find out what's going on there." Seth was tempted to just go and kidnap Ethan and sneak back before anyone knew he was there. "Consider the message delivered. Tell them not to manhandle my sister or Sir Knight and me are gonna stop being wee. Get back to the other side. Can you lurk in the woods? Pinch some food and keep a look out?"

"Of course. Do I look like a poncey knight to you?" Louis asked.

"Wasn't sure with that hair cut which side you were picking," Seth said, disappearing back into the not-so secret tunnel.

He didn't find Sir Knight immediately. Sir Percival and Daraby were there with the men-at-arms, Caleb was with Gillam and a few others on a scouting mission. "When's he going to be back?" he asked a goblin lieutenant, who was uncertain.

"We are back," Rodney called.

"Where's Ethan?" Caleb asked.

"Can I talk to you?" Seth gestured to another room in the burrow. There were people there, but they were promptly kicked out. "Louis was waiting on this side of the lake. A bunch of knights showed up, sounds like Ethan and Lily got . . . what's it called . . . detained."

"What colours were they flying?" Caleb asked.

"I don't know, it's dark out. Louis said to say that there was a Sir Lionel there, and you needed to know," Seth said. Caleb's puppet brow tensed, and he turned away. "Hey, clue a guy in."

"Something's wrong," Caleb said.

Anne returned around that time, seeking Seth. "They're not letting Ethan come in here," she said. "I was instructed to inform you to go to the camp immediately, Seth. You too, Sir Caleb."

"We're not doing that," Caleb said quietly.

"If I go, they ain't gonna let me back in," Seth said. "I can sneak around, but if they cut the ferry line we're hooped until I make a little sailboat."

"What is going on out there?" Rodney asked.

"About thirty or so knights and squires arrived," Anne said. "They were arguing with Wilfred about your plan. Sounds like they want to pull everyone out."

"And abandon everyone else? We can do it without Seth if we had to," Gillam said.

"This plan works with Seth here," Daraby said.

"If Captain Evander is satisfied, he'll write to the prince and send an army."

"If we pull out now, there's no one left. Assuming we leave five men behind, the way may become compromised," Daraby said, glancing at Percival.

"We need to discuss our options," Sir Percival said. "I'd go discuss this with them myself if the barrier wouldn't incapacitate me."

"Promise this doesn't leave this room," Caleb said. The older marionettes glanced at one another, heads nodded. "In two days, a dragon will attack the castle. It is a small one, and will not destroy it—he knows there are innocent people in here."

"How . . ." Daraby began.

"Because I told him to get rid of the dragon," Percival snapped. "Last thing we needed was for them to set their flying, fire-breathing monstrosity on our stringless." He gestured at Seth.

"You didn't think to mention this earlier?" Daraby demanded.

"I wasn't told about that, I suppose a little dragon slipped my mind."

"A little dragon?"

"Daraby, can you get that drawbridge open without being at your normal size?"

"Of course," the captain said. "I reckon it'll be easier with us being full-sized but, I've had . . .er . . .I've gotten out of worse . . .okay, I've never been this small before, but it'll be fine."

Seth looked at Caleb. Judging by that furrowed brow, he was planning something. "They've only just arrived," Caleb said. "When we do send someone out, we need to make it clear we know where they've sent Lily."

"That girl's not a priority right now," Daraby said.

"She's safe for the time being," Caleb agreed. "We don't want her falling into the clutches of whoever did this. I say we take our time responding. Let them sweat it out."

Sir Percival nodded. "I need to go back on string for an hour or so regardless. Don't do anything until I return."

~*~

Waiting paid off. After an hour or so, Lily was more or less forgotten. She wished she'd brought something besides her mandolin to do, but figured making music would be a good way to have people notice it was getting further and further away, or stop completely.

Something pricked the hair on the back of her arms and neck, and she knew something was wrong. She stuck her head out of the tent, and there was no, "You, girl!" so she hesitantly stepped out of it. Knights and squires were about their business. She realized that she wasn't being watched, and part of her was tempted to make a break for the town. She made her way to the bush nearer to the lake.

From her vantage point, an open carriage made its way to the camp ad she could see the back of Madeline's head. Lily kept to the bush, edged around.

Someone offered the puppeteer a hand down; they also had her satchels. Lily felt queasy, knowing the masks were likely there. Ethan was speaking to the captain and several others; they were trying to restore someone that was brought out of the castle.

An acorn hit the back of Lily's head. "Pssst!" Oliver waved at her from the woods just beyond where several hobbled horses grazed. Following him, she learned that he and Louis had a great vantage point and, judging by a half-eaten rotisserie chicken (and no fire in sight), had their own camp. "I was just coming to save you!" Oliver said. "What did they say to you and Ethan?"

"They want to know what's going on in the castle," she said quietly. She could feel a strange rhythm in the air; that woman . . . "I'm going to go give myself up and stop whatever she's about to do," Lily said. "I'll be fine. I'm going to probably sneak away when they put their guard down in a few days. They want to send me and Seth to some Fort . . . started with a B."

"Fort Beldys?" Oliver asked, his nose wrinkled. "You can't go there. It's a fortress on an island."

Lily didn't think she could break out of the ranger's headquarters. "I don't think it matters where they'd send me," Lily said. "I can't leave them to her. Thank you for informing Seth and Caleb."

"Wasn't anything," Louis said. "You sure?"

"They need a warning," Lily said.

"We'll watch your back," Oliver said.

Lily wasn't sure what good they were going to do, but she strode out of the bush towards Madeline unarmed. Madeline was performing the ritual of transformation on a horse. Knights and squires squawked as it diminished, and one of the younger ones was ordered to retrieve the now miniature horse.

Madeline looked over her shoulder at Lily. "You want to do the next one for me?"

"She's not supposed to be here," Sir Lionel snapped.

"She might as well stay," Madeline said.

Lily kept her shoulders back and marched to Ethan. "How much proof is it going to take?"

"Let me get this straight," Sir Goren said. "You made this woman turn you into that," he pointed at the small puppet horse, who'd escaped his squire and him and two ranger apprentices chased it into a nearby tent and then the far bush. "To sneak into Castle Mirador?" He gestured across the lake.

She nodded. "This woman came to my village asking for help," Lily said, pointing at Madeline, who seemed pleased. "She asked me to learn a song, and something changed in me. I don't want any part of it, to be honest. Sir Caleb said my eyes glowed yellow when I sang it."

Madeline nodded. "Close enough."

"What all can she do?" the captain asked Madeline.

"I taught her a song for lulling, another for summoning. She has a song of revealing, a song of fear, and a spell for turning living creatures into puppets. None of which will work on herself."

"All right girl," the captain said. "Let's hear a song."

"I could put the entire camp to sleep, sir," Lily said, and took out her mandolin. She was a better player than singer anyway. Thing was, part of her knew she could target someone or play for in general depending on the song. Afterall, Mama Fern didn't react in fear. "Be specific."

"Fear never killed anyone, sir," said Sir Lionel.

"Are you volunteering?" Lily asked, strumming. The blond knight nodded and stepped forward, arms crossed, like there wasn't a little wooden horse squirming in a squire's grasp feet away. Lily looked at him. Was this man responsible for several murders? She had no idea. She doubted she'd get a confession out of him. She strummed and part of her knew something was missing. She started to sing; no lyrics but her voice entwined with the melody, and she let her suspicions influx with the metallic sounds of her mandolin. Several knights gasped as she felt herself flow with the song.

Sir Lionel, who had seen battle for longer than she'd been alive, staggered backwards, and colour drained from his face. He drew his sword and several men drew theirs on him, and stood in his way. Lionel's cheeks flushed and he was sweating. "Liar! You're a dirty liar! You shut your mouth!"

Lily realized her mistake as Madeline had edged towards Ethan during the performance. She slapped a mask on his face. Ethan tried to get it off. Madeline let loose a strange melody.

"Seize both women!" the captain ordered. "Ethan, calm down—"

Ethan responded by throwing the first man who touched him into the second one. Madeline meanwhile had other masks at her disposal— how could they have been so careless? Blood sprayed the air.

Ethan was a monster when he fought. He'd send one man sprawling and move to another; it only occurred to Lily later he wasn't even trying to kill. Madeline masked an injured man, then another, singing again each time and Lily watched as their wounds healed and those in the strange masks turned on their fellow knights and squires. The new knights and squires weren't nearly as fast or as deadly as Ethan.

Madeline donned the spider face, and grew. Lily knew the song of fear wasn't going to work on her. Men shrieked as spider silk flew, trapping some and blinding others. Madeline barrelled down on her. Lily's hands were gobbed, then her feet. Madeline went after the others, but Ethan—he seemed to be able to jump higher and further than possible and use his spear to balance and evade just like . . . just like when she'd knocked away an arrow, only he was trained for battle. Not trained, *moulded.*

People screamed. Knights and squires fled towards town, scattering horses. Madeline crooned that song of fear. Lily would have run if she'd half the chance.

When at last all that were left were masked besides Lily, Madeline looked to Lily, satisfied. She climbed a tree and made an appropriate sized-web, before she dragged Lily from her sticky trap. She put the mandolin aside gingerly, whereas she roughly forced Lily against the elevated web. Her spider silk wrapped her waist and left wrist, leaving her right with the bracelet exposed, dissolving the gooey stuff before she left Lily dangling.

"We'll have to do something about that bracelet." Madeline fussed at her wrist, and they both seemed to realize that there was no way to get the bangle off. Except for cutting off Lily's hand. The spider seemed to contemplate that. "I'd rather keep your hands." she said. She frowned, noticing one of her minions limped. "Be right back."

She descended and sang, his wounds healed almost instantly, with strange markings where cuts had been, like new, pale skin forming. The song of healing was loud enough for Lily to hear now that no one was shouting; it immediately took root in Lily's mind. It didn't seem as terrible as the others.The spider looked at her, smiling. She sang something else; a song of compulsion; another of love—not a real love, but to see things in such a way that you couldn't help but admire and want to fawn. The songs kept striking the back of Lily's mind; one of which would have been terrible; but now four or five all circled around, competing for supremacy.

"They're painful to learn, I know." The puppeteer told her, Lily tried to free herself; it would have been difficult with a weapon or a tool. "That bracelet is interesting. Pity I have to destroy it. Brace yourself, this one will be painful."

Madeline crooned a complex melody that had a strange, hollow feel that burned Lily's eyes. She felt the bracelet go red hot, searing into her skin. It was beautiful and terrible, and she could almost feel the world coming apart . . .

. . . reality came crashing back and she found herself falling as Madeline screamed in surprise. Something had struck the Jorogumo, making her recoil. "Grab her!" Madeline shrieked.

Ethan caught Lily before she hit the ground, and Lily's heart still raced with that Song of Destruction—no, it was a Song of Unmaking. She looked into the darkness where Ethan's eyes should have been, tried to pull off the mask but it wouldn't budge. He dragged her towards Madeline, who was going to hit her with spider silk again; maybe Ethan would cut her hands off and they'd be done.

He forced Lily to her knees; she struggled, reached for his face and the mask that bound him and finished the spider's own song, the power coming out of her own throat as she focused. White light blinded her as the bracelet shattered. Her first thought was she'd killed Ethan.

He staggered backwards and letting go of her, reached for his face, the mask jagged from the bracelet's shrapnel. Ethan ripped off the mask, eyes blazing at the puppeteer. He gripped his spear and ran Madeline through the bulbous belly. The other masked men went for him; there were almost ten of them. It was almost like watching him evade children, often knocking them to the side with the wood of his blade, though his strikes looked so hard the blade would have been a mercy.

Madeline roared an order. "The boy must not be harmed! Kill the girl if you have to!" She took another sling-shot rock in one of her six eyes, staggered and fell for a fraction, struggling to stand to full height.

"Lily, catch!" Louis called from behind. He threw her sword to her. He let loose another rock from his sling, and when Oliver let loose another shot, he took his sword and charged at the beast. Lily pulled him back from being crushed by a massive tendril, then released him and they both brought their blades down on it, making the spider recoil and focus on them, opening up Ethan for another powerful strike to the bulb.

"Get away from this thing!" Ethan ordered Oliver and Louis. It only occurred to Lily later that Madeline was trying to pin him, not seriously injure him. For a moment she succeeded, trapping Ethan's left leg in a mound of sticky silk. Before she could incapacitate the squire Oliver shot her shoulder, making her stop to sing and heal herself.

Lily went to Ethan's side. He used her as leverage to pull himself free, but losing a boot didn't slow him down. He threw his spear and skewered her. The jorogumo crooned the healing song, and pulled out the spear, attempting to patch up the damage they'd caused her. Lily struck another back leg and Madeline fell and tried to rise on her tendrils.

Ethan found an axe that had been dropped by another knight, and screaming, leapt up higher than he should have been able to and hacked. The spider tried to buck, but he moved with such fluidity it terrified Lily to watch. After several strikes, blood no longer came but the sound of cutting wood. The mask fell and the spider shrivelled, aspects of her tendrils and extra eyes wisping away like smoke in the night. All that remained was a large, plain-faced, human-sized puppet, which almost let out a gasp.

"You don't get to die so easily!" Ethan grabbed the wooden head. "What did you do to us? What were they trying to do to us?"

Oliver and Louis hooted before fist-bumping. The knights who were masked, those who weren't injured, let loose shrieks of panic as they tried to wrench the cloth from their faces. Lily went to the nearest; a squire.

"You're okay," she said, catching his eyes and making sure he nodded. "Help me," she ordered, and they went to the next, a knight who had scratched his face to the point of bleeding trying to get the mask off. "It's over. Just breathe."

"That was so epic!" Louis cheered. "Seth's gonna be so mad!"

Ethan didn't look like he'd just saved everyone. Staring at several knights and squires nursing broken arms and lingering in the grass and dirt in various states of pain, he looked back at Lily, tears streaming down his face.

"Boys, help the others," Lily said. She approached Ethan, tempted to sing the Song of Admiration, but somehow after she acknowledged the thought she hated herself for contemplating it. He breathed heavily but refused to meet her gaze. "Hey," she said, touching his shoulders. He jerked away. "Look at me."

"What did I do?" he asked quietly. "What did they do to me? To us?" He looked to the castle. "I didn't think. I just . . . I just . . . "

All she could do was wrap her arms around him. "Ethan, it's okay. You saved us. Everyone is alive and free because of you. I don't know what she—or they—did to you. But we're going to find a way to stop it."

"Lily," Oliver called. "This guy's pretty hurt."

"I hurt them." Ethan's voice was barely above a whisper.

"I summoned and transformed my own villagers. I didn't want to," she said quietly. "I don't know you or Caleb that well, but I know that's not you. I have to help them. Wait for me." She turned her attention to Oliver. "Go to the infirmary and get as many bandages as you can." She retrieved her mandolin. "I hope this works," she said to an injured man. She focused on warm thoughts as the song poured out of her. This was so much easier than wrapping an injured ram's leg. The man stared at her in bewilderment.

"Don't trust her!" another formerly masked man said, drawing his sword. "She's one of that monster's—!"

"Touch her and I will kill you," Ethan growled, his voice different. It gave Lily pause but she couldn't dwell on it. He and several others stood around the fallen spider's form. All that remained was the wooden form of a human. Lily got the impression she had been human, once, reduced to . . . whatever she was needed to be. Was Madeline's face her own? Was it a better version of what once was? Lily had no idea. She moved the healing song to another knight. His wounds were patched, but he'd lost a considerable amount of blood, he still seemed weak when she finished.

"What do we do about the current sorceress?" one knight asked another.

"I'm not a sorceress. I'm a tainted shepherd," Lily said. "Anyone else hurt?"

The remaining knights conversed; one squire quickly mounted and took off towards the town. Captain Evander spoke to Ethan. "Did you know what this girl could do?"

"Sort of. We didn't really understand it," Ethan said. "Still don't. Lily, you got it under control?"

"I think so?" Lily asked, uncertain. The remaining knights made short work of cutting the wooden mannequin and throwing it into the fire, minus the head and masks. "Someone ought to go in and update everyone on the inside. Do not detain my brother. I'll . . . I'll go with you willingly if you promise to leave him and Caleb."

"Why was I forced to fight against you?" a formerly masked knight asked Ethan.

"You were under compulsion," Lily offered. "The woman did the same thing to me in my village. Kill her, and I guess the spell wore off. Why am I still able to do this?" she asked, strumming her mandolin.

There was a strange tension in the air. She frowned, looking to the castle. The spell Madeline had put on the men was over, but the one on her lingered. That meant that Madeline's master, the real master, still had talons dug into Lily.

How many more hooks were in Ethan and Caleb? She looked at Oliver, remembered what Esther said. *He wants to help them, he can't wear the armour. The armour allows them to un-string.* What did Caleb call them? Enforcers?

"Lad, what you did was incredible," Captain Evander said to Ethan.

"I need to update Caleb and the others," Ethan said lowly. "I want to bring Sir Percival out. If we send Seth, Rodney or whoever can talk to you normally, but you cannot detain Seth. He is crucial." Ethan licked his lips. "If we get that drawbridge open, will you march your men in there?"

"Not until we know what sort of sorcery is going to hit us," the captain said, then gestured to Lily. "Unless you think she can counter-act it."

"Then that's what I'm going to find out," Ethan said. He looked to Lily. "I need you to transform me. I know you can do it. I'll be okay by myself."

"If you get caught by yourself, no one is left to warn the others on the inside," Lily said.

Oliver spoke up. "Garett won't slow you down."

Captain Evander nodded. "We should knight you in the meantime."

"It doesn't really matter," Ethan said quietly.

"Yes it does," Evander said before gesturing at a still pale squire. "You go get those who ran off, tell them we're fine now, and that we need Squire Garett. We'll knight you both together. Won't be fancy, you understand. We'll do a proper accolade cer—"

"I know," Ethan said. Lily sat with Ethan, and didn't say anything for a while. Ethan watched the flames take the last of the mannequin, before he broke the spider face in half and threw it into the flame. Then the centaur mask, then another. She wondered what other tricks the puppeteer had, if she should tell them no, she might be able to .

. . no, she wasn't like Madeline; she didn't want to transform into a monster, even if it would help she wouldn't know how to move as a Jorogumo, she imagined the best she could do would be fall down and crush an enemy.

They sat in silence for a short while before Ethan broke the silence. "Cay suspected something was up. I could tell when we were doing drills. Garett wasn't a knight in there for very long, he couldn't keep up with me."

It never occurred to Lily that Garett was anything but a goblin. She'd ask, later. "Caleb was carrying a lot of weight on his shoulders he didn't have to."

"He doesn't like making people worry," Ethan said. "Thanks, by the way. You're good for him." Lily wasn't sure what to say, so she just sat quietly with him.

It seemed like they took forever for the squires to return with Garett and other riders. The burly squire raced over, looking like he was upset he missed a fight. "You're late." Ethan said, only standing when Lady Beatrice dismounted.

"What's this I hear they're knighting us real quick?" Garett asked. "Then we go and tell Percy we already took out the major threat?"

"Watch it buddy," Ethan said, grinning. "Oliver took down the major threat while you were trimming your toenails."

"Are you all right?" Beatrice asked, touching Ethan's face and looking him over. "Did she hurt you?"

"No more than they did in there," Ethan said, looking over the lake to the shadow of the castle. "Sorry to anyone I hurt earlier."

"What about Asher?" Oliver asked.

"We didn't think to bring him," one of the squires admitted.

"Can she have us recite the vows?" Garett asked, gesturing at Lily.

"It'll be fun to lord over Cay," Ethan agreed.

"I'll have you recite the vows," Beatrice said, giving Lily a smile but it was a warm, *thank you.* "I'm married to a knight, whereas you are courting a squire, so I outrank you."

"Knight," Lily said, giving a slight nod of her head and deferring.

They went down by the lakeshore. "Do not throw anything in the lake at this hour," Lily told them when she noticed Garett's gaze was lingering a little too long over the water.

"Oh, come on." Garett complained.

"All right you lumps: Kneel and somebody give Beatrice a sword. Ready? We're gathered here at the side of a lake to raise these squires to knighthood," the captain said. "By accepting these vows these young men will join a brotherhood of honour to which he will spend the rest of his life attempting to uphold."He gestured, and Lady Beatrice stepped forward. "Ethan Levi Davian, son of Sir Simon and Lady Maeve; Garett James Darrow, son of Sir Albert and Lady Elayne: do you accept the seven tenets of knighthood?"

"Yes," the pair chorused. Garett's nerves started to show, his confidence replaced by visible blanching.

"Was Caleb pleased to be knighted?" Sir Lionel's voice caught her off guard.

"I think so," Lily hesitated as Lady Beatrice had the boys affirm the vows. "He insisted for it be done in the church where his parents were married. He said he didn't deserve it, but it was done before we could argue."

"That boy . . . " Lionel muttered, his gaze on the squires kneeling.

"Let all who stand here be a witness." Beatrice held the sword and Captain Evander took it, and tapped Ethan's shoulders, then Garett's. "Be thou a knight, Sir Ethan of Mirador. Be thou a knight, Sir Garett of Mirador." They didn't move for a minute.

Lily started to politely clap whereas Oliver and Louis let out shrill whistles and a *whoop whoop*, to which several other squires joined in the bawdy noise.

Upon standing, Beatrice kissed Garett's cheeks, then Ethan's; both had to bend down for her. Their fellow squires rushed them and offered them congratulations. Lily watched, but Ethan seemed sombre.

Garett ambled over. "I don't suppose it's too much to ask for . . . " Garett blushed a little.

"Oh," Lily said, and standing on her toes, kissed him on the cheek. "Caleb won't mind. Congratulations, Sir."

"He shouldn't!" Garett said.

"Just a hug is fine for me," Ethan said, joining them. Lily gave him one.

"All right knights, time's a wasting," Lionel said. "Tell Caleb to get out of the castle."

"Ugh. Goodbye, ability to generate body odour," Garett said. "Little Goblin Brother! Look after the magical minstrel in our absence."

"You got it, Big Goblin Brother!" Louis called back.

Before Lily retrieved her mandolin, a roar sounded overhead, making everyone pause and look up. "No way . . . Oliver . . . all of you, stay here," Ethan said, gesturing at Garett. "We'll talk to Peanut."

"Peanut?" the captain asked.

"It's Varian," Lily offered, and the younger boys made it their solemn duty to protect her, before abandoning their duty to go get as close as they dared to the dragon who landed on the road. Lily watched Garett and Ethan converse with the dragon.

"They," one of the squires pointed. "Let that out?"

"Better out here than waiting for us in there," the captain said. "Leave it to that smartass Percival to befriend a dragon . . ."

"Lily!" Louis called. "The dragon wants to speak to you!"

Lily walked to where Garett and Ethan stood, but the dragon spoke to her before she joined them fully. *Do you like my scale?*

"It's beautiful," Lily said.

The dragon studied Lily. *The songs that are in your mind will weaken with time. You won't be able to summon that terrible one by the dawn.*

"Thank goodness," Lily said, then thought about what he told her. "You can hear them?"

This is most strange magic. Ethan, you are right. They were doing something to you, and Caleb. And others too, I think. Hers is different.

The opening of multiple minds was terrifying. She could sense that the two new knights were also mortified that she'd have an inkling to their thoughts—and now they were pretending like they viewed her as a sister, Caleb's intended, nothing more and . . .

Humans have very strange hang ups. Would you not be more insulted if they found you undesirable? You seem hale, though you seem unlikely to produce large eggs.

"Stop already," Garett said. "And we don't lay eggs!"

Don't be absurd! I know only females can.

"Any idea what is going on in there?" Ethan asked, trying desperately to change the subject.

The dragon snorted. *I think they were turning you into a living weapon,* then he gestured at Lily *or a tool.*

"Can she use that healing spell to break whatever is binding me?" Ethan asked.

I do not think so. What flows through you is different than healing cuts and broken bones. Lily, if you can play that Song of Unmaking, in the Nest, you may be able to break the hold on the castle.

"I sang a few arias and thought I was going to die."

It may kill you, yes.

"What?" Garett demanded. "We can't ask that."

You sang and it hurt you. Play it on the mandolin. It will act as a diffuser. Other things would work in harmony, spread the energy out.

Like when I sang and played at the same time. "You're saying that if I go up there, and find where . . . the main hold is, and play that song I used to shatter the bracelet, the castle will lose its curse?"

I do not know. You could sing and play at the same time, in harmony, and the song will unmake what is there. But it has to come from you.

"Can you take me to it?" Lily asked, her voice quavering slightly. "Will you fly me to a tower? I can't go the same way as them."

I know about where it is. I can burn the areas around you, make them . . . distracted.

"We don't know what sort of sorcery is up there," Ethan said. "And you aren't going without an escort."

When they weave sorceries on you, she can counteract them. Simple.

"No, not simple," Ethan said.

"If we break the hold on the castle," Garett asked. "That's our smarter play. Instead of bringing out one person at a time, we can unlock the curse on everyone."

"Someone has to warn Percy and Cay," Ethan said, as if he'd already agreed to this asinine plan. He looked over to the knights and squires who had just arrived. "None of these guys are used to being puppets or would know where to go."

"We are," Louis chirped.

"Yeah," Oliver said.

"Absolutely not," Ethan said.

"Why not?" Louis asked.

"I'm old enough to be your squire," Oliver said lowly. "Physical strength matters less in there, anyway."

"And we'll protect her," Garett said. "Ethan, either we take a chance now or she might not be able to protect us in a few hours. Between that and Varian's fire, you and I might be enough to take out the big guy upstairs. We strike before they have a place to retaliate."

"Captain?" Ethan asked.

"I don't like sending you," the captain said. "I also saw what Ethan's capable of. He fought like a small army. If Daraby gets that gate open, we'll ride in. We can't fight sorcery, you understand?"

"Give us about a twenty minute head start," Oliver said. "In case we don't find Caleb right away."

"All right," Lily said. She didn't like casting the song, and the knights and squires balked at the transformation. It wasn't even done before the pair fist bumped, stole the scissors, tied them to Louis's back, and made their way towards the ferry line. To add insult to injury, they were nimble like Seth, doing flips and cartwheels, quipping that Seth and Caleb weren't going to save themselves.

Nineteen

The only good thing about bugging out in that little hidey-hole was that Ethan and Caleb made their own board games and smuggled in playing cards. Seth could tell that Caleb and the others were getting more anxious. They eventually decided Rodney and Anne would go speak to the others outside. Assuming the scissors were handy, Seth suspected after twenty minutes of awkward dialogue, Rodney would at least be able to look the knights in the eye and tell them to shove off.

Gillam and Seth tried to distract Caleb by playing a board game called Vinda-Voorta to pass the time, and it was obvious Caleb wasn't really into it. "Lily and Ethan will be fine," Gillam assured.

Seth was using their being distracted to take an early lead only stood up from his master strategy when he heard a familiar, however squeaky voice.

"Why are you back so—Louis?"

"Heya, Seth. Caleb we need to talk." Somehow, it was more bizarre seeing Louis like a marionette version of his usual self than as a goblin marionette.

"I'll say," Rodney said, dragging both Louis and Oliver in by their arms, though Oliver dropped his pinned one and helped Louis do likewise, the pair cackled as Rodney realized that he was only holding parts of them "Very funny." Someone brought Sir Percival in before Seth could press Louis. "Tell them what you told me."

"We are in phase one of—"

"Sum it up," Percival said.

Oliver nodded. "There's a dozen knights and about eighteen fighting-age squires that arrived in town. You know that, right?" Oliver waited for Percival to nod. "They detained Lily and Ethan, and brought that Madeline woman to the camp, and she attacked. She masked Ethan and a bunch of other knights and transformed into that spider-woman-thingy."

"Are Lily and Ethan all right?" Caleb asked.

"Getting to it," Oliver insisted. "Madeline taught Lily some other songs, and Lily made that bracelet explode and it unmasked Ethan, and he killed Madeline. She was a puppet, too! Madeline, I mean. Well, sort of, she didn't really have a face."

"We helped, but it was mostly Ethan," Louis said. He and Oliver started to reenact the battle, to which they were prompted to finish. "Madeline became some sort of a mannequin when she died, and that freed everyone she took over still wearing a mask. The captain got Garett from town and they knighted him and Ethan. They were supposed to be in here telling you this."

"But?" Caleb asked, sounding a little nervous where this was leading.

"Peanut showed up and he said Lily can use that Song of Exploding and take down the castle's curse. Lily shrank us down to puppet size. She can't do anything for herself, but they gave us these scissors," Oliver pointed to Anne, who had them strapped to her back. "Peanut said Lily would only be able to call up that bad spell for a few hours, and said he would fly her and Garett and Ethan to one of the towers. Peanut's going to set the briars on fire and, if they can, Lily's going to make the hold on the castle go KABLOOOIE! They want you to open the drawbridge."

"How long does it take for you to reach the armoury?" Percival asked Caleb.

"Five, maybe ten minutes," Caleb said. "Doesn't matter if we're seen at this point."

The older knight nodded. "The scissors will see me back to human form in twenty," Percival said. "Squires, help me suit up. Caleb, you take four volunteers with you to the armoury that are going up. The rest of you are with Myron."

"We get that drawbridge open," Daraby snapped, turning his attention on his men.

Seth thought it was silly that Percival was among the ones who got one of the four suits of armour they'd smuggled in, but he knew not to argue. His job was taking the five going with Caleb to the armoury to regular size, and then double back to those on the main door.

Their group went first. Nothing stopped them, though the armoury wasn't in great shape. They'd inspected it during the day, taking to the halls it didn't seem like anything had changed inside the castle, save for the quietness didn't feel like neglect. They were nominally faster as marionettes, so Seth returned everyone to normal size only after they were outside the main door.

"You going to be able to walk in that?" Gillam asked. Though he'd taken a shirt of mail, he was among the lighter-equipped, mostly because he refused to let Caleb help him with the fussier pieces that required another set of hands to put on properly.

"When you're not a skinny little prissy boy," Rodney told him, if anyone looked the part of heroic knight it was him. "All things are possible."

"Except for brushing your hair."

"Shaddap!"

Caleb helped Rodney gear up and then others—still used to being a squire, Seth supposed, and to his surprise, he saw Muffin staring at them from a corner. Then, another kitsune; once they made eye contact, they got up. Seth followed them into the hallway, having donned a mail shirt.

"What do you want? We're kind of busy," Seth told them.

"They know you're coming."

To Seth's surprise, Gillam followed him into the hallway. "What in the actual—"

"We can't follow," the other kitsune said, he sounded like Top-Knot. "We'd like to. Can I speak to Caleb, please?"

"Cay!" Gillam went back into the room and bellowed. Caleb looked annoyed until he spotted Muffin.

"They said they know we're coming," Seth said.

Muffin nodded. "You won't be able to follow, Seth."

Caleb turned and pulled his sword when a thousand blue butterflies converged, and became a figure in a blue mask down the hall. The kitsunes growled and stood before them; instead of forest foxes they became fierce and terrible, nearly the size of wolves.

"You may take the ones below and leave the castle; those that you can manage you can keep. The castle is ours. If you remain when the gates close, you will be added. You may leave of course but you," the figure pointed, speaking to Caleb, "know where you belong. Go to the master."

Boscoe stepped forward towards the figure and was his teenage form, making several of the others back up. "Let us up there," he bared his teeth.

"We are not addressing you, kitsune."

To Seth's surprise, Gillam let loose a shot, and it sailed right through the figure, though blue butterflies dispersed in its wake. The arrow clattered down the hall. "Choose wisely, for it may be your last real choice," the figure said, and at once collapsed into a thousand blue butterflies, and disappeared in a swirl down the hall.

"All right," Rodney said. "Enough blah blah blah, let's take back the castle." He proceeded down the hall, barely casting a glance at the kitsunes. He then stopped with a thunk, then put his hand out. "What in the . . ."

"We haven't figured out a way around that yet," the other kitsune said. Rodney looked like he was beating his fist against the air, but he couldn't move it past a certain point. It was like there was an invisible wall in front of him.

"My arrow show past there," Gillam said when two others confirmed they could not progress down the hall. They backed up, and Gillam fired. The arrow now stopped in the middle of the hall, suspended in air.

"There's got to be someway . . ." Caleb muttered, stepping forward, and they could all feel the glow. It was green, like a barrier, which made Caleb back up.

"Interesting," Muffin said, cocking his head. "We can't help you up there."

"Can you help them down here?" Caleb asked. The other kitsune nodded curtly. Seth watched Caleb's jaw square and brow tense, then step through. He did not collapse; instead he frowned, looking back at Rodney and the others. He looked at the arrow almost hovering from his angle. He reached a hand across, but he couldn't pull anyone to him.

"Caleb, they can handle it upstairs," Rodney said. "You don't have to go alone."

"Maybe, but you'd go if you were me," Caleb said. "I don't have time to waste. Get the drawbridge open. If this goes to pot, save who you can." He went back to the armory, and quickly donned on a partial suit of armour.

Seth didn't like this one bit, but looked up when he heard what sounded like roaring. He caught Caleb's eyes when he went by. "Take care of my sister."

"I will." Caleb hesitated slightly, but moved through the barrier.

"Cay," Gillam called, and Caleb paused. "What if it's a trap?"

"I don't know," Caleb admitted. "I've . . . never been summoned before."

"Summoned?" Gillam asked.

"Yeah. It's weird," Caleb said, then turned around. "Thanks for following me in." He looked to Seth. "Thank you especially, Seth. Find Tiffany and get her out of here."

Seth watched the knight disappear down the hallway. "We're all dressed up without a party," Rodney said.

"I wouldn't count on that," Top-Knot said. "It's started. Well, shall we?"

"How many of you are there exactly?" Seth asked Muffin as they made their way down the hall.

"We sent out the kitlings. There's only about six of us left," said Top-Knot. Seth frowned, he assumed there was only about seven or eight of them before. "We can help, but we can't fight everything they're about to throw at us. Best we can do is make a distraction, hope they take out the hold upstairs."

"Distraction?" Seth asked.

"Buy Lily and the others some time. Shame we'll miss the one-two punch," Muffin offered, but his sly grin disappeared as a strange pulse was felt in the halls. Seth realized despite being cursed for days and using that silly talisman, he'd a lot to learn about magic.

Butterflies manifested more figures, which animated the decorative suits of armor that were previously collecting dust. Rodney and the men at arms clashed, and Seth realized that they weren't fighting physical beings.

"Throw me!" he told Gillam, who had been shooting. He shrank and Gillam launched him to where he'd gestured. He wished he'd more time to practice with Gillam, the ranger wasn't bad but they weren't quite synched when they workd together.

The pair of kitsunes seemed to be distressing the magical binding of one suit of the armour, but the men at arms were taking damage from an enemy that wasn't bleeding. Seth landed on a breastplace and launched up, pushing open a visor he slid into the helm, and shooting, took out a collection of butterflies. His small arrows caused them to vanish, the armour fell about him. He clambered out and became full-sized. Rodney gave him a nod.

"Get to the drawbridge, Seth," Top-Knot snapped. "We'll hold these off."

"Seth, don't die.We got catching up to do," Muffin said with a grin that was more befitting a coyote, and raced after his uncle.

Rodney gave him a nod, he and the men-at-arms chased after the kitsunes. Gillam gestured he'd come with, so the pair transformed to marionettes, sprinted down the hall, away from Rodney and the kit-sunes. Gillam didn't know the castle as well as the others, but still knew how to find the courtyard.

Captain Daraby had a team of five, the captain had obtained one of the smuggled suits of armor, Seth wondered where Louis and Oliver were. "What took you so long?" The captain barked, but neither Caleb nor Gillam answered nor did Daraby press. Seth returned his team to human. "All right, we make for the bridge room. No fear, men."

Seth shrank and rode on Gillam's shoulder, who took the rearguard and watched their backs as the team progressed through the halls. He could feel the heat as they neared the outside walls. Seth hoped Tiffany had the sense to keep her head down and let the bucket-heads do their thing.

They moved from the halls to the courtyard and arrows shot at them from above. The men used their shields to form a wall and worked together to press on towards the gate. Seth could no longer see the night sky, as it was blotted with smoke. Eventually, the arrows became so overpowering, the men came to a standstill.

"Gill, wanna mess 'em up?" Seth asked. He became human only long enough for him to transform himself and Gillam. No one shot at them as they barrelled towards the room. Gill secured an arrow with a small rope and shot into the small open window, Seth hoped they were quiet enough as they climbed the rope and entered the keep.

There was only one puppeteer; he was of a nondescript age and commanding mannequins to shoot crossbows at the men. He didn't hear Seth or Gillam, and even if he did he was focused on the armed men in the courtyard. "Get me close to him," Gillam said. Seth nodded, and creeping up behind him could touch the hem of his robe before he looked to Gillam. Returning to normal, Seth seized one arm while Gill another. They wrestled the man—he was stronger than he looked, but with the pair of them it was no contest. His machinations stopped, and after a few wallops to the face, the man relented. Seth bound him and Gillam got the door, hollering. Seth was glad they knew where they were going.

"You got a talker?" Captain Daraby asked as his men took control of the room. "Let's hope so. How many of you are there?" The man said nothing, so the captain socked him in the gut. "I can make you chatty."

"Sir!" one of Daraby's men called.

"Gillam, Seth, get to the windows and watch for movement," Daraby ordered as his men scrambled up the winding stairs. Let's get that bridge down."

Seth wasn't sure where the men were all going, but he watched for movement where he was told. It felt stupid to be sitting around waiting with his sisters unaccounted for. He wondered where Louis was, and suddenly he heard the sound of chain and a strange rumbling despite the thick stone walls about them, and shouts of men from above.

The drawbridge came down and light spilled from the other side, smoke visible as men in full armour and large horses wearing brilliant livery thundered into the courtyard.

A strange vibration struck the castle. Seth and Gill moved from their window outside, and stared up at one of the towers. A strange dread filled Seth's stomach, then suddenly, a large explosion came from a tower from the southside. *Lily and Ethan, and . . . !*

"Squire," ordered a knight to the team of younger fighters. "Get up there. I'll be there as soon as I hand off my horse."

"Sir!" another voice called. For the most part the squires had less elaborate armour; many of them had suits that did not match or were obviously a size or two too big, and required padding to fill out. The leader led a team into the courtyard and through a large set of double doors while the knights used their warhorses to take the space in the courtyard.

A strange trill took Seth's attention away from the tower.

Horses backed up and knights dismounted. Several horses reared and at least two ran back the way they'd come across the drawbridge as a great silver gryphon flew out from one of the castle halls, not quite attacking, but its tail knocked a knight off of his horse.

Seth scrambled out to the courtyard. The gryphon's claws were massive, and it had a face not unlike an owl; Seth knew at once from the old sketches this was a Northern Nightclaw, judging by the plumage a female. "All right men," thundered a knight. "Spears at the ready!"

"It's protecting something!" Seth threw his hands in the air. Where was Lily or his mother or even Uncle Freddy? He stood between them. "Easy, easy." The foxhead medallion suddenly felt heavy. "Shiny, look at the shiny," Seth called, holding the talisman. The gryphon was momentarily entranced but growled again. "Come on out. Just a little further, and you can fly out, away from these goons. Look up! Clear sky, yes?"

More trilling. Another gryphon—this one was brown, and then another, smaller and grey.

The gryphons trilled and lowered their head feathers. "Don't hurt them, let them go," Seth coaxed. The gryphons followed after Seth, needing space to open their wings, especially the great silver gryphon who was protecting her young. Seth felt stupid for not knowing more about the majestic creatures, but as soon as they could they took to the air and disappeared into the sky.

No sooner had the gryphons taken flight, more shouting—a centaur kicked and raced down, then another. Long-faced and with hair like a horse's running down their backs, they ranged in age, though the majority of them appeared to be warriors. Seth was glad they were unarmed; most centaurs could be vicious fighters.

There was only a dozen of them, but they rode past the knights, who stood defensive, the few faces Seth saw wide-eyed.

"You there!" a man called from another part of the courtyard. Seth thought he looked familiar—he was wearing black armour, and had an atrocious moustache. "What in the blazes is going on?" he demanded at the knight nearest.

"Sir, get back here!" a woman ordered. There was an air of nobility about her, and judging by her stiff-necked collar and regal plum ballgown, she was of some importance. "Do not leave me to this chaos!"

"My lady," another knight said, dismounting and rushing to her side.

Seth gawked, so much was going on around him. He had to get up to that tower. He knew his sister was there and . . .

A heavy hand fell on his shoulder. "You, boy," he said levelly. "What's your name?"

Seth's mouth went dry, but Lyle's voice caught him off guard. "Milo, really? They just got here and you already cheesed off the bucket heads?"

"Oh, lay off," Gillam said. "Shinies ain't happy unless they're grousing."

"The boy's your apprentice?" the knight asked the rangers, his grip still on Seth's collar.

"Yeah? Unless you want him, he's not good for much," Lyle offered.

"Nevermind." Seth never saw his face, his tabard was grey and blue and the knight disappeared into the growing crowd; other people congregated in clusters, Seth looked for Tiffany and Louis to no avail. The other knights and squires didn't look at him twice.

"Stay with Gillam," Lyle ordered Seth. "Gill, if things heat up, get him out of here."

No one was making him go anywhere; not knights, not rangers; if his own mother showed up he wasn't going to listen until he knew Lil' and Tiffy were safe. "My sister is up there." He didn't know the way, but Gillam might.

"Half the guard will be up there soon," Lyle told him. "You want to join her in Fort Beldys? Keep a low profile, you'll do her a world of good if you're not in the same cell as her."

"They'll have to catch me first," Seth said, and went to transform. He stayed the same. " . . . oh."

"Good to know," Gillam said. "Come on, let's go flush us out a critter or ten. Ol' Reliable will look after Lily. What's your other sister even look like, anyway?"

Twenty

It felt foreign being in halls he'd grown up knowing but hadn't been in two years. Caleb heard the occasional roar and the lower halls were warming up. Uncertain if friend or foe greeted him first, he decided to carry his helmet, lest he be attacked by someone he knew.

"Jayden!" Someone jumped him from behind, but it was more of a strangling hug than an actual attack. She was back to wearing her peasant dress, complete with wooden clogs, though she had a mail vest on top. "What's with the armour?"

"Hi Tiffany," Caleb managed, she was kind of crushing his windpipe. "I'm not Jayden."

"Tiffany, I'm over here," Jayden called from behind.

"Oh, you're decent?" Tiffany said, releasing Caleb.

"Yup. Oh, heya Cay. Do you know what's going on?"

"Who—oh, it's you," Tiffany said, looking back and forth. "Bit of a family resemblance."

"Lady Bee and the other ladies used to think we were brothers," Jayden offered. "Called us little Jay and little Cay."

"It's almost like we had the same grandfather," Caleb offered. "If you would go back down the hallway and exit the castle. Wait, how did you get here?"

"Come back, I want to compare you." Tiffany grabbed at Caleb's arm. He pulled away from her grasp. "This won't take a minute."

When they were boys running amuck their own mothers had to dress them in different colours, but up close there were a ton of differences. Tiffany pointed them out. "Jayden's just a little taller, your hair's the same colour and texture but yours is shorter and has a different part," she said. "The big difference is your eyes. Jayden's got better lips, jawline, eyebrows, general complexion, earlobes . . ."

"Thank you, Tiffany," Caleb said, putting his helmet on. "We'll continue this when I recover your sister and I get do the same thing to you."

"You pervert!" Tiffany said. "Lily and I look nothing alike!"

"You have the same nose."

"Eeee!" Tiffany covered it.

"You have a cute little shnoz."

"It's a shnoz?" They were still following him, and would match his pace when he tried to pick it up a notch or two.

"Where's Braden and Caiden?" Caleb asked eventually.

"Heya, Cay!" Caiden called from up ahead with Braden. The 'Aidens all came from different families, so there wasn't any confusion there. Caiden was the shortest, but Caiden was also the pretty one of the trio. "We're human again!"

"Did you finish?" Tiffany demanded.

"Finish what?" Caleb asked.

"Shoving Sir Justin in a broom closet upside down with Sir Hector," Braden said.

"You told me you all had to pee!" Tiffany complained, tapping her foot.

"I did," Braden said. "I guess I was holding it for two years, and before I really had to start breathing again, I *really* had to go."

"Where's Sir Hector?" Caleb demanded.

"He was up that way," Braden said, pointing. "We were just goofing around and suddenly the strings released but we felt . . . called, you know. We could enter the halls and we just started changing back."

"What's going on?" Caiden asked. "Cay, you said you'd let us know when you had the chance."

Caleb nodded. "Ethan and Garett are upstairs with Lily. I need to get to them, do you know where Hector was going?" The boys shook their heads. "I want the three of you to go back down the hallway, and get Tiffany out. Rodney and others are here, they're getting the draw-bridge down."

"Why's Lily upstairs?" Tiffany asked.

"Apparently they're going to try to hit whatever's caused this. I need to go," Caleb said. "You guys protect Tiffany."

"Who's gonna protect you?" Braden asked.

"Yeah," Jayden said, "You're not an army, Cay."

"And I am not leaving without Molly," Tiffany said. "You're going up? Boys, escort a lady."

Caleb sighed. "Guys, if you're doing this you need some better gear. I don't need plate over mail. Tiffany, you're an archer, try not to shoot any of us. Braden, you and her will be the rear-guard. Braden, watch our backs and tell me if anything's coming from behind us. Jayden, Caiden, mid-guard?"

The pair nodded. "Puts you in the vanguard," Caiden said as they divided their gear up. "Be nice if we had another person to balance out."

"Then let's get to Ethan and Garett," Caleb said. "Hopefully Percy's already with them. If I fall, Jayden's in charge and you book it out of the castle."

They agreed; Caleb didn't know this part of the castle particularly well but Caiden knew the way. Moving away from the outer walls of the castle it was cooler, but without warning crossed another barrier, and the world around them changed. They were in a different part of the castle, older the parts of the stone walls were darker here and the ceilings taller. Caleb looked back and realized that they were no longer behind him, but then Jayden stepped over, shouted, "I made it!" and reached a hand that disappeared, then pulled Caiden across. Tiffany and Braden jumped over holding hands, knocking Caleb backwards in the process.

"I don't remember this part of the castle," Braden said.

"I think they remodelled it," Jayden offered.

There was only one way forward, the room was unfamiliar to all of them, and entering through a large door, they entered a long hall lined with armoured figures holding spears and shields between tall mirrors. Caleb frowned, looked back at the others, then he and Jayden moved ahead quietly. Everything remained still, so the other three followed. They were near the middle of the room when the mirrors behind Tiffany and Braden shattered, then the mirrors ahead of them. Instead of falling to the ground, the shards flittered, like butterflies, and took on humanoid form. Tiffany shot an arrow at one, and it sailed right through. Headless, the figures stood taller than a man and took swords and shields from the still armoured figures.

"Run!" Caleb ordered, and hung behind with his shield up as the other four sprinted ahead. He wasn't sure what he was going to do other than try to buy the others time.

He met the sword of one of the mirror creatures and instinctively struck, but the shards glittered like a hundred diamonds. Slicing through the form of an arm, it shattered just to reform. Caleb knew there were more ahead, Tiffany called out and . . .

A strange vibration struck the room and the shard warriors stopped reverberating; instead they seemed to congeal and become solid, and a figure larger and more heroic than Caleb remembered bowled into the room, smashing the shard warriors with a mighty mace. This time the shards fractured; their swords and shields clattered to the ground.

The shard warriors all turned on Sir Hector. Caleb went to help him, but to his surprise, someone else ran the shard warrior through.

Martin, the sell-sword. "What took you so long?" Caleb recognized his voice; he wore a helm where he could see his lower face, but he moved before Caleb could get a good look at him. Hector was brute strength; Martin was a dancer, fluid and nimble.

There was shouting up ahead. Something else was going on but Caleb joined the older men in the struggle.

"Finish them off, then pull back," another voice ordered, not entering into the fray. "Martin, to your left! Do not pull ahead!"

"We're working on it, Percy," Hector called. Though neither man could see the other's face through his visor, Caleb felt Hector staring at him. "And just *when* were you going to let me know?"

"I was working on it," Caleb told him. "Heard you shoved Justin in a closet."

"Upside-down," Hector affirmed.

"And you didn't invite me?" Martin demanded.

"It was a spur of the moment thing," Hector explained, moving ahead Caleb and Martin needed to back away and give Hector room to swing. When at last the glass warriors stopped, Hector put up his visor. "Better late than never, sir."

Percival stepped forward. "Where's Rodney and the others?"

"They couldn't follow, sir," Caleb said. Whatever was going on in the other room was finishing up. "Did you find Lily and—"

The strange vibrations in the air stopped with a sound Caleb hardly registered. It felt natural, like it ought to be there. "Cay, why'd you bring Tiffany?" Ethan's voice.

The current helm had no movable visor. Caleb needed to take his helmet off so they would see his face. He raced ahead to where the others were with Selene in the other room, "What happened?"

"Helmet on. I need your head attached to the rest of you for the next half hour or so," Percy ordered.

"Where are we?" Caiden asked. Braden moved to the window. Caleb could see that they were several floors up, smoke blotting out the darkened night, he couldn't look down and see the castle courtyard or the surrounding lake or town.

Garett by her side, Lily's eyes were glowing; she appeared not only unharmed but . . . did she call them? No, she wouldn't . . . Caleb wanted to do nothing more than grab her and get her out of there. "You all right?" she asked him, putting the mandolin over her shoulder.

"Excuse me," Tiffany called. "I've known you my whole life."

"Tiffany, I'm glad you're okay. Why'd you bring her?" Lily asked. Caleb grabbed Lily and pulled her into an embrace. "Caleb, I'm fine. Ethan and Garett took care of me."

Garett gave Caleb an affirming grunt. "Glad you made it."

Tiffany somehow managed to get between him and Lily. "Why are you up here?" Tiffany asked.

"I'll explain later. Tiffany, you shouldn't be here," Lily said.

"I don't understand – Lily, you need to hear me out, Molly's up... well, maybe not up here, but she's upstairs somewhere," Tiffany said.

"I'll help you look for her when we're done this," Lily assured her.

"Wait, you came from that way?" Percival asked, gesturing to where he, Tiffany and the 'Aidens had only just arrived. "We came from the other way."

"We just stepped through a . . . well, we were in one place one minute then another the next," Jayden said. "I watched Cay disappear, then I followed him." He pursed his lips. "Not sure why, come to think of it."

"You lads chat like ladies over tea, Martin's got another nick on the arm," Hector called. Selene and Martin wore leather armour with metal helmets, more like when he'd first encountered them as sell-swords.

"Was wondering what we all looked and sounded like," Martin said as Lily approached him. "It's not that bad."

Lily nodded, and played her mandolin. Caleb stood next to Martin, then stepped back in surprise when the bleeding not only stopped, but pale skin reformed over the cut. He regarded Sir Hector. Hector wasn't as slow as he was; then Caleb remembered what Demetri had told him about the curse causing old scarring to disappear. Had the curse fixed his bad knee?

Am I still poisoned?

Selene approached their group and spoke to him. "You could have told us what you were up to. I was wondering what Ethan was laughing about."

"Did Louis and Oliver tell you what happened?" Garett asked.

Caleb nodded. "I'm glad you and Ethan were able to make the call. You sure about this?"

"Not at all," Garett admitted. Ethan was off on his own, scanning constantly. "Sir Percival? What next, sir?"

"You lads," Percy told the 'Aidens. "You'll be guarding this girl with your life. Understood?"

"You guys take her, I'll take Tiffany," Braden offered.

"No, I'm guarding Tiffany!" Caiden said.

"Guys," Tiffany snapped, "she's my sister. *Keep her safe or else.*"

Percival snorted. "We can't see below with all that smoke. Hector, what are you feeling now?"

"I think we're in the right spot," Hector said lowly.

"You can sense it, too?" Caleb asked Hector. Sir Hector nodded.

"We all can," Selene offered. "I lost Jace's troupe. Hopefully they're all right."

"We'll worry about them later," Percival said. "Young Lady, when you're ready."

"Anyone need cuts healed before I start?" Lily asked. No one said anything. She nodded, and played a melody. It was different, and didn't make the air reverberate. Caleb didn't know what she was doing, but something bit deep when the melody entwined in the air. This was a song of revelation.

Caleb felt it, Hector must have, too; he, Martin, and Selene all looked up.

"What happens if she becomes possessed?" Garett asked.

The ceiling in this room had no mist, but Lily's song was bringing something into focus. It was a sort of sphere, like a gem only with a milky texture. "What is that?"

"I could shoot it," Caiden offered, but Percy all but took his bow away.

"It's a sort of . . . talisman or focal point," Selene said. "Sometimes, mages manifest their power into an object. The spell radiates from that point."

"Think there's more than one in the castle?" Martin asked his sister. She shrugged. "So what happens if we take it out?"

"Won't know until we try. I don't recommend anyone touching it," Selene offered.

"All right girl," Percival told Lily. "Once you start, you don't stop. It'll probably throw stuff at us. We fan out, we'll keep you safe. Garett?" The tall knight nodded, and hoisted his shield. Caleb wanted to take his place, but glancing at Ethan, knew they were better off working together. Garett had the 'Aidens; they'd protect Lily.

"I suggest everyone find cover." Lily didn't wait for her eyes to stop glowing, and started to play. At least she seemed like herself. The song sent a strange chill in the air—different than the thing that was in front of them, and part of Caleb strangely wanted to stop her. Then he saw a sudden dent that sounded with a crystal *chink*.

The song intensified, the same chorus again, and the mandolin appeared to be changing as well—and not in a good way. Lily's fingers sometimes became uncharacteristically troubled; and her notes weren't perfect. She stumbled and her brow tensed. "You having trouble, girl?" Hector asked.

"If anyone else has any ideas, I'd love to hear them." Lily continued to play. The song became faster, more complicated, and then another crystal fracture sounded.

"You're doing it. It'll be like an avalanche," Percival said. "Little pebbles before it cascades."

A masked figure manifested itself at the end of the hall where Caleb and his squad had entered. This one was taller than the others. It wore a mask but shadow consumed the face. Lily alone kept playing, eyes glowing and fixated, everyone else staring at the figure.

"You wanted answers," it said. "The master will speak with you."

Caleb glanced at Percival, but Hector was already striding towards the door, Martin and Selene behind him. Ethan shot Caleb a stern look. "We deserve to know."

"This is the priority," Percival said, gesturing at Lily and the nest.

"Cay, back me up," Ethan gestured.

"I need to stay here and protect her."

"She has us," Braden said, gesturing at Garett and the others.

"He is only doing what he was instructed to do," the masked figure said.The others halted in their tracks. Caleb scrunched his nose. "You mistook the urge to keep the tool safe for affection. Perhaps it did manifest in some sort of crude imitation. You have done well, Wolf."

"What are you talking about?" Caleb asked lowly.

"You have a remarkably strong will, but ultimately it is still as mouldable as the others," the masked figure said.

"Show yourself," Hector ordered.

The figure obliged. Caleb expected something sinister or evil, but the face was beautiful—pale with strong cheeks and jaw, and grey eyes that looked at them intently. "I can take many forms." He stepped, and grew suddenly, and white feathery wings sprouted from his back. Again a change, and he was a handsome older man with dark hair.

"An angel?" Martin asked, incredulity.

"Not quite," the figure said. He watched them. "You may call me Asmodean."

"I don't care what you call yourself," Percy spat. "You forced my boys to kill for your sport."

"They required training, discipline. Young ones are more mouldable, not like you." He smiled at Percival, but Asmodean's gaze settled on Caleb and Ethan. "You won't believe me. I must show you."

The world shifted, and Caleb found himself alone. There was no spinning mass, there was only the castle around him, but it was . . . so different. If he wasn't standing in there, watching the room remodel, he might have believed he was somewhere else. *He* was different; bigger, stronger than he ever could have been. He was wearing a better plate of armour, but he knew he was he was still in Mirador, in that room in the tower.

The space hadn't really changed, he somehow instinctively knew time *had*.

He moved in powerful, purposeful strides, and found that his body was not weighed down, instead moving fluidly as if his armour was a second skin.

His only skin.

And the master was calling him.

There was no running away, or getting away from where he was called to. His will was aligned with The One; his name was only spoken in perfect reverence. He strode and the lesser saluted him. A million memories hit him at once. A thousand battles, a thousand victories; he revelled in slaughter only because it expanded the kingdom.

The hall to the throne room was lined with tall masked figures;

most larger than he. They were clad in armour from head to toe, and they no longer had faces; their skin was the armour. He knew them, a lifetime ago. They were called things, names that were long dead; anyone who knew them by those were long gone, and their descendants perhaps whispered them in fear. Who they used to be before they were perfected. He himself was called many things, but the only name he answered to now was the Wolf.

He was dragging someone. Some pitiless child, really. He wasn't much older than someone he once knew named Oliver, but he had that strange look of defiance. Caleb thrust him to the throne before him, and looked up at the One. Asmodean, his will always perfect, always right. He would take the sins of the world, he was goodness. Even when he gave an order that made no sense, and their troops perished, the One stood triumphant.

Mortals lived such brief, senseless lives, afterall. They could win battles, pathetic victories that were like an itch in the long game.

After all, Asmodean made weapons before he'd started his conquest.

He, and now so many others, were perfect blades in unison to the greater will.

A figure all too familiar to Caleb stepped out of his place among the chosen. He caught The Wolf's eyes, his mask manifesting a jester's smile. He moved forward, drawing a slender knife.

"Why do you resist?" Asmodean asked. "Can you not see all the good I have brought in my kingdom?"

"You have enslaved us!" the youth cried out. The boy was someone he knew—his brother squire from a lifetime ago. His old friend was both tortured and was the boy at the same time. "Call off your machinations!"

"Wolf, you have done well. This is unpleasant business, isn't it?" the One asked, standing. He was so beautiful, so . . . right. He had raised the kingdom out of the dirt. His old body would have long since returned to the dirt if he wasn't fixed. "Walk with me."

Even the Wolf's breathing was perfectly in control, but when they moved from the torture, parts of Caleb came back. He had some semblance of control. He lurched for his blade and thrust at the One, who dispersed in a shower of blue butterflies.

"Do not be like that," said a beautiful female in front of him, wearing a pink veil and dress. She was ethereal, a face he'd known once. She was a vision in pink, no longer human but something . . . something better.

Still, the nearby kingdoms rallied against them. Why? Why did they fight? Why couldn't he remember? It hurt to think about that; he just had to submit the One's will and . . .

"Wolf?" Another voice, one that he knew. Her eyes were gold. "Wolf, what's wrong?"

She was allowed to keep her face. It was some sort of comfort, from some time, long ago. She was a vision in silver armour edged with gold as she came towards him. She comforted him, reminded him that it was all right. Her touch was a sweet caress, like she was petting a beloved dog. Her sweet voice that broke armies, beguiled them into submission, made them know what fear was, also called out and seethed his nerves when a small part of him wanted to rebel.

For a moment, he was able to control himself. He was Caleb of Mirador; this was not him. This wasn't real. "Lily?"

She blinked, like she knew what he was talking about, but that he was wrong. "It's okay," she said, catching his gaze. Why couldn't he recall the real colour of her eyes? "Sometimes you remember things you shouldn't." She went to kiss him; he knew if he allowed it, he'd fall. He grabbed her wrists, but the pleading look she gave him made him be gentle in the restraint. "In this world, we're together?"

"I nurture the feelings you think you want," Asmodean said, as what would become of Lily stared at him. Her look soothed the monster wrestling to break free. Asmodean stood just out of reach. "Breaking her will was much easier than breaking yours."

"Why are you doing this?" Caleb asked Asmodean.

"To put an end to the chaos, bring order."

"By enslaving our minds?"

"I can play with your mind, stimulate your emotions, but your will. Your will is the problem. You need to submit it."

"Why not animate the glass like you did? Bring machinations to life," Caleb said. "They bleed less than us."

"I can only use what already exists. I cannot create life."

"Only taint," Caleb snapped through grit teeth.

Lily somehow got out from his grasp. She was taking off his mask, exposing him. He didn't really have a face for some time. Her touch was like a balm on a wound, hands that played songs terrible were also soft and reassuring. "Wolf, it's okay. He takes away your flaws, replaces them and makes you better. You won't notice."

The tingling in the back of his mind that was screaming, reminding him of everyone thrust into the last world, crying and screaming to go home; that they didn't want to be a puppet. He was stronger than he ever could have been as a human, but the body didn't matter; he was a puppet without strings, his will aligned to something so dark, so terrible, he had no words to describe the terror welling up from the bottom of his soul.

There was something alluring; a small reward that nibbled at his core. He had her. "So in this world, I just do your bidding, to whatever ends. And my reward is you'll let her love me?"

"She doesn't have a choice, Wolf. Neither do you, but if it's what makes you finally submit, I will break everyone you hold dear. The end result will feel like love."

Caleb screamed and threw her back and attacked the One, but he was back in the real world, to his real body, that shook and ached and wanted to vomit and run away in terror. Hector was on his knees, breathing heavily; Selene was holding her brother, looking broken. Ethan looked distraught, and eventually threw down his spear.

"Did anyone submit?" Percival asked levelly. "Speak up so I can knock your ass out."

"How are you so calm?" Caleb demanded.

"I'm too pissed off to be bought," Percival snapped. "You were a complete monster in my dream, for the record."

"He couldn't have been as bad as I was in my vision," Ethan growled.

"You were a very close second," Percival told Ethan without influx.

"All right, monster: we're not yours to shape and mould. Leave this castle, now. Whatever you were planning we're not—"

Hector's morning star raked the side of Percival's head, and the slender knight went spiralling, blood spattering the wall. Percival did not get up.

"Percival!" Martin drew his blade on Hector, but Selene slashed the back of his heel. Martin was a superior swordsman, but down to one leg he was no longer the dancer as his sister attacked.

"Stay with Lily!" Garett told the 'Aidens, approaching Hector. "Sir Hector!" He narrowly dodged a mighty swing. Caleb went to help him, but Ethan crouched and picked up his spear, and moved towards Lily and Tiffany.

"What are you doing?" Caleb asked, getting in his way.

"There's a chance all of this might have been for something if we see this through."

"You do not mean that," Caleb said. Ethan's jaw clenched, and Caleb knew he was about to drop into an offensive stance. "What did he promise you?" Caleb asked. "Whatever it is, it's a lie."

"You should have let me burn!" Ethan snapped. He brought down his spear and the breastplate saved him. Caleb knew his moves, knew his friend was distraught. "What did you expect, Caleb? Wasn't I always weaker-willed than you?"

He could hear the 'Aidens getting ready. "Protect Lily!" he ordered. "This is a distraction!"

He heard Selene and Martin struggling; he suspected one of the 'Aidens had moved Percival and he heard Hector call out as his mace was stuck in the wall. He struck Garett backwards with a fist.

Caleb had to focus on Ethan. If Caleb fell, Ethan would mow through the others; they'd buy Lily a few seconds at most, and if she stopped playing . . .

He pushed Ethan back. Ethan was taller but they were almost neck and neck for strength; Ethan had him for agility and reach, and . . . Caleb would not kill Ethan; doing so might actually break him.

Tiffany shot at Asmodean. His form melted and and the arrow moved through him. The One laughed lowly.

"Ethan! Don't forget who the real enemy is," Caleb said when they got close, but Ethan kicked him off. Caleb almost staggered backwards —but launched himself at Ethan.

Ethan blocked him but let him get close. "Controlled by him, controlled by you, what difference does it make?" Ethan asked through grit teeth.

Strike. Strike. Caleb grit, and felt the blows come at him. They weren't killing blows, Ethan knew how to render his enemies to pain or incapacitation. Caleb felt his strength giving way, the armour absorbing most of the blows, but he couldn't take them indefinitely. Ethan struck him suddenly, and knocked him to his knees. Ethan wrenched off Caleb's helm and punched him, landing him on his backside. Caleb rolled, knowing that suit of armour was better to get up from his stomach, but he found himself being dragged by his leg towards the One.

"Do not kill him. He just needs more tampering."

"Get up, Burkotta," Ethan yanked Caleb to his knees. *Bur- Burkotta?* Realization struck Caleb like a bucket of cold water. "Give me the honour of breaking him for you later." Ethan knelt beside Caleb. "I'll dispatch Martin, then Garett."

"Do not get ahead of yourself," the One said. "Go break the mandolin, and bring me my puppeteer."

Ethan nodded and stood. Caleb had never seen him move so fast. Ethan struck through the One, impaling him with his spear through what should have been Asmodean's heart. They were met with hollow laughter, and Asmodean moved, his body shifting around a blow and he was healed, but blood splattered the ground behind him. Caleb lunged up, defending his friend from the One's retaliating strike.

More hollow laughter; somehow this pleased Asmodean. "You pair really are a two-edged blade." Asmodean's glow became shadow, lapping up the light and with a strange rumble the one was suddenly feet back from them, out of reach.

He could still smell the spray of blood, and glancing at Ethan, who nodded, they started to move in unison.

They stopped when Tiffany screamed, "Molly, no!" and the music stopped abruptly.

Lily's hands were bloody; shards of the mandolin impaled the flesh of her fingers though most of it was on the floor. Molly stood before her. Lily paused only for a second, then started to sing that same melody.

Hector stopped fighting, and let out a sob, as did Selene.

Tiffany raced to Molly, grabbing her friend's shoulders. "No, you listen!" Molly snapped. "I want a better world! They're knights, aren't they? Aren't they suppose to serve something greater than themselves?"

The orb was glowing very bright. Lily's eyes were no longer yellow, they were glowing like Asmodean's.

"Molly," the One called. "To me. The castle is lost, we will continue and reclaim the pieces elsewhere."

Molly pushed Tiffany back, and racing through Caleb and Ethan, Molly embraced the one.

"Everyone out, now!" Ethan ordered, rushing over to Percival and dragging the fallen knight away with Caiden.

Caleb grabbed the shield of a fallen shard knight, and raced towards Lily, her eyes widening, and as the song reached its final crescendo, Caleb sung out, joining her in that final verse, grabbing her and using his own body and the shield to try to absorb the resulting force of the explosion.

He wasn't sure if he lost consciousness. The ringing in his ears told him he was very much alive. That, and his throat felt like it was on fire and he'd swallowed gravel.

Tiffany and Caiden were with Lily, and Jayden and Braden sat him up and he almost kissed the floor a second time but they caught him. They were speaking but it was like listening through a wall. "Look around the area," he said. His own voice was so muffled, he hoped his teeth and mouth were okay.

Ethan picked Lily up. She reached for Caleb, but Ethan took her from the room. Braden was . . . removing his pauldron? "You can have it. Just ask next time." Caleb just wanted to sleep . . .

Caleb slumped forward, dark spots welling up in his vision as he fell into the arms of the wrong O'Connell sister.

~*~

Of all the knights in all the kingdoms Tiffany didn't expect to be holding Sir Jerk in her arms. "Get him off of me!" Tiffany demanded at Jayden and Caiden, who were busy trying to take off Caleb's pauldrons.

"He'll be easier to drag with all of this gear off."

"I know you can't hear me very well," Ethan said from the room he'd taken Percival moments earlier. "Sing, please. He's going to die."

Lily's voice cracked and she coughed, but she sang a different song. Caleb was also coming around, groaning and coughing. "Ethan, hurry up," Tiffany called. "Caleb's not doing so well, either."

"Percival! Percy!" Sir Hector was beside himself.

Lily sang, then coughed, then sang again. It felt warm even from the other room. "Good job," Ethan said, helping her stand. "Okay, I kind of beat the crap out of Cay, he's next. Stay with Percy," Ethan ordered someone.

Lily tried to walk but Ethan carried her back. Kneeling beside her sister Lily sang. Her voice sounded painful, and Tiffany thought she was going to pass out. Caleb snapped to attention and touched his ears. He forgot Tiffany and grabbed onto her sister, and held Lily like she just didn't make the room explode.

"No, my sister," Tiffany said, trying to pry them apart. "Geez, were you smooching earlier or something?" Caleb gave her a smirk. "Oh my gosh, Lily!" Tiffany hugged them both and let out a joyful squeal.

"You don't mind?" Caleb asked.

"Don't push your luck Caleb," Tiffany said. "Oh, your poor hands!" she said to Lily and tried to clean them.

Ethan looked sombre and didn't meet anyone's gaze. "Cay, I'm so sorry," he said finally. "He was looking at me like I was already beaten. I knew she'd fix you. Geez . . . can't do nothing for yourself, huh?" he asked Lily, then helped Tiffany wrap Lily's hands with bandages she'd brought. "Hope you don't mind mittens."

Caleb grabbed Ethan's wrist, raised it to face level, and then slapped it with his other hand. "You got him. You brilliant Dalzen."

"I didn't stop him," Ethan said with a wince.

"You made him bleed," Caleb said. "Does anyone have water?"

"I can't believe you saved the day by singing!" Jayden said getting a flask, handing it to Lily first, then his cousin. His eyes widened and he went into an offensive stance towards the open doorway.

Ethan raced ahead; Caleb was a step behind him, the 'Aidens coming to really save the day as several armed and visored figures spilled into the room. Tiffany went for an arrow, but on both sides their aggressive stances changed and everyone put down their weapons.

One raised his visor. "Braden?"

Another extended his arms. "Garett!"

"Gavin!" Braden crowed.

Back-slapping and fist bumping; it seemed most of the squires knew one another. Tiffany helped Lily to her feet, but she was still unsteady so Tiffany pulled her into an embrace.

"You all right? You're bloody," one of the new squires told Caleb.

"Bad nick, haven't had a chance to clean it up yet," Caleb said. "Who's squad leader?"

"That would be me," said one with dark hair, she thought he might be Gavin but it was hard to tell. "Everyone okay?"

"No, we're not," Garett said. "Percival's lost a lot of blood. Get a stretcher."

"Sir Caleb, Sir Ethan," Sir Hector said, entering the room from the far side. The squires all stood to attention. "I believe you have somewhere to be."

"Right," Caleb said. "Got a good ear?" he asked Lily loudly. She seemed to understand, and nodded, pointing to her left one. "We have to go."

"Brass ordered us to check this area," the squad leader offered. "They'll be here soon."

"Distract them," Ethan ordered.

"We already told them you're up here."

"We need to go," Ethan said to Caleb and Lily.

"What's wrong?" asked another of the new squires.

"We can't be detained for questioning," Caleb said. "Can you distract them? We can sneak around."

"I'll take you," said one of the squires. He gave Lily and Tiffany a faint smile. "Come on."

"Let's go Tiffany," Caleb said, taking Lily's hand. She seemed steadier by the minute. "Can you run?" he asked into Lily's left ear, she nodded.

"Can *you* run?" asked one of the new squires to Caleb, brow arched.

"We can sneak you down," another said. "Can't get you past Daraby."

"Daraby won't be a problem," Caleb said.

"What we need is a distraction," Tiffany said. She beamed at her boyfriends.

"Tiffany," Caleb said levelly, stopping mid-stride. "I promised your sister I would get you out of the castle. Come along."

"Shush."

"Don't shush me!"

"Shush!" Tiffany did it again. "I'm going to waltz out when I'm ready, not skulk around like you three." She grinned, looking to the new squires. "Tell them to hurry up—that Sir Caleb won't stop making out with this girlfriend."

"What?" Caleb squawked.

Tiffany draped herself on Jayden, batted her eyes, then motioned for Caleb to run along now. Caleb looked like he was going to argue the point, but Ethan grabbed one arm, a different squire the other, and they dragged him out.

They were not going to improvise to an original story, but all the squires approved. One even ran off to go get another actress to help. They'd barely rehearsed when their lookout snapped his fingers to get their attention. "They're coming."

"You're about to see why I'm the greatest actress in Stagmil," Tiffany said, then pounced on Jayden, knocking him over, kissing him everywhere on his face but his lips. "Watch the pawing," she told him as she heard heavy armoured feet enter the room.

"What in the blue blazes does he think he's doing?" asked one older voice.

"Sir, with all due respect, he's a teenage boy," said another.

Jayden and Tiffany stopped, shot them both a cheeky grin, and went back to going at it.

"They were like this when I got here, sir," one of the squires said.

"Get up," the older knight ordered, and it took Jayden a little bit of rocking, but once he was on his feet, he took Tiffany's hand, and they skipped towards the knights. There were about six of them, most of which were chuckling. "Sir Caleb? You . . . geez, it's been two years. You look younger, somehow."

"It is I," Jayden said. "This is Tilly."

"Tee heee hee!" Tiffany waived.

"This isn't the same girl I saw outside."

"Were you seeing another girl on the outside?" Tiffany demanded, grabbing Jayden by his shoulder.

"Uh, Sir, I don't think this is Sir Caleb," one of the other knights said.

"It's him," said a squire.

"He gave me this scar in the training yard," said another, pointing to his behind.

"I know who I am," Jayden said. "And shnookums, I can assure you you're the only one for me." He bent on one knee. "Tilly of Taralee, will you marry me?"

"Oh, Caleb of . . . " What was this place called again? "Sir Caleb the bold! The daring! The loaded! Of course!"

"Not so fast!" Caiden crowed, coming in from the side door that the real Sir Caleb and Sir Ethan had gone. He'd found a rather rich-looking shirt with lace at the collar and the sleeves, and had his sword drawn. "She is mine!"

"What ho, blaggard!" Jayden said, pushing Tiffany away with some force to meet his rival.

"Excuse you," said another beautiful girl, coming up from behind Caiden. "You said I would be your princess."

"I tell girls a lot of things," Caiden said. "Have at thee, knave!" He and Jayden did what was clearly a very scripted set of strikes on one another. She wished they had more time; poor Braden was feeling right left out.

"Oh, whichever one will I choose?" Tiffany simpered, before looking at the knights. "Come on, help me pick. Both have castles, but it's not an easy decision, you know."

"Stop this nonsense at once!" bellowed another knight. The two squires stopped their play fighting, but then decided to fight over the other girl. "Caiden! Jayden! Cut it out!"

"Sorry, sir," Caiden said.

Jayden nodded, and kept his eyes closed. "Who is this Jayden you speak of?"

"You can't recall your own cousin?" the knight snapped. "Jayden pulled this prank once because the squires got to go on a little day trip the pages didn't. I just about made the real one cry, he had no idea what was going on."

"Honest mistake, sir," one of the squires said.

"It has been two years," another said.

"Why were you pretending to be Caleb and Ethan?" the oldest knight asked.

"Prince George of Oobadon," Caiden clarified. "And we tell girls lots of stuff that isn't true."

"We're all guilty of that," one of the older knights offered.

"What?" Tiffany demanded, slapping Caiden and Jayden. "How dare you!"

"Where are they? Don't you two slink off," the elder blond knight said to Jayden and Caiden.

"I've put them on a mission," Sir Hector said, coming in from the other room. "I've wounded men, so stop worrying about my boys. Get a stretcher, and find that old Coot Demetri."

The captain muttered something Tiffany didn't catch before

gesturing at her and the other girl. "You boys, escort those girls out of the castle."

"You liar!" Tiffany said, going limp and making her new squires do all the work. She waited until she was dragged into the hallway. "What's this I hear that there's beautiful dresses for the taking around this joint?" She batted her eyes at the new cute squires. One blushed, the other cocked an eyebrow, but grinned.

~*~

Thanks to the chaos below and ditching their armour, it was almost too easy to move around the castle. Caleb thought their goose was cooked when, despite his escort's best efforts, they ran straight into Sir Goren. Instead, he just gave him a nod and gestured, and allowed them to continue on their way.

Horses ran amuck but other squires were using the apples they'd smuggled in to bring the large horses out of the small rooms, leading them towards the castle courtyard.

"These horses are a lot bigger than the ranger ones, hey?" Ethan asked Lily, who was staring up at one who was sniffing her. She did that cute thing where she pretended not to be afraid, but her eyes widened. "The grey one with the spots on his rump is Slipperjack, the roan is Figaro, and the yellow mare is Butterscotch."

"This is a mare?" Lily's throat sounded *awful*.

"Don't head towards town," Daraby said, pointing once he walked them to the drawbridge. "Ride like you mean it, don't look back. We'll be fine. I'll send some boys to mess up your tracks if the brass starts talking sending a ranger or two to track you down."

"Thank you, sir," Caleb said, shaking the captain's hand.

"I don't want to know, just get going," Daraby barked. He frowned slightly at Lily, but said nothing; Caleb caught his eyes and gave him a nod, and the captain replied in kind. "You keep that girl safe, understood?"

"With my life, sir." Caleb wanted a better look at her hands, but they weren't bleeding through the bandaging. Thankfully, the guys delivered and he got her a pair of riding gloves. They were far too big for her hands, but they were better than nothing. "You're riding with me until we get some distance between us and the castle. Okay?" he asked Lily. She hesitantly nodded.

Ethan boosted her behind him and hitched Butterscotch so the mare would follow him on Figaro. "Just hold on to me. Little taller than your farm horse?"

Gill found them before they left. "You sure you don't want a guide?"

"We know the way," Caleb said. "Make sure you get Tiffany and Louis to us, we're heading to Port Garanby. Where's Seth?" he asked as Ethan mounted Figaro.

"Your brother's good, Lily," Gill offered. "Guy knows a lot about flushing out these little grey shrieking things . . . nevermind. Don't linger in port longer than you have to. I'll get the others across somehow. Lily, take care of my shinies, I'm partial to 'em."

Caleb gave Gill a nod before he looked to Ethan. "We'll go casually, then sprint before anyone notices."

"What do you mean sprint?" Lily asked, her grip tightening as their horses started to trot across the drawbridge. Ethan shot them both a grin, Caleb returned it. "*Guys.*"

He wasn't sure if anyone really noticed them peel off in the dark, and by the time someone would have said something, they wouldn't have been easy to spot. "Okay, you can open your eyes." They slowed the horses down to a canter. "You want to ride by yourself, or are you happy with me?"

"Tell me we won't have to do that again any time soon," Lily said.

"So long as we shake them," Caleb said. "Think you can ditch the sirs or urge to bellow squire until we catch a boat?"She nodded. "Here's hoping they didn't have any other dragons in storage back at the castle."

"What all was in that castle?" Lily asked. Caleb and Ethan gave her their warmest, most reassuring smile, but they were glancing at one another too much to be convincing. "*Guys . . .*"

"Try not to worry about it too much," Caleb reassured.

"Maybe Peanut will snatch up some abomination for a snack," Ethan offered. "Where is he . . . ?"

Twenty-One

After several hours of uneventful travel in the dark with starlight as their guide, Caleb noticed that the other two were yawning. If they ran ragged they were going to make a dumb mistake. The night was thick when he informed the others they were making camp. He insisted on taking first watch, and then quickly remembered how bored he used to get on watch.

He poked at the fire while the other two slept under their saddle blankets; the horses, too, seemed grateful for the rest. Thankfully, there weren't many clouds and he could see a full array of stars, and told himself stories from his childhood like his mother used to tell him. He tried not to think about her; she was going to be livid no matter his excuse for fleeing the castle. He felt himself drifting off to sleep more than once, so he bit the inside of his cheek, eventually getting up, doing some squats and push-ups to prevent that heavy-eye feeling.

Raising her head, Lily sat up and stretched her arms. "My turn."

"I was just about to wake Ethan," he insisted.

"I'm awake. He slew one monster and wounded another, let him have another hour or two."

"How's your voice?"

"Better, the rest helped. You need some, too." It seemed like he barely put his head down before he heard the other two laughing.

"You should have woken me for the sunrise," Caleb said, staring at the pink and orange glow. Ethan was in awe of it. Lily was brushing out her mare's coat and seemed content. The horses grazed but they gave them the oats regardless; Lily said so long as they could find a farm they'd likely acquire more, but they'd likely make Port Garandell before noon if they didn't dally.

Lily made a sort of bread she wrapped around a stick. She made it look easy; Ethan's attempt was a little crispier but they didn't care. The coin they had was pretty much a negligible amount besides what Lily had, and they split it between them evenly.

"I don't like taking your money," Ethan told her.

"You're good for it. Besides, you don't need to come running to me if you want to get something. Just remember this is all we have access to until one of us gets a job or sells something." They didn't have much to sell; Caleb didn't want her pawning that jewellery again.

"How long did it take to sail here from Shelkie's Bay?"

"About a day," Lily said. "I'm not sure how long it'll be before we can get passage. We can either go to Shelkie's Bay, or press on closer to my home up north at Port Redmaw. It's a longer walk from Shelkie's Bay, but we're likely to miss my parents if we sail for Port Redmaw."

A roar sounded overhead. Caleb and Ethan stood up at the same time. The dragon didn't commune; just beckoned. He wanted to meet them at the sea.

They didn't go directly to the port, but instead followed the road north of it and listened for Varian. He thought they'd see the dragon before they reached the sea, but when the blue horizon came into view they proceeded to the beach. Caleb assumed just standing in the ocean would be enough. They didn't bother to hobble the horses and soon there was real sand between his toes, the spray of salt and no dragon in sight, he stood in awe of the real horizon.

"We made it to the ocean," Ethan said quietly. The dumbest grin spread across his face and he laughed quietly. "We made it to the ocean!" He hugged Caleb, and a rogue wave knocked them both into the surf as Ethan belly-laughed.

"It's a sea!" Caleb said. "We don't have changes of clothes!"

"So?" Ethan said, peeling off his tunic and chucking it back on the beach. "You stand around, I'm enjoying it!" He waded out into the deeper water and dove in.

Caleb laughed, and looked to Lily. "You mind if we act like giant children and go for a swim?"

"If you don't think it's indecent," she said. "Can I join you?"

Lily at least had practical clothes but she didn't last long, citing she needed water. When he and Ethan had enough of crashing into the waves, Caleb slowly realized that swimming in salty water stung and Lily likely felt it from the cuts on her fingers.

They returned to find her combing out her hair with her hands. "You're going to get sick of us real soon," Ethan said as they picked up their tunics and dusted off the sand.

"I doubt that," she said, but she squawked a little when a rogue wave hit her. They'd barely belted their weapons again when Ethan heard Varian call, and they followed him further north of the port, then away from the sea. Leaving the horses with Lily, the knights went to bid farewell.

I have an idea where to go from here, Varian told them. *Too bad I wasn't able to bite off anyone's head for you.*

"Hopefully there won't be a next time," Ethan said.

You know this isn't over.

"It is for you," Caleb said. "Go home. Er . . . should we wish you many eggs or . . .?"

Happiness, the dragon said. *May you both pursue and find happiness. You are likely poisoned?*

"Yes."

She can help you? I can carry you over the sea.

"There's too much of a chance we'll miss her parents," Caleb said. "Although, do you think you could take us flying? Just for a minute."

They didn't get to fly all that much as puppets, so much as when it made sense, and now, without strings, it highlighted how the dragon had been so incredibly crippled. The world seemed endless from high above, and even riding in those talons, in the cold, the land and sea seemed to stretch on forever. Part of Caleb was tempted to fly across the sea, but he knew that there wasn't any outrunning what was hurting him. Besides, the most beautiful girl he'd ever laid eyes on was waiting for him on the beach. The dragon seemed to sense when they were getting cold—these bodies were stronger, but at the same time, in a certain sense, had some weaknesses he'd forgotten about.

He got the idea that the dragon was up to something when he started to take them back down. "Varian, what are you doing?" Caleb asked.

You wanted to use me to impress your female earlier, Varian said.

"You're the one who gave me the scale. No! Do not—"

Next thing he knew, he was flung—with affection—into the deep waters.

Caleb surfaced, and saw that the dragon was much more gentle in releasing Ethan to the beach, and by the time Caleb swam in, Ethan received a golden scale from Varian's knuckle.

Lily rushed out to meet him, seemingly unconcerned about the dragon. "Are you okay? What was that for?" she yelled at the dragon.

"I'm fine," Caleb said.

The dragon seemed amused with Lily. *I don't understand human preferences, but I like her. She seems adequately fierce and will tell you when you are being reckless.* The dragon nudged Lily not unlike he was petting a silly hissing kitten, spread his wings, and took off before Lily was done giving the dragon a piece of her mind.

"That was incredible," Caleb said. "I wish you weren't afraid of heights."

"She is?" Ethan asked.

"I'm not that bad," Lily said. "Do you know how high you were?"

"I know, it was great. Until he decided to be funny, anyway." Caleb cocked his head to try to get water out of his ears, watching the dragon swoop as the mind link shattered. Caleb got the impression he was getting a snack. Caleb looked towards the port and ships coming in from the distance before he gazed to the northwest and the open sea. "I guess the practical thing would be to find a ship, get passage, make plans . . . " He looked to Ethan. "Get a fresh change of clothes."

"I don't think either of you are ready for practicality," Lily said. "I'll head towards town and make polite inquiries. You two catch up when you're hungry."

"I am hungry," Ethan said. He mounted Figaro. "Race?"

"I'm not ready for racing," Lily offered. "I'll catch up."

"I like her," Ethan said, waiting for Caleb to mount, making the roan back up. Caleb helped her mount before climbing in the saddle himself.

"To town then back to her," Caleb told Ethan. Ethan spurred his horse before they agreed, and Caleb shouted, "Cheater!"

Prompting Slipperjack to a gallop, Caleb felt the rhythm of the canter and pressed his stallion faster. Wind spraying surf as the heavy hooves plunged into the sand, they tried to stimulate the wind and for a minute the young knights forgot they were racing, as they enjoyed being alive and free.

Twenty-Two

No winner was declared. Instead, they stopped outside of town to water their horses at a well and Ethan chatted up a caravan of peddlers that was heading up north. Upon catching up, Lily let her mare drink before filling up their water flasks.

They led their horses down the streets. Caleb tried not to gawk at the market stalls; Garendell was busier than Mirador, except perhaps when there was a tourney.

Caleb felt like a page again, experiencing things like street performers and artisans for the first time. He kept glancing at Lily; she seemed patient when Ethan and he got excited over simple things, like one sailor having a monkey on his shoulder. Ethan found them street food of spiced snapper and vegetables on a stick and they wandered the streets as opposed to heading towards the docks.

"Tell us if you're getting bored," he told her.

"I'm just happy to waste a day with you," she replied.

"We should get matching tattoos," Ethan said, admiring some on sailors after they passed by. "All three of us."

"Gill threw a fit when he didn't get a shirt," Caleb said.

"My parents would kill me," Lily said. "What would you get?"

"I don't know," Ethan admitted. They paused by several travelling musicians who were playing tambourines and pan flutes, several people dancing with veils of purple and crimson. "You two tell me if I'm interrupting."

"I feel like I'm the interruption," Lily said. "Tell you what: I'll head down to the harbour and see about getting passage, you guys can wander."

Caleb didn't want her going off by herself. "I'll come with you."

"I'll go see that parrot over there," Ethan declared, grinning like he was half his age.

They took Figaro and pressed on towards the docks. Though neither knew the way, the streets weren't overly complicated. Caleb overheard more than a handful of folk talking about a dragon spotted north of town—others cited it was balderdash, that the sea dragons wouldn't be near until nearly the fall.

Caleb was glad the townsfolk were hesitant to believe tale of a dragon, and tried to take in everything that had happened. That monster had been trying to break him. He could trust his own mind. And what he said about Lily, that was just to mess him up. He was here because of her.

"You're deep in thought. Want to share?" Lily asked.

"Nothing." She didn't press, but she didn't look like she believed him. "You . . . heard what Asmodean said. About us, I mean. It was a lie, obviously," Caleb insisted.

"I didn't see what you saw. I know what he said about you wanting to protect me, but . . . I like you. I'd like to think it's because . . . " She blushed slightly. "I don't know why I like the taste of blueberries over strawberries, or why I prefer one song over another. I just do."

"I keep thinking if someone else ran into you first," Caleb admitted. "He showed me what he was trying to do. Turned us into his monsters, all of us." He shook his head. "You were there."

"It didn't happen."

"It won't have happened for over a century," he said lowly. "How are we going to know if this is real? Not you standing here, but . . . us. You know what I'm getting at."

She kept his gaze, did that smile where he wanted to save her from the world. "I don't know," she said finally. "Let's take things slow, and figure it out. If one of us starts . . . to know it wasn't real, we don't spare each other's feelings." He bristled, and she furrowed her brow. "I watched you make a vow of truth. You promised not to lie, so I won't lie to you. We'll figure the rest out." He could tell looking into her eyes she felt something. He didn't want that to go away. If that was a hook in him, he'd allow that indulgence. He'd be strong enough to overcome the rest.

"'Ello," said a figure, coming up beside Lily and getting a little too close. Caleb almost removed him but the young man had pointed fur ears, covered by a wide straw hat. He looked like a traveler fresh off he boat, but given those golden eyes, Caleb knew better. "You got money? I am starving."

"You're . . . " Caleb stammered.

"And you owe me more than a beer and some chicken wings there, bub."

"I promised my first free beer would be with Ethan—" Caleb began, but the kitsune gestured. Ethan was coming up another street; he'd acquired some ridiculous flower tiara. The kitsune grabbed Lily's arm and led the way into a nearby pub as Ethan caught up to him. He had no tails, but there was something fox-ish about the way he moved. The tavern wasn't Declan's, but it smelled good and musicians played tunes that definitely didn't belong in a musical. The kitsune gestured for Lily to find a table, and then returned with Caleb to help hitch the horses.

"Who's your friend?" Ethan looked at Caleb in question. Caleb waited for them to be making their way back inside before he gestured pointy ear gesture and mouthed, "Kitsune." Ethan's eyes widened.

"Do I tell all your secrets?" Boscoe demanded. "Hey Lily, did you know that Caleb and Ethan once . . . "

"Order something with cheese," Caleb said hurriedly.

"You mean it?" the kitsune asked, his eyes widened at the menu. "It's never as good as the goat cheese from home. Oooh, something I can dip bread into. *Platter*'s a funny word."

"Do you know where my brother is?" Lily asked.

"He's on his way with your sister. I took a short cut." The kitsune grinned. He grabbed Lily's hands and unwrapped the bandages. "Some-one was playing in the sea." Boscoe put a small leather satchel on the table and produced a balm. "It stings, but it'll heal quicker." He shushed down when the waitress came over and took their drink order; the boys all asked for the house ale, Lily cited it was too early for that so she opted for lemonade. "You really should learn to like ale, Lily," Boscoe said, blowing the foam off of his. "Although you do seem to like vanilla." He snickered at Caleb.

"What's that supposed to mean?" Caleb demanded.

"Nothing," the kitsune replied. "See my mom if anything's lingering. The hold seems to be lifting, but it'll take a few days, assuming you don't keep tapping in."

"So . . . she won't be able to do those songs again?" Ethan asked. The kitsune smiled and nodded. "And we'll just be normal guys again?"

"Lily left home not even a month ago. Do you really think it's over for you?" Boscoe asked.

"No, not at all," Ethan said, crossing his arms. "Cay, Dani could be in Mirador."

"She could be," Caleb said, "but Seth intercepted a carriage with almost forty people *leaving*. They might have moved her."

"Answers are back at the castle," Ethan said. "And across the sea. I don't know which way to go."

Caleb nodded. "You go one way, I'll go the other. I need to go across the pond, so assuming I'm healthy when all is said and done, I'll head up towards Taralee and look for clues. You might be detained and stuck in Mirador for a while."

"They can't lock me up indefinitely," Ethan said. "I'll join you over-seas as soon as I can. If you find Danielle, tell her I never stopped looking for her. Don't tell her about . . . "

"I won't."

"Interesting," Boscoe grinned. "You'll give yourself up for ques-tioning?"

"What's another week or two?" Ethan asked. He looked to Lily. "You need to tell me if he . . . you know . . . gets sick and dies. Or even if you fix him. I need closure."

She glanced at Caleb, then nodded at Ethan. "I'll keep you in the loop. Where should I write to you?"

"We can send letters to my grandmother's home south of Mirador," Caleb said, "They can pass letters along to Ethan. Rodney will know where they send him."

"They won't be alone," Boscoe said, gesturing out the window to the street. "Look: it's the squires."

Gill was arguing with Seth and Tiffany, but Louis and Oliver were looking at an outdoor vendor. Lily stood and made her way to the street, so he followed.

"Louis, Oliver!" Lily called. She then saw her siblings.

Tiffany looked a little sullen, but she'd procured a fantastic red riding dress. "Lily!" Tiffany said, and she and Seth raced to her. The twins embraced their sister in a group hug. "Why's your clothing damp?"

"I wasn't able to pack your new wardrobe, but I got you and Ethan a change of clothes," Gill offered, walking over to Caleb. "Glad you snuck out, everyone who wasn't accounted for like you is holed up."

"My cousin, Sir Hector . . . ?" Caleb pressed.

"A lot more," Gill said. "Lots of people; and not just from Mirador but from abroad. Know how you said a thousand? I think it's closer to two. And creatures. Some stuff peeled right out, the woods around Mirador's gonna get a reputation fast. Where's Ethan?"

He gestured to the pub they were just in, and Louis and Oliver raced ahead. Boscoe got up, and took his cheese platter and a bucket of wings with him. "Tell Seth I told him not to worry about packing for tomorrow. You know, I'll tell him myself."

Gill followed the younger boys to Ethan, and Caleb watched the O'Connell siblings converse on the street. "We have to find Molly!" Tiffany protested.

"I know," Lily said. "But I have to get back across the sea as soon as possible."

"Why?" Tiffany asked.

"It's not for me to say," Lily said. "Come on, come meet Ethan and Caleb properly."

"Mom and dad are coming here," Tiffany insisted. "Louis said you told them where you went. You could miss them if you go back across the sea!"

"I know," Lily said. "We're not abandoning Molly. Do you know where she's gone?"

"No," Tiffany said. "Which is why we shouldn't be sailing back home."

"Come on, come sit down," Lily said. "This is Caleb—"

"We've met," Tiffany said levelly at him. "You can make me feel better by helping me into this pretty dress I got!" Tiffany said. Tiffany grabbed her sister, and they disappeared; Caleb hoped Lily would at least resemble herself when they returned.

Louis and Oliver explained the trip as they enjoyed the food and Caleb was glad the others spoke so he didn't have to come up with a plan.

"We all don't need to go back over the sea," Gill said when Ethan said he was going back to Mirador. "I'll help Tiffany find Molly . . . really?"

Tiffany showed up in a beautiful cream ballgown with golden brocade. Lily was still in the same clothing that she'd swam in. "How do you style a snood?" Tiffany asked.

"You're asking the wrong guys," Gill said.

"I think it's pretty," Ethan offered.

"You're going to need to pin the train or you're going to get it filthy," Caleb offered.

"I somehow thought you'd be less annoying now," Tiffany said, examining a headdress that looked awfully heavy. She slapped Louis' hand after he twanged it.

"How can I make it up to you, Tiffany?" Caleb asked. "I'd like for us to try to get along."

Tiffany wrinkled her nose. "I'll think of something. Oooh, remember how I compared you and Jayden? You said you'd compare me and my sister. Well, go ahead."

Caleb wanted to be really careful with what came out of his mouth. Tiffany had a natural talent for misinterpreting everything. "Your father is both a very lucky and probably incredibly concerned man to have two such lovely daughters," he said finally. "The dress shows off your shoulders."

"I guess that's okay. Shoulders are important," Tiffany said. "I was expecting my hair. Caleb, will you help me find Molly? I'd be forever in your debt and we'd start at zero."

Caleb stammered. "I could try. Any idea where she's gone?"

"No, which is why we should have stuck around the town!" Tiffany explained.

"Caleb has to come with me over the sea," Lily said. "I'll explain later."

"Well we all don't have to go overseas," Tiffany pointed out before looking to Gill. "How about you, forester?"

"Ranger," Gillam said. "Tell me where you want to go and if we need to backroad, and I'll get you there. Might not be best to tromp around in that get up."

"You ain't trotting off with this ranger," Seth said.

"You're not the boss of me," Tiffany said.

"I'm coming with you," Seth said, then looked to Louis. "You go with Lily and Sir Knight."

"Downplay the 'sirs,'" Ethan quipped. "Especially you when you're overseas."

Louis's eyes lit up, and he raced out of the pub. Lily stood but he gestured he'd do it. Stepping outside he saw that Louis was hugging a man with the same colour hair as him. "Dad, that's Sir Caleb! He helped me escape the castle! Dad, the others are just in there . . . " He gestured from Caleb to the pub.

Seth and Lily were only a few steps behind him. "I'll go right, you go left?" Seth asked Lily, who nodded, and they fanned out. He went to follow Lily, but Louis and his father approached him.

"Sir Caleb?" The man asked, and extended a hand. "Victor Phorsythe." The man had a strong build and was taller than Caleb. "Thank you for helping my son. Louis, you should have come home straight away with Dale."

"They needed me here," Louis said, taking his father into the tavern.

"Let me introduce you to Oliver and Sir Ethan and Gillam! You know the O'Connells, they ain't special."

Caleb started down the road after Lily, but he heard Seth's shrill whistle. Seth had found another group of four men and a woman.

"Caleb, meet the folks from home." Seth introduced them as Louis' uncle and his wife, Freddy and Juniper; Molly's father, Morgan; and Elias. Elias was obvious, though his hair was a little more orange he looked like a rugged, older version of Seth. In the time it took for introductions, Lily returned with no one in tow, but her father rushed to her, and after he pulled her into an embrace, they spoke quietly.

Tiffany lit up seeing the people from home. She walked up to her father, and almost burst into tears when she looked at Molly's father. "What's wrong?" Elias asked, embracing Tiffany.

"Where's Molly?" Juniper asked.

"I don't know," Tiffany said, her voice quaking slightly.

Their party had grown and there were things that were needed to be spoken in private. Caleb spoke to the bartender, and they allowed them the use of a side room. Before he could inquire about the rooms upstairs, it occurred to Caleb that the folk from Merilon might already have lodging, so he joined the others.

Seth was the one to lead the tale, though Tiffany and Louis interjected when he tried to get creative with his storytelling. Lily and Elias went to another part of the inn. At times, Elias glanced at Caleb, nodding and frowning, eyes widening, but Lily did most of the talking.

"And this is where we come in!" Louis said. "We woke up in boxes and strings in this castle!"

"I ain't even across the ocean yet, hold your horses."

"No one cares about you goofing around, they want to hear about what happened to us," Tiffany said.

"Where's Molly?" Molly's father asked.

"Molly . . . kind of . . . didn't want to leave," Tiffany said quietly.

"Don't you say that about my daughter!" the man boomed. "She wouldn't want to be away from her family. And now what, you're abandoning her?"

"If I may?" Gill asked, raising his hand. "We're not to the part where the curse was broken, but we had to get out before we were detained. The plan was to send a bunch of 'em back overseas and the rest of us would look for Molly."

"I'm returning to Mirador," Ethan said. "We need to know who's accounted for and who's still missing, right squire?"

"That's right," Oliver quipped.

"And you think you'll find answers in the castle?" Juniper asked.

"I don't know," Ethan said. "The woman who kidnapped Louis and Tiffany fled from Taralee, and that's where Caleb's headed. I'll join him as soon as I have more information, or he'll join me if there's no leads overseas."

Caleb felt a hand on his shoulder, and he followed after Elias and Lily as Tiffany tried to tell her part of the story. "My daughter said you're the one who's poisoned. You're uncertain and might have been poisoned by one of your own people. Are we correct?"

"Yes, sir."

"We received Lily's letter and my wife is on her way to get . . . what is needed," Elias said. "I would appreciate if this doesn't go further than this immediate circle. Including my other children."

Caleb nodded. "Thank you, sir."

"I should be thanking you for helping my children," Elias said. Caleb got the impression that he was being appraised. Caleb wasn't certain what Lily had told her father. "This is not done lightly, but I appreciate everything you did in keeping my children safe."

"Did you tell him about us?" Caleb asked Lily.

"Not yet," Lily sounded relieved he brought it up.

"'Us'?" Elias asked.

Caleb took Lily's hand. "I've asked your daughter if I could court her. She's allowing me that honour."

Elias' lips thinned, but soon hinted at a smile. "Really, Lily? You go off on one adventure . . . "

"Dad!"

"Let me guess: First boy you met."

"No," Lily said defensively. "First one I liked."

Before Caleb asked Elias let out a *harrumph*. Tiffany approached their group. "I don't want to leave Molly," Tiffany said.

"I'll find her," Elias said with a curt nod. "I'll take the ranger and Fred and June, the rest of you can go home. I knew they shouldn't have come. I should have been here days ago."

"I'm coming," Tiffany said. "Did they fess up about the courting?"

Elias nodded. "Somehow, you became the daughter with more sense in her head. Unless you tell me you're being courted by one of those two."

"Ew." At first Tiffany beamed but it was short-lived. "Why shouldn't I be the sensible daughter?"

Caleb looked to Lily while Tiffany and Elias conversed. "I guess we're pretty much home free."

"You've been human again for less than a day," Lily said. She seemed distant.

"What?"

"Nothing. My mother will meet us in Shelkie's Bay." She hugged him suddenly, surprising him. Resting his head on hers, it felt good to have her in his arms; he didn't care what Asmodean said. This was real. "She won't be halfway home yet, but we have a backup plan. Hopefully we won't have to use it."

"Back up plan?" Caleb asked.

Elias was paying less attention to Tiffany now, and cleared his throat. Lily let go of the embrace but held his hand. "Tiffany, go back to story time."

"They're not even telling it right," Tiffany muttered, rolling her eyes and sauntering back to the main group.

Elias crossed his arms and addressed Caleb. "You will go to Shelkie's Bay and wait for my wife Sylvia. You could miss her on the road; do not go any further than that. She has kin there you can stay with. In fact, we arrived on his boat."

"Where's Larry?" Lily asked.

"He said he needed a break and to clear his head. Him and Alfred shouldn't be far. I'll fetch them myself."

"Alfred's here?" Lily asked.

"Who?" Caleb asked.

"Isaac's son," Lily said.

"What's the back up plan?" Caleb asked.

"We fight venom with venom," Elias said.

"Dad, we can meet mom in Taralee or Stagmil," Lily said.

"You don't know how long he has," Elias told Lily. "Stick to the plan."

They seemed to know what they were talking about. "Can someone fill me in?" Caleb asked.

"Shouldn't your parents have to ask me and Syliva for permission before you knightly types are allowed to court?"

"I'll ask my mother to draft a formal letter of introduction if you'd like," Caleb said. "That might not be a bad idea, actually."

"Oh, Syl would love this," Elias said.

"Sir," Caleb said. "My intentions with your daughter are pure, but that's not what I meant. You're going to be over here, but you might need friends. I can write you a letter of introduction. My family isn't wealthy, but we know people."

"We're self-reliant people," Elias said.

"I gathered that from Seth and Lily," Caleb said. "People talk more when they're with friends."

Elias nodded before he spoke. "Can you let me speak to the knight alone for a moment?" Lily walked to the other side of the room to listen to the rousing tale, though she kept looking back at the pair of them.

"I won't say that I don't care that you're . . . courting my daughter, she asked and I delivered. I want you to understand a few things, and why it's so secret."

"Unico—" Caleb began.

"We don't use that word, for starters," Elias said. "People start looking. Burn the house down, slaughter your herds looking. Kidnap your daughters send your son's ear back in a box looking."

Caleb nodded. "Lily said that you sometimes go by a different last name. What should I call you?"

"Given the circumstances of you helping my family, this is the least I can do, but I would appreciate it if you didn't go blathering." Elias frowned. "Honestly, Elias is fine, but read the room; if Fred or June start calling me Jack, you follow suit. We go by Brathwell in Taralee, mostly because it helps sell our fleece, but I don't think going by O'Connell should be such a big deal anymore. I haven't done anything interesting in years. As far as you're concerned, I sell fleece and my wife makes ointments. Capisce?"

Best to not bring up the wyvern, then. "Yes, sir."

"Enough with the 'sirs.' You're the knight. Couldn't tell by looking, but I'm glad you have enough sense to downplay during travel," Elias said. "I've given my daughter basilisk venom. In the event my wife is delayed, Lily will inject it into your bloodstream. That will cause petrification." It took Caleb a moment to remember what that word meant. "I don't want her to downplay the seriousness of the situation. Partial petrification can kill, and if done in excess of say, fifteen years, it's almost impossible to nullify." Elias scratched the back of his head, looking contemplative. "That's more of a question for my wife and the whack jobs who figured it out. Syl's normal compared to them."

" . . . fifteen years?" Caleb asked.

"Shouldn't take that long to cure you. I'm saying: In the event that you are succumbing to the poison, this will keep you alive long enough for Syl to fix you. I've never been petrified but Fred over there has and it's not pleasant, and coming out of it is worse than going into it. Understood?"

"Yes s— Yes."

"Wait in Shelkie's Bay. When Syl say she'll do something, she will. Lily will likely want to rush back home, but if you succumb on the road, she'll panic and pick a bad spot to turn you and it'll be harder to find you later and it's better for you to recover in real shelter not a tent if the weather turns sour. Are you showing any signs of being poisoned?"

"No. Took about another day last time. I don't know if it'll react the same way or how long I'll have."

"Last time?" Elias asked.

"I almost succumbed prior to my castle being cursed," Caleb said. "Technically, the curse kept me alive."

Elias had a crooked smile. "Interesting. I'll send my son to find Larry and Alfred. You'll have to ask them when they can sail back for Shelkie's Bay." He studied Caleb, let out an extended sigh. "Thank you for protecting my children. No whirlwind craziness concerning my first born until I retrieve Morgan's daughter and have a chance to get to know you."

"I'll try my best, Elias."

Twenty-Three

The knights penned Elias' party's letters. Neither Caleb nor Ethan came from enough wealth to see them completely comfortable, but the letters of introduction would see them at least be welcome by folks like Rodney and Wilfred when they made it to Mirador.

Ethan suggested Gill's group travel to Yarrosfeld first, as Asmodean had fled Mirador and it seemed that their aid had come from there; perhaps Darius had gone that way and Gill knew people there.

Although they spent the night in the cramped sleeping quarters, Louis and Caleb were amazed at the small sailboat, and Louis's dad, Victor, cited that this was getting to be too cramped and he wouldn't mind another day or two in Ivancia, but the winds were favourable and the others were leaving for Yarrosfeld anyway.

Lily hugged her family goodbye. "I hope you find Molly and bring her home."

"I'll miss ya," Seth told her. "You're the fun sister."

"I heard that," Tiffany said, pushing Seth out of the way. "Thanks for coming after me."

"Hey Seth," Lily called, then handed her brother her sword. "You might need this. Don't bend it, I want it back."

"About time," Uncle Freddy said, grinning at Elias. "Let's teach the twins the art of the sword."

"Me?" Tiffany squawked.

"I hope your mother doesn't dally," Elias said, wading out to help them cast off.

Caleb got the distinct idea that Boscoe would be with Seth, even though he hadn't seen him. No sooner than the wind caught the sails, a small competition to help Larry sail started, Louis and Alfred engaged in knot-tying competitions. Caleb stood in awe watching the coast shrink until all around them was endless blue. The wind was in his hair; this wasn't flying, but he might as well have been.

"We made it," Caleb said to Lily. She seemed sombre, looking over the contents of the vial in the leather satchel her father had given her. "You're not happy about that, are you?"

"I just . . . you just got back to being you, that's all," Lily said.

"I trust you," Caleb said, taking her hand.

"I'm supposed to keep you two from doing anything naughty," Louis announced. "When you're in Stagmil, you can stay at my place!"

"There's room at my house," Lily said.

"Your parent'sll love that," Victor said. "We'll make sure Caleb's got a place to call home in our neck of the woods. He can stay at Fred and June's place if he's spending any time in Taralee; they live just north of the city."

"Their house is so close to the mountains. What are we investigating in Taralee?" Louis asked Caleb.

"People disappeared from there, and I think that's where Madeline's from," Caleb said. "See if we can find leads or an accomplice. Maybe after your mom knows you're safe she'll let you help me."

"You're coming at the best time," Louis said. "After shearing we'll have jigging days and there's a festival in Taralee practically every other week! There's a rodeo in Summerset and the strawberries should be ready in a few more weeks!"

"One step at a time," Victor said. It seemed that everyone on the boat knew something was up with Caleb, and it was imperative that he get to Shelkie's Bay. They didn't discuss particulars. Caleb wondered if they were all rushing for nothing. So far he felt fine.

Favourable winds drove them west and he was happy to no longer be stuck in that castle. He thought of Ethan, of Esther, of his cousin and all those left behind. Who was free? Who was still missing? He told himself he'd find Asmodean, and end this.

Tiffany felt like maybe she ought to trek out on her own with Seth and her father.

Gillam was more than easy on the eyes, but once he figured out her dad and Louis' aunt and uncle were has-beens, he completely ignored her and asked a bunch of stupid questions—about their exploits from before she was born. At least she had five pretty dresses and accessories to amuse herself with; her father still made her send most of the clothes home. Thankfully accessories took up far less room.

"You'll have to wait for Syl to catch up. She was the lore master," Juniper said.

"Yeah, we were kind of there for heavy lifting," Freddy said.

"None of this has to do with how we're going to find my Molly," Molly's father said.

"We will find her," Elias said before looking to Gillam. "Please stop inspecting my arrows. They're nothing special. I make them in my spare time. Seth, go fetch water."

"Why me?" he grumbled, getting up.

"Just be careful—this lake gets deep," Gillam called. "If you fall in, we may never find you."

Tiffany's attention went from the fire to two—no, three yahoos, one of which was holding a goose under his arm, stumbling up the road towards their camp. She could only see two, but she could hear three voices.

They were singing, loudly and off key, staggering more or less towards them. "Na na na na na—HEY! Na na na na! Na na na na na— HEY! Na na na na!"

"We are in the middle of nowhere," Tiffany muttered, arms crossed. Everyone scowled, until they realized that they were sort of staring at Seth, where their eyes widened.

Several coins braided into his hair, Seth was topless, sunburnt, with a matching tattoo across his bicep to the fellow beside him. They both wore flowing robe-style pants. Seth's were red to the other one's blue. The other one had two fox tails and pointed furry ears and a near-human face, the sort that was more wrong the more she stared at it. Their third member was a rowdy gnome riding on the kitsune's shoulder.

"Hey dad," Seth said, stumbling in.

"I just—" Elias stuttered, and they all looked in the opposite direction, at a very confused Seth down by the lake, buckets in hand.

"Uh . . . hi me?" Seth asked.

"Yeah . . . I'm me," drunken Seth said to himself, holding onto his associate for balance. "Shoot, we got back early. Don't worry, you had . . . gonna have . . . a great week."

"What is going on?" Tiffany demanded, turning her head to look from Seth to Seth.

"Funny story," said the gnome, jumping down. "We'll tell it over omelettes. Gimme dat goose."

Tiffany looked back and forth at the two Seths, though everyone else wondered why the gnome was squeezing the goose. "Dangit!" the kitsune said, holding up a golden egg. "We can't eat this!" He pitched it into the lake.

"Get out of here you stupid goose!" Seth said, tossing the goose after her egg.

"No no no no!" Elias chased after the goose, who honked before flapping her wings and flying off over the lake. Tiffany looked back, and saw that while they were watching, a large black swan had landed. Larger than any horse Tiffany had ever seen; it had two riders, a sober version of the other kitsune and another one, a girl about Tiffany's age, speaking to Seth and motioning for him to climb onto the swan.

"Wait," Gillam scrambled to his feet, hoping to join, but Seth smiled devilishly at the campers, and jumped on the oversized swan. It swam off, opened its majestic wings, and took off just as fast, disappearing into the starry night.

"There we go," the newly arrived Seth said, watching his past self depart. He hiccupped.

"Is that ambrosia?" Juniper asked, swiping the coconut cup from the kitsune. Freddy grabbed it, sipped it, confirmed, then downed it.

"Seth!" Elias said, taking his son by the shoulders. "Where and *when* did you go?"

"I dunno. Some island. There were like . . . rocks and stuff," Seth said. "Nice beaches, palm trees, a cursed temple . . . and a very grumpy hippocampus." He put an arm around the kitsune. "This guy right here . . . he's my best friend. Say hi to Boscoe everyone."

"Hi to Boscoe everyone," the kitsune waved in a most intoxicated state, clinging to Seth to stay upright.

"Liar," Elias said. "I know Boscoe. Which one were you . . . Digger or Pookie or Muffin . . . ?"

"Lily thought I was a girl!" Muffin complained, shrinking down to fox-form, causing Seth to fall over.

"He really is your son," Freddy said to Elias.

"I never . . . got caught," Elias said, then grumbled. "Celestial foxes."

"Huh?" Tiffany asked. "Aren't they just shapeshifters?"

"No, they've got three feet in this world, one foot in the ether," Elias explained. "The most powerful ones are capable of messing with time but," he frowned. "Not the first time these two somehow figured it out."

Seth found Tiffany's sleeping roll, immediately became unconscious, drooling heroically, a two-tailed kitsune in fox form snoring on his back, their gnome friend sleeping in one of Tiffany's wooden clogs.

"What just happened?" Molly's father demanded.

"And why didn't I get to go to the party?" Gillam demanded.

"Some party," Freddy said. "He came back in his human form. Remember that time when we were nineteen, Elias? With the phoenix?"

"I still got the scars," Elias said, "and I was hardly cursed, that was you."

"Ugh," Tiffany grumbled. "I should have stayed in Mirador. My boyfriends would have come up with a plan by now."

"Boy *friends*?" Elias asked. "Plural?"

"I'm still the sensible daughter," Tiffany pointed out as the goose that laid golden eggs swam behind them in the lake.

Twenty-Four

Caleb enjoyed sailing, even though he started to get a slight headache towards the end of the voyage. He assumed he was just over excited and overtired; he ignored it with the coast coming into view as the sun was beginning to set, casting the sky and waves in red and orange. They never sailed to the town or the castle in the distance, instead to where Alfred said was his parents' land. No docks, instead a picturesque cove with trees surrounding a beach was where they came in.

"They won't be expecting us so soon," Alfred said, removing his boots. Caleb and Louis did likewise and joined him in jumping into the shallow waves to bring the sailboat in.

"How far is it to your farm?" Louis asked.

"Less than a mile from here," Alfred said, gesturing once he had a free hand.

"So we came through the town back there?" Louis asked once Caleb offered Lily a hand down.

Lily nodded in affirmation. "How was your first voyage by ship?"

Caleb thought she was talking to him, but Louis beamed. "I hope to do a lot more of it and sail someplace exciting."

"If they let us our of our sight, I'll happily take you," Caleb told him.

"Promise?"

"If I can, let's do it."

"Don't forget me," Alfred said.

"You're gonna need a ship for that," Larry said gruffly. "Let's offload, we'll return in the morning and shut it down proper."

"We can handle that." Alfred gestured to Caleb and Larry. "Come on Larry, you know you want to take us."

"Catch," Larry called. He pitched bags at them, and they pitched them to Louis on the shore and Lily shuttled them up the incline. Caleb thought he heard something splash, and giggle in the water. He peered and thought he saw a large pink fin disappear into the water on the far side of the boat.

"Caleb, hurry up!" Louis called. Caleb stopped staring at the ocean and shifted the bags he was to carry over his shoulder, and followed after everyone else. Lily waited for him. They listened to the others prattle; Alfred and Louis had similar ideas of places they could sail. When they neared the farmhouse, two children, a girl of eleven and a boy of nine, rushed to meet them.

"You're back so soon!" the boy rushed to Alfred.

"We thought you'd be gone for a week," the girl said, embracing her brother before racing to Lily. "We miss Rebecca already—we're gonna go visit her in a month. Can we see your lambs?"

The Sprites' home was a comfy cottage-style dwelling, and they had a large barn as well as a new chicken coop. A woman met them outside, and her elderly parents hovered at the porch as they approached.

"Lily, I'm so glad to see you made it back safely," Nora said, embracing her. "And you must be Louis!" It seemed that she'd already met Louis' father Victor.

"And this is Sir Caleb of Mirador," Louis introduced him.

Nora's eyes lit up. "Isaac told me about you! He's out, as is my daughter Esperanza. Please, everyone, come inside. I've got leftovers and I'll figure out the rest. You just sailed in? Larry, you've spent more time on the water in the past week than Daphne."

"She should be in the water not on it." Larry still followed Nora's direction. Louis disappeared with the younger kids into the back pantry. Caleb on the other hand was directed to a comfortable trestle table. It smelled homey.

"Where's Seth and your father?" Nora asked Lily.

"They went to try to find Molly," Lily said. "They'll send letters here.

My father said to wait for my mom here in Shelkie's Bay. We'll press on; can you direct us to the inn in town?"

"Nonsense—you're staying here, we have the space," Nora said. He thanked her for the cup of tea. "I'd love to hear what happened, would you prefer to wait for Isaac? Larry, sit for fifteen minutes before you go home."

"Is Catarina well?" Lily asked.

"She's helped everyone who needed it get back to Taralee. They went with the people from your village," Nora said. "I'm a little surprised to see a knight from overseas here."

"We like him okay," Louis said with a grin, coming in with a basket full of eggs with the younger kids as well as what looked like mushrooms and the earliest of strawberries. "Gonna miss him when he's done his investigating and he charts on back home."

"Maybe you'll have to come back and see me at Miradah," Caleb said, covering his mouth instinctively. He hoped no one heard that. Everyone was chatting, so thankfully no one caught on.

The conversation around him continued about what had happened, Louis explaining that Seth and the others went to look for Molly, then began to relay the harrowing adventure from his perspective.

"You're being quiet," Lily said to Caleb. "Everything okay?"

He nodded. "I'm fahn."

She raised her brows and he gestured not to worry about it. *I made it across the ocean. She's coming with a purifier.* He tried not to think about it to much.

Lily took his hand and led him outside. "What's wrong?"

"'Ith nothing." It was all he could not do to cuss. He looked at her pleadingly. "Do not thay anything. Please."

He was expecting her to be angry, but instead she seemed genuinely concerned. "Why . . . don't you lay down and get some rest? That might help."

"I don't want to upset anyone. I had a good few hours after this started," he said. "Tell them I went to town or something.I don't know. I'm supposed to pretend to be normal, right?"

"You're with friends. We need to press on. I need a wagon . . . If I sleep during the day we can keep going throughout the night."

"Donkeys have to sleep some time. You're panicking."

Foolishly, they didn't check to make sure no one was watching. The family matriarch Vivian caught them. "Is everything all right?"

She squeezed his hand, it was strangely comforting. "Can . . . we talk someplace private?"

"Of course," Vivian said. She gestured for them to follow. Lily looked at Caleb, expecting him to follow.

"I'm not staying on bed rest," Caleb told her. "This is my first time across the thea. Sea."

"You're not on bed rest," Lily told him. "You're making a plan."

Caleb's gut reaction was to run as fast and as far as he could, but he followed the elder woman into a room that boasted a sewing mannequin and a half-finished shirt on the table. She instructed the pair of them to sit down. "What is going on?"

Caleb looked at her, then at Lily, then bowed his head. "I was poisoned. I'm okay right now, she's just worried about noffing—nothing"

The elder woman put a hand over her mouth, then nodded. "This won't go further than the room. That's why Sylvia turned around and went back north," Vivian said. "We couldn't figure it out. What happens next?"

"It's okay," Lily said, taking his hand. "You're with friends."

"I . . . last time, I passed out a few times and they hauled me to the infirmary. I'm okay right now. I don't want to be a bother."

"Yes, you're the first person to *bother* other people with being poisoned," Vivian said. "You're starting to show signs?"

"Yes."

"Okay," Vivian said. "I've seen poisons kill next to instantly and others linger for weeks. I'll speak to Nora and Isaac . . . "

"No one can know that much," Lily said.

The older woman nodded. "You were injured and we sent for an herbalist that will help you. Understood?" Caleb looked to Lily, who nodded, so he did too. "I know someone in town who can brew you up something that'll . . ."

"I don't want to be drugged for days," Caleb insisted. "That's what they did to me last time."

Vivian's look was more sympathetic than he expected. She gave him a warm smile. "You two sit here and behave. No running off to town or getting a wagon and pressing north, understood?"

He waited for Vivian to leave the room. "I didn't come across the sea just to sit around. Did you see how amazing that coast was? And that town?"

"I know. We'll meet up with my mom on the road. After she fixes you, I promise we'll come back here and you can explore the coast for a week if you want. Longer."

He wanted to tell her she didn't know. But when he looked into her eyes, and saw the concern, he relaxed a little. "Your dad said to stay here. You said we needed a plan, then let's make one. I really don't want to burden these people. I can tough it out for a few days."

"We might be able to find an herbalist who won't make you delirious," she said, then frowned. "And you are not a burden, ever." He almost withdrew from her touch. He caught himself, she must have noticed him stiffen. "Not used to it being the other way around?"

"Not at all," he said.

"Which is why we're going to keep you as healthy as possible. I think we have to let Louis and his dad know something."

"Can you think of something?" He didn't want to compromise her family.

She mused. "During the battle you got a cut. You jumped in the ocean, it must have went sour. You'll be unwell for a few days," Lily said. "We're waiting for my mom to come back with the proper medicine. There, no technical lies."

Nora came back with Vivian. Nora seemed much more concerned than Vivian. "How are you feeling right now?"

"Okay. Trying not to be poisoned."

Nora nodded. "We've dealt with worse."

"I haven't," Caleb muttered.

"You were cursed for two years," Lily said.

"That'th totally different," Caleb said.

"Do you know how long you'll have before you start to succumb?" Nora asked.

"A few days," Caleb said.

"Okay, you need to rest. Hopefully Sylvia won't be that long."

Great. He finally made it across the ocean, and now he wasn't going to be allowed to turn around without someone critiquing him. "If I turn in early, will you wake me to see the sunrise?"

"If you're well enough for it," Nora assured him. "Are you hungry at all? Larry said you were going to eat once you got to his place."

Caleb remembered how badly he started to vomit the last time. The less stuff in his gut, the better. "I'm not hungry. I think it was the thea." He doubted anyone believed him.

"You're going to take it easy until Sylvia gets here. I hope she hurries. Wait here, I'll go back up the guest bedrooms." Nora went off without Vivian.

Vivian watched her daughter go, but turned back to him and Lily. "Do you have a backup plan?"

"Yes," Lily said.

She nodded. "Good. Let's hope you don't need to go that route."

~*~

Lily told herself that he was just tired from travel. He slept solidly, and when they were roused before dawn by a rooster, Caleb seemed more lethargic. She reminded herself that not everyone was a morning person. They walked to the cove to see the sunrise. He fell asleep waiting for it, and Lily let him sleep through it. He was a little sore at her that she didn't wake him, but said they'd try again the next day. Her mother said something about making people who were sick and injured have something to look forward to. Gave them a reason when things got hard.

The adults were made aware of the situation, and Caleb offered to help with chores around the farm; he wanted to cut firewood and help secure Larry's boat and ready it for its next voyage, but he was relegated to simpler tasks, which Lily could tell irked him all the more. Louis insisted on bringing Caleb to see where he and his father were staying. Caleb went with Alfred to go visit that afternoon.

Alfred didn't come back with him. "He turned green on us. Even Larry got worried." It was hard not to march there and check, but Alfred swore up and down that Caleb was just nauseated and seemed to be content finding some backwoods to suffer in silence.

Lilyhurried there the next morning and found Larry and Sean out back, doing their chores, caring for the oxen and readying a wagon. Victor and Louis weren't far off; Louis was pumping water for the oxen and came to greet her. "How's he doing?"

"Good morning to you, too." Larry didn't seem surprised. He took her inside to where Catarina was busy working her loom. Caleb was awake and making idle chat with her over tea. He looked terrible, bags under his eyes and his cheeks looked gaunt as opposed to their normal healthy glow, but Lily suppressed the urge to lecture him."Did you need breakfast?"

"I ate," she lied. "You had me worried."

"Sorry." Caleb didn't sound sorry, he was looking through family records. "There's a lot of Brathwells. What's it with naming firstborn daughters after plants?"

"I'm not sure," Lily admitted. "I'm an O'Connell, so I don't have to."

"I like the name Sakura."

"Really, at my kitchen table?" Larry demanded. "Where I eat breakfast?"

"I need to go stretch my legs," Caleb got up slower than she anticipated.

"You take it easy," Catarina cautioned. "Lily, if he starts sneaking off again we're slapping this cat bell on him."

"I have thumbs."

"*And these mittens.*"

"I am a knight of the realm and will not be subject to—" Caleb trailed off when Catarina gave him the stink eye. "I'll behave, ma'am."

"There's a lamb." Caleb let out an annoyed *baaaah* behind Catarina's back once she was out of earshot.

Sean and Louis were waiting for them with a cart. "Where are we going?" Caleb asked once they'd climbed on to the deck.

"Thought we'd go to a place I like to pick blueberries before we head to town, then back to the Sprites' Farm," Sean said.

"We're not in blueberry season," Lily said.

"No, but Louis' dad says you'll feel better with some fresh country air," Sean pointed out.

"I hope you feel better soon," Louis told him as the wagon started to plod along. "The port here got messed up, but the beaches look amazing! Sean and Alfred said they'll take me to explore some of the woods north of town, I said we'd wait until you were feeling better because some of the paths you can't take by wagon. Too bad you were too sick to finish the board game last night."

The younger pair mostly prattled on the bench. Caleb seemed quiet and in slight discomfort but nodded and asked questions when Sean pointed things out to them. Lily's mind wasn't on the ride; her mother would still be a day from Taralee. She could be back in four days. The reality of the woods and the road came back when suddenly Caleb jumped out and ran into the bush.

"Is he okay?" Sean asked.

Caleb coughed and sounded like he was wheezing. Lily got up, told the boys to stay behind. "I'm fine," he said, eyes watering.

"I know," she said, and offered him the flask of water.

He rinsed his mouth. "I didn't want you to see me like this."

"Would it be better if it was just the boys?"

"No," he admitted. He seemed unsteady on his feet. "It comes and goes. I'm better."

Caleb refused her hand and tried to make it back to the wagon, seemed uncertain about climbing on, then pretended like he was still down to help her. She didn't notice when he drifted off to sleep, until a rough bump gave no response. They had some blankets and she used them to try to keep him warm. He shivered despite the warm sun and the blankets. She used her sweater as a pillow, and watched him breathe.

How long do we have?

"Is he going to die?" she overheard Louis ask Nora once they were back at the farm. Caleb balked at being sent to bed but didn't put up what would have been a normal fight.

"We're going to do everything we can to help him. Just . . . let him rest. He's strong."

Being strong was probably the only thing Caleb had going for him. There were times he was almost normal, but Lily couldn't tell if it would last for ten minutes or two hours. Vivian and Nora didn't let her stay with him all the time. He was better when she was there, just stroking the back of his hand when it looked like his eyes were fluttering and he was having a fever dream.

If this is what it's like watching you die from an injury, Lily thought. *I don't think I could stand it.* She didn't think she could stand to let him do it alone, either. When he seemed to settle, Nora and Vivian kicked her out, one or both of them would take over, and at least someone was there to ensure he didn't die alone.

Her mother had to hurry. When Caleb was awake he was lucid enough to have simple conversations and make decisions, but even his focus at simple card games was getting weaker by the hour. *Wait in Shelkie's Bay. Do not go home. She could miss you on the road.* She felt stupid, sitting there, waiting, watching him get weaker.

Sylvia wasn't there in four days.

~*~

"You don't have to be here with me," he told her. While Caleb slept, Lily had been reading a book Alfred had loaned her, about a knight betrayed by his lord as his lady love and best friend united to rescue him. "There's an entire world out there."

"I like reading books," she said, standing. He looked sombre and he slept more than he was awake, but he looked exhausted.

Caleb sat up, then launched into a coughing fit. "I think we might have to consider the venom," he told her once he caught his breath.

"It could take months or years to fix you," she said. "Caleb, I'm sorry.We should have left. We could be in Taralee by now."

Caleb watched her quietly until she caught his gaze. He understood, but he simply said, "Tomorrow, if she's not here by noon, you do your venom."

"I could try to transform you with the song," Lily said quietly. She caught his disgusted look. "It'll buy you more time. No bones to break, or poisoned blood."

"Let's assume you still could . . . I'd rather be dead."

"Caleb—"

"You make an excuse just this one time, you'll find a reason for another. I know you want to help, but . . . " he trailed off, blinked. "Not like that. I don't want you to be bound to Asmodean. We have another option."

"I healed every scratch on you but I couldn't touch what's going to kill you," she said. Besides, what about the next time? What if he did take an injury? If all she had to do was play and he'd be okay. Was he even lucid enough to have this conversation? "It's not your decision to make."

He went from looking sickly to scaring her when his brow furrowed. "You're not giving me a choice?"

"That's not what I meant." She tried to match him in tone but her voice cracked.

"I don't want to be a puppet," he said firmly. "Not Asmodean's, or yours." He bowed his head. She went to touch his shoulder, and he shrugged away from her.

"I'm sorry," she said quietly. She wasn't going to cry; he was the one dying. How stupid could she be? She figured he'd be better off with some space, but he grabbed her hand when she got up to leave.

"Lily, if it wasn't for you and your brother, I'd still be in that castle. I never thought I'd get to stand in the ocean or ride a horse again. I'm grateful. I don't want a half life, and I don't want you bound to this mess any more than you already are."

She blinked back her tears, nodded, didn't look at him until she was sure she had her emotions under control. Well, perhaps reined in. "Okay. When you're ready, we'll talk to the others. You want me to bring Isaac here or . . . ?"

He stood, though he had to lean on Lily for support.

Finding Isaac outside, they explained the back up plan in more detail. Isaac mostly nodded, but his eyes widened when Lily produced the venom, and looked like he was going to ask what else was in that kit. "Matter of where. We own this land, and there are caves near Larry and Catarina's that almost no one ever goes to."

Caleb shook his head. "Not a cave. That cove we were at was nice. And it faces east . . . so . . . " he zoned out. "I'm getting sappy, thinking about home and sunrises."

"Outside in the elements?" Isaac asked.

"What kind of soft rock are you turning me into?" Caleb asked. "I could go haunt a graveyard, no one would notice."

"The cove should be fine," Isaac said, then looked to Lily. "We'll keep an eye on him while you're brewing the antidote."

"Okay. When your mom shows up and you make a plan, let Ethan know," Caleb said levelly. "Tell him I said if I'm still frozen in ten years, to break up the statue. Scatter the pieces in the ocean."

"You can't mean that," Lily said.

"Your dad said it was virtually impossible to fix after fifteen," Caleb said. "You'll all have moved on by then. I'd want you to. It wouldn't be any different if I was still cursed at Mirador or the poison took me out. But if you can't fix me, I don't . . . I don't like the idea of . . . you know . . . What if someone does figure it out, and it's like a century or two from now? What if they do something sinister?"

"Ethan doesn't have to be the one to do it," Lily said quietly. "He's been through enough. I'll see it done."

The instructions were relatively simple. This batch was already proven potent; Caleb and everything he was holding would petrify. That included clothing, and even some of the grass he'd be on. She wasn't sure exactly what the younger ones were told; Louis was told that this was going to help him. Louis hated the idea, and refused to help or even say goodbye that morning.

Caleb managed to get himself onto the wagon without help. He wanted to walk, but looked like he was going to pass out again.

"I can put my hands out and you can use me like a clothesline or to hang a hammock."

Lily wondered how big of a wingspan he assumed he had. "I'd need two of you," she said. "It'll be easiest if you kneel. That way when you come to, it's easier to brace you."

"No heroic poses; got it."

"When she uses the horn, you're going to want to keep your eyes closed. Coming out of petrification, your eyes and skin will be super sensitive. Well, at first. Some of you may be numb for a while. Someone'll talk you through it, probably me or my mom. Using the horn isn't the same as a unicorn using it, so it'll be an intense shock of power. The euphoria won't last long though."

She wasn't sure how much of this was sinking in. She'd explained that this could take years to get the ingredients, and even then, Lily didn't know if she could make the potion right. Without her mother or someone who genuinely knew what they were doing, Lily or anyone else was more likely than not to make something that wouldn't completely work, and coming out of it, half-petrified, could be a death-sentence.

"Think Ethan's found her?"

"I hope so."

"I guess it's time, huh?" He'd gotten his sword out and dug the tip into the ground, and knelt.

It has to be me. "Give me your arm." It was easy to find veins on him. "It'll take about a minute. I don't know what it'll really feel like going into it. I'm told it feels really warm. Coming out you should be numb and blind. You'll get your vision back within a week or so."

She scanned the farm for a sign of her mother. Just the Sprites watching.

Caleb ran a hand through her hair, and pressed his forehead to hers, then keeping her gaze, moved his hand to press the venom in. "There. I did it to myself." She didn't move when he took his hand away from her hair. "You can't be touching me," he said. "Let me go." She hated that he was right, and backed off as his breath quickened and he winced. "It. . . feels funny like . . . " he trailed off, looking up. "The sky is beautiful."

She thought he'd look up at the end, but instead, rested his forehead on the hilt and closed his eyes as if in prayer, and seemingly all at once, turned to stone.

Twenty-Five

The day after she petrified Caleb, Lily went out to sit by him and the sea. Two mermaids were in with the tide, mostly examining Caleb. As she approached, the one with the green tail retreated and dove away, but the one with pink and purple scales didn't seem afraid at all.

"What's his name?" the mermaid asked. She seemed young, perhaps about fourteen or so. "He looks like a Jeremy. He's real, isn't he? I mean, this isn't just a statue. My friend Espy told me."

"His name's Sir Caleb."

"I shooed away a bird," the mermaid said. "Oshiera, come on back. She's sad, not angry."

"You are way too trusting with humans," the brunette bobbed her head out of the water.

Lily sat down next to her friend and hugged her knees. "We saw you together, on the beach when you sailed in. He seemed happy. Espy said you came from across the sea, and that you broke a curse on a castle," the blonde said. "And he came here because he was hurt and you are going to try to help him."

"It's a long story." Lily looked at Caleb, then at the sea. "I don't think I helped all that much."

"I like stories," she said. "I'm Daphne, by the way."

"He's a knight?" Oshiera asked, swimming closer before beaching herself. They moved rather quickly on their elbows, but they didn't seem hostile. Lily knew the average mermaid was relatively harmless, and she had the advantage of being on land.

"He is."

"Are you two in love?" Daphne asked.

"I think so," Lily said. "I've never been before. Don't tell him that."

"Come on, Daphne, we'll let them be together for a while."

"Bye, Lily!" Daphne said, and the two mermaids went back to the water, and swam off.

"How do you know my name?" she asked, but they were gone. She looked to Caleb. "You wouldn't believe me in a hundred years." She frowned. What if it did take a hundred years? What if it only took five? They'd all had moved on with their lives. He told her he wouldn't have blamed her, but all the same . . . *Mom, why didn't you hurry?*

She tried to imagine it—he spent two years trying to get his life back, only for him to go through this; in ten years he'd end up younger than Oliver would be. She imagined she'd be married and have kids by then. If not, would he want her? Would he see her as pathetic and holding on to something that wasn't even real?

I never thought I'd get to stand in the ocean or ride a horse again. I'm grateful.

"You're not scared of nothin', are ya?" Louis called. He was up by a collection of trees, and seemed nervous. "Are they gone?"

"Ocean's a big place," Lily called over to him. "How long have you been there?"

"I . . . don't know. I saw the mermaids. They didn't look scary but Caleb's told me lots of stuff looks innocent. Why do so many monsters prefer to eat men?"

"Maybe you taste better?" Lily offered. "How are you doing, Louis?"

"Okay. Dad says he's only going to wait another day for your mom before going home," Louis said, and stood next to Caleb's statue. He looked sad. Lily was so much in her own head, she'd forgotten that Louis and Caleb had become friends too.

"Miss him?"

"I guess. Not like you do. Um . . . " Louis looked hesitant. "It'll be weird, if I'm older than him when we speak again."

"Yeah," Lily agreed.

"Hey . . . nevermind."

"Talk to me," Lily said.

"It's just . . . not that I could be a knight and everything. I'm not, you know . . . what's it called . . . born to it and everything," Louis said. "But if I was a knight, do you think I'd be a good one like him? Caleb said he could teach me to do stuff squires do, and that I was good at it."

"No," Lily said. "One of him's enough. I think if you were to do all that, you'd be a good knight like you." He looked away. "Sorry, was that kinda cheesy?"

"Do I look like a guy who would turn down cheese?" Louis asked. "Thanks. I don't want to leave you here waiting for your mum."

"Your mom needs to see you with her own eyes," Lily said. "I'll be all right." She looked to Caleb. "Give me a minute."

"All right," Louis said. He didn't wander far, so Lily spoke quietly. "Just in case . . . we are separated by time. I'll leave you letters." She couldn't let the letters be boring. "I don't think you can hear me, but if you can, I miss your stupid jokes. I guess I'll go see things for the two of us." She bowed her head. "I'm sorry if I forced you to like me. I didn't mean to."

She and Louis made their way back to the Sprites' farm, and asked where, if anyplace, she could take a sketchbook.

"Love, I don't think you should be alone and wandering in the wilderness," Vivian said to her.

"All right. Louis said the coast was amazing. And there's caves around here. I don't want to mope."

"Yeah, I kinda wanted to take Caleb," Louis said.

"We'll leave him letters, just in case," Lily said. Louis nodded. Setting out to the town, they ran into Alfred and Yolanda, who took them north of the city, and they prattled on about the castle and the battle in the harbour. The day went by faster than she had imagined, and thought she heard singing in the wind.

"It's the mermaids," Yolanda explained. "They're not that bad. Not like how the sailors talk about them."

Lily listened to the melody, and tried to commit that song to memory. This time, when the song played back in her head, it felt inspiring. She wished she had her mandolin, or her bouzouki. She laughed, realizing she really was Stringless.

~*~

The next day, Lily set out early to see Catarina and Larry, with Sean and Catarina taking her to see parts of the woods that were not so much great for logging as scenic. Catarina brought food for a picnic. "You doing well?"

"I'm fine," Lily said. "Do you think I should have pressed on home?"

"No, love," Catarina said. "You had no idea how long he had. He's safe at the Sprites' farm."

That afternoon she found Shelkie's Bay did have a library—it wasn't very big, but it was fun to read over music theory. She missed her mandolin, and writing down music, returned to the Sprites' home to help make supper and ask to borrow Alfred's banjo. It wasn't the same, but Catarina was so busy preparing for more people across the sea that Lily didn't want to bother her and ask if there was a mandolin or lute she could borrow in town.

Lily recognized the mare's nicker before she saw Stella grazing, and she forgot all about the last two days. It took her a minute to compose herself. Lily could have had a wagon and gone up to Taralee and Caleb would have been just fine. She never should have listened to Elias. She checked the mare over; Stalla had been rubbed down, and found her mother inside at the trestle table, speaking with Vivian, her dark hair pinned and still wearing her riding gear. "What took you so long?" Lily asked.

"Is your brother all right?" her mother asked, rushing to Lily. The two embraced, but Sylvia noticed Lily's stiffness. "Lily, talk to me."

She bit her lip. "Seth and Tiffany were fine when I left them. They're across the sea. Father is with them. They're looking for Molly."

"Lily?" Nora asked, coming in from the side room.

"If not them, who? Louis?" Sylvia pressed.

"Why did you take so long to get here?" Lily asked. "I wouldn't have had to petrify him if you'd hurried!"

Her mother sighed, and took her daughter's hands. "I came as fast as I could. Stella is not a young mare."

"We should have kept going, or sailed for Port Redmaw, or . . . "

"Do you know the poison?"

"No. We think one of his own people stabbed him in the back. I wrote the symptoms down."

Her mother nodded, looking over the list. "How bad is he?"

"We probably had a few more days. I never should have listened to him or dad. You brought one, didn't you?"

"Lily," her mother said. "I'm not going to do anything until you tell me what happened."

She sat down and told her mother everything; her tea went cold before she touched it, her mother mostly nodded, Vivian asked questions mostly to clarify. Nora intercepted the younger children when they came in, and started to make supper around the time that they arrived at the castle and Seth found Tiffany. Well, she didn't say all of it; she didn't say that they were courting. Were they, or were they just doing what that evil monster made them do?

"So your father is still across the sea," Sylvia said once Lily concluded the tale. "Any news or updates?"

"You're not even listening to me," Lily said. "They're fine."

"Okay. The petrification certainly throws in a complication," Sylvia said. Lily felt her eyes burn. "Lily?"

"I'm so sorry," Lily tried to choke back her tears. "It's all my fault." She breathed the way Zin taught her and tried to compose herself, but let the tears flow when her mother embraced her. "Molly's gone because of me."

"No."

"Seth could have been killed. Rebecca was so frightened."

"Lily, none of what that woman did is your fault," Sylvia said firmly. "She deceived all of us. You kept your head, I couldn't ask for more. Like you did with the wyvern."

"You were angry about the wyvern."

"I'm angry that you were in danger, not at you," Sylvia said. Sylvia stroked Lily's face lovingly. "You knew something was wrong. I missed the warning signs—the way the dogs acted when she first showed up, that she didn't seem to want help back to her husband or Taralee. You tried to tell me something was wrong. I'm sorry I didn't listen to my team. I was trying to keep a firm hand on the people in town, I didn't see the forest for the trees."

"I'm sorry I was mad about the wyvern hunt."

"I told you I needed you at the home front and I meant it. And it sounded like you and Seth put up a decent fight, or we would have lost more children," Sylvia said. Lily realized that her mother likely heard the story already from Rebecca. "The letter from Larry was fine, but I didn't have enough information to just turn around. I took longer than I anticipated in case I needed to sail across the sea and un-petrify your brother." She held up a vial. "Now, how long ago was this young man petrified?"

"Three days?" she guessed, and the others nodded. Lily covered her mouth with her hand. "You brewed an antidote?"

"Of course. I couldn't tell how long I had to get to you, and I can't make one without . . . you don't want to hear it, these are incredibly difficult to do well. Where are you staying?"

"She's been staying here," Vivian offered.

"I told you to stay with my kin north of town."

"We insisted, plus the Phorsythes are staying there. Lily's a gem," Nora offered.

"Thick-headed rock like her father. What's your plan for his recovery?" Sylvia asked.

"Um . . . well . . ."

Sylvia sighed. "Would it be all right if the young man were to stay here and recover for two days? The first twenty-four hours are the worst. He's young, so that would mean a swifter recovery time than if it were someone like Elias or myself."

"Yes, he was here before," Nora said.

"We need to come up with a plan. I'm chasing off after Elias overseas, that means if you're not coming with me, we can fix him, but you're going to have to care for him until he gets to Taralee," Sylvia told Lily. "If he's well in three days—that is, two sleeps—you can start heading north. He's going to need a companion for about the first day, after that he'll be relatively independent."

"He'll be blind," Lily pointed out.

"So? He can recover on the back of a wagon just fine. Once you are in Taralee, you will hand care of him over to my old instructor. She is likely to toss him after another two days, and from there he shouldn't go too far for the next three weeks, but she'll decide what happens next. He's young and I made this myself so I doubt there'll be any complications. What are the crucial times for de-petrification?"

Lily felt her heart race. "If more of a handspan of the petrification restarts in more than just the peripheral limbs, allow the patient to re-petrify for at least three days. Ideally, we do not allow them to re-petrify for the next six months. A healthy patient would be . . . able to use their vision again without danger in about a week?"

"In three days, he'll be able to walk around without visual protection, but he won't get his full vision back for about a week. You should have been learning the information instead of moping," Sylvia said. "You can go home and get busy with the fleecing. The neighbours are managing the shearing—your grandparents are coming down, but I'd appreciate it if you oversaw the season while I'm dealing with your father and the twins. Your friend can help, so long as he's got proper pain receptors back and that shouldn't be a problem. Think you can handle that?"

"Yes."

"Good. Don't encroach on these people's good graces any more than you have already."

"We'd take it as a snub if they didn't accept our hospitality," Nora pointed out.

"I don't want my daughter to burden you," Sylvia said.

"People are not burdens," Lily told her mother levelly. "I said I'd help him, he's my responsibility."

Her mother chuckled. "You know my meaning."

Lily nodded. "You give me back my friend, I'll make sure he stays as safe as he'll allow himself to be."

"Sylvia?" Nora asked. "How are you getting across the sea?"

"I was going to make arrangements with Larry, but my daughter thinks this is important, so we're dealing with the knight first."

The rest of the family returned for supper. Lily was too anxious to eat; instead she offered to go and get Louis from Catarina and Larry's to help, but Alfred said he'd do that after they fixed Caleb. Besides, the less people who knew how they fixed Caleb, the better.

Syl and Isaac talked while Esperanza helped Lily ready the wagon and blankets, and a flask of water. Syl laughed a little bit when they made their way out to the wagon.

"I had to tell you something to keep Seth from mucking about and turning you or anyone else to stone. He would have to, just to see what it was like. Petrification is serious business. One of your father's friends had to give up deep mountain hunting; he got turned to stone six times, we weren't sure if he was going to survive another go."

"How often have you done this?" Nora asked as they walked out towards the cove, leading the donkeys.

"More times than I've cared to," Sylvia admitted. "One of our requirements in the lore final exam is dealing with a petrified animal. Making this vial can be finicky and tedious. Don't worry, when I'm home I'm going to take Lily to find everything we used."

"We?" Lily asked.

"I might have brewed it in Taralee at my mentor's home. I didn't want to contaminate our fleece."

"You had all the ingredients on hand." Lily had been to said mentor's house; made her mother's store room look like a pleasant pantry.

"You're replacing her stores; money will not cut it, young lady. Some of it preserves well, but the vial itself is only good for a few months before losing efficacy. Use it incorrectly, and you have partial re-petrifications and it can get tricky fast. Which is why we don't rush *anything.*"

Strong winds made it a relatively cool day, and Sylvia even joked about waiting for the weather to improve. "All right, this is going to take a few minutes," Sylvia said. She and Lily had a strange set of goggles made of a sort of strange dark glass, but even that wasn't going to be enough protection if she stared. "Everyone besides my daughter: Keep your distance, and when I tell you, you cover your eyes, no exceptions." She poured the potion onto Caleb. For a second, Lily thought it wasn't going to work. That she'd gotten her hopes up for nothing. But, this was her mother. This was going to work.

"Ah, he's starting to breathe. Steady him. Like we practiced."

How could she tell? "Caleb, can you hear me? Nod."

Nothing. "Talk him through it," Sylvia coaxed.

"I'm putting a cloth over your eyes. Keep them closed." He still felt and looked like stone.

"Hold him steady. The inner parts will come alive first. Just because he's not moving doesn't mean he can't hear you," Sylvia said levelly. "The de-petrification process will be unpleasant for him, so try not to make it worse by scaring him."

She felt his weight and he moved, stone flaked off like a hatching chick. Color returned to Caleb's cheeks and Sylvia pressed the silver unicorn horn to his forehead. Lily remembered she had to close her eyes, then just braced. The power jolted through them both, and her mother, and she felt a surge from inside her—different then when she sang. It was like it was purifying, drawing out every bit of disease and sickness.

"Lily open your eyes, everyone else keep them shut. Where was the site of poisoning?" her mother asked.

"Back here." Lily gestured to his back, and Sylvia pointed the horn. Lily clenched her eyes again but just held him tighter; the jolt wasn't painful but it was too powerful to be considered pleasant. She heard Caleb grunt, but mostly exhale. "Cautiously open now." Sylvia backed up and the horn was still glowing. "Caleb, speak if you can hear me."

"What . . . should . . . I say?"

"Young man, you've just undergone a de-petrification followed by a very powerful cleansing. Say whatever you'd like," Sylvia said.

Lily thought he'd be okay, but ended up just guiding him to the ground, and cradled his head on her knees. "You're okay." He reached towards her, she guided his hand so he could touch her face.

"Lily? How long?"

"Three days."

"Thank you. Both of you. Uh . . . " He rolled and tried to stand, and fell to his hands.

"Take his sword, and young man, I don't care how you normally are, you are the equivalent of a newborn kitten," Sylvia informed him. "Most of you will be flesh within the hour, little parts of you will be slow to turn. But, you'll be right as rain in a week so long as you get your eyesight back."

After they gave him a minute, Alfred and Isaac grabbed Caleb's arms, steadied him, and boosted him up to the cart. Lily belted his sword, then climbed into the back with him.

"Is it better or worse coming out of the puppet spell?" Sylvia asked, taking his arm and checking his wrist for a pulse, then instructed Lily to do the same. Strong, a little slow, but a nice consistent rhythm.

"I . . . guess worse? I feel . . . clean but . . . "

"Lily, stop fawning and give him something to drink. Not too much, and not too cold." Lily did as she was told. "As for you, Lily, are you meaning to tell me you would be as you are if he was middle-aged and balding?"

"Mother!"

"Nice to meet you, Sylvia." Caleb extended an arm as the wagon lurched.

"Nonsense, I've met plenty of folk like this and none of them are happy right now. Perhaps not plenty, but I didn't meet Elias down at the pub," Sylvia said. "What are your intentions with my daughter?"

"I asked her if we could court and she said yes. I want to get to know her better," Caleb said. "She says you live in a hilly wooded area near the mountains. I was thinking of building a nice shack in the woods."

"A shack?"

"More like a comfy hunting lodge."

"Just to court my daughter?"

"Might pinch a sheep or two if she's ignoring me."

"You mean my sheep."

"You're not being very witty right now," Lily whispered.

"I tried," he said. "I have to return to Mirador eventually. That's where I'm from. She told me it would take time to heal from the petrification. Thank you, Sylvia."

Sylvia snorted. "I have to thank you for keeping my children safe. I would appreciate if we agreed none of this ever happened. Curing you, I mean. Court her all you like, but leave my flock."

"I am going to Taralee to investigate an unrelated incident. I was delayed in the south when a wound became infected." He smirked. "And I didn't see anything."

"Good," Sylvia said. "Against my better judgement, I am leaving you to her care. We've made arrangements that the day after tomorrow, you can go to Taralee. I've written a letter to my old instructor. She's expecting someone, Lily, so help me if I have to hear from her that you didn't go there first you are going to spend the summer cataloguing and cleaning her home. The fresh mountain air will do him good."

When they returned to the Sprites' home, Sylvia gave Caleb a more thorough examination and taught Lily how to check his pain receptors. He was still numb, and insisted he was fine, but that was before the headache started.

"Is it normal for my face to feel kind of . . . ow . . . "

"Oh, the euphoria is wearing off. Do you know where the phrase 'splitting headache' originated?" Sylvia asked. "I can extrapolate, or you can drink this sleeping tonic." He opted for the medicine and promptly passed out. For the first time in days, Caleb seemed peaceful when he slept. "This is why you don't rush the healing process," Sylvia explained. "You'll have a real human being back in a few days. Now, come join our hosts in the main room. I want to know all about the handsome young man we just saved."

"He said a lot of people were kidnapped in Taralee," Lily said. "He'll be investigating there, and then returning to Mirador."

"That's jolly well and good. He can go home in a few weeks, but if he finds himself in Stagmil he can help dip sheep," Sylvia said. "What's he like?"

"Well, he's a knight, and he's from the Kingdom of Ivancia . . . "

"No, what is he *like*."

Lily knew her meaning. "He pretends to be tough, but animals and children like him. Has a morbid sense of humour at times, and he's one of those guys who knows he's smart and can be a little cocky, but generally looks out for other people. Can hold a decent conversation when he's interested." She bit her lip before she continued, "All of this might just be magical infatuation, too. We don't know."

"Oh?"

Lily frowned. "The thing that cursed his castle told him he mistook an urge to protect me for affection."

Sylvia's lips hinted at a smile. "And what do you think about that?"

Lily crossed her arms. She'd like to think he liked her because of . . . well, *something*. "We could spend the rest of our lives asking if it was a lie," she admitted. "I guess we'll just have to decide whether or not we like each other when the infatuation phase ends."

"Lily Nell O'Connell," Sylvia said, crossing her arms. "Did you force a boy into a relationship by magical means?"

"If I did, it wasn't intentional." Lily tried not to blush, her mother's laughter made it worse. "Mom! We agreed to take things slow."

"Good. I'd like to get to know him. I made arrangements in case we're away from home for an extended period. Your grandparents will be down soon if they're not already running the ranch." Sylvia paused. "Caleb's an Ivancian Knight; he'll have to return overseas." She took Lily's hand. "It doesn't matter that you helped them; you won't be one of them. Is he of a noble line or . . . ?"

"He's among the poorer families. I don't care."

Sylvia nodded. "That might work to your favour."

"Mom, I haven't thought that far ahead. We haven't known each other that long."

"I know. Just . . .think about what sort of life you want before you get too attached."

Lily considered his and Ethan's plan to lay low for a year or two. His home was back there, and she knew he'd probably be considered a hero when he returned. She was a shepherd from Stagmil. What could she possibly have to offer him?

"We'll figure it out."

Twenty-Six

Caleb wished everyone would stop making a fuss. Yes, he was blind, kind of numb, everything tasted like sand, but that wasn't any reason to fret; if anything, if he was partially stone, so logically it should have made him tougher than normal. He could handle Sylvia's instructions and warnings; but not the lukewarm food for the next week. Not that anything tasted good but he was told that would improve. Louis had his back and had already agreed to sneak him whatever he wanted.

He submitted to the examination in hopes they'd believe he was an ideal patient. Thankfully, upon realizing he had to take off his tunic, Sylvia sent Lily out of the room, and she told Louis and Victor what to look for. She'd seen him and Ethan topless before when they'd swam in the ocean, but that was completely different than her mother poking his armpits.

"Not prone to rashes, are you? If you see anything," Sylvia explained. "You let Lily know. She'll know what to do."

"He'll be in good hands," Victor insisted.

He didn't remember much about coming out other than the euphoric bliss coming to, and then a dull, terrible headache that followed. Sylvia was probably the most normal member of the family, and since she was leaving overseas that day to catch up with the other O'Connells, Lily and the Phorsythes would see him north to Taralee in a few more days.

"You might as well stay here," Sylvia informed him as she and her daughter were gathering her belongings and going over what all needed to be done back in Stagmil, putting together a care package to send overseas. Sounded like Lily had a lot on her plate: gardening, arranging for this neighbour but not that one to spin the fleece, getting a new sheepdog puppy . . . well, that part sounded like fun.

"I can handle a walk," Caleb insisted. He and Louis had already found everything he could possibly trip or bang his head on.

"Are you certain he'll be good to travel by tomorrow?" Nora asked as they made ready to leave.

"He can sit on the back of a wagon just as good as loafing about here," Sylvia said.

It was a little cooler out but a good day for sailing; he was starting to understand how to tell when the tides were ready. "Are you getting sick of sailing yet?" Sylvia asked Larry.

"Perhaps, but Alfred's just getting started," Larry said. "This is nothing, Sylvia. I was once on the sea for nearly a month before setting foot ashore. Bigger boat, mind."

Caleb smiled fondly remembering his own voyage, but he was glad to be on this side of the ocean where he was a relative no one. He heard Catarina and Sean speak to Larry, and Lily give her farewells to her mother. He was a little upset he couldn't help cast them off. He wasn't surprised that Catarina and Sean returned with them to the Sprites' farm for tea and an early lunch. The conversation was pleasant enough; thankfully it wasn't all about him or what had happened in Mirador. Life was going on. Lily and Victor talked about shearing and what needed to be done back at home without Elias or Sylvia present.

"Heard you're leaving tomorrow," Catarina said when everyone else was served up a steaming bowl of warm vegetable and beef soup. "You have to come back when you're better. You could stay a week or two, before frittering off north."

"I'm helping dip sheep," Caleb said. His bowl was barely warm. "What does that mean, anyway?"

"Oh, you'll find out," Victor said with a chuckle. "Lily's quite fast at shearing, came in third last year at a county fair, I think."

"That was two years ago in the junior division," Lily clarified. "I'm competing with the adults now; I don't normally even place."

Caleb would have been happy to go for another nap after lunch. To his surprise, it was Esperanza who grabbed his arm. "Can I borrow him for an hour? My friends want to see him."

"Ask him," Nora said.

"Please?" she asked Caleb.

He wanted to talk to her anyway. She led him outside. "I'm under the impression that you were turned into a puppet up in Taralee." She didn't say anything, but her grip tightened. "I didn't mean to upset you. You don't have to talk about it if you don't want to."

"It was really scary," she said. "I was put on display, then Sean and Daphne found me and wanted to buy me! I have the weirdest friends."

"They can't be worse than mine."

"How long were you like that?"

"A little over two years," Caleb said. He stumbled on an uneven bit of ground. "We stopped the curse. I think everyone in Mirador is okay now. I'm going to Taralee to find out more, and if anyone else is effected."

"Daphne was there, she can tell you what happened," she said. He had no idea where they were going but the spray from the sea picked up. "Can you sit on the beach okay? We'll be near the water."

"Sure." She didn't warn him that the ground would get uneven, but he could smell the sea and hear the surf; it was windy out, they needed to dress warmer than the day they'd arrived in Shelkie's Bay. "My friends will be here in a little bit. Are you still hurt?"

"I'll be perfect in a few days."

"That's good. Is it scary to be blind?"

"Sometimes."

It didn't take long for her friends to show up. He heard splashing, and Esperanza called them over. "Oh, he's young!" said a female voice; he assumed Esperanza's friends were all girls about her age.

"I'm older than I look," Caleb said. "How many . . . ?"

"She said you were blind. I'm Daphne, and this is Oshiera."

"There's just two of us. Three counting Espy," said the third female voice.

"Isn't it a little cold for swimming?" Caleb asked.

"Not for us," Daphne said with a giggle.

"You're a real knight from across the sea? And you lived in a castle?" Oshiera asked.

He nodded. "The castle is called Mirador. I'm from the Kingdom of Ivancia."

"And you have a horse and you save people?" Daphne asked.

"Sometimes."

"Are you and Lily going to get married or are you going to go off and have adventures?"

"Are you suggesting both isn't an option?" Caleb asked. They giggled. "I want to get to know her better."

"She came to see you every day. She talked to you, and sang a little. Did you hear her when you were a statue?" Daphne asked.

"I don't think so. The dreams were pleasant. I can't remember them, but . . . it doesn't matter."

"Tell us a knight story," Esperanza said.

"You want a scary one or a boring one where they punished all of us because of something dumb one of my friends did?"

"No!" they laughed. "We want something fun and adventurous," Oshiera said. "Derring-do and romantic. One about you and harrowing feats of adventure."

"I'm not that interesting," Caleb said.

"You were a statue yesterday," Oshiera said flatly.

"I got better," he said. "Actually, I was wondering if you could tell me about what happened in Taralee. Daphne, Esperanza said you were instrumental in stopping the woman who tried to turn her into a puppet."

"Yeah, I might have done something," Daphne admitted. "Er, where should I start?"

"I got time. Don't neglect anything like kitsunes or magic bracelets, I think I can handle it."

"Then you're going to tell us a good story about knights?" Daphne pressed.

"Maybe not one about me, but I grew up listening to knights who've sailed to faraway kingdoms." He thought about it. "My father romanced my mother from another kingdom, you might like to hear that one."

"Fine, but you have to tell us something romantic between you and Lily," Daphne said."Like, how her eyes are bottomless pools of beauty."

"And her smile rivals the moon and stars!" Oshiera said.

"I called her a lake monster once." He'd have to come up with some better petnames. *Lamb Chop* seemed appropriate . . . but he still liked *Stringless*. For two years, he considered it synonymous with *Freedom*.

The girls laughed, thinking this was hilarious. "Come up with something better, or else. Okay, my story started when Oshiera and I were swimming with our dolphin friends and we came across these whalers . . . "

"Your dolphin friends?" Caleb wasn't sure he heard right.

"Wanna meet our orca?"

Twenty-Seven

A passenger ship arrived with refugees from Ivancia the morning they were supposed to leave, so travelling North to Taralee was delayed a day. Folk arrived, dazed and confused about what had happened, looking to go home now that they were on the right side of the sea. Not everyone was going north, but Isaac helped Victor and Lily organize those that were.

Victor offered several people jobs and Lily agreed to help others find work in Taralee. One girl Lily's age age seemed out of place amongst the refugees. She didn't know how to plant crops or spin, didn't have any real skills to offer. What was sadder, was she didn't have a home to go to; from what Lily gathered, her family had sold her.

"Doesn't matter a lick," Lily told her. "We can teach you, help you until you figure out if it is where you want to be."

"Aye lass," Victor agreed. "We always need extra hands just for the shearing, we'll figure out the rest."

Louis and Caleb spent the extra day having Caleb learn to ride Stella more or less without assistance. Caleb joked that he was going to get incredible senses for fighting in the dark, only to immediately trip on *something*. Lily questioned the sanity of having a blind rider but, Stella was well-seasoned and tempered, and would follow the road instinctively.

The night before they were to leave, Catarina and Isaac took Lily and Caleb for a victory drink at the tavern. Without Seth or Larry it wasn't quite right, and Caleb was more interested in listening to rumour. He took in the information from home. Rumours conflicted as to what was going on with the sudden influx of people arriving in Shelkie's Bay. Victor had spoken with Catarina at length to send more people up their way.

Lily rose early in the morning and said her goodbyes to the Sprites, thanked them for everything they'd done. Caleb in particular was grateful to Isaac, and said to give his best regards to Larry and Alfred. "Come up and visit us for some of the festivals in Taralee," she told Nora and Esperanza. "I'll have room at the house if you make your way up there."

"Rebecca's invited us to visit her as well," Esperanza said.

"We'll come in a few weeks for a festival," Nora agreed. "You've got shearing and we've got strawberries to harvest."

Catarina saw them off and gave them a wicker basket of fresh bread and scones and she'd made Caleb a sweater for those 'cold mountain slopes' in spite of the days getting progressively warmer.

They set off within an hour of sunrise, Louis riding Stella while Victor took the lead reins on the first wagon, Sean on the second. The second wagon where Lily rode with her knight had more goods than people, but she found it more than comfortable as blankets were laid out and it seemed like people were trying to make the best of it, chatting about their experiences being captured, their journey overseas, and where they were going.

Caleb was starting to be able to see shapes again, a good sign he was on the road to not only Taralee, but recovery. "Think I'll get my vision back in time to see Taralee?"

"I hope so. I'll spend a day or two with you, then I'll go home. Once things are under control at home I can rejoin you, or you can join me in Stagmil depending on what you find."

"While we're in Taralee, let's get you a new mandolin."

"Save your pennies. I have a bouzouki; good excuse to get good at it."

"We're courting. I need to get you *something*. Love to see you tromp around shepherding with a bonnet and one of them frumped up skirts. A matching ribbon for your favourite lamb?"

She poked him in the ribs—not painfully, as she'd learned where he was ticklish. "I'll have to get you matching shorts with overalls. Show some leg. Louis can teach you to yodel."

"Don't make me fall out of love with you saying that sort of stuff, Lamb Chop." He tried to use that firm voice, he couldn't hide his smirk. "Are you going to be spending the next month at a spinning wheel?"

Lily laughed. "There's not enough time in the world for me to spin all the wool I'm going to be shearing. You let me worry about the raw fleece market and who's going to be busy spinning. I'm more of a 'watch the sheep and shear'em' sort of girl. And save them from wolves and creatures that go bump in the night."

"Not all wolves are bad." He nudged her.

"So long as they don't bother my herd," she said. He took her hand and kissed the back of it. "Behave."

"No."

Someone in the first wagon started to play a wooden flute, and people started to clap and sing to a rowdy song more fit for a pub than a slow wagon ride north. Many grew overly-excited when the next song began, an even stranger number, about passing a lumberjack's hat about.

"Do the lyrics make any sense to you?" Caleb asked, somehow ending up with a tambourine.

"No, but they don't always have to," Lily said, watching out the back as a fox trotted from the woods to the middle of the path and watched them. She wondered whether or not she ought to wave or see what she wanted, but decided to be present with her blind knight. Lily joined in with him for the chorus, her voice completely ordinary, her mind free, and her heart content as the kitsune grinning on the path.

Acknowledgements

Acknowledgements

If you enjoyed this story, you can thank Scarlet Cianflone for the direction this book took early on. Scarlet requested a duology, she wanted a character to betray the good guys, she wanted to know about the "Client across the sea". I pitched ideas at her and the story is better because of her feedback. It's weird that I spent time turning her into a reader, and now, she's well-read and is more than happy to let me know when my work ain't stacking up.

Thank Breanna Cianflone for naming the heroine Lily; I wanted a heroine with a plant name and Fern was my forerunner. Drafts change drastically from their original concepts (if they didn't instead of kitsunes there would be two redneck fairies kicking about). Technically Scarlet named Seth because she kept reading "Sean" as "Seth" when she was eight, and I'm a jerk who thinks she's funny.

Thank you to Darlene Mickey and R.J. Hore for the feedback. YA books aren't Ron's jam but as always, he's the beta reader one who tells me about sailing and other technicalities. Dar, I appreciate you letting me know the long ending worked and the segments that slow the story down were okay.

Thank you to Samantha Beiko for editing. Thank you Hannah Sternjakob for the beautiful cover. Thank you Jessica for the beautiful internal art of the fox and the mandolin.

Finally, thank you for reading. I'm blessed to be able to do this. If you can, please leave a review online: good, bad, indifferent; it'll help other people know if this is the right kind of story for them.